Now I See Clearly

When you open both
eyes you see clearly

Robin Reed-Poindexter

outskirts
press

Outskirts Press, Inc.
http://www.outskirtspress.com

Paperback ISBN: 978-1-4787-7484-6
Hardback ISBN: 978-1-9772-0551-3

Library of Congress Control Number: 2019901288

Cover and interior artwork by Frank K. Reed II. All rights reserved - used with permission.

Outskirts Press and the "OP" logo are trademarks belonging to Outskirts Press, Inc.

PRINTED IN THE UNITED STATES OF AMERICA

EDITING BY
I Cheng (Maggie) Choi
Shanta D. Smith
Chantell L. Tarver

ILLUSTRATION BY
Frank (Tchallah) Reed
Frank K. Reed
Brian A. Bland Sr.
Kinna LeBlanc

Contents

Acknowledgements

I give God the glory for allowing me to share my story with everyone it needs to reach. I'm thankful for my family, friends, godchildren and supporters that are always there in so many ways, encouraging me. It is through faith and prayers that I am still here. There were times that I thought I wouldn't make it. I beat myself up more than the hits that I sustained in my fourteen years of marriage. What man has made bad, God turned it around to make it good. I was blessed with a career in the fire service for over thirty years. The verbal hits and imaginary punches I received from the Fire Department were nowhere near the abuse that I encountered from many years in my marriage. I'm thankful that I was able to give back what God has given to me. God blessed me with the opportunity to love others and share my story. I hope it can help someone who needs to understand that you can alter your life and change your own story. The person that you look at in the mirror can smile and, with the willingness to change, can have control of their own life.

I would like to thank the readers for believing in me enough to purchase my first book in the Middle Maddy series. When I started writing and finishing some years later and my hopes were that these books would reach one person and make a difference in their life. Now I See Clearly, (my adult novel), did reach one person - that was me; it helped in my healing. I hope this will encourage and inspire more people to write down their thoughts and someday become authors. (runawayreader@gmail.com)

"Dear Readers,
Names, dates, places and incidents in this book have been changed or omitted for a variety of reasons, including but not limited to the security, safety and well-being of the people, places or agencies involved. Any resemblance to anyone living or dead is purely coincidental. I will leave it up to the reader to realize what is what, who is who and where is where. With this in mind, this book is listed as a work of fictionalized biography.
The Author"

"Am I pregnant?" Rita wondered anxiously. Naively, she tried to convince herself she had indigestion. She didn't know how to tell her parents, let alone her abusive boyfriend, Bill. She trembled, agonizing about what could happen next; repercussions and punches from her boyfriend, judgment from her parents and letting down family, who had such high hopes for her future. Rita felt alone; the last thing she wanted to do was go back home. "Now I See Clearly" is an eye-opening peek into the life of a young abused mother and how she escaped her abuser with new hope.

"The writing was great; it had such clarity that it kept me captivated into what was coming next. The episodes of Rita's daily life were heartbreaking at times but you knew love was there. It showed how families dealt with what life threw at them. Rita showed her commitment to her marriage and family but also her hopes and dreams of what she wanted her family to become. The characters were full of life and that made me reflect as I was reading on experiences others may have had in their own past. This was a great debut novel and I look forward to finding out more about the lives of Reva, Courtney Diane, Robin and Loren in future writings."

– Jo Banks, Professional chef

"I appreciate the literary skills, her creativity, and the overall story line. I am not the artistic type, but I do recognize talent and good sh*t. It was impressive the way the author gave her characters depth and personalities. She exposed their background, families, affiliations and interactions, very fluid and transparent. Her scenarios and dialogues illustrated how clearly she created instances of humor, sadness, and seriousness. I found myself trying to anticipate what's next, with very little success. Lastly, I felt the story line was solid and entertaining. The various interactions among characters and how they seem to fit and interface made the scenarios real."

J. Crain, retired Fire Chief

"Hey readers, I'm telling you all are not ready and I say that with much love, respect and adoration for the fun and laughs that you'll get from the characters in this book. Okay let's start with fun...this is what you will get when you get to read what and who the characters are; what's funny are how the characters react to different situations. They come together with love, tears, smiles and support for one another in their own special way. There are parts where you will laugh, cry and rejoice in the outcomes. This book had me intrigued from the beginning to the end. I could or would not dare have missed this opportunity to speak on or give my opinion on this amazing read. To all who will read this book-I believe that you will enjoy it as much as I have. Ms. Robin she did just that... you go girl! You knocked it out of the park-grand slam and home run. Let this be the first of many more to come. Don't stop doing writing because I look forward to the next one."

Ms. Bay Bay, Transportation specialist

"A fun and engaging read that invites you into a world of colorful characters. You feel you already know the snappy dialog and seemingly crazy situations. The author was very creative in making you feel as if you were in the room or engaged directly with their conversations."

B. Wilkerson, Professional seamstress

Robin Reed-Poindexter was born and raised in Omaha, Nebraska. She worked at the City of Richmond Fire Department for over thirty years. She was the first African American-and only woman in the City of Richmond Fire Department who held the ranks of Fire Inspector, Deputy Fire Marshal and the only woman Chief Officer on the west coast (in the rank of Deputy Fire Marshal).

Although she was in an abusive relationship, she transformed her pain into strength, which she instilled in her three children, two daughters and a son. Miss Reed-Poindexter is also the author of a children's book, Middle Maddy series , which she penned with encouragement from her granddaughter, Mackenzie "Mackey." Ms. Reed-Poindexter lives with her family in northern California.

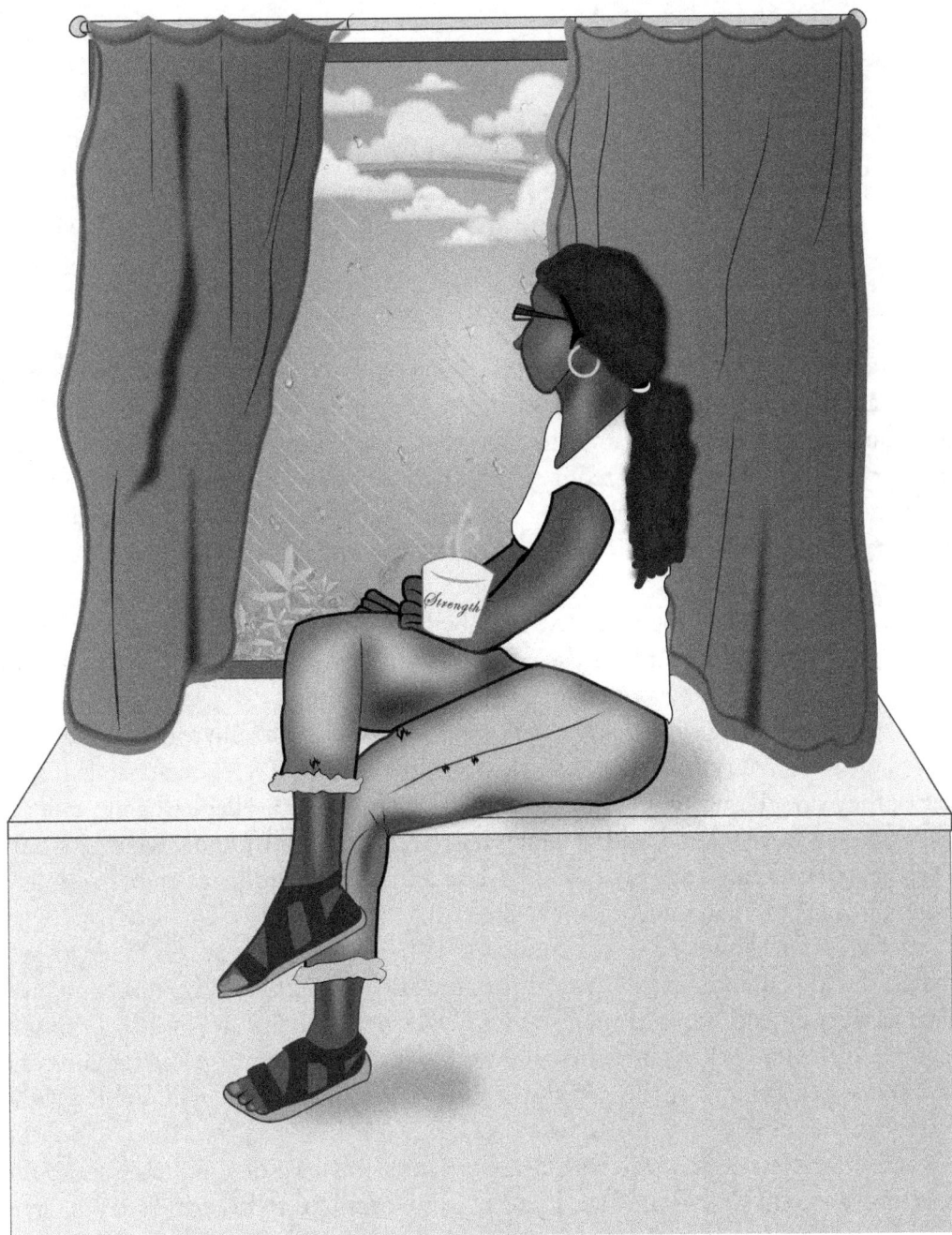

Back When I Knew My Name Was Rita

Chapter 1
My Humble Beginnings

I'm here looking at the rain fall and thinking back to the number of tears I shed. It's amazing how tears flow just like rain. They have so much in common. They both flow continuously and stop just like that. Sometimes I had to laugh to keep from crying. No one ever figured it out. No one knew how much pain I was in.

I was getting better at disguising my feelings. You could say I was a master of disguises. That made me feel pretty good. It always felt good when I got through another day.

Oh, my face shows someone trying to be happy, but I knew I had misery in my soul. If only they looked into my eyes, and saw the wounds, scars, and punches of my injured soul. I really was a prisoner of my silent misery.

I remember being asked by a new neighbor Vicki, and my other concerned neighbor, Miss Mary (or Mayla). Although they were a few years advanced than I was, they saw the writing before I knew the words were available for me to read. How could I leave when I had so much fear inside and didn't know what was outside the doors? How could I leave someone I love and who loved me? I sigh as I turned toward the window looking at the rain.

Only I knew those confusing answers. Why don't you leave? Why don't you snatch the kids up and sprint toward the front door? Just thinking about it would start anxiety attacks accompanied with a headache. As I turn toward the window looking at the rain it just continues to flow. I'm just staring into space watching the rain stare back at me. Yes, the rain flows just as my tears and my pain. Where is the sunlight in my life?

Life wasn't always that bad with Bill. It wasn't always the fussing, cussing and the belittling I would hear from him. I had become immune to his criticism and start looking at myself as not being any contributions to society or my family. My family never knew about the life I was living. After having four kids you would think we were in love I thought kids represented the love we shared and made. I was popping them out. I had one almost every other year. The last one was a surprise because

I thought everything had dried up and production was closed down. Sometimes I wondered how we had four kids. Bill was always gone, and I was left to raise the kids. He had so many affairs I thought I was the other woman. Wow, what a silly thought. All I knew was Bill. My kids were my life. Sierra, Sabrina, Shaurice and the last surprise baby Bill, "Sonny boy".

I met Bill when I was 16....young and in my first year of college. He was sitting at a table in the library and I asked if I could share the table with him. Only other choice I had was a nerdy looking guy and that didn't do anything for me. I would always see Bill leaving the classroom as I was entering or sitting alone in the college cafeteria. I used to hang out in the cafeteria with Trina looking at men. After all, we were both single at least Trina (aka Katrina) was. As for me, I was not quite single. I was doing, the long-distance dating with a man six years older than me by the name of Mason. We started dating toward the end of my senior year. I met Mason at a burger place where my high school group hung out after school. He played and sung in a band and they were pretty good. I'd never really been around a live band before and it was exciting and so new. I was young and just having fun. Oakwood really didn't have a lot of places to hang out and have some fun, especially in my age group. We would hang out in another city going to clubs. That was where I learned how to do the hustle. I made it home in time without violating my curfew. More bars than clubs and I would use my sister's ID to get in. Wow Rita are you dating yourself or what. I had one drink it was pretty good...but one was enough. Alcohol never really did anything for me. I didn't like the smell or how people acted when they got drunk.

We enjoyed each other. Mason was smart and kept me on my toes. Sex was not in the picture just kissing and hugging. Mason and his band moved to California, where there were more opportunities. We tried to keep the relationship going, but we both were young. California living is a big difference from mid-western living in Oakwood. Mason and I had about a five to six-year age difference. I was kind-of surprised my mother let me date someone older than me. Maybe she knew it wouldn't last. Or maybe the fact that my dad is three years older than her and she understood the age difference and interfering wasn't on her mind. She allowed us to enjoy our relationship respectfully. Time and distance happened and we both moved on. No good byes just moved on. I wonder what Trina is doing. For some reason, she just popped into my thoughts and I can actually see her face. Trina was slim, 5'6', with light brown eyes and long curly hair. She still sported her cheerleading look. Myself, I had the 5'4' track/pompom slim short look. I didn't realize how small I was until I had my first child. Even though she was a cheerleader and I was a pompom girl, we played each others' high school but never met until college. We used to tell people we were cousins because we both had the same last name. College was a new experience we both shared. Trina was studying to become a teacher and my major was nursing. We would laugh as we both tried talking to various men whether we knew them or not. Bed hopping was not an option. We were just girls wanting to have fun. We really didn't talk to anyone on a serious level or basis. I met many men that were interested. It felt pretty good when two reporters were interested in me at the same time. I didn't know, other men were interested, or checking me out until later when I would have a conversation with them. I was young and naïve, really, when it came to dating.

Trina had her share of guys, especially the ones she went to high school with. Wow......we were so young and immature. We both worked at McDonalds. I started working there when I was just 12. They found out my age and allowed me to stay although I was too young to work. I talked to my manager about hiring Trina. She was of age, fresh out of high school and in college. Actually, that was where she meant her first husband. Eventually, Trina and I separated because we started spending more time with our boyfriends, aka future husbands.

It was kind-of different attending classes with so many different ages and personalities. Some of the classes were easy and the others that were important offered challenges. This was a new eye-opening experience. There were so many choices in classes and in men. I had so many choices but didn't know what I wanted. I had a head start by graduating early from high school. But mentally I was still young, and I should have been more focused on my education. All I wanted was to experience the college life. Thought I knew all the answers and was opened to a new independent college world no more high school rules. With no parents monitoring my grades, I felt grown, and liberated. I spent more time hanging out in the student union than class. There were only a few classes I did well in and enjoyed; psychology, biology, and bookkeeping. I was always good with numbers and challenges. This freedom I enjoyed, and house rules had liberated me a little. As long as I came home at a decent hour in other words "respect the clock". Campus parties were fun and made me feel older. I remember working with a fraternity, frat party being held at a club. The funny part I was only 16 and they had me checking identification. Hmm they didn't know that I had graduated early. I guess I was good at acting older and keeping my mouth shut. I didn't drink but had a really good time. Bill knew my age we would just smile and laugh.

Bill was 22 and impressed with my personality. I was impressed with him being fresh off the plane from Chicago. He was 6'2", with a slim athletic built, gorgeous bowlegged, deep dimples that showed when he smiled. He had almond shaped eyes that just twinkled when he looked at me. Just thinking about how fine he was still making me get a little giddy. He was perfect to me regardless of what people would say that no one is perfect. My eyes couldn't find any flaw in him. All I knew that how he made me feel. He only knew a few people in Oakwood. And that made me feel pretty good because he wasn't someone else's boyfriend. For that moment,

I was the only one he liked. I had Bill all to myself with no drama and no history. Just thinking about Bill being fresh just lifted my spirits. It reminded me of when a family from the east coast invaded our high school. Wow the girls were pretty with various hairstyle lengths, looks, and innocent pretty smiles. We didn't hate them we just couldn't stand their beauty.

Hum, now I'm forcing my thoughts on trying to remember their names. Let me think, there was the oldest one they called Sister now what was her real name think Rita hmm Velda,Arlene,and there was Retha Lolita, Annette, Normamae, their cousins identical twins um Wilma and Reneta,their cousin's Francine, Lydia and Sharron attended the school, traitors, they should have given us heads up or warning or something (laugh). They came in variety of sizes boys were tripping and falling all over them. Now we weren't too mad because they had some fine- looking brothers Ward, Ronald and Nelson. Just thinking about them boys still puts a smile on my face. The local girls boo woo and woo woo until they saw their fine, fine brothers. They stayed long enough maybe just one year. Just when the thrill was gone, and the naivety was wearing off they were on the plane returning to the east coast.

Now their replacements were not too bad we called him Chisel Charles and woo he was just that, (hmmm and hmmm). Valerie's boyfriend Grady took it kind of hard when she moved back east. He never really got over Valerie. She's very happily married back east to her hubby, Adrem. I saw Grady one day after we had graduated, and he still was talking about Valerie being his girlfriend. Hmm I thought she was still on the east coast. He said she was, but she will be coming back. Now I remember her, and her sister came back for her Aunt Wila Ann and Uncle Porter's 50th wedding anniversary party. Then they returned to the east coast. He didn't look too good, but he was trying to hold it together. I heard some years later he never recovered. It's strange how somebody can linger in our mind, body and soul and stop you from functioning.

Hmm we hide behind a smile to cover up the truth. I do wonder what happened to those fine brothers and their fine cousins Gary, JC, Brian and Spike. Ooh could they sing. I can still picture them on the stage to this day. Wait a minute Melody and Gary I think did hook up. Anyway, those boys came in a variety of sizes and they were fine and very athletic looking, tee hee. Hmm hmm and hmmm, (sigh). I wondered if Gary and Melody are still together. They made a cute couple both fine and very athletic. They probably are still together. When the group of us girls, let's see…. Sharon Denise, Debbie Ann, Claudia and Betty, would go out we always tried to sound older didn't know I would be auditioning for my role acting older while I was trying to impress my future husband.

Its fun being in high school we always used Debbie Ann's sister Brenda's car while she was preparing for the bar exam. She studied a lot, but we had to get her car back to her and plus be home before midnight. We called ourselves Cinderellas. Funny when I think back, we would have to leave the party just when it was starting to get jumping. When we would leave, we could see and feel the boys checking us out and wondering why we were leaving. We all had a rehearsed line either we had to get the car back or we were going to check out another party, hee hee. At least it sounded good we didn't want to tell them we had to be home before the clock struck twelve.

Sharon's mom, Mrs. Rebecca wouldn't wake up when Sharon came home late. All she would do is just unplug the clock and wake up the next morning and knew what time she came in. We always had to drop Sharon off first because she lived the farthest and her mom was mean. Every time we dropped Sharon off, she would always fuss about being the first one dropped off as she exited out the car. We referred to the boonies because it was so far. I still talk with Sharon and I love her mom dearly, but I tell her I'm still scared of her mom, even at this age. I still tremble hearing her voice. From time to time we talk and laugh about when we were playing on the phone and the operator disconnected the main phone line to the house. Now we were all scared and strong friends we couldn't leave Sharon hanging. With fear and fast talking we got that phone turned back on before Mrs Rebecca came home and we got the heck out of there with sweat and fear. We laugh about it and the things we did, but her mom was the enforcer just like a lot of parents trying to keep their children out of trouble.

Needless to say, it worked for us. I had to add that my parents were no joke either. Debbie Ann's mother, Mrs. Evelyn, had love and a sense of humor for us all the time. She would tease Debbie Ann and the family if they didn't act right, she would leave her teeth at home, and smile as much as she could at everyone. They laughed but that put the fear in them. There was one time when we went out and Debbie Ann's mother Mrs Evelyn looked at us and smiled giving us a wink and we nervously laugh because we knew the inside joke. Humph if I didn't make the Cinderella mid-night clock, I would just shake my head and hope my dad was sleep. When I pulled up to the house you couldn't tell if anyone was up until you unlocked the door that needed oil. There was only one way in and that was up the stairs. I would enter really slow with my heart racing, brain numb, while thinking about the staring mole in his eye and dreaded the noise indicator of him being up. It felt like instant punishment without the jury. When I opened the door if I heard the stool at the kitchen counter scoot back, I knew he was up and there was one way out. Running was out he ran track too and played first base on his adult baseball team. So, I knew I wouldn't make it to the squeaky door that didn't open fast at all. So, hmm, when I heard that stool make that noise, I would walk up the seven stairs, as if I was walking up twenty just taking my sweet time. I didn't know what to expect. I can laugh now but it wasn't funny then. I still hate to hear that sound flashback flashes quick thoughts. Just thinking about childhood friends makes me laugh and cry because I miss them and still remember the times. Funny how I still drift off into the pass but I'm still part of my present. Fading away helps me but at the same time probably confuses others.

When I was with Bill I tried to sound and act older as much as possible. Bill was older, and I felt insecure in our relationship. I didn't want him to think I wasn't ready for a relationship or for him to look for a more mature woman. I guess I was pretty good at disguises then and didn't know that I would have to compete for someone I thought belonged to me, after all he had my heart why I should share his. I never knew how I would get better at pretending that I had it going on. Bill was my first love and that's all it took. He had my mind, body, heart, thoughts, and soul. I fell in love with the same eyes that penetrated my brain, numbed my emotions, and made my insides shrink-along with my pride and dignity. From that day on the only person I knew was Bill. I ate slept and breathed for Bill. Bill Bill, Bill, Bill. I missed his voice and his touch. I would sometimes toss and turn in my sleep thinking about Bill. When we were apart, I missed hearing his heart beat and his embrace. I loved and missed the scent of his cologne.

My parents hated hearing Bill's name because all I did was talk about him. It was Billmania in my bedroom. I had pictures, posters, and cards everywhere. His name was on anything and everything I could write it on. I would write "Rita loves Bill" in a heart or "Bill + Rita = Love". When we would take a drive, I would look over at him in the driver's seat just being thankful we were together. There was only room in my heart for him. He would always say what are you looking at and I would smile and say nothing. I was in awe of Bill so much. I was always thinking about him. How silly the things we say and do when we are in "love". At least I thought I was in love. My parents saw something different. They saw a big mistake. When you're young and confused, do you care what your parents think? No. When you are in love nothing else matters. Now when I think back, all the signs were there. There were times when Bill was very jealous and controlling. I thought it was because he cared and didn't want to lose me. So, I convinced myself to not focus on how mean he was being to me. It's funny how you look at things and you make up excuses despite the blind truth. It looks like it's going to rain all day. I always did like the rain. You can go outside and cry and no one knew no one knew. No one could see your tears your shame or pain.

I loved my Bill. I thought I was getting the best thing that could have happened to me. What a nightmare. I can't tell when the abuse actually started. I was blinded by love and how fine Bill was. I realize now that I should have looked beyond the looks. I thought if I read the book before judging the cover, I would have left book. One day we were walking up a small hill next to some ricket steps at his Aunt Wilma Kaye. Her brother Uncle O T G, Grand-dad Holister and Mama Helen all lived in that house. Hmm sipping this coffee and just got me to thinking why did Uncle OTG, aka Uncle Thomas have so many initials, hmm different. Anyway, I remember being pushed down by Bill and he tried to convince me I fell. Was I in the twilight zone or what? I knew the difference between falling and being pushed. Maybe this was the first sign of abuse. It is starting to rain harder. Just like my cries of pain. My disguise was making up my pretend world. The world where I tried to convince everyone everything was okay.

My first disguise was making up my face with a smile behind my bruises. This was the first time I had ever experienced true fear. As a child we were taught not to go down dark alleys or talk to strangers. This was something beyond that fear. One day when Bill and I were talking he just hauled off and hit me. That took me totally by surprise. I had my share of grade school fights but was never hit by a man. It hurt inside as well as outside. What kind of love was this that he could hit me and walk away? He said it was because I was talking to James. But why should that matter he knew I was in love with him and only him. We both were friends of James. I admit I had a crush on James at one time, but he wasn't the one I knew. We had talked briefly before Bill, and again James was an old crush. James was more into his education and more mature than I was at the time. And we just didn't connect. Hmm I wonder what he is up to and if he is still fine. Stop Rita stay focused.

I had my share of grade school fights but never hit by a man. Well that one time at McDonalds' getting smart with Kenneth and it happened so fast I couldn't remember hitting me just felt the pain later. He numbed me, and I don't know or remember what happened after that. Thinking back my friend Crystal's boyfriend jumped on her when we were in high school. I just remember her crying I didn't understand her pain then, but I understand now and happy that I didn't judge her but was a friend. I don't remember the conversation too much. I look back and think on what you could expect from a 16-year-old that was sheltered and just wanted to have fun. I was too scared, ashamed and embarrassed to tell anyone. I didn't want anyone trying to talk me out being with Bill. I still loved him and wanted to be with him. It happened so fast I didn't have a chance to even cry. I just remember driving home in awe state. I went into my room and just sat on the edge of my bed wondering what had happened. I was so confused but even still, I just didn't want to lose him. We belonged together. I think I lost myself and turned my soul over to Bill with a red bow.

After that incident with Bill I barely looked at James or talk to him let alone thought about him until now. This was just a passing thought, and please mind, allow this thought to keep on passing, (don't need no more trouble). Looking back, I realize this was his way of controlling me. I was allowing him to redirect my steps and at the same time losing control of a life I was just starting. I thought it was my fault, that I made Bill mad or upset or always altering his mood. I couldn't understand why he would get upset with me for just caring. I was always taking the blame for any anger or pain he was going through. But still, I wanted to be his all and all. I didn't want him looking for a replacement for me.

Afterall, we had times that when they were good; they were very good, fantastic even. Going out to eat, going to the movies just hanging out and enjoying each other. We would laugh at any and everything. We'd smile and embrace each other. I just knew he loved me in his own way, and I needed to be there for him. He was jealous, and he really did love me, he really did! Bill was just trying to hold onto me in any way he could. This must have meant we were going to be together forever. When I think about it, how silly was that thought? Ooh this coffee is hot! Sipping this coffee slow should have been the same approach I should have taken with Bill. Let me try blowing it off so I can take little sips. I'm looking at the steam grow onto the window-blocks my vision. I guess my eyes got foggy just like the moisture on the window. I just couldn't see I just couldn't! Not only could I not see I started to become numb to my feelings and soul.

My mind, soul, and whole wardrobe changed. I just wanted to be invisible, so no one would see me, and Bill wouldn't hit me again. Just be a good girl and keep my mouth shut. Silence my thoughts. They might come out through my mouth. Another secret!! Don't tell anyone. Don't talk to anyone. I had to learn how to just stay numb… at least for now. My feelings would eventually come, back-and they did. Bill would call, and it always touched my heart in the right place to put a smile on my face. I could smell the flowers again and come back to life where the numbness went away. The sound of the phone ringing opened my joy and my heart started beating for him again. I needed to see him I needed that "Bill injection". Then there were some days where I didn't know if I was coming or going with Bill. Was my life some type of movie? Maybe: was there an audience somewhere laughing and eating popcorn watching my life unravel.

In such a short period of dating how was this relationship slowly turning into my nightmare? I just couldn't understand how a small-time girl could end up with an angry person. We both came from nice families. Both of our parents worked hard and grew up knowing some of his family members. Both families had steady incomes, comfortable savings. Not rich but surviving like everyone else. How did this man become so evil? Why was he so mean? Bill and I shared a lot of good times with laughter and joy. We enjoyed each other's company. We sometimes dressed alike and were inseperable. I looked at Bill as my best friend. We shared intimate secrets, family laughter, and our goals. There wasn't a topic off limits that we didn't discuss openly and honestly. Coming from different states we shared and grew with each other. If we weren't together, we were talking on the phone. I felt we couldn't live without each other. Well at least that is what I thought. How did the love we had turn into hatred toward me?

Did my innocence or lack of life experience and naïve nature get me into this situation with Bill? I was so into Bill and all the signs were there for me to turn around and just run away but maybe it was just too late. Now I found myself being late. I was in love with Bill not only was I love with Bill but found out I was six weeks pregnant. I thought, "Me a mom at this age and not married?" Just great… I tried taking the home pregnancy test. Back then, the results took a whole day to come back.

Chapter 2

Indigestion Sounds Better

That was the longest twenty-four hours I ever experienced. Funny but not ha-ha, it felt like a rusty cartoon clock that had a very slow, slow click. So, I tossed and turned wondering about my results.

Well, my test showed positive, but I still didn't believe the results. I had convinced myself that this had to be recall or outdated box. Oh, silly me and my wondering thoughts. They remind me of the rain, hmmm they both can throw you off. I had convinced myself this was just a bad or a recalled package. Well, I needed to confirm that I wasn't pregnant. Oh no not me?? I gathered enough strength to go to the clinic. From the outside the clinic looked like it had been forgotten. Dull grayish in color, and when I went inside the decoration confirmed that no love or thought had been shown to this forgotten clinic. The clinic was full of many young women. I looked at around the room and some of them had the same expressions. Expressions of what I felt inside scared and uncertain. Actually, it was like looking into a mirror. Again, numbness was all in the room it was some type of crazy feeling going on. I walked slowly and quietly down the corridor. Nurse Meredith, (my thought was nurse moody), handed me a clipboard with forms and attitude. I look down at what she had handed me, a cup was inside the package and she said that the bathroom is down the hall. She didn't even look at me, no eye contact and no type of human feelings. I nervously smile telling her that I was here for indigestion problems. Hello! Knock, knock is there a human inside there. The nurse next to her by the name of Ovada kinda made a grunt sound and I watched her roll her eyes. My thoughts were how were you involved in this conversation? Now, that I think about her bark and bite were the same no type of smile. Nurse Ovada had a mean stare. Heck why not throw in a woof or growling noise too. I wondered what ever happened to her to act so angry.

Nurse Meredith really didn't look up. She just said to fill out paperwork and leave a sample down the hall to the right. As she was giving me instructions, she turned her head to address the next person in line. I looked down the hall leading to the bathroom, which was down the hall on the right. I just remember that walk seemed so short yet very cold and Nurse Moody was so mean, and my insides were so numb and so empty. Fear was shivering with me with my every breath and step.

When I returned, I didn't see Nurse Moody. I guess she must have gone on a break, because I was met by another emotionless nurse by the name of Irma Jean. I smiled again and told myself that this must be a nurse requirement to work here. She took the clip board and told me to take a seat until my name is called. Again, there was no smile, no eye contact and no emotions. As I walked slowly to take a seat, I looked around the room at an uncomfortable hard chair.

I sat next to a woman that looked my age by the name of Reva. She had firm no nonsense look, no smile as I asked her name. We started talking with my insistence in talking to her. She went from vague answers to telling me her story about why she was sitting in this clinic. I looked and listened to her. She was very pretty. Reva was just natural pretty with a little gloss on her lips that enhance her corner smile. She was very careful with her words. Reva still had a touch of, innocence covered with some life experiences. Life experiences that I would hope not to ever encounter. I thought to myself that she was there because she might be pregnant. I smile saying to myself I'm here due to indigestion. She gave me a look as if she was startled and confused by my response. I unknowingly and being nervous I didn't realize I said indigestion out loud. Reva looks at me saying, well Miss Indigestion everyone else is here because they are pregnant. Hmm imagine that as she turns her head back to staring into her on space and thoughts. As the conversations went on and she started to feel a little more comfortable with me we talked about a little bit of everything. I guess I was so nervous and kept bugging her she just gave into our initial small talk.

Well as we talked, she said that all she wanted to do was to save her virginity for her husband. Her girlfriend Chris talked her into dating a popular nice-looking athlete. He was a star of track and field, basketball, football and all of that plus some more. She said girl he likes you a lot and he could have anyone he wants but he chose you. My response to Chris was I'm sure he had a lot of anyones. I'm just trying to stay focus and get out of this school, so I can get my career on, and get out of my momma's house. Don't have time for Mr. All World and his conquests. I thought the same thing about Bill without the conquest thoughts. My vision was on how fine Bill was and maybe that was the deal breaker for her. He chose me out of the sea of fish. Reva said that Chris kept saying, why save yourself for your husband he won't be a virgin. Silly girl, who saves themselves in this day and time?? Girl you're crazy if you don't go out with Maurice. If you don't somebody else will. My thoughts were who cares, not me. My focus is on me and my career and I didn't have time for his high school nonsense or antics.

Then Chris felt that she had to give me the rundown on Maurice's every move

NOW I SEE CLEARLY

and every breath he took. She started with, you know that Wanda been looking at him up and down and add sideways too with her glasses on and off. Now Maurice just broke up with Eva. I saw Miss Rah Rah Cheerleader like five minutes ago, and a matter of fact I saw them talking at track practice. But that probably meant nothing cuz they weren't laughing and hugging on each other. Chris kept talking and talking about him. What she was telling me about Maurice and Eva over and over again saying, they made it through the whole day not talking to each other. Chris didn't know I didn't care like that. I don't care if it didn't mean anything because it didn't mean anything to me, because I didn't care. Chris added that in one day Maurice should be so over her. Coach Goins cancelled track practice, so everyone was just decided to hang out. I thought again why I should care about track practice being cancelled. Chris said because I would have seen them together if we had practice. I could only look at her Rita and turned my head and went back to minding my own business.

As she spoke, I thought about how when we were kids, we used to race each other in the streets, from one end of the block to the other. Not realizing we could have gotten hit by any cars coming or speeding through. Humph…. drivers had more respect for the neighborhood then and more than likely they knew the parents of the person speeding. Running was fun, and I enjoyed racing the neighborhood girls and boys. After all I was fast in junior high and high school, the street races got me ready. But my thoughts are not fast enough to get away from this silly indigestion. Man, what did I eat that gave me such severe indigestion hmm? One good burp is all I need.

Well back to listening to Reva as she was saying that she told Chris so what. Chris told her that she saw him talking to Marla too. Chris laughed Marla likes girls that don't count. Now I heard that Pam, and even Ofelia. Oh, add Ellen, Diane, Bisa, and Yvonne woo all those girls were trying to move in on your man, girl. Chris moved her head around saying that she had almost got some type of whiplash looking at the revolving door of girls moving in on your man. In class turn it around Terri was passing him notes and giggling, and you know she is straight up trifling. Patricia, Carrie and Cynthia kept smiling at him in homeroom, grinning and cheesing and Kristi was blowing him kisses. Lisa and her sister Bertha were hanging around after school to talk to Maurice, so I heard. Now you know Terri is known as "Trailblazing or tail/tell Terri and she hangs around with drop to your knees Vernale. I thought about what she was saying. Terri and Vernale were known for given it away and add a box of dime candy. They were part of a joke get it, then get gone and leave it alone, don't go back or look back keep it moving as far away from them as you can.

All Chris did every opportunity was to tell me about some girl he was talking to or flirting with. This happened, pretty much all day and all the time, shish. I sometimes wondered when did Chris take her ass to class or did, she has some type of access to some hidden cameras. Come to think of it I very seldom saw her with books, let along using them to study. It's always that one person that knows everyone's business but don't talk about their own. But Chris was still my girl. Sometimes I liked seeing her going than coming. Her first words would be "Woo girl", I did see Maurice smiling talking to Janet by her locker. Chris had me tripping and flashing back to what she said about the other girls. I really didn't have too many choices in boys, and Chris reminded me every chance she could.

She started naming off a few potentials. I wasn't really feeling her roll call of confirmations. But she started the roll call with Luchan is still dating Janice and it looks serious. My thoughts were so what!! Doug just started dating Barbara and Larry been looking hard at Eunice, Joann finally got tired of Terrance chasing her and so they are in separable, and Brenda and Terry been together forever. I could only look at with a "and so what". Then a name change got my attention. Haven't heard her talk about Rennwick and Boots or about the eyes they only have for each other. Inside my thoughts was blah, blah. But I had to pause and ask what "Boots" real name boots was. Miss Chris had the nerve to look at me as if I asked a duh question, while interrupting her endless roll call. I just remember looking at her well??? She gently smiles at me saying no her name was Rolanda no, no Romolia, and sometimes they called her Ro. She smiles again saying, hell I guess she loved wearing boots. Now she gave me a look requesting permission to continue. I looked at her with this is so boring and annoying look.

I asked myself the question of when Chris is going to stop. Oh, I guess never. Then she goes deeper talking about Roger and Alan are both into sports and school. Marcus can't make any decisions he's too scary. He was so scary that he had been checking Vernita out all year and the year is almost over. He couldn't even decide on how he is gonna to ask her out. I had to add saying that you know Marcus is and Chris spelled out s-l-o. I just had to look at her and ask with knowing it's something I should have passed on where is the "w" … Chris response was because he took too long, and the "w" got tired of waiting. Now the tortoise and the snail were sitting on the side because they had a little side bet going on. They looked at each other shaking their heads and said hey really this is our competition. You know that ain't right as they dap each other. I had to look at Chris and her imagination working, while at the same time showing very little expression.

Do you believe that girlfriend scratched her head saying do we need to have a classroom session or study hall on what you got to work with sister girl to get with Maurice? She was serious and asked again with girlfriend what you gonna do? I could only glare at her. Was she really trying to tell me that my pick from the pool is now a puddle, oh wow? What was Chris thinking that I needed a splash of water to wake my ass up?

Inside I had to admit to myself those were the only guys that act like they have some type of sense. Since she put it that way, I had to ponder my options. So, listening to Chris and given into peer pressure I dated Maurice. I watched Reva show that corner smile adding that it did feel pretty good beating out those other girls. Rita right before we went to the prom we had been talking on the phone and just hung out a lot. I hate to admit I liked hearing his voice on the phone it was so soothing and walking with him while the lookies look at us walking side by side, sometime holding hands. Strange about that was I never held hands like that before not like that. I felt that we had a good connection we talked about a lot of things and anything. There was no topic we couldn't tap into and no arguing just pleasantries. We both talked about what and where we wanted to go in life. He wanted to own his own auto repair garage and I wanted to be in the performing arts. I love singing and acting.

One day Maurice came to me and said that we needed to talk and kinda scared me which was hard to do. I guess I really did care a little something, something for him. He approaches me with such sincerity that got my immediate attention. He said that he really liked me, and I shared that I liked him too. Maurice wanted to share something with me about his family, and you know that really touched me. See our family didn't share a lot of family time or talks just yelling, cussing or silence. Our dinner time was dinner is ready you better come in and eat and that was it.

As I listened to him, he had my full attention. He said that his older two brothers couldn't have any kids and coming from the south where there are big families, they felt embarrassed. I'm looking at him and I feel bad for him because he says that it's something generic and that he couldn't have any kids either. I thought maybe he was kidding and just saying that to get with me. As I looked into his eyes, I realized that he was crying, and I took what he said to heart and for that instance I felt emotions. I thought good, because I didn't want to have any kids either. I wanted to pursue my singing and acting career and perform on stage one day. I embraced him and felt the warmth from him. We had more in common than I thought. He had me and I looked at him different way from that day on. I felt that he had a big heart and he could possibly be for real with this confession. After all who would share and cry about something so intimate.

We went to the prom and when the night was over, he said we need to know each other better if we are going to be together. I told him I didn't want to get pregnant and he needed to use protection. He said Reva I told you that I can't get anyone pregnant my brothers and I have this thing we inherited, and we can't have any kids. For some reason, I had to hear it again for re-enforcement. I thought well he can't get me pregnant and no one would know, right.

He sighed and said let's do this. Well we did this and now here I am. I remember asking her how she felt after doing this. Well there wasn't fireworks or enjoyable or all that, yet not boring. We both hadn't been around too much and that's what it felt like. Well anyway (sigh) I missed two months of my period, and I knew something was wrong. That dark secret, you know the one that brings so much light and more attention, surface. I could only shake my head thinking "damn. My girlfriend Chris is one of the reasons I got my butt in this clinic. I should have gone with my own thoughts, morals and not give into a pretty face and girlfriend's pressure. Hell, my mama drilled and told all us constantly, about she wasn't trying to me nobody's grandma or grandmother. Nope your new little additions, wasn't scheduled into her life, not now or into the future. But for at least eighteen years they will be in your lives. She says she look too good and too young to have some grandchild hanging off her hip. She wasn't ready for that shift. Then the bell ding in my ding dong brain that Maurice said they all had the same father, right?? How in the hell did his ass get here, duh Reva? I agreed with her Maurice came from somewhere. His dad had to be okay to have three sons. Hmm even as naïve as I am that didn't make sense to me either. I set there with my eyes watering to keep from laughing, but she had a good duh point.

As we sat there, I told her what happened with me and Bill. I'm here because I think I might have some type of indigestion. Reva looked at me like I was crazy as she paused her thoughts. She responded indigestion, oh really, hmmm that's different. Wow that's all and all you need is a good burp humph, then she turned her head and just smiled. Maurice left me when I told him I might have indigestion, (she laughed). He went back to Eva, talked briefly to Pat, hung out with loose hips, hit and quit it Lola and tapped Trailblazing Terri and made a cameo with Delilah and Alma. I watched Reva as she told her story. Those thoughts took me back to junior high or high school. The 'tail or trail blazers', like Vernale, Lola and Terri would be called nasty scants or just rachet. You wondered, if they are being paid professionally.

I tune back into Reva continuing saying that her dumb butt is sitting here in this clinic, just because her ears listened to someone else. She shook her head with that corner smile with a slight chuckle continuing beating herself up with her words. I watched her slowly looking around the room saying that she should have went with her first thought of don't do anything. Her words were clear about her dumb butt sitting in those hard ass chairs hanging out in this youth clinic with all these young ladies with indigestion. I asked Reva was she afraid to tell her parents.

She said she lived with her mother and three sisters and two brothers and had very little contact with her dad. Two of her sisters already had kids and her brothers were dealing with baby mama's drama, which was becoming annoying. She said that mom Aberlynda aka Ms. Aberlynda. She said with a straight face that when her mom transformed her eyes merged into one. And that one eye would just hypnotize you. That one big giant eye smack in the center of her forehead would sometimes close slowly. Like some Cyclops eye showing the mirror to her soul. She talked about how she would be disappointed if one of us bounced in her house with ball in their stomach. She made it very clear when her time was available for us. Ms. Aberlynda set down with my other two sisters Joyce and Carol and gave us a verbal beat down of just don't. She said in such a motherly heart felt icicle way, in her normal groughy sounding voice 'Just don't get your ass pregnant". Took her longer to say the sentence than the thought process and landed in the air for our ears only. That one sentence, with a quick second pause as she puffed smoothly on her cigarettes, (while that Cyclops eye rotated slowly and looking at me and my sisters). It felt like that eye looked at us at the same time. Hey Rita, I think it did blink one time slowly.

Reva says out as she looks out the corner of her eye, I think it was me and my sisters that didn't blink, because we were still hypnotized. She had such a warm motherly touch. I used to always be afraid of being frostbitten. In the back of my mind I was thinking she was sharing a little sarcasm with me.

She says with a quick humph my sisters and I slowly looked at each other as we turned away from her hypnotized eye, what was that all about, was she feeling motherly? Next time we should time it. I know that feeling oh so well from the mole in my father's eye that hypnotized us into confessions. Reva said the bottom line was clear from her mother with that one liner, she was gonna get some gone, you were on our own and leave her the hell alone. Wow can you believe all she said was don't get your ass pregnant. What type of sex prevention talk was that? She most had felt some warmth and added, beware of the dogs lurking and hanging out. Again, we thought what was that all about; she just left us hanging in a trance.

Unfortunantely, we had to find out the hard way and that's why I am here. Reva looks around the room and stated how many of us in here are here, because of that one liner sex talk or no talk at all, just leaving us on an assumption that we knew. Rita some of this could have been prevented by just making a little effort to put their feelings of insecurity aside and talk to us. Just because their parents didn't talk to them is no way an excuse to hear or accept. Life is still filled with sex and lies for us to innocently encounter. No direction just you out there blind trying to find light in dark places. We are learning from them about life. We don't know about all this crap. Now here we are starting an extended family, just because no one took the time to say something more than just don't get your ass pregnant. Except for you Rita, you are the exception you just have indigestion.

As I listened closely, I felt her concern, her pain and her disappointment. I could have raised my hand because I had to learn the hard way too. What if this wasn't indigestion?? Man will I be in trouble, and this would be far from confinement to my room and no outside extra fun. Reva said that when her mother finally finished that long puff on her cigarette the damage was already done. Her mother puffed and said that we are done with this conversation and she was on her way out to the club. No hug, no by, no frostbite just the warmth that came from the ice from her heart. My sister Katherine was too young for the talk she still was playing with dolls, it was good to see her innocence was still in her. One thing my siblings agreed on that we will protect her as much as we can.

My baby sister will not end up here and she will get more than that one liner. My Aunt Mildred, (my mother's sisters), did try to tell us and Aunt Little tried to warn us. Only her thing was that the timing was off. We needed that talk sooner. That lack of conversation left us guessing. Just a few more sentences would have prevented us all ending up here in this fine clinic. She told me that my body was precious and don't become someone's used book that has been passed around with unknown owners. But in the back of my mind my thoughts go back to hearing my mother's voice saying if your ass gets pregnant you will be raising your own child. I did my time did my commitment until you all turned 18. Party over for you and now it's party time for me. It's time for me to shake this groove thang, while it can still groove. Now it's my time to party, real time on lady's nights and not rushing home because of a babysitter. Ooh I'm surprised I remembered this hmmm this coffee is good, boy was Reva thoughts real and entertaining. Well, she told them yaw went out there and had them babies then go out there and either get on welfare and parade yourself with your sisters and the other majorettes and march down and get some type of government assistance, (I kind of chuckle on the march thinking back when I marched with the Elks).

I can picture Miss Ruthie yelling, pulling her shorts from between her legs as she was running as fast as her short legs could go. She could have played a nice part in the Wizard of Oz, but always before practice was over, she would be shouting at JoeJoe and running toward him saying he was playing too fast. While her son Yule would just stand there being patient, sometimes just looking at both like they were crazy, or this was a normal activity with them. She kept us all in check, but we all appreciated her because she was the only adult working with us training us on marching, keeping in step and looking good and professional. She made me one of the leaders of the group and I enjoyed it. Miss Ruthie saw something in me at early stage of my young life that I didn't see or feel. My cousin Michelle told Bonnie and myself that they were looking for girls. Miss Ruthie taught us how to stand on our feet for long periods of time because we would be marching far. That training helped when I worked the long hours standing on my feet at McDonalds. Actually, she taught us all about patience, love, team work and life's trials. I was sad to hear that Joejoe had died. I had spoken to him that day after years of not seing him. You never know how close you are to death. Yule had married a good classmate I had known for years that had died as well. I felt for Miss Ruthie and Yule. I can feel my chuckles turn into a smile thinking about the fun we had marching as I look at

Reva, (she wasn't feeling that chuckle and puzzled by my smile). I pick up on Reva repeating her mom's words, on get some money or some jobs, get something cause your asses gets nothing from me, not a thang. No diapers, no pampers, no huggies, no child support just no. And while you out there your butt needs to get some type of child care, because this is not a child care center or your personal daycare. I am and will not be your live-in babysitter, nanny, nanna, granna, granny none of all that and that she would keep it moving. Yep making moves on the dance floor, snapping her fingers, and shaking her ass.

She always called me Dorothy from the Wizard of Oz. In her grouchy rough sounding voice, would cough out, Miss Dorothy it's not that kind of party. I got places to go and men to see. Miss Dorothy it's not that kinda party up in here not now, not today and tomorrow isn't promising either and don't look for it next week either, so you know that next year is probably out uh. I don't know why she repeated herself I heard her the first time she coughed it out. That lady really needs to take a cigarette break. She raised her kids and there was no more room in her life to keep taking care of someone else's problems. No child, no tears, not today, tomorrow not looking good either. Then she added, oh did I say next year that my calendar was booked too. Then she would add this isn't Oz and I'm not Dorothy or the wizard and we are not in Kansas and neither are you, (while she tried clicking your heels and see if we both disappeared). Don't you know my momma closed her eyes and clicked her heels as said nope I'm still not Dorothy, but you are looking like her right now Dorothy and we are still here looking at each other.

She said her mother showed a corner smile and direct eye contact ask where's Auntie M aka Auntie Myrtle. Reva says with her corner smile, (thinking and trying not to show what she was really thinking in her eyes), wanting to ask her a simple question. While her mother yacks, she wanted to ask her where's Glenda and was she missing her broom??? Reva acts like she's licking her finger pretending to check the wind direction and flight schedule for her broom departure. She adds an added touch of looking at a flight schedule book saying oh she flies; Monday thru Friday and the broom flight is scheduled for anytime. But add a new co-pilot on weekends in form of a hoover. That hoover will get her to her mental destination faster. For that instance, I thought about how my mother would lend her broom or hoover to my niece Marqate. Maybe she got tired of borrowing the broom and invested several more on her own. I think she upgraded to customized brooms in a designer type fashion. She started young with a play broom, but the attitude didn't match a child that was playful and behold she made it before the age of two to top flight flyer.

Reva went on about how her mother went on and on about this Wizard of Oz movie. She was in to this movie. Then she started on me about that if the boy left you hanging then he left from just being a Total dog and turned into the cowardly lion, then skipped down the road to become a scouny scared crow then turned right into just an empty tin man. Then her broom swept as she added tin man without no heart, woo, woo and woo. In my mind I was saying I get it Aberlynda. I hear you I'm standing right here, mommy. She kept talking with adding that now you had to grow up and handle your business your problem, your turn Dor-o-thee I wanted to say Miss Dorothy please, since she kept calling me Dorothy. That what's done in the night got you nine months to life. With that line she paused added that's a long ass sentence uh. Hell, add another eighteen years plus ten to that because they don't leave as she looks over at her sister and brother's pictures.

Now follow that yellow brick road, go on Dorothy ease on down the road because you missed the curve and the yellow brick road should be a straight shot. Don't you know she was trying to dance like they did in the movie? I was not being amused as much as she was. I got the hint and the warmth from that mother and daughter quality and story time. Actually, I had to step away, so I wouldn't get frostbite from the chill coming off the ice sickles of her heart. Every now and then I saw drips from the ice melting. The Oz uh wow mom got jokes maybe she should be a comedian, right nope. Just thinking about what Reva's mom said made me chuckle then, just like it's doing now. When I laughed, she just looked at me with a straight face. She wasn't feeling no humor just like she looked at me when I said I had indigestion. To this day I still remember the expression and her response. She didn't find any humor, nor did she ever laugh through our conversation. Reva occasionally strectched a corner smile. Although I didn't know what my mother would say but I don't think it would be those words.

Reva said she loved her mother, but she could be a cold piece of work. Especially with some wine and a new boyfriend. I couldn't believe how calm Reva was and the peace she had on her face. Like this was a part of life and hmm she got caught when the lights came on and accepted the consequences.

I looked at her as she was telling the story and wondered how many other women were in the same situation; how many could raise their hands saying how they got here. As I looked around the clinic, I saw dull gray walls with faded painted flowers on them walls and dried plants. The place did smell of pine sol, lighting was bright and was clean but there was no warmth coming through. Everyone was dressed in clean colorful scrubs which brighten up the room, but everything seemed routine and real old outdated pictures covered the gray prison color walls and out dated boring magazines spread out on the tables.

Well the conversation ended when Reva's name was called. I watched her get up without hesitation. She looked at me and said well you should be rid of that indigestion in about nine months, (showing that signature corner smile), and don't forget to have a boy or girl name for your indigestion and a social security number too why not. Humph, why not that indigestion might need a job one day. Reva handled herself very well as she walked down the corridor as if she was just walking down the hallway to class. I heard my name called right after Reva. To me that corridor looked long, dark, cold and silent. The only noise I heard was the echoing of my fast beating heart. With my eyes, wide open and one big sigh for the road I was hoping she was going to tell me it's was just indigestion.

That's right they give patients privacy and she didn't want people to feel embarrass for me being silly and sitting here this long for indigestion. Yep that's it but why does this corridor still look long dark and cold. Snap back Rita its just indigestion. Reva didn't know what she was talking about a name humph and social yeah right. They just need to give me some medicine, so I can have that one big burp and I will feel so much better and no will know my close call. What was wrong with me making up excuses and hiding behind fear? Was my naive thinking starting to surface? Silence entered the room as the closing of the door sounded like a vault slamming closed with a loud echoing sound that out beat the pounding sounds of my heart. My body felt like an out of body experience and my mind took off running.

I remember seeing Nurse Rochelle wearing flower top scrubs and I was laughed about maybe she should take the flowers from her scrubs and place them on the wall. Oops, no reaction, not even a smile from her at all. Well she took me into the room and closed the door. I remember the echoing sound as it shut. With that loud echoing sound, I knew it wasn't for a how are you doing. She stood there motionless. She didn't have any type of expression. I found myself an unsettling feeling surface. I looked slowly around the room. The white walls were bright, but the room felt so cold and empty. Woo just thinking about the coldness makes this coffee feel and taste good. Looking around this cold room I noticed and read some of the posters. One poster said do you know why you are here? Other posters showed newborn babies and pregnant women, some had smiles and others had frowns. When I looked up one said did you use protection and if you did then why are you here?? I laughed at that poster. I knew why I was there because I had indigestion. I kinda smiled to myself and as Nurse Rochelle looked at me. Again, her face showed no emotions as if this was a routine discussion.

I tried to make small talk to ease my nervousness. I told her that her name was pretty. She said thank you without looking up. I asked again to try and ease my anxiety, the meaning of her name. Inside I was thinking well Miss I hear you but don't see you finally grunted a response. Her response was short/brief and direct. She said in a low voice that her name means little rock. Ooh, her tone was very professional, and again with no eye contact and now add no volume. I replied with hmm that's interesting to know. Hmm I didn't even hear another grunt noise in a response from what I said. I thought to myself hmm I sure would like to hit her with one of my imaginary rocks, or just thump her. If I thump her with my imaginary rock, then Miss Meany then maybe she will hear me. I bet that would get her attention. She took that nervous thought and smile from me.

I just sat there and continued to look around the room and kept my thoughts to myself. Nurse Rochelle asked me when was my last menstrual cycle? I sat there trying hard to search somewhere in my brain when was my last period. Were there any events that would remind me? It's been such a long time I thought I had one last month, but that's not the case because I'm sitting here with this emotionless nurse waiting for an answer. Then just like that my brain cells returned, and I recovered from my heart attack with a clearing of my throat I told her. She glanced at me saying that my test came back positive. What did she mean, me not knowing for that instance what that meant? Until she took out some type of wheel and told me I would be due January 27th or 29th.

I don't remember the conservation after that or the sound of the nurse leaving. She just left the room and for a few numb minutes I just sat there. No thoughts and no emotions. I found myself slowly walking down the cold corridor. I paid little attention to hearing them calling the next victim by the name of Pearline. As I left the room gathering my thoughts, I glanced at Pearline and watched her slowly rise from her chair. She had the same look of fear and uncertainty in her expression. We both glanced at each other with a nervous type smile. Before I left, I had to take a break. I set down not noticing the lady sitting next to me. My thoughts were racing, and emotions were numb. She looked at me with a big howdy and started talking. Charlotte introduced herself with a southern drawl and high energy. She looked at me with a beautiful smile and said you're pregnant huh. My grandma Ruby and my mama Sybil knew before I did those silly ladies and I thought I didn't have a life.

I gave her a puzzled look thinking wow is she related to my mother. Charlotte burst out laughing they both kept an eye on the tampon and sanitary napkin box like they were looking at their favorite soap opera. She laughs as the world turns around my silly self. I really wasn't fretting about much of nothing. Girly I didn't know those boxes had collected that much dust. I pretty much had forgotten about those monthly reminders with my silly self. They had so much dust I coughed as they blew the evidence on me. Missy I got the hint. I was busted like I just got caught falling on the pig. Those, ladies had a heap of laughter saying have you ever seen a dusty tampon box. Girlie you suppose to use them every month no dust supposed to be there if you were using those napkins/tampons. Heck girlie the box should be empty that's why we only buy them monthly girlie. Boy they even put a dot on the calendar when my period started. My dumb butt saw those dots and just thought they were printing mistakes on that silly oh calendar. Again, it's just me being silly. My goodness I didn't know those dots represented me. Hmm who would imagine that, but them silly ladies? Well those two-little old ladies ganged up on me like ants on a pile of sugar. I knew this morning sickness was more than I just needed a big burp.

Well my beau, Johnny Lee and I talked about baby names when I told him I might be having a baby. Heck girlie I didn't know if I was or not, I just knew I wasn't feeling right. Smells had me feeling kind of dizzy. Johnny Lee smacked his leg and grabbed me like he was hugging a bear lifting me off my feet. She laughed and said Johnny Lee if you don't stop squeezing me this baby gonna pop right out. He let out a big laugh when he finally let me breath again. He was cheesing so much his teeth were blinding me. I laughed yelling at Johnny Lee close your mouth you are blinding me JL. Charlotte starts rambling about so many names with a lot of energy. Well, if it be a boy, we gonna name him Reese Edward or Monroe Joe or maybe Williamlee, if it be a girl Tammijune or Glynda Rose or maybe Linda Sue. Now Johnny Lee daddy, Robert Joe and mama Inajoy would be happy about a new one running through their home. Actually, they wanted a whole heap of grandkids. He told them before I even knew. That phone was ringing off the hook being happy and all about the news. Good grief did everyone know before the baby carrier knew. That's why I'm here either I is or is I not expecting a youngin. Either way I just need to prove to them that they might be wrong or right. Or maybe I might have that indigestion too. Don't matter me cuz Johnny Lee amd me will still be stuck to each other. Two of Johnny Lee's brothers Frank and Turner (aka Truck) already talking about getting the baby ready for horseback riding. His Uncle Albert and Uncle Erwin want to get a horse ready for his nephew or niece. Aunt Inez wanna know what the baby will be, so she could knit a blanket. His other Uncle Carol and Aunt Lillie and grandparents Grandpa Fletch, and Miss Zonnie were happy that they are alive to see the next generation. Uncle Daniel and Uncle Aaron and Cousin Wesley or was it Cousin Butch and Cousin Carl wanted to cook up a feast to celebrate this youngin being born and me being pregnant.

They were wondering which son out of seven was gonna give them their first grandchild. A course Johnny Lee wanna get a couple of dogs to grow with our baby. He wants to name them Tommy, Hammer and Day and I thought why not have a girl, pup huh and call her Nala. Wow I can't believe I'm gonna be a momma. A little somebody is going to be calling me mama, girlie that would be great, me a mama. How about you? Before I could answer she just kept on talking not skipping a beat or breath. Charlotte's laugh had so much energy and love. She really was very happy about her having a baby. The daddy was happy, her family and his were happy too. It was good feeling to hear all that support she had. I needed to talk to Charlotte because for that instance I took my mind off me and my situation. She had to me cracking up.

So, her ma made her come to the clinic to start taking care of their grandbaby. Charlotte continued with her boyfriend Johnny Lee gonna be happy cuz he wanna marry me and raise a bunch of more youngins. Have all of us living on a farm with fresh air and room to run, raising horses and milking cows. Oh, heck girly why not I guess I'm gonna do it. It's not like we didn't think this might happen. We were using protection; I guess it was supposed to happen. Now that's a big oops. Oh well that's why I'm here missy. We both love each other and why not we family and all. Johnny Lee and I been talking to each other since we were knee high. Couldn't imagine we would be hitched and joined at the hips like this. Funny, missy how you think you just playing in the pond and now we both will be playing real house. When they called Charlotte's name she hopped up and switched and twisted right down the hall into the room like she had been asked to dance or milk a cow, I guess. After talking with her I realized it doesn't make any difference of your background or culture as a mom we are all the same. As I was leaving, they called out the name Penny. I watched her jump up and we made eye contact I smiled at her and she whispered thank you.

Chapter 3
My Mom Knew

As I approached my car, I pondered the thought of how I was and had to tell Bill. Sure, wasn't indigestion, damn. Where should I go from here, yep straight to see??? I got the courage to tell him that I was pregnant with our first child. When I told Bill at first, he didn't believe me. I didn't believe it myself. Wow was I ready to be a mother at the age of 19 young. Well at least I was out of school. I just remember us arguing about the pregnancy. I remember him saying he didn't come here to get married and I replied I didn't know you were coming here to get me pregnant either. This is not always about you…

In the back of my mind I was thinking how I can tell my mom and my dad about this. I wasn't showing but my mother kept a good eye on me and watched my every move. Her eyes stared, and my mind was saying and screaming "you're right I am and stop staring at me go away" while running and pulling my hair out. I stayed away from the house, hoping I would not encounter my mom alone. I tried to avoid home and her. I found things to do and reasons to stay away and places to go. I was still in college and working so at times it wasn't too hard but on the other hand. Sigh, that was really becoming hard she seemed to be everywhere in my mind, my thoughts and presence. When did she tire, when did she take her body to bed? Why was she keeping her eyes on me? This coffee still is too hot, just like my situation with my mom aka Sheryl. Now Sheryl didn't play, by time you realized she was there it was way too late. Like some type of magic poof. Mom could have easily shared the same ice heart as Reva's mom, hmm could they be related and not know.

There was a time when she told us to clean up our room. A course being young and silly adding not listening didn't give too much thought to my mom telling us to clean up. I was just a kid and I just wanted to play outside. She eased our troubles she burned all our toys in a fifty-five-gallon barrel in the backyard no thoughts and no emotions. You could see the plume of smoke. We thought it was leaves burning, but the smell was different, it was our toys that were up in a blaze. I can still see the embers floating in the air. She burned our toys, every one of them Christmas, birthday, all toys up in smoke. Now our toys turned into a pile of ashes and melted plastic. Did we learn from that oh yes? Instead of smelling autumn leaves burning I smelled melted hard plastic. I remember running upstairs looking under the bed for my dolls and my toys. I look at her probably with confused eyes and mind asking her about our toys. She looks like a mean mother with the broom, with drips of water melting from around her heart. All she did was look at me while repeating I told you to clean up your room. Inside I remember thinking who really looks under the bed. Only the rude lady with the broom and I don't mean taking flight or sweeping either way just rude.

My thoughts were that maybe I needed to step back so I wouldn't get frostbite. I should have done the act Reva said she did by taking her two fingers across her mother's heart checking the moisture level. But her mother replied with you thought it was blood. Reva response was no ma'am it was just the preparation coming from your heart and I had to assist with the dripping moisture. Surprisingly her mother response was oh you think that shift is funny, (as she sashays away the same way that Reva did in her walking occasionally around the clinic). Now if I did that type of movement to my mother, those two fingers would be in a sling. My mother really didn't have a sense of humor and very seldom laughed. I guess with her grandmother sleeping with a gun, hammer, switch blade with razor strap under her pillow, I guess there wasn't much room for signs of affection. We hug but anything other than that nah. My sisters were close, and I was the insert in the middle. Man, my mother very seldom took my side. There was one time I remembered Bonnie and I were playing with the burning leaves in the fifty-five-gallon barrel. We would play in the fire heck we were bad and not thinking while playing in the fire with sticks. Then my sister Bonnie accidently hit me near my eye with the burning stick. Now I didn't get this concept of getting chewed out about my eye getting hit by a burning stick. My eye Bonnies' hand and I got chewed out, wow. Bonnie and I are three years apart how did I know I was a kid. We both were playing, and Bonnie hit the burning stick near my eye. Didn't leave a physical mark but left an everlasting one mentally. I still remember it so many years later and can still visualize us playing in the barrel. Yep we knew at an early stage that my mom didn't play. Still to this day she still doesn't play or display any sense of humor or laughter neither does my sister Bonnie. That is something you just don't forget and make sure you listen. I don't think conscious or care ever crossed my mother's mind as she dumped the bag of toys into that fifty-five empty gallon barrel and lit the match. She probably did each toy one by one smiling. Just thinking back my mom face flashed and really was my mind playing with me.

The more I tried to avoid my mother the more it seemed as if my heart would race every time she came around. It would be just a matter of time before I get cornered but until then I had to remind myself to keep it moving Rita. I just kept the same routine going to class, work, and trying not to be caught sleeping too much but, I was so tired and hungry. Wow its going rain all day. The rain is just not going to lighten up today. Just like my big secret. I wished it would lighten up, so I can see the sun. I just had a gut feeling she knew. I wore the same clothes hoping no one would notice my stomach. Only I could feel how tight my clothes were getting. They were beyond snug it was more like help me out here Rita at some point we really need to breath. Every time she passed me, I would look at her with a nervous smile. I had very little eye contact and tried holding in my stomach, and slow down my breathing. Actually, I tried holding my breath and stomach in at the same time and that was a serious ouch. My mother and I were not close and had very little conversation. Hmm to this day we still aren't close and still very limited conversation. I guess somethings just don't change. I love her, but we just don't really like each other. In a small way we are almost alike. I was hoping she would keep that routine up shop, rest or something. My heart would beat so fast I just knew my mother could hear it as it echoed and thumped as hard as my eardrums were pounding. I thought my heart was going to run out of my body and cave in my chest saying this is just too much pressure no really. I can't take this anymore see ya Rita. As I tried to slow my pulse down and hold it together the clock kept ticking. Good grief Rita what are you going to do other than scare yourself with these thoughts? I could only shake my head I really didn't know what to do. How do you tell your parents when you have so much fear inside that is beyond trembling and causes your whole insides to shiver and want to take off? I tried to avoid my mother as much as possible which was becoming harder each day. It seems as if she would pop out of nowhere, which kinda of scared me actually no it did and added more pressure. She normally goes shopping or something why change her routine now, man.

Then one day that I was home with her alone and that day seemed very long. My thoughts and mind felt like a clock ticking slowly like some type of cartoon clock. I felt something strange and that was it my mom approaches me with that dreaded question and the mean look accompanied with her broom. That was when everything left, mind, thoughts, brains and they didn't have time to tell me where I could pick them up. Courage gone, fear stayed, thoughts gone, brain gone, fear stayed and lingered. I was so numb what was left inside didn't shiver. Why couldn't she be out shopping why couldn't I stay gone just a little while longer?

The opportunity that I was so desperately trying to avoid had finally arrived. The question that gets your heart beating faster, followed by headaches, blood rushing through your head, and feeling a little light headed. A nausea feeling set in adding a possible fainting spell to throw off the questions. This was a time I wanted to snatch her broom and fly out of there. That's it she can't ask me anything if I faint come on legs either buckle or run don't just stand there like a possum to the head lights. She said you're pregnant and her words, her voice shattered everything inside of me. I thought I left the building without my luggage or a brick being thrown at a glass window and everything just shatters. I don't remember breathing or taking a breath. All thoughts, feelings I mean everything left fear got the heck out and left me standing there with mid-air, mid-day adding numbness, wow another nummy attack. I just looked at her and her words followed with the words echoed that I heard all my life I'm gonna tell your daddy, aka Little Eddie. My heart started back eventually enough to combine with my feet and brain saying get the heck out the door. Right now, I heard it yelling to rush out the door right now get some gone honey go and don't look back run like you did in high school. Courage had left, and I saw it running in front of me, coward. As I think back then what I know now I wouldn't have made it. How could I out run an angry pissed off track star. I was going against family history. Mommy who could run, who knows how old she was maybe in her seventies and, my mother wanted to be a PE teacher and in good shape and let's add pissed. You would have thought I was running the 100 like I did back in the day. Yes, if I sprint to the door, she might not catch me, but with my luck the door would be locked. Nah she'll hit me in the back of my head with her shoe before I make it the door. She was always popping me with those shoes, and would she pop me again?? She moved so fast I never saw her hand reach down to her foot. When she gave them to my daughter, I burned those boogers with a fast gladness. Wow I cut out so fast I don't remember hitting the door or hearing it slam, or anymore words from her. I just remembering I got in my Vega and jetted to Bill's place. Not looking behind, me and with a stiff neck I kept my eyes looking forward. I was too afraid to look around. Courage was still running as I passed up coward.

I told Bill what happened and ask could I stay there. Bill let me stay but he treated me like a live- in lover really kinda too late for all that. Maybe his thought was the damage was already done. All I heard replaying repeatedly in my mind was I'm gonna tell your daddy. That just played over and over like a broken record those words just wouldn't go away no matter how hard I tried to alter my thoughts and words. Those words kept returning echoing in my soul and consumed my thoughts. I knew what came with that was punishment, but this was a situation that sending me to my room wasn't going to work. Actually, it was more of the unknown that really bothered me because I never been in this unknown and it was evidence, I did something in the dark that surfaced to the light. When you think back how much pain could be inflicted when you are already an emotional wreck and your body and emotions are constantly changing. How do you wake up from this nightmarish dream? Woo I just wanted to wake up and open my eyes sit up in the bed from a cold sweat saying man that was a bad dream. Then lay it back down with a smile pulling the covers over my head and go into a deep slumber and a warning don't sleep with Bill again. This wasn't a dream but my reality. This was not a dream, not girlish thoughts of having a family this was very real and you can't run away. I had to open my eyes and see clearer of what I was going to do. Now I had to wake up, stand up and face them and the world on the secret I kept for weeks that lead into months. Courage came back on its' own and actually was lying right next to me saying what are we going to do. My mental response was now oh it's we. My parents and my family had high expectations of me more than I had for myself. I was the first child to graduate early and go straight to college. I had a taste of college now I will savor in the flavor of motherhood.

How could I face them with the shame and this disappointment of my actions? I was so ashamed because I saw how they treated my sister when she had two children out of wedlock at a young age. As I'm looking at Bill with all these emotions and questions going through my head, I got enough courage to tell him I would do this without him. I don't think he had a clue of what I was physically and mentally what I and my mind and body was going through. It seemed like each part of my body was competing for attention. I had to dissect this, so my mind and thoughts wouldn't make me a basket case. I stayed at Bill's for a few days still going to school and work as if nothing happened, but the fear inside was still there. Although, in the back of my mind I knew so many things were happening I just needed a mental break. I had to calm myself down, so I could redirect my thoughts and my new focus. I really had to do some real heavy thinking. It wasn't like the security you had when you could go to your parents and they help you out. I was scared of them and everything that went with it. As I arrived to work nervously looking around for my dad to pop in at the bank as he had done some time ago when I worked at McDonalds. What would I do if he showed up? I remember one time he came to work when I let Bill drive my car and my father saw him. Both my parents were upset. I didn't understand then what I know now it was about the insurance, liability and responsibility. My dad showed up at my job when I worked at McDonalds and just set in the lobby watching me.

I eventually left Bill's place and went home to face the firing squad. After all I did miss home and being in my own bed. I wasn't happy living with Bill because he was being so mean, and this living situation wasn't working. We both had to look at the reality. Only one thing I was feeling the pressure and I couldn't walk away and throw my hands up and move on. He lived with his aunt and grandparents and there really wasn't any privacy. His Aunt Tracy moved in with her two set of twins. Twin girls were Joann aka JoJo, Judy Ula aka JU and the baby boy twins Sean Terrell aka ST and Marshallee aka LeLe. She left her husband umpteen times and moved in. Her children were very polite just like everyone in the household. I never felt like a stranger when I went there. I guess that was why I went there, my other home. They didn't judge me but accepted me with love and hospitality. It was an embrace I still get from them, nothing but love. Not that we needed to hide our situation of us it was now in the light. They really didn't worry me they were actually very kind as they understood and respected me and my situation. I was blessed to have Bill's mother Naomi accept and not judge me. She was down to earth, beautiful inside and out still to this day. I have nothing but love and respect for her. Her husband Phil was nice and very straight forward. He kind of intimidated me and to this day he still does but I loved them both. I was afraid about being pregnant due to the fact everyone in Phil's family were twins and his mother was a twin. There was Phil, Paul, Pat, and Pittman, and the girls were Ruth and Rose. Naomi told me that she had always had concerns about getting pregnant and how many babies she would be delivering. She had the two children my Bill and his sister another Rita.

Bill was kind of numb to our reality. His parents were happy about having their first grandchild. I had to go and talk to my parents and looked at the disgust on their faces. I always thought my parents looked so good together. They too made a beautiful couple and worked long hard hours together. My mother had my brother early and somehow, she forgot or maybe she didn't want to remember. Did I repeat her history or was I starting my own? How soon we forget and block the visual from coming into the present as a reminder. My mom just kept saying what about her. I felt her pain and tried to understand her disappointment, but this time it wasn't about her it was about me and my unborn child. Just thinking about that as I slowly sip this coffee, I looked just like my mom even had her personality. She was looking at herself in me with being pregnant at a young age. That reflection of her past scared her as she looks at her reflection in the present in me. My brother Charles or Chuck who ever come first was present at the wedding, but no one could see him until about less than nine months later. Hmm imagine that little hidden secret that lurked behind that beautiful white dress. Then I thought really Sheryl aka Mom did you forget about the white dress. I saw the wedding pictures now this is a really and come on now. Can you cast that first stone? Somewhere in there we stopped holding hands and just skipped totally around the issue of history kinda repeated itself not once both at least twice, EJ and now me. Some where we should have had a serious conversation about preventing history from coming back. Not a history moment but a real reality check. I reflect on what Reva said about how many girls in this clinic missed that talk. Not the talk from Reva's mom Aberlynda/Theresa of don't get your ass pregnant, but a real sit-down conversation and setting all pain aside.

The thoughts rushing through my head was can I have a me moment and couldn't concentrate on my mother's words. I have something growing inside of me. I can't eat what I want and feeling nauseated all day and can't sleep on my stomach. Actually, I felt myself tossing and turning trying to sleep, it felt like a wrestling match with my mattress and pillows. My clothes are getting tighter and I'm stuck on dumb right now. I had nieces and nephews but that is not the same as raising your own child. I could always send them back to their mamas or daddies.

The pressure was on me pressure from my parents, school studies and my job. My body was now changing and growing every day with a bigger food appetite. I now had someone depending on me. Rita now it's time for you to grow up and get real with your situation. Welfare was not the answer or option. I now had to accept my responsibilities and turn this situation into a better one. I would talk and read to my child while gently rubbing my stomach. I knew she liked it because I could feel her kicking. She was my incentive to want and need to work extra hours at the bank and hit the pavement for another part-time job. Not too many people wanted to hire an eight-month pregnant woman. Well Sears did for the Christmas season. Working both jobs kept me busy and my mind off Bill and focused more on taking care of my child. The rain finally stopped just like my concerns about what Bill was doing and who was he doing it with.

The part-time job consists of me working with another pregnant lady wrapping gifts. Another lady worked there by the name of Sheri she kept us spiritually grounded. I made it through the hot, humid Oakwood summer and was entering the winter months and my due date was late January. I worked with a lady that had a different but similar story from mine. She was a teacher and had put her husband through college and when he graduated, he left for another woman. How rude could that be? When she needed him the most and made so many sacrifices he just up and left. Now she is bringing a new life alone. I guess we both had the same thing in common only difference was our age. Pregnant and single wow really (sigh). Her mind was must be going crazy and emotions racing too. On this nothing really separated us. I couldn't point the finger because it came back on me. He left her pregnant confused and broke. I couldn't understand her situation too well because I still had the security of living at home with my parents. How could he leave knowing she is bringing in the world their first child? Her and her husband had a love connection coming into the world in form of their child. Once he finished medical school, he left her for a younger nurse graduate. I really couldn't understand but hurt for her.

Well, I cut back on my class schedule, so I could prepare for the birth of my child. Driving was becoming difficult, so I was limited in my travel. Walking was becoming difficult due to water and weight gain. I felt and looked like a walking bell with a head attached. I remember one night my mom had to come and pick me up from work because I couldn't drive. Bill wasn't available, and I really didn't want to call him but had to get home. The store was closed, and he did not answer, and my mind started wondering what he was doing and who was he doing? When my mom picked me up all she did was fuss about Bill. I was so tired, and my feet were hurting. So, all that fussing sounded like Charlie Brown's teacher, blah blah, and blah. I remember trying to hold my breath slightly, so she wouldn't hear the sighs and my thoughts wouldn't accidently flow out and tell her how I really was feeling. I really didn't want to hear it. I was just as tired as she was mad. She wasn't saying anything I didn't already know or haven't heard on a continuous basic. The sun is trying to come through. Well I made many purchases for my baby and started saving as much as possible. I didn't want to depend on Bill for anything or burden my parents anymore. It wasn't easy, having to deal with the looks, stares, criticism from family, friends and the community that really hurt. They act as if I couldn't hear them nor at one point did, they really care. It wasn't about their feelings and opinions. I had to constantly redirect my thoughts from their pain and disappointment. I'm pregnant now and I had someone depending on me, Rita aka mom in training. The people you loved didn't know the pain of hearing again and again and over and over, their on-going criticism. The hurt of hearing their disappointment as if you couldn't see or hear, feel their verbal thoughts. I had a head start by graduating early from high school. College bound then I pushed myself back. I didn't need anyone to continue to push me down. I needed someone to help me up and understand what my mind and body was going through. Sometimes I would kick myself. I didn't need anybody else's foot embedded in the center of my back.

All Bill did was watch as if he was viewing me from out in the audience in a comfortable theatre chair. I didn't see him too much while I was pregnant, and my parents watched to see if Bill was coming around. I was hoping that he would prove them wrong on their opinion on him. Why does he always prove them right? As my body grew and the girlish figure ran away, I now looked like a bell with a head. I was feeling like a ding dong and the chimes rung inside my head. I was butt and gut and couldn't see my feet but could feel them swell. I had to wear slip on shoes because I couldn't bend to tie my shoes. I ate everything in sight. I had a huge appetite especially for a big bag of homemade fries from my favorite place called Bronco's. Hmmm big bags of French fries and double cheese burger had to get my meat group and starch in there. The greasier the bag the better the yum. Occasionally I would call Bill just to hear his voice and hoping that he is alone. I didn't want to hear any giggling in the background or try and visit him only to be asked to leave because he had company.

I took a chance and I toiled with that voice telling me not to go over to see Bill. My inside voice quieted down, as I walked into Bill's house. What could it hurt? After all this was my second home and plus, I'm carrying our first child. I walked in smilng and hoping to get a smile from Bill in return. I walk into my second home only to see two shapely women talking to him as if I wasn't in the room. They looked through me as if I was invisible. That was a thought I had all my life didn't like the feeling reoccurring now this was not the time. I don't think they even gave me a thought with their glances as they continued with their conversations. They made me feel invisible again, along with ignoring the pain displayed on my face. Inside my pain held hard to my insides and then my heart cried for me. They wouldn't let the tears show on my face they had me covered. The numbness helped me show dignity as I was preparing to leave. Before leaving I looked at their figures and remembered how I used to have one similar. I didn't know which one was dating Bill; there wasn't time for an introduction because at that point I really didn't matter to them or Bill. I was treated as if I had never entered the room. I felt the annoyance from him, as he rushed over to ask me to leave. Right in front of them I hear their laughter with giggling and small chatter about me. Yes, my insides had my back as I cried inside the tears never surface for their entertainment. No show time today but I should have left him and exited with a real good performance. That was always something that kicked me in the butt of what I should have done or said to make me feel better, but no Rita you let others benefit from your pain. To this day their faces are still a blur just as mine was to them that day.

Sometimes it's hard to see through the storm. Hmm, starting to rain hard just like the storm that made a cameo into my life. I always heard that expression of not knowing when to come in from out of the rain. As silly as I was, I didn't know where the umbrella was and plus, I enjoyed having the rain hide my tears. But the rain couldn't hide the redness in my eyes. One thing Bill's company did know I was pregnant with his child. Now, that was my small victory and I was large enough for them to tell I was very pregnant. Wow, what battle did I really win, considering I still had to leave? As I left Bill's place feelings hurt, stupid, embarrassed, and wondering could this get any worse? Yes, it did as I walked out the door feeling like crap, I look up just to see my grade school friend Joel. He was smiling as usual with his country accent saying that he threw ya out again huh. As I looked at him with a half nervous smile, thinking I wish your country butt would shut up. Like I really needed to be reminded of being asked, to leave, (what I called my second home) again. I often wondered did Joel watch and wait for me to come out just to greet me with that. Unfortunately, this happened a lot. Eventually I gave up and stop making cameos at Bill's place. My reality set in that it was going to be me and my child. I guess Bill seeing me reminded him of what happened, and he didn't want to be reminded of his responsibilities. I remembered how I would just smile and went home feeling defeated, tired and mentally exhausted. I wanted to be with Bill, and he made me feel unwanted.

There were so many nights I cried myself to sleep. Didn't know then this would be my way of life living with Bill… My parents were not happy with me or the other relatives that I disappointed. I had to see the disappointment on their faces. They didn't know that the looks, comments were embedded in my spirit. And from time to time their expressions would resurface in my thoughts and occasionly display visual replays. Through my pregnancy, I would talk to my child. I wanted her or him to know that she/he was not a disappointment. We grew together and shared emotions. My child was not any type of disappointment to me. I was confused about the delivery and scared at the same time. I heard from other women I went to school with saying the delivery is not bad. Then an old girlfriend of my brother name, Kathy made it real plain direct and sounded so painful. She said Rita they are pulling something from between your legs, how do you think that might feel? Wow that gave me a big sigh, eye and mouth opener with an ouch. Now I'm scared and even more confused.

I kept up with all my clinic visits and prenatal vitamins the various doctors that examined me, said my baby was sounding and looking good. Although it felt lonely going for my visits, I wanted to share the good news with someone, anyone to let them know how happy I was feeling with this new life developing inside me. So, I had become to know the nurses and enjoyed their enthusiasm with me. Now that I think back, they were human too and got caught up in the same old routine. So, when I went to the prison looking clinic with faded flowers, I greeted the nurses by their first names. They would look at me in shock that their names were mentioned. I watched other patients come in look at them and they would look back without a word other than saying their names for their appointments. It's like when you go to the store and they tell you to have a good day, not looking at you and in the same breath saying next before you even gather your bags. I learned from the clinic people really do like to hear their names. Okay Rita think of some of the nurse's name. Ooh it's been so long, now there was Ovada, Meredith, Velvet, Delores, and my favorite Marsha. They took an ultra sound and gave me a copy of my baby. Wow, to see the life in you in black and white was an uplifting feeling. I saw the head, stomach, fingers and a smile. It was good to see that he/she was happy. To hear the heartbeat sound so strong and watched the movement. I saw and captured the life that I was bringing into the world. My reality into motherhood was being developed in black and white. Sometimes I would hope that Bill was here to share in the excitement or be there, so I wouldn't feel so alone. It was lonely going to the classes and clinics by yourself. I wasn't too alone there were other ladies sitting solo, but that didn't help with the empty feelings.

It was important that I attend these classes for myself and my child. I didn't know the sex of my child. Just thankful my child was giving a good sounding heartbeat. They said it might be a girl due to the rate of the heartbeat. I prayed for a girl. When I did talk to Bill which was very rare, he wanted the baby named after him. My dad wanted his name in there somewhere. Wow, now a new different type of pressure from two people that couldn't stand one another. Yep, that just added to the pressure that already existed. I prayed for a girl that would settle all of this. Regardless of my fear my child will be arriving when he/she is ready. I managed to save money along with purchasing baby supplies. Storee and Stacy from the bank threw a surprise baby shower that helped a lot. I worked up to one week before my due date. When the date drew nearer the support started to return. My parents started showing love along with my family and friends. The rest of my family and friends watched me, as I grew up and handled everything with style, energy and determination to make this situation better. Prayer helped, and love sealed it.

Well I went passed my due date, now it can happen at any time. Anticipation was killing me and not knowing the sex of my child added to the emotional high. I was too scared to go anywhere thinking that my water might burst and deliver in some supermarket with dirty feet. I sat there wondering what the delivery would be like and holding my daughter for the first time. Hmm said daughter and the ultra sound said a girl. But that wasn't a gurantee because mistakes can happen. I had a friend that thought she was pregnant with one. Then all sudden she gained weight found out she was having twins, but when she delivered, she gave birth to triplets, because one was hiding. Ooh I still had to keep in my mind how twins ran in Bill's family. Pretty soon I will no longer have to rub my stomach and talk to my daughter hoping she could really hear me but will be holding my daughter for the first time. I will finally get to see what was growing inside of me. What would she look like? What would her voice sound like? Would she like me? Will I be a good mother? Just like a cloudy day I'm glad the storm passed over. You just don't know when or if it is going to rain. Will I know the time? All I heard you will know.

Well, I knew at one o'clock in the morning it was time. I told my mother I think it's time. Out of habit I was going to take a shower. I was told your feet and underwear should be clean. When I closed the door, my mother was yelling let's go. I called Bill and surprisingly he met me at the hospital. I was hoping I would get Doctor Deck. He was my favorite doctor, but there was no guarantee what doctor would be on duty. As I was being prepped, Bill and I went into the delivery room leaving my mother outside and upset. I was in pain and wasn't dealing with her emotions. I just remember that it felt good to see Bill's face. As I was told to push, and I saw the smiling eyes of Doctor Deck and I smiled and pushed. This pushed felt like a long bowel movement with back pain and strong cramps. I didn't scream just kinda ooh and hum. But pain was there and crying and screaming wasn't an option for me. I had to show Bill that I was okay. Bill's smiling twinkling eyes were now focused on me as I pushed our child into life.

When Sierra was born, she looked like Bill's twin. I remember saying all that work and she looks just like him. She had his beautiful almond shaped light brown eyes that blinked at me as I smiled at her, wanting them to hurry up and give me my daughter, so I can hold her, embrace her and give her a big hug and kiss. Sierra's expression was why did you take me out of my comfort, and who are all these people.

Bill saw the birth of our first child and fell in love with her and I saw love again for me in his eyes. I saw him hold her with a tear coming from his eye. I watched as she held his baby finger and Sierra didn't let go. I watched Bill's eyes fill up with water as he just broke down and said that she is so beautiful. I didn't know he was capable of having those kinda feelings. Now that was pleasing to see. She was so beautiful and smiled with deep dimples like Bill. While I was in the hospital the nurses were very nice. When I held Sierra for the first-time emotions over whelmed me and I cried, because it was all worth it. It was time to prepare to leave and I had packed the clothes I once wore before Sierra was born. I just knew I was going to leave with that girlish figure again. Actually, I was looking forward to putting them back on again. Again, my naïve nature really thought I would be going home in the clothes I wore before I was pregnant. Wrong I had to wear my maternity clothes home. I would take Sierra to a freshly painted neon bright pink bedroom and a baby bed ready for her all done by my dad. During my pregnancy, my dad was cool, disappointed, but he still was my dad. I probably could have shared my feelings, but I didn't know how to talk to him like I used to. Guilt had a good hold on all my emotions and had out beat fear. We were always close and once the disappointment went away, we both laughed again together. I reflect and still smile of how my father would look in the mirror at the same time singing how fine he was and pause and turn his face from side to side singing again yep I'm still so fine. I would watch him as a child shaving. Funny I still like watching men shave as I hear the song playing in my mind of my dad singing how he was so fine.

My fathered picked me up from the hospital. Really wasn't surprise Bill didn't show up. Sierra and I were finally going home. As my father drove, I held my daughter looking out the window thinking about my future with my daughter. I was so overprotective I barely put Sierra in her baby bed my dad assembled. She slept with me sometimes lying on my chest. I wanted her to hear my heartbeat as I felt hers and the warmth that came from her small body. I was so afraid of crib death and I wanted her near me. I wanted to feel and hear her heart beat and feel her breath on my face and inhale that baby fresh smell. I'm a mom now play time is over. Now I had an alarm clock called Sierra and my life has a new beginning. When I held her, I would feel her love just filled my heart and again I tell myself that it was all worth it. Now, I was finally holding a tiny body that was formed inside of me and made me realized I was blessed. Sierra was tiny and beautiful, and I always enjoyed holding her and watching her sleep.

I stayed at my parent's house and my mother helped me so much with Sierra. She would always come into the room just to give her a kiss before she went to work. It felt good to see my mother happy and smiling before she went off to work. I saw that she had some warmth in her. I fed Sierra and did the best I could, with what I observed with my nieces. I would warm the bottle in a hot bowl of water or on the stove. My mother asked me when you do you give her water. I just fed her milk again I didn't know. I guess people just assume you know. I didn't and I'm glad she asked. Classes weren't available for new mothers, but I was open to assistance with raising Sierra. In so many ways I was on my own, learning and growing. Bill's lack of actions and no interest became an eye opener and I moved on without him. I missed him but couldn't afford to savor on that emotion. Someone was depending on me and I wasn't going to let Sierra down. I went back to work full-time as a teller/new accounts working everyday, but in need of a babysitter. I didn't want to be on government assistance. I was able body and save that option for when I really might need it. Mommy thought I was going to have the government support me and I told her my reasons why I wasn't. She smiled and understood my stance. EJ had been on assistance so Mommy just assumed I would too. Nope I had a job and I had work to do starting with finding a babysitter for Sierra. EJ watched Sierra until she started working and I didn't trust Sierra with just anyone. That was when my father strongly suggested Bill. Bill was living at his grandparents' house and there were plenty of family members still living there. So, that was my answer. I really can't remember his reaction at that point I didn't care. I wanted to keep my studies up and realized that nursing wasn't going to cut it for me with a young baby. So, I always enjoyed working with numbers and did well in accounting. I was working full time at the bank, so I decided to major in banking and finance.

Commercial bank was so impressed with my work and personality; they had me doing commercial for them and advanced me to new accounts. I enjoyed working there but dreaded Saturday classes in Bellvue. My parents watched Sierra on Saturdays while I attened classes. When I would come home Sierra would be knocked out. I didn't know if they fed her full or they just wore her out. The sound of her tiny snores allowed me to do my homework with a wonder of what did they do to Sierra. During my work and class schedule I didn't drift off into what is Bill doing or who is he doing? I really didn't miss him; he just didn't fit into my schedule. I very seldom thought about him again there was no time and no energy allowed in my program for Bill. Diapers formula, work and school were now my schedule. Sierra's birth accelerated my maturity level. I only saw Bill when I picked up Sierra from his grandparents' place. Surprisley I didn't hug or kiss him just give me my daughter, so I can go home. I thought briefly that at some point maybe watching our daughter would assist Bill in growing up and stepping up to be the father I hope he would be. I guess at some point Bill will realize he had a child. Sierra needs someone that needs to be active in her life. Bill has a daughter that looks just like him and needs to see him as her father. As my thoughts grew so did I and I realized that it was time for me to move on.

I had a few old boyfriends that wanted to date and be a father to Sierra. I wasn't ready for dating. I had to take care of my baby, Sierra. Bill realized that the scene changed and was he ready to step up to be what I had been waiting for. Now he wanted to be married and raise his daughter. Bill needed his own visual that life moves and not just around him, my, my what a nice surprise. Not by my planning just a simple karma. One time when Bill came over to the house unexpectedly an old boyfriend Mickey was holding Sierra. I saw the surprised/shock look in Bill's face and the pain that came with it. This was a quick face emotion, probably to quick to dissect for him. For some reason, it didn't faze me not one bit. There was no humor, no emotions and I offered no excuses. Now he realized that I too had a history and that someone else was paying attention to me. I didn't have my high school figure, but I could hold my own. Now I had company, tee-hee-hee hee followed by a silent chuckle, and it made me feel pretty good and alive again. The difference between me and Bill's giggling company I introduced Bill and didn't make him feel invisible or unimportant. Bill left on his own I could only imagine what he probably was thinking. Who cared I was thinking about formula and diapers. No time to feel his feelings or burp him or change his diaper. I had to grow up and now it was his turn. I couldn't help him or hold his underwear for him to put on. He had to put on his own big boy underwear. For once reality hit Bill that someone else would step up to the plate if he didn't. Sometimes you have to bring more to the table than just an appetite and a chair.

Chapter 4
Was the Ring a Bong or a Dong

Bill told his parents we were getting married, but my parents weren't happy, and it showed in their expressions that they didn't try to hide. My parents were a whole different story. The funny part about getting married I don't remember giving him an answer to the question. Well he did ask but that was four months into our relationship, and it was like well okay, I guess. So much had happened since that proposal it kind of just faded away with so many other thoughts. My father's mother, Mama Sadie supported me by telling my father he had to ask. She had open mind and wisdom and my father had much respect for her. I remember telling her that this particular seasoning tasted good on chicken and she tried it without a saying any words her expression showed that she liked it. I was impressed that she was willing to try and had an open mind at her age.

Mama Sadie was short on words and had given birth to ten children. She lived to be one hundred and eight years old. Wow can you imagine living that long and the changes she lived to see. The only times she had been in the hospital was for birth and cataract removal. She had a sound mind and moved better than I did. With her blessings, my father agreed and gave Bill my hand in marriage. Well we did get married and it was a small church wedding, small crowd. Bill's cousin Loren drove up from Chicago to be in our wedding, yep our wedding. Didn't know how much he would help Bill and I grow. Well Bill was going to grow but just on his time. At the urging of my Uncle Danny my father escorted me down the aisle. My father had on dark sunglasses because his eyes were red from drinking the night before and so yep, he was drunk on residual in church. Only thought I had was that I'm getting married and I love Bill. Hmm I don't remember if we had a wedding march or any music. I just wanted to make it down the aisle to my husband that was looking and smiling at me. Funny how you think about these things, and funny how time and changes either fade or blend in together just a passing thought. I'm married to Bill and that was my only thought.

While we were exchanging vows, we both watched the sweat dripping from

Pastor Williams's forehead and follow the sweat travel like a tear from his forehead to his eyebrow and drop right into his eye. He kept blinking so hard Bill and I looked at each other and smiled, we really wanted to laugh. Pastor married us without our marriage license because it wasn't ready ooh another sign. Once we finished exchanging vows Bill's ring was too small and we had to place it on his baby finger, wow another sign. All I knew I was Mrs. Bill, yeah. I guess I should have noticed that sign, but again I'm in love with Bill and wanted to do what is right for my family. Sierra needed to be with her father, and I wanted to be with Bill. I thought about the many people telling me I need to marry the baby's father and be right in the eyes of God and your family. I wanted to prove my cousin Elvin Clevon wrong aka EC or El or Clevon, just Elvin or EC or Cliffy. Those were the only names he normally answered too. He said that Bill wouldn't marry me. I can still picture Elvin Clevon's face saying it. I can also picture his face when he attended my make-believe wedding, ha- ha- ha. He meant well, he was just protecting me. I think he might be on his 2nd or third marriage. Oakwood had old fashion beliefs you stay in the marriage, you don't leave you make it work. I've seen loving relationships and I've seen business relationships with no love or no compassion. Hmm I still hold the philosophy of mommy saying go back because we don't do that; stay in until your finish. Out here in sunny side of California their outlook is a little different. I still love seeing EC/ Cliffy through his marriages and enjoyed his visit to us from time to time. It was always good seeing him and the many varieties of conversations we would have. He was family and it felt good to have family around in this new unfamiliar environment. Some were very challenging but, in the end, we were family and we loved each other.

So, Bill joined the armed services to provide for his new family. It happened right after he saw Mickey holding Sierra. I guess that again was a wakeup call that someone was willing to take his family, woman, child and all with no questions asked. The ironic part Bill didn't have a clue that they were the farthest thing from my mind. While Bill was in boot camp he would write, and I loved reading his letters. When time permitted, he would call letting me know he was coming for his family. He had been looking for a place for us outside the military base. I could hear the excitement in his voice and the happiness knowing that he would be seeing us soon. That made me feel good, I was finally his wife and we were a family. I was really married and comfirmation every time I looked down at my ring finger. Something I had always dreamed of happening and it finally did. Becoming Mrs. Bill was a wonderful feeling. While taking care of Sierra and like looking just like Bill reminded me that we were a family. There were no parts of me in her at all she was all Bill. I was happy about leaving and being with Bill, but still not understanding the outcome or how it would affect my family. Many were happy for me, but I still didn't' get it. You never really realized how people especially family of how they love and look at you. They show their emotions or concerns in their own special way and sometimes you don't understand their ways. Something's you just take for granted and sometimes they think you understand their thoughts through their actions. Hmm being young and learning and sometimes I didn't understand and just went with the flow. How many times do we go with the flow because you are too embarrassed to let them know you don't know?

Chapter 5
We Made That Move

I left my comfortable living and comfort zone in Oakwood, Nebraska and moved to the sunny side of California. I'd only been there once to sunny side of California and it was hot and smoggy. I was hanging out with my cousin Cliffy and most of the time my parents were doing their thing. My father was happy and hanging out with his sister Aunt Martha and she had a lot of energy and my mother enjoyed her as well. Cliffy knew my secret and it stayed with him, because if he told I would have been buried out there in sunny hot California. So here I am again in the sunny side of Califorina with palm trees, beaches, no friends, no family and adapting to a whole new life style of a total environment change. I only went on one vacation to California and that was with my family. This was weird and so new with them not being here. My comfort zone was slowly fading away and it was scary. I never had been too far from my parents or my family. I left my great- grandmother Mommy and Grandmother Hazel and Mama Sadie who encourage me to go. I was thankful that I could call on their strength because they were women of much courage. Including my mom and many other women I would encounter. I never thought I would call on my ancestral strength as much as I did. But I was thankful for their available strength. Just thinking about Mommy brought tears to my eyes she didn't play at all and still showed us her kinda love. She would sleep with a gun, switch blade, razor strap and the biggest gun I ever saw underneath her pillow for just in case. Mommy's just in case never, never happened.

My great- grandmother Mommy went into the hospital before I left. It was hard looking at her and seeing her age in front of me, but her smile was still warm and needed. Her skin was still smooth, and her smile was still gentle, but her heart was growing tired. She told me she was going to be okay. I trusted her smile to let me know everything would be okay with her. I really missed her and my conversations I used to have with my father. My grandmother, Mama Sadie, helped me pack; man, she had a lot of energy. I watched her wrap and pack with a serious swiftness. What would have taken me weeks she did in a few hours. That's what I'm talking about that kinda strength. They didn't have a lot of book knowledge, but they had plenty of life experiences. I didn't know I would soon join the ranks. Well Bill came home from boot camp for his family and it was time for Sierra and I to go. We said our many good byes but the hardest one was when it came to leaving home. I remember as we drove away, I watched the tears flow from my family's eyes. Was that another sign I missed? As we turned the corner the faces faded away as we look forward to a hopefully a new beginning. My tears had to dry up because I'm someone's wife and mother no longer daddy's little girl. Bill and I looked at each other with a smile as we took off with a U-Haul attached to the Vega and headed west. His smile always did warm my soul just like this nice cup of coffee during the rain.

During the road trip, there were times when Bill did fuss and cuss like this was my fault. He would get frustrated, but it would go away. I guess he would catch himself and exercise that military discipline. I was sitting next to him and I was experiencing it with him. This drive was not a solo run. We would look at each other and smile that has always been our way of soothing any anger or bad choice of words. We had agreed when we married that we would not go to bed angry or stay mad at each other. I always thought that was so insane living in the same house and not speak or look at each other. We were clear on not being mad at each other, exciting to know this was our first decision together. So, Bill would smile and say your crippled leg daddy and I would smile back with a response your crazy mama. We would both laugh and said that response for many years. My dad was short and bowlegged, and his mom wasn't crazy but very sane and kind. Then it was times where we enjoyed the scenery, we both saw for the first time and say wow look at that or did you see that. Growth is hard, but it comes together when you communicate and stayed determined to make it work. I felt that we were trying to make it work we just didn't know how. Bill was happy in his own way of being in charge and trying the best he could to take control. He did all the driving and I attended to Sierra who would be sleeping comfortably in the back seat that my father had put together. There they go with that comfort and putting Sierra to sleep, and it wasn't Saturday. She was only eight months old and had no clue of the new world she was being exposed to. Sometimes I would sit in silence and look and think about what did I get myself into and there was no turning or running back. Turning back meant failure and that was not an option. During our drive, we called our parents, so they knew we were okay. I could still hear the sadness in their voices as they heard the joy of us seeing and sharing with them so many beautiful sites and experiencing new scenery.

Occasionally I tried to understand what I could have done or said to trigger some of Bill's angry outburst. So, I would just be still while sitting in the car looking as the scenery changed and try to keep my tears from flowing. So many thoughts were flowing through my head. I remembered trying hard not to let one tear flow down my cheeks. I had to grow up I'm married there is no turning back. I told myself in silence that you will make this work Rita. I had to keep reminding myself repeatedly don't cry. While still driving, I remember Bill fussing at me hard on my birthday some present huh. I thought what a birthday present, no presents, no parents, no family out in the middle of nowhere with no air conditioner in a Vega in this dry heat.

Well, we arrived safely to a beautiful city in California called Oceanview. As soon as we start entering California, I heard songs from this group called 'Maze' I never heard of this group. While we were driving, I looked over at Bill and the song "You Make Me Happy", was playing and it put a smile on my face and erase the trials times on the road. Then another one of their songs "Happy Happy Feelings" was playing as we drove up to our new home. Funny both of us were singing off key trying to say the words we didn't know. We arrived at our new place because neither one of us ever been there before. Every time I heard those songs it would put a smile on my face. Now I just try to rock and move to the beat. Huh that song took me back.

Well Oceanview was the city where the base was located and here, we were happy feet and all. Wow, this coffee is good and the happy, happy feeling just had me rocking to the tune playing in my head, oh yes. With big eyes, we both saw palm trees, beaches, sunshine and people I just didn't know. I have never been away from my parents. As I glanced out the window looking at the rain, I realized that Bill never traveled much either. When we did travel, it was always to a family member's house. I think we both were scared and just didn't want to admit it. I had to embrace my faith and hope that Bill would take care of us. His new little family was here to stay. My place was with my husband. We pulled up to our apartment building we looked at each other with nervous smiles. With sounds of sighs coming from both of us we realized that this is our new home. I looked at Bill and seeing his smile and sparkling eyes looking at me it was all worth it. We are married, and no one can take that away from us. We are in this together.

Bill carried sleepy Sierra upstairs to our new place. As we walked up the stairs I looked around at the people as we entered our two-bedroom apartment. Bill handed sleepy Sierra over to me as he bought our little possession into our new home. As I carried sleeping Sierra I looked into each room. Each room was covered with bright white walls and empty, waiting for us to move in. It reminded me of the bright room I was in when I discovered I was pregnant. I remembered how I glazed at the poster reminding me of why I was there. I chuckle with the answer of humph indigestion. It seemed like so many years ago. Yet, we are all here together. I smiled at how it would look with furniture that Bill and I would be looking for together. The place was empty only filled with what we bought from Oakwood. No bed, no table, no chairs or couch, one television and an empty refrigerator. This was our new place and we were happy we were a family. We slept on the floor without a complaint just looking at each other as the television looked at us, laughing as we fall off to sleep snuggling up with each other as Sierra lay on her father's chest. Sierra had her bed, but we laid on Bill and fell off to sleep. As we lay on his chest I listened to his heartbeat and realized we both had the same beat this was good. Bill smiled as we laid on his chest saying he was happy that he had his girls with him giving us a big hug at the same time. I smiled, and my head felt more comfortable as I laid on his chest. Yes, we are his girls. That was so soothing to hear. As we closed our eyes from exhaustion I smiled again thinking yes, we are his girls. This is a new beginning and it's gonna be okay because we are a family. I'm Bill's wife. For many years, I would lay my head in the same spot on Bill's chest that was my mark. When we slept on our sides, we would still embrace each other. If we had our backs against each other, we still would touch in some way. Hmm I missed his touch in years we grew further apart, and our backs didn't touch, and I lost my spot on his chest.

Oh well anyway the next morning we were awakened by the sound of a rooster crowing. We both jumped up what the heck?? Neither one of us had ever been around that type of sound. We both went to the window and saw a rooster and many chickens. Bill and I looked at each other and busted out laughing at the same time. The first day hearing the rooster was okay every day we just wanted to cook it. Bill took off from work, so he could help us get situated. Our next-door neighbor Michael and Melba had a little girl the same age as Sierra. Her name was Michelle and her brother name were Mickey Jr. Michael was a corman in the navy (male nurse) and Melba stayed home. The families' downstairs were Tina and she had twin boys Trent and Trace. They were two years old. She stayed at home also. Her husband Benjamin was in the navy too. The other neighbors I would come to know them later. Let me see there were the sisters Maria and Gina. Now Maria kids were Nia, Mia and Gia, her sister Gina kids were Rena, Ria, Tia and Crea. Their husbands' names were Bruce and Wayne. They made me think of batman Bruce Wayne that's how I was able to remember their names but couldn't tell them apart. I couldn't tell their children apart either. Every member had round heads, big smiles and apple cheeks. Bruce and Wayne were brothers and they all grew up together and married the sisters around the corner from their neighborhood. Together they form one big happy family. They did everything together. I remember when Maria and Gina had baby boys at the same time and named them both Eric. I had asked Michele how do the Eric's know which is which, when their names are called. Michele laughed because others had asked the same question. Gina's Eric is Eric Keith, or his nickname was EK and Maria because she was a nurse in emergency name her Eric, is Eric Richard or ER. My response was okay then, that was different. All I remember it was a big celebration and they invited all the apartment residents. We met their parents Mr. Bert and their mom they referred to as mutter or Mama Dreia. I asked them what did mutter mean. They all laughed almost at the same time. They said when they were little, they couldn't say mother, and they called her mutter. So, the whole neighborhood would refer to her as mutter. They both had a lot of energy and seemed so happy together. It was refreshing to see a large happy family. They allowed us to join in their celebration, food, games, music, much fun, and everyone was laughing and dancing. That was how I met most of the people living in the complex. Toni was married to Javon and they had two girls by the name of Fendi and Chanel they were toddler age. Miss Clovis and Reggie Coy known as RC had just retired from the Navy and their younger sons Floyd and Lloyd were in the service as well and both were being stationed overseas. There other sons Boyd and Troy and their daughter Veretta were all doctors on various air force bases in the Midwest. That was one of the reasons for them moving. So, they decided to move back to the mid-west I think it might have been Kansas. There was also Rod and Shelia they didn't have any kids and they both worked on base. Upstairs were single mother Shirley and her daughter Shannon. And Lynton had two daughters Bernice and Jacqueline he was raising while his wife Harmony was away at boot camp.

Toni and Javon lived right underneath us. I would hear Toni's cries when the windows were open in which what would become a routine. I didn't know how to help her, but I knew that I could pray for her. Javon would jump on Toni every payday Friday and pass out on Saturday and Sunday and be ready for work on Monday as if nothing happened. I couldn't understand why no one would help Toni or talk to Javon. Melba told me many people in the complex tried and would get cussed out by Toni and Javon. I really didn't understand then, but I learned to understand now. Time and experience will teach you. Now, I understand what my daddy and my grandmothers were trying to tell me. All you have to do is keep on living. Melba and I kinda hit it off since our kids were the same age. I spent a lot of time with Bill before he returned to work. We explored with Sierra the sites of Oceanview oohing and looky at the beautiful beaches and palm trees. It was definitely a military town. The weather was beautiful, beaches were a wow and the palm trees looked like something you see on television. While we were sightseeing, I was hoping to see a familiar face, but it didn't happen. We were here together no mom, no grandma hands, and no family to run to. We had to make it and that was only going to happen by communicating and working together.

Going to the store was fun because we never shopped for groceries. We were like kids getting what we wanted not purchasing in preparation for meals. We had money from savings and what the family members had given to us. Let me see great-grandmother Mommy gave me money in a pill bottle for my headache. Hmm did that headache come oh yes, Mama Sadie gave me money in a handkerchief with a knot tied at the end I thought she was gonna pin it on me, ha-ha and grandmother Hazel grab my hand and put money in it and whispered you gonna be alright. We also received money as a wedding present and the money I saved while working at the bank. Well when it came time to cook neither one of us knew how to cook. To this day, it's still trial and burnt errors, laugh. Bill was good at breakfast and for me hmmm. I remember at his grandparents/aunt's house upstairs was a small apartment. It was equipped with small kitchen, bathroom and two rooms. The only thing we did cook was breakfast. Now house playing was over and real life was our beginning. It was scary yet fun being with him and watching Sierra learn about herself and the world around her. She didn't have a clue that she wouldn't see her cousins or grandparents for a while. We realized we wouldn't see them either. No more running to my family when things didn't work out, we both had to grow up and faster than we wanted to. Neither one of us ever lived on our own. This was going to be an experience that would either bring us together or separate us. Bill and I had Sierra depending on us. Everything was so very new, no snow, no autumn leaves, no watching the seasons change. We both came from states that had all four seasons. We had to get used to seeing our mailman or delivery man around Christmas in shorts instead of being all bundled up. The weather was the same pretty much every day sunshine or rain.

While playing outside I ran into another neighbor by the name of Dina she had two teenage (not twins) daughters, her hubby Bradley was stationed overseas on a temporary assignment. Her daughters, Carolyn and Sharolyn both were active in sports. So, I didn't see them that much. It was a combination of families' older and younger kids. Not too much room for playing areas. One big area in the center, where the children played, and their parents could keep an eye on them, as they sat around talking and watching everything that was going on. We had a walker that Sierra would move around in outside and would hang out with Melba and Michelle. Thinking of Sierra in wheels it's funny because she couldn't' stand riding in a stroller. One time when we took her to Sea World Bill was tired of carrying her as I pushed an empty stroller. He mouthed to me on the count of three, when three came we stopped abruptly and put her in the stroller. Sierra had a surprise look on her face and the rest is history. The parents would sit around and look at the fun the kids were having. I think they were happier with them not bugging them, so they could have some time out or me thoughts or just adult conversation with a little laughter. I looked at them play so innocently without a care in the world. The kids were in eye sight of their parents. I enjoyed looking at them play, laughing, observing and exploring their surroundings made me feel so warm inside. Just like holding this hot cup of coffee in your hands keeping them warm and the insides feeling the same way. As the days passed, I had question and doubts of could I be a stay at home mom. If I did this would just be temporary because in time I would be working. I have always worked and just seemed boring. I thought how I could sit at home while my husband busts his butt. We were in this together and I wasn't going to have any undue stress on him or our family. We had a little money we both had saved and what was given to us. It was nice surprise that so many family members pool some money together before we left. We were able to drive from Oakwood to California without worrying about money for gas or food.

We stopped one time at a hotel and registered as Mr. and Mrs. Smith the clerk looked at us strangely, we laughed because that was our name. We laughed with would he had preferred Jones, wow that would be a change humph. Well, we could have used another last name with color like green or brown hmm that's funny too. That added a little ooh to the road trip. That Maze song plays again in my head again "you make me happy". And I found myself smiling as I hum that tune. That flashback has me humming and rocking as I drink this coffee. Housework was easy clean up because we didn't have any furniture. That was soon to change. Bill returned to work and I became a home wife or joined the ranks of apartment boredom. It was okay the first week and the second week was okay. I started getting bored going into the next month and missing my family. We really didn't have a phone because I would run the bill up. Really didn't talk to the neighbors. When I did it was only in passing. I didn't have a car because Bill drove the Vega to work. That was a good ole car. It made it from Oakwood to Oceanview with no problems. They don't' make them anymore but it hung in there for many, many years and long drives. That was my graduation present from my parents, and they gave us the title. When we ha-ha-ha, traded the Vega in and we both laughed hoping it would start. I traded in the fun memories I had with my friends and the long ride to the sunny side of California.

The following month Bill was tired of coming home to an empty place. He had a few friends over. I don't remember their names they all went by their last names. To this day, I don't remember their faces or their names. In uniform, they all looked the same. They were cute, in shape and I was afraid to look at them.

Well, Thanksgiving was approaching, and Bill wanted to have some of his friends over that couldn't go home for the holidays. Hmm funny I couldn't cook then and still really can't cook now just a few specialties. I had to ask my Mother for some recipes, and she laughed and laughed until she starts coughing. After hearing the laughter at my expense, I asked well do you have any?? She sent me some recipes and I still have the paper for Thanksgiving dinner. Well this means that we had to fold up our table and iron board that was a big thick white blanket and get some real furniture. We went to the local furniture store and established an account. Our first bill together as husband and wife this was good. We looked at furniture, but we were used to grandma looking furniture and that is what we purchased. This coffee is getting old time for a fresh cup. It was refreshing looking at the apartment finally being furnished. Now it was time to cook, ooh cook a turkey, and other items. Ooh this was going to be a challenge. People were coming over and the pressure was on, because we had to get additional plates and silverware. This was going to be interesting. I tried making jello and it never jelled. I tried baking a pound cake the first one was dry and was a heavy as a brick. I had asked Miss Clovis how to bake a pound cake and, I asked her to be very clear. She told me to use three cubes of butter. Me not knowing cubes of butter I took one stick of butter and cut off hee-hee three cubes. That pound cake was dry, and very, very, heavy. Not to add that I couldn't serve that watered un-jelled-jello, laugh. Well pound cake was out. Thank God for cake mix and frosting and the abiliy to read. My sister Bonnie gave me a recipe for peach cobbler from the can, but she was the better cook of the family.

I started the turkey early in the morning. My dad told me to cook it on the breast side that sounded easy. What about the other food entrées, well hmm green beans from a can "Green Giant" he helped with the corn too. Dressing by taste which is hard when you don't know how to cook, but mom provided me with a recipe. Mashed potatoes hmm came out kinda of crunchy. The macaroni and cheese, hmm I didn't try it but everyone else seemed to enjoy the entrees. Bill came into the kitchen while I was cooking. I asked him how much longer for the turkey he looked into the oven and said fifteen more minutes. My response was okay sounded good to me. Neither one us knew anything about cooking a turkey. As I looked back on that moment it was funny and memorable. Now the dessert hmm I could read so they were okay not dry or raw. Well we had four people over and Bill was smiling from ear to ear. I could see the proudness as he showed off his family and apartment.

Sierra was on her best behavior. Bill and I were so happy that she didn't put any food in her hair or, hiding food in her lap and happy that she didn't put any corn up her nose. It's funny we had served corn. Bill had banned corn from the table. One day we were eating and enjoying dinner. Sierra didn't put her food in her hair like she always did. This time we noticed she was picking at her small nose. She wasn't crying just picking at one side of her nose. She couldn't really talk. Funny when she learned how to talk was very well. She would just look at you like your mouth wasn't moving and she wasn't hearing you. Hmm she still has that habit to this day. Bill and I were talking and weren't watching her and looked up her small nose and a saw a piece of corn. She had stuck a piece of corn up her nose. Wow, as young parents we panic and could see it but couldn't get it out. Sierra was just looking at us with no emotions. I ran next door and to get Michael (he was a corman) and he came over with a pair of tweezers and removed the corn. After that episode corn was banned from our menu. So, we were hoping that Sierra would be on her best behavior. After Bill blessed the food, we ate slowly nervously because we wanted to keep an eye on Sierra with the corn. She looked at us as if she knew we were scared. Her almond shaped eyes would follow us as we followed her with occasionally looking and talking with our guest. That was a long meal. Sierra ate all her food which was surprising. One thing she was good at was hiding things. When we went to pull her out of her high chair all her food fell out. Everyone laughed, and she just looked at us and smiled. She had a beautiful dimple smile and was very active little kid. She took off and acted like she was being released and she was escaping to freedom. The guests love playing with her and she enjoyed the attention. Well, we made it through the Thankgiving, and Bill was back to work.

Chapter 6
I Don't Want to Stay Home

I wanted to get ready for Christmas and I had to ask Bill for some money. My savings were very low, and we were now depending on Bill's income. I found enough courage to ask Bill for money. He responded with why I needed any money and what was I going to spend his money on. Wow what a quick blow his money and not our money. Now, that surprised me I wasn't used to asking for money. I have always worked and couldn't understand then what I figured out later. I gave it long hard thought about getting a job and escaping from this apartment boredom. I had some bank training, but I didn't want to leave Sierra with just anyone. There were a lot of banks in Oceanview almost one on each corner. I talked with Bill about working a part-time job. He really wanted me to stay home. I was lonely, bored, no friends, no family in an unfamiliar city. I really did try to adjust to being at home and having dinner ready, and sewing socks, keeping the house clean, taking care and raising our daughter. Bill wasn't home much and a part of me was lonely. I really didn't know where he was, and we didn't have a phone. I would try and stay awake so when he came home his dinner would be hot and ready. Sierra was sleep and the minutes turned into hours. I wondered where Bill was and when was he coming home. I wanted to be awake for him. Sometimes he would come home so late Sierra would be sleep. She had a bedtime routine, dinner with us if dad was around followed by a bath and putting her toys up. To this day, Sierra still falls asleep early. When Bill did come home sometimes, he wasn't hungry. I would put dinner up and finish cleaning up the kitchen. We were still a family. I had to keep convincing myself of that. Although, Sierra was there with me I would sometimes feel the emptiness of being at home alone. I thought that Bill should be home more often with his family.

My dad always came home, and we ate dinner as a family. What was happening with Bill and our relationship? Bill and I always were able to communicate. I didn't know what was happening to us. Here I was in a place where I didn't want to be. I left the comfort of my family to be and support my husband and our small family.

Inside I wanted to wake up and run away from this dream that sometimes felt like a nightmare. There was no Vega to take off in or nowhere to run. Then I started thinking about another Maze song "Joy and Pain". Was joy and pain starting to happen? I didn't know this would be an anthem for me and our marriage. Holding this new cup of coffee was a new beginning of learning about life experiences. Sierra would eventually fall off to sleep after I would read her a bedtime story. I couldn't read it the way her father did, and I think she missed him. He used such creativity while tickling Sierra as he held her close to him. Sometimes after Sierra went to bed, I would just sit on the couch looking into space as the television looked at me. My thoughts were as empty as the pain in my heart. Only sound I heard was my heartbeat slowing down and my mind becoming numb to confusion. Holding a cup of coffee tightly wondering what was happening just like I'm doing now. Funny, how I like coffee now but didn't like it growing up. It's strange how you pick up habits and they follow you for life. I would sit and sit in silence trying to figure out how to keep my husband happy and raise our daughter. Sometimes I would go outside at night and just sit on the steps by myself or with Sierra looking at the stars. I think back to I wished I paid more attention to the class we had on the big dipper and so forth. I would be able to follow the stars and point them out to Sierra. She didn't know the loneliness I was feeling or the confusion that was trying to take over my soul.

Well, Christmas came, and we had a small family Christmas. We really didn't have much money at least I didn't Bill made sure of that. We were able to buy a few presents for Sierra and Bill bought me some skin-tight polyester pants and a purse ooh I don't know what it was made of. I had purchased him a nice sweater. In which he liked. Bill still didn't want me to work and we only had the one car and Bill had it all the time. So, Sierra and I would walk to the park or around the neighborhood just to get her out of the apartment and fresh air. Fresh air was needed to refresh my brain and thoughts. Every now and then Bill would go with us to the park or we would just go for a ride. I would look over at Bill just wondering what was on his mind. We still slept together but for some reason I felt we were becoming roommates. I had to keep talking to myself saying you are a big girl now, and you can handle this. I looked at Bill as my provider, a leader, my protector, my best friend, and the head our household. Was I becoming boring to him since he has been around these California women and I was just a Midwestern bore?

All I knew was Bill. I just married Bill how could I lose him to something I didn't know I was battling. I thought I was exciting I just took my role as a housewife very serious and wanted to be the best for my husband. Was it the way I dressed or looked? Bill would have to let me know. Just like this coffee I know when it's too hot to drink. Was my marriage becoming lukewarm before our anniversary, was it simmering, or did it just get cold like an old cup of coffee? Even with coffee you can reheat the cup, but could we reheat our relationship? Hmm I remember one morning Bill woke up foul. I tried to smile to ease his foul mood. I always cooked his breakfast before he went to work and made his lunch. Maybe the smile I placed on the lunch bag will brighten his day. He told me how his co-workers would always tease him about bringing his lunch to work. He would laugh but he liked the fact that he had someone home taking good care of him.

Any way he just kept fussing and I just wasn't doing anything right that particular morning. As my eyes watered, I wouldn't let him see me cry I fought back the tears. Taking a big breath and said what you want from me a divorce. He stopped and just stared at me, (it was a look of what did you just say). I was missing home and ready to go back. He looked at me and said yes. My heart dropped but courage and numbness responded. Okay let's do this. So, we loaded Sierra in the car and went to the base lawyer. Man was this military lawyer dedicated to Bill. I can't believe they wanted to pay me $50.00 a week for Sierra. Food and a place to stay and any other essentials were not included. I just broke down because I didn't have anywhere to go. My Vega was gone so that leaves no transportation. The fear that came in was in a different form. I said I didn't want a divorce and Bill just looked at me and laughed. I felt small and empty. Going back home to Oakwood just wasn't an option for me. I could see it now a failure in marriage with a young child. Well, we left the office and that was a long ride home in silence. My brain just went into a deep, deep what are you going to do? It wasn't a we, it changed to a me. Bill just kept saying you thought you wanted a divorce huh. As I turned my head just staring out the window wondering where do I go from here. Bill dropped us off and he went back to work. No good bye, no kiss just stopped the car long enough, so we could get out. Thank God for brakes.

As I carried Sierra up the stairs for some reason our complex was quiet, just like the pain my soul was feeling. Why bring me, us this far to treat me/us like this. I tried so hard to be a good wife and mother. What happened between the altar and arriving happy in Oceanview? For a quick minute my brain stopped talking to me. I tried talking to my mother and they just wanted me to come home. I talked to her more married than I did growing up in her house. I kept thinking I just couldn't go back this way; I had to make this work. He is the father of my child and my husband. The phone was working but he didn't call. I remembered picking the phone several times during the day to make sure it did have a dial tone. I tried to hide my feeling from Sierra. Yes, putting on my best performance again. When she finally took her nap, I started cleaning up the apartment. Trying to avoid thinking just kept it moving through cleaning. My mom did it now I know why she would sometimes clean the way she did. As I was washing the dishes I just broke down and cried. I cried so hard I had to drop to the floor. My head was hurting, and my stomach was in knots. Where can I go? Should I go to a shelter, or just pack up and call it a defeat and just take my family up on their offer to bring us home. I got up and walked to the window and set down and just stared out the window. It wasn't raining like it's doing now. The sun was out, and it was a bright day. Was this bright light for me and what was happening to us?

When Sierra woke up, I started dinner for Bill. Hoping he would come home so we could talk. For some reason, I was in a slow-motion move. Sierra and I baked cookies. She loved putting puzzles together she wasn't a cartoon television child. As I looked at her, I see Bill in her eyes and her face. Well, Rita what are you going to do. I looked in the mirror trying to figure out what changed on me. Was I looking tired, was I not attractive to him anymore, was I too big, what was it? Well Bill came home I looked at him with confusing eyes. I didn't know what to say or how to say it and didn't know if I should approach him or run away or what. He smiled at me and pulled me toward him and embraced me all at once my emotions took over. I felt love from him, and my heart sighed and my spirit rejoiced. Bill kissed me and asked what was for dinner it smelled good. Sierra told him she made cookies in her child like language and tone. He laughed and smiled again at me. I start thinking is this for real or is this a set up for a let down? As I prepared his plate, he grabs me by the waist and said that he loved me, and he was sorry for what happened this morning. I smiled back and said I love you too. We are family and we need to keep the line of communication open. We have never had a problem with talking. After dinner, he said don't worry about the dishes let's sit down and look and television. As we sat on the couch, he held Sierra in his lap like used to. She would lean into his chest and I would lay my head on his shoulder. Yes, we were going back to being a family again. We are still his girls. That night was special again and I found my spot-on Bill's chest to lay my head. It felt good and I was in love again as if we first met. Bill didn't want breakfast he told me to sleep in.

One thing Sierra and I used to do was kill roaches in the morning. This apartment was infested. I never saw flying roaches before. I would wake up with a shoe as Sierra pointed them out to me. The landlord would bomb only when you complained. So, the roaches never left, they just relocated to the next apartment unit.

I was looking forward to our first wedding anniversary and hoping Bill wouldn't forget. I haven't purchased clothes in a while and had been looking at my clothes for months trying to put together the perfect outfit. I wanted and needed something that would just wow Bill when he saw me. I had picked up a little weight so finding something to wear was hard, but I had to look good. I had to find something that fit. Bill is my husband and we made it through the first year. It was a good day for a one-year anniversary. Bill had asked Melba to babysit and that surprised me, and I manage to put a nice outfit together. I wore a beautiful red clingy dress with 3inch heels. Red was Bill's favorite color and I practiced walking just right in those high heel shoes and I practiced falling gracefully. It's funny I still have those sit-down shoes. Bill had paid to get my hair done and I had a flower in my hair the way he liked it. I had his favorite perfume on, and the night was young. He bought me flowers. This was a first because Bill never bought me flowers. I felt all giddy and girlish. I felt like I was going out on our first date with no curfew.

Bill took me to a nice restaurant. I asked him had he been there before because the people were very friendly as if they knew him. He said that he had heard about it. I wasn't gonna let my thought and mouth ruin this night. But one particular waitress by the name of Gail kept looking at us and when I turned to look at her, she seemed to vanish. Hmm, funny I learned to become familiar with the many unfamiliar women. I wondered who knew me and I didn't know them. I glanced at Bill smiling and nervously my emotions were racing. I had a feeling Bill had been here enough times that they knew him. We had a nice streak and shrimp dinner followed with a nice glass of wine. The restaurant bought a small cake to our table for our celebration. I fed Bill a piece and he fed me as well. I sipped a little of wine. I didn't care for wine and Bill wasn't much of a drinker either. We looked at each other after sipping the wine saying ew. Bill smoke some weed but not heavy into anything else. Bill proposed a toast to us and held my hand. I looked into his twinkling almond shaped eyes and they were smiling at me. It had been a long time since I saw his eyes sparkle. I had seen more anger than the twinkle in his eyes.

Today I felt like a queen again sitting here with my king. How long would this reign last? Would my hope for better years turn into a fantasy of lies and disguises? I kept glancing at that waitress, and she was glancing at me. All I knew was I was leaving with my husband and watch us leave whoever you are. I put my arms into Bill's and laid my head on his shoulder as we walked out with a little switch in my hips. My dad taught me how to do that and when to do it and this was that time. I felt her eyes on me as we walked out. As we drove home, I wasn't going to ask Bill or mention that waitress. This was my night and she wasn't riding in the car or coming home with us. We talked about our future and how we wanted to grow old together. Bill laughs and says I need to have someone to squeak to. Then we talked about what Sierra would be when she grows up. Maybe a nurse or doctor, either way we would provide a healthy environment. Well the honeymoon in months was over and Bill was back to fussing and complaining. I guess he was getting me ready or training me for growing old with his squeaking. Wow I can't wait!! He was now letting me take him to work, along with getting Sierra ready. I either had to drive while he rolled his joint or I had to roll it for him. I didn't smoke anything. If Bill was running late, I had to speed up to get him to work on time and get yelled at for his weed being spilled. Darn if I did and darn if I didn't, I just couldn't win. I would get yelled at for not driving fast enough it was a no-win situation.

Sierra and I had fun now that we had a car. I still wanted to go back to work. I was still bored and didn't know what was bothering Bill. Maybe if I worked that would help him with the bills. An unfamiliar feeling came upon me again. This time I knew what it was, and it wasn't indigestion. Pregnant again, wow how or when did this happen. Bill wasn't home much, and I guess it must have been one of those special nights we had. I still loved Bill and wanted to make this work. Funny how what you want is not always good for you. I told Bill I was pregnant when I picked him up with Sierra. He smiled and seemed to be happy. He wanted to move to a better place and larger apartment that was free of flying roaches. Just when I was getting used to our complex it was time to look for another place. This time it would be special because we were looking together. Our family was increasing, and we were still married. A new beginning, just like a fresh brew cup of coffee. Hmmm, so good and yet so exciting. No more flying roaches and no more sounds of tears. We went looking for apartment and it was fun. That day we were driving and talking again.

I had to go pick up Bill so Sierra and I started off early. We didn't have much money, so I stopped at the PX just to look around. In just an instance Sierra disappeared. My heart dropped, and I went frantic looking for her. I lost my baby and Bill is going to kill me. I didn't know if Sierra ran off because she saw a stuffed animal. She was very afraid of them or was she hiding and playing a game with mommy. She was always good at hiding. One time when we were running late for a Christmas party, she was sitting on the couch, and I turned my back and next thing I knew the present was missing and Sierra was sitting on the couch looking at me. Now little girl could talk when she felt like it. I asked her did she see the present and she just looked at me and said nothing. I went through the apartment looking for the present hurriedly because we were running late. I found the present in the closet where Sierra had hidden it. I laughed, and she smiled because that was all I could do. I was hoping this was the case she was hiding in between the racks. I called out her name as tears formed in my eyes praying my child would surface. She was hiding in between the clothes rack and my fears left the building. When I saw Sierra, I just picked her up and kissed her while holding her close to my heart. Now I had to hurry over to pick up Bill and hope I wasn't late picking him up. I made it and waited out in the car for some time before Sergeant Miles Lee and Sergeant Deforest both approached me and told me Bill had left. I asked where he could be this late and they looked at each other and said he was on assignment. They showed no emotions just look straight ahead. I smiled and thanked them both but at the same time my stomach wasn't feeling this answer. Something wasn't right. Why would Bill leave knowing I would be picking him up?

Well, we went home, and I did the routine of dinner waiting for Bill and time just kept going. It was time for Sierra bath and bedtime. Another night she wouldn't see her dad before she went to bed. I stayed up waiting and trying to keep his dinner warm. I fell off to sleep to be awakened by a kiss on my forehead by Bill. I asked him what happened, and he said he was at work at another location. I thought to myself that wasn't what his Sergeant told me. What was really going on? Who was telling the truth? What reason would Bill have to lie to me? As we went to bed, I started wondering who this stranger was laying next to me. As I moved toward him, he said he was tired. Hmm, strange never heard that from him before. I didn't take Bill to work after that. The Vega was still hanging in there and I was home again being bored and confused about the days before. I still wanted to work and was home schooling Sierra. I wanted to go back to work. Every time I asked Bill for money his response was what do you need it for. He bought some clothes for Sierra, but I had to mix and match her clothes, so it looked like a new outfit. Something for me was way out of the question. I knew some of my clothes were out dated. My mother had given me some of her clothes, but why would I need new ones Bill really didn't take me anywhere. If he was home, I wasn't allowed to spend too much time talking to any of the neighbors or spend any time at Melba's place. Some people thought I was numb and quiet. I guess through their eyes I would appear that way. I talked very little and smiled. Not too much on conversation. Bill and Sierra was my world and the outside were on a limited time table. Bill told me that his check was short. I couldn't understand why I didn't think you could have your check docked due to office hours. I didn't understand what that meant. That was some type of military talk that I wasn't familiar with. I laugh now but it wasn't funny then. How could he be late for work I would take him, or he would leave early enough not to be late. So, I pressed the issue of what was office hours and why was his check docked or short? I thought I was being supportive. Bill told me to leave it alone. I just couldn't, and I kept asking and he said he was disciplined by Sergeant Miles. I asked what for and he said very sternly Rita let it go.

My stomach said let it go but my mind said this doesn't make sense. Bill said that when I came to pick him up, I told them I had to leave. Someone said that they saw me leave with a woman and they have strict rules about fraternizing. As he tells me this, I'm trying to understand about the term fraternizing. I asked him what woman did you leave with? Bill said it's done let it go. I stated let what go?? I still can picture Bill's face with frowning eyebrows and anger in his eyes. From his tone, I told my brain and mouth to instantly don't say it. I couldn't give into this fear I needed to know, that's my paycheck too. Who did you leave with I asked with a stern sound? Now, my tone changed and with a glance it surprised Bill. He said some co-workers and I went out for some drinks. I looked at him with anger and said why didn't you call me and who or what people did you go out with. Before I knew it, Bill hit me, and I saw flashes before my eyes. I stood there in shock and felt the burning in my face. This was a feeling I had felt before. I just cried and walked into the bedroom and just laid on the bed. Bill came in behind me and said I told you to leave it alone and snatched some cover off the bed and slept in the front room on the couch. I was trying to understand what is going on as I shivered in fear and my emotions comfort me without saying I told you so. This was the first time we didn't sleep together. I didn't like rolling over and not seeing Bill sleeping. It was an empty and sad feeling that I didn't like, but curiosity slowly laid next to me. Who is this woman that is trying to take my place or was it just an innocence happy hour after work? I laid there crying and bundling myself in what cover that was left on the bed. I prayed please don't let me be like Toni and Jovan. I didn't want to match her pain or tears. Bill left the next morning before I could get up and make his breakfast or his lunch.

Chapter 7
I'm Going Home

As I prepared breakfast for Sierra, I received a phone call from my mother. For some reason this ring felt strange and when I answered a feeling of pain rushed in. My mother was calling to let me know my beloved great-grandmother Mommy had passed. I dropped down holding the phone in my hand looking at it. For some reason, I couldn't let go of the phone. I stared at the phone trying to figure out what to say. I cried for my Mommy and I cried for myself. This was too much at one time. The last vision I had of Mommy was when she was in the hospital letting me know that she would be okay. I wanted to go home I needed to go home. I couldn't stay I needed to go home. I wanted to call Bill at work to tell him, but fear consumed me. A smile came over my heart thinking about when Bill met my great- grandmother, Mommy. Mommy wasn't hard of hearing but when Bill would talk to her, he would always yell. She would look at him like he was crazy. I would have to remind him that she could hear stop yelling at her. I can see Mommy sitting looking out her front window. She would just look out the window with such peace and calmness. Maybe that is where I get the habit of just looking out the window. Looking out the window does have a calm, peaceful feeling. I'm doing it now and I feel calm as I enjoyed this cup of coffee. When Bill came home, I told him my great-grandmother had passed and that I wanted to go home. I needed to go home. For once Bill understood my pain. My heart lost a very important person in my life. I thought how much of my pain do you care about. My family pooled money together for me to come home. Sierra and I took the train. When Bill took us to the Amtrak a song was playing and to this day, I still have that vision of us leaving as we said good-bye to Bill. The song went every time you go away you take the biggest part of me. I looked at Bill did he know and feel he was losing his family. As we boarded the train Bill hugged and kissed us both. I looked at him and the only thoughts I had was that I'm going home. Going home married and carrying another child.

The train ride took a few days and Sierra loved her new adventure. I enjoyed looking out the window and hearing the conductor coming through announcing the various stops. As we arrived closer to Oakwood a feeling of relief filled my soul and gave my spirit a joyful kick. I started remembering how Mommy would love and spoil us yet kept a firm hand on us. Mommy couldn't read or write but she raised us with integrity and what hard work was about. I see and picture her washing using old fashion machine where you had to put the clothes through the wheels spinning to drain the water and hang the clothes outside on the clothes line. Saturday was her laundry day and she worked while we played outside. She would heat up milk and put it in a bottle and, we would laugh, as we suck the milk from the bottle while rolling in the bed laughing. It was funny because we were grade school age. Oh, she could make a mean peach cobbler and hamburgers with grilled onions. Just thinking about those hamburgers gives me a yummy thought. I haven't been able to find that taste in a burger for years or good peach cobbler. As we pulled into the station it was a joy to see my dad again. As we drove home, I really didn't say anything just looking out the window enjoying being back home and feeling the strength that filled my soul. I arrived home to see my mother trying to smile through her pain. Mommy raised her, and she was the only mother she knew. While I was there, I tried to make my mother smile. Every Sunday we went to Mommy's house and whatever we did we always shared it with Mommy. We would play our piano lessons and read her stories and tell her about our day.

As we prepared for her burial, I spent more time with my mother than I have ever before. We laughed together while singing and for the first time enjoying each others company. This was strange because my mother and I were not close, but this time we were. It felt good that she remembered she had another daughter other than Bonnie and her family. She didn't know that she was treating us the same way she hated that her mother Hazel did. Sometimes it's hard to see clearly the reflections of yourself through others. When we went to the wake, I looked at Mommy, hoping that she would take one big breath and come back to us. She laid there beautiful and peaceful with a smile to show me she was at peace. How could you take that away from her? I reflect on her strength and the many lessons she taught us. Great-grandma's hands were now at rest. She is finally at peace. I loved and missed her. I smiled at her with a sigh and just said I love you as I placed my hand on hers. I wanted to hug her one more time and smell her scent for the last time. She couldn't read or write but she did share her life experience and taught us not to quit and those thoughts keep reflecting in my mind and had absorb into my soul. There will never be another mommy for us.

She told us about her husband leaving and she said that she was still married. Mommy's husband had left some 30 years ago, to go get some cigarettes and never returned. Mommy later found out he moved to Oklahoma and started a new life but when he died the lady, he was living with recieved the house, but Mommy enjoyed receiving his pension. She was left to raise three kids, my Uncle Allen, Aunt

Retha and my grandmother Hazel during the depression with limited education and money. Mommy survived depression, leukemia, breast cancer, mastectomy but her heart grew tired. We didn't really know how old she was because she didn't have a birth certificate. We figured maybe she might have been either late eighties or nineties. She would walk a lot or rode the bus and walk downtown and used tobacco and yet never had cancer. Prince Albert tobacco was always inside her cheek. As we said our good byes it was time to move on without our Mommy. That move was so very hard to do. It was so hard to let go of mommy's hands. I miss her love and kissing her on the side of her cheek where she had stored her tobacco.

The aroma of her place was gone. She was gone we wouldn't see her wave at us as with drove away or see her sitting in the window in her favorite chair, just chilling and looking out the window. The smell of Lysol, tobacco, fresh peach cobbler and the homemade hamburgers no longer lingered. The harder part was cleaning her place. I looked at my younger sister Bonnie and we both looked at each other with a sigh and realized that mommy wouldn't be sitting on the couch we slept on or sitting in the chair just enjoying her moments by just looking out the window. My Uncle Raymond and his kids raided her place and left what they thought was junk. It was treasures to us. Junk like the table my mother made when she was young, the cake pan that held the cakes she went downtown and picked up for us, the spice rack that looks like a book on a chair that I to this day still have. Yep to them this was junk to us it was Mommys', and our memories. It's sad that if something happens to our parents Bonnie's kids will be the ones taking everything and leaving my brother Sonny and sister EJ will be left with claiming junk to them but treasures to us. We love one another but it is what it is. Again, there that reflection that you just can't see, but it does exist. My Uncle and his family were those same people that hardly spent any time with her. But were the first one in line to gather up her belongings.

I looked at the doors and remembered how Mommy chased after my sister EJ when she had sassed her. Emma Jean, sometimes we called her EJ, always had a habit of talking back. Hmm she stills does always have to have the last word. You would think as she grew older that she would have stopped by now. She talked back to Mommy and tried running out the back door. Mommy was pretty good runner for her age and caught Emma Jean. We laughed at Emma; EJ didn't think it was funny. EJ in return took her teeth when we were picked up and Mommy chewed my mother out. I just remember my mother saying that she didn't have her teeth, until my brother Sonny and I were laughing at EJ trying to put them into her mouth. What could my mother say through the laughter in the background? Mommy response was bring me back my teeth and they bet not be broken. One thing we all knew about Mommy was she didn't play. So, EJ found out the hard way that Mommy had another secret. We didn't know about her being a sprinter. But later we found out that she had passed that gene down to our mom. Looking back another thought comes into mind with my sister sprinting home because of her mouth again. Some girls were chasing her home and she forgot to turn into the gate. My mother watched her while she was standing in the door. She watched EJ get the end results of her mouth. Hmm, EJ was able to sprint away from the girls. But she ran too fast and ran past our gate. Needless to say, that the girls caught her at the corner and finished what her mouth started. My brother said he had different memories behind Mommy's door.

My brother Sonny had a different story. He said he had gotten into a fight and the boy was getting the best of him. Opportunity presented itself and he took off running back to Mommy's place. She looked at him and pushed him back outside and locked the door saying we don't' do that. I found out later from Sonny that she pushed him out the door with a look and a shove and told him to go back and finish it. He laughed now but not then saying pick up where we left off at the fight, I was getting my ass whip. Sonny said after that fight they had become friends. That pretty much what happened when we fought either you become the best of friends or just acquaintances, or just ignore each other but you lived. What I took from that was finish what was started even if you had to go back. You are stronger than that, and finish so you don't ever have to look over your shoulder. I was in this marriage for the long hall. Mommy taught us that finish what you started. I loved when we would spend the night and how she spoiled us big time. We always helped her set up her homemade alarm, by placing newspapers on the floor by the door and at the end pop bottles. Whoever came in the door or window would slide onto the newspapers into the pop bottles making all type of noise. One thing Mommy was a light sleeper. Whichever, item she reached for from under that pillow that was what they were going to end up with either slash, shot or beating it just depended on what her hand grabbed first. Like my brother always said he felt sorry for whoever broke into her house and funny no one ever did.

As I continued to absorb and remember the places where items and furniture were placed I could only sigh and smile. I looked at the spot where her television was located. Every Saturday night we would watch the "Lawrence Welk Show'. She loved watching ballroom music and dancing. Her other show she loved was "The Fugitive'. As we look around the room sharing or remembering our memories, my mother set in the chair Mommy used to sit in as she would look out the window. My mother was looking out the window knowing this would be her last time too. It's hard to say good-bye but Mommy's heart didn't suffer any more pain. Mommy washed her clothes with an old fashion washing machine and hung her clothes on the line. She always kept it moving. As I looked at the sofa bed, I remember how all three of us slept in that bed fighting over the covers. And being in the middle the cover was just on top of you with no type of comfort, while my brother slept in the room with Mommy. I looked at what might be trash to others were treasured memories. We looked over at her phone and realized that we wouldn't be able to call her anymore. I still remember her number. I remember my little fingers dialing on a rotary phone and then advanced to a push button phone. I thought if I forgot the number, I would forget Mommy. She still lives in all of us and it's been almost some thirty years ago. My mother still misses her and we still to this day talk about her. She has been embedded in our hearts and memories. I felt Mommy's strength and my problems seemed not to really move me. I wasn't thinking about Bill or what he might be doing. It was good to be home.

Yes, I was back home, and it was good seeing friends and familiar surroundings again. I kinda of ignore Bill's phone calls after all, what would we talk about. I was away from the pain and confusion. Sierra was enjoying the attention and playing with her cousins. Yes, it felt good to be back home again. I enjoyed going to places with my family and friends as my parents enjoyed watching Sierra. I was back home with familiar faces, places and back with my family. Being back home felt good but I started missing Bill. This was home, but my place was to be with my husband. Although, it felt good to be home and it would be so easy to stay and pick up where I left off, I had to go back home. But like Mommy said we don't do that, finish what you started. As it was approaching time for me to leave, Bill called with concern in his voice. He was wondering how my family was doing, how I was feeling and when will I be returning home?? Funny, but not ha-ha I didn't talk to Bill that much because I was out having fun. I hesitated with my answer wondering do I want to return, and to what. What would I miss? Many family and friends were happy to see me and wanted to hear about California living and my heart was happy to see them too. California was nice, but it wasn't home. I pondered leaving Oakwood, because here I was laughing and smiling again. My thoughts were did I want to leave my comfort zone and family. This time the innocence had changed me. I wasn't the same person I was when I left Oakwood, or would I be the same person returning, (if I go back), to Oceanview. I just didn't know what it had turned me into. I still was exploring my options and my thoughts on my living arrangements with Bill. Bill pleaded for me to return it was like he knew or felt my inner thoughts. He wanted his family back and he missed us.

My Aunt Martha and Aunt Adele talked to me and said that I should give it another try. I heard my mother's voice stay here, I heard Mommy's voice saying finish what you started, because we don't do that. Although, it hurt my dad to say there is nothing here for me and your family is in California. That had to hurt my father saying that but, he was telling me to grow up and that I was no longer daddy's little girl but now I'm daddy's daughter. I talked to Bill and told him I would be returning but things had to change. I had to repeat that emotional roller coaster of leaving my family again. They didn't know how much it hurt me to leave or the hurt that I was receiving in California. This would be my secret but, I had to see this through, so I wouldn't have any regrets later.

Chapter 8
Well What's Up and Who is He

Well, we went back on the train and as we pulled into Amtrak station in Oceanview. I looked out the window to see Bill looking for us. As I exit with Sierra, I heard that song playing in my head. Every time you go away you take the biggest part of me. Sierra jumps off the steps and runs to the waiting arms of Bill. He picks her up and swings her around and just hugs and kisses her as she laughs and tells him she mised him. As, I walked slowly toward him I'm having mixed feelings. Who is this man, and should I have stayed in Oakwood? Was I given another chance and blew it? He looks at me with a big smile and stretches his other arm to hug me. He kisses me and says how much he misses his girls. That silly song just kept playing in my head. I looked into his eyes thinking what do you want from me? I'm not who you want any more why prolong this? Why bring me back from my comfort zone. I didn't have much there in Oceavsion and he could have kept those items or threw them away. He says I love you Rita. For once I felt his love again and enjoyed his warm embrace. I could hear the voices of Aunt Martha, Uncle Cully, Uncle Duckie, Mommy and my dad's voice saying it's going to me alright. As we walked toward the car, Bill held my hand; that was something that he hasn't done in a long time. I felt that we were merging again into one.

This was random move just like when he held my hand when we left the mall. Guilt must have set in after that stant sales clerk had tried to sell him shoes two sizes too small. Yep, what random act did he do while I was away??? Was this the same man that I had to ask permission to touch his hair, to hold his hand, yet he grabbed my hand? Again, who was this man? When we made it to the car, he opened the door and kissed me again. I had forgotten how sexy his lips looked and how soft they felt against mine. Maybe this was the reason I came back. My heart and soul needed his warmth again. Could this be my imagination or was I watching our life on television and all this was not real. What channel was I looking at? As he closed the door, I look at him as he walked around the car. At what point will he change back. I almost went into shock when Bill held my hand as he drove. I just knew we were on some type of caught on camera segment, because this was not the man I left. Who or what was filming us as I absorb and meditate on his actions? I had to look around to make sure I didn't see any cameras filming us, is this real?

Maybe Bill was happy having his girls back. Maybe we did take the biggest part of him when we went away. My thoughts were going in so many directions as I stared out the window wondering what is really going on. There were no cameras, no taping and no camera crews. I had this funny feeling and it was tearing me up inside. Those family voices kept popping up just give it a try or just watch he will do something to ease your mind. I was trying to digest all this and try to remain calm and loving. Here I go again with disguises. When we arrived home, dinner was waiting with flowers for both Sierra and me. The food was pretty good. The roast was tough and the potatoes a little crunchy. I guess he picked that style of burned meat and crunchy potatoes from me. Hmm he was paying attention, I guess. We both laughed, it was kinda like last years' Thanksgiving dinner. Sierra laughed because we were laughing, and we just couldn't stop. When we did it ended in a smile. We both looked at each other and said let's put Sierra to bed. I listened with a smile in the next room Bill telling Sierra a bedtime story. He did it often that was their daddy and daughter time that she looked forward to. I could see and feel the joy of listening to him. Bill would combine so many characters from books and cartoons that it confused Sierra to sleep. I think it just wore her out trying to understand and picture all the characters. I really don't think Bill knew that he was adding so many random characters. Sometimes I would just laugh in silence as the view of them together warmed my heart. Bill had his own way of reading, playing and talking to Sierra. It seems as if as he read the book or tells a story in a way that they communicated and understood each other. In the back of my mind I was wondering why he didn't just read the books that were by her bed.

The night was wonderful yet different. Listening to Bill tell Sierra a bedtime story and enjoying the family time was my picture to capture. Bill did things that surprised me. Our night was wonderful and filled again with love. But something was bothering me. When I put my head on his chest something didn't fill quite right. Hmm, something happened but tonight wasn't the night to try and figure it out. As I think about that night Bill was trying to add some spice to our life. We were becoming an old young couple. It's hard stepping out of that comfort zone. Even to this day I'm hesitant to switch from coffee to tea. Bill had taken a few days off, so we could go look for another apartment and spend some time with us. I admit I didn't like the flying roaches, but I did like our complex, but our family was increasing, and more space was a must. We would be leaving familiar faces and the families that had become to admire and adore. Well we went to several locations and found a nice three-bedroom apartment. Wow, Bill was serious about his family again. It felt good being Mrs. Bill and walking together as a family. I wasn't showing yet, but I did have flash backs when I first became pregnant with Sierra. Was he going to run with other women and allow them to come into our picture? I would look at the women and wonder how Bill was looking at me. They dressed sexy and had no hidden secrets when it came to their bodies. I felt uncomfortable seeing their very revealing clothes with much attitude. I remembered the one-time Bill was holding Sierra when we went to the beach, and two women came up to both of us saying how cute Sierra was yet glaring and smiling at Bill. I thought that was a bold move with showing no kind of respect. My mother used to always try to get me to dress sexy and I have always been a conservative dresser. Well, I dress conservatively, and I felt good about it. Ooh what a flashback when I went back to Oakwood and came back slimmer. Bill said why I waited to go to Oakwood and become pretty. I thought what a jerk, what did I look like while I was raising our family. Was Bill becoming bored with my attire and look? Well, I thought if he was, then he needs to invest in my wardrobe. Ooh was that courage trying to creep in? Hmm, I was feeling that ancestral strength coming on a taking a front row seat. Bill used to always say when you go home you get some courage and bring it back. I guess I did. Then the strength said girl you are pregnant. What outfit do you think you can wear? Ooh that drop kick that thought. Oh well look at me now I got it. Well this place was three-bedroom apartment located downstairs. This was nice because I didn't have to load things up and down stairs, and I could sit outside the apartment and watch Sierra and the next one coming. I tried packing a little each day moving slowly through the whole process. I guess I really didn't want to move to another unfamiliar area and I really didn't know how to pack. My grandmother helped me the last time as I stood there and watched. I sure could use Mama Sadie but that is not going to seriously happen. Now I had to grow up again and figure this out. Everyday Bill would ask how the packing was coming as he would come home late from work. My thought was can't you see, we both live in the same place.

I really didn't have the nerve yet, to voice that thought. Was he still doing the office hours? I was still trying to figure out what that meant. He was expecting dinner, a clean place and plus take care of our family. Now, don't get me wrong he did spend time with Sierra especially on the weekends. Let me see think Rita oh yes, he made time for me when he fussed, cussed and complained. Was that considered my quality time? I guess it was some form of quality time. Well at least we were communicating. I had to wonder is this how married couples live? Where is the sunshine? Wow it's still raining outside and in my life. I know there is a rainbow coming through, but when will the rain stop. From time to time I thought about the older couples and what they might have went through to come to this point. Were they happy or just learn to tolerate each other? Some of them you see with smiles and they look like high school couples, and others look bored and just too old to leave. I guess they were in their own comfort zone they created. I guess it was better growing old together with love and/or some form of squeaking. Something that Bill was trying to convince me of he wanted, to have someone to squeak to. I want to be that happy couple looking back on the years of the joy and pain along with raising our family. Minus a lot of squeaking, because I didn't want to do a serious snap. Seeing our children grow up, date and someday marry. Hoping, we would be seeing our next generation of grand-kids and then some. But first I had to get through our trials and problems. I had to continue to be the adhesive to our family. I had a gut feeling I had to fight. But I didn't know what battle I was was preparing for. Funny thing was why???

Hmm time was approaching and move out day was coming. Some of the families had moved out so in a way it was easy to leave and finally saying goodbye to the flying roaches and their acrobatic teams. Melba watched Sierra maybe for the last time. So, Bill and I okayed for Sierra to spend a night. Sierra always had fun playing with Michelle and Mickey Jr and Melba watched her from time to time. We said we would try and stay in touch, but friendship doesn't end it just eventually fades away. I wonder what Melba is doing now and what her kids look like. Bill stepped up and helped with the packing. Some of his soldiers' friends arrived looking mighty fine. I knew them by their last names now he was introducing them by their first and last names. All I saw was their fine chiseled features, oh how they were in chiseled shape. About five came in tight ooh baby jeans and white t-shirts showing the strength in their bodies, with that clean-cut look. Fresh haircuts always turned me on. Kinda of reminded me of fine boys in high school singing and the fine cameo cousins. To this day, I remember them their faces as they were singing, Markel, Brian, Marcus and his brother, wow. I just glanced at them when Bill introduced them, but that was a good memory glance. There was Erwin, Tavis, Stan (the man), and Michael, (aka aw ooh). I asked shyly what does aw ooh mean. Everett says because he is always getting injured. I chuckled, and everyone laughed but Michael. His response was that he could play a mean game of pool but put your knives up just in case. I smiled and said we are having chicken no knife required. They saved the best for last in walks in the one they called 'Z' for Zmarkus. He shakes my hand and looks at Bill telling him that Russ and Hornsby had to work on a special assignment. I thought hmm never heard those names before, but we were here in California. They all had the same smile with pearl white teeth, trimmed mustaches and dimples to set off their lips. Oh, yea baby the military haircut was on all of them. I had to talk to myself by saying, Rita stop before your mouth drops open staring and Bill catches your eyes. Hmmm, just thinking about them with a nice cup of coffee, sure does feels good.

I would glance out the corner of my eyes as they picked up the boxes flexing those muscles. A couple of his friends looked at me. I nervously smiled and kept it moving. What could they possibly see in me? I guess first part of your pregnancy you do look a little sexier with bigger boobs, until your stomach catches up with everything. It's funny how you can tell that a woman might be abused in some way by how they respond when you talk to them. They give you very little eye contact and conversation. Sometimes they come across very nervous and anxious. I really didn't want to look at his friends for fear, and not knowing how Bill would react. He kept me pretty much away from everything and people. Sometimes, when I would go over to Melba's place or talk to the other neighbors Bill would come looking for me because I was gone too long. I would see him through the window walking and looking around and I knew it was time for me to come home. I would just kindly excuse myself with that nervous smile and say I have to go. So, I'm so familiar with that smile and nervous reaction. Again, I'm gaining more of life's experience. Well as we were moving, I went to our new place so when they arrived someone was there. I picked up some food, so I could cook for Bill and his friends. I knew at some point they would be hungry, and it was only the right thing to do.

So, I fried up some chicken with biscuits, green beans, macaroni, corn on the cob and Mrs. Smith deep dish apple pie. As they were bringing in the boxes and furniture, I was busy trying to unload some of the boxes and cook at the same time. His friends would make comments about there was something that sure smells good. My thought was you just don't know how hard I had to learn how to cook this meal. It felt good to hear a compliment, because I really didn't hear them often. Actually, it kinda scared me when I did get one. Bill heard them and responded yeah Rita can cook. Wow, his response sent a shock wave through my soul and penetrated my brain. He invited them to stay for helping us move. They gladly accepted they pretty much said at the same time they can't remember the last time they had a home cook meal. As they set down to eat Bill blessed the food as he always did. They couldn't wait to dig in. As they ate and talked about sports, back home and work. 'Z' had mentioned how he was glad that Bill recovered from his office hours. At that point everyone and everything just went quiet. As I looked around the table at everyone's expression it was something that slipped out. I thought here we go again with the office hours. I really didn't say too much at the table just when someone directed a question towards me. Michael compliments me on the meal and told Bill he was blessed to have a fine humble mid-western woman like me and that could cook too. The meal reminded him of his mom cooking back home, and that he was thankful for the invitation and enjoyed the meal. Bill smiled with a smirk and you could tell he really didn't like the comment and said yea man I know.

I thought no, no, no and please don't say it, ah man. Rita is a good wife, mother, soulmate and my best friend. I don't know what I would do without her. Tavis said he has one of those home grown mid-western woman. At that point I quickly finished my dinner and excuse myself from the table. I thought this is my 'que' to get up before the conversation becomes too focused on me, don't linger go now. The guys stood up as I left the table. Bill acted like he was getting up, but he never made it fully up. Hmm, I can't remember the last time he opened a car door for me. I thought what gentlemen. For Bill the thought was right try again soldier boys. I again did the nervous smile while thinking that Bill was a good liar. Since when did he ever call me a good wife, let alone his best friend or soul mate? The other men at the table co-signed what Bill and 'Z' had said. They gave me a toast, not gesture but…. For some reason, I felt more embarrass. I really didn't know how Bill was going to react after they leave. My gut feeling sent me back to what happened with James during our college years. Man, I didn't want to argue, or fight about something that was nice and innocent or ruin a nice day or spoil our evening. After dinner, they stayed maybe for about an hour or two just hanging out in the front room since the furniture was set up. I nervously washed the dishes as I listened to them continue their conversations they had started at dinner. Sierra was spending a night at Melba's so the night was ours. I kept thinking did I look at his friends too much, did he see my mouth drop open when they entered the apartment, did I say anything wrong, did I come across as a flirt trying to be nice? I had a lot of 'did I's" racing all through my head. My emotions were racing, and my brain was thinking so fast I could dissect my many thoughts or my many questions.

I really wanted to ask about the office hours. But I knew that was definitely a no, no or a not. That warning in my head move right up front and said strongly don't do it, do you remember what happened the last time. It sounded like sirens ringing in my head. Life experience set in again. After finishing the dishes, I started going through our new place trying to take advantage of Sierra not being here and have her room set up. I miss her, but I knew she was having fun playing with kids around her age. I kept as quiet as I could not to bring any attention to my presence. My thoughts switched to looking into each room enjoying our new larger place. The master bedroom had its own full bathroom, how nice. I really didn't know how much the rent was. Bill took care of all the finances. While Bill was still entertaining his friends, he sounded happy. They were all laughing at looking at the fights. When they finally left, Bill called me to let me know that they were leaving. They all thanked me, and everyone gave me a hug. That was not good for me, man. Ooh that made me so nervous and caught me off guard. I know they meant well and were just happy being with a family and being off the base. My thoughts were how Bill was going to take me being hugged by not one but five men, and co-workers. I admit those hugs felt good and the scent of their cologne lingered into my nostrils. It felt like I was human and could feel again. It startled me when they hugged me. Inside I was thinking I'm gonna die for this hmmm, warm embrace and hugs.

This coffee sure is hot not only did it burn my tongue it just numbed my senses. Again, emotions raced and how was Bill going to react when they finally left. I was really nervous about his reaction. It felt like arriving home way past your curfew and you make it worst by coming home later because you knew you were in trouble. My gut feeling or life experience was setting in as Bill walked them out to their cars. I watched them walk away laughing and joking. I was hoping that Bill would keep the laughter and joy going. I didn't know what to expect when he walked toward me as I was looking out the door. Why did I go to the door, in my mind I was standing there looking proudly at my husband? I looked around the neighborhood/complex and it seemed so quiet and calm. If there were any kids, they must be inside. Tomorrow, I will have my baby back and we can explore our new environment. As Bill walks, toward me I notice his smile and I smiled back. My insides said don't fall for it. So, my smile became nervous and my insides became scared. Until, we went inside, and his mood changed just that quick. All I knew was I all of a sudden, I was holding my cheek. It happened so fast. I looked at him and wondered if I could make it to the door and take off in our beat-up car. Now, I remembered and flashed back to how I wanted to run out the door at my parents' house, when my mother asked me if I was pregnant. Now, here I am pregnant again and history somehow repeating itself. I tried running for the door for fear set in. We both made eye contact on what my next move might be. Fear entered my soul and rage came out of Bill's eyes. I felt something hit my back as I ran toward the door. It was the rolling pin I used for making the biscuits. Bill, grab it and threw it at me to slow me down. I made it outside the door and all I could feel was a hand grabbing me and pulling me back into the apartment. I tried screaming. I couldn't hear my own voice, and no one responded. Maybe my voice or cries were silent. My shirt was torn as I was pulled back inside. Terror entered my soul and fear was shivering behind me. What could I have done? I kept a low quiet profile around his friends. I tried avoiding any type of eye contact and didn't smile or glare at them. So, what was the problem? At least give me a chance to either explain or give me a get out of beating card. Some type of pass should be given to me. Because I really didn't know what I did wrong or what I did to upset Bill so. In my thoughts, my brain was racing to try and find an answer. Now, I know how Toni felt when she and Jovan would fight.

Like rain calm before the storm comes and the storm was coming quick with no signs of sun light or a rainbow. Well he brings me back into the apartment fussing about them hugging me. I responded with how was that my fault. He hit me again for mouthing off. Do you think that they would be interested in someone looking out of shape like you? Have you looked at yourself lately? He dragged me all through our new apartment. As my feelings meet my fears and tears, I felt my body hit the walls. And I heard the sounds of my body as I was thrown against those freshly painted bright white walls. I felt his foot in the middle of my back. My quick reflex was to protect my stomach. I couldn't feel my body. It felt like it just took the hits without the pain. I had an out of body moment. I couldn't hear my voice. I felt the boxes crumble as my body landed on them. When was this going to end? He complained about what I wore. I had on a long jean shirt and a blue blouse that fit real loose. What was sexy or appealing about that? To me my wardrobe was crappy. Sexy had left the building long ago. He said they said that you were nice, and you had it going on. Going on where my clothes were old and fit tight because I didn't have any other clothes that I could fit and look half way decent in. When the hitting stops, I got up not looking at him. Bill left as I went into the bathroom. As I grab a wash cloth to wipe my face, I'm here again. I turned on the cold water and just let the water run on top of the facecloth. Looking in the mirror at a face I didn't recognize anymore. The cold towel would help with the swelling. I knew how to aide myself. But I didn't know that I would have to aide myself physically and mentally. Wondering how an almost perfect evening could end up this way. I wipe the tears and emptiness came over my soul. What should I do? Why bring us back to have history repeat itself with the beatings again. I didn't want to go to a shelter with Sierra. I didn't know anyone here to go and stay with and moving back home was not an option. Go back home with one child and one on the way. How was I going to support my family? Welfare was out and who would hire a pregnant lady.

Funny how history repeats itself? Here, I was due around January 27th or 29th again. Only difference it was too early for Christmas to be a gift wrapper job, and how would I get there and who would watch Sierra. What about my prenatal care? As I left the bathroom pondering all those thoughts, I saw the blue dye from my jean shirt all over the hallway white walls. I was tired and told myself that I will get it off the wall in the morning. I'm going to bed, because it's been a long day and I'm mentally and physically tired. I crawled into bed slowly not because I was in pain because I felt my spirit leaving me. I felt so drained what a long day. I laid there crying and so many thoughts were forming. I was still trying to figure out what I did wrong. When Bill came home, I heard him fumbling in the kitchen a bit. Then I heard the main bathroom door slam closed and eventually he came to bed. I didn't make a move not even turning my head to look at him. I felt his body pressure only so slightly. The kiss good night was out and when we turned our backs toward each other Bill would kiss the back of my shoulder. That I knew was out, he used to pull the covers over me to tuck me in that was out too. No conversation and no apology. We just went to sleep as if nothing had happened. I laid there as still as I could. He told me that I wasn't a good mother or cook and that I wasn't worth anything and meant nothing. Those guys filled your head with all that nonsense they don't know you and you just kept smiling and loving all that attention you were getting. You liked all that attention, didn't you??

Only if he knew I was trying my best to not have any type of attention directed towards me. So, Bill was feeling left out. Bill thinking was so narrow he didn't realize how big of a compliment they were giving him. I don't know why he was so mad he invited them, it was his party all I did was just cook. So, this is about his crushed ego or feelings. Here we go again it's about Bill, woo, woo, and a tear. Should I kiss his booboo and tell him it's going to be okay. I muster up enough courage and said you weren't anything either hitting on a pregnant woman. I'm your wife not one of your girlfriends. Why did I say that Bill hit me twice in the face? I immediately shut up. The tears flowed but I laid there too scared to make a sniffing sound. Snot rolled down my nose and met up with my flowing tears. Once Bill went to sl eep, I wiped my face with the cold towel I had used earlier. I eased out the bed moving real, real slow trying not to wake up Bill for any more rounds. If I moved slow, with very little movement, he wouldn't feel me easing out of the bed. I just couldn't lay there like this. I made it out of the bed and Bill didn't move or reach for me. I felt bad inside and out, empty bruised and scared. I ran the water slowly not looking in the mirror. I really didn't want to see what I looked like. The reflections were becoming frightening. I got back in bed trying to ease with little movement looking at Bill with so many thoughts running through my head. At that point I realized you can hate a person and want to smash a pie right in the center of their face and at the same time show love by wiping the pie off their face. I laid there playing Bill's words back over and over. He also had the nerve to say that I cry too much. I cried because his hits hurt. Now, I had to go to that ancestral strength on where do I go from here. One thing I knew I wouldn't do was cry again. From that day on the tears wouldn't flow. Maybe my eyes will fill up with water, but the tears will not ever flow again. This is something that I had control over not Bill. I learned how to become numb to my feelings. Show no emotions and show no pain. Weeping may endure for the night and joy comes in the morning. What happens when you weep during the day?

The rain hides my tears, but it can't hide the redness in my eyes from the pain my soul is feeling and crying out for help. I needed my mom and my family. I missed my conversations with my dad. Most of all I missed my great-grandmother Mommy. To this day, I still remember her telephone number. I still want to dial her number and hopes she answers. I just couldn't let them know they would only want me to come back home. If I told them they would make me feel bad and I had to make this work. This was my family, and something is wrong, but I still don't know what it is. Eventually, my mind rested enough to put me to sleep. I laid there with the cold towel on my eyes hoping that all swelling would go down. I didn't know what to expect in the morning. All I knew was keep on praying because trouble doesn't last always. Hmm to this day people don't understand my strength because I show no emotions or signs of pain, but it doesn't mean I don't hurt. This was from life experience and I learned not to display emotions. Do I feel? Of course! Just like anyone else I just can't let go enough to cry or show any emotional reaction. I know this coffee sure taste good, I can feel the soothing taste with each sip. The rain is really my friend, because I can hide my feelings as the rain cries for me. I wasn't interested in his friends, they were just being polite. They must have filled Bill's head up about me for him to be that mad. I guess he had to face the fact that someone else might want me and was looking at me. That I am still capable of turning heads. Why not he married me, I can't be that much of a bow wow. I can still turn heads ooh, now that felt good.

Well I knew I had to get up early and try to straighten up and pick up Sierra. Bill did help with cleaning on the weekends, so we could do family stuff. I woke up to the smell of bacon and biscuits and Bill mixing the eggs in a bowl. When we first met that was Bill's specialty along with cleaning. I guess with working he put the cleaning on me even though he did complain about my cooking and cleaning. Neither one of us look like we were missing a meal. Bill kept in shape, but he could do some damage to food. I walked slowly into the kitchen. Each step was accompained with fear and wide eyes. I didn't know what to say or how to react. My emotions were behind me looking over my shoulder. I looked around the apartment and some of the boxes were empty and thrown away. Even the crushed box I landed on. There were no traces of the anger from the night before. It was as if he tried to erase what happened. Here I am again with Bill trying to orbit me to think that I was back in twilight zone again. Just like he tried to do when he pushed me down and tried to convince me I fell. He looked at me and smiled. I looked at him and rolled my eyes. He asked how do you like the way the apartment looks. I said it looked nice even the blotches of blue dye on the hall way walls. I guess he missed a spot. Bill walked toward me. My thoughts were oh you said too much again Rita. Girlfriend, you are gonna have to learn how to bob and weave and block and cover your face. I didn't know rather to run or block. He stretches arms out as he walks toward me. I'm confused about the kindness he is displaying. What was this all about? He kneels and grabs me by the waist and puts his head onto my stomach. Bill looks up at me with sadness in his eyes. He said he felt that when they hugged me that his space was violated. Rita, you belong to me. I'm the only one that should ever hold you like that. They thought so highly of you and yet I didn't think that much of you. I felt embarrassed and ashamed. I really disappointed you and myself. My thoughts were you could have said that instead of throwing me around the apartment. That would have felt so much better. Bill almond eyes sparkled as he said that he didn't want to lose me. You and Sierra and our baby are all I have. You are my strength. When I come home, I hope you are still here and Sierra's in her room playing.

I told him I have no interest in them, but why do you cuss and fuss at me so much. He said I wanted you to be as mad as me. I responded with you seem to be mad enough for both of us. I heard my friend Doug voice say I rather deal with the headache I know than the ones I don't know. Hmm words to live by. Why would I want another unknown headache? I asked him what do you want from me?? I just know that half the time you act as if you have so much hate for me. Bill stood up and embraced me and said how could I hate the one that gave me a new life and put up with so much. I still couldn't grasp what was going on. Was my mind gone away again? I was hearing the words but had to look at his mouth to make sure it was moving. I just couldn't or wouldn't believe his words. My heart wanted to, but it just didn't feel right. How can he look at me with a straight face not noticing the bruises and scars on my face, arms and legs? How can you not notice in my eyes the pain my soul has been suffering by your actions? If we are one how can you not feel my pain? Where was his mind or thoughts? Bill just looked at the food. With all that happened all he could say was that he was hungry. He smiled and said let's eat breakfast. I smiled and stuttered and said it sure smelled good. Bill nervously smiled and said, it should I burnt so many pieces of bacon and biscuits. I wanted it to be perfect, but you know we are used to burned food and he gives me a smile with a wink. I was going to feed you breakfast in bed, but you woke up too early.

Chapter 9
The New Shoes Experience

Bill said that he noticed that I needed some new shoes. The ones that I have been wearing looked as if I walked all the way from Oakwood. I thought good, because the only pairs of shoes I had were one pair tennis shoes, one pair of boots, and one pair of dress shoes and the walking shoes he talked about. He wanted to go to the mall and I will be there with him. Now this was a surprise only time I went to the mall was to look around. Was Bill really trying, but through it all I don't remember hearing an apology. Rita just enjoy the day and see what happens. Joy did come in the morning. As we walked out Bill ran into a friend that told him about the apartments. His name was Clarence and his roommates name was Keith. Clarence and Keith both worked at a place where they made 747 air plane parts. Hmm, to this day I still can't remember the name of that place. They had another roommate I didn't see him much. His name was Darryl Alan. He was a theatrical actor, so he was on tour a lot. I did have a chance to see some of the movies he acted in, but very seldom saw him. I just remembered they were nice, and Keith loved cooking. I didn't hug them I learned from that last lesson. I saw a father throwing football too I guess they were his sons. Now let me think the father's name was Amos his wife name was Monica Monique and they called her Momo. They had young sons look like they were many different ages. Their names were Bert, Chris, Craig and Ryan. I remember when Momo saw Sierra she fell in love with her. As I think about Momo at first, I couldn't understand why she yelled or talked so loudly. At first, I thought maybe she was hard of hearing and thought everyone else was hard of hearing, but she had to yell so her sons could hear her. Actually, they all talked loud except for the dad. I guess they got so caught up in their sports world they would lose track of time.

Every now and then Momo would bake special shaped cookies for Sierra or buy little outfits or little toys. I welcomed the love she showed for Sierra and our family. I picked up a few recipes from her and she would laugh at the outcome of me trying to duplicate her creations. Momo would treat me and Sierra like we were her family.

She always wanted at least one daughter but said it was too late. She was happy with all the men in her life. They treated her like a queen.

I tried to look my best going to the mall because I was going with my husband. Maybe he will treat me like a queen. I took the ponytail out and let my hair hang down. Bill comment that he forgot how long my hair was. I threw on some lip stick and a little perfume and it was on!! Bill had on some nice fitting jeans with a denim shirt. I thought it looked nice on him and Bill thought the same thing. I would look at him in the bathroom mirror prepping himself. He spent more time in the mirror than I did. I was thinking can we go now. How much can your looks change in five minutes standing in front of the mirror? Bill opened the door for me which very seldom happened. As he drove, he was doing most of the talking. I listened to him as if he was the receptionist at a doctor's office. I answered occasionally then sometimes I just listened to the music as if I didn't hear a word he said. I learned that from my mother. You can be sitting right next to her and she might answer, or she might night. She showed no shame or any concern. If you didn't hear yourself talking you would think you were invisible to her. I did always enjoy riding and just looking at the scenery change. When I was younger my parents used to take us for rides. No reason just to get out of the house and a change of environment. As we park and enter the mall it was seemingly crowed. It was full of noise and many conversations. Bill and I kinda look at the various stores. Out the corner of my eyes I saw that same woman, Gail or Gayla something like that. I remembered seeing them at the restaurant some years back with another lady. They both seem to look at me as if I just arrived from some farm. I observed them staring in our direction as they whispered to each other. If Bill saw them, he didn't show any signs of concern. I looked at the clothes they were wearing and I visioned what I had on. I punished myself mentally by comparing them to me. I used to wear shorts and shirts, but Bill said my legs looked like baseball bats and strongly suggest I not wear them. So here I am in this long jean skirt hiding my legs. Right when I was kicking myself for my lack of a wardrobe Bill grabs my hand and suggests that we go into a maternity store. I glanced at those ladies and smiled as we entered a store that they knew the purpose. Again, I kept wondering who these ladies were. I asked Bill did he know them, and he glanced at them and said nope without hesitation.

We looked and made our purchase and went into a shoe store where another woman looked at Bill as if she knew him. My gut feelings said that they knew one another. Hmm what is her name, Allison hmm that figured. He smiled at her as she asked if we needed some help. I told her that we were just looking for now. As I look at shoes and feeling pretty good about being out with Bill, I found a couple of pair of shoes I liked and wanted Bill's opinion. It felt like I was moving in slow motion as I turned to look for Bill to find him laughing and talking with the sales clerk that originally asked to help us. When they noticed my expression, Bill grabs a pair of shoes and asked if they had them in a size twelve. Allison notices my expression and she asks him if he would you like to try those shoes on and in what size again? My thought was what is going on here. Life experience was setting in. Now, I wasn't that bright about certain things, but I knew this situation didn't look or feel right. Now Bill smiles at me nervously. I responded with a yell right. He knew by my look that I wasn't pleased. Well Miss Thang or Allison or Alice didn't matter I didn't like her, she bought his shoes out in a size ten and I looked at the nerve he had in trying them on. I had to watch this act of Bill trying to force his foot into the shoe like he was auditioning for the role of Cinderfella. With eyebrows raised higher than they were before when I saw them talking. I just looked at him with a duh look. Bill looked at me and said she said they would stretch. I looked at him and said you got to be kidding me. They are not going to stretch two whole sizes. A course she bought a pair of shoes she liked. Hmm they both were playing the role of idiot, except one will be coming home with me, minus the size ten shoes. In my mind, I just want to pop him in the head for trying to add me to his idiot movies or episodes. In my mind, I just wanted to pop him in the head for trying to add me to his idiot episode with that nasty co-star and there was no movie sequel.

I just had to shake my head and re-adjust my thoughts from wanting to grab each shoe make them airborne into his face, so he could smell the leather and tell me what size it was. Also watch the magic stretchable ten shoe fit the size twelve feet. This woman or thang wasn't going to have any power over me not this time. I thought about propelling both shoe boxes at her and wonder which size hit her first. Yep, my ancestral strengths were cheering me on with getum girl, you got this. They didn't look like the two pair of shoes I had given her. I just looked at her with; you should be interested in my business and not my husband. I gave her a look that I didn't think I was capable of giving. It was a look I grew up and developed from my father and my mother Sheryl. He had a mole in his eye that when he stared at you were hypnotized and didn't know if the eye or the mole was staring at you. All you wanted was the stare to go away. My mother gave you a look that pierced right through your soul. Now, if my dad had on his glasses that mole had another all together different look. All those glasses did was magnify his eyes and the mole and forced you into a trance, and you would confess to every and anything to be released from his spell. I guess my dad strength kicked in with a little mixture of moms.

Bill watched me walk away and for that instance he listened to me. I made sure that walked made him realize who and what he had. In my mind my high school figure came back for a brief cameo and ancestral strength didn't abandon me. Work it Rita walk slowly and make this walk count. I looked at him with that lingering look why waste it and asked slowly for clarity do you know her. His response was a course nope shaking his head saying nope slowly for clarity. Here we go again with the nope. What is this a new word he learned from Sierra and shaking his head in the same manner. Well we made the purchase with another clerk. As, we walked out Bill grabbed my hand. For that moment, it meant nothing to me because I really wanted to slap the full idiot out of him. I held his hand, but it wasn't with a grip. It just didn't feel right. We walked the mall and just window shopping with very little conversation. I just glanced in the windows to avoid any more meaningless conversation. In the back of my mind I have flashbacks of those girls at his place and the thang that he allowed to take my seat. I watched how some women would say how cute Sierra was while looking at Bill, as if I was the friend of the family or invisible. I would look at their eyes and read between the lines and he just didn't get it. On this one I did get it and just didn't know how to deal with it. Sometimes I felt I was all alone with my thoughts and no one would understand the inner me that is confused and bruised. I said its time to get Sierra and bring her to her new room. As we walked toward the car another set of women looked at us or Bill as if they were waiting for a hello response. He walked right passed them and so did I.

Today was not the day to try and figure out nonsense. It will take too much energy, effort or thought and today wasn't time for it. I wanted to go get my daughter and prepare dinner and just forget about this whole weekend. As we drove home Bill just kept talking. I talked just like someone in trouble and was trying hard to hold some type of conversation. I just looked out the window and put my mind back into the doctor's office not hearing the receptionist. Today Bill was the receptionist. We pull up to our old apartment and my heart is filled with joy of seeing the neighborhood kids playing outside, and the smell of dinner filled the air from various apartments. I looked up at ours and it seemed so empty. Well duh Rita it is, and I smiled at that thought. We both walked up the stairs to Michael and Melba's place to pick up Sierra. When we walked in Sierra's eyes lit up as she ran toward us. Bill reached down and picked her up throwing her in the air. I smiled as I listened to her tiny laugh and voice. She yelled mommy and daddy I missed you and I made this for you. She gives us a leaf that was glued onto construction paper. The colors were pretty but the love that was put into it made it a classic picture. We told her that we were going to put it on the refrigerator, so everyone can see it. She giggled and laughed causing everyone to laugh and smile with her.

For that moment, the sun smiled on all of us just like the sun is trying to come through the rain. As Bill carries Sierra, he glances at me with a smile and a wink. I glanced back at him with a smile showing my teeth. I just want to go home. Sierra looks as if we missed our turn. Her expression was one of confusion. Where are we going daddy she blurts out? Bill says we have a surprise for you. When we arrived home, she ran through the apartment with wide eyes and an open mouth. She somehow found her room and liked how her toys were displayed. We took her picture and placed it on the refrigerator, and it seemed to brighten up the whole room. As I smiled, I glanced down the hallway and notice the blue dye on the walls. Sierra innocence and learning her colors said mom there is blue on the wall. The blue did stand out on the fresh bright white walls. Bill and I both looked at each other because we knew how it got there. I waited for Bill's response. He reached for her and said it came from mom's pretty blue skirt. I looked at him and added with dad's assistance. Bill looked at me no expression just a don't do this now look. I went into the kitchen and prepared dinner. Thinking about that blue stain until the thought faded away in preparing a dinner menu. Bill and Sierra went back to her room and played with puzzles and read some books. I liked hearing her voice asking questions. One thing Sierra love to do was put puzzles together. Now that was her quiet time and she didn't want any type of interruptions. I would look at her expressions that showed a childlike serious concern on completing her puzzles. I guess it paid off to this day Sierra is very good at solving situations.

While cutting up some potatoes Bill comes behind me and gives me a hug and kisses on my neck. I guess he felt my uneasiness at the mall. I smiled and said it's not good to sneak up on me while I have a knife in my hand. He steps back and said you would cut me. I smiled looking dead into his eyes no someone needs to be here with Sierra. He steps back even further and asks what time dinner will be ready. I told him in about one hour. He says he will be back. I really didn't care at that point. Hmm I always loved it when our family ate together on Sundays. Thinking about Sunday always includes some type of family thing. Rather eating dinner or going over to Mommy's house for her famous peach cobbler, yummy. Hmm I can go for a slice right now to go with this cup of coffee.

After putting the roast in the oven, I noticed that I didn't hear Sierra playing. When I went into her room, she had fell asleep on her puzzles. I picked her up and put her in her bed. She was so tired she didn't wake up at all. As the hour approached dinner was ready the aroma filled the apartment. There was no sign of Bill. I checked the phone for a dial tone, and it was working. I didn't use the phone much because I would run the phone bill up and it would end up becoming disconnected. So, I had to refrain from calling home. I was isolated and felt like I was on an island looking at people enjoying themselves on land. I looked out the window for any signs of Bill arriving home. I stepped right outside the door and just looked around the complex. I watched a lady and her I guess were her daughters carrying bags from their car. She looks at me and her daughters with a very pleasant smile. It was very warming and needed. I was feeling a little down and that smile was welcomed. I watched the girls carry bags that probably weighed more than they did. The little one said momma this is heavy. She replied suck it up walk, talk and move. We are almost home, and you are hanging tough. Walk with me don't drop my hand. I always wondered what that meant it meant walk with me follow what I am saying. I smile now because I use it often. I admired their strength and their politeness. Their mother came for the last group of grocery bags but stopped to introduce herself. She said her name was Robin and her daughters were Denise and Nicole. I had to ask how old they were, because they were carrying them heavy bags and didn't complain at all. They showed such discipline. She laughed and said that you don't see them behind closed doors. Denise is nine and her little sister is Nicole is six. I listened and watched how she was developing strong, independent women. As I remembered I watched them grow into very manageable, polite, beautiful young ladies. They reminded me of a young Carolyn and Sharolyn very athletic and busy. Robin welcomed me to the neighborhood and went into her apartment. As I heard her door close, I looked around for Bill to arrive at any time for Sunday dinner. I had to wake up Sierra, so her bedtime schedule wouldn't get thrown off. One hour went to two hours and the clock kept on ticking. I woke up Sierra, so we could have dinner before it got too late for her. Sierra stretches and struggles to open her eyes and looked around and asks for her daddy. She asks again for him and I told her he will be home in time to read or tell her a bedtime story. Sierra said grace and she did such a good job. My heart smiled at hearing her say words that she didn't yet understand. She looked so serious and said amen at the end. Sierras added bless my daddy's food too.

I smiled but I wondered was he somewhere eating or what. The phone still had a dial tone, so what was his reason for not calling. Where was he? Bill never missed out on our traditional Sunday family dinner. I thought did something happen to him. My mind raced to the welfare of Bill. Well Sierra and I ate dinner and she helped with the dishes. I washed, and she talked. Some of her words I understood and struggled with trying to understand the other words. After dinner and dishes, I put a plate up for Bill and ran Sierra's bubble bath. Time was still ticking, and Bill was still missing in action. I got Sierra out the water and ready for bed. She wanted her dad to read her a bedtime story. Where is my dad? I told her I don't know but I can read to you today and dad will read to you tomorrow. She fussed and cried because she wanted her daddy and she wanted him to tuck her into bed. She definitely was a daddy's girl and she knew it. As she cried, inside I was crying too, because I didn't know where he was. It was very hurting not knowing and not allowed to ask. I had to do something to keep my mind from wondering.

Sierra finally cried herself to sleep. So, as I walk down the hallway frustrated and concerned, I look again at the blue dye on the walls. I stare so hard at the stain I thought it look like it was moving. The spot looked larger and darker. I turn my head from side to side looking at it from different angles. I stared at it until the stain became a big blur. I went into the bathroom and collected all types of cleaning supplies to try to scrub and scrub the blue stain away. As I scrub flashbacks of my body hitting the wall flashed over and over. The sound of my body hitting the wall echoed and turned into a ringing sound in my ears. My head starting pounding as I scrub harder and harder on removing the blue dye off the fresh painted bright white walls. Where is Bill and why am I scrubbing this stupid wall. Anxiety set in and I felt myself feeling light headed. I stood up slowly and at that time Bill walks in. I look at him with such a puzzled look and said what happened. Why couldn't you call home? Dinner had been waiting for you and Sierra cried herself to sleep waiting for you to come home and tuck her into bed and read a bedtime story. He said that Dennis, Michael and Russ were stranded, and they had to make it back to the barracks before curfew. I asked why you didn't call, and he said that he lost track of time in picking them up and trying to make it back for dinner. I told him I had a plate waiting for him. His response was that he wasn't hungry because he had grabbed some food with Dennis and them. He just got caught up and lost time and track of everything. I just went to the oven and pulled out his plate placed it inside the refrigerator. I really didn't have anything to say after that. I turned and walked down the hallway to check on Sierra and gave her a kiss goodnight and headed toward our bedroom.

I listened to the footsteps of Bill. He set on the couch looking at the television. The volume was very loud. I thought I heard him on the phone but as sleep set in and I nodded off I thought I was just hearing things. Why would Bill be on the phone this late and not in bed with me? I started to get out the bed to go into the front room to confirm that he wasn't on the phone. As I started slowly to remove the covers, I heard Bill coming down the hallway. It sounded like he stopped and paused in the hallway and headed toward Sierra's room. I hurried and threw the covers back on me and closed my eyes pretending I was sound asleep. There you go again Rita working on your Oscar. Hmm, I learned to perform very well. He went into the bathroom and closed the door then came out and set on the edge of the bed. My eyes were slightly open looking at him. Something was bothering him; I didn't know what or how to ask. I watched him put his head into his hand and just sat there. Something was bothering him and inside I wondered if he would share his thoughts. If so, come on Bill let's talk. He set there for a while and with a big sigh he took off his clothes and got into the bed. I felt his eyes on me and I tried to lie as still as I could and look like I was sound asleep. I guess it worked he leaned over and kissed me on my forehead. Was my mind playing tricks on me I thought I smelled Chanel perfume? I knew it wasn't me wearing Chanel, because I always thought it smelled old, but I smelled that fragrance somewhere before. I laid there fighting with my brain where or who had on that perfume. Where did he really go and who was he with. Dennis and the crew weren't available for me to ask and I don't think they wore Chanel. Nor was I ever going to ask them. I eventually fell off to sleep with those last thoughts. The next morning Bill got out the bed before I did. So, I didn't get a chance to prepare his breakfast or make his lunch. He kissed me on the forehead and hurried off to work. He kissed the forehead that developed a headache from his actions last night. Somehow, I had to relax my thoughts to stop my head from aching. What was wrong with Bill kissing my lips? I long to feel his lips press against mine. He was such a gentle good kisser and I missed that too. Was someone else experiencing the pleasure of his lips?

Since I was up, I prepared Sierra's breakfast and planned our day. I didn't have a doctor's appointment. At least two to three times a week Sierra and I would ride the bus to become familiar with the area. Minus the blue stain on the wall we were finally settling into our new apartment complex. Sometimes we would transfer buses or find out where the local parks were, or local libraries were located. Sierra was going to be starting school next year and her brother or sister will be in need of a big sister. She was looking forward to bossing someone around. I would laugh and smile as she spoke to her sister/brother by talking loud to my stomach. Bill went back to his routine of working late some days but was home for some of the weekends. I still needed to find out what is still bugging me this thing called office hours. I'm still puzzled about what does it mean and who can I ask without it getting back to Bill. As I grew larger Bill became scarce. I made it to my appointments and walked often. This time I saw the same doctors on base. It would be either Doctor Warren or Doctor Jerome. They both were patient and thorough with me. Actually, I looked forward to seeing them and the nurses to have some type of adult conversation. It still was lonely not working. I really missed working and having my own income and less restrictions.

One day in route to the bus stop Robin saw us and asked where we were going. I said we just ride around for a few hours to become familiar with the area and get out the apartment. She asked if we wanted to ride with her because she had a few errands to run and she could show us another mall or children's fun center. I smiled at her kindness but was embarrass about my limited funds. I had a bus pass and just enough change to get a little treat for Sierra. How do I tell her I have no money and still save face? I really didn't like not having any money. I remembered before we married, I had a savings account and friends. Now I have no money, no friends and no first name. I'm a wife and mother and Bill's friend. Wow, all I have to show after four years of marriage is this! Where did I lose myself? Robin looks at me as if she knew what I was thinking. I smiled and said maybe next time. Inside I really wanted to say yes please take us somewhere anywhere. I wanted to run and jump in the car with Sierra and say hit it lets go. As the bus pulled up, I told Robin thank you and can I have a rain check. She smiled and said I will hold you to it. As I got on the bus, I watched Robin turn the corner and I just wished I would have said yes. Sierra looks out the window describing everything she was seeing. I heard her, but my mind was on the freedom Robin displayed and the joy in her voice. Since moving from our old apartment, I haven't really had anyone to talk to. As Sierra talks with so much energy and joy, I thought about where my joy went and when will the rain stop falling on me.

Occasionally, I would look out the window hoping to see Robin to either talk to her or cash in that rain check. When I was younger, we would go for rides without any money just enjoying the scenery and conversation. Bill would ask what you are looking for, and I would sigh and say just looking no reason. Occasionally, Keith would come over to borrow some ingredients he needed for baking. He loved to bake and whatever he baked he would bring it over to the apartment. When Keith came over it was either for eggs, flour, sugar some part of the main ingredient needed to complete his recipes. Now, Bill didn't mind him coming over as long as he was there. When Bill wasn't there Keith kinda knew the rules and understood when I would bring what he needed to a cracked door opening. Actually, I looked forward to tasting his creations. I would always tell him he needed to open a bakery, and we would be his first customers. Keith would smile and rush back to his place to finish his baking smiling and laughing to himself. Sometimes when I would come outside with Sierra, Keith would come out and keep me company. We would just talk about nothing in particular. His roommate Clarence would sometimes join in on the conversation. I really didn't see Darryl Alan the other roommate but look forward to talking and seeing him too.

Chapter 10
The Rain and Check Arrived

That rain check came finally in a form of rescue on a Saturday afternoon. Robin might have heard Bill yelling as she passed our apartment. I stood there looking at him like a child getting scolded by their parents. I showed no emotions which was hard being pregnant because all, your hormones are all over the place. I heard a knocking at the door a welcome relief from Bill's routine blah, blah and blah. I thought really Bill if you wanted to go out, all you needed to do is change your routine from always starting an argument, just leave. Just go like you normally do. Don't let your lonely pregnant wife stop you from being bored for the weekend or week day. I opened the door and who do I see Robin smiling asking if I wanted to go with her to run a few errands, before I knew it, I said sure and told Bill I will be right back. He looks at me leave with a surprise expression at the same time Sierra says dad come and play with me. Sierra's timing was perfect, thank you Sierra. Now that's my little girl watching out for her momma. I smiled and grab my empty flat purse and dashed out the apartment. Robin looks at me with a smile with keys in her hand and a purse on her shoulder. She probably smiled because I accidently stepped on her feet trying to hurry up out the door. I apologize and thanked her for asking.

I hopped in the front seat fastening my seatbelt like a child getting into their car seat. I didn't care where we were going, I just was happy that we were going. Wow and yippee and my thoughts were turn on the radio and let's do this. Hit the pedal sister and make this car move. We went to places that the bus route never had taken us. I rolled the window down and let my face feel the wind hitting it. For that time, I felt the fresh air of freedom I saw in Robin. She was very pleasant, and her demeanor was calm and confident. As we talk girl talk, I really wondered what was Robin's story? I never saw any type of male figure around her apartment. I would occasionally see her working on her car. I thought wow she is very independent. She didn't come over to our place or any other male person to ask for help. Her daughters Denise and Nicole were pretty, kind and very respectful. She talked very proudly about her daughters. You could hear the love for them in her voice. She said they were the reason she had to leave their father. She went on to add that almost every generation repeats some type of action.

Ramon's Uncle Glooly, (aka Gluman Lee), was called that because he stuck to many women some at the same time. He was happy with being a womanizer yet when he died, he died alone. They didn't even show up for the funeral I guess the glue dried when Uncle Glooly or glue stick died. When he was in a nursing home, he had two women fighting over him. Always the glue stick until the end. Ooh my thoughts went racing on all types of reasons; one thought was I really could be friends with Robin. I haven't had a good friend since my grade/junior/high school and college years. Robin noticed my expression of just kinda fading away, yet I heard everything she was saying. She asks if I was hungry because we heard both of our stomachs growling. We both laughed with Robin insisting that we go and have brunch/lunch and talk a little more it was still early. I laughed and said when is a pregnant woman not hungry. My silent concern was being away from home too long, but I was enjoying talking with Robin. She listened to me as if my words were important. Wow I felt human and real again, not invisible. While I was in deep thought, I could see Robin pondering that thought of a pregnant lady being hungry and with a delayed response she starts laughing. She laughed so hard she made me laugh with her. It felt so good to hear laughter that was not at my expense and we both were laughing.

We stopped at a restaurant called Blue Wave seafood. Seafood was their specialty but had a large menu of other items. As I look at the menu and at the ocean view where we were seated the place was warm and atmosphere felt fresh. I noticed a light crowd with each occupied table involved in their own conversations. I slowly looked at the menu again and everything looked good, smell was slightly killing me, and hunger was there, but reality set in. I didn't have any money and couldn't afford any meals on this menu. All I had was a bus pass and some air even the spider left and all I pretty much had was just an empty flat purse. I'm now carefully looking at the menu because I only have a few dollars that really won't add up to buy a soda or cover a tip. With a big sigh, I said I thought I was hungry, but I changed my mind as my stomach grumbled saying something completely different. I knew in my mind I got caught up in having some adult freedom and being paroled from Bill, kinda like being on a few hours' furlough. I had to get home before warden notices I'm not in my bed or passed curfew. I just smiled, and Robin said this is my treat and don't be acting all shy. We are girls out just having fun and conversation. Robin goes on to say it feels good to be out of the office and enjoy my day while the girls are at their Grandma Phyllis Ann's house. My thoughts were what are your working hours, because I see you at various times throughout the day. She said they were doing the spoil me weekend with her. She thinks I don't know how she spoils them rotten and sends them back. I'm thankful for her, my sister-in-law Donna and my parents that still live in northern California in a city called Valley View. I told her I never heard of that city. She said it is between Oakland and San Jose. As I look at Robin talk, I noticed she had one slightly deep dimple that showed when she talked or smiled and small mole by her nose. Thinking back her smile and demeanor reminded me of my Aunt; Martha, Barbara, Inez and Jo had the same calm personality and the smile at the beginning and end of a sentence, laugh or joke.

I enjoyed their conversation just like I'm enjoying Robin's. Her eyes kind of twinkle when she laughed, and she was fairly attractive and maybe 5'4 and medium built. Her hair was curly dark and shoulder length nails manicured no make-up other than wearing light layer of lipstick. If she had on make-up I couldn't tell. She spoke with clarity and had a gentle but firm nature. You could hear the confidence in her voice. I started to ask why she was single. That was when the waitress Bershonda (or Bee) came for our order. I really didn't know what I wanted. Seafood sounded so good and so did the different sandwich combinations. I really didn't know what an avocado was, so I decided to try the turkey cranberry sandwich on sourdough bread and a glass of water. I really wanted a soda but, I didn't want Robin to think I was being disrespectful. Robin says hmm that sounds pretty good, I will have the same, with two glasses of fresh squeeze lemonade as she smiles at the waitress and winks at me. I look at Robin and told her I never tasted fresh lemonade. She smiles and says you will enjoy it. As we continue with our small talk, I love looking at the waves from the ocean. I gathered enough courage and asked what she did for a living. She told me that she used to be a CEO for a marketing company and just took a temporary leave because they refused to let her resign. Right now, she is kinda on an on-call basic, consultant with benefits with her firm and from time to time she does free-lance photography for the local news stations. She was saying that she didn't realize how much she enjoyed taking pictures. It started out taking family pictures and cataloging her daughters Denise and Nicoles' moments as they grew. See I like how they capture the moments and you can smile as you look at them later. Your mind can capture the moment, but the pictures hold the time. She laughed and said that I needed to take pictures of my family. I agreed since we really didn't have any type of family pictures, especially updated ones. Robin said she loved photography and still like the fact that could stay with the firm she had been with for many years. I asked so you are a consultant now? Robin laughed yes something like that. When they need heavier guns, they call me. Then I come in with my weapons and go back to whatever I was doing. They made me an offer I couldn't walk away from.

She must had noticed my puzzling looks because, she said let me share something with you. My puzzled look confirmed my confused thoughts on her comment. Robin leans toward me, (as if she was going to whisper), saying that we have a little time for a story you might find interesting. I didn't understand then what

I now know what she was guiding me through. She starts by saying she had been married to her college sweetheart for twenty-five years and some change. We both shared the same dream of being some type of marketing executives. We both went to school in northern California and when we graduated more opportunities were available in Southern California where Ramon's family lived. So, we moved there with bright ideas and goals that we were going to reach together. We started out pretty good. We both landed jobs with the top marketing firms. I advanced and Ramon kinda lingered behind because his heart was no longer in it. By that time, we had leased a house with the option to purchase and the house was large enough for our future family. We thought it was a good idea at the time. Our family grew by two daughters and we had money in the bank and life was looking good and very comfortable.

We both were making good money and had comfortable savings accounts. Ramon came to me one day and said that he wasn't happy. Robin said it kinda startled her. She thought things were going well and why would we be talking about a divorce. If he was asking for one, I didn't see that coming. I smiled but I was thinking the same thing. As she talked, she remained so calm and poised. He said he wanted to get back into the entertainment field. Okay his dream his heart desire why not after all we are partners in marriage and co-partners in his business. Being the good wife and supporting my husband you know why not. Being a CEO of well-known advertisement agency, I was able to fulfill my dream and I believe in if you're in a marriage or relationship you work together. By putting my hand in the middle of his back, and not my foot on his throat I will be there to push him up the hill and in return he can reach down and bring me up standing by his side. I said with a big sigh lets go for it, you have my total support. After all, Rita we were in this together.

It started off slow but later it picked up in a matter of two years. Through the ups and downs, it didn't matter because we were in this together. I carried the bulk of the weight because I had to support my husband's dream in supporting him supported us. He was happy which meant we all were happy. But in the entertainment field there is always some type of women temptation. You can only imagine that there is someone always auditioning trying to replace you or advance in their career at anyone's expense except their own. There is always a woman out there that wants to take the short cut at someone else's expense. I never really thought that Ramon would be unfaithful, I thought he was stronger than that; it never ever entered or crossed my mind. Until I started noticing his hours became longer, his temper shorter, phone calls to the house at all late hours and they were always in some form of a whisper. Ramon tried to start little arguments and my response was I'm not going share in your frustration or play ping pong with your arguments. I firmly told him that I will listen and discuss whatever is happening like we both have sense, but if you yell you know exactly where you can take that. I'm listening as if I was looking at a movie that was filled with suspense. Right when she was getting into the plot the waitress Bershonda brings our food. I was thinking not now I want to hear the rest. Robin breaks and asks the waitress for more napkins. I sip the fresh lemonade and I close my eyes and sip again and again and I like it, and Robin can tell by my expression. She smiles and says I knew you would like it. They make the best lemonade and sandwiches. I'm thinking finish the story I must get back home soon because I left in such a hurry, I don't know what type of mood Bill will present. Robin says now where did I leave off at. I said you said he changed. Ooh yes Robin looks as if she is trying to put the thoughts together. His mother told me she loved her son but would have divorced him four years into the marriage. She knew how much I loved him and wanted the marriage to work. I would just smile at her statement, because I was still crazy about her son.

His sister, Donna who was crazy about her brother too but one day she pulled me to the side and said she wanted to talk to me about something that was very sensitive. She reluctantly said that when I go out of town for business, he brings the girls over to the house to spend a night. He claims that he must take care of business. Donna breaks with a big breath firmly saying that, she didn't like it definitely didn't support it and she didn't care who it was. Robin says I'm looking at Donna and there was a cross between pissed and pain. I could hear the disgust in her voice as she was telling me about it. While she was telling me, I was trying to remain calm, but I was boiling inside. I'm looking at her and I can't believe what I am hearing could this real. She had to be telling the truth because it flowed so smoothly and precise. Donna said the Ramon hangs out at the mall picking up whatever, whoever and there is no good coming from his roaming. He was just as trifling as those scants, he trying to talk to, and you know those nasty ho-hos know he is married. All of it equals trouble that you don't need in your life or my nieces didn't need to see or hear about. Donna reinterated that she loved the time she spent with her nieces but, it wasn't right what Ramon was doing. She said that she didn't, wouldn't, couldn't, support that type of party. Donna repeated, I love my brother and you know I do. But his craziness is not right from any angle. He's not right and I didn't know or if I should say anything. As I listened to Donna, she didn't know that this was tearing me up the inside. Robin said as I listened, I felt my mouth hanging open along with my mind, this time it wasn't close.

Donna said you are too kind, I've known you since I was four and you deserve to be treated better. Now, my eyes are slowly opening and really hearing what she had to say. I took the long way home listening to some soft jazz. I had to gather my thoughts and just simmer on what Donna had said. I had to get my thoughts straight. I found myself thinking about the strange things missing or out of place at our home. He was making me think I was crazy when things were out of place. So,

I start thinking about, with visuals on how there was hair in my brush that didn't belong to me. The hair color was a slightly different color, or make-up pads in the trash basket that he said belong to his sister or the girls were playing in my make-up. I knew this was untrue because I barely wore make-up. I wore make-up only on special occasions and, why would Donna come all this way to apply or play in my expensive make-up.

I really didn't think about questioning Ramon over and over about the strange things happening. My first thought was he would think that I'm displaying some type of insecurity. I didn't have time for any type of a useless argument and no room future tripping, just don't trip it's all in your mind. Sometimes you have to pick and choose your arguments. For some reason time wasn't made for that argument, but twenty years plus should mean something. I must check Ramon on this. Respect is something I was raised on. The more I thought about it the more I just refused to be disrespected in any way. So right when you think you are going crazy or starting to replay instances and sort thoughts and process what's really happening. While I'm trying to sort out my thoughts, my next-door neighbor First lady Janice who I love, and respect dearly notices me outside by myself. She pulls me to the side and inside I was thinking now what? I just want to get inside and chill with a nice glass of wine and my soft jazz. Get my thoughts in order and relax my emotions today and this moment was not a good time for me to have another sensitive conversation. In the back of my mind was now what, this isn't really a good time. I don't feel like talking or being nice I just want to relax and chill for real. I know too many people that had been placed unwilling in a role of their spouse infidelity, and I wasn't going to have that role played in my life or heart. I don't believe in sharing my man. You can call me selfish but don't call me a fool. At that point the waitress brings us more lemonade with additional napkins. I'm sitting on the edge of my seat as I listened while sipping on my fresh glass of lemonade.

Miss Janice words were gentle she didn't want to pry into my family business but felt strongly about talking to me. She didn't want to hurt me, but she looked at me as if I was her daughter. My thought was would this waitress please go away I am on a time clock and enjoying this story, but keep the lemonade coming. Robin continued to smile as she talks showing her dimple saying that this was my last duh performance on this act. You would have thought we were at a bar the way we were drinking lemonades. Miss Bee didn't mind she kept her smile and she kept them coming. We both looked at her with smiles of thank you but please must hold the ice I think it's becoming too strong. My smiles had an added taste of thank you much but please go away. As I said my prayers I bit into the sandwich and it just melted in my mouth and how good this slightly warm sandwich tasted. I roll my eyes back with a sigh followed with a hmmm. Robin bites into hers and the cranberry sauce just flowed out. Now, I see clearly why she needed more napkins. I take another bit as I listen and my cranberry squirts out too. We both laugh and sip our drinks at the same time. So far, I am really enjoying my time with Robin. We dranked more lemonade and laughed as if were knew each other for years. All this drinking didn't help my bladder, but it was all worth it. Robin said that her and another neighbor came to her one day and told her that a woman would come over there and spend a night or two. Last week when I was out of town, that lady came over three times or was it she stayed for three days humph. This was the confirmation that I was told to me by first lady Janice. I trusted what she and Donna had said because they had nothing to lose by telling me. They didn't want to inflict that type of pain on me. I saw the pain in their eyes as they were sharing what had been happening while I was innocently away taking care of business. They took a chance on how I might react and, that showed me how much love and respect they had for me. When I look at her telling me I saw the pain in her eyes similar to how Donna's facial expression would had displayed. For that instant I felt like everything had left me even my sense. I became very numb as I shared in Robin's pain and story.

I knew that what everyone was telling me wasn't a coincidence, but I'm a visionary and I must see it for myself. Rita, I'm that type of person that must touch, feel and see. In the back of my mind I hope I was wrong. In my mind we as people make up excuses sometimes to avoid the truth. That hair I knew wasn't mine or that used make-up pad, but I said it wasn't worth the question because; I didn't really want to know the answer. Why look for an answer you really didn't want to hear or prove true. My mind was so numb to what might be. My mind was trying to avoid connecting the vision to my heart. How could something like this happen? I mean really this was my family, my husband and I just couldn't phantom him, Ramon seeing or being with someone else. One thing I wasn't going to do was to make my life and marriage an ongoing investigation. I heard about it and seen it but didn't think it would invade my home, my house, my family, and how dare them our marriage.

You see Rita you invest in your marriage, family and future together hoping that the investment will pay off. Then you have someone else that wants to cash in on your dividends without applying any emotions, money, time, energy or effort into making it work. Look at it this way we both invested in stock. We invested in our marriage and were expecting returns in form of love, life, and staying together. He cashed in our stock and for some reason forgot to tell the investor, which was me. I listened to her words on stock and investment and wished I would have paid more attention to Mrs. Covington while she was explaining how to read the stock in the newspaper. At that time that was the furthest thing from my mind and here it shows up some years later. I'm able to follow along but it just gave me that flashback of I should have paid more attention. I wondered how Bill viewed our relationship. Robin is not bitter just venting and as I li stened, she shows the same expressions. How could Ramon allow this violation to happen in our house? How could they wake up seeing my face smiling in the pictures? It made you wonder in the back of your mind were they laughing at you. As Robin was talking, I felt her pain and watched her expressions as she told her story. I could tell she was still bothered by it, but I can see that she kept it moving. She said she had to really do some soul searching on what direction to go. Robin firmly said that she had to resolve this situation and be prepared with a plan of action and act on her plan. She went on to say she had a gut feeling and that feeling is a form of a warning especially for you. Robin closed her eyes as she took another bite from the half- eaten sandwich. I ate mine as I listened to her every word with amazement. I felt I was in the front row looking at a movie that had a lot of drama and had me seating the edge of my seat intense with her every word. While I'm on the edge of my seat eating my imaginary popcorn, I wait for her to continue with her story. She takes a sip and said it wasn't about her anymore it was about her daughters Denise and Nicole. Would I want them to be subjected to the abuse of an unfaithful boyfriend, spouse or the unhealthy environment that would come from this drama? I had to put my feelings to the side.

So, I decided to change our environment and create a new beginning for our daughters. I put everything into motion. I talked to my mom Miss Shirley Jean aka grandma and asked if my daughters could come and stay for a month. Why not, since school was out. The girls could start enjoying their summer early with their other grandparents. They could be in another environment with another set of grandparents to spoil them, and of acourse Ramon didn't mind since it was just for a month. Don't get me wrong he loved his daughters and was a good father, Bill just couldn't be faithful.

I had to think of a place that would allow a good time away with a quick turn-around time. So, hum I told Ramon that I had to go out of town to Chicago for a week and will be back by Friday or Saturday. I forced a smile and told his sorry butt that I was sorry for the short notice babe, but work had to be done. I knew this would give him time to do his business. I looked into his eyes and saw the wheel in his mind working like a hamster spinning in an empty wheel. I smiled and said honey I will be back Friday or Saturday and maybe we can do a getaway, you know spend some time together. You know real quality time especially while the girls are away. I was working the room. I insisted that we needed some cuddle time. Maybe go somewhere nice and romantic while sipping on wine. We needed a change of scenery. While I was talking to him, I had to convince myself to keep performing this charade. Ramon smiled and said that a little vacation sounds good, and that he was looking forward to it, but the wine nah you know I don't like wine. Its funny I could see the lies coming through his eyes. He asked questions to reassure himself that I would be out of town for a long period of time. I looked at him and smiled with a wink and said let me start packing. I blew him a kiss and he grab it as I turned around and crossed my eyes. All the time we both knew in our own world that we both had plans for the week and weekend. I reminded Ramon that he didn't have to take me to the airport because the company would pay for the long-term parking and that way, I wouldn't have to inconvenience him in any way. He smiled and said that's my baby and he was going to miss me. I smiled responding with I will be thinking and missing you too, as I blew him another kiss and he pretends he catch it and place it on his heart. We both should have been given the academy awards for outstanding performances. We both laughed. Robin had my full attention and I had a mouth full of food. So, I kissed him on the cheek goodbye while rubbing his beard gently. I really wanted to knock the mess out of him, but I had to remain calm and get ready.

I pulled my bag out the closet and with my bag in hand I wink and took off. He really thought I was going to the airport. Nah, I went to the local Embassy Suites. I told Ramon I would call him when I arrived, which wasn't a lie. I checked in and took a nice long bath, while taking slow sips of wine. While I gathered my thoughts in my bubble bath and chilled with some soft jazz music and scented candles. It felt good just to relax and try to gather some peace of mind. In my rush, I always took showers and didn't allow anytime to sooth my body in suds. As I listened to Robin, I thought when was the last time I lost myself in some suds? I too thought about how I rushed by taking a shower. I needed to get back to some me time. Robin went on to say she kept listening to her music, sipping her wine while bathing and kept it going when she finally let the bath go. With a sigh out of nowhere, Robin said that she forgotten to make a special phone call. Yep, I had to make that one call to an old associate, and I hope he was awake.

You see my assocaite has been waiting for this call for some time just waiting for Ramon to hmm. Rita looks at her and says been waiting for what? Robin looks at me and said I was going back to my house that morning. I had to give Ramon sometime to think that I was gone. So that's why I took my sweet time. Funny, I took my time when I looked at my watch. I almost studied my watch so long, that the numbers started to blend together, and I lost focus. I had to regroup and refocus, and remind myself, that there was something that I had and must do. I snapped back like someone had slapped my wig on straight and placed the part back where it's was supposed to be, (we both chuckle). I thought enough time had gone by so now it was time to call Mr. Ramon. I called and told him that I had made it to the hotel. He asked, how was my flight. I laughed telling him that flight was bumpy, yet we had a smooth landing. As we were talking, I paused in the middle of the conversation and pretended that someone was at the door. I said, ooh dear someone is knocking at the door. Honey it must be room service bringing my luggage. Well, hate to cut this short but, I do have an early morning. I will talk or see you later, hun. As I hung up the phone, I don't think he caught on to my closing words. He missed my outstanding statement will talk and see you later. I could hear the joy in his voice of saying how was your flight and small talk ending with I miss you and I love you babe as we both click the phone good bye.

Hmm, what did Ramon think he was providing me with accomondating affections? He was right on cue when needed. The affections that are convenient rather in words or an unexpected kiss for show in public or private don't matter. Just know there is a hidden agenda but don't forget this one key point it could be a distractor. You must be alert to those accomondating affections wasn't Jesus betrayed by a kiss. I love you, right as he hangs up to redial his local scant who is in all ways on standby to accommodate. I thought I'm sure you do and when did you start calling me babe, hun. Certain feelings happen for a reason and that reason is that gut feeling. Normally that gut feeling is not usually wrong. He used to call be Nibor which is just Robin backwards. Ramon must be in time warp if he thought I was going to step backwards with his childish boy games. I said why not play along with this game. For this will be one time and one time only where we are both game pieces and why not amuse myself through this curtain act. He didn't know that I had my hand on the door knob waiting with hesitation to open the door and walk out, but I had to continue this curtain act. Humor us both in rehearsing our imaginary lines. I couldn't believe how convincing he sounded when he said, honey I miss you too babe. Here we go again auditioning for the Oscars again, and the winner is… Robin continued laughing, while holding her hand to her chest, as if she is at the podium accepting the Oscar, (while pretended to be wiping away tears). Hell, Rita he should have done all that auditioning with those scants before we made it to the altar. Ramon should have gone with the understudy, so I could have had a real leading man in my life.

When I arrived at my decision a fresh feeling filled my lungs and, I exhaled with freshness with a good spiritual cleansing feeling. For some reason, I felt a strange kinda freedom with that breath of fresh air. Guess you could say like a confirmation on my decision, a sort of peace. I knew I had to make that call to Ramon. So, after I did me, I did use the room phone to make another call. I wanted the number to give confirmation that I was at the Embassy Suite. I knew that this would ease Ramon's mind. Let him feel relax with thinking that I had arrived in Chicago and the sun is shining and he has all week. A whole week for Mr. Ramon to feel confident enough to bring Miss Trixee to the place I once called home. This way they can confirm my suspicion and why not spend longer time together. I said to Robin you know her name. Robin laughs and says ooh no, no there is a Trixee everywhere their specialities are tricks and treats. They are sexual performers' only one talent. Working to take yours because, they can't get their own on their own. One thing else, they are real good at accommodating affections. You might see some of them at the mall or down on Hill Street looking for an investor or in some cases a sponsor.

So, I thought what a good time would be to arrive home because I wanted to make sure that they were well rested. If I went around 7:00am that morning it might be too late because that is around school time for some people, and other people would be leaving for work. Plus, too many witnesses might see him with her, and he would have to explain. You know just entirely too much traffic and too many distractions. So, I thought 5:00 am sounds pretty good. They should be in a deep sleep around that time before that morning bathroom run. So, I laid out my blue jeans, sweat shirt, tennis shoes and placed my earrings in my purse no earrings were needed for just in case. After making my call to my associate I knew he would be there to pick me up. I went to bed not feeling bad at all about my decision. Actually, I was enlighthened about a new beginning. I had awakened before the alarm clock sounded, really couldn't sleep, I guess I was anxious, but the thought came across I don't mind being wrong. I put on my clothes and loaded myself into my S500 Mercedes. Robrier meets me at the Embassy tired but happy seeing me again. He was fussing while lecturing me at the same time. He takes me to the place I once called home. As I looked at Robin, I thought wow a Mercedes that's a nice car. Well, of course anything to me would be nice other than my left and right feet and my unlimited passenger vehicle called a bus. I listened as I watched Robin taking occasional sips from her fresh glass of lemonade. I mentally took notes to store in my archives for my own just in case. Just in case I had to pull the file out, and hopefully I won't have to but it's good to know it's there. Robin smiles gently showing her slight dimple with wholesome features as she tells the story and I'm in the front row paying good attention.

She said that they pulled up to her house and saw an unfamiliar car parked next to their driveway. Robin said she had to take a big breath. She had to be ready to see what was on the other side of this door. I listened and she that, I told Robier I will be okay. He insists that he could stay if things get out of hand. I told him I got this in so many ways I'm so okay. While exiting out of the car I sighed and looked at Ro as he looks at me with a heads up because, he understood the strength I needed. I look at the brake lights as he drives off. Wondering if I should run behind him saying hold up, I thought I was ready. Rita inside I wanted to run hard after him and say never mind, but my strength wouldn't allow it and my mouth opened but no words came out. My voice was a silent as the morning dew. Was I ready for this? I walked up to the door slowly hoping my thoughts were wrong. You don't know how I wanted to be wrong. I shook my head hoping I was wrong. For that quick second I found myself trying to convince myself that I could be??? As I listened, I reflect on trying to convince myself that I had indigestion but, I couldn't laugh because this was a serious situation. I was listening to and didn't want her to think I was crazy. I tune back into her saying…. I unlock my front door and entered a quiet house, but something didn't feel right. My stomach felt like butterflies were flying and landing all in my stomach. My leg felt like they were trying to give out on me, but fainting was not my option.

The master bedroom door was closed as normal. We always closed it before we went to bed. Some habits are hard to break. I didn't know if it was locked or not locked didn't care my house. You know it didn't matter he didn't know I had a key and why wouldn't I this was my house too. I placed my hand on the door knob and turned it slowly. I didn't know if I turned it slow to stop myself and turn around or I really needed to see what was on the other side. The door opened with ease not making a sound to the sleeping souls. I walked into the room to see them both not covered laying there naked in our bed. Inside my stomach rumbled, my legs wanted to give out and the butterflies took off. But I had something I had to correct, and fainting was not one of my options. I looked around the room and saw empty wine glasses on both nightstands, ooh I thought oh what a night hmmm. I saw clothes thrown about on my light blue carpet. I saw our pictures on the dresser and walls smiling as they laid there sleeping from the empty bottle of wine. Funny, but not ha-ha Ramon didn't drink wine, but this night I guess he did. I saw her outfit hanging on my closet door knob as if she was paying the rent up in here. Robin sighs and says she had her stuff lying around our once scarred bedroom like she paid the rent and Ramon allowed it. Miss Trixee probably thought we owned this beautiful spacious house. He didn't tell her the whole story. It stopped being a home when he bought that trick into our marriage and into our bedroom. He allowed this trick to disrespect me, our daughters, our family and our home, idiot. I looked at her as she was telling the story and my mouth drops open and my eyes water, but the tears wouldn't come out. I could feel her pain at the same time not knowing what I would do if I was in that same situation.

She walks over to sleeping Ramon and pats him on the side of his leg and says what's up. I look at my robe laying on the edge of the bed as if she had it on. This trick is trying to see if the robe fits her wide ass. I remembered leaving my robe hanging on the hook on the back of my bathroom door. Ironic she wanted my life so much that she wore my scent, stupid. I stepped over to sleeping Trixee and grab her big toe and I say good morning. I looked at her, but I didn't give her any features because she really didn't matter. Another recycled regenerated scant. She doesn't respond but, Ramon wakes up startled that he is seeing me. Yes, I wanted him to see the rage in my eyes through my sunglasses. I raised eyebrows because the pain left a long time ago. I saw the big surprise look in his blood red shocked eyes and he couldn't see mine. I guess that they must have been drinking my wine all night and jamming to my slow jazz. Which is ironic because, Ramon really didn't like wine he would nurse a beer, because he wasn't a drinker? As far as trixee she had no value to me. I didn't look at her as being a woman because I didn't see her as being human. Glancing at her the bell ding what she was talking about not being human. Kinda what Courtney Diane said I'm glad when a beach reminds me that she is a beach that way I don't forget she is a beach. In this case I think she was referring to Trixie as a beach but in a Robin sophisticated fashion.

I watched her as her eyes fade into her vision and just talks about it as if it just happened and eventually faded away. Just some object to supply numb boy needs. Ramon should have thought this through but, how can you when you are numb. With his nummy dumb butt. As I walked out of the room Ramon jumps up out of the bed grabbing his robe and trying to explain what I saw. Wow, like I woke up drunk. Funny, on this one my eyes didn't lie just Ramon. He stuttered as he tried to form his lies or thoughts as he tripped on his own words. I had a few glasses of wine, but I was nowhere near drunk or buzzed. My mind was clear, and my thoughts were not in any type of battle of should I be here. Kind of made me mad, for trying to play me for just total stupid. He watched me walk slowly down the hall and he thought I was going into the kitchen for what a knife, nah.

Their blood would not be on my hands. I looked at him and said my mother always told me that I should walk in like a woman and leave like a lady. I walked out proud and stronger than I ever had been. That ancestral strength whispered we got this and kept it moving. I walked out saying I will not be your entertainment. I'm scarred on the inside, but I refused to be scarred on the outside. I was determined not to show them any fear that was being held down by my strength. This was not worth jail time and no more of my time. With each breath and words my courage grew stronger. He watched me go toward the hall closet and not one time did I turn around to look at this weak lying man. This little boy, I once called the love of my life and a big part of my happiness. Ramon concerns were about the bat I had in the closet for just in case. Mom always says if you are crazy enough to have it you are crazy enough to swing it. Yep, at any time you could hear that theme batter, batter swing. He watched with real concern, I could feel his eyes watching my every move. I could hear his breath racing to try and catch up with his thoughts. I felt the silence in the air of wondering what was my next move? This was a side of me he was never introduced to. This was my reserved that he triggered. You see this was about me now on my terms in my way. I only showed him the me he needed to see. Now, the other me surfaced and it wasn't the one he thought he knew. He awakened a dormant surprise. Ramon had a supportive loving wife that believed that I was his side rib and we were one. I opened the closet door slowly and again slowly looking up and down. Then I paused he couldn't see the smile I had on my face only if he could read my thoughts. At that point I was far removed from any type of anger this situation was not worth that emotion. No "s" no emotion. I said oh here it is??? I just did that to mess with him and Trixie if she was listening. That heffer probably moved a lot last night, but she sure didn't move while I was there. If she did, I might have snapped and battered up on both of their asses. I reached into the closet and pulled out my packed luggage. As I left, I set a pair of keys on the counter with my back still turned and I walked out and closed the door.

Ramon shouts so you are leaving the keys to the house. I told myself that I was looking forward to a new life. There wasn't anything behind me, only my past. Ramon runs behind me yelling what you are leaving me the keys to the house trying to (get this) raise his voice. I smiled as I walked away then I hesitated turned slowly looking at the covered car. Then I gave him direct eye contact and said that we both took marketing class, together right? As I looked and listened, I imagine how smooth and calm her actions were throughout this whole ordeal. The main thing or subject Mr. Richards would always say that was enforced in every lecture and that was that you should know your product.

This was the only time I looked, and I smiled and said there is a song that I heard that had some lyrics about Tyrone. Well you don't have to call Tyrone because you are already in this leased home. I hum some words as I walked slowly just glancing around; looking as I passed the covered car that belonged to Ramon. I got back into my black on black S500 Mercedes no smile, no feeling showing and no emotions. Ramon repeats louder as he runs glancing at the car that's covered asking so you are leaving me my keys to my house. Hmmm, oh this is his house, right. I put my hand on the door with a pause as I heard Ramon's voice for the last time. I start the car up and slowly pull out of the driveway that at one time belonged to us. I asked Robin did she do something to the car. She shook her head no and said slowly I didn't do anything to the car. I looked at Ramon's expression out of curiosity of what was under his car tarp. The handsome face and the spirit I loved in this man were gone. I saw the ugly of his soul through his eyes and his face I didn't recognize anymore. You see the tarp was a little loose where it is normally tight and fitting. Robin laughs I bet that took his wine high and whatever else they had planned for that day. I guess no sex today!! As I pulled out to head down the street, I stopped and give him one more look, in my rear-view mirror as I drove off.

Robin starts laughing again and I'm trying to understand the laughter in this sad story. She says I looked in the rear-view mirror with a slight smile, as Ramon raised up the tarp. That tarp seemed more like slow motion in the breeze. I see his mouth open. But I couldn't hear his words. His arms go up in the air and he drops down to his knees holding his head in his hands. I asked again, you didn't damage the car??? I put my hand over my mouth with wide eyes looking at Robin and her expressions. No, I keep telling you I didn't do anything to his car as she shakes her head again nope didn't do anything to the car. Now, I could have taken my bat for just in case and bashed that car down to a six pack, recycle the rest but nah, I didn't do anything to that car.

She looks at me with a straight face to show that she is telling the truth. Robin, occasionally, closed her eyes as she responds to me consistently responding with saying that she didn't do anything to his car. Her cool and calmness while she was telling the story had me admiring her strength and her demeanor. I was very impressed. She has strength that seems quiet but when you look at her you see it there before you even talk to her. She did what Mommy used to always tell us finish what you started because we don't do that give up or run. I had replaced his or mine other S500 Mercedes with his old lime green Pacer. He didn't realize that I drove off in his car as he gazed at the tail lights. I bust out laughing lime green really didn't they stop making them some twenty years ago. I haven't seen any around for years. Robin laughs yes it was his original car with the same color tarp for the S500. The tarp for the S500 was in the trunk. Robin says now I was kind I could have left him a gremlin or a pinto or a ducted taped up hoopty. I wanted to leave him something he was familiar with.

You'll see Ramon's lime green antique was his classic. We purchased identical S500 black on black Mercedes. We were in love and she squints her eyes, (still showing a smile through them). Something told me to get that gremlin back. See you should always go with that voice that's talking only to you. I remembered the dealer looking at me laughing and asking was I serious. He had the nerve to negotiate the price. In the back of my own mind I had to laugh at myself too. So later that day I went back to the car dealer and purchased it as the dealers laughed holding my check in his hand and I caught myself laughing with them. I kept it at a repair garage called Robiers Auto care. I had helped him market his business and it grew into a large business enterprise. Robier or Ro let me store the car there and I paid for storage and he kept the maintenance up for me. He would start it up and take it around the block. He teased me saying I owe him because people would point, stare and laugh at him in that round lime green out dated car. I told him it could have been a pinto or gremlin. He responded is that supposed to make it better as they both shared a laugh. Ro said it was like driving in a big green balloon with wheels and that he had a reputation to up hold. I meant Ro at his garage, so I could pick up the Pacer and he was so relieved to finally get rid of it. I left my Mercedes back at Robiers garage with the same agreement. I asked why she didn't say anything to trixee. Why did you allow her to to get away with being with your husband? Why did you give her that power? I stuttered as I stared at Robin response with concern and some form of anger. She wasn't worth the time, energy or effort. She had no power over me. I had control of my actions, thoughts and I would not allow her to see or think in her little world that she had some type of prize in Ramon. My hand was on the door knob their actions allowed me to turn the knob and walk away. Now, she thinks she has advanced to my life, my world and become his wife. Nah, she did me a favor in allowing me to give her my problem and my headache. Now her trifling ass will need the aspirin.

Chapter 11

From Mistress to Good-Bye

You see I'm not looking back or going back I have too much a head for my daughters and me. Ramon loved us, but he should have loved us and his family more, how weak was that? She wanted to move from mistress to wife. She wanted my life, but mistresses very seldom get promoted. They really think that they might become a wife. Not even if she rehearsed it in her dreams. Somehow, she convinced herself with her limited vivid imagination her ranking order would change. They believe their own lies and the lies that Ramon probably told her dumb butt. You know it's rare that they become their wife. Usually, they marry someone else and the scant/trick gets played. She left signs of being there and she knew what she was doing. The trick tried raising her leg like some type of puppy trying to mark what she thought was her territory. Mr. Trix tricked the trick. If she didn't know she was more stupid than dumb. Whether it was knowingly or unknowingly he allowed her to disrespect our home and violate our vows. Trixie had no reason being in our house like she had some part in paying the rent/bills. Her dumb ass probably thought we owned that big house. She knew there was an-us.

Twenty-five years of marriage and he only thought about his own selfish needs. Ramon took off his ring rather it was physically or mentally. He removed our commintment the moment he opened that door. How easy that was just a simple twist of the ring I placed on his finger. Ramon removed his allegiance with just one twist. He confused lust and love at the expense of our family. Ego had a high priority over his love for his family. The love he had pledged years ago, left don't know when? If love was still there all this crap wouldn't have happened. The lust is just a temporary emotion it last as long as the feeling, but real love lasts a lifetime. Ramon went from us and we to all about him. I supported our family while he was getting his freak on what a serious slap and it wasn't on my ass. Ramon was supposed to protect my feelings, but I realized that I was responsible for protecting my own feelings. I don't share my heart, but he shared his heart and thoughts and much more with someone else. I felt so violated in passion and hurt by the betrayal to his family. I had more questions like what he shared about something as special as our intimacy. Did he share thoughts with her he should have shared with me? I pushed him up the hill for our family and hoping he would pull me up, so we could stand together. Because, I really believed in us and that we would continue to grow and be together for twenty plus more years. I guess he got bored and I was thinking this was just the beginning of us finally reaching our goals. Quality time for us was really going to start. Heck, I thought that someday we would be playing with our grandchildren and travel more. Travel back to Barbados or rekindle the love we had while visiting in Paris.

As I listened and thought about it then as I'm thinking about it now while enjoying the rain I long to go to Paris and Barbados. I don't really know how much it would cost or if we could ever afford to go, but it did sound fun. I thought I was doing something big when we moved to California. I dreamed with a slight smile as I continued to enjoy the interesting conversation and time with Robin as she continued. She said that the pain that was inflicted on us, me our family was straight up on the wrong. Pain does fade away into tomorrow's memories. It is up to you if you want to stay stuck on that same channel or thought. This trick didn't care because Ramon didn't and showed her how not to. That was all taken by one trick or there could have been more. I'm not going back and make myself sick behind her or any other nasty women. She knew I existed. She saw my picture on the walls, the dresser in the bedroom she knew we were married. She saw our couple pictures and wedding photos. She saw our family pictures, so she knew. She knew my scent, the perfume I wore my shoe size probably my panty size, she knew me on an interment level. She shouldn't have been allowed to know and he shouldn't have allowed her to get that close. It wasn't fair for her to know me and I didn't know her or what she looked like. In her world, she wanted my life including Ramon and my wardrobe. How can another thang call a trick because I can't put her into a category of human, that thang was nothing but somebody's filler.

I found out later that she wasn't the one that had spent the three days at my house/inn. Living freely off someone else's sweat, tears and heartache, she didn't realize she gave me a compliment with her weak selfish dumb ass. Robin looks at me and noticing my perplexed look. Inside I was feeling her tears and her pain because I have been there. I wanted to wipe Robin's invisible tears for I had them also. People sometimes think that if you don't show pain that you are not in pain. That is a crazy thing. She wanted everything about me, so she had been looking at how she could get my husband, house and all the glitter she thought Ramon had. Trixie didn't realize what happens in the real behind closed doors may someday swing open. She was too selfish to know we struggled to get there. She thought she was getting a gold mine her ass did get a mine; it just wasn't gold it was a mine that would eventually explode on her. Now, she can live the life of looking over her shoulder and wondering who the next candidate is or canidates he will date to audition for her vacant spot. If you tell me or show me, you are a liar or unfaithful I believe you. Sometimes you are only as faithful as your options. I want to live a life free from infestation, diseases that scant may transport.

See trix have many cable connections and I just wasn't going to be one of those extensions. That is just straight up nasty, not for me. Didn't want to take that chance with my life, because I don't know how much time God will allow me to be here. I want to be here for my girls. So, let her sweat Ramon as for me I'm so Audi as she puts her fingers up to her lips showing a peace sign. That house she slept in is under lease with the option to buy and we never agreed on a price on the house. I did talk to Miss Mary the owner and let her know I will be breaking the lease and moving out. She wasn't too happy because she looked at me as a daughter and she always took care of whatever was needed. Miss Mary shared pictures with us of her grandchildren and invited us to many of her family affairs. I didn't want to move but I had made my decision and she reluctantly but with love supported my decision. Miss Mary was like a mother to me she was beautiful and filled with such a positive spirit. As I listened saying the name Miss Mary reminded me of my godmother. The godmother I grew up with I didn't know she was until she left Oakwood and moved to Minnesota and died. What's up with that mom? When I was young, she was my beautcian that would have been a good time while drying my hair to tell me. I was very grown when I was told and wished I had known this information earlier. The conversation with my mom was just by chance. Funny ha-ha if I didn't' ask she wouldn't have told me. Robin went on to say as I snapped back that Miss Mary told her she understood after she shared with her the reason. Miss Mary said that she had a tenant that would be ready to move in by the first. Robin smiled saying oops in the mist of the confusion I forgot to tell Ramon that the new tenants were moving in on the first. That was such an oops on my part hmm I'm sorry, got a little distracted. Strangely the first was in less than twenty-four hours, oops my bag again.

Robin smiled saying that the house we shared was nice, roomy, large backyard four bathrooms, five bedrooms located by all levels of school, freeway and the mall. I really loved shopping at that mall. I left with just what belongings that meant something to me, some of the girl's things and oh I took my bat, you know for just in case, (as she smiles). She or he can have the rest. So, I looked at Robin and asked so you are not mad at her. Nah, she said Trixee was her best friend. She allowed me to walk out of this relationship on my terms in my way with grace. I came in like a woman and walked out like a lady. We had stopped a long time ago being a married couple. Girl we slept in the same bed, but we were so separated we almost fell out the bed being so close to the edge. Our bedtime became a routine of no touching, no feelings, and just a routine good night. Our snoring was the only noise we made until the alarm clock broke our snoring sounds. If Trixee would have asked I would have given her Ramon with a red bow. But this trick disrespected me, and I had to do me. I later found out that they had been dealing with each other for some time. That was so selfish on both their parts, like I or the girls didn't have any type of feelings. Why go through all that, why get married if you can't be faithful? No person deserves that. Now I see clearly, I opened both eyes to see clearer. Now I'm happy. No sweat, no tears, no headache, heartache and no Trixies lurking around. Oh and no looking under the bed or no one hiding in the closet, nope no time for that drama. I'm not going to be the watch dog, nope, no watch dog on duty.

I like living in the apartment complex because it offers a since of security for me and my girls. They are not in the house by themselves. I don't have to worry about the upkeep in maintaining a home. I will buy a house or condo when the girls get a little older. I listened to Robin and realized she had grown from this life experience. I looked at her and said so are you still married. She laughed and said no he found his divorce papers on his front seat passenger side. I also left him my ATM card too. I couldn't contain myself in asking why she left him any money. She said well I didn't want to be the bad guy, so I left our ATM card with the bank statement showing a balance of $100.01. That should fill up his lime green Pacer for about a good month and .01 was the interest I am not without a heart. He earned it as she continues to smile. We both laughed about the balance. You see, Miss Rita, I handled all the family financial business and I had opened a mad money account. You know for just in case. I left him the bankcard to our joint account. I'm still comfortable and I'm still employed with benefits.

Ramon made good money on paper at the time of our divorce and waived child support in lieu of spousal support. One thing Ramon was not good at was managing money. After I did, they mental flow chart of; did I do that, and did I do this my mind was clear and thoughts were free. I'm pretty sure trixee was in ah when she saw the lime green Pacer and not the S500 that she probably was attracted to and hope someday to drive or continue to sit in the passenger seat. We both laughed as I try to visualize what Robin had said about Ramon and Trixee. As we finish the last bite of our sandwich I glanced at my watch and said I need to get back it's getting late. Robin looks at me with understanding and a kind smile.

I thanked her for her story and company, and she said that we would have to do this again as a girl's day and next time we can bring our daughters. I started laughing and said lime green Pacer. She laughs and yea girl lime green. I now know how it felt to have some of Robin's temporary freedom. It felt good that day, it warmed my body like a hot cup of coffee. The sun was out and shining and the sky was clear. As the day comes to an end it was time to go home and face whatever attitude Bill might have as I enter the door. Until then I continued to enjoy Robin's conversation, the music and the wind blowing in my face. This freedom felt good and I wanted to feel this freedom again. In the back of my mind the words Robin uttered let's do this again stayed as the wind continued to blow into my face. Robin talked about accountability saying that we must be accountable for our actions and the consequences from them. Ramon's actions were a contributing factor in this unethical equation, Courtney Diane voice chimes in with your dumb ass. Ramon filled his heart and mind up with knowing or unknowing he pushed what we had out, it was too crowded no more room. Much too crowded for me and I don't share a heart. I remembered her gentle smile finishing up with he didn't realize that I had left a long time ago and that was why he had that additional space. With those words, I feel the freedom in the continued form of fresh air. I see the peace in her soul and the renewed spirit. God has created in her a new clean heart and renewed her spirit. She wasn't going back, too much to look forward to. Funny how she said that part of my past can kiss her ass. She went on to say that this is the freshes form of freedom. She didn't have any pressure from parents, no being a watch dog trying to keep up with Ramon's trifling butt. I now have fresh air and my girls.

As we pulled up my heart beats with panic of what type of mood Bill might be in. My fresh air of freedom was slowly blowing away into the wind. After all, I had rushed out in such haste without allowing a response from him or telling him where I was going. I was so thankful that he didn't act up with a witness present. I thanked Robin again and she smiles as I exit out closing her car door. I take a deep breath and sigh for it doesn't seem late. I'm home before the street lights came on and before Sierra's bedtime. As I walked slowly to the door, I fumbled with my empty purse looking for my keys, and dread what is on the other side of this door. From the outside I noticed that the kitchen lights were on and the rest of the house seemed dark. Wow, what is really waiting for me on the other side of this locked door? As I grabbed the door knob, Robin walks past asking if I was alright. I looked at her with nervous smile saying I'm okay. I really didn't want Bill to hear me talking. I watched Robin walk up the steps to her apartment. I heard her door close, and that was good. Then here comes Craig and Bert and their cousin Manly passing the basketball to each other with high energy. Chris is kicking the soccer ball and Ryan is whining about Chris not sharing the ball. When Chris throws the ball to Ryan's tiny hands, he misses and runs to catch the rolling ball. Amos just walks behind Momo who, is yelling at boys to go into the apartment and clean up. Wow could she get any louder? Really Momo this is not the time. I thought now what? Good grief, and oh no, here comes Keith out of his apartment saying he just baked some fresh banana bread and asked was I ready for the first hot piece. Although, my mouth was watering for his fresh baked goodies, I just wanted to get into the apartment to face whatever is waiting for me.

For some reason, I felt that I was being stalled for some reason or was it the paranoia that started playing tricks with my racing pregnant hormones. As I entered the apartment it seemed so quiet. The television was on and I tried to be as quiet as possible. I saw Bill lying on the couch and Sierra passed out on the other couch. I went to check on her. I glanced over at Bill and he looked like his eyes were closed. Sometimes it was hard to tell if his eyes were open because they were so small. I glanced, at Bill and he looked as if he was in a deep sleep. As I walked to the back, I heard a voice say you finally made it home Cinderella. I haven't heard the name since high school hanging out with my friends partying. At first it startled me since the room was dark and had that haunted house kinda feeling. I just smiled and said I had a nice time and that Robin was a nice person. I thought it was still early... Plus I felt that he had enough time to start an argument and leave and we all can have an enjoyable evening. My thoughts got bold with just do you and leave us in peace. Go on and just get. He slowly set up and said so what did you do for ten hours? Now, I knew I wasn't gone for no ten hours. Well we went on some errands and I saw a lot of places the bus didn't go, and it was good just getting out of the apartment. My energy was high and nervous, but I felt that Bill was fishing for something. It bothered him the fact that I left him, and he had to play dad for ten imaginary hours. I admit it was early morning when I left and early evening when I returned. It's like coming home late from a party. You enjoy it while you are there because you know you have passed curfew and punishment will follow.

So, now I had something to think about and enjoy for a few minutes. At that time Momo knocked on the door and the knocks echoed all through the apatment. Bill opens the door with a quick hi. Momo starts saying that she saw this cute dress jumper for Sierra and at that time the telephone rung. The phone ringing was unusual, because the phone very seldom dings or dongs. As Bill went to go and answer the phone, I laughed and thanked Momo for thinking about Sierra and that the jumper was gorgeous. At that point Bill yelled telephone!!! I guess you are Miss popular today. The way he said it didn't sound too nice. Momo said well that's my que to leave and you are so welcomed. She said I just couldn't resist it and knew it would look adorable on Sierra. I told her thank you and excused myself to take the phone call. I skip to the phone passing Bill who is looking at me like I was crazy. I was just happy that I was about to hear a friendly voice. Bill is trying to listen and the only thing he is hearing is the laughter from my joy and the taste of freedom I'd experienced today.

It was good to hear from Melba and filling me in on the old neighborhood. She told me many had moved out and many had moved in. It wasn't quite the same, but it was home to them until they maybe someday move into their own house. As I hung up the phone, I felt myself smiling, laughing and it felt so good. I saw the snarl on Bill's face and that couldn't take my joy away either. I told him that Melba had invited us to Michelle's birthday party. Next Saturday mid-day and she is looking forward to seeing us again. His remarks aren't we the social butterfly two Saturdays in a row of outings, hmmph. I laughed saying, well do you want to go? I had the tone of boldness telling him that Sierra and I will be going. Now you can stay here but I'm going. He looked at me with such surprise that I could tell he didn't know how to respond. Wow another day away and around people. It's strange how when you are around someone with strength you kinda tap them and receive some of it. I felt courage as I responded to Bill. I felt like I could roar and growl. He said well, how are you going to get there because I have to work? Well I said just drop me off or I can take you to work and pick you up when the party is over or when you get off from work you can pick us up. I could see from his facial expression he didn't like any of the choices.

I really didn't care. Another opportunity was presented to escape to fresh air. I had another chance to get out the apartment, and Sierra had an opportunity to spend some time with kids around her age. Just the thought of going back to the old neighborhood took my mind off what Bill was thinking. The fear that I had when I came home left. The fear and concerns all just ran away by one phone call and a knock on the door. It was like the last bell ringing on a boxing meet ding, ding and ding. I felt like a champion and I was Rocky for one moment. Just sitting here and enjoying the rain and this cup of coffee and the Rocky theme playing in my head. Sure, does feel good. The rest of the night kinda went by the wayside, no arguing, no fussing and no cussing which surprised me. I just knew I was in trouble for coming home after the street lights came on and I wasn't in his view.

As the week days followed one after another, I mentally counted the days to the birthday party. I gathered enough nerve to ask Bill for some money to buy a present. So, on our weekly bus ride we had more money. I had a big twenty dollars Bill gave me to look for a present and the twenty included bus far. I was looking forward to seeing everyone again. It's strange how you think about the old neighborhood and finally get a chance to see familiar faces again. I saw Floyd walking around my complex looking for a certain apartment. When I saw him, my eyes lit up! When Sierra saw him, she ran right to him. He smiled and called her 'little bit' as he embraced her hugs. Now, it's funny about that nickname for she was tall for her age. Floyd lifts her up as he is tall. He was telling me that he was still in the service and enjoyed med school. I had so many questions for him like a little girl trying to get all the questions out and one time not letting him finish the first one before I ask another one.

I asked how Reggie Coy and Clovis were doing. He said they both were doing fine. They had moved back to Ohio until they got a good taste of Ohio winter. Mama Clovis was happy to move back and be with her sister Aunt Beverly her husband Uncle Montez, and my dad Mr. Reggie Coy brothers Uncle Will/Wilbur, Uncle Randall, Uncle Leon, sister Aunt Deforda (aka Aunt De), Aunt Debora, Aunt Ava and cousin Francis. Floyd laughs they enjoyed being back home with family and sharing the old times stories. Last year winter was the coldest one in

Ohio. We both laughed because we knew how California weather can spoil you. Well they stayed one winter and said they needed some warmth. That cold air woke them up. So, they moved where mom had two other younger sisters Aunt Tamara and Aunt Grace. Dad had some old friends that moved there after getting out of the service and his sisters Aunt Susan and Aunt Karla were living there too. So, they loaded up and moved to a small city in Florida called East Sea Florida. They still have their place in Ohio they call their summer house for when it gets too hot in Florida. I laughed at them calling them booze. They love it mom has her gardening and dad has his farm he always wanted to return to. Mom and Dad are hanging out with family and traveling like they are in their twenties. I thought what's wrong with traveling and not allowing grass to grow under your feet. That was a phrase my father would always say to me, to get me out of the house while Bill was away at boot camp. He said that they live on about three-acre farm with horses, dogs and plenty of room to grow. They have been talking about building houses on the land for each child. Floyd laughed and said to his dad what's it gonna be called Reggieville or Clovis clusters or, (as he laughs harder), RC colonies. His dad laughed and said hmm not a bad idea. We both looked at each other now with a serious face and thought and said hmm not a bad idea...

Chapter 12
Hello Henray

At that time a tall slender young man walks toward him smiling saying hey Henry you made it. I have seen this young man around but didn't know his name. I had seen him with I assume his mother because they look identical. I would occasionally see them leaving early in the morning. She was in uniform and he dressed as if he went to a private school. He always seemed kinda shy yet polite and spoke very well. When the young man reaches him, they give each other a strong brotherly embrace followed with a hearty laugh and what's up Mr. NBA and whats up Dr. Scaring me. Floyd introduces him as his good friend, Henray. Henry come to find out later had a full basketball scholarship and was majoring in business administration but got drafted to the NBA while in college. Yes, yes and say yes again labor and pain paid off and college tuition is probably what his mother shouted. Henray the way Floyd said it sound funny. As I looked at the very polite Henry and noticed that they had similar mannerism. He said his mother, Courtney Diane had nothing but good things to say about me. This made me reflect on what my parents would always say someone is always watching you. I guess I was being watched, it beats the negative dissection I would receive from time to time from Bill. I asked him if his mom was in the service. He smiled and said yes that she was being transferred to Fort Marshal located in Florida. Floyd was here to see them before they get on the road to different destinations. He was glad he made it back from being cleared from his assignment overseas to continue his medical career in the service. As they say good bye, they leave hitting each other like they were in grade school on the playground.

Just ear shy and a nose away I heard Floyd say Henry, Henry, Henray what happened to Melinda, he's laughing as he is asking. Is she still trying to get her MRS degree via baby boy? Henry looks at him with a smile out the corner of his mouth the same way his mom smiles. Man, I had to cut that crazy girl loose and why you got to go there. Aren't you still shivering that near miss with Veronica? All you know that moms could not stand her ass at all. Floyd interjects you mean your mom said with her dumb ass or just dumb ass. Henray continues saying not skipping a

— 107 —

beat, I barely escaped that I'm pregnant trap man that shift don't feel good at all and that MRS marriage wasn't happening either. He raises his eyebrows saying I'm too young and still innocent. I still remember how I boohoo to moms when I had to tell her. I showed all signs of punk that bought that little boy in me front and center. I did one of those ugly I'm in pain cries. That incident had sucking my thumb wanting my teddy bear and my mommy. Moms was disappointed, and I couldn't stop crying glad pops wasn't around just my best friend my moms.

Floyd, I didn't mind moms seeing me punk out because that was the least of my concerns, but I knew the big wet puppy eyes would work. It wasn't like I was pretending this shift oops was real. Floyd was listening and chuckling at the same time, but in a fun and compassionate boyish way. Henry laughs as he talks you know my mom's been saying some strange stuff. Floyd agrees adding that, man your moms, man would say stuff that turned you into a punk and make you mentally run and go hide somewhere and shiver like a kid. She would take all man away daggling my stuff on her ear lobes. I had to use my hands to try to hide them from unforeseen danger. Then depending on the time of day or if she is pressed for time, she might just snatch them and place them on her earlobes. Does she still keep that drawer of balls she has collected? He laughs holding his hand to his face saying she makes your voice go soprano. Yep, soprano and howlla!! I know moms can get to you, but she definitely is not any part of joke, but that's my mom's. I know somtimes you have to wait for the icicles to melt around her heart but she's cool in a mom type way.

Floyd continues with, you remember how she and your Aunt Robin tagged team us told us both about not making any deposits to any of those scants. And we better make an early withdraw. Floyd, man that made us feel comfortable talking to them… I listened, because if I said anything she would just go on and on. Then you had her and Aunt Robin always saying know your product. Man, they just remove or take all compassion from it, making it sound like a business transaction or a marketing move. Saying other stuff, like don't be merging with those fast tail girls. Detour that vehicle car whatever because I'm pretty sure you aren't the only car that has driven or drove up that ramp. Floyd says what holding his hand in a fist motion up to his mouth. She called your stuff a bumper a car?? Yep and called them a road ho, dude. Another friend by the name of Ian joined in saying his mom called them road ho is that like a freeway freak. What's Melinda's number I'll settle for a highway ho or interstate idiot, detour do not enter, or enter at your own risk. But I'll hold still so she can bump as he goes through the motions, (they didn't know I can still hear them, they are still in my site). Henry no you don't, you don't want to fool with that freebie cuz it ain't free. Melinda had me sweating and sick, but she was good man. But I had the wrong brain started whispering to me like what can it hurt, the damage is done and who would know, she already pregnant. Then the voice got softer with you do kind of like the girl. Well, so what she nasty that's what you liked about her. Someone in the crowd group shouts out wasn't because of her boxed shaped. I end up arguing with myself saying just hit it Henry.

Then sex thoughts kept talking and the urge started stretching, man. As he looks and raises his eyebrows hell, she knows I'm broke. They all chime in we all know that your ass is broke. Henray pauses while looking at them as if they interrupted his train of thought. He acted like they had to pause with as I was gently saying' all I know is when Melinda said she was pregnant I almost tried one for the road, just one more time man. Hey, it was good I figured what the heck she is already pregnant, bumper need to bump. I saw my mom's face and heard her words echoing all around me, saying with your dumb ass scared me. Shift she had me mentally stuttering. I had to put that car, laughing in neutral and let it roll on back down that ramp, and detour from that dead end and get my dumb ass off that road ho. Can't believe I'm sounding and saying what my moms have been drilling into me. Damn she has arrived in me.

I am still standing just an ear away and don't hear too much, but enough. And it was just good seeing their relationship show in their conversations. Moms tried to tell me about her. She would say don't bring that fast tail girl, road ho around here. Watch her; no don't watch her, stay away from that boxed shaped scant. Moms was right, damn again. I pictured her giving me that look that I just straight up can't stand. Hey, Henray what's up with you and that fine-fine girl, Keyana, (as he motions the top part)? I never heard him called Henray this way so many times by his friends. The way they said it sound kinda funny and country, (like they were calling a chow line). Said she didn't need me and said a few more words that could make my momma blush. She flipped that pony tail and switched her ass on. But her moves were like an ocean flowing when she walked away, and I wasn't getting sea sickness. She kicked me to the curve when she found out about Melinda. Ooh ooh what about Peacola with that (he motions figure eight) with body that makes your head turn totally around with their mouths open. Now, you know she can't stand to be called Peacola it is either Cola or Peaches. I made that mistake and my boy Rodney caught it in her presence. She giggled and smiled at him and snarled at me and they are still together. Now, did he pull some Jody got your girl. What I got to do with this, but as he laughs, I did get your girl Celestine. She didn't talk bad about you other than calling you some type of lying heathen. Hey man she kicked me too, for your dumb ass Ian. Ian says my bad but hey we were young, and I liked her. She into religion man I'm not touching that. So, your famous dimple white smile didn't work. Henry smiles at Floyd saying is it working with your dumb ass. Floyd laughed harder saying oh snap fool you aint kidding. So, she wasn't your girl and now she's Rodney's lady ooh did she punk your dumb ass.

I saw Rodney the other day at Safeway and he and Peaches own some type of business don't know, don't remember and don't care. But she's still looking good, dudes. She could have been yours if you said her name right dude. You too cold Floyd, and that's not nice as he continues to chuckle. Speaking of running Morris are you still running from Debra. Ah man you had to go there. You forgot about when you left her at that party and when she saw you what a week later. He laughs something like that. She chased after your boy here with a knife. Shoot, he was running so long the boy stop to slow up and looked behind him she still was running after his ass. Thinking back on that conversation I heard that his wife would chase after him with knives and tree branches.

I guess he didn't learn or stayed in shape, so he could run. I looked at them and as Floyd talked about the girls or young ladies. It always started out with unk hum with his eyes closing looking bored but amused at the same time. Ah some of them fine girls we drooled over either like girls gained a lot of weight or looking for a daddy for them babies. They all say we don't have any time for diapers. Dude they should have heard your mom's, aka Miss Courtney Diane calling our shift a car and accelerating those cars up those fast tail's ramp, road ho's. Where does she come up with this shift? Henry holds his fist up to his mouth saying I backed my car down from that ramp. No idling and no babies here not ready to be no body's daddy or baby daddy or your daddy laughing pointing to his friends. Oh, you are going there you got jokes, huh. Yep how's your momma? Speaking of big booty baby mommas Roshunda with that baby got much back, still got back. Didn't she drop kick your ass Floyd, nope dropped kicked me, you and your laughing asses over there. I think my sister saw her over at the mall. What about Sondra the one that looked at you crazier than moms, not sure what happened to her it's like she disappeared. What is your mom up to? Still crazy and making sure that I stay focus. She didn't know at one point it was too late. How about knock out bam-bam Shieleen, nope won't even return my calls and I think she blocked my number. At that point they both agreed that they are passed that high school nonsense.

At that point three more young men around their age looks at me with smiles and hi's and whats up to the boys. The way it was said made me feel old but respected at the same time with a ma'am was thrown in there. They embraced Henry and introduced Jody, Ian and Morris to Floyd as he daps each of them. Hey, we were just talking about Henry's high school rejects. You know roll call of our once was. You know Joann, married I think to Terrance Raymond, TR, she is some kinda chef at hmmm. I guess you weren't her type of recipe, huh. Ian asks what is up with fine ass Ursula. She had body, but not no more she lost a lot of weight and it landed right in the middle. Ursula fine ass is, (sigh) she's pregnant man, but she still looked hecka fine and sexy. Morris says it ain't mine. You wished man. Wow Shanita ah man she finally got that bull's eye she had placed in the center of your big ass forehead.

Okay what about Camile. They all say remember her, but she had too much tude. She was fine, but the girl was crazy, and straight up rude. I remember I took her to the movies and she just talked and talked through the movies. We had people shushing her and I had to mean mug their asses. I didn't come there to leave fighting for the honor of that scant. I looked at her thinking why don't she shut the hell up? Is this shift worth it? I just wanted the coochie from this dumb ass hoochie. I thought she was cute until she opened her mouth. Not only did she have no home training she made me think about my moms and it was oh hell to the no. Jody says she just needed to be understood you know take one of those anger management courses like your momma is taking. Except she and your momma both need at least one course inside the classroom with people attached to computers and a desk. Did you understand when she slashed your momma's tires? Ah you had to go there. I'm still paying for those bald ass tires and busing it. They both break out laughing man you sound just like your moms. She always uses either two or four words, and they both say it all at the same time pointing at each other. It's either with your dumb ass or dumb ass. I know man somewhere in that conversation you don't know when she will trip out and go south, or just left the building, just don't know.

You all know moms have a heart you just had to chisel it away from the ice. You know once that ice melts she's cool. They both say yeah right. Now who took the chick to the movies and when you set in the front row, she uh took her boots off and sprayed perfume on her feet? Hey that would me, (as he pointed proudly to himself) I took oh trifling, what was her name, other than scant. Oh, oh um um I just saw her, umm June the other day too and saw the crow feet in sandals. She thought I was looking at the ass nah; I was looking at that line she was leaving with those toes. But that made me think about her, but oh umm Lynnie, Leslie no, no Viana too that shouldn't expose the world to their toes, yuck.

There were so many conversations going on. Henry went on about his mom with that she had asked me some crazy ass questions about Melinda. You know she asked me if I liked Melinda or heard about her. I looked at her and said, what's the difference? Okay if you like her that's good you bring her home to meet me. Now, if you heard about her that means she is well known if you know what I mean. I look at her with a huh. She looks at me and ask is there a problem? You like her you bring her home because you know I don't want no tramps/ tricks or whatever up in here. So, let me break it down to y'all with your dumb ass.

Then here we go dumb ass, she saw a neon sign flashing right in the center on your big dumb ass forehead. Oh, really moms what did it say. Well it said dumb ass, dumb ass. You moved from having the duh attacks to acting like a little dumb, dumb. Then celerated full throttle to smack dab slid into dumb ass. That's my boy my onliest son and your mom wants you to do right. I laughed she looks at me and said are you finish now yep, then get your dumb ass out of here, (then she starts laughing and we laugh together). Moms is my moms. I listen and inside I laughed at their conversation. Because it was not only funny but made me think about how men or boys do talk about us. Well Henry you got to be a fugitive go where they just don't know your name. At that time the brothers Klay and Kyle walk up saying hi and looking straight ahead.

They hug and dap, saying guess who we just saw? Kyle says that scant Rene. Boy did she pick up some weight with a grocery cart full of kids with Lars. You all remember your women competition and track buddy. I watched them enjoying and sharing memories as they set on the picnic table. No one loved him better than himself. Now he has many loves and they were all in the grocery cart. Did they look happy? Nah, they looked bored and broke. They all laugh and say nah. They look over at Henry man that could have been you. How would you do your famous jump shot with babies on your back your arms, hanging off your neck and any limb they could get to? Henry responds oh you got jokes huh. We saw Melinda on the bus stop. Man, she did look bad. I heard she was doing drugs and tricks and she looked every part of it. Henry sighs woo as he wipes his forehead saying that he was sorry to hear that, because she was a good person just trifling at times. You know that they said I was a dog and if they looked me up, they would have an 8x10 glossy with your picture cheesing and all. Klay teases him singing bow, wow, wow, and ah ooh. Henry woofs at him (shaking his body). What can I say I wasn't me? Hey what about green, green eyed Angela or was it her sister Angelita. You know the one that cuts her eyes at me as if she is slicing and dicing me in mid-air. Last I heard she moved to the east coast. See what you did made that girl move and he acts like he is wiping a tear. Laughing he says my bad, that tear evaporated, poof. That wasn't me that was Jody, and before you go any further down your memory lane dumb asses. Has anyone seen Piere I miss her and that accent? Do you really miss her? Remember how pissed off she was at you calling, you a lying dog? I don't know why and she sicked that little sawed off dog Simba on me. Can you believe she said me and little mut were related? Man, that dog looked at me up and down as if it was going find a spot to piss on me. I had to look before I ran his teeth were bigger than his body. That mut got to my foot raised his leg and lower it as if I wasn't even worth pissing on or acted as if we were related. That dog gave me one slow woof and ran away, no actually man I think he slowly walked away, looked back at me now was some tripped-out stuff. They laughed and woof, woof at him.

Now, that was some strange stuff, and Angel thinks I'm a heathen. Wow man. Henry looks at him and said I just wanted to help you out. Kyle says I not talking about that I'm talking about the dumb ass. Oh, my bad moms just creeped up on me from nowhere so don't go there, (as he leans back). Yeah, you were man they cut and pasted your picture in the dictionary. Tell me, you couldn't have forgotten that shift? That was funny when they put it all over the school posters too. Ok ok I got it, but I wasn't bad boy come on moms would kill me. Yeah, she would kill all of us if were in her sight. I still fear your mean ass moms. I laugh to myself because I'm still scared of Sharon's mom too. Miss Courtney Diane you're right, she doesn't play that messing over on women, girls, whatever just don't make her a young grandmother. They laughed saying dumb ass, as they look at each other slowly getting up and walking away. They were asking, when are we going take a ride in that Benz? When you are leaving? Henry said in a few days, Jody and Ian look at each other next week right. Floyd laugh with saying that my leave and back to my reality ends Sunday.

Let's go shoot some hoops before Henry goes pro. Henry motions a hoop shot. Do your dumb asses think ya got some game? Let's make that move and get some gone. I got to pee man is your moms home. Nah, she out then let's make that stretch. Why her car here I see her Mercedes. Nah, she out hanging with my Aunt Robin and some friends doing that cougar crap. She says its lady's night and ain't I a lady so I'm going. Morris says I can be their cougar, (he purrs and puts his hands up like a kitten fighting a ball of yawn). I will treat her like a lady as he smiles raising his eyebrows up and down. Henry responds hey that's my moms and aunt. Your ass acting as if I can't see you know I'm standing right here dumb ass. What you got flash backs. Yeah, your moms hella mean man I can't even picture her like that ew, (as he shakes and looks around). The others chime in we can your moms got body and your Aunt Robin got bootey.

Do you remember how my moms rip a hole in my butt because of y'all dumb asses? Ya knew I had passed my curfew. Oh, Ian I was out with ya dumb asses and told you ya had to get my ass home before curfew. But, nah ya fooling around with those chicks and did you at least get the numbers. They laughed and looked at each other we got more than that. So, so sorry, we left and went by their place we knew you couldn't go. No that was Kyle and Morris. Don't matter ya knew I had to get home. Ian laughed why saying that we had made up good reasons. They sounded good to us. Yeah until I got home and ya heard moms jamming me up against the wall. All I heard was feet running and the door slamming. Where was my back up? And when I told her the story it had all sounds of stupid, even to me. We had your back yelled Henry back at home. They all laughed we know. I had to laugh at myself too. Then I made a mistake and answered her question. That dreaded what if, Ian and Kyle add Floyd too if they were to jump off the bridge would you?

Without thinking or remembering who I was talking to, I said yeah with Ian in a head lock. After the words came out, I knew she had heard my dumb ass. I didn't know, if I was going to experience death or dying or just kill my ass which ever came first. I closed my eyes and didn't look at her. I had to close my eyes in preparation to soften the blows. I knew the blows were coming and I had to think quick. While thinking, I thought about landing on Melinda or maybe Camile. Not quite thinking about the fall but thinking on what body I woud be landing on. Hmmph, that would be a mighty sweet landing! I don't know which one said that I would land on your mama. Henry snapped back with no worries she already landed on your daddy.

It went like ah you got joke, (the snapee, snap). And Henry said yep, and I'm funny too. Then Ian with Morris says in syncs what about her sister Veeva yeah. That would be a nice landing too. Henray looks at them as if they were dreaming about the girls, busting them out saying not going to happen. But I would have landed one of yah girlfriends if yah asses had one, so Braelyn and Veeva is asta la vista buddies. With eyebrows raised do I've your permission to continue? But when I didn't feel any gush of wind coming toward my face, my dreams of landing went poof. I was thinking maybe this was a time delayed blow. As I wondered would she go left right or right left. Don't matter blows are blows uh.

I slowly opened each eye at a time and saw her corner smile with both eyes cracked open. She had laughed in her way on my answer. I love to hear my mother laugh which isn't often coming from her corner smile. She said she had to tell me something. Moms said she had to check out the window to see if there was a car running with me spinging up to her. She was impressed and that was my option for giving me that dumb response. I must admit moms was impressed with my dumb ass quick response. Ian squeezes in raising his eyebrows with didn't your moms talk about shrinkage. Henry goes into motion of squeeze this and catches himself. Although I'm ear close and vision shy, I appreciate the respect they are showing without knowing that I'm not that much older. Henry quick response if you gonna interrupt my life round it up right with your dumb ass. Now, y'all the shrinkage came from when moms went to look out the window to see if there was a running car waiting for me. She paused during my eye closure to see if she shrunk. Moms said she had to check to see if she had some shrinkage happening to her. Because I had talk to her like she was my child. Man, ya moms had to recalibrate her thoughts and actions why she like that. Ian gathers himself through laughter saying she needs to retrain and take that online anger management class again and put her ass in a desk and sit on the front not the back of the room. I don't think that on-line class is working has she ever thought about refund if not she should. Nah, she just needs to take her ass to class, hell we did as they slap hands. Henry glances into the group and one other responded with what I didn't say no ass I said take her ass; sit it down at a desk. With everyone laughing Henry keeps going on with his story looking over at Kyle smiling oh you are getting in on this with my momma.

Smiling and calling Kyle aka "Togo". Morris snaps back oh snaps that's what your girlfriends would tell your ass to- go and don't mean you being a sanmich either. Kyle chuckles through his slight embarrassment saying you know the routine Togos in public and to- go when it's us and all you all can as he stops kiss my Togo ass. Kyle smiles saying that's just all the way wrong and that happened in high school. Why ya bust me out like that? I'm a changed man saying trying not to choke as he spits out the words. No, it ain't shouts out Floyd what happened to that brief interlude with Chaurice. Was that nontin, she told your dumb ass to- go not now but ret now? I think she meant was getting your shift to- go, my oops sorry man get your ass out. She wanted you out she lost all grammar. Ret now is that like fitna or gonna what the hell!! All we knew was you got to- go. With a quick response Kyle chokes while saying why yaw got to bust out my business, I do have a rep. All the guys were pushing one another, as if who was going to say it first. His own brother drops on him saying you're right you do represent. Then they all chime in you represent Togos!! Ian and Morris saying and not the sanmich and you got to- go. No no someone shouts out I wants my sanmich ret now to- go. You hungry Henray as they laughed making smacking sounds. Wees sure is hungry. Kyle laughs nervously but without pain saying I sure am hungry too. He rubs his stomach smacking his lips and join in on the laughter. I chuckle silently not to disturb their conversation and bonding time. Henray continues while other conversations are going but they are still somewhat paying attention. Klay comes out of nowhere stop he's a little sensitive about Togo meals. Kyle starts to say what he really wanted to say, but realized I'm still shy of hearing them. He looks at them pretending to wipe a tear saying this hurt, ouch, but y'all still all the way wrong. I'm so enjoying their conversations just entertaining as they cover each other in snapping, and the list of girls and their memories.

Henry continues and explains one of the reasons for not dying or coming to death was I think that one emotion she was saving stepped up. With a smile added to her expression, she had to admit I was her son and Mother Florrie's grandchild that gene had to surface sooner or later. Moms told me that her boy took the lollipop out of his mouth and learned how to walk and chew gum, humph. There is some part of me in there somewhere. Moms said she looked at me with my eyes closed smiling and said out the corner of her mouth, (showing that dimple), probably was thinking about that box shaped scant and landing on her with your and her nasty asses. Humph, Mother Florrie came out I guess she had to show up at sometime. What fear and thup-id can produce and add a deep duh attack too with my dumb ass. After I thought about it, I had to corner smile myself. I couldn't wait to get to my so-called buddies' curfew my ass. Moms gives me a spine but, will take it away with other anatomies in a heart beat and take my breath away in a second. Listening to their stories the bridge headlock answer was a good one. To add they laughed at Courtney Diane adding you spined up and common sense left, and sense of humor stepped on in. She added, boy don't do too many crazies you're my on-lilist child too old to get a new one. I can picture them both doing a corner smile together embracing each other with hugs. They probably never revisited it but at least they used common sense right and not like Rhona confusing common sense with "common scent". Just for the sake I wondered what happened to Aunt Brandi and Rhona.

I remembered when my brother came home late and I heard the stool scoot back and his friends coming in with him. We all knew what that stool scoot back meant, and no one wanted to hear that sound. My pops grab my brother and jammed him against the wall. I heard his friends Donnie, Martin and Ivan take off. I heard feet thumping as they sounded like they were running into each other saying words get off me man that faded into the wind as the doors slammed closed sounding like a vault slamming shut. And that was a no-no my parents hated to hear those doors slam closed and listen how the sound echoed through the house. With their voices on the end yelling don't slam my damn door or either stay in or out. I think that was a universal statement. My short dad standing 5"6 had my tall brother standing 6"2 off his feet on that wall. What a sight to remember as Charles looked down as if he was afraid of heights. Hmm, I wondered if Charles still remembers.

I'm still listening to them. Oh, you got jokes again. Man, I'm scared of your moms. I'll just wait and use the bathroom somewhere else, like that nasty ass gas station down the street. There is no stress and all I need is a centerpiece. Someone shouted, hey is that moms pulling up? They all gave a quick glance, except Henry who is laughing, no man I told you she wasn't home. See man we got to get some gone from here y'all play too much. You could see the love and respect they had for each other as they talked about each other's family members. Hey, Kyle what about you and Hope. He shakes his head no hope. His brother says he's hopeless. Kyle looks at him with a crazy look of why are you dogging me out, like that brah. Where's your lady Mr. Togos. Everyone oohs him. I'm not the dog they look over at Henry again in which he responds with a howl. Then they all left and gave a howl out. We called it the dozens, now they call it something else. Just hearing it made me kind of chuckle. Sierra sees Floyd leaving and jumped off her big wheel and runs and gives him a big hug for the road and now she was ready for her bus ride. I listen to Henry and his friend's names thinking maybe I might use one of the names for my unborn baby.

The others are still talking about what happened to Lydia, have you seen Lydia with her fine ass and what's up with Desseret is she still looking for your tired ass. Klay burst out laughing oh Henray you could have been with that spice girl. At that point everyone pauses and turn their heads at the same time. As if they were waiting for a response. Henry, oh you got laughter huh that spice girl known as Ginger turned into a cookie and snapped on me dude. I only went out with her because the twins other there, as he motions to Klay and Kyle that they wanted to take out the flavor girls. At that point they all turned their heads to Kyle and Klay. Klay burst out what?? Klay says hell who could forget Monaye Monee known as mmm, mmph and her fine sister Halina Manee, known as hmmm and humph. They just roll their eyes with a big smile. As if their minds were roaming and memories were replaying snaps were flying. Hey, Henray someone had to take out their cousin and we know that you are always available. Every now and then I glanced over at them giving high fives, jumping back and just young men hanging out and laughing not knowing what awakes then in their adult world. Actually, I really don't know what waits for me as I grow into this adult reality either. Martin widens his eyes and motions his heads up to Ian asking about crazy Loona. Is she still circling around mars? You know the loona module. The response was quick, and the expression was funny as he responds with, she is more of a looney tunes and that's all folks, and on that note Henray says, lets bust a move.

Henray and Martin ask with a slight smile just want to know does your mom have a special ball drawer with men body parts she opens every now and then to admire her collections. Yell man your moms can wow out a boy, a young man, an old man, any man or human breathing. At one point, they stopped talking and looked at each other. Then they looked at their watches then they looked at each other again and Klye says in as deep voice and slowly what time is it. They all say in sync is it time to care, with a pause adding with our dumb asses. They all crack up hitting and dapping each other that must be an inside joke. Floyd motions a hoop move and Kyle says let's hit some rims. Morris chimes in saying I'm in. Floyd and Klay both look at him like what you gonna be the ball, bounce your ass full court. Henry well track season is over and somebody ani't been running. Humph I guess jogging is out too. You do look like we could bounce and might roll over just reaching down for the ball. Morris cracks a smile saying oh you all got jokes up in here uh. Well let's all bounce our asses up out of here. Henray mouths to the others then turns his head toward Ian hey man you still got to go man? His response was nothing changed. Henray says let's go before mom comes home. Floyd takes off like he was getting ready to run saying man here comes your momma. Before Ian can glance, he motions to take off. One laughs harder as their laughter slows up to chuckles. As they walk away their conversation slowly faded away from my ears. With Ian saying ya play too much. But, before I take yaws asses to the hoop, I got to take my own ass to that service station and forget you Henray all of you. Henray laughs saying the last time you tried to hold it. Ian gives Henray a look saying because of your ass gave us ex-lax that looked like candy. Henray snaps back it was your greedy ass that took a big piece thinking it was chocolate candy!!

He looks over at Ian saying that you almost made it, and do you want to have that little expisode happen again my friend. Ian just looks at him saying how he got his butt back when he gave him the dog beef jerky. Henray laughed saying yep that kept me up, then he howls, and they all start laughing. I enjoyed their youthful conversation and their love they displayed for each other. For that quick second, I felt old yet still entertained by laughter and the mutual respect they had for each other. I love hearing the love and respect he had for his mother in her absence. He reminded his boys that when my spine weakened, moms made me spine up and straighten up and stop acting like a dumb ass. He laughs saying she so sentimental. The walk seems shorter this time to the bus stop. Sierra was rambling about seeing Floyd and it was just good to have his kind humble spirit remember us.

Chapter 13
Back to the Old Neighborhood

We greet the bus drivers by this time I knew their names. Today Fred was taking us for a ride. Sometimes the drivers were Ralph, Cornel or Milt. I haven't seen Nick in a while, but it was good seeing Fred again, his big smile and kind conversation was appreciated. Sierra hops on the bus with her beautiful smile greeting his. I smiled and asked him how he was doing, and he said okay and that he had missed us. He had been out of town enjoying a different type of sunshine and look forward to going back to Hawaii. I told him it was good to see a familiar face and listen and see through his eyes. Places I long to one day go see but don't know if it would ever be possible. Sometimes when the bus was empty, I would have small talk with the drivers. Fred said that he was in a singing group and he would talk about the songs he wrote and the different venues they worked. I could see him and his group wooing the ladies. He had the bedroom eyes with long eyelashes, with white teeth, a gorgeous smile and soothing voice. As I listened to him, I looked out the window just like I'm looking out now at the rain, with the condensation on the windows, while enjoying my Chai tea.

Reflecting on Henray's tale of shrinkage and Courtney Diane's perception on that incident were funny. She said that when he said he would put Ian in a head lock, she went into punk mode with a quick hit on the cheek, imaginary sucker punch. She smiled saying I had to snap back and stroll over to the window knowing inside my ass wanted to run to the window to see what his exit plan was spining up to me. My thought was what the?? My ass had to know. Looked out the window nope, no running car that options out, nope on the camera crew from "punked" nah no people, no cameras and no action. Then I passed a mirror just for the sake of making sure I had to check myself to make sure I didn't shrink when I got punked. I had to blink twice to make sure that I didn't shrink into his child. I know I didn't shrink girl but for that instance I thought I saw my ass as a child with barrettes and ribbons and shift smiling. I had to step back because I thought my ass was or turned into a dumb ass little me again. Had to back it up one more again to smile to make sure it was me!! I had paused at the mirror to make sure it was me looking at me. I thought I touched the mirror expecting to fall through like Alice in Wonderderland and shift. That shift really messed with my ass. I chuckle to myself because in her fussing I can hear Robin saying you don't have an ass maybe Rita could give you little of hers. In my mind I wish I could, but I got to keep my heritage alive in my mind. I slap my own butt saying here it is.

Courtney Diane said she had to look at Henray dumb ass and he up there smiling and shift grinning one of those stupid goofy ass grins just waiting so calmly. I don't know if it scared or impressed me. That boy put me in a duh thought in what the hell. I had to look at him again opening and closing my own eyes. Blinking making sure I wasn't in Oz with Aunt Brandi. When I opened them one at a time my thoughts came back to my brain. Where his thoughts might be, and I knew his trifling ass was thinking about one of those nasty tail scants with his nasty ass. Then I put it all together and had to fess up he is my son and Mama Florrie's grandchild it had to surface sometime in his life. I guess Courtney Diane must have forgotten or didn't want to remember how she had mouthed out, (or aka another known action), in her own words spined up to her dad Papa Cleve Jr. Oh don't forget you must add the junior just like you have to say Courtney Diane's whole name. Her dad had struck her on behalf of her mouth. That tap crossed her eyes and caused her to lose her educated grammar. Then I throw in there Reva using two fingers to take the dripping preparation. With a corner smile talking about her mother Aberlynda/ Theresa and her mother frostbitten heart. Courtney Diane said that her sisters or brother never ever mouthed off to our parents. Surprisingly, my sister EJ didn't either she always had something to say but nope not even her. We all knew the consequences. I guess sometimes you forget that actions of your actions came quick. Fred talks as I fade in and out of listening to him. As I try to envision Courtney Diane and Henray having that conversation as she moves toward the window and he closes his eyes for situation for just in case. Why not add when she had place set him in the corner for tee-hee time out and she heard noises coming from his room. She opened the door Henry had his arms up in the air imitating riding a roller coaster what an imagination took the learning experience and time out away.

Funny I can picture his small frame laughing and learned at a young age how to entertain himself. Here we go again an aka, another known action humph. I don't think he noticed because he was focused on driving and my mind was just taken to a place where laughter placed me, and my spirit enjoyed the lift. Fred has always been so kind to me and not really knowing me just by riding on his route. I looked at him as a brother and riding friend. He would drop us off as close to the door as possible. Fred would also let us know what time he would be back through and would keep an eye out for us.

Sierra walked and talked as we looked at different items in different store windows. She wanted everything she saw. Inside she didn't know I wish I could buy her a portion of what she asked for. If I could I would purchase it right now. She was innocence in our broke world. I told her we will come back but inside I knew coming back was not in the picture nor in the future. I knew one day it would come where I can shop without looking at the tags with big sigh and hoping it will happen someday. I want to help support my husband and our family. I had my own money before we married and financial freedom to purchase almost anything and everything for Sierra and myself. Those days seem so far away that the purchases are just blurrs. Oh, how I long for Bill to lighten up so I can go back to work. Be amongst adult conversation and working my brain. No more just staying at home and allowing my brain to be massage when Bills talks to me without the hidden jabs. It's gotten where I don't know what type of mood Bill will be in when he comes home. We needed the money and I needed to be around life and among the working living. I didn't realize how much I missed working until it was no longer available. At first it was fun staying home but I come from a family of movers. The only time they were home was to rest or sleep. Mama Sadie would travel and visit the nearest senior center regardless of what state she was in. Mommy walked everywhere and traveled downtown to shop and walked a lot. They both lived long and healthy one close to 100 and the other one 108 years and they both finally had a good talk with the Lord saying I'm tired. I remember my dad saying walking is never crowding. There will always be room to walk. We walked so much didn't realize how much Sierra's little legs had traveled. She was too busy looking in the windows of almost every store we passed. I was doing the same thing longing to someday make a purchase just one without guilt.

Our walking was getting longer in the mall for we both were getting tired. Luck has it we found a store that had a huge sale and clearance items. My Aunt Carmen, Aunt Vanessa and Aunt Esther taught me how to shop fugal and dance, just free your spirit. Not a bad thought something I will learn later to appreciate. Oh yes and my mother, Sheryl taught me to dress in my own style and spend a little or more to not look like someone else. Who wants to see themselves across the street in the same outfit, especially if it looks better on them, no way? Our clothes were always unique and different where people would ask where did you get that outfit. We were taught not to tell because they would go and get the same outfit. Didn't want to see yourself across street and do a double take. Especially, if the outfit across the street looked much better. The owness is on you because you told them where to purchase the item that was, a not. My mom philosophy was if I wanted you to look like me, I would have told you, or picked two up just for us. I remember she said she did it once not following her own rules and the person went there and purchased the same pair of jeans. When she saw that she stopped wearing them. When she told me that, I understood the seriousness of limiting your conversation. Now, what she meant then you must be different, so you don't blend in and get lost in the crowed shuffle. Especially if they look better in the style than you do, in other words they are wearing it too well. Mommy taught us not to run and strength comes in different levels and my mother taught us it was okay to be different. I really miss them and being at home. I found a nice toddler outfit on sale with an additional 40% off making the purchase $6.00 leaving us $14.00 left whoopie. I smile and said Sierra we are rich. Sierra looks at me and giggles and I laughed with her. She didn't know how much this meant the time and watching her grow and learn her surroundings and still displaying her innocence. This is time that you can't get back. I purchased her a little toy and we went to the restaurant with a $1.00 menu. Now, I can get my soda and Sierra a kid's meal. It wasn't the mouthwatering turkey cranberry sandwich that melts on your tongue or a tall glass of cold fresh lemonade, but I could afford the menu without a sigh. As Sierra started to tire out, I looked forward to Michelle's birthday party with a present and seeing everyone again. Although I haven't seen Melba in a while, it was nice hearing her voice.

Sierra was full and ready to go home so we both could sleep it off. When we arrived at the bus stop bus driver Fred opens the door with that huge smile. Saying someone looks sleepy and one is sleep. I smiled it didn't click at first that he was talking about me. I guess I didn't think about my little one would be tired too. Sometimes I keep moving without thought. Mommy would take the bus downtown and walk for hours and walk to the local grocery store, and Mama Sadie went to the local senior citizen center regardless of what state it was in. Now, I see why she lived to be 108 and her baby sister Auntee Etta 106 and her cousin Bula lived to be 106 too, (she never married or had any kids). I guess that was her choice. It sounds kinda lonely but the times I saw her she never looked bored and was always happy. As my dad would say no grass was going to grow under their feet and it didn't. They kept it moving at any age until their death. I tried to keep my eyes open while looking out the window as Sierra lays her head in my lap. I look at her sleeping so peacefully while looking identical to Bill. I realized I really did love him and whatever problems we may be having it to shall pass. I don't think either one of us knew what was wrong or how to fix it. How do you fix or add parts to a relationship when you don't know really where to start or know what part is broken?

As we approached home Fred lets us off as close as he could to our apartment complex, which helped because I didn't have to carry Sierra too far. While she was sleep, I gathered thoughts on what to prepare for dinner and have it ready by time Bill arrived home. Hopefully, during that time, I would be able to take a little cat nap. Bill arrives home and I greet him with a fork of spaghetti. He smiles and gives me a kiss and I tell him dinner should be ready in about ten minutes. At that time Sierra hears his voice and the jingling of his keys and rushes out to greet him with a big hug and a kiss. I look at them with a smile on my face and my heart. My little one inside of me felt the warmth. He/she kicked in the evening going into late night and early mornings. I took Bill's hand and placed it on my stomach, so he could feel our child kicking at the sound of his voice. At first, he snatches his hand back I could tell it kind of scared him, but he placed it back and embraced me while holding Sierra. My family may be small but it's my family. Well he said dinner looks and smells good. I laughed now if you are ready and Sierra mocked by saying now daddy now. Bill laughed as he took a seat at the table. I place the food on the table so we all can join right on in. That felt good just like resting in bed on a rainy day. I told him that our baby was doing fine. According, to Doctor Brooks and I might know next month what we will be having. Sierra laughs when is my brotha or sissy coming, I want to play with them. We look at her at the same time laughing and enjoying the moment of dinner time. I reminded Bill about the birthday party and told him that I had found a nice outfit for Michele. Surprisingly, he didn't ask about the amount and that anticipated sigh didn't happen. It somehow turned into a loud smile.

Bill helped Sierra get ready for her bath and then bed as I cleaned up the kitchen. Watching Bill carry Sierra out in a wrapped towel just brought so much joy. Just like when he helped her balance herself on her bike with training wheels. I watched them both as they put the bike together, (team work and daddy and daughter time). Bill was a good father and Sierra had nothing but love for him. While he was getting her dressed, they were still playing peekaboo as if she was two years old. Sierra still laughed as if she was two years old. Warmth filled my body as I watched their father and daughter time. I listened as Bill read her a story which was so much better than the stories he tried to quote from memory. I could hear Sierra asking questions almost after every sentence. It seems not to bother Bill he was in no rush and you could hear his patience. After cleaning I sat down on the couch for some television time. Not really looking at anything in particular, it was more or less looking at me. I was just enjoying the sound of laughter and the love coming from Sierra's room and thankful that my baby was doing fine. When I no longer heard any laughter, or reading I look into the room to see that both Bill and Sierra were sound asleep. Now that was a Kodak moment. They looked so cute and peaceful. I still look at my kids when they are sleep or just doing nothing. They would look at me and say "what" and my response was nothing. They didn't know that I was saving that mental snap shot for later. I still have those snap shots replay every now and then. That's something I'm glad that my mind can store and replay when I want or need to have an instant replay. I took a picture of them and they never knew that someday they will see their shared special moments.

As I sit here looking out the window at the rain flow, I'm staring and thinking about a snap shot in my old archives. I went back to the couch because I just wanted Bill to hold his daughter as long as he wanted to, that was his right and his choice. I didn't want to ruin the moment. I sat back on the couch this time with a small cup of hot chocolate and enjoying the quiet time. I lean back and place my tired feet on the coffee table just doing nothing, just chilling, enjoying and smiling about nothing. If someone was to look at me, they probably would think I was crazy, but if they could see into my mind the image, I was focused on they would take a seat with a cup of something warm and soothing and just lean on back too. Life can be so fast it is up to us to slow it down. Right now, I just want to enjoy the scenery of flowers and smell the roses and slow the car down. I love and enjoy the rain and how fresh it makes everything look. As I get close to the last sigh and sip, I feel something warm next to me. Bill cuddles up to me and just says I love you and thank you for our daughter and being there for us. I know I can be difficult, and you put up with so much, thank you. As my mind goes into shock who is this man or did, I venture back into the twilight zone. I smiled back and told him you are welcome. I add that I love and appreciate our little family, and that he is a good dad. He lays his head in my lap as we continue to enjoy our quiet time. Bill fell off to sleep while we watched some crazy movie. Now, I didn't want to ruin this moment and it felt good but that hot chocolate ooh had me getting up. He jumps with me are you okay? I told him I'm fine your child has had enough of the hot chocolate. He laughs as I run to the bathroom. We go to bed and just embrace each other and enjoy the moment, with a smile. We had each other, and our family was increasing. This was something I had always wanted with Bill since our college days and now we are here.

I wake up that morning excited about going to see the old neighborhood while Bill and Sierra bring me breakfast in bed. It was a nice surprise and they both cooked. Sierra said that she scrambled the eggs and dad let her hit them open. I knew she was talking about cracking them open and scrambling the eggs. Bill smiled and just said good morning. That sound was soothing to my ears and heart. The baby liked it also. I put Bill's hand on my stomach, so he could feel the love coming from our child. Wow, our child and now we are already on the second one, woo. I never thought about having kids when I was in college let along being married with two and moving out of Oakwood. I thought I would always be there near my family and growing old with my friends. I still miss them after all these years of being out here in California. After the big breakfast in bed Bill tells me that he will clean up and get Sierra ready for the birthday party and he looks forward to seeing the old neighborhood too. Wow, breakfast in bed plus a family outing to a family affair. I give one good stretch in bed as I wake up slowly from this special morning. I feel my baby stretching inside too. I guess she/he liked the breakfast in bed and the late sleep in. The sun is shining placing warmth on my face and it's a good day for a birthday celebration. I showered while Bill and Sierra discuss in detail what she wanted to wear. He listened and looked at her as she coordinated many colors and patterns that didn't quite match. Bill smiled and gave her fashion freedom. I laugh as I captured the mini discussion on "why" whatever answer Bill gave her she kept following up with another question. I had to come to his rescue, or he would be there all-day entertaining Sierra endless imagination. We were going as a family and people will see that we are still a family. The sun was out, and the day was clear and perfect for a birthday party and the neighborhood gathering.

I missed the fun we used to have, especially with Gina and Maria's family and their parents Mr. Bert and Mutter. I hope they come. When we arrived, it was like arriving to a mini carnival. Two large jumpers for the kids, a few booths with face drawings, hot dogs, cotton candy, the smell of fresh popcorn popping, music, kids running all around, clowns and large amount of energy. Half the street was blocked off. There were many adults sitting around playing cards and laughter was in the air. There were many tables and chairs and all with their own conversations of laughter and joy. Mutter and Mr. Bert were trying to hula hoop with their grandkids. There were a lot of kids there that I didn't know. But as the day went on, I end up knowing all their names with the help from Sierra. Carolyn and Sharonlyn had a booth drawing faces on the kids. Sierra rushes over to the jumper where Lynton and his girls Bernice and Jacqueline are helping. A beautiful slim woman comes up to him and grabs him by the waist and kisses him on the cheek. I assume she was his wife Harmony, and she was holding a little boy. While Sierra was rushing over to the jumper Bill and I join her. That's when Lynton introduces us to his wife Harmony and his son Thomas. Bill shakes his hand with that a boy hugs and congratulation on his son. Bill proudly tells him that we might be having a son soon too. Lynton smiles with an alright hug and a high five. I smiled because I won't know until next week what we will be blessed with. As I looked around at all the fun and excitement Melba walks out a little thicker than normal. Wow, has it been that long? She smiles telling me that she is pregnant. I grab my mouth with amazement and watered eyes and yell out you too!! She said yea girl Michael finally caught me. We both laughed as we touched each other's stomach. At the time, Mickey Jr. comes around and he is talking and walking wanting to hang out with his sister, the birthday girl Michelle. Michelle was running around and made it over to the jumper when she saw Sierra. They hugged each other as they both jumped together.

Bill kissed me on the cheek as he hugged Michele and left. He rushed over to the table where the guys were laughing, drinking and playing cards. I liked the glances Bill gave me as he played and talked with his friends. It felt good to see the love and support he showed me with just a smile and a glance. Melba laughed and said I see that you guys are still on your honeymoon. I thought what honeymoon what she saw that I didn't feel. They say it's in the eyes and for that moment I looked at Bill a little different. I didn't notice the look, or the special heart felt smile. Sometimes it takes someone from the outside to put a warm feeling in the inside that can just make your day.

Just like the rain flowing and flowing and life keeps on moving. Some people love the rain, and some can't stand it. Right now, I'm enjoying it and my moment. I sit down with the other ladies in the apartment complex and met new neighbors. Melba was filling me in and assisting me with meeting them. Melba said that her Aunt Richardine and cousins Zena, Benita and Sandra were bringing more food. I thought how much more food do you need. Melba laughs and says that another cousin Catrice was bringing her nine kids. Ooh, I said people are still having that many?? Melba responded yep her name is Catrice. We both laughed as we look at the hula hoop. Mr. Bert grew tired from hula hoop. He just didn't have the rhythm to make it work and gave up. He smiled as he grabs a beer for him and his brother Lawson. They both sit down and take sips from their beers and just observed and talked. Lawson's wife Ms. Timia was double dutch jumping rope. At some point, turning the rope tired out her and she dragged herself to the area where we were sitting, (making huff/puff sounds). Through her laughter said that some odd ten years ago she could do some serious double dutch. She took a big sigh slowly saying that when she catches her breath, she's going to show them how we do it. The funny part she never got to show them, and that second breath never came just the huff/puff sounds. She looks over at her sister and yells Dreia (Andrea outside this complex) whenever you are ready, we got something for these youngsters. She laughs back and says I'm still looking at Della trying to get those hips working with that hula hoop. Timia laughs saying wasn't there much more space between you and the hula hoop. She laughs back and says the hips still work its this hoop that has the problem. They just don't make them how I remembered them. Dreia chimes with, girl that was when we were playing jacks and younger. These kids don't know nothing about that. I laughed because I knew, and Melba laughed, we all do remember. We miss watching that ball drop as we counted. Melba says I used to hate when I stepped on those steel jacks. We both laughed it was fun then but probably boring to this generation.

As we laughed and talk, I asked where was Toni and Jovan? There was a brief silence and sigh as she talks about Toni and Jovan. Well you know what almost every Friday consisted of with them. Well it was one Friday too much. Toni was doing pretty good and looking even better. She didn't look drained or abused. You could tell she was starting to feel better about herself. The girl had more pep in her steps. You could hear her singing and her voice was angelic. Everyone agreed as they nodded their heads. She had start working at the gas company part-time and going back to school. We all took pride in seeing her and the girls carrying back packs. Chanel and Fendi were pre-school and kindergarten age so she had more time and freedom. Jovan supported her, and it seemed as if he slowed down on his drinking. The Friday nights had become somewhat quiet and less cameos from our local police department. Thank God, we thought we were going to have to install a police substation in our complex. As I listened, in my heart the fear speeds the beat up as

I wondered what was coming next. Everyone was calm no one was interrupting just peacefully listening. Well the company liked Toni so much they wanted her to go full-time and send her to school for her new position. We heard her and Jovan arguing about the position and that she wouldn't have time for him or the girls. Melba sighs and said Toni had thought this would be a problem but really wanted to take the position. Jovan wasn't having it her being gone and not at his arms reach. She was tired of staying at home and there was more out there for her than just staying at home and dreading the weekend fights. All his antics had gotten old and she needed a change. Toni wanted to move into a house one day where the girls would have room to move around and not be confined to this concrete jungle. This was an opportunity that she didn't want to pass up not today or any day. Jovan knew the pay was more than he made, and he didn't want to lose the control he had over her. Shirley, Carolyn and Sharonlyn mom slowly take a chair and sits down with us. I look at her with excitement of seeing her. She reaches over to me and gives me a big hug. I look at her and notice she hasn't age at all she still looks the same. Shirley says Toni was going to take the position that it would help the family financially and offers an opportunity to purchase their own home. Dina and Melba both say if you are in it together then you both win and grow together. Why couldn't Jovan see that? If he would have just put as much energy into his family and as he did in chasing after those other shirts. Now, Toni has always been more faithful than Jovan could ever be. I thought back to what Robin had said you are only as faithful as your options. Dina interrupts by saying I would have left him some time ago. Shirley adds after that first hit. Jovan is creeping on Toni blurts out from Coura, say it isn't so. With that statement, they both look at each other with raised eyebrows and a sigh.

So, she decided that day she was going to try and convince or just tell Jovan to support her as her husband and friend on taking this position. It would offer more opportunities for their daughters and their marriage and get out of this apartment complex. She wanted to keep everything positive and in a loving way. I remembered how she rehearsed over and over what and how she was going to say it. Well it was Friday and payday. Jovan had his weekend injection of beer or some type of hard liquor. Coura comes in and says that he thought he had stopped and thought that they were doing better. I looked over at Coura wondering, who was this insert. She was new to me but old in the apartment complex. She smiles saying my name is Coura and those teenagers and the younger ones over there our mine. We all paused from the story to look over at the kids and the different booths where they were located. They all laughed saying that she has nothing but girls. They added laughing how many times you tried, trying to get that one boy. She laughed back responding with, we tried five times and the sixth time was a no show, false alarm. She laughs it didn't bother me or Jack we had fun, (wink wink), I told my husband Jack Herman that you will have many sons-in- laws one day. The one handing out the hot dogs and checking out Tina's sons Trace and Trent with attitude is Myra and the one trying to figure out how to make the cotton candy, (and she has more of the cotton in her hair) is LaShaun, the little one Carolyn is drawing a flower on is Bonita, the one approaching us to tell on her sister Latressa and the other little one is Rhonda. We watched Rhonda as she runs over yelling, I'm gonna tell momma. And she was right on que. As she runs up to Coura her daughter tells on her sister and she is almost out of breath but uses every breath to tell with convincing eyes. Coura looked at her but you could tell by the look she had the mother look of I'm listening but not hearing you, especially not now. She amuses her and says I will talk to her and with that it seems it was enough for her and she runs to her sister laughing telling her I told on you. She glances at her and Coura with hutched shoulders and continued playing and laughing with Mutter and the other kids in the area. Melba laughs saying that Mutter is going feel that joy tomorrow. With that statement, everyone laughs.

Melba breaks the news that she will be moving back to Oakland. She wanted to be near her parents and Michael has less than three years left and will be transferred back to San Francisco. She wanted to help her sisters and brothers with their parents and look forward to returning home. For that instance, I wish I was in her shoes. How I longed to move back home and be with my family and familiar friends, environment and with my family. I snapped back to reality when I heard familiar voices. Gina and Maria had been talking for how long, I couldn't tell you. I had just mentally checked out for that quick moment, they had picked up on what happen with Toni. We were all sitting around talking but everyone was in support for Toni and no jabs or negative energy was in the air. Toni gathered enough courage to take on Jovan on her decision. I thought then and now she probably called on her ancestral strength like I did from time to time. Dina said I heard the calm before the storm came in. Everyone said we all heard the calm. That made me think what they might have heard coming from my apartment. Did they hear Bill and I when we fought? No fight I didn't strike back just took the hits. I really hope not and hope I don't get added to this discussion. Well we heard the yelling from both which was not normal because Toni didn't argue or yell back. She was yelling this time and so was Jovan. We were thinking go Toni that's what his ass needed. We heard noise that sounded like things were being thrown. Those sounds were not uncommon coming from their apartment. So, we thought Friday night as usual followed by Jovan going to sleep and waking up to go to work Monday. We called the police so much we knew them by their first names, and they knew us by our first names too. This was just one big family weekend with nothing unusual. They all agreed this was normal.

Melba said we heard hits and crying followed by don't do it followed by a loud siren type scream. This was very scary and unusual sound and we all rushed to their apartment. We didn't know what to expect. As we walked to the door of the apartment an eerie feeling comes over us. We walked into the apartment very slow-ly, looking around at the damage furniture, broken beer bottles, the smell of fresh blood and blood all over the walls. Tina rushes to her apartment to call 9-1-1 and get a first aid kit. Dina and Gina grab Chanel and Fendi from their bedrooms where they were hiding in the closets in fear. We walked into the kitchen and see Jovan eyes wide open with a blood-soaked shirt. We are all nervous and scared at the same time. We yell out call 9-1-1. Tina runs to the nearest apartment and calls 9-1-1. Jovan tries to talk and says I didn't mean it, I really didn't mean it. I'm sorry I really didn't mean it. As we listened, we wondered where was Toni? Benjamin, Bruce and Mr. Bert go back to the bedroom looking for Toni. You can hear them yelling for her with no type of response. The back bedroom is dark and cold. Wayne stayed with Jovan and Michael had applied pressure to him saying you are going to make it and yells at Melba and Tina to grab his first aid kit. Michael tells Jovan to hang in there and where is Toni? Jovan kept saying as his voice was growing faint and breaths were becoming shallow. I really didn't mean it. Wayne says what do you mean where is Toni. Bruce wondered what happened to Toni. At the same time, Mr. Bert turns on the light not knowing what to expect. The walls were smeared with blood, and where was Toni. Benjamin calls out in soft voices for Toni. They move slowly into the master bedroom calling for Toni looking around the room in ah, at what they see. Maria walks back to the bedroom she puts her hand over her mouth to muffle the scream, as Bruce finds Toni in the closet with blood all over shiver-ing in the closet holding a knife. There was very little color in Toni's face and her hands are gripped so hard you can see her veins. She is not wearing her big signature glasses and her blouse looks shredded. Maria rushes over to her as Wayne tries to pull Maria back. Toni is not saying a word her eyes are fixed and staring straight ahead. When her name was called, she stayed motionless, without even blinking her eyes to respond. All eyebrows are raised as Wayne moves toward Toni pushing Maria away making room. Mr. Bert stood next to him as they both moved closer to Toni. They didn't know what to think. Benjamin calls her name and she doesn't blink or respond in any way. Toni's body is covered with blood as her hands shiver. They are almost hypnotized looking at Toni holding the knife tightly in her hands. They couldn't tell if she was injured. Everyone was in their own form of shock. As I listened to all the conversations going on, I can only imagine the horror that was present. To hear them say they stepped on and over broken glass, the pictures on the wall were all thrown around and the wall was smeared with blood. I had to wonder what type of rain storm was Toni and Jovan weathering?

What was only mintues felt like hours when the police, fire and ambulance arrived. We kept trying to talk Toni into letting go of the knife before the police rushed back to the room. We were hoping and praying that would have a familiar routine officer responding. We heard the paramedics working hard trying to save

Jovan. We heard words like defib; eppy and we all knew what cleared meant. It meant they were shocking him. We heard get him on the gunnery he's coding. I heard Michael and Bruce saying hang in there, man just hang in there. We heard people crying and screaming while the paramedics were counting compressions. Everyone was talking and telling the story. Confusion and chaos were in the air.

I looked around and the men are still playing cards along with dominos, the kids are playing innocently, the elders are just chilling and laughing. The teenagers look bored but enjoying the boys as well as the girls enjoying looking at them. Officers Michael and Clyde arrived on scene, which was a relief seeing familiar faces. Officer Jonelyn or Joycelyn arrived which made it better accompanied by Officer I Kuan. Her sister Officer I Cheng was on another domestic call. It was good to see women in this situation. They entered with guns drawn as Jovan is rushed out of the apartment. At that time, Rod and Sheila arrived with Toni's dad Hollingsworth. As her dad looks at the paramedics working on Jovan fear comes to his face of where is Antonelle. He rushes in looking at the blood and the damage. While the officers' motion for him to move back. He yells that's my baby daughter Antonelle that's my Toni. He yells Toni, Toni can you hear me it's your poppy, (from the front door)!! The officers move in slowly looking around the apartment. They have been there before but this time it was different. Everyone in the back was yelling and pleading with Toni who is still in a daze. Maria kneeled and prayed as she pleads with her to respond. The officers came in and told everyone to move out and clear the area. This was real and not a movie we all were scared. Everyone was moving slowly except for Maria. She tells them I'm not moving. She pleaded with Toni to hand her the knife mamacita. Toni is still not responding. Maria pleads with her in a soft voice please Toni please. The officers tell Maria to move as they pulled her away. By this time, Bruce is yelling at Maria please come out, please babe please. The officers are trying to control the scene and keep people from coming in. Hollings is yelling and crying for his daughter and the crowds are gathering outside due to the red lights sirens and many other officers arriving on scene. Their weapons are drawn, and everyone is still pleading with Toni. Officer Michael moves in closer while Officer Clyde backs him up. Officer Jonelyn/Joycelyn not clear on name so much going on moves a little closer with her weapon drawn trying to talk to Toni. Officer Kuan arrived and stood to her right side with her gun strap unfastened and hand on her weapon. I'm listening and visualizing the concern on the officer's faces. She is pleading with Toni and telling her if she doesn't drop the weapon we will be forced to shoot. Those words bought horror to our souls and fear to the sound of the clicking of their weapons. At that point, another officer removes Maria from the room as Toni continues to stare straight ahead. Then a whisper is heard in the mist of the confusion and noise. Toni stares as she says I didn't mean to do it and just kept repeating in a low whisper. Officer Jonelyn reaches slowly and gently grabs the knife not losing any eye contact as she calmly spoke to her.

Toni is soaked in blood, scars on her face, hair is in a disarray, blouse shredded as the officers slowly lifted her up. They turned her around and put handcuffs on her as they read her rights. She repeats again I didn't mean to do it. Where is Van where is Van. The sound goes from soft to yelling out for Van. She looks up and sees her daddy and yells for him and asks where is Van, where's my Poppy? The crowd separates as Toni is lead out in handcuffs looking around. Melba says the paramedics knew him and let Michael ride in the ambulance with them while CPR was being conducted on Jovan. Hollings walks into the apartment with his hands in his pockets shaking his head. Mr. Bert accompanies him just for support. He looked at Bruce and Rod and with tearful eyes asks where are my granddaughters? Melba and Gina had taken them to Shirley's place and her girls kept them busy. Then Rod and Sheila's came over and took them to their apartment to play games with their niece Daphne and eat late night pizza. Maria comes out with tears and a little shaken. Her husband Bruce embraces her and the crowd leaves because the event is over. Melba said she walked over to Toni and said we are here for you and the girls are with your dad. Toni turns her head slowly and looks at Melba with tears in her eyes my girls are okay? Yes, they are with your dad. Where is Van, I don't see him. She looks at her and says Van is on his way to the hospital. Toni becomes dazed and the expression is one of confusion. The familiar officers looked at Toni and told her we know you didn't mean it. We are going to take you to county hospital just to have them check you out. She looks at them in a soft voice saying thank you officers you have been very kind. As she repeated, I'm okay and Van is okay, I'm okay and Van is okay.

As the last police car drives away, we all looked at each other and agreed we couldn't wake up to this. We needed to take care of this apartment. So, everyone goes into their apartment for cleaning supplies to put the apartment together as much as they could. I listened to them and realized this was a village in action. Looking out for everyone and everything and not asking for anything in return. They said that they scrubbed walls, swapped up glass and turned furniture back over. Benjamin and Wayne left to go to the hospital to check on Jovan and pick up Michael. When they arrived, they are meant by Doctor Strudwick and he had said that it was touch and go and he had coded twice, but he is in intensive care and we will know something in the next twenty-four hours. Michael comes out exhausted and happy to see them. Nothing is said just silence in the hospital lobby and on the way home. No one had anything to say they just looked out the window and was in silence until they arrived home. When they arrived, they noticed everyone cleaning and straighten up the apartment discussing about pooling a fund for Toni's defense. Melba looked over at Tina and asks her does she know any good lawyers, since she was a court reporter. Tina says I will talk to Mr. McNeill he has firm McNeill and

MacKenzie associates. I have a good rapport with Mr. McNeill and will check with him tomorrow.

They all agreed together that Toni was going to need prayer, a good lawyer and her friends. Jovan is going to need prayer for his recovery. Michael agreed and said it didn't look too good for him, but we will know tomorrow. Dr. Venus is the best in his profession. We needed to go to county and check on Toni too. Wayne said that might be hard because she was in police custody. Gina says to Bruce can't you call your friend Marvis or Santos or Thurman, or Alva/Eva even Jimmy and ask them or somebody to check on her, anybody? Come on now we need some serious help. With a big sigh and an expression of uncertain all he could say was I can try. When she said Eva, I flashed back to Reva's story and remembered she had mentioned an Eva. I kind of wondered if they were the same person. Wow that would be a wild chance.

Hours passed, and time moved on as they talked cleaned and sighs on what happened in this apartment. They did the best they could, and all departed and went their separate ways to their apartments. They remembered as the sun rose and the day was calm. Michael received a phone call from Dr. Dewey saying that Jovan was doing, better but was not out of the woods yet. He had lost a lot of blood and was weak and not in the best of health but will keep you informed. Mr. Hollingsworth or Hollings and his wife Lynette returned that morning to pick up some items for the girls. We were glad that we had cleaned up so, they wouldn't have to see the disaster in the apartment and be reminded of why they had their grand-daughters. You could see the surprise in Mrs. Hollingsworth or Mrs. Lynette eyes as she entered the apartment. They didn't bring the girls they had left them with Toni's sisters and brothers. They didn't need to see their place and ask questions about their parents. I remembered I only met one of Toni's sisters, Sheridan and brother, Howard and they both were looked identical to Toni just older and very polite. All they knew was that they are getting some help, and everything would be okay. Before they left them, both went into each apartment and personally thanked everyone for their help. His heart was so humble, and kind and you could tell by Toni's parent's mannerism that was the way she was raised. They just walked slowly while holding hands. We all watched as he took her hand and opened the door leaning in and giving her a kiss on the cheek. She smiled as he closed the door. He didn't move fast but he wasn't slow either. We watched them drive away knowing that they were truly a loving couple. We all sighed saying that we hope that we end up like that. Later that day we heard the news we wanted to hear. Wayne told us that Nurse Muang said Toni was doing fine. She just had some cuts, scraps and bruises, but they have her under psychiatric watch for next forty-eight hours. She is under police custody and can't have any visitors and all she had been doing was sleeping. He went on to say the officer with her Officer Perlisha is good people she will keep a good watch over her. Melba said that she had heard that name before but couldn't remember where she heard it.

Well as the ladies continued the guys were still playing cards and eating along with everyone else. As we talked time seem to stay still what felt like hours was only minutes, the day was still young. It felt good being around them again but sad to hear about struggles that ended up with so many injuries and casualties. I looked over at Bill and hoped that we will be that couple holding hands and growing old together. I hope are hope will show up wanting to be, waking up seeing each other while enjoying breakfast and holding hands.

We all wondered who would go to Toni's job and tell them she might need some leave time. Should we ask her parents'? Who would step up and convince them that Toni will be returning? No one wanted Toni to lose her job and have to start all over. This was a chance in a lifetime for her and a new beginning. We all agreed we had to at least try for Toni. Tina did talk to Mr. McNeill about representing Toni just in case it went to trial and the possible cost to represent her. He said it depends on what they were going to charge her with, the county she lived in and who was the prosecuting attorney. He also stated that he could go talk to her while she was in custody and see what direction they might be going in. That was better than not knowing at all. We knew this would-be baby steps for all of us. None of us have ever been exposed to this type of situation. This was something that you either read about or show it in some type of movie. How do you recover from this? We all agreed with prayer and love. Time passed, and it seemed like years and everyone agreed. But in reality, it was only months. Jovan slowly recovered but it was a long way. We visited him, and he seemed different. It was for the better. He was missing his family but was not allowed to have any contact with Toni. Her parents stayed in contact with Jovan for the girl's sake. They never really cared for him but put their feelings aside for their granddaughters. Jovan's parents would visit him from time to time they were a little up in age and it was hard for them to get around. Michael, Wayne and Bruce would visit him and take his parents to see him. During his stay, Jovan had a chance to re-evaluate his life, what happened that night. He had deep regrets he harbored about not being the best husband, or father and always felt at any point in life that Toni would leave him and take the girls.

He said he hid behind the beer and hard liquor and knew if Toni grew, she would not want to be with him. He found lust in other women to fill any and all voids he thought existed as an excuse to be unfaithful and Toni didn't deserve it. I didn't care if she knew or not. Being with those other women made him feel good because, at any time he could leave them. Now, the crazy part he said was that they could never measure up to Toni. It was strange to hear a man say that he had insecurities. Jovan didn't want to press any charges, because it was his fault everything, for many years. He said he tried to make her happy but only saw sadness he inflicted on her in her eyes. He hated seeing that look and would get frustrated. The weekend indulges allowed him to make it through the weekend and not be reminded by Toni's tears. He just wanted to sleep it away. During the week was easy because the days went fast. Because all he had to do was just come home from dealings at work, eat, sit down and go to bed and wake up and do the same routine. There was no routine on the weekend too much time. Time, he had to look at his family and wanted more than just coming home, but just didn't know how to say it. His parents were loving, and his brothers and sisters all had good marriages and he would look at them and just couldn't figure out how they did it. He was hard on himself and extended it to Toni in words and hitting her. Knowing that he cried showed us that he was human and really had regrets.

During Jovan's recovery, Toni was dealing with her issues. Officer Perlisha seemed to be with her more than any other officers. She would come in and visit her on her days off. We were able to keep up with her through Nurse Muang, and Captain Marvis. From time to time the other officers that came that night would check on Toni too. They would keep us updated on her progress. The doctor that was evaluating her was very nice and easy to talk to; I think they said her name was Doctor Ranjana. She said that Toni was doing better, the hospital just had so many series of psychiatric evaluations before she could be released. They couldn't tell us if she was going to be charged or not. We thought since it had been so long maybe that was a good sign. Unfortunately, we spoke too soon. Officer Jonelyn and Officer I Kuan came by and told us they heard that she might be charged…. With a gasp and fear racing through our hearts and minds we thought no this was self-defense as we looked at each other with fright mouthing it was self defense trying to convince everyone within the sounds of confusion. They didn't know Toni like we did. We never ever heard her raise her voice and she was trying her best to be a good wife and mother. Toni has never, never hurt anyone. She was always on the receiving end of getting hurt. What type of system was this? The officers really didn't have an answer and just chose not to respond. They were just happy that no one died, and calm was back in the apartment complex. But how much calm was needed you could see the guilt in our expressions that we should have done something sooner but sooner came quicker than we thought. No one could ever fathom that this would happen in this complex. We tried to focus on what the officers were not saying. If they heard anything else, they would let us know. Melba said that she was glad to hear from Officer Perlisha. She told us that Toni asked her to contact her and told us she was going to be released from the hospital and transferred to the county jail to be charged on attempted murder. Melba repeated attempted murder you got to be kidding. She just remembers how her heart dropped and cried how could they! Then she contacted Tina about Mr. McNeill representing Toni and hoping he wouldn't be too expensive. They had heard he was good and no-nonsense attorney. We still wondered how much, would good and no-nonsense cost. We all got together and made an appointment to go see Mr. McNeill. So, all questions about Toni's charges could be answered. When we arrived, we saw a man with a gentle handsome face, hair of maturity and a walk of confidence. We knew he was the one. We all spoke and told him what happened that night and would like to hire him because Toni needed the best. We had heard that she was being charged with attempted murder. As he spoke, we listened hard to his every word. He said he would go to the jail and see who the prosecutor is and what she is being charge with. At that point, we can discuss his fees.

In a few days, we heard back, and it was true Toni was being charged with attempted murder. The reason for the charges was that, Toni was aggressive and could have walked away. Jovan was stabbed more than once. We gag at the thought of walking away. She was defending herself. There should be records of many domestic violence calls. Mr. McNeill listens to our concerns and says that this case might be assigned to an aggressive prosecutor Renee Ray and she looks for some serious time. We all looked with a-ah what kind of time. He said 15 to 20 years and out in 7 on good behavior is what she is sometimes known for, sometimes longer. Also, it depends on the judge assigned to this case. We all yell you kidding this can't be happening? Wow, what will this cost us? He said I will go and talk with Toni and I will get back to you. We asked when we can see her. He told them the visiting days are Thursdays and Saturdays, not sure of the hours.

Melba called Officer Perlisha and asked if she could get a message to Toni. Please tell her we are getting her a lawyer and don't worry about the cost. Perlisha asked the name of the lawyer representing Toni. We told her Mr. McNeill and her response was he is good, expensive but you get what you paid for. Those words were soothing and just hope he lived up to his reputation and free Toni. Melba said her, and Maria was able to see her. They wanted to see and show Toni she wasn't alone. It took a long time to be cleared to see Toni in jail. The line and the process were so long. We didn't imagine it would be that long. They had so many rules and we didn't want to do anything wrong and not be able to see Toni. By time we made it through that exhausted process we finally saw her. It felt as if it had been years since the ordeal happened and seeing Toni again. She looked rested but tired with some residual scars that healed but left some marks. Toni looked smaller than her normal petite size and wasn't wearing the big glasses she had hid behind for so many years. She tried smiling through her pain. She told us that she didn't want her parents or her kids coming there. We told her that her family was doing fine. This was not the place for them. She didn't want the attorney either she did it and didn't want anyone to cause any financial burden because of her actions. She would be okay with the public defender, save your money. Maria and I spoke firmly that you would be just a case number with a Public Defender. Please think about Chanel and Fendi, they need their mother.

At that point, she asked about Jovan as she tried to look at us. Her voice was low, and she looked so scared. The months that she had been there showed in her face and emotions. We both looked at each other trying to hold back tears and be as strong as we could for Toni and for us. We both said he's recovering. For that was all that we really knew and didn't want to add any more stress to Toni. What time was allowed for visitation we kept trying to convince Toni to talk to Mr. McNeill and allow him to represent her? The place was very noisy with many conversations going on at the same time. Not much privacy we strained trying to hear and convince Toni about Mr. McNeill. We didn't want to pressure her but only try to persuade her to reconsider her decision. By time the visiting hours were over Toni accepted with hesitation the offer only if we allowed her to pay us back. We agreed but we knew that we would not take the money.

We spoke with Mr. McNeill and his assistant/intern attorney Shasa. She was very professional through her occasional smile while taking notes. We were glad to see a woman. Mr. McNeill and Miss Shasa had interviewed Toni and were impressed with her. When they left Toni everyone was in agreeance, and they accepted her case. Whatever, Miss Shasa said to Toni it was a blessing. He told us that the prosecutor Renee Ray was assigned and reminds you that she is very aggressive especially against domestic violence. His retainer was $3,000.00. We didn't say it but we both thought wow $3,000.00 and that was just a retainer. That was like having a lawyer on a layaway plan. How many installments would this involve? We both said at the same time a slow okay. When we walked out of the office, we said that we would have to do some heavy praying and needed a ram in the bush. If each family could donate $500.00 to $700.00 a piece, we might be able to pull it off. While we were talking about the lawyer the ride home seemed like this all couldn't really be happening. We tried to make conversation, but the small talk turned into random silence. This ride felt longer than the ride to the county jail. Michael and Bruce were staying in touch with Jovan and his progress.

Jovan was recovering, convalescing and reliving that night. He had asked for Wayne to be his sponsor in a twelve-step program for his alcoholism. He also requested Reverend Goodlet; we had to remind him through his medication that he had passed away over twenty years ago. Jovan then snapped back requesting senior Pastor Turner or his brother-in law Pastor Ward and at first, he, said Pastor Jones. We had to correct him in saying get those women out of your mind it's Minister Baltimore he married your sister nut. He shook his head back into reality and went on and said I need some religion up in here in order to make it. This was an eye opener he had wanted to stop for a long time but didn't know how to do it. He said it was not Toni's fault. He cried as he said that he drove her to it and she just snapped. He knew about the new position because he overheard her talking to Melba. I approached her after hearing her talk about it and she sounded so happy. I haven't heard her sound that happy in years. It had been a long time since I had heard Toni laugh. Man, my ego, pride said oh hell no way! She will get the big head and realize who she was married to. I knew one day it would come so I tried to prolong it as long as I could. I knew I was a jerk. Michael and Bruce laughed and agreed. Jovan said man I didn't need a-amen on that, (he kind of chuckles with them).

I know you both set me up with that Nurse Hilda. Bruce points at Wayne saying it was him. Wayne eyes enlarged as he looked over at Bruce, (who looked over at Jovan). Wayne said that Nurse Chanae and Nurse Anita had our heads going from left to right and then right to left and our eyes met. Bruce and Wayne said in sync, that was a- oh hell no! That would not work for Jovan. So, Jovan glances at Bruce so it, was you? They both say in sync it was Dr. Ranjana. Jovan eventually smiled and went on telling what had happened. Then I heard Toni's voice laughing and happy about being asked to be trained for a new position. Guys really, I thought hard and long. I looked around our apartment and I had always wanted more for my family. I just couldn't figure it out how to get there. After thinking about his family and wanting to do better and wanting more for them. Jovan would just look at the progression of his brothers and sisters. He felt it was about time for him and Toni to move into a house for the girls. Jovan voice cracked as he tried to fight back tears to tell what happened. He moves very slow trying to find some form of comfort and, you can see and feel the pain he is experiencing, as he again tries to adjust himself in his hospital bed.

Jovan admits that he had been doing his normal weekend crazy drinking. He needed just a little courage to tell Toni he supported her promotion and that he was really, happy for her, for us for our family. He was ready to progress to the next level. He actually embraced and was happy about maybe moving into a house. Buying new furniture and get rid of the hand-me-down out dated furniture that just didn't match. He took one big sip from his glass filled with Hennessey and set it back on the kitchen counter glancing at Toni while she was cleaning. The girls were back in the room sleep and he thought this would be the perfect time to talk to her. Toni was in the front room cleaning up my beer collections that was spread all over the table, on the floor along with cigarette butts accompanied with ashes embedded in the carpet. I watched her as she cleaned, and I asked could I talk to her about her promotion. I was a little buzzed but coherent. While walking toward her thinking about what or how to say it, I paused for that second at how Toni looked so beautiful. The look of how I remembered her when, I first saw her in grade school, beautiful. Guys you believe I gave her a toy ring from the bubble gum machine. It took all my allowance money to finally have the ring roll out. Even as a young kid I knew she was the one. I don't know if it was my tone man or what was up. Did I frown when I approached her that she felt I was going to hit her? Hell, I don't remember,

I really, really don't remember. I heard her tell me she was taking the promotion regardless of what I said or thought....

While, I was trying to adjust my hearing to what, how, and the way it was said! Because I just knew this woman didn't tell me, what she was going to do and now she is wearing the pants and draws. She must be some kind of crazy talking to me like that! Did this woman take a sip of my Hennessey too? She snaps again and says she is taking the promotion rather I liked it or not. Then she followed up with a humph. Now, that through me off and I had to take a step back where did all this come from? Then I snapped back with the drink and my ego pushed up front and yelled back at her some things that were not nice. All that kindness went out the window. Next thing I knew she is throwing and breaking things in the front room. I'm trying to process what is happening, but everything seemeed to be moving in slow motion including my brain and reflexes. She must have smashed a bottle, or it broke when she hit me. Because, before I knew it, she had cut both my arms as I tried to block her swings. I felt the pain and heard my flesh getting cut. I yelled, Atonelle what the?? She runs back into the bedroom. And I run after her thinking what the heck is going on, she must be out of her rabbit mind. I look at the bed and she is by the bed. I don't know where this strength came from. Toni had flipped the mattress over. I run behind her and with quickness I get hit with a lamp. I feel a sharp pain in my chest and my shirt feels wet. I looked down and it's bloody, man. I placed my hand on my stomach and look and it's full of blood, my blood! Can you believe it she stabbed me as I get up, she stabs me again? I step back looking at her wondering what in the hell is going on. I'm still trying to dissect the first cut, now they just keep coming. I didn't realize that I had screamed and when I screamed again, she stabbed me again. My mind did step up to the plate and said dummy stop screaming, shut it up now. I think at that point I staggered down the hallway falling and trying to balance myself. Man, even the Hennessey left me running down the hall screaming and stuff. Michael and Bruce kind of chuckled, but still paying attention with deep concern. Can you believe me screaming man like a little girl? I felt myself falling, but I made it back up to my feet and I slide down the wall. Everything that was on the wall I knocked down as I tried to balance myself.

I thought which was silly; if I could get to my drink everything would be okay. I couldn't believe this crap, just ani't happening not now not to me. I must be looking at some movie wake up Jovan and change the channel. I just need a good strong sip after all its Friday. Just needed that last drink, (he smiles), you know Hennessy its not cheap. You know me, I only dranked that only on paydays, (that was my payday special). You know the other days I consumed only that cheap beer and I couldn't let my payday Hennessy go to waste. I go to grab the drink and the glass falls out of my hand and hits the floor and I follow it. My legs buckled underneath me. It felt like some type of slow motion you know like you see in a movie with a slow song playing. Only thing is, I can't hear the theme music only the sound of me moaning. While down I rolled back and forth in pain. I felt the broken glass on my face at the same time holding my stomach and my chest is hurting. All I could only think about was my Toni. I didn't mean to make her that mad. I never had seen her that mad before. The only thing missing was her spitting out pea soup.

Next thing I know is that I thought I was looking at you Michael and Wayne. I heard noise, but I couldn't make out the words. I felt my lips moving but I couldn't hear my voice. The next thing I remembered was waking up in the hospital. I had a visit from the police and prosecutor and didn't know for what? I was in and out sleeping. As I opened my eyes slowly, I tried adjusting my eyes to this tall lady with legs that kept going into her fitted suit. She was attractive but not my type. She was a site of relief from Nurse George and Nurse Julius. The only male nurses that seemed to attend to me other than Nurse Hilda. Who gives me a sponge bath with her arthritic hands and aroma of bengaid or some sort of medicated smell? Man, what happened to the women nurses. I would take ugly one over medicated smelling arthritic Nurse Hilda. Which seemed like she was always on duty and ready to give me a sponge bath, yuck? When does she go home dude? Michael and Wayne snicker because they saw Nurse Hilda. Now man I heard women nurses out there why they keep sending these male nurses in along with on duty Nurse Hilda that doesn't go home. Come on now I just wanted to look, not thinking about touching. I need some sweet thoughts to put me to sleep other than this medication. I just needed a nurse or nurses to rock me to sleep. You know that could help with my healing process, (he winks with a chuckle). They wink back with a ha-ha and hell no! Michael and Wayne laughed saying we saw Nurse Chanae and Nurse Anita and you know, and we know that wasn't going to happen. You want some type of eye candy. You don't need no eye candy you need to get rid of that sweet tooth nah really man.

Now I got my tall order of legs. I had to blink twice to make sure I was here. So, it was refreshing to see that prosecutor by the name of Renee Ray. She came in sweet, smelling good and looking fresh, legs for days. I told her I wasn't pressing any charges and that it was my fault. Come on this one I had to man up. I had started the fight and had abused Toni for many years and that was something I wasn't proud of. She tried to tell me Toni was trying to kill my ass. I told her I had killed Toni's spirit many times over. I was there, and you weren't. I wasn't pressing any type of charges and turned my head away from her and towards the window, shaking my head that wasn't a good feeling. Reality really hurts a man and it hurt me. This prosecutor wasn't feeling my answers or thoughts. This lady of legs didn't show any type of feelings. Her eyes showed anger, disgust, and disappointment in my answers. She says some words in which I had tuned her out by then and, I thought I saw her spit out pea soup and fly off on her broom. Man, I think I heard it reviving up like a motorcycle and varoom off. He chuckles in pain with Michael and Bruce. I didn't tell her what happened because, I knew it would hurt Toni and I had hurt her enough. She deserves better and the girls need her. As Michael told Melba what happened he said that Wayne and I were stunned. How do you respond from what he said? He numbs us both and we just stared at him as he spoke. I think we both were in shock and perplexed. It sounds like something out of a movie not something you see live, but we knew he had to get it off his chest.

Melba told him that Maria and she had spoken with the lawyer and the retainer would be $3,000.00 gettas. Michael said $3,000.00? Well if each family can contribute $500.00 to $700.00, we will have it. Now, we just have to adjust our budget, but we will be fine, and you know it. Michael smiles and all the ladies laugh and said Michael always smiling. What do you be doing to him?? Right then Shelia says her family comes from hitting men with items. She said her grandma Ernestine hit her granddad with a phone and heard the bell in the phone tone and stepped over him. We laughed saying ding ding dumb. Granddad heard ringing for a bit and stayed away from the phones, and my momma Pandora hit my dad in the head with an iron and watched him shake, as Shelia looks over at her husband, she laughs good thing we have cell phones and permanent-press clothes. Everyone laughs as they look over at the men still playing dominos and cards eating and drinking not knowing we are talking about them. I thought to myself they are probably talking and laughing about us too. I can only imagine the ammunition we give them to joke about. Melba smiles as they continued with the story. Dina says okay Melba speed the story up. Okay, okay everyone is still assisting in the story. Well between hospital and jail visits time went on and the judge assigned was originally Judge Dexter, but he was convalescing from surgery and he was the judge we needed. They reassigned Toni's case to Judge Jerrold. We heard he was fair but didn't know too much about his reputation. Mr. McNeill wanted to go to court with a jury. He talked about plea bargaining as another option. He was going to offer three to five years because Renee Ray wanted Toni to do 15-30 years due to the nature of the crime. Renee Ray was charging attempted murder due to the severity of the injuries. She said at any time Toni could have walked away but she chose to stab Jovan several times and had a knife hidden in the bedroom and waited for him to enter. You're kidding Mr. McNeill simple battery assault. Mr. McNeill states that if we plea for 3 years Toni could be out in 18 months on good behavior or take a chance on a jury trial.

So, we meet in Judge Jerrod's chambers to discuss a plea. Mr. McNeill had talked to the prosecutor Renee Ray about 3-year sentence. She was very set on 15-30 then bargained down to 10-15 years. Michael and I were allowed in the chambers while the rest of them waited outside. We were allowed inside his chambers, because we represented the invested interest. Renee Ray was well aware of who we supported. Jovan was there in a wheelchair on leave from the hospital and was recovering very well. He looked tired but more concerned about Toni. Both Toni and Jovan's parents were there too. So, she seemed very rigid as she passed all of Toni's supporters. We noticed that as she entered into Judge Jerrold's chambers, she slowly closed his door.

We were very impressed with Mr. McNeill calmness and brilliance. He stated that here we have a woman sitting here that is result of domestic violence and she snapped. We have her evaluations from the county that I and Miss Renee Ray have reviewed. We have laid everything out nothing is hidden. Toni sits listening looking at him as he speaks with no expression occasionally wiping her tears. She has no criminal records; pillar of the city and she is attractive mother and wife. Mr. McNeill pointed at the door stating that she has the support outside these doors. Miss Toni's husband is out there in a wheelchair with their parents. Let me add that she would make an incredible witness. Toni will not be returning to her apartment, so she won't be returning to that environment. She was employed and attending school and she is still employable upon release. His recommendation was to plead this down to a simple battery assault. Renee responds you must be kidding?? She stabbed him serval times and there is no record of her ever calling 9-1-1 to help save her bleeding husband. She did more than assault her husband, while their children slept in the other room. You're talking about a slap; a slap didn't draw as much blood that was left on the walls and floors of their apartment. Look at the pictures of the crime scene. After she firmly voiced her concerns you could see the aggressive expression change from Miss Broomstick Renee Ray. She was really in deep thought and angry at the same time. Reray, (they chuckle at the nick name), had her feelings hurt and insisting on how insulting this plea sounded. This woman snapped to the point of attempted murder. Mr. McNeill calmly responded, we are not saying she isn't guilty, and she needs to be punished. Let us not take her opportunities away from being a productive part of society. My request on behalf of my client would be to have her of being incarcerated for 3-5 years. If we went to jury, she would be a good incredible witness. Your Honor, if you would take a few steps and just look outside your chambers you will see her supporters. Yes, a lot of concerned voters out there Miss Ray. Judge Jerrold listens and asks us to leave so they could discuss amongst the lawyers about the plea bargain. Whatever happened inside we don't know. When we could return, we were informed that the judge accepted the plea bargain of 3 years. Reray/ Renee Ray wasnn't happy but this wasn't about her or her happiness. Toni had to tell the judge if she accepted the plea what happened that night.

Toni tries to fight back her tears and her voice trembled, as her body shook. Miss Renee studies Toni and her every word. Toni looks at the Judge and says first I'm sorry for what happened and apologize to everyone here. That day I had talked to Melba and Gina about the position at the gas company. I talked about the new position to everyone who would listen. I never thought I could be in such a position. I didn't believe in myself enough to believe that they wanted to promote me. This position would offer so many opportunities for my girls and take some of the financial burden off Jovan. I was hoping that someday we could buy a house and new furniture. Some place where the girls could have a backyard and Jovan and I could have a garden with flowers and vegetables. You know inner city farmers and stuff. I would just imagine the house and pictured the girls playing and Jovan and I getting dirty from gardening and laughing as we plant and watch the girls play. I kind of knew Jovan might not want me to take the position because this would take me from home. He talked about it because he had overheard me telling Melba and Sheila about it. I was just so excited and didn't want him to ruin my joy. For once I had my own joy and him or Hennessey or beer wasn't going to take it. This time he wasn't going to beat me because, it was the weekend. She raises her voice a little but returns to the shy tone she had before. I wanted a change not just for me but for my daughters and for my family. They had to know this is not how you live, and this is not how you show love. I had to give them an answer Monday and I watched Jovan do his normal routine of drinking.

Toni breaks with a sigh as she looks slowly around the room with her head up telling what happened. I was ready for him to say something to me and when I usually respond he hits me, and if I don't respond he hits me and this time he wasn't going to hit me. I was determined to take that promotion. I wasn't going to take any more punches, not today or ever again. I had suppressed the abuse for so many years. So, just by him approaching me and saying he wanted to talk about my promotion fear set in. I just snapped and said I'm taking it with or without your permission. I asked you as a courtesy I didn't need your permission just your blessings. I never ever spoke to him like that. I think we both were shocked at my outburst. I finally stood up, but I knew by that outburst he was really going to hurt me. That gut feeling set in and I heard a voice say ooh, now you better run. I just started throwing things around and broke one of his empty beer bottles. I snatched up so many beer bottles that were on that table. I was cleaning up that's why they were there. He starts fussing and cussing and the fear heightened. I started swinging the broken beer bottle at him striking both arms as he blocked. I saw blood and knew ooh now I know I better run. The safest place for me was the bedroom. I had hidden a knife between the mattresses and knew if I pulled it out on him, he would go away.

I heard him running behind me yelling my name and I really didn't know what to do. I was really scared. So, I grab the lamp and hit him. He looked at me with so much rage. I just knew I was going to die and not see my daughters grow up. It happened so fast. I flipped the mattress over and grab the knife. I guess I stabbed him because I heard a loud squelching sound and realized it was Van. I stabbed him again and he screamed again. I really don't know why I stabbed him again. I just saw my life flashing in front of me and the thought that I would no longer be hearing my daughter's laughter. I watched him leave the room hoping he would call 9-1-1. I was scared, and I turned off the lights and hide like a little kid in the closet. Hoping this was a dream. I heard voices, but I just couldn't respond. I tried and tried to yell out, I'm sorry I didn't mean it, but the words wouldn't come out. The room and closet were so dark, and I was so cold. I saw blood and didn't know where it came from.

Then an array of light had me in some type of trance, and I heard a voice say let go. This voice didn't scare me. This voice was angelic and calm. Did Van hit me again except a little harder something was wrong? Once I let go the voice and the light left. Then I remembered being lifted and waking up in the hospital with a police officer standing beside my bed. Toni's voice strengthens as she holds her head up with sincerity in her eyes and tone. I admit now I was wrong and didn't mean to hurt anyone especially my family. Jovan and I loved each other but that wasn't enough anymore. I could have and should have left but a shelter wasn't an option for my daughters. I didn't want them being in a place we didn't know anything about. My parents have been married for over 50 years and I wanted to reach that milestone plus add more years. I wanted the house with the picket fence. Now, I realized that our relationship was unhealthy and toxic and that we both contributed to it. I used to blame Van, but it took two. I hope that Van has or will forgive me and that I be allowed to raise our daughters and be an asset to my community. I need help to get through this and provide a healthy positive environment for my daughters and be productive adult. Given an opportunity I will not let my community or legal system down.

I thanked my friends for their support and want to pay them back for supporting and believing in me. I can only do that by you, Judge Jerrold to give me the opportunity to return back to society and continue to be productive. Time allowed me to re-evaluate my life and my marriage. The sessions I attended here in county helped and opened my eyes to so many things I never thought existed. I went from being abused to abusing myself. I had to renew my thinking and process my thoughts on the direction I needed to go in to help myself, in which would help my family. Sometimes a little bell goes off where you have to realize the value within yourself. If you don't see the value in yourself no one will either. At some point, I realized that I had been hurt a little for a long time. I should have taken a lot of hurt for a short period of time and things wouldn't have turned out this way. I'm happy that I and my husband both benefited from this tragic incident and I hope my daughters will continue to love both parents and live in a healthy loving environment.

After Toni finished, she confirmed what Mr. McNeill said she would be an incredible witness. Many eyes were full of tears and others were crying. I thought I saw a glimpse of humanity in Renee Ray aka Reray and Judge Jerrold. So, she was human and for that instance she put her broom in the closet. The judge accepted the plea and Toni received one year for time served and served eight months in a half-way house. During that time, she and Jovan divorced but remained friends. Toni and her daughters stayed with her parents. Although, Toni lost her promotion with the gas company, she went back to school and finished her bachelors. She knew she had to re-evaluate her career direction. Toni knew that she needed a new career with more job opportunities. So, she applied to the local university nursing program and was accepted. Right now, as we speak Toni will soon be Nurse Toni. Everyone suddenly quiets and mouths open. We heard laughter and conversations. When we slowly turned our heads and up walk Toni, Jovan and the girls, Channel and Fendi. The girls run to us giving us a quick hug then take off to the booths and games. We laughed and smiled at the site of seeing Toni in her scrubs. She said that she had just gotten off from work and Jovan had picked her up. Jovan was laughing and gave us all a hug as he limps over to the men still playing cards. I looked at them, and how they balanced each other. Jovan looks like he lost 20-30 pounds and Toni looks like it bounced onto her. She was a little fuller than her normal petite frame and now sported a short hair cut in place of her long pony tail and contacts instead of her big glasses. They both were laughing and talking normal. This was something I never saw during the time we lived there. The girls were laughing and not acting shy or afraid to speak. Time did heal all wounds and refreshed a new life and beginning. Hmm, I got so caught up in my thoughts and forgot about the sun trying to come through. Well sun did finally shine in Jovan and Toni's life. Their rainbow finally smiled.

Jovan said to Toni I'm going over there, babe with the boys. Everyone laughs that's not a" B" word we are used to hearing from your boo. The ladies laughed like high school girls as they say the "B" word shaking their shoulders all together saying ooh were trembling. Jovan looks at them and Toni blows him a kiss and says I got them babe. Toni smiled as she turned her head toward us with a wink. We start singing I got you babe as we all rock. Someone yells get him, get him and Toni says got him and nah ya don't hate. One of the ladies breaks out in a cheer. Saying big "G" little "O" go Toni go. Toni laughs and says no it's shish boom bah and does a little body shake. We all join in and say rah, rah, ha, ha as they throw their arms in the air and do the wave. Everyone is laughing as the men look at us as if we had just lost our mind.

During the rahs Gwen and Becca says hey Tonee where did you get that bubble gum ring from? She laughs as we look at Gwen and Becca didn't hear them come into the circle. Just doing that cheer and wave and listening made me think about when I was a pompom girl cheering with Doris, Lisa, Sandi, and the other girls on the squad. I don't remember all their names, nor can I remember their faces, but oh well. Man, that brought back memories just like it's doing now. Those were the fun years no care, no worries just boy issues. Hmm this coffee is good, and the sun is still trying to come out. Looking over at the guys table they all jump up with a hugs and excitement of seeing Jovan. They offered him a drink and he refuse saying he has been sober, for two years and I had to usher at church tomorrow. They hug and dap him in support and offer a seat at the table for the next victim as they all laughed. This was the first time that we saw the family.

Toni asked about Miss Clovis and Reggie Coy we told her that they had moved back to Ohio until that first winter got to them. Everyone laughed and said now they are enjoying the sun in Florida with a lot of property. Their daughter Missy Veretta finally married. Say it's not so, she did what? Yeah girl Retta got married someone finally nab her, an officer, girl. Yes, some officer I think his name was Gerald or Jerry or Jeremiah, or Jeff something like that. All we know is that she is married, and he is in the service and Veretta is some type of doctor. Miss Veretta/ Dr. Veretta paused enough to have a bunch of babies. She was popping those babies out, pop, pop, boom. She had three already and went for the last, last should have avoided last surprise. They had twin boys to add to their three girls. I thought back on my mother-in-law Naomi and how she was always afraid of having twins and the fear extended and stayed with me. I smiled as they laughed because inside, I was hoping that Bill and I were having just one. As I looked around at the families and the fun, I didn't realize how much I missed our old neighborhood. A lot of the families moved, and the memories faded away with the names and the fun.

Watching everyone dance with their own signature dances and laughing re-minds me of when my parent's card games that turned into an impromptu party, with family, friends that were invited or just came by when they heard the music. The original house or block party with dancing, laughing, eating and just being happy and no one showing any stress or problems on their faces. To this day my mom and dad still do the same side to side two steps. My father twisting a little and my mother side to side then she throws up that one arm as she and my dad, both get into the music. Mom always just throws up that one arm straighted as if she is hitting a high note. Dad watching and smiling at her moves with the proudness of love, wink, and wink. Trying to add his off tune singing with his arm stretched as if they were performing a duet from afar. Some of the people were dancing on beat some were singing off beat to their own tune. I would sit on the stairs watching them trying to be as quiet as possible. I quietly watched, until I was told to go to bed or asked to get a glass or whatever the request may be. All I knew was that it was an honor and plus I get to stay up and watch the adults having fun. When I hear those oldies, I think about the dances that they did, like the jerk, the twist, the pony and the mashed potatoes. Funny how my generation was doing the chicken then it went to the funky chicken, then to the funky four corners. All those dances from many generations didn't require partners or energy and very little rhythm. I can almost feel the heat from them dancing, smell of cigarette smoke, the aroma of beer, liquor mixed with home baked dishes with an added fun and no fighting. Where people made sure you made it home safely and lived and laughed to talk about it the next day. To this day when a certain song comes on my mind just relaxes and I'm there smiling until the song goes off. That was my quick memory me moment.

Clarence said that when his parents partied his dad did a side to side step too. When Marvin Gaye was playing you would think he was in concert with the man. He would stretch out both arms above his head and act like he was on stage with a mic singing off key with Marvin. I laughed because my father did the same thing, but it was when he was in the mirror singing that he was so fine. The song he made up should have added another line that I'm so vain. Clarence looked at me with his eyebrow raised on that wasn't funny but to me it was. I can picture Clarence raising his eyebrows in the same way his dad, Jerry probably did. Clarence does his two side to side dances singing off key and doesn't realize that he is his dad Jerry. Now new families move in and the cycle continues. Right when we were laughing about Veretta and her enlarged family, we heard the sound like herds of cattle approaching us. The sound of cattle with voices running toward us was coming closer. We didn't know if we should run or really run as the noise grew louder. The herd was Melba's cousin Catrice coming with all her kids plus some added nieces and nephews. We wondered how all them fit in that one minivan. Really was there another van on the other side. Catrice was beautiful but looked too young to be having nine kids. She was medium built her frame didn't resemble any parts of having nine kids. When she opened, her mouth the looks didn't match her voice. Her voice and mannerism made me think of Charlotte. I wondered how many children Charlotte ended up giving birth to and with the combination of first names. She probably has a house full of children just like Catrice. Catrice's frame would be hard to convince me she had nine kids. She is very pretty, petite with short hair and slightly big boobs. I laughed because I thought of timber, because she was kind of top heavy. Either way I bet their house is never boring. Melba greets her as she introduces all her kids and nieces and nephews. The children were coming and, and, and continued coming. We lost our thoughts and our minds, and our mouths were opened as she said all their names.

Let me see the triplets were May, June and August that covered spring and part of the summer seasons, (the sun will always shine with those names with a taste of rain). I would like just a taste of rain in my life not the clouds that seemed to be trying to burst into a storm. Well anyway hmm there was Miriam, Vernon, Janay, David, hmm man this has my brain hurting and the babies were Clarice and Robbie. After they all introduced politely introduced themselves, they all take off in different directions yelling and running. Her husband Greekum follows behind her moving in slow motion. I guess after having nine children he is probably was tired. He was flat everywhere just straight up and down, no muscles, no butt, and no chest impression. He looked like a walking hanger with clothes hanging off it. Melba yells Greekum and he gives a heads up to all the ladies. He tells Catrice that he's going over there where Michael was playing cards. As he turns his head back toward where the men folk were, he even turned his head slow. Catrice smacks him on his butt in which he pays no attention as if this was their norm. We laughed and said that action might get you number ten. She laughed hey why you think I smacked him it's the fun part of getting there. Catrice smiled and said I love that man and he still looks sexy. We all laughed telling her she was nasty and that was just too much information. Catrice laughed you mean TMI, too much information. We all continued to laugh as the next set of nieces and nephews come up for introduction.

I asked Catrice was does Greekum mean because I never heard that name before. Here I go again maybe her response will be different from the Nurse Rochelle. She said that he comes from a family of twins and that he was a twin. Momma was a twin, grandparents, aunts, uncles and cousins were all twins. They didn't know at the time his mom Anuna was caring twins because Greekum was hiding, surprise!! But some of the twins died and the grandmother Rosetta would call them her Greekum babies, because she didn't give them a name. Now, Greekum twin brother died at birth, he was stillborn, and they thought Greekum was going to die too, but he survived. Greekum even survived after giving me these nine babies and she chuckles. You know I had to love that man to carry all those big head babies. His sister Malia had twelve of her own. Anuna tried to tell me about Greekum, (or sometimes she called him William), that he was potent I now know what she meant. I thought she was trying to say he was important she had such a strong accent. Silly me grinning, smiling and knodding and agreeing to a word I didn't understand. Everybody busts out laughing. I should have really paid attention to the twelve brothers and sisters Greekum has. Heck Anuna came from a family of twenty. I guess I didn't get that clue either. Coura said you should have invested a little more in her interpretation see what lack of knowledge got you. With everyone laughing saying now you know what it means. Catrice laughed with us saying yep now that I know what potent means, (as shes says it slowly), it was important to know. I thought she was saying important and I thought I repeated it and she nodded yes. Coura laughs with, ah girl me too with all these babies. I got nerve, don't I? Catrice said Miss Anuna, should have went in a little more detail. Don't you think ladies and said her boy or the men in the family or very, very I got to say it again ladies very fertile? Now I understand that word with or without an accent. No way would I have thought I would be counting these many heads at the dinner table. I thought I was having twins that's what the ultra sound showed me and surprise one was hidden. That ha-ha surprise gave me those identical triplets over there, with spring and summer names. After four I stopped counting. Yep they got me with that hidden secret surprise. I looked and listened to Catrice and she sound so loving. She enjoyed talking about her family. When you looked into her eyes you could see the twinkle of love she had for her husband. I wondered if Bill and I will be happy regardless of what number we stopped at.

As I thought about Bill, I still wondered what was on his mind when it come to having more kids. That was something as I think about it now, we never really discussed having them we just had them. No questions no answers. That question made me think again, about the ultra sound next week. I hope it picks up any hidden surprises. Catrice had me thinking about Bill's mother, Naomi's concerns about having twins. Now, I'm becoming concerned again about twins or triplets. Ooh, that sounds so so scary. The babies playing hide and seek in your stomach hmm, that thought scares me too. Then Catrice calls over the next set of kids and finishes the next set of nieces and nephews. They all had the same concerns, asking can we eat and play. She smiled as she introduced them. Here we go again the ands are coming with commas. Her brother Bryan's kids were BJ for Bryan Jr, Brazil and their little sister Breoni, and her sister Wynoma kids were little Larry, Larelle, Lizeht and Lazel, Lacy and Greekum sister Keoni best friend Tiziana's son Leonard. They were very polite. They all said in sync, it was nice meeting everyone,) while looking at everyone with beautiful smiles). All the new arrivals were pleasant and polite. As I tried to remember names I never heard before, it just reminded me about family and how they all supported each other. I'm sure there are times where they get tired of being the crowd. The atmosphere was a village raising many children and a blessing that we were invited to share in their family antics.

Keoni was very gorgeous no kids and was pursuing a career as a pediatrician and was doing some part time modeling. Well with twelve siblings she had a lot of practice and with the endless number of nieces and nephews. Keoni is accompanied with a tall slim athletic looking fine man call Anthonye. As Keoni yells for Tony we ah with our mouths open looking at this gorgeous man with deep dimples striking dark features. His presence was making you want to know, what his daddy looks like, where is the momma and are they happy?? Shirley laughs point at each one calling them cougars. Dina laughed hurt me love me make me write bad checks. Then another one chimes in give me reason for insuffient funds, make me overdrawn. I don't mind having a negative on my statement cuz I got memories, tee-hee and it was worth it, (as she winks). Yep a voice comes in she must be feeling the seconds and moments. Lalita chimes in saying give me a reason. I don't mind being insufficient funds too, with that cutie. I can make him grin, show those teeth and put a nice big smile on your face. As she cheeses make me smile and cheese too, hurt my account. Give the bill collectors a reason to call on me. I can utilize my caller ID for bill collectors. You know they are my fans every month. Oh, and stop me from paying my bills cuz we can live on love,love,love and loving! Can I get a high five or a got it girl, ladies? She and everyone laughed and agreed we can do that. Dina looks at them saying we, no this is about me.

Gwen and Becca laughed forget all that what does his daddy look like and is he happy and where is the momma. Funny because they said it so slow as to understand I will take the daddy. I don't mind saying dad-dad, or calling him poppy, (as she stands and pops her butt), screaming ow. Becca laughed as she calls everyone nonees. Who is Nonee does she do nails on First street? Nope. Does she sell that that you know those CD's that skip or have no kinda of sound? Nope. Gwen looks at her as if she is crazy and says girl who is Nonee. Now, what in the heck does she have to do with this conversation? Girl, where did you grab that from and what are, and what does that mean. She shakes her head trying to figure out what the heck does Nonee mean. For that second, we all were trying to figure out where did that come from, too much punch with too much ice and sitting too long. Becca tries to say it through her laugher, no need to hate and cracks up as we just continue to laugh. Sheila looks around and says getting back to our bid on that fine man over there. Now, I got my check book with me let us get back to the business at hand on Mr. Fine over there. We all are acting like we are looking at our imaginary checkbook.

Dina laughs saying make me howler. Aunt Flossie looks at her with those deep than deep dimples and her beautiful smile and laughed adding hurt me too. Now, sister girl saying don't your hubby Bradley make you howler. She looked over at her nah, he makes me sing, as she hums closing her eyes, but every now and then I need an outburst!! She pauses and startles everyone with a loud scream, make me howler I'll sing later. What about Catrice's cousin Spence. He made the calendar with one child for each month, who does that? Shout out saying twelve women did. A pause was there as if this was a station identification break or news flash. Catrices laughs nah ten women twelve childerin. I know I have a heap of them, but they all have the same daddy, my sweetie, Greekum. Sheila pauses saying hmm maybe we could practice on next year's calendar. If he has energy, I'm good and if he's tired, I'm still good. She stands up working her body like Momo would. I can work it for him, work it baby and work on it. Dina comes in saying what you gonna do your well is dry and that's just nasty. Sheila responded with your point is, I hope he still can get nasty that way I don't have to use my checkbook. Aunt Flossie laughed a new calendar doesn't sound too bad. But this one January oh I mean Anthonye a new beginning. Let's get back to the original bid on that fine man. Now, we need to get back to our orginal negotiation. We got to handle this business. Now, ladies stay focus on January new fresh of the year Anthonye.

Lalita's cousin Christine comes out of nowhere adds so smooth and calmly, saying I can give him a reason to howler again, again and one more again. Howling is good for the lungs and other organs sister girls!! Some of the ladies made howling noise, and then they laughed in sync. The men looked over at us as if we had lost our minds. Only if they knew as they continued to talk. I'm enjoying them while still laughing. I said according to my portfolio if we do spaghetti week. I can afford him for at least a good month, and I laughed because I wanted to too. This surprised them because I usually don't say too much. Sometimes, I just like listening and observing. My father always said you can learn a lot about a person by just looking and listening they will tell you who they really are. Although, we laughed about spaghetti week my kids hated that week. Every day they came home from school the question was what's for dinner? I would laugh is the week over yet?? They would say nope, or I would then say we are still in the spaghetti week. They would ah mom I would ah yes. With little money and growing family, you had to stretch money in many ways. Bill didn't really eat the whole week of spaghetti because sometimes he wouldn't be home in time for dinner. Huh office hours again. I'm gonna find out what that is all about. Coura raises her hand extending her arm. Christine tells Coura to put your hand down you are not in class, although we all wanted to school that baby cougar. Coura says I want to add as she smiles. Okay, Gwen says it slow let me or we understand you are adding okay, (as she smiles raising her eyebrows mouthing cuckoo). They laughed harder and Coura adds, I got you the following two months Rita we can do top ramen week. I can't remember who said I got you all beat I don't have a job. I can love him until my unemployment stops, and then all we can do is look at each other. Although, looking at him all day would not be bad on my eyes. Oh, and if we did everything in the dark, I could show him a few things. I want him to know this lady got it going on hey hey. I rhyme see what that man did. Hey, hey as she acts as if she's riding a horse. Come on don't nonee me.

I laughed as I flashback on when I first started learning how to cook without my mother being a step or phone call away. I had made some Manwich and thought hmm this might work over some noodles. When Bill saw that Manwich mixture, he was not impressed and said he wasn't going to eat it. At that time, I thought can you do any better or is there someone else you know that can? Thinking about it now it looked like yuck, and I couldn't blame him. I tried it and it didn't taste good and never ever tried that again. When I think back on how our parents tried to show/teach us how to survive, you learn a new form of appreciation. It's like learning knowing how to swim, (a self-taught method), and they put you in the water and leave you either to drown or work those arms for survival. That's pretty much what my parents did when I started working at McDonalds. I was only making $1.65 an hour twenty hours a week at the most because they wouldn't let me work nights. With that modest income, I had to put gas in my car and buy my own school clothes. Well, that didn't leave much money left for fun. But just like being thrown in the water I learned how to budget and make do with what I had to work with. Some things in life are free.

My insides are filled with laughter as I looked at everyone having fun. They all are cracking up as Gina returns from fixing a plate. She joins in the laughter and asks are they twins, the ones over there talking to Sharolyn and Carolyn? Melba's says no that's Tayoni. We call her Tay and Leilani we call her Loni. They are Catrice's husband sisters. That litte baby boy Khary is their brother. Catrice finishes her drink and says they all look alike uh. They come in small, short, tall and they all look alike just in different shapes and forms. If you don't believe me look over there where my kids are. We looked, and everyone oohs and ahs and laughed because she is right. It was good to see kids' not acting crazy and behaving with manners. As I looked around, we were the village. This was a safe place and healthy environment for them. I'm so glad that my family came and was included in this family fun time. Everyone was laughing, and all the kids had high energy. We ate well and were full to the rim. There was plenty of food for many hungry appetites. No one left hungry or empty handed for there was enough to take home. As the hour gets late the younger kids are growing tired. We all know that's our que to go home. I watched Sierra slowly rubbing her eyes and I knew she was tired but wanted to stay. Bill looked at both of us and said, babe are you ready to go? Wow, I haven't heard him call me that in a long time. I said sure babe and smiled, as I gathered up Sierra who was tired and fighting sleep. Bill grabs her from me and carries her to our car. We walk away as a family to go to our home.

I still think back on the fun we had and watching the elders' hula hoop, talking and playing with the youngsters and grown folks just chilling in conversations and stories. On the way home that's when Bill and I had our best conversation. Sometimes, I like it when he takes the scenic route home, because we are in no rush to get home. Bill talked about Jovan and Toni. He said he was glad they had gotten it together just a shame they had to go such a scenic route. Bill said how good Jovan and Toni looked and it was good to see that they weathered the storm. I smiled and thought the sun finally broke through their storm. Jovan told us that he fell in love with Antonelle the first time he saw her. We laughed when he told us he spent his whole allowance trying to get a ring out of the bubble gum machine and the male nurses that took care of him. I laughed with him and laughed, adding so that was why she was wearing that bubble gum ring. Yeah Rita, he said it was a promise ring and that they will never put either one through that again. I laughed telling Bill that he should spend his allowance on me for a ring. Bill smiles and said I would give you the world plus my allowance. My thought and only a thought, was hoping wouldn't show through my eyes. The thought of why don't your cheap ass give me an allowance.

Bill is really into Jovan and Toni's new-found relationship. He said that they were dating and into the get to know you phase again. Maybe Rita you and I should have a date night. Here comes that thought again, smile because first you have to be home in order to date Bill…

Chapter 14
Now Were Home

I continued my thoughts with I have dates with myself every night when Sierra goes to bed, Bill. Funny but not ha-ha, Bill is just in a conversation mood. He smiles and looks at me with sincerity saying that he knows that he hasn't been the best. My insides agreed with him. But I had to force my eyes not to show my thoughts. So, I smiled and closed my eyes and just listened to him. I listened to him tell me that I had put up with a lot of his mess. My insides agreed again. Ooh, not again my thoughts were telling me this might be your que to exit and run. Because, he is being too nice and what is he setting me up for? He talked about how fun it was getting out and seeing everyone. We were laughing at you ladies laughing and having fun. Bill and I were enjoying our quiet evening. There is no interruption of the phone, knock on the door, no yelling/fussing. Bill did make his normal simple continuous request of can you get this; will you bring or can I. During his requests he kept the conversation going.

Bill goes on to say that Michael's friend came over trying to convince us of all that he thought he knew every and anything. Sometimes, it's okay to be wrong but not cool to be right all the time. His friend Angel Lloyd/ AL couldn't admit he was wrong on the meaning of Greekum's name. How can you tell the person what their name meant now you Mr. Google or Mr. Bing? Greekum known as William tried explaining and eventually shook his head and just gave up. That was 'cc' yourself. Until we all noticed Greekum's sister Keoni. We saw you ladies noticing her male friend. We laughed because we could only imagine what you cougars were saying. We said with our old butts we could only be sugar daddies or sponsor a young headache. Nah, they don't say that you got to. 'CC' yourself what in the heck is that? Come current or come correct. Those ladies want responsible sponsorship. She looked high maintence and we have low maintaining money. We all laughed as we looked at our flat pockets and agreed that they were mighty flat. Which meant all our asses were joke broke? Then I said oh really Bill you or we are broke. No babe let me finish.

Don't know who said it man at least she not one of those Leegirls. I had to ask and wondered if this was a no need to hate word?? No not like that you know ugly. I just shook my head. Bill said I had to ask where all those acronyms were coming from. Really, Lee girl's bro that was funny. Now, some men will talk to anything. Then they all turned their heads slowly towards Leslie Carl/LC. He said hey, how did I get pulled into this, I do have standards. We then laughed harder at Leslie Carl/LC trying to convince us, what he could do for that young thang, and his standards we called him "fly paper". I looked at Bill fly paper huh. Yell, he sticks and talk to anything that moves in a skirt. That sounds like your cousin Steve, he laughed sure does. Steve made me think about Robin's Uncle Glooly. He was glue to woman too.

I asked Bill so when do men like that get tired and grow up. He was silent at first and later responded I don't know. I know that Steve won't. He likes his cigarettes, liquor and much sex. He will save up his money to buy it under the guise of dinner or a movie with his broke ass. Steve was so cheap and was good at using other, people's money. Remember a time when he came over and said he needed to go to the store. Funny he left our house with a bag full of groceries. Then had the nerve to tell us we had a few items that were out dated. I guess Bill needed a pause break too. Bill said that he needed that space and chill out time with the boys. We didn't argue we just shook our heads because it wasn't worth the energy with the deniable truth. I told Bill that I really enjoyed this day and he agreed. Bill and I talked but not as often as I would like. We get so caught up in everyday business and sometimes forget to see the beauty in the flowers and adore their scent. I was enjoying the time that we spent together and played the words over again in my mind about Bill telling me he loved me and knew things weren't right. That felt good and made me feel like I wasn't going crazy or tripping. Can we just end this evening with some form of intimacy?

As the evening slowly was ending, I reflect on when we arrived home. I love watching, Bill getting sleeping Sierra out the car, as I go ahead and opened the door to our apartment. I was so glad that I had left it clean. Because, now all I have to do is spend some cuddle time with Bill. I watched him carrying Sierra as she laid her head on his shoulder. I enjoyed that snap shot picture. That memorable picture put a smile on my face and warmed my heart. It made me wonder could I have nine Sierras, hmm maybe. Right when I was thinking of my Bill and, ready for our cuddle time that moment changed. Bill returned after putting Sierra in bed and tells me he is going out with some friends. My insides were saying yep all that long conversation was just a distractor. It happened so fast it left me stuttering okay, I guess. Now, I kind of knew how he felt when I dashed out the door with Robin. I said I was hoping to spend some cuddle time with you. It's quiet and Sierra is exhausted and probably won't wake up until tomorrow. He looked at me and smiled as he exits. I caught him before he closes the door and asks where is my kiss? He smiled and gives me a kiss saying he got to go. In my mind, I'm wondering what was the rush? Where was Bill going and with whom? Normally he tells me the names of the people he hangs out with or where they will be going. This time he barely said good bye.

I'm trying not to get emotional with these racing pregnant hormones, but the mind is working overtime with the emotions and I don't like it. The baby didn't like it either. I felt him/her doing their normal routine of playing sports again in my body. Whatever I'm giving birth to, he/she is going to be very, very athletic. I just wished their activity would happen during the day and not at night. Ooh, this baby has a lot of energy. I hope it is just one, ooh Catrice, Coura had me scared. I didn't need any type of hidden surprises.

As I go and sit down, I blurted out just one Lord, please just one. For that moment and that night, I watched the television watch me. Back to my ole familiar date night with the television again. I wondered where was Bill, and what was he really doing? I thought about it again how can I fight for something I don't know. I remembered what Robin had said I can fight for my family and my husband. But it's not fair to be in a fight with air. I can't fight him who is in the inside and a woman on the outside that I don't know. That numb nut of a husband failed his family and allowed her, (Trixie), to put me, and my daughters on their battle field. As I thought about it why should I fight a battle that turns into a war that I didn't care or didn't ask for? I wasn't having any part of our family becoming casualties. Who wants to be in that kind of dangerous situation? It's not fair.

I felt lonely again after such a fun family day. Just television, swollen feet, TV guide, sleeping babies and me fussing and having conversations with the television. I sighed as the thoughts raced through my mind of who is she. What does she look like? He had me flashing back again to when I was pregnant, and the two ladies were over his house and he put me out. Your right Robin! I say as if she is in front of me responding back to me, saying it's not fair. But am I being fair in what I'm thinking?? Bill could be out with some friends. Then I wondered is it Allison the clueless sales clerk, or Gail the staring waitress, or the soldier he had left with. Who is the one that wore Chanel or was that just a coincidence with the perfume? Or did someone just happen to give him a hug. Nah, why trip on the unknown. I remembered Leeler/Lene telling me that her family would talk to themselves and answer and then get mad at themselves because of their answers. I don't think I'm doing that. But I am mad and tripping with myself. Come on Rita really don't trip don't fall and don't be added to Leeler/Lene tales and family adventures. Leeler/Lene did have some good ones. I missed seeing her at the birthday party. She could tell you some tales and wouldn't bust into laughter like everyone else that was listening.

Everyone had a good day. We had fun and Sierra played with many kids around her age. She was so tired she went to sleep with that flower painted on her face. Why wash it off let her wake up to a pretty flower with her own memories before we wash it off. I sit staring at the television and waiting for the phone to ring. I'm watching and waiting for something on the television that will get my attention. I needed something to take my thoughts away from what Bill was doing or seeing. I don't think I'm insecure, but Bill doesn't help me feel secured either. Is he oblivious to my feelings? Robin avoided an argument to not let her hubby think or use that as an emotional excuse to belittle her. We know what we feel and think. Majority of the time we are right. I guess I still have a lot to learn. There was no book I could read and believe about a perfect marriage or relationship. I think back on Pandora and her family hitting husbands with whatever was there, and they stayed together.

My thoughts continued to distract and takes me to when, my brother Charles told me that when EJ's boyfriend tried to get front or straight up disrespect him in front of his girlfriend. He told him that when he goes into his trunk and the first thing, he puts his hand on he was going to beat the shift out of him. Hmm, sounds familiar same thing we said about Mommy if anyone broke into her house. The first thing she put her hands on will be her weapon of choice. I wanted to call home, but the time difference they are probably were sleep. I didn't want them to know what was really happening out here and I how I really felt. They would only try to convince me to move back home and that wasn't an option I wanted to entertain. I didn't want to be a failure and hear my mom's mouth. I had to grow up and be a big girl. No one needed to know, it was our business and not theirs. So, I pretended again that I wasn't hurting, and I kept it moving.

I flashed back on a story told to me by Elaine years ago. She said her father was a hard-working quiet man. Come from a family of many brothers. She said that she only saw her dad get mad one time and that was when he told her brother, Kevin Casey to rake the yard. In those days, you only were told once. Well, Kevin Casey, KC, didn't rake the yard. He was fooling around in his room. Well, while my brother was chilling inside his room, outside dad had stepped on the rake and it smack him hard in the face. I just remembered Elaine's expressions, while she was telling the story. She was so animated. Her dad knocks on Kevin's door when he answered he just remembered waking up seeing his mom Goldie. She was sitting on his bed looking at him, while dabbing his face with a cold towel telling him you will be okay. I kind of chuckle and ask did your dad hit him. She smiled with adding mom was there when he woke up. I remembered grabbing my mouth laughing. I guess parents had different ways of getting their points across; mine was the burning of our toys.

Elaine said that she saw her dad slowly pack a small suitcase and she heard him telling her mom that Uncle Eudell was acting up again. Mom didn't ask what was wrong or how long, he would be gone. They just had the unspoken understanding and trust. See when love is for real you have trust. Knowing my Uncle, he probably was acting a plum fool, chasing women, not going to work, arguing, fussing, drinking and fighting. His wife Edna had enough. She didn't want to make the call, but it was time for a change. So, the brothers gathered themselves for a weekend run to see Uncle Eudell. Her dad treated it like a job no emotions just going out of town to take care of some family business. Well they took care of Uncle Eudell and after he bandaged himself, they all ate dinner as if nothing had happened. Uncle Eudell acted right until his wife had enough of his drinking, womenizing and left him. The brothers only made that trip, one time to straighten up their baby brother. It lasted for a while but too much and a little too late, Aunt Edna was done. She loaded up the family and moved back home. I heard she was doing good and never re-married. Where do you draw the line of enough?

I didn't know where my line was. I just knew that I was confused. Did I need to call my uncles or brother to straighten Bill out? Silly I would only bandage him up and get his dinner ready, (sigh and laugh). Why isn't the phone ringing and where's Bill it is getting late. I lay on the couch trying to stay awake, but sleep was kicking in and took me right out for the count. Why doesn't he bring his butt home and stop playing? Now, I remembered when we used to go out together. Then I realized that there is nothing out there for me anymore. Especially, since I am married with children. I didn't want us to become some old couple that stays at home and there is nothing to do but look at each other and television. Just thinking about that sounds boring. But when do you stop the partying and start being a husband and family man? We are looking at increasing our family and I didn't want to continue this guessing game of where he is or who is he with. Robin was right there are trixies out there I just hope she or they didn't find my Bill.

I stayed on the couch until I just couldn't take being uncomfortable. My bed was calling me, and I was listening. As I walked down the hall, I picked up the phone to check for a dial tone and the phone wasn't off the hook. I coluldn't fight it or what Bill was doing it was time for me to just lay it on down. When I laid down into my fresh cool bed, I melted into the comfort of soft pillows and the smell of freshness. I thought I should have done this sooner. After all Bill will have to come home to our bed. I fall off to sleep without any type of fighting and my baby allowed me to sleep. Only thing I remembered was waking up to Bill lying next to me. He fell to sleep with his clothes on. I guess he was just as tired as I was. Good to know he didn't take a shower before getting into the bed.

This morning I wasn't going to get all emotional. I wasn't going to fuss or fight. Nope, not today there will be no fighting, and no fussing. Today and today only Bill had a free pass. No snooping for numbers or sniffing for the smell of some type of cheap perfume and no searching for unfamiliar items in our car. My morning wasn't going to be ruined not by Bill or any outside sources. Not today, nope, no way not today. Today is my day no pain and no arguing, (today is a just because). I walked over to Bill and I gave him a hug and kiss as I go prepared breakfast for my family. Bill is kind of startled by my lack of emotions about wondering what time he came in. I saw his look but today was my day. I'm just going to let him wonder, because today is my day, no pain, no fussing, no arguing just no. I had the best rest and fun the day before and I am going to savor every moment. Just like now as I'm enjoying the rain and my hot cup of coffee that is how I enjoyed that day. Bill looked at me and asked why I was rocking. I just smiled because I was singing and humming and didn't know it. I guess that was the day I learned to hum through my pain and just enjoy my thoughts and put my own joy in my heart. Today I have joy, sunshine and the rain yep.

Throughout the day, Bill kept watching me as if he was a child waiting for the parent to say something or issue the punishment. I thought you deal with your own conscious; becuase today is just not the day. Sierra wakes up rubbing her eyes trying to wake up to the smell of frying bacon. Bill grabs me by my waist as he says good morning. I say it is isn't it. I smile and say how was your morning. He snaps and says what do you mean by that? I look at him with a smile but in my mind, I realized that I am performing again. Just asking that's all, what time did you come in? I tried waiting up for you and I fell off to sleep. I'm trying not to sound as annoyed as I felt. Our hugs were far and in between but when we did Sierra always insist that she wanted to snug with us too. We would just look at her and open our arms as she hugs our legs. Reflecting on my mother, her mother and her mother's mother weren't really huggers and not very affectionate. I kind of inherited that trait until I realized a hug and a smile can go a long way. Put on the smile Rita you don't want to be hit or cussed out not today it's too early. His response was babe I don't know hanging out with Sulli, Bragg, (aka ow ooh). I had to stop him there, whats a 'ah ooh'. Yell hmm, babe he is always getting injured and if you called him by that name he will answer. I know this had to be a funny distraction. Bill laughed saying you know, you say ah ooh when fall or get hurt. Funny we did say that as kids and its still funny hearing again. Bill said you might not remember Reed, Farrel, Gilmore, Poindexter and old good time Smitty by their last names. He was right regardless; if he told their first names or last names, I couldn't tell the difference or remember their names. These are the buddies I went through boot camp with. Bill smiled with when we are with Smitty we are guaranteed a good time. So, we call him 'Good Time Smitty'. He couldn't dance, couldn't sing but is always on the dance floor doing some type of dance. Some awkward move only he knew the name. With moves that were hard to duplicate but fun in trying.

We laughed drank and share stories probably like you ladies do. Bill said that he missed going out and hanging out with the boys. My thoughts were good grief then, where do you go when you come home late? Now, I was afraid to ask didn't have that much ancestral strength. Change your expression quick Rita before he sees your eyes, because that will tell how pissed off you really are. Bill said the time just got away babe. I really wasn't planning on staying out that late and didn't want to call and wake you up. I know how hard it has been lately for you to fall asleep. I hmm and asked did you forget your watch. Don't say it out loud what Henry and his friends said about time. Is it time to care?? My thoughts were, I think its time to stop? Oops that slipped out, oh oh here it comes.

I told him I didn't know your friends by their last names. I missed that verbal bullet. Z showed up with Dennis. Don't you remember they came over for Thanksgivings? Babe we were just boys just gone wild, in an over the hill juvenile kind of way. Ooh no, I said it doesn't matter you made it home and breakfast will be ready soon. He said that he was sorry coming in so late. He just wanted to have a couple of drinks with the fellas and time just got away. I thought I heard you the first hundred times who are you trying to convince me or youself. I really did want to spend some time with you. I enjoyed yesterday and realized what I had and what my boys don't, a family and a good wife and mother. Wow, Bill was really stretching telling me about his night. His night should have been our night and not his morning, I'm home stuck and slept alone. That was something we talked about. We promised each other that we would never go to bed mad and wake up to each other.

Sierra runs to Bill with arms stretched out reaching for her daddy. She was and still is a daddy's girl, oh and momma girl too, but daddy was all hers. Sierra eyes sparkled as she looked up to her dad as he raises her up pass his shoulders. I hear their laughter combined and that it another snap shot stored in my archives.

I see the joy in his eyes as he lifted her and gave her nothing but hugs and kisses as she laughed and giggled showing her dimples. They both laughed together as he started tickling her. I loved hearing the laughter and seeing the love between them. I told Bill this is the week that we find out what we are having. He laughed with saying watch it be another girl. I laughed; responding with then you will have two daddy's girls. He laughed as he snatches up a piece of bacon. Sierra was getting bigger but, not too big for her daddy to pick her up and swing her around. She shouts out that she wants some pannicakes. I laughed pannicakes will be coming soon. Sierra says daddy help me set the table pees.

I looked at them and remined myself that today is my day. Bill says I'm going to take Sierra for a ride and to the park, and did I want to come. Nah, this is daddy and daughter time, because they haven't done it in a while. Today is my day and I'm just going to enjoy the quiet time with just me and my daughter or son. Knowing Bill, he will probably go by Melba and Michael, and from there Michael and Bill will take the kids and keep them busy all day. So, Melba will get a break too. Now, I can get an early start on the laundry without worrying about Sierra and the rest of the day. This day was all mines for the having and taking, wow. Laundry room here I come! I watched Bill watch Sierra pick out her clothes. Although, the colors and patterns don't match she was determined to dress herself. I smiled as Bill tries to convince her that she should reconsider. He lays out several outfits and she looks at them and shakes her head no and says daddy I got this. We both looked at each other she got this? I mouth to Bill she got this. She looks at him because she doesn't have a clue what reconsider means, and she knows what she wants to wear. Sierra decides on her outfit. She is now dressed, happy and ready to spend the day with her daddy. The baby moves as if she/he wants to go too. I rub my stomach and say in due time. It's funny seeing Sierra developing more independence. They say that when they do, they are getting ready for their brother or sister. I guess in this case it seems right. Bill notices me rubbing my stomach as I smiled at Sierra's independence and he places his hand on my stomach as the baby moves.

He smiles showing his deep dimples and is no longer jumping when our baby moves. We make eye contact and I still see the love for me in his eyes and Bill looks happy and proud. I look at him and wonder what was he thinking about?? We never really shared the first pregnancy under the same roof. It does feel strange but good at the same time. We are growing older and learning together. When I think back on our relationship, communication was not ever our problem. Sometimes you can grow apart, but it is up to both parties to come to happy middle and try to get back or reach out to each other. As Sierra runs to me to give me a kiss, she pulls on daddy to go. Bill hugs me with a kiss and asks so what are you going to do with all your free time. I laughed laundry, stretch my legs and rest. He smiled as he grabs the keys while Sierra is pulling his hand toward the door saying come on daddy we have to go, hurry up please.

Chapter 15
I Finally Meet Courtney Diane

I watched her small hand get lost in her dad's hand. As I sorted clothes it felt good to be in a quiet place with just good thoughts while enjoying my day. I told myself that nothing was going to get in my way. As I sorted and checked Bill's pockets, I was relieved that I didn't see any numbers. There were no phone numbers in his pockets or match books from some hide away rendezvous. Ooh nothing, I felt bad for just thinking something like that might be hidden. But, after listening to some of the women that found match books with hotel names on them or receipts for lingerie made me wonder.

I loaded Sierra's wagon with the laundry basket and some magazines for my short laundry trip. As I looked inside just to make sure there were enough washers and dryers for me to do all loads at the same time. I struck gold and yeepee they were all available for the taking. Now that's what I'm talking about washing with no interruptions. Yep this was my day. I loaded up the washers and took a nice seat outside to just relax until the washing finishes. While listening to the sounds of the wash cycles, I had time to glance through the pages of my Home and Garden. I always looked forward to looking at that magazine when I used to go to the clinic for my prenatal visits. I had it made I was able to relax and feel the warmth of the sun on my face.

I watched a beautiful slender lady approaching and she smiles at me as if I knew her. She walked slowly with a military style presence. I tried to focus on her face to see if I knew her. She is about 5"10, pretty tall but anyone could be taller than me, with real short haircut and muscular slim, wearing blue baseball cap with black flip flops. This lady had a body, but minus a butt. She carried a medium basket load into the wash room. When she came out, she introduced herself asking if it was okay for her to join me, (showing a slight corner smile). Not wanting to be bothered I smiled back saying a slow okay. Inside I was thinking heck no I just want my me time and enjoy glancing and reading my magazine. I politely smiled and welcomed her to have a seat.

She introduced herself as Courtney Diane a friend of Robin. I smiled and told her that I met her son Henry. I told her I met him through a young man I knew by the name of Floyd. And that Henry seemed to be a very nice and polite young man. She said that Henry and Floyd have been best friends before their voices became deep and mustaches developed. They used to tell people they were cousins. Couldn't say brothers because they knew Henry was an only child. Her facial expression changed when she said that she is going to miss her boy. But she was grateful, that her son had received a full four-year basketball scholarship. With a corner smile she added that helped her out a lot. Courtney Diane said she couldn't afford four years of college and didn't want him just hanging out and working. Too much temptation out there and I need for him to stay focused and stay away from them fast tail girls.

I watched her smile fade away as she called me by my name. She transformed with a different tone in her voice. With a calm but stern tone, she recalled one scant that was not ripe. I watched her eyes move as she tried to remember her name. She called out saying ooh her name was Melinja, Melinda, something like that as she rolled her eyes after getting her name right. She said that she couldn't stand that nasty ass scant. Melinda tried calling her Mother Courtney or mom and clearly that scant was and never would be her daughter. She said that she tried to smile but the corners of her mouth wouldn't allow it, (adding I heard whole beach). Woo that came out of nowhere um huh, (as that corner smile developed). Courtney Diane described her shape that just looked like a box with a head on it.

She didn't do anything for me she was a pint size box with big boobs, no waist and short legs; I'm sure opened a lot. Her face had no knock out glare and I thought it must be the bootey and not the beauty. Henry only saw the top and not the brain. I thought take your eyes off her I heard tot-tots and don't think with the wrong brain with his dumb ass. I was hoping he would see through that trifling ass tramp. I felt that she really needed to release some type of built up piss off toward her son and ooh and that scant. Hmm haven't heard that word in a while. Courtney Diane is not short on words especially the strong one's ooh. First time I heard scant was when I was talking to Reva in the clinic, (trifling scant or rachetted scant most be old).

Henry came home saying that he needed to talk to me. His dumb ass was boo hooing like some little punk at the beach swinging snot. I told that numb nut idiot about his and her lower parts communicating and forming some type of bond. I told his dumb ass that he needed to merge with his real girlfriend or wife. I had to remind him and his little dum, dum too many cars had been up that thang's ramp. You know that she is road, (ooh I heard hohoho). Ooh never heard of a road ho. Did he really think he was the only car going up or driving up that ramp and doing some type of temporary parking? That was a parking ticket he didn't need and couldn't pay for with his broke ass. I told him over and over don't be making deposits withdraw fool. If you want to be a fool practice on being your own fool, dumb ass, (since Henray was good at it). She thought Henry would be her bank and life time personnel ATM.

Ooh he made me so sick that my butt aches before my headache. That boy, Henry, still trying to tap into minutes of my life with his dumb ass. Whatever time I have it will be a minus twenty mintues, because of Henry's dumb ass antics. Dealing with his dumb ass twenty minutes will be deducted off my life. So, let's do the math?? I get 2/3rds dead and 1/3rd time to finish off my drink, thanks to his dumb ass before the 2/3rds sets in. Did he think for a second, I wanted to give up my twenty minutes? I might want to sip slowly on my drink before my last breath. Thanks to Henry it will be minus twenty minutes. Mr. dumb ass got to act, no pretend, no hell he's just a dumb ass. I told him that that trick saw that neon sign flashing on his big dumb ass forehead, and I asked him do, you know what the sign is flashing?? I had to help my boy out I said with your dumb ass it said dumb ass.

I pictured Henry standing there very tall and slim very handsome looking at her with water filled eyes. With expressions of confusion and frustration that shared in with his busy thoughts. Thoughts that were racing all through his mind and hoping that his mother wouldn't kill him, at least not that day. I had to debrief myself to calm down, so I don't take the boy I brought into this world out. Only thang I could think of was to pop him on the back of his big ass head and remind him of this is the head you think with your dumb ass. She said I saw his innocence was genuinely showing and was converting him back into a little boy. You know little boy just wanted his mommy because he fell and got a booboo. This was more than a damn booboo with his dumb ass.

I pictured Henry and he didn't have a big head, but he did have some of Courtney Diane's features, especially when he smiled, (nope he didn't have a big head). Henry probably was popular like Maurice was in Reva's time. Courtney Diane continued with those tricks scants just get recycled/regenerated with different names. She looked at him with his red puffy eyes swinging snot and hunched his shoulders stuttering I don't know. Hell, that was a hella delayed answer about his neon forehead sign. I had to slowly repeat my words to my only born dumb ass and his numb nut. The neon sign on your big ass forehead said dumb ass, dumb ass. Now don't get me wrong I'm glad I have a relationship with my son. And that he could come and talk to me and I didn't have to hear it from someone else. You see Rita, pissed off and anger didn't have time to take a seat and wait for their introduction. Those two stepped right up to the front. Hell, they moved my ass out of the way, because they had something to say. Now don't get me wrong it did hurt. Henry is my son, my only child, my boy. My little dum dum accelerated sliding, rolling, stumbling and advanced to dumb ass, (duh). I didn't have time to tick, tick, tick boom it was a quick tick boom. I wanted to hug him, then pop him on the back of his big ass head or just thump him in his throat and tell him/we were going to get through this. I knew in the back of my mind I knew that scant wasn't pregnant. She was just trying to keep some type of selfish connection to Henry with his dumb ass, (I laugh inside because I remember Henry and his posse talking about two or four words she would say, and it came out), and because she knew his potential and she didn't want to work.

That boxed shaped heffa. Whatever her story was, she wasn't going to be our problem or our tear, nor were we going to share in her story. Rita, it wasn't that kind of party especially not with my son. Now, the boy could play some basketball and it paid off, but no baggage was needed to tag along with him in form of a baby. Especially with Miss Thang's gum popping, gold hustling stant tail heffer. I listened and really wondered what I would do if I was in that situation. I just listened as she vented. Maybe I shouldn't have said anything about Henry. Her face showed the anger she still harbored along with the pain and disappointment. Whatever she thought she loved her son and only had his best interest. Oh, well I learned not to do that again.

With eyebrows up, she added that little girl didn't bring her dumb ass around here either. She knew better, not to bring her stanky ass around me and calling me some Mama Courtney or Miss Courtney. That scant didn't know me like that but, if she came around, she would know the old school in me. Courtney Diane said she was glad that she attended that online anger management classes. She proudly said that she learned to, re-learn, refocus, and redirect her energy. Then breathe and recover, re-group, re-connect so she could refocus from whooping up on her ass, to relaxing and recovering her thoughts of beating her ass. I would have beat her ass later but I 'm learning in my transition to beat her ass now as she closes her eyes and inhale and exhales slowly, (as if she was smoking an imaginary cigarette, but she didn't smoke). I was thinking maybe Courtney Diane needed remedial training and need to be inside a classroom for those on-line anger management classes, for some re-direction with re-thinking and live feedback.

Courtney Diane always said she was keeping it real. I wondered does that give her the peace she needs or does the on-line management helps her with the pieces that she complies in her emotion with no "S" and thought process. I don't think those classes are working, seriously. She shakes her head saying with the corner smile that no more whooping ass no more "F" word, but I still wear my flip flops and cap. Rita let me tell you I used to like to use the "F" word. Every now and then it does slips out, but I do know that I'm saying it. I liked the way it felt and feels good saying it. As the word welled from my stomach, channeling through my throat and bounces soothingly off my tongue. While it is making its way out of my mouth, with force, making echoing sounds to my delicate ears. But the way I may say it, depends on how I feel that day. I just like the sound of how it echoed in my ears and the sound it made as I said and heard it. Every now and then she substitutes it with a-freshness.

Yep, Courtney Diane confirmed again that she isn't short on words or thoughts. I thought to myself if this is the new school, what was she like in the old school days. I had to chuckle because I was a fighter in my days in school too. Hmm, how sometimes we forget but the residue still lingers until it's time to surface. Yep, when it's time to show the other you they will see the other you. Courtney Diane said she told him he took at least twenty to thirty minutes off her life, with his dumb ass. So, when it's time that extra time is gone due to Henry's dumb numb nut butt. Courtney Diane added that when I die know and count on me being ah, I will be minus twenty-minutes fooling around with his dumb ass. I'm trying to live, and Henry was trying to kill me again minus twenty minutes. I was not trying to deprive him of his adventures or his journey. Now, I had to do something, mindless task to keep from choking his dumb ass and looking for that boxed shaped scant. Something, mindless like playing pin the tail on the donkey or Henry dumb ass or some laundry. She chuckled as she glazes into the sky as if she is in deep thought. I listened and thought about playing a little mind game with myself let me count on how many dumb asses she will say. So, far the count should be at around five dumb asses or so. I've been substituting her words of profanity I should go ahead and keep count on that too. It's funny to this day she still uses those terms.

She went on saying that her Henry acted like a possum to the light. With his dumb ass saying, I can't see whose coming man I'm blinded by the light, what an idiot. I love that boy but that was a dumb ass move, (there goes another one), it's not like we didn't talk about sex over and over. I felt like I tied him to a chair, so he could listen without interruptions, (she glances at me showing her corner smile). No, I didn't tie his dumb ass up just trying to get a much-needed point across to his two brains and wanting one to stay numb while the other one was listening and thinking. Especially when that box shaped scant saw how he was not only good in basketball, but track and football he could have went any athletic route.

Then a few months later Mr. Henray comes in skipping and smiling at me. I had a feeling he was going to tell me that junior Trixie wasn't pregnant. I'm surprised that she didn't say she was pregnant with twins that seem to be the going con lately. She probably told him she had a miscarriage sometimes that is the oldest trick to trap a person. Something her gold digging momma probably told or taught her or one of her trifling rachett scant girlfriends. They will linger on until either that thang really gets pregnant or just say it was a false alarm. Then acts as if she is depressed, and his dumb ass feeling sorry for that trick and re-start the cycle of numbing up again. I needed to stick a straight pin in his ass and make him howler to wake his ass up. Well he smiled saying, moms Melinda is not pregnant she had a miscarriage or false alarm. All I knew was she was what I thought she was a trick. Time changes but a trick is a trick no new games, just different faces. I thought nah, really as I rolled my eyes up in the air. I looked at her and she rolls then again as if she had Henry right in front of her. Now, that boy needed to run to the hills or mountains or just hide from her. And don't look back because she is like a game piece that says try again. Oh, hell no run Henry run as she raises her eyebrows. Rita, it doesn't matter what age or time the trick is a trick. Tricks just like scants they get regenerated or recycled. We talked about avoiding this scare and keeping his focus on his education.

We both laughed, and I love his laugh. My son looked at me with those big eyes looking like a little boy. Henry always tells me that I got to take care of you moms' cuz you're my girl. We both laughed, and he said moms I got you are my moms and my best friend. I laughed and said, and you know it. I just love him, and he always adds I want to marry a woman just like you. Courtney Diane tee-hee-hee-la-ha-ha, whatever, I don't know about that do you?? His response was you do have a point? My response with much love was hey you...

I noticed that she doesn't really laugh it's a tee-hee or la-de-da-ha-ha; I guess it depends on her mood. Henry had to pause at that statement and scratched his head then rubs his chin left the room laughing. I love my son and you can't be every-where, but you can put thoughts or visual out there to help guide them. I appreciate that he was going to try and do the noble thing, but it was with the wrong horror. I want him to know that person is out there to share that type of compassion just hold out, but if you can't I'm not naïve just know your product and don't get caught up in looks, needs or pressure.

I reflected on Reva and Maurice and wondering if her mom is still calling her Dorothy. How could Reva avoid pressure with her girlfriend yelping in her ears? I come back into Courtney Diane adding to walk away, no run away. If you walk into something you can't walk away from your dumb ass needs to run!!! Try to just think about how you can change or alter the situation. If you are not ready to deal with the consequences don't line up for the task. The time will come when you will know the time is right. We made some mistakes ourselves I know I did, and I just don't want him to fall short of his goals not mine, not his dads but Henry's goals. This is his life and he have to live it, but I will try to be there for him in any way or capacity. I can't keep him from falling, but I can teach him how to land on his feet. She smiled and said I can't go behind him blowing his noise, I just hope I showed him and talk to him enough that he knows when to blow his nose and where the Kleenex are located.

Well I thought after that long short story, and I guess the need to vent un huh, (I raised my eyebrows with an ooh and hmmm). I think after that story my little baby was ready to go to sleep or church. I said to her that he seemed to be very fo-cused and a polite young man. While she was talking about Melinda I thought and wondered what Bill had said about me to his mom Naomi. Naomi told one day that Bill told her that he had found a girl that was different from the other girls that he dated. He said that I was really kind, cute, (meaning me wow), and I might be the one. With that thought I smiled to myself and warmth had filled my heart. Bill told his mom that I came from a fine family and he thought I was the one; she seemed very smart and focused, (again he's talking about me). Bill told his mom that he liked my eyes and dimples. He said my eyes had an unusal twinkle with compassion. So, different from the other girls he had been around. Naomi said that he showed her a picture of me and said that was all my hair. I forgot how long my hair used to be. She said then you should go for it before someone else snatches her. She also said he was really excited about meeting me. I remembered how excited I was when I talked about Bill to everyone and anyone that would listen. I still love this man and that it was nice to hear good things about me, and not be referred to as a scant and that he wasn't swinging snot.

Courtney Diane smile reminds me of Robin. I can tell why they are friends they almost have the same mannerism minus the profanity. She gave me a good mind workout on substituting her words. I asked was she related to Robin. She said no just y good friends. We worked together as marketing gurus and grew up in the same neighborhood. We would just talk about how we wanted our life to be like. You know cute husbands and two or three kids and a huge house and maybe a maid, making good money so we could take trips and retire while we were still young and looking good and can still move around. I thought about what she was saying. I laughed and told her how we talked about the same thing growing up, different states apart but the same dreams. I told her in Oakwood we thought large families were like twelve kids. Families and working were all we saw in our parents and that would become our lifestyle. We both laughed. She said I don't know about twelve kids?? But hey, think about the fun in trying to reach that number, (she gives her corner smile and a wink). Good thing we were kids. Can you picture yourself with twelve kids?? Not today in this time and age I can barely take care of myself. Then the childhood script was flipped, and something happened in your life and changes everything. Yeah, we all grew up and somehow lose our childhood innocence and dreams. Sometimes you don't realize it's gone until it's gone. Now it's no longer childhood innocence the name changes to naive. Circumstances created in life changes your thoughts, your attitudes just alter all your goals and sense of direction.

Robin and I used to hang out until she went off to college. We had the same majors and goals just went to different colleges. When she got hired and eventually promoted to CEO, she invited me to come and work with her. I leaped at the chance and opportunity to work with her and change my scenery. She is the one that told be about this apartment complex. I'm getting ready to move but I'm thinking about letting my sister and cousin stay here in my apartment. Just take over my space in case I have to return. I'm moving to Florida to Fort Marshall base; don't know how long but a change sounds good. The army is transferring me which is good and bad, either way I got to get some out. I need the change, but this change is taking me out of my comfort zone. I lived here almost all my adult life now I have to up root to another life and career. I have a few army friends that I was in boot camp with that will be transferred there as well. So, I won't be too lonely. Just missing my big head boy, but he won't be too far from me he is going to school in Florida and just a drive away. He is a momma's boy and I must cut the strings, so he can become the man I know he will become. I can't walk behind him anymore blowing his nose. Now it is time for him to wipe his nose himself and he can do it. But I will have a box of Kleenex for just in case.

I set there listening to Courtney Diane and really enjoyed our conversation, with no interruption and no rush for time. Just very relaxing and no thoughts just listening as the sun warmed our bodies and the quick breeze cool our minds. I asked how she liked being in the service. She hesitated and said this wasn't her choice just something that kind of fell on her. She shared saying that it had the structure and discipline that I was raised in. Thought I escaped it, but it did a full circle and came back and picked me up. I looked at her I guess with a puzzling and confusion on my face, and Courtney Diane added I guess it does sound silly since I made the decision to join. I gave up my Prada for multicolor green fatigues wow. Too bad they couldn't be a designer camouflage uh. Now tell me that is not some type of tripped up shift. I laughed you really would be styling. We both chuckled.

She went on with; you see I really enjoyed marketing and welcoming the challenges and seeing the end results. I spent four years in school and busting tables as a waitress putting myself through college to become a marketing guru. My parents didn't have the money. They provided a good healthy environment for my sisters and brothers. They gave us what they didn't have, opportunities. My father worked for the railroad and my mother went to college to become an educator. So, college was the only choice we had. Structure and discipline were to extend our education by attending some type of college or trade school. Out of the eight of us five have college degrees the other three hmm just doing or existing. Matter of fact I have been going back and forth about letting my baby sister move into my place or my cousin with all her babies. I just don't know. It's not about her but about my baby cousins. They didn't ask for this life that my nutty cousin been giving them. Bouncing from pillow to post, they need some type of stabililty. Maybe this will help her get focus and become some kinda responsible.

Any way I worked with Robin for about twelve years plus she was already there when I arrived. She was an executive and I really enjoyed working under her and 1 learned a lot from her and was hoping to someday be an executive with her or another company. Well it didn't happen. I have no regrets, but it was an eye opener. I responded sometimes we see what we only want to see. I thought where in the heck did that come from? Did I just say that woo even that surprised me?

She said that she was an accurate punctual person. She was always on time you could set your clock by her. At 9:00 I would be sitting at my desk, noon walking out the door for lunch, 6:00 pm I was shutting down my lap top or computer. My father Cleve Jr and you must include the Jr., he wouldn't hear it any other way or you will feel the look and hear that thundering voice that make you shiver in your own shadow. He worked on the railroads and keeping on schedule was very important, along with making meals as if he was feeding a football team. I remembered my mom saying that he is so punctual that if she died before him and if you aren't there on time Cleve Jr. would probably say well babe it's you and me and get this started. On the other hand, mom would say if he died before me its okay if you're late I'll wait baby. I just remembered as a little girl looking up to my dad and would watch him with his pocket watch and I wanted to be just like him. On the other hand, Mother Flo would look at her watch and us being silly, innocence or naive would look with her looking at her watch. Our heads would turn slowly to her watch then look at her then again look at her then her watch. Then out of the blue she would ask what time was it? Now we are both stuck on a duh attack thinking a course too scared to say hell you have the watch don't your dumb ass know. Remember this was just our thoughts. I started early with my choice words and thoughts. But on the other hand, mom's response was I'm looking at my watch to see if it's time to care and it would be followed with a tee-hee-hee. How do you respond to that shift but move quickly or slowly but you get your little ass out of the room and don't look back. As I listened, I see where she gets her quick wit from. Courtney Diane pauses to say I wanted to get a hold of a hammer and smash that dumb ass watch.

Courtney Diane reflected on a few classmates that just kept picking at her and talking about time, wrong move, and wrong time with no pun meant. Asking me shift like are you in a hurry why you keep looking at the clock and your watch. I ignored ingornance. They kept on as I glanced at them like you are so pushing your ass into my foot. Why are you looking at me you both should be looking at the book with your dumb asses? Then ooh they said oh you are rolling your eyes at us. Now at my young age I really tried to avoid being violence but, in this case, the warning just didn't catch on. I calmly responded with I don't roll I cut. After that I smiled and turned back to my own thoughts and my own business. They just couldn't shut up. Then they offered me that challenged again saying we can meet later.

Inside I tried but oh what the hell here I go. Why meet later the same results in the confinement of the classroom with a small audience will have the same results with more space and the whole school as spectators watching me kick your dumb asses. Since we were in class, go for what you think you might know. Now if you want to meet later according to my watch, I will have more space more time to wear your dumb asses out. Let me make this clear text don't make me regret holding back on your dumb asses. I made it very clear that if I heard that you ran home telling, don't have your momma call my Mother Florrie. Because I will lose sleep making you both my highest priority and my finish will be so wonderful. I guess she meant it when someone told them after school they will meet. Which sounds like what we used to do after school was to meet to fight? She smiled as she glanced at her watch, saying that I have time now. I pictured her looking straight at them without blinking with her corner smile displayed. Courtney Diane sounds like her talk and bark worked well together actually it was usually an impacted one liner.

So, that's where she gets that time thing from Mother Flo and Papa Cleve Jr. We had more in common than I thought. Such as fighting in school and after school and our mother's holding on to an-item we just wanted to destroy in Courtney Diane's case her mother's watch. The same thing I thought with burning my mother's shoes she would pop me so often with. Burn them flip flop shoes like she did our toys and watch the plume of smoke fade into the air just like our toys turned into ashes. Poof, in a puff of smoke shoes gone memory gone. Now my pops had patience of Job. She pauses saying her brother Cory Davon had patience and a habit of saying a quick yell with a pause following with a slow okay in a duh kinda way. He just showed signs of brain numb he was beyond dumb ass.

Now walk with me I'm switching thought gears right now about my brother, because he's on my mind right now. I love that man. He did that yell pause okay too many times and it caught up with his numb ass. When his girlfriend asked him to marry her, his response was yeah okay. And before he knew it, she was preparing a wedding with four big ass gangster looking brothers. You know that family you stay away from because you will be fighting for days continuing with the next generation and more would keep coming when you thought you were done. You might as well add the overbearing mother-in-law and the father-in-law I didn't know how to say anything other than hi. Come to think of it, Cory Davon don't say too much of anything, like if you said the sun is shining his response would be yes. So, you see he would answer, but you weren't getting any more words added. One thing he did do was he stopped that yeah okay response.

I listened as I thought about my brother Charles and cousin Frank how they would answer with no more or no less. Funny Charles would always say about work I'm here to make ends not friends just make sure that the name is spelt right on my check. I fade in and out on what Courtney Diane was saying about her brother, but I knew by the way she talked about him they are still very close. She talked about the woman he should have been with but oh no one too many slow okays with his present Miss Thang. She says that whenever she gets a chance with Cory Davon, they laughed later about it. He said that was a stupid move and I added-er. He laughed are you saying studiper, is that a word? My response was yep with your dumb ass. He responded in a brotherly way I rather be your dumb ass brother than a fictious name called stupider. Is that word listed in the dictionary or your dictionary? How you going to make that word, is that what you went to college for. At that point, we both looked at our watches then each other then back at our watches then we looked at each other and said in sync is it time to care. We laughed, and he says I'm telling momma about your improper modification or alteration of words. I had to finish this don't forget to tell her I said with your dumb ass too my brethren. That's important too, dumb ass.

After all that we ended with an eyebrow raise from both of us. Cory Davon seemed to be just an eyebrow raise with a smile on every response. Casee his wife trained him well probably got pointers from her momma a tag team act. My brother did a holt on that yeah okay response. Nope didn't say that no more. Sure, did and said much of nothing. He continued to be short just on words. After his tee-hee break, he said that he needed a fifth of something, vodka, rum; gin something strong to drink straight. Funny ha-ha he wasn't a drinker but now and then and again he occasionaly drinks a fifth to tolerate the house full of girls. Trust me Casee keeps popping them out to make sure his tired ass didn't think or exercise any option of leaving. Casee saw him in junior high and kept close tabs on his dumb ass. She made sure of no competition and no affairs. My dumb ass brother didn't see it coming.

I had to ask out of curiosity, how many kids does he have. Right now, noisy girls Coree, Courtnee Danette, and Lillee are a year apart then Semaj and Casa are eighteen months apart. Since I only had my son Henry Luis, Miss Courtnee is the one closest to my heart and a clone of me. Reesee three years, Marlee four years and Bailee six months is his baby in his arms. There goes my family with those matching names, twin's names crap again.

Now, she's pregnant again with maybe a boy. Casee needs to plug up that outlet for reals. He will not or cannot go anywhere. What's that song cheaper to keep her or you leave hmm not too many options because, Casee removed all of them. She laughed adding that she tried to help a brother out when they would go out and women would be checking him out. But me being me I would bust him out with I love you baby brother and my eight nieces and nephew it just those seven trifling scant mamas I can't stand. That ran them off and leaving my brother with his eyebrow raised and mouth open with no words and no attempt, to correct me. I was right on the kids but funny on the mamas. That corner smile has more depth as she says now when I really want to funk with him, I asked, how was that issue with the back-child support going?? You know that some places give you jail time, I hope you got that right baby brother. Why not, say it that just cuts the unethical equation and funk with him during the process.

I made a mental count of the names she ran off so fast I came up with seven and a half; yep that is a mini platoon. I'm sure that he was a willing participant. As Courtney Diane tee-hee-hee with a corner smile said, that when the mini village comes in, they sound like a herd of locust or cattle. Their running sounds like an army platoon marching or running in sync. When you hear the noise, you try and run and get away before they notice you, then damn it's too late they are grabbing and pulling at any or every limb they came in contact with. As she talked, I imagine the sound of marching and cadence in a miniature version.

The miniature platoon was lined up introducing themselves by sounding off yelling out their names. In which it sounded like a bunch of loud ass echoes. They are loud and bad, older folk might say mischievous. Their momma disciplines them as she comfortably sits on the couch yelling out all their names. I love them, but they are some bad ass noisy kids. Hmmph, their lazy ass momma yells at them from the couch, or from wherever she is sitting, not to do this or that as Corey Davon slowly sips on his fifth of whatever, to avoid saying anything and having no direct eye contact. While our parents looked at them with would you get that child off the table, stop the others, ones from jumping off the couch, or running through the house. In the midst of all this noise my parents' just stop, and they looked at each other and their watches and wall clocks. This time no time to care comment just saying with their eyes when in the hell will these little bad ass grandkids and trifling momma and our nummy son go home. Those acrobatic minis might hear her, or they might numb up just like their dumb ass dad.

Now my pops I love that man just like my mom, but I am a daddy's girl and a momma's clone. He stood tall and strong and his deep voice had the strength that filled the room and was immediately called to your attention. His smile calmed your nerves, but you knew he was a real professional. As she talked, I thought about my dad, he wasn't tall but strong in his respect, demeanor and his smile calmed me as well. I still remember how I liked to watch my dad shave. As a little girl, I looked up to him too. Courtney Diane went on to say it was only when he was upset that you wanted to run, and she repeated shiver in your hiding place holding your breath. Only one time and I mean one time that I mouthed off to him and you remember deep about that one time, ooh that shift stays with you. He asked me to go to the store I even can't remember what he asked me to get. I just know I really didn't want to walk all the way to the store. Shift we were always walking everywhere like cars weren't invented. Yet, you know in those days, no was not your option. I laughed because I remembered when my mom asked me to go to the store in the deep snow for bread with a 10-cent reward.

Courtney Diane glanced at me as if I didn't need a-amen with my story or back up. My thoughts were ooh she is having her sensitive moment with that one feeling again, ooh okay. Well, I went and got the wrong fricking thing and my dad let me know by saying that I should have sent JJ. Me not realizing my voice carried just like his said, then you should have.... before I could finish the sentence, my father slapped me, and I felt my eyes cross. When they finally straightened out, I thought to myself quietly, while blinking my focus back in. I didn't want him to hear my thoughts, that slap changed my grammar to, I ain't gonna do that no mo just totally took the "re" off, of more as I tried to refocus my vision. At that point, I thought I might need my glasses to assist with decrossing my eyes. He is the only man that hit me, and I made sure of that.

So, when you see me, or Robin cross our eyes that means, we are getting smart and to slow our role or a silent whisper and that's just our inside joke. See if any man tried to hit me, box or fight, pick any one of the mentioned choices the only choice I will give them would be a whip on his ass. When he took his punk ass to sleep that mother of friends would wake up with all type of knots on his dumb ass forehead. Now my mom, Mother Florrie orginal name was supposed to be Floyd. Her daddy just wanted all boys and their names were ready for each birth, so her mom altered their names a tad bit. I didn't think much of what Courtney Diane said about her mother's name. After all, my great- grandmother was named Douglas and her parents didn't change or alter her name. I don't think her parents considered that option.

Courtney Diane said that, my mom was a teacher and she loved her students as if they were her children. Now Momma Florrie was about as tall as my dad she stood proud and gorgeous at the same time. Her beauty was a distractor because she didn't play and what she said she meant and didn't repeat herself. Her bark and bite were the same. She didn't play in no way shape or form. Oh, and my parents could be rude you just didn't drop by and when they were ready to go to bed, they did with you still there talking to them. Now let me back up this was how they treated family just let your imagination go with how they treated others that stop by.

Girl I remember when my mom was sitting in the back seat while dad was driving, and when they pulled up her sister Gigi's she just looks at my mom. Her name was short for Geneene, her original name was supposed to be Gene or Eugene, (granny altered her name too). So, my Aunt Gigi said Florrie why are you sitting in the back seat. My mom responded because I bought the whole car. What is it to you I can ride on the bumper if I want to it's my car and I didn't purchase just the front seats. I laughed when she told me, but mom kept a straight face. With Mother Florrie, you better had heard, and I mean better had heard her the first time, shame on you if you didn't or if dad heard her call you and you didn't respond that came with a double beat down and a long ass speech. Explain this shift to me, why they got to talk while they are beating your ass?? The longer the speech, the longer the connection if you know what I mean. I think just shut it up, so we can get this over with. I go to my room hurt and pissed and they go back to reading the newspaper or looking at the news. Now don't get me wrong I did some crazy ass shift. Plus, my dumb ass got away with some shift you don't want to talk about. I had to agree with Courtney Diane that I got away with some things that my parents need not to know now or then, unt un.

Chapter 16

The Courtney Diane Story Continues

I looked and heard the strength and confidence her parents passed on to her along with the height. She could be a basketball/volleyball player or a model. She displays a hidden dimple that comes out when she talks or when she shows that corner smile. Only thing Courtney Diane sure likes to do is cuss. We were just talking then all of a sudden, those special words come out. It happens like a sudden cloud burst. Just like this rain before the sun comes out you just don't know which will linger the rain or the sun. That's what she reminded me of. Now I wasn't a virgin to swearing, this is my day and I heard it enough from Bill. Just like Courtney Diane I never knew what triggered Bill when he would swear at me. Sometimes I pretend to put my finger in my mouth to test the wind direction on when Bill will erupt with the blah blah and blahs. I always felt if you cuss you are short on words for that quick second and need instant filler. Bill would cuss, and fuss and his words just became one big blur of words.

I asked Courtney Diane if she liked her job and it offered her career opportunities why did she leave. She said that she was always very punctual and paid attention to details. Robin needed a file I had left at home, so I had to run home. This was some weird shift, (I just bleep the fillers from her in my mind). I was trying to follow her, but I had to insert my own words, so the swearing wouldn't block out our conversation, but it took a lot of work. She said all that she had to do was run into her house and quickly grab the file and get back on the road. I knew Robin and I would be working late on a big client's job so leaving gave me a break. So, I arrived home off schedule to see something I wasn't expecting to see it blew the "f" word hmm change to I heard fun out of her.

I opened my door and it's an eerie quiet and funny feeling. This type of quiet puts a funny feeling in your stomach, but it wasn't a fright or flight situation just a funny feeling. I heard the shift again. I looked at Courtney Diane's expressions and she has a puzzling look and she gathered her thoughts. After hearing about Robin and Ramon story was history repeating itself in the day time. I put my hand over my mouth and said it wasn't another woman coming out of the room or lying in your bed, she said oh hell no!! I just responded with an oops. What happened? She said blue skies make up in the trash can, hell Robin didn't wear or need make-up. How would he like it if his dumb ass found used for the sake of not sounding nasty condoms in the bathroom trash can? In clear view and Robin told him in her always calm, clear voice ah just the girls using them when they had their water balloon fights how would you like that shift. If Robin really wanted to piss Ramon off with his dumb ass say so calmly, nicely honey they weren't yours they were super excuse me magnums. With that there is no room for mad just a quick distracter and thought of wow no she just didn't. Now with that you would smile and walk away knowing you have just silently pissed him off. With that I grab my mouth to hold back my laugh, but my eyes watered in laughter's place thinking at the same time what's magnums. Then something inside hit my head saying didn't she just say condoms; the other voice goes oh yea real slow. Inside I just screamed thinking no I'm not turning into Rhona. What timing, the washing machine stopped and time for the dryers.

This story had me really wondering because Courtney Diane sounds like she would walk in like a woman and leave as a mad woman with some causalities. I can show you cuckoo more than you would like to see crazy. If she didn't get them with some type of combat battle, her looks would make you want to insert the bullets yourself. If not with her looks and actions would make you inflict your own pain just to get away from what might happen from her looks or actions. The way she talked about her parents she inherited that look and demeanor. As we unload the washing machine we talked as we threw the clothes in the dryers. Not paying any attention to people walking in or around us. She said it was another woman and it wasn't. She glanced at me to see what my response would be. I thought and said is that like being a little pregnant or just indigestion. I kind of chuckle for this is an inside joke I knew and not many shared with me. She laughed indigestions uh. Courtney Diane paused to address Robin's situation.

When Ramon started leaving the room to talk on the phone, I would have sat my ass right next to him and encourage him to continue with his conversation. You know I would give him a look of I insist that you continue you, punk ass bitch. Tell that hoho to speak up I can't hear her dumb ass. If he started an unnecessary argument I would have paused and lean back and ask what this shift is really about, and what trick you trying to impress or trying to meet at my expense. If he wanted to play games, then get the game board out and go ahead make that move. Talk to me because your acting, like some little cowardly punk ass I heard bitches again. Develop some type of spine you rude, I heard mother of friend. How you going to disrespect me by getting up and doing some whispering like I can't hear your dumb ass. Then I would calmly tell him to get your shift and get your ass some serious gone.

Since he like phones as soon as he came around that corner, I would hit him with the land line phone. Let him hear a ring since he like ring tones. With that line, I had to reflect on Pandora and her family history of hitting their husbands with anything readily available. Courtney Diane added that, one time a woman set next to Malcom David when she had just got up for a moment, damn. When she came back, and the other woman acted like she didn't want to get up. So, she does the corner smile I'm going to make this trick quick with this bitch. She said she slowly looked at her throat and at her boot. We had a mutual understanding without words. She gathered from my look that I would hit her in her throat then stomp her with my boot end of conversation. Now get this because she was much larger than me, I guessed I should have done some type of shiver move. Oh, hell no my move was on my terms get your ass up or the other choice you will get your ass up.

I had to ask out of curiosity because I needed some pointers in case that scant Verlene or any other women try that move now I know what actions to take. She acts like she was mad and got her ass up, and Malcom David didn't have a clue on what had just happened. Now getting back to him, he would be getting some leave of absence from my presence. I will nicely tell him that you can use those hefty bags there strong and sturdy and there are plenty of them. See I 'm packing your shift like a lady. I will throw your shift being nice in a bag because I'm working hard on my anger management class. Take a trip to your trick. Malcom David's voice can't go that low and it's amazing how the fine tuning of your ears can pick up every word. So, he would have to kiss my entire wide ass in the huddle position, (I heard bitch), with no regards.

She said I would have reversed all that shift. First, I would have walked in the house that night why lose a nights', sleep flunk that. Miss Rita, I would lose sleep thinking about getting them. So, I would be selfish I won't lose sleep, at least not that night. I would handle the business now then rest. That I heard bogus blue skies hmmm. She said she would open that damn closet door and grab that bat in preparation for swinging like I'm ready to hit a home run!! One swing two heads take Miss Trixie out too. Since she wants to play games and sleep next to him, bitch. You see tricks have emotions they are self-serving on the other hand I only have an emotion without no "S". Yep her butt would be sleeping alright, right next to Ramon's knocked out ass and I wouldn't blink or flinch. As I walked to my closed bed room door in my house, I would lean that bat against the wall. Oh, hell no I would open the door with one hand and hold the bat behind my back as I entered. It would be battered up and the baseball theme in the background dum dum dum batter swing! The only dilemma I would have was who to knock the shift out of first. Should I first start from the left to right or the right to left? What the hell eedie meanine minie which ho should go first. Sometimes it's hard making decision on who to knock I funk out first. I would be so mad I would really want to lift the mattress up and flip both their asses out, then run and jump on top of the mattress trying jump on every lump my foot or the bat felt under that mattress, while screaming. Wow I look at her and I believe she is serious. I heard funk again and pausing I heard shift. I would do one long swing hitting them both.

Then I would call the popo. Then leave out screaming, don't hit me ow, ooh, why you hitting me, why you got that naked woman in my bed Ramon, why babe why??? You got to throw in an emotional connection, and then add a tear and cry as ugly as I could woo, woo, oh no stop oh, tearing I heard shift off, twisting my hair to make me look total crazed, throwing stuff around the room, throwing my body against every and anything I encountered heading toward the front door. Saying to the police oh help me please oh stop hurting me, (a tear a tear). Why you are hitting me, why you and that woman in our bed, why you do that Ramon, (while crying, then she winks at me). Get that woman off me why ya both coming at me that ain't fair ow!! Then she motions with her had a countdown of five, four, three, and two, one I'm on, as she grabs her throat forcing a scream. I'm screaming as loud as my choking would allow. I will be saying uh stop choking me I can't breathe, cough cough, I feel like I'm passing out then make gurgling sounds with one big exhale.

Woo Courtney Diane is a good performer and she deserves an Oscar and plus she has a vivid imagination ooh very scary. Wow this would make a good movie. She added that she would hang up while screaming and crying with strong sounds all the time. What a performance and the call the popo again. But sound like I am out of breath, help me please, help me, (cough, and cough), as if I'm trying to catch my breath. I then would make it outside screaming/yelling, of course, so the neighbors could hear me. I would position myself you know like I just collapsed. So, if you're looking at me, I would look like I've just passed out on the ground. You know like a drunk on a Saturday night binge. Position myself just right, you know pose looking really stiff and mumble saying I was assaulted, they jumped on me. Moaning, oh no why they got to hit on me I didn't do nothing but come home, and keeping my eyes closed until popo or someone lifts me up and ask me if I am okay. Depending on my mood maybe come out swinging like I'm trying to fight back thinking it was them coming after me again. This one I would play by ear. I would start mumbling and stuttering, shivering and rambling and all that shift. I didn't know that woman was in my bed and all I was trying to do is defend myself from both, (a tear, and a tear). I would conveniently and sincerely, (smile) ask are they okay?? Again, adding another tear, a tear with a boo hoo woo ooh. I came home tired been working all day. I'm so very tired humph. I would be looking up with puppy watered dog eyes and sounding sincere. Then I would shiver and look around saying that I'm so scared. I watched her as she shows she would be trembling. Again, adding a tear, a tear oh while swinging snot like my boy did yea, I forgot about that. Adding they really hurt me, (ow). Why they both had to jump me, (while rubbing my arms and neck), ooh I feel so sore and say oh my head and right into my conversation just pass out.

Why did they have to hit me with that bat? I didn't do anything they were in my bed, (ouch and ooh)? I looked at her performing and she was very convincing and funny at the same time. It made me think about Bill's buddy they called 'ah ooh', because of his injuries. Courtney Diane goes on with a look of sadness in her eyes as she continues performing her story. I sit there with my imaginary bowl of popcorn laughing as she performs as the imaginary ticker tapes flows underneath her reading for entertainment purposes only don't try this at home tee-hee-hee. Now see my bruises will show up faster on me than Robin. I would put on such a performance that I would have to nominate myself for best performer. She cracks a smile out the corner of her mouth as she continued. As for that car, that shift, would become somebodies six pack, and I would mail it to him in packages, (using her hands to show small). Let him drive that shift in form of a six pack. I had to tip my head off to Robin though she walked out like a lady and I would walk in as a straight up bitch right into an assault charge.

Another thing I wouldn't have left my house. I would have put Ramon's trifling dumb ass out and put my foot up that tricks ass, oh rachet scant. I was substituting that word for ass but what the heck Jesus rode on one, Samson used a jaw bone for defense and some people can act like one so oh well. For that quick instance, she made me think way back about Reva. Listening to Courtney Diane she reminded me more of Reva and less of Robin, but you could still tell that they were good friends in sister form. She made me think about what Reva might be up to did and did she ever get a chance to pursue her singing and acting career? As I snapped back Courtney Diane goes on with sounding out the pain and crying cute. While trying to keep my eyes shut with no flickering of the eyelids until I feel someone shaking me asking if I was okay. Then I would break out the moaning and shift batting my eyes real slow, and maybe throw a little cross eye motion. I couldn't believe how dramatic Courtney Diane was. She was not only entertainment on a boring day but scary at the same time.

She said that, just say that if the police didn't believe my performance and when they regained consciousness and I my assault time hopefully would be converted to temporary insanity or misameaner, I'm done. Well let's just say if they tried to charge me with attempted murder that would be a not. I would make sure that they took good pictures of my body for my evidence. All I was trying to do was let them continue to snuggle and snooze in my bed since they found my bed so comfortable. I would add how considerate I was by letting them sleep together a little longer in comfort. Now you must admit that was a kind thought considering the circumstances. Then she smiled innocently with eyes that showed something entirely different.

I would let them continue the thought of being sleep passed out together. Let them stay all comfy, snuggly and cuddling. Now if they arrested me, hmm another factor I need to consider. Along with controlling my adverbs and she gives a wink. Get one of those over worked pissed off public defenders and help them out with my plea bargain. Rita girl it's like this if it did work, and they change my felony down to a misdemeanor through my creative bargaining from my public defender, (as she rolled her eyes), I'm out and reformed, (she winks). Of course, I will continue to attend my on-line anger management classes and shift. Oh, damn sorry I mean shoot, because I'm reformed. After my quick sentence time, (if I receive time tee-hee-hee), I would refresh on the fact that I knock their asses out. Batter batter swing and you're out; try to step up to that plate. Now how you like that shift. I can say it now I'm not in court. After my stinch in Singsing I'm out for a slow day of pampering for me. Oh, I forgot I would be driving my Benz back to my refurnish home.

I would fumigate that house get rid of all that furniture including that imported bed set, nasty girl might have left her pets she carried called bed bugs. All that shift would be replaced, because I don't know where Ramon and that nasty bitch been in my house and what she set her ass on. Just start all fresh with no Ramon memories lingering. Redecorate my house and the wardrobe to match. While still sporting both identical Benz's parked in my driveway. I would send his car in pieces, but it wouldn't be the Benz I'm not stupid. I would send a substitute in form of his lime green Pacers he used to sport in college with a pack of cigarettes. Oh, and Robin talking about that scant is a friend oh hell no she's not a friend and sure anin't no buddy. That bitch needed to be airborne via my right foot.

Well my situation was a little crazier she said that her husband, that mother of friends had me all confused. This mother of friends was dressed in my clothes and stuff/shift. I really had to pause because this threw me for a curve. Maybe I should have borrowed Robin's bat for just in case. Before I cussed his ass out, I had to refocus on what the funk I was looking at. I was so mad I made up words to say to him. He made me forget all my vocabulary. He had me substituting words and shift. Rita, I had a paused moment girl as I had to check it out, I was in a-ah or a hell no. I had to look at how this mother of friends had accessorized by jewelry and scarfs and shift.

At that point, I had very little residual of compassion. It was more like wet bath tub of the remaining concentration of what was I seeing. I was trying to refocus but all that dit was going fast. I had to snap back after I said what the funk is all this shift about and really had to give him kudos on how he put my shift together, but the ending was still hell no! Hmm I never thought about that could work with that color, but he had better not stretch any of my designer outfits or shoes. Of course, my husband, Malcom David, was startled by me coming home so soon. Hell, my ass was startled too. This wasn't a solo act. This was out of character for me. My blind dumb ass didn't see any signs of this shift coming. Knocked my thoughts in all

ROBIN REED-POINDEXTER

different directions where they had the nerve to ask me what's up. He was walking, parading and strutting his shift, technically my shift. Then I had a me and I moment of what the funk you a bitch now you got my thongs on too. We both looked at each other with our mouths and eyes wide open, both thinking what the hell!

I said what the funk you bastard. He said I wanted to tell you for the longest just didn't know how. So, you show me better than you could tell me you, coward ass bitch. Then the fool tried to comfort me by trying to blow smoke up my ass at the same time trying to convince me my ass wasn't on fire, or better yet cigarette smoke and my taste in clothes was good. Hell, I know my shift is good that's why I paid the price to get my shift right. I invested in my designer clothes. I didn't need comfirmation from his tired dumb ass. I got my shift right I knew I had damn good taste. Obviously, he liked my taste in clothes too. I don't play when it comes to my shift. I didn't purchase it for someone else to borrow or loan it out. This is my shift and my shift were in my closet with the rest of my shift!! Did he really think that I was this fool that belong to him? I thought what the funk obviously I and me was a fool in my choice in men. Hell, he had pants on at the wedding when did he put on my slip and that something needs bleaching. I need to send him back to his mom Miriam. Malcom David selfish, mother of friends should have said that stuff before he married my ass. What the funk??? She went on to say that bee, itching I heard beaches, but beeitching fits the tone and this word that rhymes with witch. Where do we go from here? Once everything inside decided to come back, I had to refocus on what the funk was going on.

Now Rita I can handle another woman, because a mistress is a trick with a name. You see I know some tricks of my own. The only trick she can do is being some idiot's sex toy and a hidden fool waiting to get funk. She laughed saying in between her venting that saying the funk the stronger she makes it sound the better it makes her feel. I can tell because she said it as she was popping mints into her mouth, refreshing. After the pause for the 'f" word identification she continued calmly. Very seldom will they get promoted from hotel ho. There are no emotions no face and no commitment. I can't compete with a woman wanna be or I don't know yet. I'm the woman I don't need another piece or part of any type of drama in my house and especially not in the bedroom.

Malcom David used to throw me some affection which left me wanting and confused on what was really up? We had very little intimacy, very little kissing or hugging. This was different from the beginning of our relationship and marriage. In midst of working we became friends with very little benefits, and I didn't get the memo, card, or text hell not even an email. Our life was a full course meal with short ribs. His selfish ass ate all the ribs in our relationship and had no problem leaving me the dried ass bone. That selfish something needs bleaching. See Rita he threw me crumbs of affection which left me starving for more emotional attention. Why can't

I have a piece of the cake instead of the dried-up stale leftover and crumbs. Crumbs that weren't even moist enough to gather onto a fork. I had a hearty appetite day and night. I didn't want what he felt obligated to give me a snack. Something with no flavor, no taste just indigestion. I couldn't short change myself like that, I knew I deserved and wanted better. We were talking about a lifetime together. That's what I thought when we were up at the altar. What the funk was he thinking? I didn't want the cameo with the affections the site for eyes to think we had it all together, but behind closed doors the lies go away, and the truth prevails. I didn't want to feel that I wasn't good enough. I wasn't going to do the affair crap either too messy, nasty and I honored my vows. It's just not worth the drama and too many lies to try and remember, and I didn't have time for that shift. Not worth it!! All I needed to do was just send him packing and let him be gone. With my dumb ass when I think back trying to down it with with my sexy thong while slowly working my nighty thinking he was impressed. Nah he probably taking it off me to put it on him, ain't that some blue skies. Now don't get me wrong I could get a dill pickle from any-where. I wanted my husband not some, one-night number that I wouldn't want to see ever again just do the thank you ma'am and get out. That wasn't for me. I didn't want some random desperate dill pickle.

With her corner smile she proudly states that Malcom and she will not be to-gether today, tomorrow it was infinity of ever. I learned the hard way using the "N" word of never for some reason brings it to existence. And in no way shape or form do I want any part of that act or party. Today the forecast says cloudy, but my ass did see clearly until I opened both eyes to see clearer. The rain came out and showered all over my dreams. Eventually the sun did come out. I no longer felt the chills from the clouds but the warmth of the sun on my new life. After listening to Courtney Diane, I was amused. But her mouth wouldn't send sailors out they would buy her a drink in a way of showing some type of respect. I guess with that type of unpredict-able mouth and gorgeous looks she had them hooked.

She said when she went back to work Robin thought I had accident. My crazy insides must have surfaced to my face. The collision I had was going home and run-ning into my outfit on my husband. I did, I accidently went home and saw some crazy ass shift coming out of my closet. She said Robin laughed saying all those clothes finally started jumping out at her. No really Malcolm David came out of my walkin closet wearing and styling my clothes. Robin looked at me with blank eyes I guess she couldn't believe that shift either. Hell, I was in disbelief myself and had to have a special me moment. I had to find a quick seat. So, I sat down on Robin's desk in which I knew she hated. She knew something was wrong as she looked at my butt and me as to what is up really. With a big sigh and shaking of the head I had to tell her again that I couldn't believe this crazy ass shift happened to me. Shouldn't this be a movie moment or some shift. This shift shouldn't happen what the freshness is up, I just knew at any moment that some type of camera would come out saying this was a punk skit. Had to tee-hee-hee because damn he wore and accessorized better than me and make up was tight. The last picture of him was him wearing and prancing around in my shift. Shift why did he have to look so damn good and the vision of that shift was still replaying in my head. He's a fine mother of friends. I knew one thing I told Robin that I needed a drink, a fifth of something, gin, rum something straight and strong, or little mixture but strong on the main ingredient. Now, I knew how my brother Cory Davon felt. I could have added a slow okay myself. Now, I'm feeling stupid add a 'er'. I needed to cut this short, so I could get gone or something. Robin laughed oh a new dictionary word stupider. What would your Mama Florrie think about your new word?? Robin smiled adding girlfriend, next time keep your flat ass off my desk and position it in a chair. I'm sure it will fit and that is what they are for heffa.

Robin looked at me kinda crazy saying that sounds like the ingredients for your long island iced tea. What a coincidence, hmmm. We both laughed because we knew that Robin couldn't stand to have people sitting on her desk. She knew I needed something crazy and strong. I could only say right now with my-me moment happening, I needs something. Courtney Diane kinda shook her head as if she is still in the moment of the incident. I had to tell her his dumb ass said that he loved my foundation from Maxx Factor, and we are running low. Robin said Maxx Factor uh well let me know when you will be going shopping. Hey, I might want to tag along. Courtney Diane ugs and said don't give me a reason to stretch my leg and foot. With that said, we both cross our eyes at the same time. Robin agreed being my girl and we left early and got our drinks on. Just to put a numb on but very able to drive home. While Courtney Diane occasionlly asking whatever in the hell just happened when I went home. Did my life switch to some type of Twilight zone shift or did I open the wrong ass door? What kinda time zone did my dumb ass step into and was it being viewed by the audience on TV.

I had to make some type of decision soon, why wait for later. This was some nightmare shift never could have imagined. Why couldn't it have been another woman all I had to do was kick her ass? I'm thankful for my on-line courses. My anger management on-line course taught me to hold my role? Don't repress, regroup, recover, reconnect and redirect my energy all the "re's" that's why I got to retake that dumb ass class again shift. I had to grab my mouth to keep from laughing out loud, but my eyes watered showing my insides were really trying to hold it in. Even Courtney Diane had to tee-hee-hee, la-la and ha-ha-ha, whatever. She or him had to get some gone and leave me and mine alone. Now how do you compete with this shift?

Malcom's younger sisters Hannika and Kwanza were beautiful cool and not over protected by Madame Miriam. I thought how different two different cultures birth by same mother, but his mother was cuckoo as hell. With adding, now that's just my opinion. I asked her, what were their nick names. She paused and looked at me as if I interrupted her train of thoughts. She laughed and said guess. Because their names represented the Christmas holiday their nicknames were Holly and Hally. Why can't I get away from all these creative names in my family and my dumb ass married into the same doggy poopoo? I paused and chuckled, ooh that makes sense. I didn't like the way his momma talked down to me as if I was new at being an adult. I love his gorgeous sisters and love their names, because they were unique. But I still can't stand that momma.

She babied her boy so much and thought he was her extended husband. He was always doing for her needy ass and I fallen and can't get my butt up. She was a please help my lazy butt up because I don't want to do anything not a thing to help myself. Rita, you believe on our wedding night she followed us everywhere. When she couldn't follow us anymore, I felt her eyes watching our every move. I thought what kind of bogus booboo was this shift? Did I marry her and him?

I laughed and told her my mother- in- law Naomi was cool and didn't take no mess and kept her smile through everything. I thought to myself, wow count your blessings. Naomi and I talk but Bill is not a momma's boy, woo I'm so glad. Courtney Diane looked at me as if I interrupted her story. Oops excuse me. She says nah it's not like that just thinking about her and Malcom still, but just thinking about them pisses me off with his dumb ass her too. Now, she has someone she can go shopping with and polish each other's toe nails, and wax each other's back yuck. Rita I can deal with him being obsessed maybe wanting to be so much in my life, but not being in my shift. I wouldn't know whether to go shopping with Ramona to help me accessorize or hide my shift, so Ramon wouldn't wear it. I gave his ass a secret thought that he was looking better in my shift than I did. So, I asked what happened. She said I couldn't live that kind of secret life behind doors because eventually the knob turns, and the door opens making that squeaky nosie and shift like some crazy ass scary movie. I wanted and married a man not someone that looks better in my clothes than I do, until you look at his mannish ass big feet.

We laughed as I tried to picture what he might look like as a man and dressed in her clothes. I said especially because this man, I mean really Rita he looked better than me in my own suits. Yes, Malcom David was slimmed built with a small waist but size twelve feet. Now I hate to admit he did look good and applied his make up so well. I wanted him to apply my make up on me. I didn't want a girlfriend I wanted and married my best friend. Don't you know he had the nerve to tell me, (now hear me), we needed some more make-up because the shadow and foundation was getting low and maybe we should consider this brand instead of the one I was using via him? I had to grab my mouth on this one, what the hell we need more make-up and we need to change from my Maxx Factor. Hell, I just purchased Maxx

Factor it's in my purse your ass needs to buy your own or go to your mama's house.

See I had to shut up because I couldn't think fast enough of what I really wanted to say. His ass had my mind studdering and shift. My mind and speech had me gasping. Gave me the feeling I had to hit myself on the back to cough out my own words. I was trying to say shift or utter forcefully my favorite word. You know express my feelings and that her corner smile was in full effect. I told you I had to give him his props for the way he coordinated my shift. I would have to wonder if I bought clothes would I have to hide them to keep him out of them or shop with him, because he was that good. I couldn't live that life of hiding my shift every time I went shopping. Just saying that does sound sick uh? I had to ask his ass, are you stepping left or right because there is nothing in between. I wanted to get it straight that, I'm not tying my one emotion in you. Are you stepping left, or right? I refused to have a question mark in my life. Ain't no little pregnant up in here either your ass is or ain't mother of friends.

I will not allow anything to mess with my mind, our son, house, marriage or the one emotion no "s" to funk with. I raised one child that has a mustache I refused to raise a grown ass man way pass puberty with a mustache. Not him in any form rather in a dress or pants. I am not sharing my slips, my thongs, my draws, bras, my scarfs, my Maxx Factor or my three-inch heels. Nope, no vision no effort, not today hmmm not ever, in my life time, hell no. I couldn't put my marriage and emotion on pause because he really didn't know. Well, he knew enough to prance his ass around in my Prada's and shift. Rita, you can't tell me that wasn't some weird ass shift. Hmmm she seemed to have favorite words along with the two to four specialty acknowledged by Henry and his posse. I kind of hutch my shoulders because no I couldn't and didn't want to ever know how that stuff felt. That sounds cuckoo; again, that's just only my opinion. Come on now we had a son and I just didn't want that type of friction or confusion for Henry Luis. If I thought this arrangement was bizarre what would Henry think? I couldn't put Henry through adults' shift that we couldn't even figure out. That's crazy and straight up stupid no "er" in the end.

Talking with Courtney Diane had a variety in her conversation with good high energy she was very entertaining and passed the time away from the tedious task of laundry. The morning went well, and I met a new neighbor and possible friend. I had to change my me thought while talking to her. I really enjoyed her conversation. She said Malcom David and I tried to do some intimacy because I had to get the dill pickle that I knew, but I just couldn't get the image out of my mind seeing him in a negligee while looking at his mustache ew. Girl I wanted to scream like one of those horror movies and totally punk out screaming and running. I can do some freaky shift in the bedroom but weird shift just not me. Malcolm David didn't know what his trip was he just knew he liked dressing in women's clothes, and he liked the way the clothes felt and applying make-up, in which that bitch told me I was out of make-up one too many times.

Take you and your purse and go buy your own damn Maxx Factor. If you saw Bill dressed in your clothes, I think that would make you rush to the bathroom and earl. I had to ask what's an earl. She looked at me like what world do you live in; it's the sound you make when you are throwing up, really Rita. While I was trying to listen, my mind wondered could I dance and swirl and drop it. Would Bill look at me like I was crazy or reject my intimate attempts. Then I thought about one of those Trixies showing him some craziest moves I didn't do or try or ever seen or know about. Morning sickness was enough adding that thought yuck. Time seem like it stood still. It was still early morning. We talked about me being pregnant. She said she wanted a couple of more babies, but it just wasn't meant. Her niece Courtnee Danette is about as close as she is going to get to having a daughter, and she is my name sake and clone. She smiles lucky kid uh. Things have a way of working out for the better. She said her son is off to school and she doesn't have to worry about child care or tuition, breast feeding with droopy boobs, altering her schedule or changing her diet. Just some scant gold diggers in training trying to snatch or trick my boy. I know I taught him well enough that he will find the right one. I might not like her because I'm losing my boy but the right one will make and support the man he will become. I had to let go so he could experience his own freedom. She liked that type of freedom of no bondage, no shackles and no Henry Luis.

We both had heard the dryer ding and slowly rised knowing we had to do some folding. When I got up, she said hey when your butt due and what are you having? I told her about three months, and that I go this week to find out the sex. Courtney Diane said I saw your little cute daughter; Robin has nothing but good to say about how smart, cute and well mannered she is. Ooh that made me feel good hearing her say that about Sierra. I thought the same thing about Robin's daughters Denise and Nicole plus more. After folding the clothes, we kind of just sat enjoying the sun and Robin sees us and walked over to us. We both jumped up and hug her as if we haven't seen her for a long time. Robin says I need to be doing some laundry while the girls are over at their grandmother Phyllis house, getting spoiled. I know the little girls are either going shopping or looking at the racing forms with her and their grandpa Richard. Courtney Diane said they still playing the horses and play-ing cards. Robin laughed and said it's like breathing when have you known them not to and they love it.

I said to Miss Robin what are you gonna do today. She smiled with I have a lot to do. She looked over at Courtney Diane and reminded her of that big contract they had with Ty West. Yep they are expanding, and they hired us again. Their busi-ness in northern California has now made its way down south to southern Cali and they want me to help expand their growing business. Courtney Diane looked at Robin asking are you still taking those fifthteen minute cardio kick boxing classes.

Robin laughed saying yep, while turning her body around to show off the results. That's why I am advertising his business. I like the results and many other people will too that can't commit to an hour class. He has a program that works and plus him and his wife, Janice practice what they preach. They work hard and are good grounded people.

Back to the reason for the class so I could kick your ass if you had one. Courtney Diane smiled wow, any way heffa we did do a helluva good job. I'm not surprised they wanted to hire us again which means another big paycheck bonus for us, (while looking at Robin and crossing her eyes). And don't worry about my ass just give me my monee, tee-hee-hee. I really miss that part do you want me to help you with it for old time sake because I did say we and not just me, (hint hint). Robin crack a corner smile saying, sure why not that way two heads can knock it out quicker, (hint hint), we and I will hook you up, (winking and crossing her eyes). Let's do this Miss Courtney or should I say Diane and she replies okay Ro/Rob/Robbie or should say Miss Lovely or should I give a shout out a tweet tweet. Robin says should I say with her flat ass. With that Courtney Diane shakes her butt smiling. They both laughed and ask if I wanted to join them. Although it sounds fun, again I had to pass and ask for a raincheck. Inside voices are saying go and enjoy your time the clothes will be there, but the reality sets in saying raincheck next time.

I watched them laughing with each other as they both let out a big silent sigh. Courtney Diane says to Robin kiss my asset and Robin said which cheeks heffa. Should I go left right or right left? Courney Diane responded with I love when you talk dirty to me say it again, (as she shakes and wiggles her body). But this time say my name slow and don't forget the "Miss". That action reminded me of Momo. The day is still young, and I wanted to enjoy my me time while I still had it. When the time arrives again, I will cash in on that raincheck. It was good seeing them together they reminded me of sisters more than best friends. I watched them leave laughing and throwing ideas back and forth as Courtney Diane carries her medium size basket of folded clothes away. I noticed that they have similar body frames, but Courtney Diane is just slightly taller.

Chapter 17
New Rejection New Reaction Moves In

As I left, I thought about Aunt Jo or Aunt Johanna always called me runaway, funny ha-ha, that's what I really was feeling like running away. I don't think to this day she remembers my real name. So, as I pulled my wagon of folded clothes, I probably look like I was running away from home. My thoughts would sometimes run away passing rapidly through my mind. I laughed at the name runaway (because my Aunt Johanna not really related to me still calls be runaway), an early label that somehow stuck. To this day, that name still fits me just right. To this day, I don't think Aunt Jo remembered my first name. Every time I called her, I have to say runaway, bcause if I say Rita, she doesn't remember me. It's funny I used to runaway to her house because the babysitter was so mean or there was a misunderstanding with my sisters and parents. I guess then I realized at a young age I didn't have to put up with people being mean to me. The silly question is why I put up with Bill being mean to me. Should I runaway? I still pondered that thought. I love him and didn't want Sierra to not be around her dad. I didn't want to picture him with someone else. When Bill is being mean to me, it just puts me back to that little runaway girl. So, I put up with it until I get tired of being tired. Right now, is not the time because our baby will be due in three to four months. I walked and felt the smile on my face, but my thoughts kept racing in my mind.

Then I saw Clarence talking to a woman at his door. Which was strange, because I never seen any women over their place or seen her before. I smiled at them saying hi to her and Clarence. I believed in always extending that respect to the significant other. He invited me over and introduced her as Anjanet/Ajay. I remembered extending my hand to her while saying it was nice meeting her. She reluctantly extended her hand with a slight smile. When our eyes meant it just confirmed the bad vibes of who is this. In my mind, I wanted to say I'm not your threat. I kept it moving while pulling the wagon behind me. Not turning or looking back. I felt her eyes slowly watching me, but I hope she could see that I am not her threat. I have no interest in another headache. I opened my door to silence not turning back to see if her eyes were still following me. I felt like her eyes were moving but her head didn't turn.

The day is still short, and I still had some me time in my quiet apartment. After talking with Courtney Diane and inserting words, woo me and baby are rather tired. So, I forced clothes into the same drawers they came out of and put the wagon back in Sierra's room. I laughed as I look around at the many clothes she left on her bed and floor. Squatting down to pick up the clothes was a little difficult but made me feel as if I was falling or tipping over. Although I felt like a tree falling and I should yell out timber. There she goes boomp. The pictures flashed back on Bill and her discussing the outfit she wanted to wear, and the outfit Bill thought was more coordinated. Which is funny, because Bill is not good at coordinating his clothes either? I looked at the bed and laughed at how Bill was playing rough with Sierra by throwing her on the bed and tickling her. They did have a beautiful father and daughter relationship. I couldn't take that joy from her or him. I just would have to suck it up and make us work. Going back to Oakwood was not an option I wanted to fall back on. I go into the kitchen and make me a nice cup of coffee grab my magazine, and just glance through like I did when I was at the clinic thinking, I had indigestion then later went for prenatal care humph indigestion. I slowly glanced at the pictures realizing that I was really bored so now its time to turn on the television. So, I can look at it and it look back at me. Thinking how nice it would be sitting here with quiet time with Bill and maybe him rubbing my back or massaging my feet and maybe me rubbing his back too.

Just some intimate time like and how we used to spend minus the massaging feet, but that sure sounded good. I might glance at television while revisiting old memories, but it would be just a matter of time that I will fall off to sleep because my child is kicking and we both need to rest. The way this baby is moving I just know she or he is going to be very athletic because it is nonstop ping pong playing, running, moving and everything in that confined space called my stomach and it always happened at night.

I just hope tomorrow when we go to our appointment that there is only one baby and no hidden surprises. Now I can feel the anxiety Naomi had about bearing twins. That can be nerve racking and scary at the same time. Not to mention the accelerated emotions and my baby playing tennis in confined space. My baby feels my thoughts and starts back playing tennis and getting ready for a track meet at the same time. For some reason, I felt I was further along than the doctors told me. There is just too much movement, more movement that I could remember with Sierra. As my baby kicks, we slowly fall off to sleep to be awakened by Bill and Sierra. I wake up to see them both smiling down at me and Sierra giggling. It brightens my day at just looking at them and the love we are all feeling. They brought dinner home which was a surprise. I just hope I can eat it. It smells good, but the smell starts to make my stomach a little queasy and I jump up and run to the bathroom. What's that word to earl, humph? Sierra laughs saying mommy runs fast. She sounds so cute, but I felt yucky.

Bill did what I thought he would do go by Michael and Melba's to pick up Michelle and Mickey to go to the park and run around. It sounds like they had more fun than I thought they would. Sierra comes to me after I leave from the bathroom hugging me and saying I love you mommy. It sounded strange because she normally calls me Rita. We always have this conversation about calling me Rita and not mom. We go into a debate at her small age about why she should call me mom and not Rita. It's funny to this day we still have the same debate. When I remind her, we both laugh but she still calls me Rita. I don't know if she was afraid to call her dad Bill but for some reason, I never ever heard them debate about Sierra calling her dad, Bill. I get Sierra ready for her bath as Bill put his feet up and relaxes on the couch. I replayed that thought of us sitting together just enjoying our quiet time. Sierra rambles on about the fun she had all day and the rides she went on. Her vocabulary is getting much better. I work hard at trying to understand her words. If I didn't understand she made sure to try and make me understand. Sometimes when she looks at me a certain way, I wish I could understand what was going through her mind. Sierra still has energy after getting out the bath tub, so we go and sit with Bill relaxing on the couch. She jumps on his lap and I trid to snuggle next to him, but for some reason he is not feeling me. If I said something, he would blame it on my racing hormones they call it being sensitive. I know I can be a little emotional and it's not because I want this. I try to control it, but I do know when my feelings are hurt. Although I smile through the rejection I am feeling, it doesn't stop the pain. Inside I am feeling lonely, fat and rejected.

Sierra says she had fun at the mall. Hmm that is something that Bill left out. I asked Sierra what you did at the mall. She said it so quickly that Bill didn't have a chance to respond. I saw a lot of big girls that fed me and played games with me too. Before I could ask what were thier names. Bill hugs Sierra giving her kisses and she starts laughing and lose all thought and mind about what I had asked. I started wondering what is at the mall that sends him there so much. Why didn't he mention it or at least try and play it off? Who were these women that were en-tertaining my daughter? I just abruptly get up looking back at Bill saying to Sierra it's bedtime. She whines a little because she wants to stay with up with Bill. I insist that it is time and Bill re-enforces me. As I carry Sierra, I feel the pain of who is it this time? Am I going back to that thought of being replaced again while being pregnant? The only difference is Joel is not outside looking at me getting thrown out of Bill's grandparents place. I tuck Sierra in her bed she hugs me and inside my soul just melts. She asks in such an innocence way when you sleep does Sabrina sleep too. I look at her with a questionable look of who is Sabrina your imaginary friend. Nah she is my "scissors". Did she know what we were having before anyone else? I kiss her good night as she warms my heart and changes the chill I had going through my body when she mentioned the ladies at the mall. Inside I am fighting tears because I didn't want her to see me cry. I haven't cried in a while, but the pain has not ever left me either.

It hurts to always second guess yourself and wonder what is going on. Again, Rita how can you fight against something that you don't know what you are fighting. Why do women want what you have and can't find their own man? Why are some men so weak when it comes to what Robin and Courtney Diane calls tricks? If the trick is dangling a carrot, (in form of her ass in front of you to catch), then try another vegetable, idiot. What a waste, just a selfish waste on both parts at someone else's expense. Why are there so many games out there which keep you from having a wonderful relationship or marriage that you seen on television or dream of when you were little girls? There is always something out there just ready to take your joy because they think they can or it's their right. Why should they care about you if your significant other doesn't give a damn? I had a good me day just to have it end in tears. I go to bed listening to the television playing as I tried to fight back tears. I find myself trying to switch my emotions, so I can cry and go to sleep at the same time not making a sniffing noise. The baby is restless, and sleeping is becoming more difficult. I wait for Bill to come in and keep me company. I just want him to hold me and let me lay my head on his chest and we both fall off to sleep. The sleep evidently came but Bill didn't. I tossed and turned to wake up to see him sleeping soundly on the couch with the television watching him. I tried to wake him up by calling his name with no response. I go to the hall closet and a quick glance at the wall and I see that small blue mark. I flashed back to that night and emotions set in as I opened the cabinet door and pulled out a blanket to cover Bill.

I feel so lost, lonely, and so confused. Where is the love we had? Is it lost, and I wasn't informed? My insides fluttered into a worrying within worrying. I still loved this man, but I honestly had to admit I don't think he loves me anymore. What should I do? He hasn't hit me in a while only the belittling and cussing. Although, I thought I had become immune to his words. They still penetrate enough to hurt and sometimes that pain lingers and slowly fades away. I had just lied to myself because it did hurt and when I had mental down time it would surface back and remind myself of the words and the pain I felt. I move slowly down the hall and place the blanket onto Bill and turned down the hall glancing again at the small blue spot as I entered into the quiet lonely bedroom. I lay in the bed clutching and holding the covers as if it is a comforter for me. I stare out into the darkness wondering will I feel the warmth of love from Bill or will I continue to be his filler when he needed attention. I felt and wondered when will this end?? What was wrong with me that sometimes I feel like he just straight out hates me and just tolerates me. Does he tolerate me because I'm Sierra's mother and this is a package deal? Am I some type of bargaining tool for Bill? This just didn't feel right, and it just wasn't fair. I felt deeply I deserved better, but I just didn't know how to act on it or what move to make.

Here I am mentally alone and away from my family. I have people I talked to, but it is not the same, and fear sets in on how they would look at me, and if Bill found out what would be my consequences. I lay there just staring as the tears rolled down my face with no sounds just tears. I wondered what would have happened if I took the seat with the nerd in the library and not Bill. He pursued me, and he did ask. I didn't have to chase anyone they came after me. I didn't realize how much I had it going on until I lost the confidence, I had in myself. Remembering and reflecting on old boyfriends and other potential suitors. I wasn't looking for Bill when he found me, I was just minding my own business trying to get ready for an exam. All Bill did was talk in which it really kind of annoyed me. Maybe that was it?? Bill liked and wanted the chase of me or had been checking me out and I didn't know or feel his presence. We would talk I would tell him that if we didn't make it, he would move out and someone would move up and we will grow old with someone else. I can't believe I had a lot of confidence then as for now hmmm nope. As I think about it, I wanted to grow old with Bill. I wanted to look across the kitchen table and look at him and reflect on our life together and the joy and pain we experienced. I wanted us together to see our grandchildren grow and compare them to our children. I wanted us to spoil the heck out of them and send them back home only waiting eagerly again to repeat the spoil part again. I wanted laugh with him and look into his eyes and see the love I used to see.

I stared into space with so many thoughts of what could or would if only I. What is he doing and with what? I stared until my eyes drew weak from staring and my thoughts tired out and the baby went into their own snore. Eventually the thoughts wore out and the brain grew tired and I fell off to sleep in a bed with one less body, no weight to balance this bed. My thoughts just tired out and it was just time for me let those thoughts wander off somewhere and bring them back another time. So, after I gave in and tried to relax into a sleep, I didn't feel coming. I woke up the next morning not smelling bacon or the aroma of fresh baked biscuits. I looked over at the couch and the blanket that kept him warm is now thrown on the floor. I looked at the kitchen counter and the keys were gone. What happened between last night or yesterday and today that he couldn't kiss me good bye. My mind drifts in maybe he had plans. My father would always say a courtesy kiss my butt is better than nothing at all because at least I'm being acknowledged. Hmm that was how I was feeling a courtesy sure would have felt better. I picked up the phone to make sure there was a dial tone and by golly it sure was. I know I am not his mother, but I am his wife, some respect should come with this marriage. It's called vows in which if I remember correctly that we both were standing at the altar. I am so tired of this guessing game with Bill. I argued with myself. Asking, well Rita what you are going to do?? My response was nothing but flexing your nostrils adding that it felt good uh. I had to laugh at myself, because I thought about what Leeler/Lene said about her family talking to themselves and getting mad at the answer. I almost fell for it. I almost got mad at my own answer now that is some cuckoo nonsense.

Just keeping the thought of what Courtney Diane would say now that's just my opinion on the cuckoo. Well it's Sunday morning and the sun is always shining in southern California. Today will be a good day. It's a good day to go for a walk and Sierra's wagon is ready for the journey. With a hearty breakfast and some sandwiches to go and we will spend the day enjoying the warmth of the sun and the breeze from the wind. We were on the road like Thelma and Louise in an adult and preschool version? As I glanced out the window, I see a familiar face. I had to focus so he does live here. I see the actor Darryl Alan wow he does exist. I smiled at him and cracked the door open to just say hi. He glances at me with a smile that looks like my dad's, but I know he is not related to me. He approaches me with his hand stretched out with a big wide smile and big bright eyes that greets me. Wow he is smiling at me. I'm not star struck type person, but he looks just like he looks in the movies. I can't believe that I'm seeing him in the flesh. His voice was deep and he's slimmer and handsome. Funny he looked more muscular; I guess it must be true that cameras add a few pounds.

Darryl Alan smiles telling me that he heard about me from his cousin Keith and roommate Clarence. He talked how they lived in the mid-west area and that Keith and Clarence parents moved around. Somehow, through their travels they managed to stay in touch with each other. Darryl claps his hands together as he flashes what seems to be his nature big smile. Now, where is your daughter Sierra that everyone just loves her to death. Keith is always talking about what he baked for her, and he loves sharing recipes with you. I love his baking too can't you tell as he rubs his stomach. We both laughed as he excused himself. He said that he had just finished his tour of being on the road for about a year. The play lasted longer than anyone had anticipated and he just looking forward to relaxing and enjoying Keith's cooking. He rubs his stomach smiling saying that he made room for his cooking. He laughed through his smile and said that he just wanted to lie in his own bed and stretch out his arms and legs. It sure feels right being back home. I'm on a little break and will see or talk to you later. He seems normal and nice. Wow different from what I've seen or thought Hollywood actors would act. As I watched him leave, I wondered why he lives with roommates and not one of those big Hollywood homes I hear so much about.

Right when I lose that thought I hear some heavy brakes. I turnaround and look at the moving truck pulling up and a little boy jumps out the front seat with an older man. I looked at him and smiled saying hi and he looks at me and smiles but said something I quite didn't understand, with a strong accent. I guess they must be moving into the downstairs apartment across from us. It sure would be nice to see some young children around Sierra's age so she can have someone to play with. Courtney Diane might be moving and there is already a vacant apartment next to her. Hmm I wondered if that one is rented as well. I check on Sierra and she is still sound asleep. Her snoring sounds as if she worked at least four jobs. The last time Sierra slept that hard was when Bill's parents, Phil Richard and Naomi visit wearing her out. They were making use of the time they could share with her, even when she went to sleep. Every time she tried to sleep, they would wake her up. Sierra was more tired than Bill and me. I enjoyed their visit it was just too short and not often as we would like to see them.

Phil, and Bill were playing basketball and Phil Richard sprained his ankle but still had energy for Sierra. Even thou Phil fussed through his pain he still managed to joke and laughed with us. Naomi was concerned about Bill constantly giving out orders having me do one thing after another without completing the first task he requested. Well not too much has changed. Let me see I remembered I saw a little drug store that might be a good walking distance that would be a good and new adventure for Sierra. I saw it when Robin had taken me on a tour around the area. I really did enjoy the time we spent and hope someday we can do it again. Bill has given me a little more freedom. This would be a good day for that and help me keep my mind from crazy thoughts that would not end up favorable for me. Now that Bill has given me an allotment, I have some bills and not change. I would take the bus but being a Sunday, it will take too long between buses. I still wondered where was Bill, and why he didn't leave a note. I looked all over the house for some type of note and the phone is still working. I don't know how many times I picked up that phone in a twenty-minute period. Its similiar to opening an empty refrigerator, to see if the contents have changed in a twenty-minute time frame. I want to make phone calls back home because I'm missing my family and friends. I had to discipline myself or another phone will be disconnected again, and I really really didn't want to hear Bill's mouth or give him any ammunition to go off or use that psychological warfare that he thinks I'm not familiar with. The only things I don't understand is the office hours and I will find out just don't know where to start. Either way I would be the one effected by whatever I do or say. Just great whatever I say or try to do Bill will be one step ahead of me.

I checked on Sierra one more time and this time I see the almond shaped eyes staring at me and just blinking without a word. I asked if she was hungry and she smiles and nods her head yes. Sierra wasn't really a television person she enjoyed playing with her puzzles and toys. She did like looking at television with us or her dad, small exception to her rule. She was a daddy's girl. Looking at her just warms my heart and I wish she could stay this age forever and she still looks like Bill ug. I asked the dreaded question of what she wanted to wear. Ug again was my thought because this could take forever then add more time. Her response was I don't know, let me tink about it she smiles and looks at me out the corner of her almond shaped eyes looking up and says Rita. Here we go again good grief. I sometimes pleaded with Sierra, to stop calling me Rita. Her response as always everyone else calls you Rita why can't me. No Sierra it's I. She laughs you're silly why would you call yourself Rita, Rita, Reeeeeta or can I call you Reeree. Thinking back when she used to call me mommy it was just like the way she was saying Reeeeeta. She would wake me up by saying mommy, mommy mommy, and momee. I would respond what what, what, what real fast. I laugh now, and it was funny then too. To this day, we still talk about why she should call me mom. No way. Ooh Sierra let's just pick out something. We both laugh because this would be an all-day event between picking out clothes and trying to convince her to call me mom. I hope this little one will not follow her sister's foot steps on calling me Rita. They just don't know how hard I worked to hear the words mom or mommy or mama something that sounds close to it other than Rita.

Breakfast is ready, and I tell Sierra after we eat, we are going for a ride. She says will that lady ride with us again. I say to her what lady. The lady dad told me not to tell. Tell what Sierra, my heart stops and resumes at a faster pace. I don't know. I found myself stuttering asking a little girl, where did you see this lady and when. The mall silly, we played games and I ate and ate and played and played I had fun, fun, fun, fun, fun. I asked was your Uncle Michael there. Sierra not knowing the confusion she is causing answer with no it was just dad and Sierra. What about the lady?? She says what lady. Come on now Sierra I thought this is not the time to go back to nursey school. I tried to pry more information out of her and she wouldn't budge. I guess with her attention span she just forgot and was ready to go on our adventure.

I try to shake my mind of what lady and what she looks like. This is my family and my daughter, nothing will ruin our day. We clean up the kitchen laughing with very little small talk. I wash, and her little hands rinsed off the dishes and place them in the rack. We made some sandwiches for lunch for our new journey. I watched her small hands spread the peanut butter and jelly with such concern about not making a mess. She's growing up and that feels good too. Watching her establish her independence makes room for her sister/brother. I try to conduct myself as if I didn't hear her ask about another lady going us. Should I ask Bill and if I do how will I ask without getting my butt kicked. After all, tomorrow, we will be going to check on our baby and find out what we are having. I sure hope it is a boy I know Bill is hoping that he has a son, so he can pass his name on. I pondered the thought of what is happening at the mall. When I go, I don't see any military men or girls hanging out. Silly Rita you don't see them because you go during the week in the morning. I laugh oh yeah right, duh Rita. Sierra laughs why are you biting your thumb does it taste good? I hesitate on responding because I'm still thinking about this lady. I stuttered on my answer oh no, no Sierra; mommy is just thinking that's all. Actually, I just had part of my thumb in the corner of my mouth. I just was in deep thoughts. Sierra looks at me with such concern asking, thinking about what mommy and what your thumb taste like. I looked at Sierra with a short laugh because she snapped me out of that far away thoughts. Does it taste like candy I like candy? No, Sierra mom didn't mean to bite her thumb. She says it's okay Rita, Rita, Reeeeeeeta. I look at her really Sierra and I run over to her and just tickle her while we both laugh with me saying Rita, Rita, Reeeta, Sierra, Sierra, Sieeeeera. Our laughter fills the room as we prepared for our adventure.

Right before we leave, we hear a frantic knock on the door. I look at Sierra and say I wonder who that might be. She looks at me and hunched her tiny shoulders and says I wonder who at the door. We had to go see huh. I look out the window to see Keith smiling with something in his hands. He smiles and says good morning I made some cookies that I kind of threw something together tell me what you think of them. Sierra and I looked at each other as to say why not?? We bite into the warm big cookies that were good and a taste I never tasted before. I told Keith now this is a new taste cookie and Sierra says Mr. Keith this is a big yummy cookie. He smiles and blushes at the smile time. Keith was and probably still is a good baker and cook. I told him that he missed his calling and what are going to do with all those recipes. He throws his hands up I never really thought about it, this is something I love doing. I told him I finally saw Darryl. Keith said yeah Darryl came in there looking in the fridge wondering what I had cooked, and he was famished and wanted a home cooked meal and some much- needed rest in his own bed. I agreed with him. I guess it is a lot of work acting and traveling. Don't let him fool you he loves it. That was something he had wanted to do since we were kids. Hey, I didn't know you guys were related. Yep we are real cousins his father and my father are brothers making us first cousins. Darryl lived here, and I needed a change of scenery and he offered me a place to stay. Clarence is from Chicago too. He moved here for the same reason. Wow that must be nice to be here with your family and childhood friend. I miss mine. The only family I have is what's inside my place and I don't have too many friends. At least ones I can hang out with or come over and visit.

A voice inside said Rita stop right there before he figures out that you are on restriction or some type of Bill's house arrest. I'm only on temporary escape because he left the keys in the door. I had the fear of Bill coming home seeing Keith not knowing if he was in the apartment and was just leaving. Fear was there but laughter had to be added to help me through this. Hee hee just a thought, now Keith probably thinks I'm crazy. I snapped back, and Keith looks at me in an ah expression. So, you don't have any family. Nope, just what you see, Bill and Sierra and the new one on the way. So, when I do go out and people get me confused with someone else, I have an easy answer I'm not from here, I didn't go to school here, and I have no family here. Keith smiles do you have time to talk I need to talk to you about something. I told him I had to get a raincheck because Sierra and I are going on an adventure. He looks at Sierra and says where you are going. She giggles and says on an adventure. I want to do this run while I still have the energy and strength. Keith smiles and says I will see you later and for you Sierra later gator. She looks at him and just smiles trying to understand what he just said and responds only with gator.

I nervously chuckle but the insides knew that I needed to go. My thoughts shiver because not knowing where Bill might be, I just didn't want him to pull up seeing Keith at the door. That was the unspoken rule. No company allowed especially men, ooh no, no, no thank you. I say to Keith that we had to go, now please. I didn't even want to think about what might happen. The hits/beatings from Bill had slowed up and I don't want to feel that type of pain. Not today or any of my tomorrows. Today the sun didn't stay away, and the day was clear. We load up the wagon and start walking. Well at least one of us was walking. Sierra is enjoying the new surroundings from the view from the wagon and not the bus. For some reason, she is pointing out everything as if it was for the first time. We would stop so she could pick up leaves, pine cones, flowers whatever caught her attention. The wagon was filling up but still room for her to be comfortable. We pass many apartment complexes and some homes up for rent. Hmm living in a house again sure would be nice. We wouldn't be too far from the complex and still in familiar area. Bill might go for it offers more room for Sierra and the new baby to play. Although our three bedrooms will work for now, I just want a backyard to enjoy.

Funny how your child has timing on how just to make your day or moment at the time you need, and not knowing you needed it. We pass by a little drug store or corner store that I didn't notice before. We go onto the main street making various turns as I try to remember how to get back. Sierra sits up and lays down in a relaxing way just really enjoying being out in her wagon and not walking. She didn't know that in her little world she was feeling the breeze of freedom. I guess I was her chauffeur for the day. I hear her describing everything around her as she asks if I seen it too. I pause every now and then because with the baby weight has placed more weight on my feet. We find a park with swings, slides, merry-go-round, really the works. I didn't know this place existed, and it's not crowded. Then a duh comes through maybe because it is too early, or this is a hidden secret. When Sierra sees the swings and slide, she can't decide on which one she wants to get on first.

As she takes short steps toward the slide she then pauses and turns toward the swing she shows her indecisive side. I laugh and ask well Sierra what are you gonna do. She turns her head from side to side looking at the slide and swing. In the back of my mind I want to help her but paused so she can make her own decision. She huffs and sighs and runs toward the slide. I had an idea that she would go there first, but it had to be her decision. Her little legs climb up the stairs with a smile and carefully holding onto the rail as she climbs. Once she hits the top, she yells look at me watch this. As she slides down, I hear the wee and the wind rush by her as her little body goes down the long slide. She hits the bottom and runs around to the steps again to repeat the long slide ride again and again until she had it down pack on different ways to slide down. Sometimes she would hold her hands up in the air, sometimes she would go down backwards or sliding down on her stomach. I enjoyed looking at her creativity in the makings. When I saw her energy slowly going down, I suggest that we pause or take a break for lunch. She leaps at that and we go by a tree with a blanket and sit down and eat the peanut butter sandwiches she made along with the cookies Keith baked for us. Everything was great. We smile at each other as we bite either into the sandwich or cookies saying yummy, yummy yummy for our tummy. Sierra licks her lips for the yummy song. As we laugh and enjoy our lunch I look around as the families start arriving to the park and they look like complete families. Both parents laughing as they watched their children run toward the play park equipment.

Sierra pauses long enough to notice that some of the children are around her age and wants to go to the swing where majority are playing. She runs I just try to walk as fast as I could to keep her in view. She looks at the little girl around her age and jumps in the swing next to her just smiling and not saying a word. The little girl smiles back, and their communication and understanding are established through their childish smiles. Sierra in her excitement yells push me mom. Oh, now its mom I laugh as I pushed her not too high. I still love going to the park I miss not being here with Bill. I am still wondering what happened to my husband today. I hope he is okay now I am concerned that something might have happened to him. Who do I call? I have no one to contact that he works with and if I did, I would be too afraid that they would tell Bill I was calling around.

I look at the father pushing his daughter and the mother looking on and watching their other kids run around as she prepares a small picnic lunch. I look at the father playing Frisbee with his children and their dogs. It was just a pleasant sight and enjoyable moments being shared. It makes me think back to when our family used to go for rides with no destination just ride. My sisters and brother would pile in the car ready to go without a care. Then we might pull over to a park or get some ice cream and go back home. We played games in the car like slug bug or reading out of town license plates. Sierra was enjoying playing with all the children at the park having so much fun. I'm enjoying the laughter and the atmosphere that time somehow just got away from both of us. We both missed our nap time. When I noticed, her rubbing her eyes I knew it was getting close to time to go. I watched her fight sleep as she was really enjoying the slides, swings and her new temporary friend. They played and followed each other as if they have known each other for years. What seemed like a few hours end up consuming the whole day it was time to start back so Sierra could take her quick nap and I can get dinner ready? As we prepared to leave Sierra fusses a little because she doesn't want to leave her new-found friend. They say their good byes as Sierra slowly falls into the wagon as her new friend waves until Sierra is out of her sight and she runs toward the slides. Sierra talks about the fun she had on her adventure ride. She wants to do it again tomorrow I just tell her we will see. As I pulled the wagon Sierra slowly cuts back talking and her words slowly fade away, because she is so tired, she falls asleep. The walk for some reason feels a little longer because I didn't have my riding buddy to talk to.

I pulled up to the apartment seeing our car, so Bill finally made it home. As I put my hand on the door something other than my child inside of me feels funny. Something is not right but I don't know what it could be. I don't know if it is nerves working, fear of not leaving a note for Bill, the place not being clean enough, or coming home too late. Fear is trying to invade my soul and rob Sierra and I of a good day of adventure. After all it wasn't me that left without saying good bye or not leaving a note. I guess I'm brave on the other side of this door. What waits for me on the other side of this door? Why am I trembling inside? After all I live here too. I opened the door not knowing if I should smile or show no emotions. My thoughts are racing, brain is aching, and my baby is shivering. I turn the knob with slow hesitation just go inside and get it over with regardless of what might happen. It will be over soon, and joy will come in the morning. I open the door to see Bill looking at me with no smile and no emotions either. What could I have done with him not being home? I slowly pull the wagon into our apartment with Sierra is soundly sleeping away. I parked the wagon by the kitchen and pick her up to put her inside her bed. My actions and movements are slow, and my heart is pounding harder than my thoughts and fears. As I walk out, he asks about our day.

Was this a trick question? How can I respond without wondering if I might get slapped? He kissed me on the cheek which gave me a sigh of relief. It didn't hurt, wow that actually felt good, now that is a strange feeling for my cheeks. Once nervousness left a breath of fresh air entered my lungs and thoughts. I said she had fun at the park that is not too far from here and we had a picnic lunch. She met a friend and played hard and long. She enjoyed her adventure ride just like the fun she had yesterday with you and some of your friends. Inside I said oops, you done it now. Bill turns as looks at me and said what friends. Bill eyes turn smaller saying in a stern tone that they went with her Uncle Michael and his children to the mall. I laugh nervously and short. When his eyes go smaller that is the warning sign, but right now I choose to ignore. My thoughts became bolder, thinking liar. Sierra said she met a lady and that you and her were laughing and playing games. Bills voice and tones changes as his looks I remember all too well when it is getting ready to happen. I humble down with saying that she was just talking about her day. Sierra was just only trying to share her day. My mind is racing and trying to get the words right before this psychological warfare sets in. Ooh recovery Rita my thoughts laugh but don't push it. How do I recover quickly enough to get that smile back on Bill's face?

I'm thinking, I'm thinking. Bill voice echoes asking was I trying to question Sierra to see what she would say? Why would you involve her in such I heard blue skies? It happened so fast and I just feel myself holding onto the couch trying to lift myself up off the floor. All too well of the feeling of pain that rushed from my cheek to my spirit. I didn't make the humbleness come fully enough for a quick recovery. I guess that kiss on the cheek was a temporary distractor. I don't remember being hit, I just felt pain on the side of my face and it's burning yet numb at the same time. I didn't make any noise as the tears rolled down my face. Although, my face feels still numb I feel water on my neck going down to my chest and that was when I realized it was my tears. Come to think of it I never made noise when he hit or jumped on me. Just keep quiet Rita because if you start crying or make a noise the hits would last longer. It somehow became par for the course. I know all to well the routine. I grab my first aid kit, in form of an ice pack or cold wet towel. The bible says weeping may endure for the night and joy will come in the morning. I just wondered when my morning will come. Maybe the morning will bring sunshine through a rainy day.

I pick myself up trying to balance myself on the edge of the couch. Bill didn't help me up and the baby feels okay. I get up go to the cabinet and pull out a face-cloth and go into the bathroom and run cold water on the towel to place on my face. Kinda routine I should just leave an extra facecloth on the bathroom counter for just in case. As I fold and roll the cold wet washcloth I slowly place on my face and eyes. I looked at myself in the mirror and watch my youthful face fade away. I wipe my face slowly looking, staring, glazing at a soul that is confused and growing tired. I mentally have a question for Bill and I'm just wondering how he can do this especially while I am carrying our child. My thoughts reflected on when I didn't notice Sierra sometimes would be standing there and her words were soothing to my ears and soul as she asks about her scissors Sabrina. That puts joy where pain is. There goes that song I heard when I first moved here. I hear the door open and close without a bye or I when he will be back. Hmm was that the reason for the cheek greeting another way to exit. I leave out of the bathroom wondering what I did this time. An answer came mentally back with the same thing last time nothing that I am aware of, just because hmmm. I check on Sierra and she is sound asleep. I open the refrigerator looking up and down on what to cook. I stare so hard my vision loses focus and the contents become a blur. My mind is resting because it has become numb again along with my feelings. I see water on the ground and realized it was the tears flowing still from my face. I didn't feel the tears due to the numbness on my face. Why does this man hate me so? Who or what am I competing against? Why should I cook for someone that might not come home or might not want anything to eat? Lately my dinner meals weren't up to his standards nor were my looks, shape, or walk. Wow with so much did I breathe right or was that too noisy.

It's funny but not ha-ha how I would sometimes replay Bill's hurtful words. He would fuss and talk about my cooking when we first married, and I tried so hard to improve my culinary skills. I never told him I was a cook or gave him that impression. He should remember most of the time we ate out. At least in my mind I thought I was trying. No credit for effort, huh. Who is he comparing me to now; again, who am I competing against? My body and mind are tired so tired I'm just going to lay it down and just let my thoughts put me to sleep again. I have a doctor's appointment tomorrow should I prepare for a long bus ride or a quick ride without my husband. I lie down and just talk to my baby, just like I did with Sierra. This night my baby and Sierra had mercy on me and just allowed me to sleep and get the much-needed rest. Sometimes you don't realize how tired you are and mentally drained can wear you just like physical exertion. I had them both and I slept soundly. I thought I was dreaming Bill holding me like he used to. It's been kind of hard with the baby and sometimes Bill just didn't. It had gotten back to the point where I had to ask permission to either touch him or put my fingers in his hair.

When he would lie in my lap, I wanted to rub his back or hair for fear of taking our cuddle time away. I felt a warm body next to me I thought I had wanted it so much that I was dreaming and didn't want to wake up, because this felt so good. I could feel my body warming and combining with Bill to keep me warm as I rub my foot on top of his like we used to. This was my pacifier for falling asleep. He would laugh and say go ahead and I would put my fingers in his hair. I love us snuggling and I wanted my husband back. I slowly lay my head on his chest founding my imprint like a pillow and rub his feet with my foot and drift off as my nostril absorbs his scent. If this was a dream it felt so real and I wasn't going to open my eyes and lose my dream. To my amazement when I woke up it wasn't a dream Bill was actually lying next to me. It frightened me because it just happened without the bed moving and keeping me into my sound sleep. I couldn't tell what time he came home because I was really knocked out. I open my eyes slowly, so I can focus and capture this moment into my memory bank for later. He gives me a hug and kiss that just makes me melt and I have to focus again to make sure this is really real. My heart fills up and my eyes water as I feel the love for him and from him.

He says good morning and I need to get ready for our doctor's appointment. Sierra is already up fed dressed and ready to go. I shower, and dress and I am ready to go too. As we drive Bill tells me about the work load that increased when the soldiers returned, and they had to be processed. I was running late by falling asleep on that couch and had to pick up Hornsby and Wilbur on my way to work. Of course,

Captain Jesse and First Sargent Farrell chewed us out and we had to stay late, and I was already tired. I listened to him but really didn't hear him. I am enjoying the ride and looking in the mirror to see why Sierra is so quiet. She is enjoying her ride and the view too. Through our conversation, I never heard Bill say he was sorry about hitting me. I guess why say sorry if he didn't mean it. It's not like I don't have feelings. I hurt just like everyone else. We had no real conversation, which still left part of me just feeling numb and tired. For now, I'm just enjoying being in the car with my family. We arrive early and sit in the lobby with other pregnant women. One thing about military hospital sometimes its hurry up and wait or sometimes you are in and out. I guess it just depends. Doctor Jerome is in which is good seeing one of my regular doctors. He greets us with his gentle smile and shakes hands with Bill. He looks at me just a little different and extends his hand with a smile.

He says today is the day we know what we will be delivering. Sierra laughs I know her name is Sabrina. Bill looks at me Sabrina I just hunch my shoulders and smile with don't ask. We both smile, and he says that's all I need. I laugh another daughter for you to spoil or a son to hang out with. As Doctor Jerome and Nurse Evenlyn set everything up for the ultra sound we hear a stronger heartbeat and my blood pressure is doing fine. Just a little off course of my weight gain but I still have residual from Sierra. At least that is the excuse I'm using. As everyone looks at the ultrasound, Doctor Jerome says looks like it's a Sabrina. Sierra yells daddy my scissor Sabrina heart makes a loud noise. Bill looks at me with a smile and says I guess Sabrina will be coming soon. As the Doctor leaves, he asks Bill to come with him, so they can talk. I wondered what could possibly be wrong that couldn't be discussed with both of us. The door opens and I'm expecting Bill, but another doctor enters.

The times I have been coming to my appointments I have never seen her before. She stretches out her hand and introduced herself as Doctor Upesi. She was very petite with beautiful big eyes that twinkled and a big smile with perfect white teeth. I felt the warmth from her spirit which puts me a little at ease by her presence. She introduces herself and says one of her specialty is with women's resources and asked how I was doing. I'm puzzled because she passed my doctor and I heard them talking as they glanced at me, why would she ask me that question. Now what is really wrong, is my baby okay, am I okay?? Nurse Evelyn is keeping Sierra entertained while Bill is talking to the doctor unlike that flashback of that mean Nurse Rochelle from my first clinic visit. I chuckle inside that I know this isn't indigestion. She smiles and says I noticed a bruise by your eye and on your cheek. I guess in my haste to get ready I didn't notice any signs of bruising or any scars or any swelling. I guess the numbness did exist. Man, I'm in trouble now. Usually, I either wear my glasses or apply a little make up in that area. Oh, my God is that what they are talking to Bill about?? Now I am so scared of the consequences I will face in the car which will turn into a long ride home or what will happen when I get home. I told them sure

I'm okay I went to the park and not paying any attention the swing hit me in the face. I was unaware that it left a mark. It did hurt when it happened, but the pain went away, and I thought nothing of it. I hope they believed this performance. As I speak, I see the concern in her face as the smiles grows into words, I really don't believe you, but I am concerned. Rita, you are performing again work harder you need this Oscar. I thank her for being so concerned and that Bill and I are fine.

I try another distractor by asking would she be one of the doctors that might deliver our little girl. I laugh and try to distract her from my nervousness. She says she might we are on rotation it just depends. I felt the warmth of her concern and really wanted to talk to her and maybe she felt that too. She lingered around but she felt my apprehension and smiled leaving the room. It felt good that I had some type of adult conversation with a woman doctor. I wanted to talk to her, spill my guts out, but that was hard with Bill right outside the door. How could I tell her how I really felt? Did I miss my opportunity for a graceful escape from his actions toward me? She smiled and said be careful of the swings we want your baby to be healthy and you safe. I told her I will duck next time. She smiles yes you should duck, and you and your family enjoy your day. In my mind, it was saying you better learn to block and weave.

She carefully hands me a card, I quickly glance at it and put it into my flat purse. I try and smile while gathering my belongings more concerned about what awakes me outside this exam room. I walk out to see Sierra now playing with Bill and he is smiling at me. I look at him not knowing what expression I need to display. I know my heart is racing and my thoughts shiver at what Bill will say to me as we leave the viewing eyes. I asked are you okay and Bill responds with we will talk about it when we get in the car or home. I want to press it, but I know when to step back and put myself on time out with the questions and the looks. I dread getting in the car. I felt like I was going home and facing my father for coming home late. I tremble as if I was hearing the stool scooting back as my father sat on as I entered the house after being out past my curfew. Didn't want to get chewed out then and just like I don't want to get chewed out now. How was he hitting me be my fault and why should I take the blame for his anger or actions or being over worked. My heart races as I tried to hide behind a scary smile. Inside I am scared and crying. I hold Sierra's hand maybe for protection which is a silly thought. Bill is walking in front of me in his uniform and treating us like we are a friend of the family. One thing about him he did always wear that uniform well. Man, he looks good, still slim, with the bowlegs showing through the uniform pants. Why does this walk seem longer when you have butterflies flying and landing in your stomach and shorter when you are not paying attention to anything? I just want to enjoy the day with a moment of no thoughts no pressure. This is the first time I can remember having all these thoughts leaving the doctor's office. This is supposed to be a family moment a fun day.

Bill glances at us to make sure we are behind him. He slows up, so we can catch up with him. Oh, now he remembers we do still exist. He opens the door and places Sierra in her car seat and leans over me and gives me a kiss on the lips this time. Am I settling for crumbs again? My thought is another distractor to throw me off for the next coming attraction. He starts talking but Sierra jumps in pointing out the ducks walking around and the band aide that Nurse Evelyn drew a happy face on. She said she had fun at the doctors and wanted to do it again and asked if she can go to the park and see her new friend and swing. She excitingly yells out daddy you can see me slide down the slide! Bill laughs maybe next time daddy has to go back to work. While she is talking, I look back at her and glance at Bill to see if I can see what expressions he is showing. Maybe, I can figure out what type of mood he is in or know if I'm in trouble again. I really want to know and yet not want to know what the conversation was about between him and Doctor Jerome.

Curiosity is setting in, but my gut feeling tells me to take a time out on this one. What you don't know will ease your thoughts to something else. After all you are having another daughter now you can plan for her arrival. Now they can share rooms, clothes and Sierra can finally get the sister she wanted and play mate. I wondered what my daughter would look like maybe, me or another Bill again. When I was pregnant there weren't ways of knowing what you were carrying. I remembered I prayed for a daughter because my dad and Bill couldn't stand one another and naming them after one of them would be a big constant argument or just feeling uncomfortable all the way around. Other than finally giving birth the joy of seeing my daughter is a snap shot that is embedded not only in my mind but my heart as well. No one could have told me that I would be married, living in California and giving birth to not just one child but getting ready to have another one. I remembered joking about how many children I wanted to have but that was just kid talk. In the mid-west that was what we knew get married, work and have a family. I couldn't picture myself having nine like Catrice or coming from a family of twenty like her mother- in -law Anuna. Their family reunions and family gathering must be fun but where do you hold that amount of people. Now Catrice didn't mention too much about the other family and the number of children they had. I bet it would be fun, no one would be bored and the just seeing all those many generations in front of you is historic. Would I like to be a part of such a large family, I thought sure? I only have the family that lives in my home that will be increasing by one. I hope to see my girls grow up and Bill and I grow old together laughing and playing with our grandchildren, but for now I'm enjoying the growth of Sierra and her little sister. Wow I'm having another baby girl. I'm enjoying the ride and just look out the window at the scenery while listening to the little conversation from Bill and Sierra high energy of talking. This time I don't have to talk or hear any negative comments or criticism from Bill, and I can still enjoy my day with Sierra.

Chapter 18
It's Family Time

We pulled into Sierra favorite place, Del Taco where she loves the shakes and I can eat without feeling sick. We used to stop there a lot especially when I would pick up Bill. I can't believe she still remembers. Sometimes when we would drive by Del Taco, she would look at us as if we forgot to stop. She's happy and knows what she wants a shake and a bun taco just for her small hands. She tells her daddy that she wants to get out and play and jump in the balls. Bill tells her next time, daddy has to get back to work. Sierra laughs telling him that they will have a lot of next times uh daddy. He laughs and says yeah, we will. Mommy and Daddy will remember the next time. Going through the drive thru had me flash on how Clarence felt going thru the drive thru with his dad, Jerry. I didn't picture Jerry laughing a lot but had a sense of humor. I can see or hear it in Clarence and can only imagine that his brother Steve is probably the same way.

When Clarence said, he hugged his dad because he hadn't seen him in a while his dad responded are you done, and Clarence said he snapped back to reality. So, as Clarence and his dad go thru White Castle, Jerry asked for a cheeseburger and hold the cheese. Clarence responds to him do you want me to hold it in my hands? Jerry looked at him, oh you got jokes huh you a funny man now.? I'm cracking up as he's telling me, and I am tempted to say I want a quesadilla and hold the cheese. Bill would flip and probably say what the uck are you doing or you funny now huh. I just kept that thought to myself. Clarence telling the story how do you tell the person to hold the cheese and keep your dad happy and not be a funny man? He said that he had to think quickly and not piss off Jerry. So, he told the lady to wrap the burger in cheese burger wrapper. She looked at me like I was crazy all I could do was smile, (as he raised his eyebrows). Jerry got his cheese burger without cheese and Clarence said that he never took his ass back there.

I looked at Bill and smiled it was soothing hearing mommy and daddy because those words reminded me there was still an us in this picture. I asked him did he have office hours today. He gives me such a look, of what did you just say. I repeated it again not knowing I was doing a duh, office hours do you have to work late. Bill laughed as if this was a relief and heads up from Corporal Lewis and said no Captain Jesse or Officer Crain gave us a break while Lieutenant Preston was on leave. We are getting ready for our two-week training we do every year. I say oh yea I forgot about that as I smiled, but inside I'm thinking no I didn't forget that gives me a break. Maybe I might do what Robin does send them back to one of their grandparents for a week. Nah just a thought I would miss Sierra and her sister. I'm really going to miss her when she starts school, she is my heart and my life.

We placed our order and we are homeward bound. Food smelling good and no bus stop or waiting for one. The ride has a smell of freedom as I listen to the radio and what comes on? Maze's "Joy and Pain" and today no pain and the sun was shining. I rock to the music and Sierra laughs look at mommy smiling and rocking. Bill looks at me as I look at Sierra imitating me. We both laugh and Bill sings off key the lyrics and we all join in trying to say the words, but we are all off. I look out the window as we sing and just enjoy the scenery and being with my family. We took the long way home and this ride was one for the archives. Bill opens the door for me and unstraps Sierra and she jumps out of her car seat, ready to finish sipping on her shake. Bill takes my hand and it feels like it is shivering as he holds it. It has been a long time since we held hands. I guess that I was feeling the warmth from his hand extending to my hand and flowing to my heart and soothing my thoughts.

As we arrived the complex its quiet as usual no noise, no nonsense hmm just like enjoying coffee and the rain. We enter a clean apartment and no work is needed. Bill gives me a kiss and picks up Sierra giving her a big hug and kiss as he tells us he had to get back to work. I asked him what he wanted for dinner and he says don't cook I will surprise you. I smiled with a little twist oh surprise okay and I give him a kiss and he gives me a smack on my butt. From time to time he would smack me on my butt, and I would fuss at him about it, but lately I liked it and didn't know how much I had missed something I thought was annoying. There I go again savoring the crumbs of affection. I guess I thought it was a form of affection that I never saw my parents display and to this day I still haven't. I guess different people have a different way of showing affection. One of the things I always liked and still liked was when I would go to sleep, he would pull the covers over me and that would just warm my spirits. I snuggled in response to him covering me as if I was still sound asleep. Its funny I catch myself doing it to my children. While enjoying their peaceful expressions as they slept. I wondered if they felt the same warmth I felt. Hmm maybe I should ask them. They probably will look at me like I was crazy or that was a random thought. We go into the front room ready to enjoy our Del Taco feast and it's still warm and ready for us to savor every morsel.

While Sierra was enjoying the meal, her eyes were slowly closing. I knew it was time for nap and that sounds good idea for the both of us. We slept deep and long until I heard a loud panic knocks in series at door. It startled me as I tried to wake up out of a sound sleep, thinking I was hearing things. I thought it might be Robin since she is usually the only one home around this time. I glance out the window to an unfamiliar face with tears and fear showing. As I open the door, she introduces herself as Natalia she just moved in from Camp Zeist in a small town in Central Netherlands, (she said that they were Dutch), and she was wondering if I had seen her nephew Tim. She speaks with a strong accent as I tried to focus and understand what she is saying. I told her that we were sleep and my daughter hadn't been outside. She said Tim has a habit of playing hide and seek and he speaks very little English. My mother Eula, sometimes we call her Helen is frantic looking for him. I looked over at their apartment and see many people speaking a language that I'm not familiar with, looking through their apartment and outside calling his name. As Natalia talks an elderly gentleman yells out that we found him. She yells okay and tells me that is her dad Heinz. When she said Heinz, it reminded me of some type of steak sauce. I went to school with a Heinz, but I knew it wasn't him, but for that moment it made me homesick.

I remembered back to high school and how fine and quiet Heinz was humph. As we speak Clarence and Darryl walk up carrying groceries with Keith bringing up the rear. Five or ten minutes later Keith's sister Kymberlyn and cousin Paulette showed up with looked like cake boxes smiling speaking in between laughter and involved in their conversation. Momo is carrying sleeping Ryan, with Manly running toward the door. Momo yells for Amos to open the door. Robin runs into her apartment and passed us saying a quick hi to everyone holding her camera equipment. I figured she must be on an urgent assignment. One thing about this complex it is never boring, and everyone is always doing what comes so naturally. Natalia looks around as everyone is holding their own conversations but pausing to say hi. She excuses herself and says she hopes to talk to me again. I watched her as she walks away with a certain type of style. Natalia looks muscular, yet you know she is a woman. Her mother and dad were shorter than her and rather stocky and older looking.

I looked at the time and know Bill will be coming home and our night will be a family night. I looked through the guide to see what a good movie might be to go with our surprise dinner. I make sure the place is straight; floor spin and span clean, dishes washed and put up. Nothing left but the aroma of pine-sol. I cross my fingers that there are no distractions and no need for any type of argument, at least not tonight, because the place is clean. I wonder off and think back to that old nursery rhyme stick and stones may break my bones, but words will never hurt me. The words do hurt they can pop in at any time and linger into your thoughts. Then the words just go away, mysteriously pop back into that hidden corner. Funny how your mind can play tricks on you just have to learn how to work with mind tricks and stop it from driving you cuckoo. The clock is ticking, and my heart is racing. I always look forward to being with my family and spending every moment I can with my hard-working husband. Only if I knew then how hard was, he was really working. Time passes as Sierra wakes up playing with her puzzles and keeping to herself, no demands just chilling in a childlike way. I guess they have their me time in a childlike manner. I chuckle at that thought because it sounds so cute and yet so grown.

As Bill enters the door with bags of takeout food, I grab one of the bags smelling the aroma of fresh seasoning and hot temperature that is escaping from the bag. I reached in to grab some food out of the bag and not really paying too much attention I accidently grab two receipts. I'm puzzled, and I look at both receipts with a quick glance and tell Bill there are two receipts here. One with dinner meal and before I could finish, he snatches the receipt from me with such force and anger it totally throws me off. What just happened all I did was ask a question with no energy or thought behind it. He yells at me calling me nosey and his facial expression didn't show any type of I was just playing. It really startled me of his reaction and how mean was that. I asked him why he was so upset about a receipt I thought they might have either accidently put someone else's receipt in there or charged you for a meal you didn't get but paid for why so nasty. He struggles to give some type of answer that makes sense. My question was innocently asked didn't require a rude response. I didn't think he even knew how to answer. Now he has me thinking how he really heard about this restaurant. Something inside is telling me that it is more to just finding two receipts.

For that instance, how dare you talk to me in that manner? I look at him with no smile, no expression but ask why you would talk to me that way. He says he can talk to me any way he wants and that he is grown. I keep it going but I am the mother of your children and I didn't deserve that. Why did I keep it going and just let it go? Sometimes you just get tired of being talked to as if you and your feelings just don't matter. I do matter, and I do have feelings and that hurt. They penetrated my heart and soul. Being pregnant I have a bunch of emotions floating, moving, dancing, and talking all to me and in all ways working their way out at different times in different ways. Sierra must not hear his voice or the yelling because she hasn't run out the room to meet him. Maybe she has become immune in her own childlike way to the fussing of her dad at me.

I took a bold courageous stance. I leave him, the food, the attitude with the receipts and go into my room and turn on the TV. I walked fast so I wouldn't feel anything hitting me on the back of the neck or being snatched back because I spoke up. That ancestral strength made a strong cameo. I laughed as I lay on the bed as if he wasn't in the apartment. Laughing at commercials whatever popped on the screen. Today was not the day Bill wasn't going to ruin another minute. We had leftovers which I will enjoy better than that stinch of food. Bill didn't really like eating leftovers, but how could it be leftovers if you didn't eat any of it. Sierra and I will eat, or you can prepare your daughter a plate of that takeout food. Whatever happens he is just going to have to do it to this body laying down getting some rest. He walks into the room and I do what my mother taught me very well I just act as if I didn't hear him. I lay there laughing as if I didn't feel his presence or smell his cologne. Regardless to the fact he was only a few feet from me. In my mind, I say go back and continue your lunch, dinner or whatever or whomever you had it with. Was this dinner a cover up for something I really didn't want to know or even think about? It's strange how you trust someone and don't think about them being unfaithful. How those words that Robin said about Ramon somehow echoed in my mind and now my mind is alert. He stands in the door way I can feel his presence and I feel him waiting for me to say something. He was surprised by my act and actions. Actually, I was surprised by my actions too, did my ancestral strength kick in unexpectanly. The eyes I loved gazing into sometime would turn into piercing arrows trying to penetrate my soul. Well today the arrows from my soul and my eyes shot back a piercing look that deflected back to him. No piercing tonight Bill. The look my brother and I learned from our dad that would just sometimes send chills through your warm soul. That look surfaced to show Bill that I can stare too. My soul reached in and grabs for that quick second the pain the annoyance from his words and looks and moved me to this unexpected emotion. Maybe I just know for that moment I was tired and just didn't want to hear it. He turns around and goes into Sierra's room and she ignores him until he calls her name. I guess she is tired right now too. She must have kept playing with her puzzles because I heard him ask for a hug. Maybe Bill thought she want to take a break from putting her puzzle pieces together because daddy bought home some dinner. She goes down the hallway looking into the room and asked why mommy isn't eating with us. Bill responds that mommy and your little sister are resting.

I think to myself you are such a dumb ass, woo did I just sound like Courtney Diane. I better stop that word because what you may practice may become permanent and I need to stop it now. Although, it did feel pretty good coming up through my stomach and echoed off my ears. As I said it, I smiled and just didn't care what he said or thought. I do matter and so does my feelings. I lay there just thinking I need to be in there with my family this is about Sierra not Bill. Just when I was thinking about going into the front room, Sierra comes in with Bill carrying a tray of food, in the back of my mind I'm not in the mood to eat. She is smiling as Bill is helping her carry the tray. He looks at me and smiles as he kisses me on the forehead right now that doesn't work. I just looked at him displaying no type of emotions but thank Sierra for being a good helper and for bringing me dinner.

As I sit up Bill set the tray down and help with adjusting my pillows, so I can eat my dinner in bed. For that moment, I smiled at Sierra and thanked her again giving her a big hug and kiss. She laughs saying daddy helped, give him a hug and kiss too. Sierra big smile warms my heart as she acts as the peacemaker. I snarled at the thought and looked at Bill as if this was a hard request to grant. He responds yes mommy give daddy a kiss for being a good helper. I looked at him again with no emotions because I didn't find any humor in him. He reaches over to kiss me, and I just want to really punch him right in his throat or smash a pie in the middle of his face. Only thing if I went through with such an act, I better have a car running with the door open ready for me and Sierra to jump in and take off, with the only sounds of slamming doors and screeching brakes. Sierra jumps in the bed and Bill takes a seat on the other side ready to eat with us. In my mind, I picture myself kicking him off the bed, again if I did that car better be running. I tell Sierra that mommy is not very hungry, and she asks why. I told her that mommy just not hungry. She asks what about our movie and family time. I looked at her innocence of just want-ing her family time in which she does deserve. She doesn't need to see or feel the tension that I have right now. So, I give in and ask her what movie she wants to see. Bill looks relieved that I seem not to still be upset or mad at him. Only he doesn't know that I learned at an early stage in our relationship of how to be a good per-former. For that instance, I felt what I haven't felt in a long time the understanding that line of hate and love. I hope our love will not be interrupted by some nonsense that I didn't sign up for. There were only three people standing at the altar, Pastor Williams, Bill and old lucky me un huh.

Sierra and Bill picked some movies or a favorite program of Sierra. I heard the title, but my mind was so far away, and Bill looked at me with some concern. In which he should. Do I know what I have planned no, not really? Just at that mo-ment I had to re-evaluate what happened earlier. Could it have been an innocent mistake and he was mad about something earlier or was it even his receipt. Did these emotions over take me and I over reacted? Nah I don't think so. I think my radar is up and I need to really see what is happening, but for now I am not going to ruin tonight for Sierra because of her daddy. I look at Bill as if I am really study-ing him. He looks at me as if he knows and feels my anger and curiousity work-ing. I think for this instance he might have a concern and he should. I didn't have anywhere to go but I am not going crazy. Seen and heard about women having a nervous breakdown and I will not put myself with those statistics. He tries hard to be affectionate but sometimes when it convenient for him. Oh, now tonight I get more than crumbs, humph how long will that last. Although, it feels good this added attention and the softness of his lips kissing me. My insides were fighting at the same time melting into his touch. Then I had to think how long you are go-ing to be mad and this is more than crumbs right now. Well I said to myself it has him thinking and wondering what I am thinking. The abuse I suffered from him taught me how to not always show emotions. At the same time, I didn't know I was practicing some type of discipline. He created these feelings and I didn't know in time it would help me through a lot of situations. It really could be confusing on what emotion to display. If I was happy, Bill sometimes would just snatch the joy away, and if I was sad, he complained about me being sad. So, if I showed a poker face there was no way of knowing how I was feeling. Sometimes I would just think is this what I really wanted??

Did I want to live my life this way on a continuous basis in our marriage? Not knowing what performance or act will need a curtain call. My insides had a meeting and we agreed that sometimes I just wanted to be invisible. I found myself wondering is Bill less married and this might be too much for him. Is less married like being a little pregnant. I started having doubts about us, our relationship, and our family. Why, Rita are you still here? If he wants out why didn't he just say so instead of being so mean to me all the time?

He would discipline Sierra which wasn't often and was rarely mean to her. When it came to her cleaning her room that was where he put his foot down. He was a good loving father. He spent a lot of time with her playing and educating, and just showing nothing but fatherly love. Bill was good at continually building that daddy and daughter relationship. That is one thing I did like and mentally captured, was the father and daughter relationship they had. I hoped that same love/discipline would travel over to our other daughter. Then crazy thoughts of if, we make it that far the love/discipline will be with our other children. Bill has his own way in trying to make up for being so mean. The words he said were hard to erase by just an apology. Does he really look at me as being nosey? How can he make that accusation, when I barely open my mouth out of fear of being hit, fussed at or cussed out? He tends to Sierra as I lay in the bed trying to calm down and not ruin the night for Sierra. He knew I was perturbed and highly pissed. No one has or will ever talk to me like that ever again. Maybe I should start living up to this name he gave me and start noisying around his pockets, dissecting phone bills and what does office hours really mean. When I find out I really can't say what I will do, but this has been bugging me for years.

Clarence and Keith have always tried to tell me something and insist that they need to talk to me. I think that it is hard for them to tell me, but they have been trying for years. Every time they tried something interferes or interrupts our conversation. I can only talk to them when I am outside, and Bill is not around. He usually gets mad when I'm either gone too long in the complex. Then he comes looking for me as if I didn't make it home at the time, he told me to be home. Bill isolates me from communicating with anyone really and especially with other men. I still remembered the beat down from that Thanksgivings that happened many years ago. Hmm this coffee needs refreshing just like nature needs to refresh itself to keep growing. Bill puts the food up and runs Sierra's bath water getting her ready for bed and read a story before putting her to sleep. All I know is that tomorrow I will take out, the take out to our local dumpster, because I refuse to eat this crap. I don't want it or what it could possibly represent and plus the smell just is not working.

I lay there flipping through the channels trying to relax my mind. Thinking of the flipping made me think about the flipping and flopping Momo always talked about ew, vision. I smile and reflected on Courtney Diane saying that I have to do some mindless task just to calm myself down to keep from punching somebody in the throat. A mindless task like by folding towels, something with no thought, no energy or no effort. Thinking back Courtney Diane might need some anger management classes, not online but in a classroom with a teacher and students ooh but I won't say a word to her about that. I guess my mindless task is channel surfing, until the channels are looking at me and listening to me snore. I don't remember what I was watching I just remembered Bill pulling the covers over me and I loved when he did that and then I felt the warmth of his body pressed against mine. It felt good and kind of ease the tension we had earlier with each other. One promised we have tried to keep but had been difficult was not going to bed mad at each other. We were the only family we had here, and we had to make this work and not look upon ourselves as failures. I do love him. I wouldn't have sacrificed my like if I didn't love him by giving birth to our children and left my comfort zone in Oakwood, to travel many miles in a no air-conditioned hot Vega. Oh, along with Bill occasionally fussing at me from Oakwood to California. He didn't know that inside I was hurting, missing my family and at some point, wanting him to turn the car around and take Sierra and me back to my home.

Occasionally, I think about where I would be if I didn't marry Bill and not move to California. I just lose my imagination and imagine being with someone that loves and cherish me and our family always doing family stuff and maybe traveling. Do what we do in Oakwood, getting together for family dinners and holidays. I would be growing old with my childhood friends, like Debbie Ann, Sharon Denise and Melody Lynn. I keep in touch with them, but I do still miss them. Wow Rita hard to realize it's thirty years later. I remembered when our parents used to put years on a friendship, and we would think wow they are old now look at us. Some friends I remembered names and some I remembered faces; time changes our looks and features for so many reasons. I've seen older relationships look happy and how the years have touched then through the test of time like the; Tarvers they had an understanding only they knew, Shepherds that have aged gracefully and lovingly together, Hollingworths that were so kind loving that when I gave them my graduation tassel you would have thought I had given them the world. I remembered how good that felt. That made me feel good inside to see and feel the warmth of love they had for each other and penetrated my young heart and soul. My childhood friends Melody

Lynn and Sharon Denise and myself we had our boys to men crushes. As we grew older the crushes did too, but Debbie Ann and Froggy oops Brian showed true long-lasting love. I was blessed to have a front seat. From grade school to so many years later they are still together through the trials and tribulation they have been married ooh long. When she developed a minor disability, and couldn't climb any stairs, he built a house no stairs just hand built with love. Brian designed and built their house with his own hands and time. Now that's love. I hope that Bill and I will make it through our trials and times like Debbie Ann and Brian.

Being out here in Oceanview I missed the opportunity to be hanging out with family, friends and living a mid-western type humble life. Seeing familiar face would feel so good out here no but nah that's slim to none in seeing any familiar faces. Well oops one time I ran into my high school classmate. He had joined the Marines and was stationed in Oceanview. I always thought he was cute, tall, and quiet and very smart another crush. Well, I remembered when I ran into him, I was with Bill. For that moment, I had a piece of Oakwood and I was happy to see a familiar face. I was so excited seeing a classmate and it felt so so good. Someone I went to school with and knew. I was excited about seeing him and overwhelmed with emotions. I guess Bill must have seen my excitement and the joy I had in embracing him. To me it felt like embracing an old friend. When I introduced him to Bill wasn't too nice, which made me feel uncomfortable but Bill for that moment or second wasn't going to take that joy from me. I felt Bill hold me tighter as I tried to move, and it felt good to know he was holding onto me and not letting me go. I guess that is like a dog raising his leg and marking his territory. Inside my mind was saying he really does love me, and he really wants us to stay together. I couldn't believe he felt insecure about a quick embrace to someone I will probably will never see again. I wondered if he had those thoughts when he is eating lunch or working late. Oops there you go again going too deep.

Maybe we will be that happy loving couple that will grow old together and laugh at our past indiscretions. Funny, how we fantasize about a perfect marriage and children when we're young. I didn't know that my life was going in so many different directions that I might need a road map. I should have read the signs along the road better. I wake up with Bill still holding me. I had to think was this the weekend, nah but what the heck, enjoy the embrace and don't say anything to ruin the moment you are so enjoying right now. I wiggled just a little to just let him know that I am waking up. He grabs me and kisses me on the back of my neck and my shoulder. Again, just feeling his lips felt so good and relaxing. Hmm he has never done that before but a change and out of order is okay. He did include the shoulder. Go with the flow Rita and indulged in the affections you love to receive from your hubby Bill. No more crumbs. I reach my arm around and grab his arm and it feels good to know he is here. In the back of my mind I just want to know why he is not at work, probably because I wanted to throw out that nasty take out. That figured good grief just had to spoil my game plan. Now, I got to think of something to get that food out of here. Okay at some point the performance will have to happen so no one will eat it and that way I don't even have to smell it. I yawn and said hmm in a soft voice, so you are spending the day with your girls. His response was, and you know it. I took a vacation day just to hang out and spend some quality time with you and Sierra. So, Bill my loving hubby what do you have planned for us today I smiled at him and he smiled back and said let's hang out and just be spontaneous. Un huh, I respond with a cute little chuckle and say that's what I'm talking about let's do this.

My wardrobe was very limited and the allotment that I received from Bill I use for household items and clothes for Sierra. So that leaves very little money for clothes for me. So right now, I made up for the lack of my limited wardrobe or shoe collections. My children call me a hoarder I call myself blessed to have the options to wear. I want and have clothes for every and any occasion. Whatever we do today one will be throwing away that take out. Sometimes you have to act fast even when you don't move fast. Today was one of those actions that I needed to do. Bill says why we don't heat up last night's dinner. I say hmm why not I go and open the fridge, and sniff one of the containers saying yuck this smells horrible. Sierra runs over and sniffs it and says ooh mommy it smells yucky and I'm not eating that!! I look at Bill with a half-smile and ooh this might be spoiled and proceed to dump all the cartons. It happened so fast before Bill could even grab one of the containers or just sniff to see what we were talking about. I said to him ooh babe get that smell out of here before that aroma fills this apartment. Ooh I feel like I'm going to earl. I motion to move that container as Sierra holds her nose saying pew. Sierra backs me up with daddy it stinks, (as she fans her nose). She looked so cute Bill could only look with hesitation and no speed in getting that smell out. I really didn't want to put my daughter in a lie, but I just couldn't stomach that food and who was there when he purchased it.

Bill says oh well let's go out for breakfast. Sierra and I smile at each other and yes flows from both of our mouths. It was rare that we went out let along for breakfast. I just enjoyed being together as a family and not riding on the bus. I asked Bill any suggestions on where we want to go. He says I going to surprise you. I think here we go again with another one of his food surprises. This time Rita don't say too much, because you didn't have a chance to test the wind see what direction his mood is in and anything might set him off. All I want to do is enjoy the day, so Sierra can have fun and get out of the apartment. Bill opens the car door which was rare, but the seat was pushed up. Now I know I gained quite of bit of weight a wee bit over you can say, but I know I didn't get shorter. As I get in, I look at Bill and say who has been up here they must have been short. For that instance, I could see how I threw him off with that statement. His comeback was I didn't pay any attention to the seat I'm just a driver and he tries to smile while making that comment. Oh, yeah, he came back with he was looking for something in the back and moved the seat up and, when I gave Wilbur and Carl a ride, they moved the seat up for leg room. I looked at him and said which one sits in the car seat. I glanced at Sierra as she fastens herself in her car seat right behind me. He laughed it off and I chuckled a little bit inside who was in our car, especially since you are the driver.

We rode a few miles in silence with Sierra and I just looking out the window enjoying the fresh air and the wind hitting our face. When we rode on the bus you couldn't feel the wind just glaze at the scenery change. Inside I pondered the thought of how far I should go with my unanswered questions. I glanced over at him and wished I had a pie just, so I could smash dead center of his lying face. That whole story was a story he just didn't think about the ending. I turn back to looking at all the cars speeding and/or just enjoying the slow lane going to different destinations. It is hard to drive in California without getting on the freeway, unless you are on the bus and that rides takes a long time. I would know I've been on the bus a many of times with Sierra wishing for a car. Now, we made it to IHOP now that what I was talking about. Finally, a familiar place with a familiar menu. As we entered the first waitress Gertrude greets us with welcome back Bill. She smiles while greeting Bill and looking at us, as an afterthought for a greeting. I smiled at her and looked at him. He was trying to avoid my looks, but I knew he could feel my thoughts. I thought back to Allison at the shoe store is this another one of those coincidences or what? Now here comes Lanelle looking at Bill not noticing the rest of his family. The way she responded once she realized that we were together her whole demeanor changed. Now my radar is up, and he has been here before but with whom.? Un huh, this just not feeling right they seemed to know him too well. Inside I'm burning up outside I show no emotions, but I had to ask.

It's that unspoken word that eats away at your soul and ponders in your brain and they come together to ease the pain and remove the confusing thoughts that are trying to tear you apart inside. I tried to be nice, but there's anger that's ready to ooze right on out. This was that moment where I had to do or say something without anger and without sounding like some insecure wife. So, Bill he looks at me after he makes sure Sierra is secured in her booster chair. So, tell me you come here often, babe? He responds with not right now Rita we don't need to go there. I looked at him go where with what? So, I come here why make it such a big deal. I'm not making it a big deal they just seem to know you well and looked at me like I am some friend of your family. Bill looks upset and responds with those pregnant hormones got you all crazy and insecure again. I respond back with hormones have nothing to do with what I feel and see. That is not an excuse I want to hear so don't go there with me either. Right when we were getting into this conversation Lanelle comes up smiling as if she was enjoying hearing our discussion and giving her some type of false leverage over me.

Today lady is not the day and my hormones are well in tack. May I take your order as she looks at Bill with a smile? I looked at her and smile yes honey looking at Bill go ahead and order for your family. I look at her as I say cuz you know what I like, and I wink at him and turn toward her to see her smile slowly going away as mine slowly surface. Now, how do you like me now, heffa? Bill looks at me smiling and says what do you want. I looked at him and say the usual you get and a small portion for Sierra. He gives me such a look that I knew some way or somehow, I was going to pay for this later. I didn't care I was tired of being ignored by the women that were always silently drooling over him. I had to admit Bill still looked good but, which sometimes made me question my own looks because he didn't look at me the same way I would see him look at other women. Sometimes, I knew it sound crazy, but I started wondering what type of women he was now interested in, for some reason I felt it wasn't me. I tried to hold up but inside I really wanted to cry but there was no room or time for those emotions. Bill would only make it worse by swearing at me in a public setting. He would sometimes make me feel as if I wasn't even in the room as if I was invisible. I still wondered how Sierra's sister happened. When Lanelle leaves, he looks at me and snarls what was that all about. Here comes my performance again. What are you talking about, I don't know that lady never seen her before? Well strange and funny leaving out the ha-ha but she seems to know you and add Gertrude too. His response comes with the sound of anger of what are you talking about? I thought I might have heard him publicly but softly say that he didn't know hmm beach sounds better. I hoped she heard that. Calling her that didn't make the pain feel any better, it might have turned her on. She brings our drinks this time without her signature smile she had flashed at Bill earlier. I guess she did hear him. I hope and in the back of my mind that it doesn't affect our food. Bill glares across the table at me and I looked at him wondering what he was thinking or see when he looks at me especially like that.

At one point, it scared me and another point I'm not going to let her or him disrespect me, at least not today. He says was all that necessary again my response was what. I played dumb very well on that one. The food comes looking good and Sierra can't wait for her daddy to cut her panicakes as she would call them. When she said that, it just eased the tension that was developing between me and Bill. She definitely was our adhesive to keeping us together. We knew we had to be there for her and the other daughter we were bringing into the world. As the waitress kept coming over just totally getting on my nerves, I still tried to enjoy my meal with my family. This was my family and why should I have to fight all the time to try and keep it together??? I wasn't alone in this marriage. Where was Bill, was he trying, or did he just give up and didn't tell me. After all he asked me to marry him and bought me out here. I was doing fine in Oakwood minding my own business. I reflect on our original conversation when I got pregnant with Sierra he didn't come here to get married and my response was I didn't know you were going to come here and get me pregnant. I couldn't believe how that ancestral strength jumped in on time.

Now, I wondered sometimes did I make a mistake leaving my comfort zone. Then I snapped back and was reminded of the words Mama Sadie said to my dad he had to ask. She was right he had to ask. Out of all those women he asked me and me alone. Now which ones of these scants are trying to replace me. Wow I said scant, woo. The thoughts raced through my mind on which one it could possibly be. Yeah which one of those scants is it, the waitress Gail or Gayla, (something like that), from our first anniversary dinner, or Allison the confused store clerk, or this Gertrude or Lanelle or the one that wears that funky Chanel perfume. As the thoughts entered my mind of Bill's infidelity my smile goes away, and my facial expression is replaced with concern and wondering who is it this time. That kind of explains the phone calls that hang up when I answered or just breathing, then hangs up, or the late-night whispers when he thinks I am sleep.

Wow, did I just get a flashback on the conversation I had with Robin. I never thought about the late-night whispers meant he was being unfaithful. So, do I take a chance and ask to ease my wondering thoughts. Well Mr. Bill how often do you eat here. He looks at me with what are you talking about. Of course, I play along with it too. Miss "Antique" Gertrude seems to know you along with her side kick Lanelle. What I heard blue skies are you talking about sound little like Courtney Diane except it sounded more pleasant coming from her, (ew this is sick). The IHOP we just left they were so busy trying to please you and grinning during the process. Sierra asked or maybe you didn't hear her ask if something was wrong with them smiling so much, I told her yes, crazy. Bill yells at me stop it we don't need to go there. I said go where crazy and what do you mean? This is bugging the heck out of me but somewhere I do need to break so we can have a family fun day. I will store this because this is not over. I looked at him with so much dislike; I really can't say that I hate Bill. My great-grandmother said if you hate someone that means you rather see them dead than alive. I don't want to see him dead I just want us to be right and enjoy each other.

I want to picture us as we grow old together, is that asking too much from your husband, my husband. Why should I share him with other women and why should I have to defend myself on why it should be me? Now, I get paranoid of wondering what type of woman he likes just taking all my confidence. It seems like I was slowly disappearing, and no one knew I had left the building. I looked at him and I know he knows I'm looking at him with disgust. I just turn my head and refocus on the drive, the wind and being with my family. For now, no scant will interrupt my tranquility for this is our time. I turn the radio up just to listen to some music and of course Maze playing "Before I Let You Go" I smile and think yea Bill before I let you go. I think he picks up on the words, because I'm singing the song and hum some parts of it as I meditate through the words. Bill tries to bring us back to happy and he joins in singing his normal off beat. I laughed because I remembered when he told me that his music teacher Miss Henton told him he was tone deaf, and to this day she was so right. Now I can't help but to laugh because he is really trying hard to find some key to sing in. I laughed and looked at him and he grabs my hand and holds it with I will always love you. I'm not going anywhere. That was good to hear and reassurance to the insecurity that I was developing. I really didn't like this feeling, just like sometimes I didn't like the rain because I wanted some type of sunshine in my life as I enjoy this nice cup of coffee. This day was sunnier than the normal sunny day. Very little wind just a beautiful sunshine day and just a little warmer than normal. I was dressed in my maternity moomoo feeling like a walking bed spread with floral print and can't see my feet. One thing I can laugh at Lanelle saw his full family one eating and talking and one very soon on the way. How do you like us now?

We drove for miles which seemed like no destination in site just driving. One thing about living on the coast you see nothing but ocean and waves. I never thought I would be living in California let alone married with children. I looked over at Bill and my thoughts come together I'm here because of him. What was he thinking about when he moved us out here and what changed along the path we were travel-ing? When I delivered our daughter, he showed up but faded in and out of our lives. But now we are family. I tried holding back the tears and the many hurtful paths I had to take to get here.

That feeling resurfaced when I went over to Bill's aunts and grandparents house to see those ladies there and I had to leave. So many years later I still remember the pain and looking at the figures on them and longing for mine to return. It's funny I agree with Robin you don't remember their faces, just the situation. When I saw them, I was very pregnant then too. It sure didn't help seeing my classmate Joel smiling as I was asked to leave, and him reminding me that he did it again asking you to leave. Hmm he is another one I wished I had a pie for just to focus on his face to find a good place to smash the pie. I know it wasn't his fault, but I had a feeling it might had felt good, just because and being pregnant I could get away with it. Yep racing out of control hormones, yep sure needed that excuse then.

What seemed like miles and hours of driving was only less than an hour. We drove through beautiful nice expensive homes to a large well kept-park. Large slides, merry go rounds, jungle gyms and many swings, and area for rock climbing. I watched Sierra look around as we pulled up. I was so overwhelmed with the many things that are here for Sierra to play on. There were many children there but not too crowded. Sierra's mouth and eyes widen as to which one she wanted to get on first. Bill opens the doors for both us as Sierra anxiously wants him to hurry so that she can run, ride, or slide down something. Then to my surprise Bill brings out a picnic basket. I didn't see him place that surprise inside the trunk. Now this was a pleasant surprise and much needed. Bill chases after Sierra over to the swings and she rushes and jumps into the middle of the group. She yells for her dad to push her higher and I see her close her eyes as she feels the wind hitting her face with the biggest grin. Bill pushes her carefully not to push her too high. I see the joy and the proud look on his face as he watches Sierra go up and down. They are talking to each other, but I can't really hear what they are saying but they look very happy. I looked in the basket seeing Sierra's signature peanut butter and jelly sandwiches, ham and cheese, many small bags of potato chips and juice just right for a special occasion. When I looked at Bill and Sierra, I'm reminded of why I am here, because of the scene that I was looking at. I don't know if there is someone else but sometimes, I get that feeling, and sometimes I feel maybe I dissect everything too too much.

I see families, but I see more women than men here we go again good grief. They are glancing at Bill and Sierra interacting together because he looks at them responds and continues pushing Sierra. Then they stop and run over to the larger slides like little children. After several slides, down they come over both out of breath and fall on the blanket. They looked at me as I asked them are, they ready to eat. They both say yeah at the same time as Sierra says daddy and I made the sandwiches and let him help me. He laughed as he reaches for my hand which throws me off again. I hold for a quick second, as I feel his warmth transfer to my hand then into my heart. I hold on to that snapshot before handing him and Sierra a sandwich with chips. With that added ingredient of nothing but pure love, I told Sierra she made the best sandwiches. I watched her glow with laughter saying that daddy helped. I asked how, and she said he was holding the bag when I put the chips in and sandmiches. We both laughed as I looked at Bill asking was this some form of child labor law you're breaking. He laughed and said she had my stubborn streak come out of her and she just had to do it herself. Everyone was laughing just like you see on some type of family commercial. Only if I could believe that type of family commercial would last in our lives. So many things were happening with no real answers or reasons on what is going on. What is Bill up to and with whom? I hate to even think about Bill being with someone other than me.

I'm his wife and having his second child doesn't that require allegiance. Has a Trixie invaded my home? Is it any of the women that I have been coming across my path? After eating Bill lays on my lap and Sierra lays on his legs out of nowhere just looking up at the trees trying to count the leaves. When asked she said I'm doing nothing just counting, but we are looking at her little finger pointing and counting with such a serious face. What I'm feeling right now makes up for the things that happened earlier at the restaurant. I haven't forgotten but this is not going to ruin our family time. I want to put my hands-on Bill's hair and just play in it, but I have to ask for permission and that would just ruin the moment again and feel all of rejected. I have been rejected from him in so many ways I just carry my imaginary band aides, my own built in medicine cabinet and just self heal myself. In my healing cabinet I use a little iodine, no alcohol that might release more pain and remember to use the neosporin to help hide and heal the scars. I learned not to cry at an early stage in our marriage. I pushed the envelope today challenging my ancestral strength. I get so confused on how he really feels about me and our marriage. Is he shopping for a new bride, replacement or just some type of cheap filler, that provides sex only and no emotions. Hmm what type of emotions could be involved when you cheapen yourself with someone else's husband? I savor the moments we have right now but ponder the thought that this may change. Not knowing what type of change is scary and just not fair.

I looked down at him while his eyes are closed and fight the feeling of putting my hand on his head, so I just place my hand carefully and gently on his shoulder. He moves just a little and it is good to see a smile appear on his face. Sierra stops counting and wants more swing time. Bill opens his eyes slowly and says let's all go for a swing. I laughed, and Sierra says come mommy lets go. Mommy I haven't heard her call me that in many years. All I hear now is Rita with no thought as I continued to tell her to stop calling me Rita. I walk slowly toward the swing hoping I can still fit the swing and not be embarrassed or laughed at by Bill and innocently by Sierra. I watched them run toward the swing as Sierra hops in one as Bill holds the other swing for me. I sit down and amazingly I can still fit, and I didn't hear any noise as if I was too heavy. He gets behind me and pushes but I hear sort of a grunt didn't like hearing that. I didn't know if he was being funny or this really did take some effort. I enjoyed the push from him as I swing to keep up with Sierra. After swinging she wants to run over to the slide again before we leave. Bill looks at me saying hey you want to go down the slide. Before he could finish my thoughts were what if I get stuck in the middle of the slide down (how embarrassing). Before he could finish his request and I could finish my fearful thoughts Sierra rushes pass me asking her daddy to watch her slide down backwards. I was so glad I didn't have to try and go down that slide and hear some type of negative comment from Bill. I didn't know if it would be mean or sincere if I did get stuck. When I would get in the bed, he would say wee wee and roll in the bed and saying thanks for the ride lady or was it the ocean wave. Hang ten now he's surfing when I jump into the bed. Either way it was mean. He didn't know how much that hurt.

I think even if he did know that it hurt, he probably wouldn't care. I know I gained some weight, but does he think I like being this size. Bill managed over the years to remain in shape and still had his wash board six pack stomach. He did still jog and worked out. When I think about it all his uncles were still slim his Uncle

Cully and Uncle Duckie just to mention a few. I never really worked out after high school but kept busy enough not to pick up any weight. I felt a little comfortable but always knew there was room for improvement. I had a nice figure and didn't miss it until I realized that I had lost it and hoping it will someday return.

Just when I was feeling better about myself and confident, he snatches it away. Now who is he comparing me too? I smiled behind my pain and perform so the day will go on as planned for Sierra and our family. I dare not climb that ladder to try and slide down. So, I detour for our picnic layout to start picking and cleaning up, so we can continue with our day. Bill notices that I am cleaning up and comes over there with Sierra to assist. Sometimes it is just hard to bend or squat with my daughter holding on inside. During this day, my daughter was calm with very little movement, but she usually waits for the evening to practice her athletic skills. Funny as I think about it now, she was and still is very athletic. Didn't know at the time she was preparing for her debut outside.

The car ride was slow yet fun. I loved when we would take the long way home. We really didn't talk much; I guess sometimes there is just not much to say. After all my days/hours/months that are spent at home, not much to say about my daily routine. I glanced back at Sierra and she is looking out the window until exhaustion took her into a deep sleep. I lean my head back and close my eyes and just relax with the music and sitting in our car. I can't relax to music or close my eyes on the bus, so this was an enjoyable change. This was very relaxing with little conversation. It felt so good just being off my feet and not worrying about falling to sleep and missing my stop. I know that one day I will have my own car and money; I just have to be a little more patient. The day was still young, and I thought we were on our way home. We stopped at a hole in the wall burger place. Bill carried Sierra and she slowly woke up. I watched her eyes, but her body said that she just didn't want to walk. This time the waitress Falless didn't stare as if she seen or knew Bill, so this was a good start to an enjoyable meal. I really wasn't feeling burgers. Being pregnant altered my appetite to burgers and soda pops. During both pregnancies they just didn't work well with my stomach. But hmm fries do, unfortunately I can eat fries like potato chips. Bill orders steak burger and we share the fries, (cute uh). He added a kiddie meal for Sierra's small hands and appetite. At least stopping for dinner keeps me from cooking when we finally make it home. Sharing fries reminds me of when Bill and I used to hang out at Bronco's burgers. I was young and very slim then and their fries were so good. I used to eat them a lot when I was pregnant with Sierra. No burgers, no soda pops but the homemade fries were on hit and Sierra loved them as much as I did. Hmm I still like homemade fries, but I am thinking its time to detour from that once I deliver another bundle of joy. Bill eats the sandwich and asks if I want a bite although it was a nice gesture, just wasn't appealing. We were sharing fries, (cute again huh). I did take a small bite and had to give him credit for trying and sharing. My heart was just set on the fries and being somewhere I didn't have to look at others look at me. Wow, how good that felt, and I can really enjoy my family and my meal.

We make small talk about family back home and maybe moving again after the baby is born. Nice thought but I really don't feel like moving and getting to know people all over again, I just want stability. Bill moved around a lot so that didn't really bother him. I moved only three times, one when my parents had their house built, then when I moved here to Oceanview and when we moved from our first apartment. I didn't have Mama Sadie here to help me like she did before. I sure did need her energy and my great- grandmother Mommy to get me started and keep me moving. No stress and no strain just the mind set of just getting it done. One thought came to mind and here I go again, but I just had to ask because my mind would not be at ease. So, inquiring minds don't rest they wonder. I wondered where we were getting the money to move. Our savings was weak, and my $120.00 allotment didn't go as far as Bill tried to make it. Maybe he had some type of magic trick he was going to magically pull off with a rabba-daba a money tree, hmm that's a thought.

So, Mr. Bill where are we going to get the money to move our car is almost on life support and a prayer. You won't let me work but I really want to help our family and take the pressure off you. He looked at me as if I just stepped on those size twelve feet. I wasn't thinking about it right now just a thought to ponder. Our family is growing, and the girls need room to play. We brought up what Jovan had said ooh that had to be years ago now. He talked about wanting more for his family. Jovan said he got tired of looking at everyone in his family with homes and enjoying working around the house. As Bill is talking, I see that he is serious and had given this some thought. Bill said he had lived in apartments most of his life, but he didn't want that for his family. How do you respond from that when you had so many doubts about how you thought he might feel about you and being married? Just when I am ready to give up, he surprises me. Sometimes, I get mentally tired of trying to either think ahead or prepare myself for whatever comes out his mouth. Like the wee wee joy sound Bill makes when I get in the bed, like he was riding on a wave or roller coaster because of my weight gain. Then he flips the script by saying he wants to move as a family. He wanted more for us and taking us out for a family drive with a surprise picnic. Does this confuse me I must say hmm hell yes?

Now, Rita don't start with the swearing. I think that I am more confused than Bill. He wants a lot, but I would like to help him, so he knows that he is not alone. We are here for each other as a unit without any division. We will not divide so other women can conquer our marriage. If my husband wants to move, we will pack and move our family together. Grow up Rita no pouting, no tears, no fussing just work with him and make it happen. One day you will work again and be there financially supporting family dreams. I want to continue to support Bill in every way and let him know that I am still his rib and back him up in whatever decisions he makes for our family.

Baby Sabrina is moving around and enjoying the ride and the day's adventure. I can't believe I called her Sabrina. I guess that's the name that Sierra likes might just work. Hmm Sabrina not bad, maybe Bill might go for that name also. We drive with little conversation and looking around and enjoying the scenery. Sometimes silence can be golden. We need to look at the roses, the flowers, buildings everything and just admire the beauty with the breeze hitting your face. Today reminded me of when I was young riding a bike down a hill and feeling the breeze hit my face and body. Just innocently enjoying the sense of freedom you didn't know existed. In our youth the only responsibility was getting home before the street lights came on. I kind of chuckle and Bill looks at me wondering and asking what I was laughing at. I laughed and said with the wind and the fresh air hitting my face made me think about riding a bike down a hill, feeling the wind and freedom and the only thing that we had to worry about was…. before I could finish, he said before the street lights came on. I laughed even harder because he lived in Chicago, yet the rules were universal. We were beoming one again in completing each other's thoughts and sentences.

We reminisce about childhood do's and don'ts and a song comes on I really don't remember I think it was a Jackson 5 oldie. We both start singing and of course Bill is tone deaf, so he was off key. I'm not in sync either but we make music together no matter how horrible we both sounds. It seems not to bother Sierra's ears. Our siren sounds in form of singing didn't wake or move her. He glances at me as he sings, and I grab his hand as we harmonize on a song, we actually do know the words to. We head home happy, full and thankful for a good family day. We pulled up and it seems like everyone is home. I see Momo outside with her niece Melinda walking in her walker, and Manly, Bert and Chris playing football with some neighborhood friends. Later with all their energy started racing each other from one end to the other. I remembered we did that in our neighborhood, playing football or baseball or racing each other in the streets not really thinking about cars. Funny that was the high point of our night and weekends. Just playing outside, staying inside was for either being on punishment or you were sick. Courtney Diane gives a wave as she drives off and Robin is carrying her photography equipment into her apartment. I would sometimes see her daughters Denise and Nicole playing with some neighborhood friends, but today they were nowhere in sight. It was nice seeing the neighborhood like I remembered mine. It really made me homesick, but this was now my home. Little boy runs over to Sierra and says hi to her and that his name was Tim. His English sounded a little better, but Sierra looked at him before responding with hi. I think him running up to her threw her off. She was always used to running up to people now had a chance to see how it felt.

It looked funny, but she was nice and took off running with him over to where Manly was playing, a funny looking two squares. Bill looks at me as I assist Robin with her equipment. Bill glances at me with very little emotion as he goes into the apartment. My mood was so good Bill's lack of emotion didn't faze me as I asked Robin if she needed any help. She smiles, and I just take a small camera case and go with her into her apartment. Bill is watching Sierra and I am still looking back at Sierra to make sure we make eye contact, so she knows where I went. Melinda and Tim see Sierra and run over to the apartment wanting to play with her. Manly looks over at them and breaks from playing football and runs over to play with his age group. Bill is ganged up and invaded by a bunch of little people. Bill didn't like when Sierra was the only girl, so I was glad when Melinda was added to the posse to hang out. He glances at me and I glanced at him with a smile. Bill's expression is one of a happy question with the invasion and what should I do with all these kids. As I walked away, I turned my head and giggled thinking welcome to my world.

I start small talk with Robin to avoid the breathing steam coming from the Bill's nostrils. I felt if I talked, I could act like I didn't really see or beware of his little children invasion. I can play it off as if I thought it was just for a five to ten-minute invasion. When I walked into Robin's apartment her place was nice, clean, and calm and plenty of pictures. There were one with her and Courtney Diane, one with her son Henry and Floyd, one with Denise, Nicole and Henry and one large group with all of them. On another wall were with a few of Robin smiling and family members you see and feel the love along with the closeness with many years of friendship. The furniture is modern, and the rooms are bright. My place could use some brightening and more modern furniture. Our furniture looked like grandma's style big and stuffed. I liked her place and the peace that I felt as you entered. It was a place that you knew women and young ladies lived there. Not like there were clothes everywhere, just a woman type atmosphere. You knew you just knew, but hard to describe. I asked where Denise and Nicole were. She said that they were visiting their dad at his parents. I replied that sounds good. Robin said its okay his parents were the ones that wanted to see them; it's not like the idea came from Ramon.

I asked if her if she missed him and do, they still talk. She laughed as little as possible. Ramon is still their father that won't change. I asked well how he is doing. Her response was calm, he is doing okay I guess he's not living in the home we once shared. He is in some condo out near his parents. He finally got rid of his old raggely green, oops lime green Pacer and purchased a car the girls call merjeep. I asked with a cracking in my voice what is a merjeep. She said I asked the girls that because I felt silly, I thought I knew a lot about cars. I grew up with my dad showing and teaching me and my brother how to work on cars. Well the girls said he had some hoopty and had a hole put on the hood and went to the junkyard and found a Mercedes and took the emblem and had it welded on his jeep. So, the girls called it a mer for part Mercedes and part jeep, so we came up with Merjeep. I laughed asking Robin why she didn't just give him the Mercedes. She responded calmly and very clear, with girl oh hell no oops, and have that rachet scant in the front seat or driving my car note. Let me add something I paid for oh unt un hmm. I would make that into a six pack before I would give it to him. Let her roll her scant ass in that cinderella green pumpkin she inherited. He would have been out of his rabbit mind to even think or stutter the words to ask. That car is over at Robier's with the same agreement. Why don't you have a car? I could only answer with; well one thing we can barely afford the hoopty we have now.

Robin laughed about her daughter Denise laughing while saying now that custom made Merjeep went with his ooh baby jeans both outdated and tight. She chuckled a little saying I guess he misses his Mercedes. Ramon should have some appreciation for that lime green big round Pacer I left him. Her daughters insisted that they couldn't ride in that bubble with wheels we have a rep to up hold to, mom. We felt like cinderella getting into a pumpkin and looking for the mice to rescue us. Rita, Robin responded, with men they don't miss the water until they need to quench their thirst. No way would his trifling butt be wearing no ooh baby tight ass pants, because his ass had plenty of suits and jeans. You know for a fact that we dress our men. If we didn't put their clothes out, and if they they could get away with it, they would wear the same clothes for a whole week. Then once they take them off the clothes would take off running.

Now I really didn't want to ask and seem naïve, but I asked Robin what are ooh babies? Robin pauses saying that ooh baby jeans are generic name for tight jeans. She said her daughter Denise came up with that phase. It's what you say when the jeans are too tight. You say ooh baby. I laughed with Robin as she said they all laughed when she got the clear understanding. The girls say he prays before he gets into Merjeep and they can feel the springs in the seats. Thank God for butt padding. I don't wish any bad for Ramon he just forgot to prepare for the aftermath. I smiled and hunch my shoulders in agreeance. I tell her as far as the car it sounds like one of the cars, we had minus the merging of two cars into one.

I told Robin we had a car like that we had to pray before we went anywhere, and if it rained, we couldn't roll into a puddle because it would stop. I laughed so hard telling her we had one car that I had to use two feet and it wasn't a stick. Robin comes back girl, we all had some type of lemon in our life rather it's a car or some trifling man. We laughed and said that they are just boys with mustaches, yep and yep, (and we gave each other a boogy dap). Just out of curiosity Robin is he still with Trixie. Rita nah she was just that a trick, just a spare tire that comes out when needed. She served only one purpose was to satisfy his selfish sexual desires and pump up his pathetic ego. Why would he marry her, he had a wife and tricks are not wife material, just something to play with until they get bored and move on. They might tell them it's over or just don't return phones calls and just leave them hanging and feeling the same misery we felt. Payback is a trip. They don't realize there are no emotions or feelings for tricks. When she thought, she was going to move up to wifey she had to go. She didn't realize it wasn't that type of party. I watched Robin smile go away and I immediately said I didn't mean to upset you. Robin smiled you didn't, it bothered me at first when I left. In the back of my mind I still loved this man and was hoping to spend the rest of my life with him and we grow old together. Sometimes I would second guess myself, but I couldn't let my mind toy with me like that. I had my boo hoo moment and it was time to let go, because I didn't want to look back or go back. I mentally agreed with Robin. Inside I knew too well about boo hoo moments. I learned so well how to silent my cry if I could cry.

As I listened, I wondered if I ever came to that point could I leave Bill. I shiver inside and just thinking about it saddens me. So, that means that I should change that channel in my mind and really readjust my thoughts. This is fun time I am sitting here being entertained in adult conversation. Looking back, you stumble moving forward miss all the signs. I just didn't want to spend the rest of my life looking under the beds or inside closets for this trick leaving signs around to let me know she had invaded my bedroom and had my husband. Who wants to live like that, always wondering what he is doing or who he is doing with what? Robin said that she still thinks about him but flashed back of him lying in our bed with that naked nasty, trifling scant was a sight that I can't forget or forgive. I don't want to bore you, but it took two and somethings are worth fighting for and somethings just are not worth the energy. I can't fight two people, regardless of how much Ramon tries to convince me that he loved me. Love wouldn't have put a naked woman in our bed, not once but several times. Love wouldn't have divided our family either. My mother of course blames me for the divorce. She said I should have forgiven him. In marriage, you give more than you take. I had to ask take what, the crap he was trying to spoon feed me? Hey, I smelled the aroma and it was foul. I didn't want to be disrespectful and held my tongue but continued with my thoughts. After all, how many times did she, my mommy, forgive dad. I remembered those cab drives to Mama Roxie's house only for dad to come and bring us back home. That wasn't the life I wanted for me and didn't want the girls to think that was okay to continue to forgive infidelity. She gets up and ask if I dranked. I told her no and she responded now I like my glass of White Zinfandel, or Merlot to mellow me out. Courtney Diane turned me on to Merlot. Now she likes her Chardonnay, ooh long island ice teas and if she really wants her buzz Hennessy. I love that girl and she can be a handful. But she still is my girl, and she can be a little cuckoo, and I'm gonna miss her when she moves to Florida.

Hey Rita, would you like to try some Chai tea. I told her I never had any and wasn't really a tea drinker. She said let me hook you up, you didn't know about fresh lemonade, but you enjoyed the fresh taste. I smiled and laughed and said and you know it, okay Robin bring it on. I glanced out the window to make sure that my place is okay so when I go home Bill will be okay. I must be okay because if I stayed at anyone's house too long Bill would come looking for me. I asked Robin how many sisters she had. As she brings me the tea, she says she has two sisters, Darlene and Kim and one brother Edward. I'm the middle daughter. I laughed nah you in the middle girl syndrome. Robin laughed yeah girl, you know we are not the first, nor the last girl. So, we are not the special daughter, more like the friend of the family. How many pictures do you have of you that you are alone in other than school pictures?

We both laughed and said at the same time we looked like the friends of the family. We are always in pictures with family members barely alone huh. Yep we are the friend of the family, just an insert. We were either someone's older or younger sister with no name. Yes, they just snatched our identity like we didn't have enough issues and no kind of feelings. We hunch our shoulders saying yep, friends of the family with no name. Now is that some cold booboo or what? I laughed that's some foul-smelling booboo. Robin paused before saying that Ramon had married again. It wasn't the same Trixie or the standby understudy. This Trixie was somebody he met somewhere out there. Now get this my mother was crazy about Ramon trifling butt and he could do no kinda wrong. Ramon's new quickie bride was a former stripper. I can't and didn't bother to try and remember her stage/first name. She wasn't worth remembering her name or the day they married. Come to think about it, didn't care then and next year probably would have the same don't care thoughts, and more than likely the following year too. Courtney Diane joins in I don't re-member seeing her come in. She says yea yea we get it move on with the story. Ooh Robin crosses her eyes looking at Courtney Diane saying girlfriend don't have me stretch my leg. Courtney Diane says with that little foot that wouldn't get me across the street. Come on I need a tickle go ahead stretch the leg from that end you call a foot, I need the laugh. Well as I was saying before someone with "an" emotion in-terrupted me. This newly married wife to Ramon would visit my mom's restaurant "Maggie's Pie". Now that relationship with my moms got kinda close. She marries Ramon now she thinks she is part of my family. My mother would hold a conversa-tion longer with her than it took me to dial her number. Plus, she would tell me she talked to this thang like she was her daughter. I had to step back and say hey mom why didn't she call Onni, that's her mother-in-law not my mother. I got kinda upset asking and saying you held a long conversation with her. Let her, Miss Thang make a long-distance call to long distance mother-in-law but no she calls you, mom, because you're local. I had to go there and ask how would you like it if dad left you!! Let's just say dad divorced you, and I became friendly with the new mommy,

mommy and I told you how we talked and talked and talked and laughed. All I heard was a long pause because now I bought it home to her. Yep I slid right into first base; humph she didn't like that feeling just like I didn't. I bet that hurt just like it did when she was telling me. If I could have just reached my mom through that phone and snatched her and placed some humanity/allegiance back into her ooh.

Then get this this strip trick had the nerve to come over to my parents' house. Now Ramon's grandparents didn't live too far, why couldn't her act be taken on the road to Ramon's grandma's house? She comes over of course to my mother's house and mommy lets her in, and she stays for about 2-3 hours. Then while my daughter was visiting, she woke her up to meet her other sister, for what a sister she didn't know and would probably not see ever again. Nicole looked at her like she was crazy, good one Niki and went back to bed. Before my daughter left the strip, trick had the audacity to tell my daughter let me repeat my child, and my mother that she will bring back Nicole's other grandmother over to meet her. I was like what the hmmm mom really, I'm not dead. Are you really listening to what you are saying? Her response was she stayed over 3 hours. My response was good, and I hope that she brings the other grandmother back over drunk.

Courtney Diane feeling her friend's pain adds, so let me understand you are still living as an insert or friend of the family. Which means that you can visit when you want to huh?? We all paused with hmmm no guilt hmm insert, sounds like there might be some benefits being an insert. Robin had to take a pause on her story and laugh. Her facial expressions said it all. We are still laughing through our pain. When I think back to being the middle sister you learn how to have your own identity. I was an insert just like Robin and others that experienced the middle child syndrome. No name used, just so and so big or little sister. Somewhere in there they had to see our expressions of no you really didn't make me just disappear. That's why I didn't answer unless they said my name or came close enough without tearing it up. How can you get Rita wrong?

I flashed back and remembered my friend Sapphire saying that her mother Rori was a piece of work and if she died, she would be the only one smiling at the funeral. Sapphire would have a nice smile and saying don't mind me I'm okay and chuckle just a little. One thing she made clear deep down inside she loved her mother, just didn't like the attitude that somehow seemed to hang out with her all the time. Funny but not ha-ha how these thoughts can go around and how they affect many daughters. Why is it so hard for some mothers to love their daughters? I mean love and like all their daughters not just the selected ones. How hard is it to remember, Robin it's a bird's name? No not blue jay but a person by the name of Robin and not a person name blue jay. Shoot my mother had no imagination spelled just like the bird no "y" spelled with an "I". I broke down saying that I'm not too close to my older sister Emma Jean or my younger sister Bonnie. I'm close to my brother Sonny.

My mom and I are not close either. Something I eventually gave up on trying. We really didn't get close until I got married. I guess we had something in common to talk about. She is closer to my younger sister Bonnie and her family. Girl we are from different states with the same situation. Wow my mother favors my younger sister Kim too and her family. Do you call your mom? I try every now and then, but she really doesn't have too much conversation unless there is a need, then that is quick and short, and we are right back where we started.

I know she loves me, and I also know that she doesn't like me. Robin looks at me and says my mother doesn't like me either. We both laughed as we both said, I'm not a fan of her either, but in the back of our minds it did hurt. We both sighed after the end of the laughter because that was our reality. The only comforting thought was that we were not alone and would make sure that our children will know that there is no division. We do agree that our moms are good to their granddaughters. We added that our parents did take good care of us and we didn't turn out too bad. We agreed that we didn't want for anything just a little more love and respect. When my mother visited, she did bring goodies that lasted long after she left. I watched Robin close her eyes as she stated that she would ever be thankful for her mom and all that she has provided. Everyone in the neighborhood was in the same boat, working and trying to survive. Now when I think about my mom, she loved us in her own way. My mom just had much to do with raising a family, working with very little social time. That part used to bother me. That is my past and now I'm grown. Living out here in California allows me to escape from separation and division that I felt growing up. We are a small family, but we are very loving and supportive. We love both our daughters but in different ways because they both are unique. I'm proud of Denise and Nicole. Sometimes I'm not the best in some of my decisions, but I try as hard as I can to be there mother and a role model they can look up to. I agreed with Robin that Sierra is my life and new daughter added to my life.

Robin says girl you are wearing your pregnancy very well. Oh, I thought.... me look good? I looked at her and asked is that wine working and blurring your vision. She laughed I just started sipping I know what I am looking at girl and you don't scare me enough to make me lie. I laughed lie huh. Robin says don't people sometimes lie out of fear. This was a strange compliment yet welcomed to my ears. Hearing someone tell me I'm beautiful while being pregnant. Bill never said I looked good during pregnancy I haven't heard a compliment in a long time. He would make a comment like after I showered and come out the bathroom saying that he was looking at the football game and the team lost. I'm listening, and he comes back with they lost because you missed their defensive line up. He laughed saying I thought you were a team player. You missed being in the line up to help defend your team. I didn't know he was referring to me, ouch. He saw the hurt but seemed to ignore my expressions and all my insides felt the pain. Was I that big and did I disgust him? I looked out the window to see how Sierra was doing and they all must be inside the apartment. I don't see her other playmates outside. Robin looks at me as if she wants to say something since, we are just girls talking. She asks" does your husband yell at you a lot". I smiled and lied and say not really his voice carries and it may sound loud. Humph did that sound weak or what? Am I some little girl lying to hide the truth? Have I become so immune that I don't hear the words anymore or trying to convince myself, and hope it would take me to a safe mind place? It used to bother me not knowing when I had to hide my tear at the same time protect my heart, but I couldn't block all his cruel words. He made me feel like a child getting reprimanded. I felt his eyes piercing my soul and his words would sometimes linger in my heart. I would feel myself shrinking in my own inner world slowly loosing myself. I no longer had a first name. I was either Mrs. or mom when Sierra felt like calling me. I felt like I was back in my parent's home being someone other than Rita. Sometimes I felt like I annoyed my parents and that is how I feel sometimes with Bill. I heard Robin and Courtney Diane talking, but the words turned into blahs. I was listening to Robin and for a minute which felt like a lifetime that my thoughts took me away.

She asked do you say anything back when he yells. I don't know how long or often she asked I just remembered responding with a smile that turned into a nervous laugh, I can't respond to something I don't hear. She laughed and looked at me with a calm concern as she sips her glass of wine, just be careful if you need to get away you are always welcome to come over here. One thing I had to add was being the middle child helped you to become independent. You learned how to appreciate your freedom and more so as you get older. Oh, Miss Rita if he, Robin laughed harder I still have my bat in the closet for just in case. We looked at each other with laughing eyes then I laughed saying for just in case. We all join in saying for just in case, (as we click our glasses together). Don't have me and Courtney Diane come over there, it will not be cute, and I don't do ugly. Ooh no not Courtney Diane. Yell girl and I will load her up with some Chardonnay or long island ice teas and you know what she will say. I laughed saying what. Robin says she will say let's go get she pauses with I'm going to say with your, and Courtney Diane joins with I'll say it with his dumb ass. Sometimes when you say dumb ass around her, she looks at you like she owned that phrase or words. The look was so quick that I don't think she even notice her pause. Ooh I can't believe I said ass, oops. This time her smile was partially there, and she had a look that a big sister would have. I smiled at the thought of her calling Courtney Diane my cousin would back me up. She would come in swinging two bats like she was some kind of ninja, with an ooh ah noise. I felt I had a friend that would be there regardless and a crazy cousin a few steps away. I looked at her feet to make sure she wasn't wearing her famous flip flops minus her hat.

I chuckle as I left thinking about how Robin said that Courtney Diane was running after the wedding planner that had played her sister, and she had on her hat and flip flops. Courtney Diane said that she had improved after taking on-line anger management courses. She toned down the funk word she loved to use and start using dumb ass a little more. Without that, there was a delayed kick ass, but if she had on the flip flops and the hat, that would be an immediate kick ass. She is so new and improved. I don't know if you noticed she does the zoop zoop as if she some type of laser eyes. If you ever noticed she sometimes squints her eyes as if she's performing her zoop zoop motion penetrating your body with her eyes. My response was uh. At first, I thought Robin and Courtney Diane were kidding about the on-line anger management course. Hmm it must be sort of working because; I haven't really heard the "friend word" in a long time, just dumb ass. Courtney Diane in her own way said that the "f" word feels good channeling from her stomach and jumps off her tongue into the air echoing to the soothing sound to her ears. Funny that she wasn't skipping a beat and going with the flow commenting how soothing those words were to her ears. She was not short on words. She smiled saying that it just feels very therapeutic and so soothing to her tongue and she throws a pretend puff into the air as if she just had a cigarette. She continued with the sensational feelings on her tongue and the melody ringing in her ears until she sighs with smile. Just words that flow right into her sentences and she doesn't realize it.

I flashed back to my youth. I did fight a little in grade school and junior high but mellowed out in high school, funny how that transformation happened. I guess there was a little Courtney Diane in me. Strange how time changes; with environment, awareness will alter your attitude and your outlook on life. All I did was fight at school, the playground and in my neighborhood. Majority of the fights were from me protecting someone I felt was the underdog. For some reason, I was always holding up the wall at the principal's office. Silly thing was I never went to the principal's office because I was in a fight. I think mainly my mouth and attitude, hmmph. I really was a tomboy loved running, climbing trees, jumping fences you name it. I guess looking at it now I was athletic and didn't realize then that I had a shape and miss that youthful figure.

Only on somethings I wish I could turn back the hands of time. I drift into us riding bicycles all over town; we just had to make sure that you made it home before the street lights came on. We took on challenges like riding bikes down alleys that we knew had dogs. We would ride, and they would chase us so far and we would just peddle faster laughing not realizing the danger. Was I in danger and I didn't hear the music to warn me like it did in the movies? Or was I that little girl wanting to be challenged. The warmth of Robin's place extended from her heart and surrounded her place. Her smiled confirmed the warmth of sincerity when I left. I was grateful for the time I had to taste a little bit of freedom and laughter with no restraints.

I really didn't have any friends to hang out with and knowing I had another one felt great and liberating. Melba will be moving pretty soon, and I really don't have anyone to talk to. Not that I hung out there either, but that security felt pretty good knowing that she was a bus ride or a call away. My world was Sierra and Bill when he allowed it. I met people like the bus drivers, some neighborhood complex associates, but no one I really could hang out with like I did back in Oakwood. Inside I knew Bill was slipping away from me and I just didn't know how to grab him and plead with him to tell me what I needed to do. This was all foreign to me with no instructions on how to translate it to something I can understand.

Chapter 19
Honey I'm Coming Home

Time was getting away and Bill came up to the apartment looking for me. I didn't really see him approach the door or come up the steps; I just heard a knock that made my stomach drop, because I had a feeling it was for me, I had exceeded my curfew/ parole time. As Robin opened the door, she greets him as she turns toward me, so he could see that all was calm, and she wasn't up here corrupting me. Bill and I make eye contact but it wasn't, a I'm glad to see you type of contact. He didn't act like he missed me but tried to act as if he liked me kind of like my mother. Hmm it's funny how life prepares you for so many unexpected journeys. I nervously smiled at him and told Robin thank you for the tea and I needed to get home. She smiled back at me with a wink as she glances over at her closet. I smiled and said just in case, but I finished it with thank you for just in case. Inside I felt so embarrass that he would do that but it's not like he hasn't done it before. I nervously tried talking to him as we walked down the stairs and he was very silent. Inside butterflies were floating and my stomach felt like Sabrina is sleeping with one eye open. I don't know what's gonna happen once I get inside, but inside my mind I talk to myself and I convince myself that I didn't do anything wrong. He gave the nod to help Robin, but now that I'm thinking about it, he didn't give a smile to go and stay so long. Ooh what's going to happen? I feel so nervous. I tried small talk again as we walked in, again no response from him.

For that second, I reflect to my friend back home hmm Joann. She stood about or almost 4"7 or 4'11 something like that and maybe 105 pounds holding a heavy book. Made me laugh when I saw someone twice her height threatens her. She moved so fast all we saw was her on top of that woman beating the crap out of her. Her cousin Andrew was slim as well and I've seen him take out the two guys that were trying to jump on Joann, without any type of sweat. Now that was some type of family support. Just remembering that sight made me kind of chuckle silently to myself. As I entered the dungeon and noticed that the street lights were on oops. Now what did I do or didn't do. Hmm or that I stayed away too long and I'm going home to my parents' house and as I entered our apartment. Mentally I heard the stool scoot back knowing my father is sitting there just waiting. I think I like the scene from Joann taking that giant out better. It seems like I can't do anything right.

Oh well make it quick on whatever you are going to do Bill. It's not like I haven't been beaten, hit or cussed out or called something outside my name. It hurts and it's sad that I had gotten used to the pain. When he loved me, I guess you call it love it was great, but when the wind shifted, I never knew how I would be treated, and what I did to trigger it. If I did, I would try so hard to avoid it. The only thing I'm thankful for is that Sierra never saw it and I hope she never heard it. Rejection is hard, but I have had it a lot in my life. Inside I think back being the middle child sometimes you are not looked as being special. Actually, you kind of fade away into wind with no one noticing you're gone. You slowly fade into becoming invisible, and people or Bill barely notice that you were missing. Your voice couldn't be heard because you were losing your body and all existence.

Bill just opens the door and keeps it moving as he goes into the bedroom. I walked into the apartment to see it in disarray from Sierra and her friends play day adventure. I knew he was mad about that considering how neat conscience Bill is. Sierra must have gotten in some type of trouble because normally she cleans up her mess. I go into her room and she is sound asleep with her clothes on, which confirms she was told to go straight to bed. I look at the peace on her face as she sleeps. I hear a slight whispering from Bill as if he is on the phone. Woo, do I walk in and try to ease drop or just leave well enough along and let this night fade into the morning. As I eased up, I feel a little uneasy. I go into the front room and start picking and cleaning up the kids' adventure of fun. No sooner than I stand up with shredded papers and broken crayons Bill is looking dead at me. His look puts the question in my mind of what now?? I don't know what happened from that phone call but for some reason it will affect me in some way. I just have that funny feeling again. He looked at me and his eyes changes from twinkling to fire. It startles me because I still don't know what I could have possibly done. He said did you have fun over that beachs, (or itches sound better minus the "b"), place. I said who Robin's??? I said I didn't stay long maybe less than an hour. He said no beach. I responded with why I have to be called that. I am the mother of both your daughters. He responded, and I heard flunk you. Hmm this is going to be long night. He said while you were gone for over two hours these kids were tearing up the place wanting this and that. Sierra got a little besides herself and I sent her company home and her to bed. I had somewhere to go. I stood there wondering what do I do or say. My body is shivering, and my baby is wondering what is going on out there and interfering with my rest. I am so trying to not show fear that is inside and the thoughts that are continuing racing throughout my mind and wondering is this a fight or flight moment. I told him you said it was okay and I didn't know I had a curfew. Aw man I thought why did you say that??? I heard beach you should have bought your fat ass back home. Only I could think of was that I was sorry as I held my head down fighting back tears. His response was you sure are sorry. Wow how do you respond to that? I didn't know he looked at me like that.

I held my head back up and responded that is one thing that I am not sorry. Strength came up from my soul and I didn't know if I said it or had loud thoughts of saying it. I really don't remember I just know that I said it was this fat ass that caught your dumb ass attention. Aw shucks did I just sound just like Courtney Diane?? Did I practice a thought that became permanent enough for me to say? I really hope this was a bad dream or was I just feeling dizzy. Something is wrong and next thing that happened goes into a blur. I know what happened to my courage buddies showed up and left. Before I could finish my thought, process rushing through my mind, soul and telling all muscles to just shut it down and don't say anything else. I felt my eyes closing as I tried to catch myself on the arm of the couch to keep from falling. I just realized that he just hit me again. I really didn't feel the pain. What happened did I become that numb or did my pain take a leave of absence too?? I just remembered looking at him as he left me clinging to the arm of the couch, looking around for the papers and trash that I had just picked up off the floor. I moved slowly as if the wind, my soul both left and somehow found me. I felt something wet and that was the tear that made its way down my face. Just that one lonely tear that finally said I can't stay in this one place anymore. I needed to come out and just for it to fade away and just fade away it did. Only if I would have cleaned up or came home sooner, this wouldn't have happened. What was I thinking? Did the whole complex hear Bill yelling or heard the sounds when he hits me? Just the thought made me feel a little embarrassed.

All I wanted was just to have a time with a friend or someone that I could just kick it with for just a few moments. I didn't realize that I was really gone that long. While I was having fun, I guess time did get away from me. Man, how could I look at Robin the same way again, plus wonder what the complex thought about our family. Right now, I really didn't care where Bill went. I just didn't want to feel this type of pain again. I just needed to rethink and process. As I walked down the hallway, I glanced again at that blue spot that seemed to not go away. Maybe it was left there for a reason. I go into the bathroom and look in the mirror at a face that looks so tired and swollen again. I get a face cloth and run cold water on it which somehow has become some type of ritual with me. I slowly wring the water from the facecloth, as I slowly wiped my face and I stared into the mirror wondering who is this reflection glaring back at me?? I looked and felt so empty. What happened to my soul, my feelings, my joy and my husband? I slowly leave the bathroom and walk toward Sierra's room and she is still sleeping soundly and still innocent to the world around her. I'm glad she didn't hear him or see his actions, she had enough for today. I go into my dark empty cold room and sit on the edge of the bed. Placing the wet cold cloth on my nightstand, as I pondered so many thoughts of where do I go from here and thankful that my daughter wasn't harmed.

I changed into my night gown, so Bill wouldn't see me naked and I wouldn't have to hear his cruel jokes that only he laughed at. I didn't even glance at the mirror sitting in front of me, because I didn't want to be reminded of what I look like and the yester years of my beauty and my youth that has faded away. Robin words pop into my mind about men and them being unfaithful. She said if you need to have more than one woman what is the real deal? Is it to score all the "oonees" you can get like some high school adolescent going through pimples and puberty, or your insecure short comings? Short comings of knowing you can get many women, but as months fade so does the ladies, once they figure you are putting on some type of facade. Meaning that is he happy behind that smile and bragging of false feelings and childish conquests, hmm that worked both ways with the women and men. In the long run, you end up alone and horny, with pictures and names that just fade away. Was it worth all that, pain and insecure conquest of trying to tap every "oonee" out there? Although, Bill was still handsome, but how long would his looks last before the women realized that he is really a mean person?

Not thinking I dropped the clothes on the floor then in a quick second, I thought girl pick those clothes up before Bill returns home to see them thrown on the floor. Those clothes were picked up so fast I didn't remember bending down or stretching to pick them up, fear entered before my thoughts came in. I picked them up and re-folded them as if they were fresh out of the dryer. As I lay down, I placed the cold damp face cloth on my eyes to take the swelling down, as I cried myself to sleep with no sound. I shivered but I wasn't cold, my thoughts are racing but my mind is numb. When I think back on that time wow it seemed as if the end was that night as far as feeling some type of love from Bill. I now know there must be another woman or women. All I know it is not me. Was I being punished for him missing his date? Was this the beginning or was I in the middle of his affairs and just didn't know. Tears flowed but I didn't cry and eventually fell off into a sound slumber. I didn't hear or feel Bill come home. Should I be happy that he always came home? Does he know how I miss him pulling the cover over me like he used to as I rolled over and laid on his chest and inhale his scent. The scent that I have always love to smell and now the smell has faded away.

I just wanted to lie on his chest where my head used to have an imprint. That imprint too has faded away just like the love he once had for me. I woke up to see his back facing me as if he didn't want to look at me. He was so far away as if he didn't want me to touch him either by accident or just reaching out to feel his warmth. I ease out the bed as slowly as possible trying not to wake him up. I glanced in on Sierra and she is still sound asleep. I go and shower and get Sierra's clothes ready.

ROBIN REED-POINDEXTER

Today I think we need to take or just make that special trip that I have avoided for years. I look through my drawers looking for that card that was given to me a few months ago. I didn't have to look long or hard it popped up as if it was waiting for me to come back and use it for that special ride. Bill was still sound asleep not noticing that we were getting ready to leave and the smell of bacon frying will not fill this kitchen today. The morning is quiet, and the sun is out as usual another California day. Sunshine and the smell of fresh air will be the freedom and courage I need today. We leave out trying not to make too much noise as we listened to the sounds of Bill snoring as if he worked hard at being a jerk.

I told Sierra that we were going for a ride, before she would go with the series of endless questions. I told her that we were going to eat breakfast out today for just because. She laughed can I get panicakes with the face on them. I told her whatever she wanted. I looked at the bus schedules as I tried to listen to her and study the bus route. I needed to see how many buses we needed to take to get there. Keith saw us on the bus stop and asked if we needed a ride. I laughed saying no thank you, but inside I didn't want anyone to know where we were heading. We both laughed as Sierra looks down the street waiting and looking for the bus. I continued to laugh, saying to Keith that he and other people would always be picking us up, because we are always somewhere near a bus route. The thought was really appreciated. I think back to when I had my Vega and the freedom to just get in my car and take off. How I missed that freedom that now that I think about it, I took for granted, never ever thought that I would be without a car. Hmm on the other hand I didn't think I would ever leave Oakwood either.

Sometimes it is frustrating being so confined to that empty apartment. I missed looking outside at my car and it felt good and was comforting just knowing I had transportation. We have never traveled to that area on the bus, so I have no clue on how long it will take and what the area looks like. I'm thankful that I have saved some mad money that my dad used to tell me to always have. Miss Lorena, my old teacher and Miss Vickie J, (my old babysitter) said that I should always have mad money where I can get to it. Seems like almost everyone likes that phrase, just in case. Well just in case came today. Hmm only two buses wow now that sounds good.

So, we load up and head out. We wait at the bus stop to see a familiar face bus driver Hector. He smiled and said has it been that long wow, look at you both. I laughed and told him I'm due in about a month or two. Sierra opening her alphabet book looking and saying the letters associated with the animals. She asked elephant starts with an "L" why it is with an "E". I tell her that you pronounce elephant. We debate back and forth on why it doesn't start with an "L" and why an "E". At that point, she tries to understand the same answer I keep giving her. With wide eyes and confusion, she says you say it e-laphant. With that everyone laughed, while Sierra is confused on their laughter. Hector smiled as he starts to talk about his family and all he had were girls. His oldest daughter Charita was attending college majoring in sociology. She is seeing this guy David James after breaking up with her long-time boyfriend Sheldon. He chuckled at how Charita would get mad when I called him Sherman. I told her hey I got close to the knuckle heads' name. Robbie was cool, but I thought they were too young for all that type of serious. Now this David James he seems to be alright, but I would like for her to focus on her schooling without distractions. I was hoping with the break-up that she would take a break. He laughed knowing from his facial expression that wasn't going to happen. What I wanted and talked to her at length about trying a junior college and you know getting her feet wet by feeling that school change. Then maybe transferring out of state in which hmm didn't want, but I want her to experience life before settling down.

This made me think about how my dad uttered those same words and all fathers have that love for their daughters. I wondered how or what would have happened if I would have taken that route and went away to school. I fell in love by just going to the library to study and chance to encounter Bill studying for the same test. If I knew then as they say what I know now I would have sprinted out that library like my great- grandmother, Mommy did when she chased my sister. Only difference was I wouldn't have looked back. Too scared to see him standing there smiling at me those twinkling eyes and beautiful smile with those deep dimples. Ooh snap back to reality Rita pay attention and don't lose focus on why you are on this bus trip.

Hector went on to say I do want some grand babies but after school and hoping she would get a chance to enjoy life. Wow did Hector and my dad share the same scrip. His other daughters Ofa and Aletha both wanted to become doctors. He laughed we will finally have two more concentrating on attending college. Now, his younger daughters hmmm, Kandance, (I wonder is it Candance with a "C" oh well if you're not writing it down, I guess it doesn't matter). Maxine and Erika, they still love playing with dolls and hopscotch. I laughed asking do they still play that. He laughed sometimes I try the hopscotch with my girls on a good day. Sometimes, these bones ache and crack but I got to keep up with my wife Shelby. She works, volunteers and runs our daughters to various activities that they are involved in. I listened and hope that I will be able to do those things with my daughters. He talked so proudly of his wife and daughters, and I wondered if Bill spoke of me with so much love and energy. I'm listening to him and Sierra and my thoughts all at the same time. Not really focusing too much on all the conversations that are going on but trying to pay attention. Not to mention that we were riding to a place that I dreaded going, but this ride was long overdue.

As the conversations fades from Hector due to the many passengers, I look out the window as Sierra describes everything she sees along with, many, many questions. I love her energy in which it has helped me in so many ways. Today I really need the distractions. I think back on my relatives and the trying times that they must have experienced in trying to salvage or save their marriage or my friends trying to work on their relationships. There is nothing wrong with trying especially when you love someone, but you must keep in mind to love yourself too and don't get lost in thoughts or dreams, or fantasies of a picket fence and perfect husband or family. The soul is there to help you do some searching. Someone has to protect your heart and it has to start with the one it belongs to. What was so different this time to make him mad at me again? The pain inside seems to feel sorry for me too. I wanted to call on somebody that would listen and not judge me I needed a friend, family to just ask questions before my brain exploded and my heart just caves in. I knew if I did, they would call and try to help but all hell would break out and would probably make it worse. Because, they are there, and I am stuck here. Longing for friendship or just to experience a little freedom like I did when I hung out with Robin and ole crazy Courtney Diane.

I knew one thing I didn't need was to lose me. So, I call again on my ancestral strength to help me with this decision. As we meet our transfer point Hector smiles as he tells us to enjoy our day. I looked at him with my nervous smile, because I have never been at this transfer point before. I thank him and looked at the marquee to see when the next bus will be arriving. Sierra says this is different where are we going? I tell her to special place but, before we get there, we are going to special place for breakfast. In the back of my mind I really didn't know where we were going and where was my mind at taking this trip and going to a strange place where I didn't know anyone.

People around us seemed to know where they are going because everyone was moving fast. I see where to stand for our next transfer and Hector showed and directed. Sierra's little legs are trying to keep up with me as I wobble carrying her baby sister. We both laughed as we rush to the next area for a new adventure. We get on the bus and the driver greets Sierra with a smile as she asked his name. He was very polite saying his name was Admiral Tate and it was nice to meet us. I smiled as he smiled back telling Sierra we must keep it moving for other people are behind us. They smiled and seemed very pleasant; maybe this is a good sign. I'm a little excited because I haven't been in this area before. Sierra is enjoying the change of scenery and her new adventure. She is describing everything and sometimes quiet as she absorbs things/scenes that just arouse her curiosity. I enjoyed hearing and looking at her happiness. I again snap the photo and store it up for just in case. I see nice houses and gorgeous apartments and many play areas for Sierra. This is maybe another area we can adventure to again but with her sister added. One day we will get will be another car, so we are not so restricted to the bus route. Everything in the area is so bright and clean and the people are so well dressed. I think back on how I used to love shopping and took pride in what I wore. I laughed when my mother always wanted me to dress sexy and I was more of a conservative dresser. My Aunt LaShondra would tell us leave something for the imagination and her brother Uncle Richard says sure your right. Yeah, but you hmm now that I think about it you got show a little something to put the imagination there. Now, I wished I would have listened that way a practice would have become permanent. If I did, would this keep Bill's eyes and attention still on me? Now the only attention I get is what I don't do. Did Bill mean sexually, sight or what, he really wasn't saying. It could go in so many directions on what he was talking about. He wasn't saying and if he was, the words and emotions were sometimes so mean I just blocked out the words.

I admit it did hurt and would surface when I had some mind down time. That was why I had to snap shot some photos in my mind to fill that void of hurt from words and sight. Or in vision some stories to take those hurtful thoughts away. I tried to tell him how the words hurt, only to have him come back angrier. The look he would flash towards me, with his fire burning in his eyes, with harsh words put every emotion into a shiver mode. The eyes I fell in love with, would sometimes penetrate my soul and infest my spirit to remind me of the pain I had been feeling for years. Maybe today this is the time or the day my life will change for the good and I will not look back but continue to move forward.

I will move to a better place in my life with laughter, that wouldn't be at my expense for a change. I look out the window and still the rain is coming down, but the rainbow is showing and shing on our new adventure. We need the rainbow to show that the rain or the tears don't last in all ways. My own tsunami of tears has passed, and the array of sun is just over the hill waiting for the right time to surface and come out above the horizon. I like the hills, mountains and the beauty of the clouds and trees that surround them. Nature looks so nice; especially when it rains it makes everything look so fresh. That is how I had to look at things as I enjoy this coffee and looking at the beauty of the rain presents in moderation at the right time. We all need some rain in our lives, so we can grow and go. I look at Sierra and wonder what she is thinking. I hope that we, Bill and I, can give her and her sister all that they need to grow and go in the right direction, knowing that we love them and that we are trying our best to provide and teach them what we know. With that thought that means we will be together teaching our children as they go into teenagers and develop into young adults. I smiled just thinking that as our children travel into adult life that they take the knowledge and experience with them.

I get a quick flash of Courtney Diane saying that she drinks because she likes to and when she gets her buzz on her aka Cory D can make a special appearance. Then she smiles saying that a quick cameo by Sonya kicks in and she likes the liquor audience that supports her. Courtney Diane said that when her drinking friends show up, they help her, because she doesn't want to apologize because that requires feelings. She said men that chase a dog, (beaches), just got to chase any tail, even their own. Because, a dog in heat knows no boundaries, tee-hee-hee. Now, I heard her add that a ho that lay with a man knowing he is married or committed is a ho. Courtney Diane made a slight grunt noise adding that a ho is a hollow ho and only knows darkness. The only light they see is when they go from one dark room onto another. They are invisible and to busy being stuck on a duh attack to know they are a ho. How sad when you get to a certain age, they feel that they still have to put notches on a belt to show off their conquest of "oonee's" they have tapped. In this case in their small world quality should outweigh quantity when it comes to a serious relationship. I had boys, but I was ready to marry a man. It's funny how thoughts pop in just to move you to smile, laugh and just have some type of comfort within yourself that only you can enjoy. I needed that reflection. If I tried to share this thought, no one would understand. They would look at me like I was crazy. They wouldn't understand my sudden outburst into laughter because of my deep thoughts. Timing is always good and today it came in handy. Never thought that I would make this kind of move, but I did. We get close to the location and I look around for some place to stop and have breakfast. Just me, (with a sigh), Sierra and her little sister, (Sabrina) getting ready for a much-needed change. With this change I don't have to ease around our place trying to avoid Bill and type of emotional swing.

I wonder what this person or thang he is seeing looks like. Nah, I really don't want to know. Now, is not the time to think about that requires energy, thought and effect and I don't feel like it. Hmm, I feel that ancestral strength kicking in and it feels relaxing and soothing. Yep today is the day. The area looks nice, people walking dogs and some just getting exercise. As we come closer to our stop, we slowly exit the bus saying good bye to Admiral Tate. Sierra and I noticed a restaurant called PataRee' Pancakes. Just what we needed and what Sierra wanted. The lot was almost full so that was a good sign; just hoping the wait wouldn't be long. Well it really didn't matter because we weren't in any type of hurry and Bill is probably still sleep or enjoying us not being there, (so Bill could do him). Maybe he might just wake up wondering what happened to his family and were we coming back home. I just hope that he was missing us and worried about his family.

PataRee's sounds good and family friendly. Sierra is excited about seeing the giant pancake holding a pancake and balloons as you entered, showing a play area for additional fun. The atmosphere is filled with many conversations of people enjoying their food and shared thoughts. I see pancakes in different sizes; colors and hamburgers that made Sierra's little sister smack her mouth waiting for an introduction of pancakes or cheeseburgers. We are greeted by a manager by the name of Leggins. He kindly escorts us to a booth with a bucket of Legos, puzzles, and coloring books with crayons. There also were adult word games located in an area that looked like it was designated for all family members to enjoy. Another area was with older families laughing and playing some type of word game on the table as they waited for their food. Our waitress brings Sierra a little toy rubber pancake with legs and for me a crossword puzzle. Sierra didn't know what to reach for first, the Legos, coloring book or just play with the toy pancake with legs. They had a menu designed for little hands with pictures, so the Sierra could see what she wanted to order. I looked at the menu and the colors and designs were eye catching. Robin would have loved to market/advertise for this location. There is a fine dining restaurant next door called 'ShaRoberts' and I chuckled then and now at the skating rink called 'Mop the Floor' with a bowling alley adjoined. That seems to be busy as well. PataRee's Pancakes what a name, never heard of that before. I guess it must be one of a kind.

They had twenty-five different types of pancakes and ten different burgers and ten different chicken sandwiches. I was at an ah at the varieties of food items listed on the menu. Sierra and I had fun trying to decide on what we wanted. We were laughing and pointing at the pictures as she enjoys playing and shaping different forms with the Legos. Hmmm, this was a great idea for a restaurant. I looked around at the people laughing and the waiters and waitress moving with ease and smiles. We are greeted by the owners Pat and Sheree with their daughter Mackey. She looks at my stomach and her dad and says she had a dream of a baby uh daddy. He looks at her and smiles nodding his head yes. I stand there perplexed not understanding dreams and being pregnant. Pat smiles at me with a little blush on his face and says she asked me about when baby is in your stomach does it come out. I told her yes when they wake up. I chuckled still trying to understand where the dream part comes in. He sees the confusion through my nervous smile.

Then he goes on to say that Mackey asked where they come from. I told her in a dream. She asked will I have a baby I had a dream about babies, and he told her no, she has to be big like us for that to happen. That answer must have worked because she didn't ask anymore questions about my dream. I watched her stand proudly by his side, looking identical to him. She is as beautiful as were parents Pat and Sheree. I had to double take again, because Mackey resembles her dad a lot. But she has her mother beautiful dimpled smile that allows her eyes to sparkle as she laughs, smiles and talks. Such a small person that was saying such big words. Mackey was amazing and very professional. I don't know her age, but she speaks very well as she greeted customers. I bet she calls her mother, mommy unlike Sierra who calls me Rita. I still pause with telling Sierra about calling me Rita. Mom or mommy or ma would be so soothing to hear. Only time I get mom when it's signed on a card, hmm.

I watched them move gracefully together and separate greeting other customers. They seemed to know the regulars' names. I always did like that, going to a place where they either know your name or face. They are such a nice looking, happy family in which was passed onto their restaurant. I wondered how people looked at me and Bill when we are with Sierra. I can see why the atmosphere is so calm, happy and busy. I watched the owners again move with such ease throughout the restaurant greeting each table as their daughter joins in with the thank you for coming. They must have known or noticed that we were new customers. I thought that was so cute and just shows the love that extends from their family onto the restaurant. One thing I liked was I had money for us to pick whatever we wanted and was anxious to taste their lemonade.

Hmm I hope it is as good as the lemonade I had with Robin. I will order some for Sierra, so she can be introduced to something different. Our waitress Vera or Vivian hmm something like that comes with a pleasant smile and not overbearing. Sierra picks chocolate pancakes with a blueberry twist and I pick chicken sandwich with bacon and onion rings piled high. Although, the many flavored pancakes looked very appetizing I'm kind of funny about my pancakes. The only ones I ever liked were my Uncle Willie's, IHOP or Uncle Cully's waffles/pancakes. Uncle Cully would make so many he had freeze them. Hmm I wondered if he still does that.

As we wait for the order, Sierra switches from Legos to coloring while I look at cross word puzzles. This is kind of a different concept and takes your mind off any possible time delay of your meal. Vera's brings us a fresh glass of lemonade. We both lick our lips as we enjoyed each swallow. It feels good introducing something new to Sierra. I slowly looked around and seemed as if the food was coming out in a timely manner, and laughter was still in the air as other children playing outside on slides. They also had papers for painting and drawing. We had good timing as I looked around watching this place filling up very fast. Mackey retunrs to our table with her dad to ask Sierra how she liked her pancakes. She looked as cute as she imitated what she saw her parents do. Mackey said that the chocolate pancakes were her favorite and thanked us again for coming, as she smiles with dimples and twinkling eyes looking identical to her father. They both walked away as she skips to other tables enjoying the atmosphere of laughter, fun and the chatter of many conversations, not to mention the children enjoying the many toys, food, and fun events that were occurring all around them. Now I see clearly why this place is so full. Vera/Vivian brings our food with steam vapors flowing into the air. The aroma from the plates I was hoping that the taste matched. She smiles as Sierra glows looking at the plate with decoration of mini pancakes with the blueberries and whip cream. I looked at my chicken sandwich piled high with the onion rings and steaming hot French fries.

Wow, this is nice I kind of bob my head as I look at everything, hmm just like my father used to do and probably still does when his meal. Just thinking back on that clears up an understanding of why he did bob his head. I hope we can eat all of this. We say our grace and we dig into the mouthwatering meal. We both smile and look at each other closing our eyes. I say hmm, Sierra says yummy and we continued eating and just enjoying our mother and daughter time. Vera returns making sure that everything is okay. Sierra is eager to tell her how she likes the pancakes and lemonade. She smiles as leaves us to check on other tables. Sheree returns to our table asking us if everything was okay and welcomes us again for our support and if we enjoy our meal. I couldn't get my words out fast enough of telling her how impressed I was with a restaurant that caters to all ages, with good food and a healthy atmosphere. I asked her how she competes with the restaurant next door called ShaRoberts and Mop the Floor. She laughs and says she doesn't.

ShaRoberts is owned by her sister Shanta and her husband Joel, and Mop the Floor is owned by her parents Gordon Maurice and Robin Denise. We are hoping that our brother Curtis Alan will join in with taking over Mop the Floor. Hopefully he will. Right now, he's a DJ interim at a local youth broadcasting station. Once he completes that internship, he wants to be a broadcaster somewhere. ShaRoberts opens when we are closed. They are strictly evening dining or special occasions. Normally, they are closed on Mondays and Tuesdays so that we all can have family time. It will be open this Sunday for an anniversary party for Richard and Phyllis. Her husband Pat passes by and she taps him on the shoulder asking did Ben and Robin fax you Courtney and Chasmine's birthday party requests/demands. She turns her direction back to us saying that Richard and Phyllis were celebrating their forty-year anniversary at ShaRoberts. I responded with wow forty years now that's love. But in the back of my mind I kind of envy anyone that celebrated that many years. In my mind and hidden in my heart I hoped that Bill and I will grow old and share laughter with our grandchildren.

I snapped back to hear Sheree say that they were just open for breakfast and lunch, and we have a birthday party today and she had Cache and Jazmine/Jazz help with the set up. ShaRoberts has a mix of older and younger crowd. They are open for dinner only in which they have live bands and on Thursdays and Fridays and karaoke on Saturdays, and the skating rink is open during the afternoon, and weekends. We run this as a family business, so we don't have to worry about invading on each other's business. I laughed and had to ask why the skating ring was called Mop the Floor. She laughed, and I looked at how pretty she is and how well spoken with eye contact and a real interest in our conversation. Sheree said that when you first learn how to skate you often fall, (with a beautiful dimple smile and raised eyebrows,) I got it. I said ah ha and start laughing with her as I think about the times, I used to mop the floor. What creativity. As we laughed, she turns toward a couple walking in and her face lightens up, and Mackey runs to her calling her TT. They resembled each other so I assume she must be her sister and brother in law. Mackey runs to her as she picks her up while she smiles at her uncle calling him Unk. I kind of chuckle as I hear Mackey say to Unk, as she tells him that we are going to find you some hair. Her uncle was bald, it seemed that was the style he wanted to wear, but Mackey in her innocence wanted to show some love and help him find some hair. They made a beautiful couple too. I enjoyed looking at the respect they gave each other with love and supporting eyes.

I hope that Sierra and her little sister will have that type of closeness. Sheree politely introduces us to them. They invite us to their restaurant. I thanked them and hope sometime in the future my husband and Sierra would love to attend. In the back of my mind will we make it there to enjoy the restaurant and look as happy as they do? Both couples looked as if they should be on some type of magazine or models. Both couples were very humble, nice so so polite and professional. This was defintely family oriented. I would have to tell Robin, Courtney Diane and Momo about this place. Spread the good news oh yea Keith and Clarence would love this place too. Wow good timing. They gracefully excuse themselves as they laughed going back to the office to continue their conversations. Their husbands greet each other with an embrace laughing and talking about last night's basketball game and who would make the playoffs. Sierra pancakes are slowly filling her up, but the excitement is keeping her busy as she draws, eats, colors and talk briefly with Mackey.

Today is really an adventure that turned into a nice and pleasant surprise. Well we must finish up and fulfill the purpose before it gets too late and I lose my nerve. I must follow through with this, because I can't continue going on the way things are going. I looked around and I wanted to be a family laughing and sharing mutual pleasant conversations with my husband like I used to. I hope it can happen, I pray that it will, but until then I had to do this. I had to make this move. The place is just a few blocks away. Not too far to walk for short or tired legs. Sierra and I can and will do this. My sandwich was filling for both of us, (little one inside of me), and we really enjoyed our meal. The only noise I heard from her was a burp via me. I looked in my purse for my billford and I had enough to cover our bill. Vera or Vivian, (something like that), comes back and tries to entice us by asking if we wanted any desserts. Wow, that menu was mouth watering, but we just didn't have any more room. I just asked politely for the bill and maybe next time on the desserts. I think there would be a next time, since I know how to get over here. This is a nice area and an easy route. As we get ready to leave Vera gives Sierra another coloring book and Sierra politely thanks her. Ooh that feels good that Sierra remembered her manners. Sometimes she might speak and sometimes she might just look at you. As we go to the counter to pay our bill which is very reasonable, and I have enough money, yeah. The cashiers Delana or Darica tells us that our bill was taken care of, as we listened to Britney and Erin greet the next group of customers. With an ah, I looked at her with a puzzled look of who do I know that would pay for our meal. We didn't talk to anyone other than the owners and their family. Sheree comes out with Shanta with their signature smile and tells us to come back again. She said the bill is on her and looked forward to seeing us again and Shanta smiles in agreeance. They both smile as they handed me an envelope. I politely took the envelope and thanked them both again for just treating us like a family member. Their looks are so familiar, and I chuckle in wondering if we might be related.

As Sierra and I walked out I just stared at how many buildings that belong to this one family. There was PataRee's; ShaRoberts and the other one was Mop the Floor. My eyes watered at such kindness from strangers, they made me feel like family. I stuttered as I accepted their kindness to us. I embraced them thanking them for showing such love to strangers. They smiled and said, now we want to see you again this way we know we will, take care. We both turn in opposite direction with task on our minds. They slowly turned back around when their names are called. As Sierra and I stand there trying to move out of the way, more laughter and hugs are displayed. We are forced into the circle of introductions.

We are introduced quickly to Carissa who is rushing in to make arrangements for her godson Ryan's birthday party. She is followed by her sister who was introduced as Chantell who tells us to excuse her sister for being rude as she rushes by. Chantell feels a need to buffer what she thought was rude action from Carissa. I told her she is just keeping it moving and trying to make it happen. She smiles and her eyes close slightly. When Chantell sees Shanta and embraces her saying she's late because Carolyn/momma had us pick up grandma and Billy because Carolyn and Deac had to run home, right both hmmm, and you can tell that they are really good friends. They continued to laugh using their codes for parents Carolyn and William. Carissa yells with a deep Texan accent come on you are walking too slow walk, talk and keep it moving. Chantell and Carissa seem to sound like they are mad or yelling at each other that must be the way they communicate. They are followed by some parents and many children. I couldn't believe that I was seeing a familiar face, and it was Keoni with some more children.

I recognized Khary, but the other ones look like they are related. Before we are introduced, I say hi to her. She hesitates, and I can tell that she is trying to figure out or try to recognize my face. I told her it has been a while I meant her at Melba's daughter's birthday party. A smile comes to her face as she still tries to recall how we meant. I tell her that her sister in-law Catrice was there. She laughs saying now she remembers. I thought to myself all the cougars remembered your fine boyfriend that made everyone want to write checks, go in debt and howler in some way. I laughed as I remembered them saying love me, like me, make me write bad checks. Give me a reason to be overdrawn with insufficient funds.

I asked if one of the littles ones belong to her. She laughs and saying, unt un, no these are my sisters and brothers. Wow it is a whole lot of them. Kenoi smiles saying that the majority these little toddlers belong to Catrice and Caset. She names them as they stand there as she places her hands on each one, she names. They are in different shapes and sizes yet identical to each other. There was of course Khary, Nalani, the cousin twins Kamaiya, and Kaila, the monthly named triplets May, June, August and another little one Maki. She said that Catrice will be wobbling through here shortly. I looked at her I guess with a puzzled look. Her response was that Catrice is pregnant again only this time with twin boys Jaseri and Jabari. At least it wasn't triplets or one hiding, woo, uh um, hmmm. This brings her and my brother Greekum, you probably know him as William going on eleven children.

I chuckle and say ooh better her than me. Catrice would always say I love that sexy looking man that was TMI for me, too much information. Keoni adds that beauty and sexy comes in many forms and perception, uh. I still remembered him as a walking hanger, no butt, no obvious muscles, just no. Greekum is holding up to being potent and not being important. Funny how I reflected to my thought of indigestion not the same but just my naive thoughts at a young age. I chuckle at every time I think about how we laughed and Catrice not knowing the fullness of that word, "potent" now her house is full of that potency. I don't think I would have the patience for eleven children, but she does have Greekum there to help her, and he loves her just as much as she loves him. I just think back how they would tag or tap one another and smile with the look of young love that has never faded away. I laughed as I look over at Sierra wondering could I have ten more just like her calling me Rita nah. Keoni responds with, no I couldn't have eleven of those boogers either, but I do love all my nieces and nephews. Right then Sheree comes over and takes her to the party room as Keoni tells me it was nice seeing me again. She pauses as little ones run up to her to catch up with the other little ones. Behind them are the other sisters I remembered Leilani and Tayoni yelling at their little cousins, Lalo, Leke, Sofia and Soco to slow down so they don't run into anyone. I thought and could only imagine how many cousins existed.

Keoni was right better her or them than me. While Leilani was carrying baby Elizabeth or Ellie that was clinging hard on her hip. I quickly say hi as they paused while Brandy yells at Boggan and Sprague, display a nervous smile and a puzzled look of who are you. Yet they politely respond as they tried to keep their focus on anxious children running to the birthday party. Tayoni looks back at another maybe sister or cousins saying Trioni come on and she yells at another cousin calling her Milani. Girls walk talk and let's keeping it moving. She responds back I see ya. She is due a month or two behind Melba. Why don't you stay for the birthday party as she looks at Sierra? She would love to but maybe the next one. I would have loved to stay but I had to keep focused on the reason why I was over in this area. As Sierra and I try to leave, we watched many more running feet enter. I slowly noticed that we are in the path of their travel. Sierra and I try to move out of their rushing path.

I listened and like the name Vanetta. I like the name Sabrina but I'm still open to other names. Chantell and Shanta embrace Fetira as she brings in her children Tre Vincent and TaRiah, not twins but cute. Telling them to slow their roll and slow it down and wait for Randy and Isaac. They glanced back and slow it up but walk a little faster without running. Breana tugging with Marquita, Ben and Andre and they are bringing up the rear. Shanta's cousins, Brielle, Tanisha, Lakeisa and Keta rush to her about their plans for tonight, and Keisa said the boys are parking the car. She laughs saying Benny Jay or BJ, Edward Shannon and Shannon Edward are outside trying to see if the two honies will notice them enough to go out, while BJ looks on. Vanetta saying I hope that those honies act like they are yawning and cover their mouth to keep from showing that they are holding back the laughter or a burp. Tanisha said remember when they tried talking to some girls at the airport all that work, and they didn't understand a word they said. Keta laughs I heard them when they walked away laughing and speaking clear English. Everyone laughs, but my thought is that I'm confused on the name reversal of the Shannons, Edward Shannon in reverse Shannon Edward, ooh this is one to tell Courtney Diane.

Chantell says she forgot to tell her that Stephanie, Shayla and Tracie will be late and, Shanta says don't worry about it I still have to go to the airport and pick up my cousin Tracy. She laughs saying that she had to pick up just one person because Kelly and Niki couldn't make it. She goes on the say that I wished my mother could pick up Tracy while she picks up her cousins. Keisha says why not give Aunt Robin a call? Shanta says she should be on her way to pick up her cousins, might be too late.

I told you Cousin Frank is going sing at our birthday party. He is the lead singer for the Chi-Lites. Yep we couldn't afford the Chi-Lites, but we could afford one so take the "s" off just, no no just the one Chi-Lite. They say in sync just one Chi-Lite, no money no "s". As they laughed and paused from the many conversation that were going on started singing the lyrics, "tell me have you seen her" and singing off key the songs they remembered in medley form and doing the Temptation walk combined with their current dance steps. I joined in on the laughter and watching how they interacted with one another. Shanta said that Robin had to borrow the van because she had to pick up Frank, his wife Stephane, and their son Frankie II, plus his brother the actor Darryl Alan and his son Brandon, (who volunteered to be the MC). I heard a voice from the crowd that wasn't familiar. Found out her name was Takeya or TK in which I thought was nice. She asked if they are as fine as their fathers or should I say daddy. The girls laughed, and then I heard another voice uh Tria saying I need a daddy. Keisha says not that type of daddy you are so nasty. Keta says girl you need to stop aren't you still will Raja. Keisha blurts out, no I'm with Roger. Keta comes back with an ooh excuse me. Hey, I'll take the daddy that's coming alone, (hmm don't know who made that comment). Now girl you nasty just like homegirl. Let's get it right I'm not nasty just freaky there is a difference. She directs this question to Keta, so where is your man. You know the one with the presidents' name um George with every name said its nah, Abraham, Adam, Thomas, Jefferson, oh yeah; it's the one with Theo. Another voice chimes in with I or she cannot tell a lie Washington. Keisha laughs that's Abraham Lincoln see what happens when you fall asleep in the back of the classroom, you come out sounding thup-id. Who stupid not you your thup-id you gave Webster another word/definition. Oh, hell no is an annoying response from Keta but she is still smiling. Oh, Herbert vacuum cleaner?? Oh, really, it's Roosevelt. After they played the name game, they look over at Kesia and what about your man?

Before she could answer Shanta asked what's up with my cousins Skip, Claude or Ronnie, Keshia. Nah that is not me that's LaFaye trifling butt acting like a hoochie with a heated fire coochie. I heard a new voice hop in, must be LaFaye. She talks with a slow slur saying that they are fine but, Miss scant I'm not a hoochie I just like to keep my options available. Unlike you all keeping your options limited to one. I limit myself to who I want and today it might be Greg or Joey. Friday, it might be Qunicy, or Lance. No telling my decision my choice. I keep it moving don't hate because I exercise my options. Ava came in from somewhere and starts it could be Dave or Scott it could be Danny or Daniel or then Lafaye interrupts it could be that you kiss my ass. Ava laughs what ass, you so flat you could stand up against the wall and there would be no kind of space. They laughed and said as if they were surprised where did you come from. Ava laughs from behind Lafaye's flat ass. Lafaye laughs and says kiss my flat ass. I had to reflect on how Robin teased Courtney Diane about her flat ass, I guess its universal statement thank God for my more than ample rear. Ava laughs are we going that route again because you have no ass left. I listened to the cousins mixing their conversations with their friends and they sound just like a family. It didn't matter if there was a bloodline or not, they laughed and laughed at and with each other, just like Henray and Floyd did with their boys.

The sound of laugher and many conversations reminded me of family gathering that might be like Catrice and Greekum's family or the shindig that Charlotte and Johnny Lee are probably throwing for every or any occasion. My family reunion would probably be similar to Reva's get togethers very entertaining and interesting especially with an added ingredient called liquor. Just listening to them made me homesick for my family, friends and wished we had times like that type of family gatherings. While thinking and refreshing the fun I had with my friends and wished I could click my heels and be back in Oakwood enjoying what I took for granite. I might not remember all the names, but I'm glad that they included Sierra and I as if we were family. When they were calling out all those names my head was turning/spinning as I tried to remember names with faces just like the gathering with Catrice and her million and one children and family members.

For now, I'm not invisible because I heard my name through the laughter and introductions. I feel life, love and the realization that I'm not that much older than they are as I remember the warmth of their embraces. It felt good being here and hope to come back again with Bill, so he can see and feel the spirit of what families do together. We need more life and energy like this back into our lives. I smiled as I looked around and glad that I'm here with Sierra, and not staying at Havens House confused. Or just riding the bus and glaring out the window remembering what I had before marriage and now wishing I had some of my life back.

At that time, Xuan comes in and tells Shanta that Tony and Chante finally set a date and wants to plan to have the reception following with possible after party; and Dennis and Deborah need to reschedule their anniversary party. Xuan adds that you can put Oscar and Carol in their place. Before Shanta can respond LaFaye blurts out it's about time because Tony was looking mighty fine. Chantell laughs saying like you had a chance. She looks at Chantell and say hey girl don't hate because I'm so beau-tiful. Lafaye responds with laughter as she shakes her body. Chantell says what candle you were trying to hold up against Chante. Keisha laughs the one she burnt out waiting for Tony. At that point everyone bursts out into an even louder laughter. LaFaye smiles crossing her eyes and says oh you got joke uh, but only a little chuckle came out. I don't know who said it, but they said it laughing don't be sensitive. It sounded funny to me too. I had to catch myself to keep from laughing too loud, even though the laughter felt really good. So, good I felt my heart laughing and my spirit just feeling over whelmed with joy. While they were laughing, I was looking around and no one was sad. There was nothing but smiles, laughter and conversations. I listened to LaFaye and at that point I wondered who either hurt her or taught her to think or feel that way. Was she as sensitive to others as she was with her own feelings, or did she stop feeling and reacted by impulse and defense against her heart and mind? We do make our choices, but we also have to deal with the consequences of our decision/choices.

You really can't judge her for standing up and clearing her throat, so her voice can be heard. Lafaye adds, why should she confine herself to one person. Finishing up with she is too young and look too good to limit myself. Plus, this gives her something to tell her grandchildren. What grandchildren no one is going to marry a ho. Lafaye smiles tilts her head saying, well if I grow old by myself hey my choice my decision. I like men and I like variety. Why not create my own buffet of men? She smiles while she is saying don't get it twisted get it straight this is my decision and my choice. They all say it sounds like a hoochie scant. She sounds like Courtney Diane minus the hoochie scant. Funny they forgot ractchet I guess that's for the hard hoochies. When we were little scant, hoochies meant that you were as Courtney Diane would say and I changed to horror. That's a long reputation to live from grade school, junior/high school and reputations keeps following you and maybe into your adult life. Unfortuantely, people only remember the bad not too much on the good. It helps to keep the conversation going. Have you noticed that when you talk about good things it doesn't last too long, but talk about something or someone that just isn't right you can go on all night?

When we were younger those words accompanied with beaches would really be fighting words. The fight either occurred; in the place where it was said, the classroom, cafeteria, or after school where everyone gathers for the bouts, but they fought and lived. They might become friends or just stay enemies Okay Lafaye shouts out, as she looks around at them calling them all heffers. Wow, I haven't heard that word in a long-time surprise that word still exist. There were so many conversations going on it reminded me of when we were talking about Keoni's male friend. Vanetta laughs as she says girl those are your cousins. Nah, uh un they your cousins. I'm family but on the other side of the family tree. Now, if they look like their daddy's I will really be your cousin, hi cuz. So that's what we sounded like. No wonder we were laughing and just having fun with no harm involved. In my heart, I sure would love to come back to ShaRoberts; it sounds like this is going to be fun. I would love to be on the dance floor dancing again. Uh Bill was never a good dancer but didn't stop him from trying. He had the looks but not the movements. It makes me reflect to our college days when I thought he could dance. I just knew that he would show me some new moves coming from Chicago and all, but no I get the one with no rhythm and tone deaf.

Going back to the original thought this sounds like a black-tie affair. I don't have a designer moomoo and Bill doesn't have a tux or nice black suit. Now, I'm wondering too if this is the Darryl Alan that lives in our complex. I asked, and she says it might be he lives in Oceanview with his cousin Keith and, she starts naming some of the movies, plays and commercial he has been in. Wow small world, now that was a hidden secret. Sheree adds that mom is always talking about her cousins. She said how she remembered her cousin Frank singing into a hairbrush pretending it was a mic. As a little girl her mom would be all geedy as she stared at her fine cousins. Remembering Frank longing to become a Chi-Lite and he fulfilled his dream. They managed to stay in contact with each other, his brother Darryl and her cousin Keith. She always said they were her favorites. As I listened, I sure would like to come back with Bill, but who would really watch Sierra and we really don't have clothes for such a nice affair or the money.

I haven't been out in a long time and I don't want to become an old young couple. I sigh as I remembered the fun times we had in Oakwood and college. We were just hanging out without too much of a care in the world. Greekum's sister, Keyana walks in smiles at me. My heart warms because she remembered me. She has three little ones with her, Aulani and Alia little feet moving as fast as they can with displays of confusion on their faces, as they tried to pick up with their smaller sister Lina bringing up the rear. Looking at them made me smile as they were trying to pick up their baby sister that was almost the same size. It reminded me of what Sierra might do with her little sister. I just chuckle at the love being shown and innocent support they are giving each other. They looked like her, so they might be her children. Keyana circles back smiling with one deep dimple and picks up Lina and slows up for her two other little ones, that are giggling as they try to keep up with her. As they giggled, I see the signature one dimple located on the left side like their mother Keyana, with a small mole or beauty mark on the other side, which confirms they are all hers. They looked as happy as they try to keep up with each other with much love. I still see the innocence and support as they join others in celebrating a birthday.

Again, as I tried to leave, I heard hi from the crowd calling the name Dante. Dante enters with big brown eyes and gentle big smile ready for the ladies. He said that Jordan, Curtis Eugene, and LaShaun had to pick up Marcin and Phillip and Joan was driving in. Mr. Woodson or was it, Mr. Wilson they both sound close was looking as he directs the looks toward Shanta saying that he wants to know how you want the tables set up for tonight. Mr. Woodson says with kind of a corner mouth smile that Coleman is going crazy trying to finish that special request of mini cakes before tonight, and you need to separate him from Miss Beth Lauren for she kills him, and Trevor said that DJ Magic is here and wants to know where you want him to set up and confirm any other special requests. At that time, Xuan says I need to ask if he might be available for Tony and Chante's reception. Mr. Woodson says humph he finally asked uh. She responds I guess so. Trevor returns asking how many guards from DP securities. Oh, I forgot his sons Marshal or Mike or Matthew, Matt said they had the wrong dates for their dad's 50th anniversary.

Shanta pauses and says call Davenport no call his daughter Crystal she would know. Joel comes out and without calling his wife's name they just seem like they pick up on each other vibes and turn toward each other and he said he will take care of it. At that time, Sheree comes out telling her that their brother Curtis Alan is on the air and wanted to know how many free dinner tickets will she be going to give out? At that point, Pat and Mackey come out and in sync Pat and Sheree both say for PataRee's we will give out two family passes. I looked at this love that was so in sync with good vibes, communication and much respect. No touchy touchy feely but able to communicate compassion. I looked at how the family worked together without sweating each other, but only showing nothing but support and professionalism. This also transferred to their family and friends. We are all gathered in the lobby of PataRee's and this time Sierra and I are not blocking the path of travel.

As everyone is laughing and into many conversations Shanta tells the group we need to get busy much to do. As they slowly disband Shanta says that she needed to get over there and deal with this mad man and assist Joel. Now I really need to go although I enjoyed meeting more people and being included Sierra and I had to get going before Sierra gets to comfortable and will want to stay. I really enjoyed seeing family laugh, friends talk and laugh with each other. This made me miss my family and my close friends back home, Debbie Ann, Sharon Denise and Melody Lynn. And how we laughed and talked about boys trying to get their lines straight before we started laughing. I thank Shanta and Sheree for their kindness and sharing and taking time to share their family with me and Sierra. Looking at them they remind me of Robin's daughters Denise and Nicole. They both are so pretty, Shanta has an exotic look and Sheree has a girl next door humble innocence. Shanta and Chantell had invited me and my husband to their birthday party tonight. Chantell said when we come that we will be able to meet her husband Anthony. They don't know how much I would love to have Bill and I come back and dance the night away. I look at Shanta and Sheree and their smiles are almost identical. Shanta and Chantell laugh and say almost the same thing at the same time, again showing how really close they are. I remember them telling that for twenty days they are the same age and we always celebrate that fact. I thank them, but I knew in the back of my mind that Bill wouldn't come back here with me for something like this. Especially, if I had to wear a moomoo and other ladies with nice shapes float around in nice fitting attire with "3" inch heels. It would be nice if we were on better terms and he had eyes for only me. I don't know if we will be sleeping together tonight or what. Something had to change because we can't continue this route that we are on. I learned a lot from this day. Sheree and Pat paid for my meal and I hope that someday I hope to repay by buying a meal for a stranger.

I want to keep the blessing going and pass on the kindness that was given to my family. Someone reached out to me and I want to reach out to someone else and share the love that was given to us from a stranger. Kinda domino blessings pass it on. The sun is out, and the day is still young. I briefly think about Bill and know he would love all the places here to eat and bowl. I doubt it if he might go skating. Well he might for Sierra. I smile at the thought of us being a family skating and bowling and enjoying this happy atmosphere that has love and joy. I don't know if Bill can bowl, but this would be something that would be spontaneous. He's always been athletic, but bowling never came into our conversations. For once I can introduce something new to Bill. We can return to a place where someone knows my name and no crazy glimpse. If we are still together, I would love to have us all come here again. This time it will be my treat and surprise.

This felt good that now I can add more names to my list of family members. Sierra thanks everyone as she gathers all her goodies from PataRee's Pancakes.

MacKenzie comes out and runs yelling Brielle and they embrace each other as if they haven't seen each other for years or were the best of friends. Walking in behind them must have been Brea's parents because she looks like both. Sheree takes the time to introduce them as Jeremy and Monique Brielle's parents. I looked at how nice of a couple they were, and they blend in with all the people I was introduced to today. They were not only beautiful but very polite and professional. Now this was an enjoyable morning and day. I still wondered in the back of my mind is Bill missing or looking for us. I hope so??? I try hard to convince myself that he is missing his family. This time let him wonder where we are. I like that feeling, yep it feels good that he is looking and missing us. While walking out a large van pulls up with a woman in it with a bunch of yelling children. I laughed for as I focus its Catrice easing out the vehicle looking like to she is ready to pop at any time, and you can tell she is having twins. Hmm it looks like an extra one might be hiding and maybe she might be having triplets again. I laughed at my thought when she said she didn't understand her mother-in law saying that her sons were potent. Now I'm sure Catrice knows that word very well now. As the many heads pop up and run out, she sees me and greets me with a big wide smile. I'm happy that she remembered me, and it was good to see her after all this time. She introduced me to a petite slightly older lady as her mother Miss Coramae. Catrice resembled her slightly by weight and sight. I chuckled to myself I bet she knew what potent meant. I said it was nice to meet her as she smiles and walks with the many other heads anxiously walking fast to keep from running inside to the birthday party. I asked her about Melba she said she still moving and wobbling along with her. She is having another boy, so Michelle will be bossing another younger brother and loving it. I told her I was having another girl. She asked if I was going to try again for a boy…

I looked at her like she was some kinda crazy and laughing saying, girl baby steps and no pun meant. I told her I saw her sisters-in-law and asked if Greekum had any brothers. She laughs and says a whole heap of them. There's Chanceller, (aka Kaleo), Vince (aka Beno), Randall (aka Auna), Eman and he has a twin Elana, Walter (aka Olajuwon), Eli/Elieber (aka Laluhah), Brenton, I guess the creativity of names ran short and my hubby Greekum or William. Oh, I forgot the baby brother Wellan. You remembered William was a twin, and the twin passed away during birth. I think we are making up for the ones that didn't make it. She flashes that gorgeous smile showing her beautiful dimples. Now all those brothers have at least five to seven kids a piece. I laughed I guess they are potent too. I keep my laughter to myself as I looked at the family members keep coming like an assembly line with labels on their chest showing their names. She laughs back I know what that word means now. Now look at my Greekum, he is so sexy, skinny, toned to me and I got the best looking one, and I just love me some him.

I laughed TMI, too much information. All I remembered as I flashback was that he looked like a walking hanger with clothes on, no chest, no butt, just no all over. But Catrice loves it and that is all that counts. Catrice gathers all the little heads and says stay in touch giving me her telephone number. Laughing saying since Melba is leaving, I know you will need a replacement, give me a call girl. I thanked her, and I told her I would, but I don't think they all can fit in my apartment. I leave feeling good and feeling the warmth on my face and ready to face whatever may be in front of us.

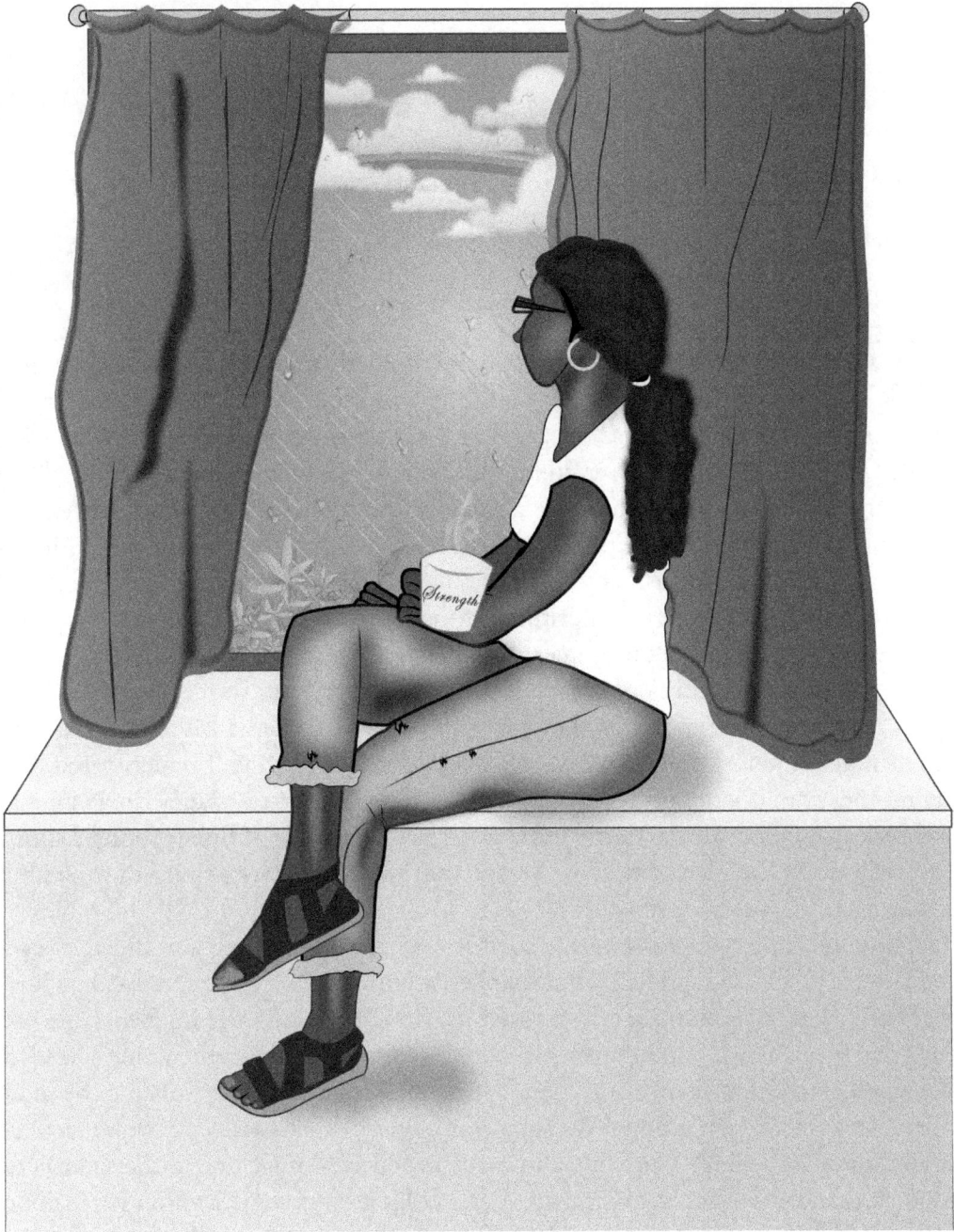

SECTION 2

Another New Beginning

Chapter 20
Make That Move

We walked down a few blocks which felt good walking off that heavy filling breakfast brunch. Hopefully, walking will keep Sierra awake. I feel butterflies replacing the sandwich as we approach our destination. This was a place that I didn't think that I would ever come to or have that type of need. I really didn't like being here after seeing so many families at the restaurant enjoying themselves. Hmmph, this is hard but at first, I was sure, but I just can't keep going through this with Bill. I think back on many older couples that lived in my old neighborhood that probably went through some stuff but managed to stay and grow old together. I've seen where if you ask one a question, they both gave the same answer, or complete each other sentences. I've seen it with my parents and other relatives. So, I know that relationships last as they grow into one. I thought Bill and I was one, but he makes me feel that he is one step away from me leaving. I remembered how my mother would leave only to have my father come over to Mama Roxie's house and pick us up and return to the same situation that we left. Being young I didn't understand but I am learning now. Maybe that was an understanding they had but wasn't what I wanted for my marriage.

How did those couples manage to stay together for so long and did they ever want to leave and stay gone?? The Shepherds and Harris's always seemed to have the look of understanding. They enjoyed just looking across the kitchen table just enjoying breakfast or sometimes in silence, but they were together. I now understand somewhat that silence is golden. What held them together? It had to be more than love and understanding. Was something special that needed to be bottled for struggling relationships like mine and many others that might be in the same confusing situation? I wanted to know so I can at least have some idea on what to do. Now, looking back at Shanta and Joel, Pat and Sheree and Greekum and Catrice tells me that young loves with no conditions attached does exist. They communicate and I'm pretty sure they don't ever have to think about a trixie trying to break into their marriages. I watched how they gently touched each other with compassion and spoke to each other with so much respect and love. I wouldn't know what that felt like. When Bill does talk to me it is as if I annoy him or he just can't stand me being in his sight or presence. How do you feel love from that? I'm only called everything but my birth name. Majority of the time he refers to me as Edith Bunker, a dingy clumsy. Wow that makes you want to rush into the bed and look forward to waking up to hear that almost every morning.

When I was younger, I was Bonnie's older sister, Emma Jean's/EJ younger sister no one seemed to know my name. They would always say how cute Bonnie was with me standing there as if I couldn't hear them or had any type of feelings. I guess then I was preparing myself for now of just being invisible. Now Rita suck it up you just left a fine establishment where they remembered your name, so you are not invisible, at least not today. It felt so good seeing familiar faces and a change of atmosphere and change of scenery. I never would have traveled to this area if it wasn't for the mission, I set myself on. I don't know what all the signs were telling me, but I know one thing it feels good to get out the apartment without worrying about getting home before the street lights came on or before bed check happened. I still wondered if Bill is looking for us or even maybe we might have left him, and he is growing scared; hmm yell that's right he thinks we might have left him. Bill could be throwing up confetti in celebrating that we are not there. Then I think back to what Reva's mom said, maybe the tin man developed a heart. Maybe he might be reflecting on how cruel he has been to me and wanting to make it up and not just a temporary fix. Maybe this will open his eyes and he will stop taking me for granted. As Sierra and I walked we were amazed at the beauty and cleaniness of this place. The buildings, the art work, the playgrounds so much. Nice looking strip malls, people walking dogs, the weather is just right with a slight wind and the walk seems faster than what I thought. We are still feeling the warmth from the sun and the continued beauty of California. We are approaching the house, and the walk didn't seem so far after all. I guess we were so busy admiring the surroundings we took our mind off the distance. We made it to the house and from the outside very clean and beautiful. Inside I'm thinking that I hope cleanliness continues inside as well....

This house fits the neighborhood. It doesn't stand out to make you feel that everyone knows your secret. Sierra and I walked slowly up the ramp approaching the stairs looking around at the manicured lawn, the van in the driveway, with some chairs on the porch and so quiet. Sierra looks at me asking why are we here? Her expression says it all. I smiled and tell her it's going to be alright. I ring the doorbell followed by an almost silent knock. At this point I shivered inside and maybe my gentle knock reflects me shivering in fear. Maybe inside I hope that no one is home and maybe I come back another time and rethink this thought.

Maybe, I was hoping that if I do a quick silent knock and no one answers, we can go. I'm not running away just a little scared about the uncertainty that is behind this door and meeting some more strangers and being in an unfamiliar environment. A lady with an angelic smile greets us. She welcomes us in and offers us to have a seat. She introduces herself as Demetria. Her smile reminds me of the Doctor Upesi who told me about this place. She knew no matter how I tried to convince her I wasn't abused, and my injuries were not from just me being clumsy or ditsy according to Bill. I'm glad she extended her love with concern and gracefully handed me a card as Robin would say for just in case. Well just in case came and we are here. I wondered how many women said the same thing and she looked at them with the same angelic smile handing them a card for just in case. The women didn't know at the time how which this was much needed and appreciated, not only by me but other women that are afraid and just didn't know where to begin. Maybe they are in the fog and/or rain and just can't see clearly. Hopefully their sun will break through the clouds and brighten up their day, so they can feel the warmth of the sun on their face and know that they are still alive. Maybe they need to enjoy a nice cup of coffee and enjoy the rain, reflect and relax. As I nervously sit down, I take Sierra and hold her near me as if I am guarding her. The room we were sitting in had a home setting, but it didn't feel like my home. The place inside is as large as the outside. They must have many bedrooms here. I really didn't want to share a bedroom with a stranger. I have not ever slept away from Bill since we have been married. It just doesn't feel right, but neither does the cruel treatment either. I shouldn't have to test the wind to see what direction he will be coming from or use my words carefully, so I don't get strucked or mean words hurled at me.

I just want the love we had at the beginning. How did we lose it and was it really all my fault for the change of emotions or the change of our environment? I still can't fix what I don't know what is broken, and how did it get broken?? Where were the instructions for repairing this mess? I saw a few women come in and out. Some were with children and some by themselves. I really didn't see any smiles. I guess it is hard to smile when you are removed from the comforts of your home, or maybe it is getting adjusted to being in a hopefully better /heathier place. No one wants to start learning all over again to love themselves, laugh and come back into society as a human and not an object for some type of abuse or a statisic. Some looked in my direction without a smile and I tried nervously to smile back at them, and some kept it moving without even glancing at us. As the last person comes through the door a woman slowly approaches us. I can feel the love and compassion she has for this place. She reaches her hand toward us to welcome us to "Haven's Place" introducing herself as Minister Tamara. With a giant peaceful smile, she says that she is the resident manager. She leads me into her office to talk briefly and assured me that while we are talking, Demetria will entertain my daughter.

Demetria squats down asking Sierra what was her name. Sierra looks at her like she was crazy debating on rather she should speak or do her sometimes normal stare. Sierra could give a stare that made you really wonder what was going through her mind. She finally opens her mouth and saying that her name is Sierra. My thoughts were thanking God, that Sierra didn't numb up. Demetria takes her hand and tells her to call her Miss D as they leave the room. Sierra looks at her and smiles as they go into a room that looks like a children's room, with many things that would keep her occupied. Minister Tamara asked me to follow her to her office for a brief interview and just to talk. Her voice is soothing and demeanor very calm. Her walk flows without effort, and with confidence.

I entered a room that has a picture of Christ on the wall and various scriptures. I mentally say to myself that, my Lord Jesus didn't bring me this far to leave me. I still know and believe that… Her bookcase is full, and the desk looks very neat and two comfortable chairs in front of her desk. She calmly asks me to sit down. These chairs are so comfortable. I feel like I'm sinking in comfort. I slowly looked around the room and how organized and fresh it smells. Everything in this place is clean and well kept. The women I did see seem to be pleasant strangers. I tried to ease my soul and mind while Minister Tamara wants to know my story. She smiles with warmth as her heart connects with compassion to know how she could help me. I sigh as I tried to say without yelling for help, but still scared about telling my business, because you just didn't do that.

In the Midwest you handle your business and you stick it out regardless. You make it work and dare not bring any shame or embarrassment to the family. I thought switch emotions, switch thoughts, brain calm down and nerves be calm, and just tell my story. I really, really wanted to yell from the belly of my soul all the pain and hurt and I needed a place to hide out. Only thing is I feel uncomfortable in an area I didn't know. Funny about I still feel that way to this day. It's strange how I had to take medication for sleeping, bath aides with sleeping sprays, just to fall asleep if I'm not familiar with the bed or environment. I reached inside and pulled out from my soul that I have been abused physically and mentally and I need a safe environment for my daughter Sierra and my unborn child. I don't work, I have no money, and no family out here. I sighed so I could take a breather as the words flowed from my heart out to my tongue. It gets lonely but taking care of Sierra keeps me busy, but soon she will be going to preschool and then what? The then what came in as a surprise, (the then meaning my daughter I am carrying). I don't want to go back home to abuse or move back home to Oakwood. I watched her as she absorbed my every word and for an instant someone was listening and not judging me. I still felt unsure of where this testimony or confession was going. She nodded and smiled as she just listened to me??? I looked at her and my mind ask what in the heck was she thinking? I am doing all the talking and all she is doing is just nodding her head smiling. She reminded me when Bill and I went to the military lawyer and all that lawyer did was nod his head. Then he said that he felt it was okay for $50.00 per week for a child in diapers that some day will out grow her diapers and grows into a little girl that needs more that one pair of underwear. Wow $200.00, what a joke but the lawyer had a straight face and it didn't move Bill and all he did was laugh.

For that quick minute, I knew and gained the understanding about that thin line between love and I can't stand him. Mommy always taught us not to use the word hate for it meant that you would rather see the person dead than alive. I didn't want Bill dead just wanted him to do right by me and our marriage. All I could do was shake my head to regroup my thoughts and somehow swallow what little pride I had left. Inside I felt Bill laughing as my soul cried. My soul was crying then, and I can feel the sniffles trying to force a cry in now. Funny how some feelings can repeat and repeat. I guess it's crazy how it sneaks upon you. Then body slam your feelings giving your soul a temporary knock out… Only thing is who's counting as your soul is laying down for the ten count. Anyway, my feelings repeated as my soul sanked. My mind went numb as my vision blurred as my reality was sitting in that I was here at Haven's House….

I continued to look at the rain outside and inside my life. That's how I feel now; I just wanted to leave. I had to hold it together I couldn't let Sierra see me cry or show any frustration or demonstrate any weakness. She really doesn't know why we are here, and truth be known I didn't really know either. When I was at home, I thought I had the thoughts all straight in my head until I came in and sat down in this chair looking at Minister Tamara. She is looking at me trying to help with my frustrated and confused mind. I'm trying to act like I had put on my big girl panties, but my eyes are showing the pain from my heart. She asks questions and I hope that I am answering them. I really couldn't hear my voice anymore as if things were shutting down and again my thoughts were numb. She probably is thinking that I am having either a duh/dummy attack. I must be saying something because I can feel the vibration on my lips. Inside I wanted to pass out from all this anxiety. I'm feeling the confusion that was taking over my mind, and my soul feels like it has taken some type of temporary residency. Was I ready to make this type of decision? Was I really in the right mind trying to do this while being pregnant? Maybe things will change when Bill sees his daughter like he did when Sierra was born. Is it wrong to hope and long for your family to be the way it was and want a family life like the ones I seen as a little girl on television? They were always displaying the perfect family. In my mind I pictured the white picket fence… I wanted my husband to come home and kiss his wife while she was preparing dinner, and the family is always happy and supportive of each other. I wanted the husband with the picket fence and the love and laughter in the air, the family vacation that I took with my parents. The simple rides with no destination just driving. All we were doing was enjoying the scenery and exploring new areas to visit later at any given moment.

I'm here???? We traveled what seemed like a long time and bus transfers to get here. For some reason time seems as if it is going slow. We continued to talk but I don't remember much of the conversation. I think Minister Tamara was talking more and at some point, I was just listening at least that's what I thought. I might have had an out of mind experience in thinking again. What was going to happen? Was this the outcome I had anticipated?

I reflected on some of the people I had encountered and what would they say or do. Before I could form a thought on what to say, Minister Tamara asked me to come with her and that Sierra will be okay with Demitrea. We walked up some steps that seemed long as the corridor. I remembered the long corridor I had to walk down when I had to hear that I didn't have indigestion. I slightly chuckle, and I had to mentally laugh about my misdiagnosed indigestion. Well uh um Reva was right I should be through with the indigestion in about nine months, and make sure you pick out a name for your indigestion and get a social security number because one day that ingestion will need a job. Now, I have another series of indigestion Sierra's little sister.

Hmm, I wondered what happened to Charlotte and how many children does she have now. Funny I haven't thought about the clinic in a while, but I see it clearly. The nurses' faces, Dr. Jermone, Dr. Hebrard and Dr. Strudwick all were nice and even Nurse Rochelle lightened up. I hope it is still open and not affected by budget cuts. Before going up the wooden spiral steps I glanced into the open door to the kitchen seeing a few women working and laughing as if they have known each other for a long time, kind of like family. So far everything seems like the up and up and feels pretty good. As I walked up the steps Sierra is still in my view drawing and coloring in the book, she received from PataRee's. As she leaves my sight I look forward as this might be where our future lies. Was I ready for this move and leave Bill behind, or was I just trying to put some type of fear in him? What else could I do to make this silent stance work to my advantage? I had to do something we can't keep living like this and Bill needs to know my name. It is the same name he heard at the altar, and the same name when we first met.

Why do I keep losing my name and my identity? I had to silently say my name. But I still felt invisible to Bill and I was only available when needed. I am still his wife I deserved some respect from him. We are on our second child must be some type of love still hidden in his heart or embedded in his mind that we still exist. As I looked into the rooms, I still wondered why we were still here. We traveled clear across town exploring another place to live and be safe and free from the hostility, and anger. I still don't understand and don't know how I got here. What happened to the promises that we would take care of each other before we left Oakwood? Did all that love and support fade away while, we traveled from Oakwood to Oceanview during the yelling. Did the passion leave our marriage? What nonsense did I get myself into? I can't be in love and get stuck into stupid.

As we continued to walk down the hall, I looked into the well-kept rooms that had two beds with two dressers and one closet. A common bathroom shared by everyone, yuck. Can I really get with this new type of life style? I look into another room that seems that it needs another roommate meaning us. The rooms looked comfortable, but I like sleeping in my own bed and knowing the previous owners. She said I would be sharing a room with Keenan. I asked where Sierra would sleep. Her response was that we would temporarily share the same bed, due to limited sleeping rooms. Now, I don't know if I can really get with this. I didn't want to be sleeping in and on bed linen I don't know who the previous owners were. Plus, adding that I was taking her away from her own bed and what happens when my other daughter is born. We would all be crammed into this one little bed with limited resources and room space. I looked around and my thoughts are now racing, and butterflies are trying to take off and leave this whole situation.

Crazy how home seems a whole lot better. I enjoyed this adventure, but I didn't really think this was us. We had our break now it is time to go back home. Maybe being gone Bill might at least have a change of heart. As Minister Tamara talks, I heard her, but was not really listening. Right now, I am listening to my senses and it tells me to go. There is no back up in my mind and now we need to go before Sierra gets sleepy and time becomes too late. I just continued to look around the rooms, the surroundings, feeling the atmosphere and this is not us. I looked at the bedspread and they looked old and donated. The rooms looked comfortable but just not home. Sharing the bathrooms with many other women, I just wasn't feeling that either. Not having anything but the clothes and very little possessions, nah not feeling that either. Now I am ready to run out of here grabbing Sierra as we dash through the door and run to the bus stop. We had to get some kind of gone from here. This is not us. I need to re-evaluate my relationship and leave more prepared. My dad always said when you leave prepared don't have your mail looking for you. I need to have money saved and leave right if that is the route I might need to take. I could tell Bill like Courtney Diane said tell that beach of yours, and get this straight, that I will cut her and rinse the knife off and if I see her on the streets, I will run her over and send the family tweezers to remove her from my tread. I thought ooh that sounds kind of rough/harsh and I remembered looking at her and she didn't blink or stutter. But she said it's okay to keep the same expression and leave them wondering. She was someone that I knew could back up every word she said. She said I took Trixie and Ramon as nothings, so for her, Miss Courtney Diane couldn't make something from two nothings. I thought woo wow that was deep.

I couldn't runaway lost, confused and defeated. I need to walk away as a woman. Like Robin said come in like a lady and leave like a woman or was it come in like a woman and leave like a lady. After all I am grown and now, I need to start acting like it. Now, it's my turn to look into a full mirror, and the reflections of me, and my life with or without Bill. I realized Haven's Place wasn't for me. The thought was convincing enough for me to leave and make an attempt to change something but, it really had to start with me. I again take another slow look around the rooms. The thought about sharing a bathroom, had me thinking no not for me. I looked down the hall at the closed bedroom doors and wonderd how many roommates I will go through before I leave this place. What would be my time frame of staying here days, months, years? Did I want to raise my daughters here and see Bill on days he picks them up? That is not what I meant when I said, "I do", for us to separate or be away from my family. As I come downstairs with Minister Tamara, I think she senses my resistance. It might be the concern from my soul surfaced to the expression on my face. I walked into the room to check on Sierra and she was playing with two little girls that must be identical twins. They are all playing and laughing as if they have known each other for years, I just chuckle and smile as I approached Sierra. The twin's mother comes in to visit her Aunt Tamara. She is introduced as Felicia and her twins are Anise and Anyiah. Now those were pretty names to but I kind of want to stay with "S". I could use those names as a middle name, hmmm.

I look at Minister Tamara and Demitrea and thank them for their time and tell them we need to get back home. They both look at me with warmth and I didn't feel I was being judged for leaving and returning to the reason I had come there. I just knew whatever happens this wasn't for me. Something else had to happen and it will. Funny how I put myself there and when I think about it now, I was really crying out and no one heard my cries because I didn't open my mouth. I thank everyone again and told Sierra we need to get back home. She didn't put up much resistance because I could see she was getting tired and she wanted to go back home too. The problem was what were we going back home and to what type of enviroment. I strongly felt that I wasn't swallowing my proud just enhancing my courage. Not that I am trying to convince myself, but this was hard to take this first step. I didn't know then what I know now that I was preparing myself for many more battles but who was going to come out the winner of this war.

Bill's heart probably didn't skip a beat on wondering where his family might be. We said our good-byes as we venture back past the sames places we passed coming here. PataRees was still crowded; ShaRoberts have their friends and relatives still entering the restaurant. I see many vendors bringing in items as many exits. Wow, I really wish Bill and I could have attended. It looked like it would have been fun and a good place to spend adult time toghther. For the time that I was there they made me feel like I belong to their family. For that instance, I felt not only I belonged but, I existed to someone else in which it was more than one that acknowledged me and a few of them remembered me. The day is not quite over, and we may make it home before the sun goes down. The ride home didn't feel confused or lonely. Sierra and

I both had fun and enjoyed our adventure. As we journey back home, I form my thoughts and think about a plan of action. How did Robin say it plan your action and act on your plan? This long ride was worth it and now I didn't feel so confined to the comfort of my apartment. We had a wonderful adventure today. I learned a lot about myself and learned how to say no.

Sierra is looking out the window laughing and calling out the names of her new friends. She remembered them better than I did, and she didn't tear their names up like I did. I thought it was funny that she was correcting me on how to pronounce them. I had to laugh as I listened to her talking with excitement in her voice and no signs of sounding tired. Too much happened today that kept her energy level up. I figured by time we get home and eat; put her in the bath tub she will go out for the count. I was feeling the same way, but I had to deal with my situation or maybe not. This time it's my decision my rules. After all we live together and share the same expenses. If there is a scant, she would just have to keep it moving because, I am Mrs. Bill and she is nothing. So, don't need to make something out of nothing. As I think about what Robin and Courtney Diane said I wink as if they are watching and co-signing my thoughts and my ancestral strength are still watching and cheering me on. Hmm again didn't know how much I would call on that strength through God's grace. Hmm my stomach is still tight from that big sandwich and even my daughter is resting. Sierra hasn't asked for anything to eat or said she was hungry so maybe I might get away with not cooking or just eating something very light. Bill is on his own tonight. Fridays and Saturdays will be my cooking break and be well rested to cook Sunday's dinner.

Hmm, I kept that tradition for some time. Ouch, out of no where, I haven't thought about my grade school friends Ora, Gail, Annette, Anita, Bonita, Rene D. and Muriel J. in years, and the crazy things we used to do. I missed sharing Muriel J. "s daughter. Later saw Gail years later and she had married my cousin Spike. That was good to hear and glad to see their family. I wished I could have shared her family as I have shared with Debbie Ann, Melody Lynn and Sharon Denise. I had fun with my friends, and they are still my friends. We used to ride our bikes everywhere. Riding down alley's where we knew dogs would chase after us. Wow we could have been mauled in today's age. It's funny how thoughts pop in and out and at the strangest time. I guess timing is everything on anything. I remembered now and saw at a young age their strength that they had even in grade school. Didn't understand then what I know now. Their parents or parent were developing us at an earlier stage than I could not even imagine. I never saw them cry, sweat or back down from anyone or anything. They weren't bullies they were just being themselves and didn't need approval from their classmates like many of us do. I can only speculate that their children are as strong as they are.

This coffee seems to get stronger with each sip as the rain comes down harder than before, mixed with a little hail. I hope at that time that wasn't what I was going home to. Many levels of strengths and thoughts came in on that long to short ride back home. Thinking back, I gave into inpulse and frustration on top of emotions. Why should I lay in a bed that probably had many occupants, while Bill sleeps in our fresh bed and the comfort of his environment? While in the interim Sierra and I are struggling to just survive along with her baby sister. I left one comfort zone did I really want to move again to a new environment with strange people with many different stories??

The thought gags me that Bill will be in his comfort of his home, throwing up confetti and partying to his new freedom. While we become shackled as we lose our freedom. I really thought I was ready to make the move but now is not the time. Only time will really tell or maybe heal the wounds. I just need to stop trying to peel off the scabs. Hopefully, the scabs and scars will fade away into faded memories and be replaced with the joy and laughter that once lived in our spirits and ran freely with our souls. I thought about my family and many other older relationships that last through the test of probably their lifetime. I think about and vision their faces as I think about how they interacted with one another. They flashed in so quickly I just needed just a glimpse of them to remember my own roots and childhood strengths. Funny how timing is everything and it helps to store memories. Those snap shots of memories come in handy. Wow neighborhood friends such as Gail, twins Anita and Annette, Bonita, Rene and Muriel J. from old Druid Hill and McMillian Jr high, Ora, Michelle, Shirley or Melody Lynn aka Mel-T hanging out with them having, while enjoying dangerous fun years. I wonder where some of my classmates are. Then there was Central High, with Debbie Lynn, Crystal, Sharon Denise and Betty. We had fun memories, silly crazy antics/games, Cinderella curfews and some growing pains. Where you were in love with the only one for a week then you break up, cry. Then the following week, or two a new relationship develops and blossoms. We felt that time was on our side and the next love of our life is already replaced by the last love or if you are fortunate enough to fall in love and withstand the test of time. The love of your life sometimes ended before the semester started over again. It balances out in the long run that adds to your life experiences. Some of us made it and some passed on, but the memories are still in form of a snap shot. I still stay in contact with Melody Lynn, Sharon Denise and Debbie Ann. Other friends and childhood memories of adolescence grow. They don't really rush away, but they just slowly fade away until some parts of your memories are completely gone. Until maybe you might need them, and you mentally search the archives to resurface them.

Sometimes those cherished memories will come in handy to one day share either with a stranger to help them along the way, or a friend or just for yourself when you need a smile or a hug. Sierra's talking started slowing up as her eyes slowly shut and the scenery she enjoyed are now in her memories and dreams. She lays her head in my lap and I rub her back as I glance out the window wondering what I'm going home to. Will Bill be home or somewhere else? Did I really want to know or imagine where somewhere else was or with someone else called trixie? As I looked at the scene reverse on our way back home will the situation be reversed? Will Bill give me back the love he had for me and remember that I have feelings and I hurt like anyone else. His words penetrated my soul like arrows hitting a bullseye and the hits did more than bruise my body they injured my spirit. This is pain that I never thought I would feel or a life I didn't signed up for. If this is a story, I had to find out a way to change the chapters and reinvent a new way of living together as husband and wife with two daughters. I don't want to live as strangers, and I don't want to live a lie either. The trip to "Haven's Place" was an eye opener to vision that was blurred by fantasy of a picket fence and bills paid. Just like this rain sometimes you can see clearly and then it alters when the storm comes, and hail is included and perspiration forms on the windows. As the rain comes, I know that the rainbow will shine as the sun tries to fight its' way through. Right now, I feel a new kind of joy and another place to come back to. Funny a bus ride in a different direction gave me a new freedom and a different direction. Freeing my spirit and my soul is flying and the wind is whirling around me and the fresh scent of change in whatever it may be flows through my nostrils and causes me to take deep breath and smile when I exhale with a sigh. Whatever I go back to right now I have no fear. It might change once we get closer to home, but it was all worth it and good daughter and mom time. With a silent chuckle that only my soul can feel. I can hear Sierra calling me Rita as we conduct our routine debate again on why she should call me mom. Maybe this daughter will call me mom and not Rita or Mama Rita. I will hear mom again, yeah. I look at Sierra sleeping soundly and resting. Maybe she is soundly in thoughts of the new names with new faces she meant. I looked at her and how she resembles her dad except she looks more peaceful. I feel the love I have for her and the love for Bill rush through my body like a frozen drink that gives you a brain freeze. That chill I just felt I didn't know if that was good or bad. Just know that I felt a strong chill rush through my body freezing my brain. Is this thought trying to numb my brain, so it can somewhat relax?

It's been a long time since I felt relaxed. I relaxed more as I sipped my coffee and allow my mind to just drift and stop where it wants to. It feels as good as this coffee on a rainy day along with my private thoughts. Our transfer point is coming up and my daughter looks so beautiful, peaceful and I'm thankful for her and her character and her sister. I love them both and only want to try and do what is best. I looked at the relationship with Shanta and Sheree and they appeared to be very close. Their friends and family seem to be the same way too (close). It felt good watching them work, conversate, laugh and still maintain a business posture. I would like to have that type of relationship with my sisters, so I could talk to them about every, and anything. You don't know who you can turn to, or who would really with sincerity would care to hear your pain or your joy. If you found someone to listen would you run them away? Sometimes it's scary because I have so many questions and wanting them to be answered quickly. The questions and stories I could tell might have them running away and not looking back. Then I feel myself maybe pausing without receiving a painful response only knowing that no one could help me. Would they understand what I'm feeling deep down inside and how I hide behind my glasses, so no one can glance into my eyes to view my troubled sad and confused soul. The eyes are the window to your soul, but my view is still not clear. I hope one day I will see clearly.

Sometimes, Bill weakens me and sometimes it is hard to take the verbal punches or hide the bruised spirit and the soul that shivers when he comes around. I never know what mood to be in. I just don't know anymore and how to feel for my husband or my marriage. I look at Sierra and gently shake her, so we can make the next transfer and be on our way home. She slowly opens her eyes and just in waking she looks more and more like her dad. Only difference is I don't want to smash a pie in her face. I only imagine smashing one in his face and having a car running outside as Robin would say for just in case. That thought makes me smile and chuckle. I miss my conversation with Robin and Courtney Diane more than I missed talking and hanging out with Melba. They are a good and much welcomed replacement. Actually, very pleasant replacement and I feel like I have known them for many years. Right now, just thinking about them I'm missing talking and laughing with them. I pictured Robin either doing something with Denise and Nicole, and Courtney Diane either with them or somewhere doing her. Either way they have their freedom.

Once Sierra wakes up, I gathered her and her goodies in route to the next stop then home, ug. She begins to gain her energy back and starts talking about her fun adventure and can't wait to tell her dad. In the back of my thoughts I wondered how much does she remember to tell? Either way I need to be ready for any questions or fillers that might leave a question mark in Bill's mind. I enjoy listening to the excitement in Sierra's voice that eases the tension that I am feeling. She is reminding me of the day we had. It was a nice adventure and a growth process for me. I wouldn't have imagined that I would be thinking about moving into a shelter just get away from the abuse. Now I have a feeling with respect of how hard it was for so many other women to leave and stay gone, or return. The exhausting confusion can wear any mind out. For this short time, thid has mentally exhausted me and Bill doesn't even know where we were. I feel the pain and visualize the fear for the women that leave and had to constantly look over their shoulders wondering where he is now. Constantly having to hide and can't really reach out to family or friends.

All is known is running, running, without money, car or food with maybe a child or children in tote.

Time changes everything but it's a mystery on when. Looking out the window reminds me of how I was just happy being on the passenger side in Bill's car thinking how fortunate I was to be sitting here. It could have been anyone, but he chose me. Life changes just like the scene changes as we pass people walking, talking or just doing nothing but minding their own business, while we look at them wondering what's happening by just looking at their expressions. I don't want to go home and hear the thunder in Bill's voice like I had to hear in my father's voice when I arrived home late, or just screwed up on something or anything it didn't take much. I chuckle at when Courtney Diane said when her hubby Malcom David tried to raise his voice she said in a very clear voice, now you think your bad ooh, humph and nod her head saying, okay real slow. Then I picture that she did her corner smile as she was telling me but I'm sure it was present when it happened. She said that something needs bleaching, Malcom David tried to punk me with his so called, thunder, and thought he was going to leave me shivering in the rain. When he yelled, I had to ask him to repeat because I had muted his ass. So sorry now come on, hold on, hold on, really come on now please try it again. Then that dumb ass had the audacity to repeat it and I shimmered and shook and said ooh and put my hand up to my mouth as if I was scared. Then since I had my hand up to my mouth I yawned, oops Malcom David try it again, I just took a quick stand up nap during your sqeaking or snapping. I begged him to please try it one more again this time I will be scared I promise. He looked at me and just walked away. I did stay there as I promised and asked him not to leave come on, no come now don't be mad, why it got to be like that? I laughed under my breath by George was it something I said, I had to funk with his dumb ass.

I guess he was trying to scare somebody up in here; it's not that kinda party. Robin laughs as I just stared at her couldn't believe she wasn't afraid. Robin said Ramon tried to pull that crap and I told him to come with me and I took him to the girl's room while they were sleeping and said those are your girls you need to raise. Oh, by the way if you need new toys K mart, Walmart and Toys R Us is still selling toys, so don't toy with me. I'm not a new adult and I can hear you better when you are not yelling. He apologized, and it never happened again. Even when he was trying to ask me if I was leaving the keys to the house. He raised the volume but not the anger, he knew better. I started to use Courtney Diane's line with your dumb ass. Courtney Diane responds back sure you're right. I needed that, and it felt good to chuckle and smile. Sierra doesn't know why I am smiling and I'm glad she didn't ask. She is looking out the window staring at the scene changes too. Her head turns from left to right trying to keep up with what she is seeing. I wondered what is going through her mind...

Chapter 21
It's Bonding Time

Off the record and thought, I needed to change. My thoughts drifted off to what Keith cooked or baked today. I sure could use one of his big baked cookies or whatever surprise he might have for us today. I looked at the people on the bus stop and reflected on Courtney Diane's sister Juanita Janise or JJ who was injured while standing at the bus stop. How do you get run over by a motorcycle that was tapped by a car while waiting for the light to change? Her leg got busted up bad. Courtney Diane went on saying that she was a trixie with a name as she called her other than a rachett, (I heard), horror scant. All she dated was married men. One she dated for some twelve years plus. She was at his wedding reception with her dumb ass, but not at the altar, watching her man and his wife exchange vows. Men don't usually marry their mistresses they marry the other woman that has their heart. She said karma came at got her dumb ass.

They would meet maybe two to three times a week for seafood lunch, (of course not dinner). Mr. Trix had to be home with his family or that other, woman her dumb ass didn't know about. If, the wife did know, she probably was numb and had stopped caring or worrying some years ago. The wife didn't care because the trick was doing what she probably didn't want to do… JJ and her male Trix would attend comedy shows at least once a week and she didn't blink twice about seeing or being with someone elses husband. She didn't have any type of shame. Here I have my hubby dressing in my stuff oops she laughs, I am drifting away my bag. Anyway, karma came around and took a seat and crossed his/her legs. When that motorcycle fell on her leg, now understand there were about ten plus people waiting for the bus and that cycle found her. So, now she couldn't work the jobs she wanted. She worked many many non-thinking jobs and managed to get fired from each one. JJ went out with Mr. Numb nut and his ass got sick, and the side effect was if or when he would get excited, he would have seizures. So there went the sex and the comedy show oops. Oh yeah on their seafood meal JJ had an allergic reaction choked the dit out of her while trying to eat seafood. So now she can't eat shrimp, scallops all that seafood she loved gone and faded away from her tastes buds another enjoyment removed. Then karma uncrossed its legs stretched and set back down and crossed its legs the other way.

The one steady job she did have was a part-time lover, aka scant, closet classic, trunk trixie and a full-time fool in which she was very good at, what an idiot. All that education, money our parents invested, and she grew up to be an understudy. An AKA, (another known action), called under someone's husband. You know t understudies' study to try to advance or receive the role of wife, with their dumb ass. As I listened, I started back counting the dumb asses Courtney Diane kept saying. I was wondering when she was going to say her famous phrase. I look at her as she continued with the issues, she has with her sister JJ. I don't think she's as mad as she was disappointed in her sister's career choice of homeraker, scant, closet classic, trunk trixie or her occasional reoccurring role as an understudy. She said that JJ finally found work, a job that supported her master's degree and not her mistress degree. Girl had worked at this nice place for about hmmm few years. Now get this dit just when she was feeling comfortable and into herself all that humblness went out the door and she thought she was some hot dit. Then her job pulled a surprise and conducted a random audit. In which they conducted a background check and went back over twenty years plus and found out she had been convicted of petty theft and fired her. Who goes back that far, really twenty years? Now, Miss Degree is back working those temporary jobs with a slight limp, with her dumb ass! Courtney Diane shook her head letting us know she was not through girl, walk with me don't drop my hand or skip around or behind me, because if you do drop my hand and run out and get your ass hit and that dit is totally on you. I remembered Robin and me looking at each other as they both sipped their wine while I enjoyed my Chai tea. Courtney Diane added that this didn't happen all in one day it was sparatic.

Since her married lover couldn't perform, she couldn't attend her comedy shows with him or eat shrimp, any type of water creature. That entire fun she had at someone elses expense gone good bye, bye, bye and no more tricks. She had to fill that void somehow with someone. There weren't any married men readily available, so one day she decided to go and walk the lake just because. Courtney Diane, tee-hee-hee laugh gave us enjoyment and entertainment. It's not like JJ was in a hurry to go home to an empty home or bed, nasty scant. Anyway, she was feeling herself and decides to feed a squirrel with some nuts she had in her pocket. JJ was really bored since she could no longer hookup with her numb nut. So, in her boredom, she kneeled to feed a squirrel and the squirrel held on to the peanut. She didn't let go of the peanut and the squirrel was holding on and flying in the air still holding the peanut in its mouth. So, JJ dumb ass was raising her hands in the air with the squirrel holding on to the peanut for dear life. She's waving and flapping her arms in the air, not realizing that she needed to let go of the peanut. That squirrel wasn't dumb just her ass. Mr. Squirrel had enough sense and didn't want to take off flight in mid air and land somewhere not knowing what it might hit. The squirrel wasn't the dumb ass; JJ was the one with the degree. For some reason common sense didn't come into play. We were laughing almost in tears as Robin and I tried to catch our breath, while listening to Courtney Diane's story. JJ had a sudden thought with her dumb ass let go of the damn peanut. Oh, yea and she did, and the squirrel looked back at her maybe calling her a dumb ass and it ran off with the peanut. I guess she got her nut huh??

After that ordeal she sits down by a tree to rest, exhausted from flapping her arms. JJ leans back against the tree. Somehow, she closes her eyes maybe, for just a quick ooh and aw breath. Then suddenly, she felt something wet and warm on her. She slowly opened her eyes thinking what the funk is happening now? It was a clear day and no signs of rain. JJ was perplexed on why she was getting wet. She again slowly turns her head and a dog was pissing on her girl. In her rush to get up she trips somehow falls flat on your face, scaring up her nose. I had to step back and look at her when she was telling this crazy ass dit. Can you really get with some strange dumb ass stuff like that? I hope her dumb ass learns from that. I hope she learns that she needs to start looking at married men like they are wearing some type of kryptonite ring. Run dumb ass run. So now she is at home looking at television with her memories of the karma that hung out with her and took a temporary seat. You can't do ugly and think that if you are cute you will get away from karma knows no face just reacts.

I thought I hope this is not the sister that Courtney Diane talking about, letting her stay in her apartment. She couldn't be that sister?? I hope it's not her, she doesn't have morals, self esteem or kids, ooh. That was one thing we didn't need, was that type of woman around me or Bill. Then it dawned on me as my thoughts, temporary spaced out Courney Diane and Robin's laughter, that it was one of the two other sisters that were close in age. Hmm what were their names? Courtney Diane laughed but was dead serious about how her parents Mama Florrie and Papa Cleve Jr. JJ's would react to JJ's practices. With her quick wit Courtney Diane said that none of her sisters were raised to act like some street ho. If Mama Florrie found out she would still be warming her foot up JJ's ass. Anyway, it didn't matter Courtney Diane was still in her talkative moment. She said that her mother didn't play. Her mom always had flashbacks about her cat that scared her. Mama Flo sent him out with firecrackers on his tail and didn't know if those nine lives helped him. To this day when she tells the story she always adds she didn't know what ever happened to that cat. All Courtney Diane could add that, I know is that Mama Florrie didn't play, and her walk and talk had the same force.

JJ should be happy that our parents didn't catch her ass fooling around with married men, and her dumb ass secrets. If Papa Cleve Jr. found out, he would make her tremble at the sound of thunder coming out of his mouth along with a very long lengthy lecture and the look that had a hypnotizing affect. When she said that it made me reflect on how my father and his mole in his eyes had that hypnotizing affect too. Twelve years of being someone's spare time or tire was a waste of time, to be a trunk trixie. Why can't she put that kind of time into her own boyfriend or hubby? No that scant had to play games with someone elses life and love. I sit back and wondered what JJ look like. What look did she have that gave her the confindence to think that she could take anyone's husband? Well let me take that back because it takes two and you can only dangle candy in front of a baby for so long. I always thought that if I did something like that it better be better than what I have, but just the thought just sounds nasty.

The time changes just like the weather today. Rain comes and fades away as the time in the day. I always did enjoy the rain it was the storms in my life that bothered and scared me. What was I going home to? I left without leaving a note or calling to let Bill know where we would be or the time, we might be returning home. The day is not over but I become mentally exhausted at wondering what I will be coming home to. Will love be shown or the look that I dread, just like the look my father would give me when I came home. Either way it was nerve boggling. Looks from my father and Bill would just hypnotize me and put me into a place where my soul shivered, and my mind went into a duh or dummy attack and shut down all thoughts and brain waves went surfing. Hang ten right, they didn't hang out at all everything inside was stuck on fear and my mouth would not come together with my mind at all. I would just listen to the yelling words that didn't have any part of my name in it. I was everything under the sun but Rita. This flashed me back to my parents I very seldom heard Rita without an attachment. It was either shift Rita, or Rita shift. How can someone tell you they love you and in the same breath make you feel hate from them. There is an imbalance between love and hate. How can you hate someone you love so much? I still loved Bill in spite of how he treats me. He still was a good father and was still providing just with strict control. I still didn't have a car and the monthly allowance did help. Well sort of after I paid some bills. This sometimes left me with very little. My dad always told me to put up some mad money, as Robin would say for just in case. This ride seemed longer even though we are just reversing the directions. This time it gives me a chance to get my thoughts and emotions together to be prepared for whatever I encounter when I get home. I feel like I'm back in high school doing the cinderella thing rushing home before I get in trouble and had to deal with the consequences. I didn't like it then or now, this was not a good feeling and just too many thoughts on the "what ifs".

When did I stop being his wife? I'm still wanting to stay married and Bill for now he is still my husband. I didn't want to go back to Oakwood as a failure and start all over again while wondering what Bill was doing. After all he bought me out here and took me away from my comfort zone, family, friends and the life I was trying to make for myself and my daughter. Could I ever leave Bill? In the back of my mind I knew the answer was no and stored there was why even play with such a thought. Like Mama Sadie told my dad he had to ask. Right and he asked me I must remember that out of all the women he asked me. I chuckled a little at what Chris told Reva about Maurice, he picked you and Reva right and that's why I am sitting here in this chair and Chris is out doing her and I'm doing baby or indigestion. I now laugh at that thought I had then and now how crazy funny calling my pregnancy indigestion. At that time, I didn't know then that I was in some serious denial. Indigestion humph that is funny. I was so young and naive. It didn't dawn on me that almost everyone in the clinic was pregnant.

I remember I looked into the mirror and worry was catching up with me and aging me fast. This part is not what I signed up for; I still want my youth just like everyone else. How can I change the looks back to the fun I had and the love of life that was inside me? I'm not dead or dying, but my soul feels like it has lost its spirit. It's time for me to renew my spirit and put some pep in my thoughts and walk. I'm fighting me not Bill. It's my soul I need to strengthen. I need my ancestral strength to get me through whatever is on the other side of my apartment door. I didn't come all this way from Oakview to fail. I came all the way out here to live and to be a family unit. I'm stronger than this situation. It's my life and it's worth the struggles and strains to continue to share my life with Bill, Sierra and my unborn daughter. I want to live and continue to love my husband and raise our family. This is my family and not up for any Trixie to take away in any way shape or form. Not today and not at any time. Just at that instant the names of Courtney Diane other sisters surfaced. She really had a issue with the rhyming of her sisters names for instance; Litte Noreal (Litty) and Latte Noreen (Latty) she laughed that was some silly names my mother's sister Aunt Gigi came up with, and moms came behind with some tripped out shift trying to make them look like or sound like twins. They were a year apart, but she would dress them alike and people really thought they were twins. Thinking back as I look at the rain, you would have thought that, Sharolyn and Carolyn were twins by their names. They weren't but they were very close in age and to each other. The last I heard was Carolyn was a good debater and chemist major in high school and Sharolyn was working on biology major and working with special children. They looked like sisters, but no way did they look like somebodies' twins. I fade in and out in thought of Courtney Diane tripping with her family names. She said just like my brother Cory Davon we anin't twins either. Oops we are not twins, let me represent Mama Florrie as she points her little pinky finger stretched out as she corrects herself. l laughed because I remembered she said her moms was a school teacher would probably give a "F" grade, with punishment and extra homework on grammar usage. Mama Flo had Cory Davon and me, paired like some salt and pepper shakers and stuff. Hell, we came in on a solo slide down the birth canal. I didn't see him or give him a dap or heads up or remember being told we shared the same uterus, ew and yuck. I thought me sliding down her birth canal was a solo run. Nope don't remember tag teaming my brother with a dap while passing him, or him telling me on my journey out to sunlight and cold air that it's cold out there. I will see you much later sis. She laughs hey bro what's up, huh, what the funk. Yeah, we are like two years apart. They paired all of us except Juanita Janise (JJ).

Papa and Mother Florrie thought they were through with kids and some ten years later oops here pops out bright eyed JJ and she wasn't paired. Well actually she was paired with Aunt Gigi's last 'surprise. Her daughter Jazelle Jalese (JJ) surprised her ten years later too. Our JJ is more like the, (Robin looks at me and we both say like the friend of the family and laughed). Oh, yea we chuckle, Courtney Diane gives a corner smile saying yep a friend of the family. As Courtney Diane sipped her drink she said, "What kind of mixed drink did mom and Aunt Gigi drink, was it some kind of coffee with a big hint of wine"? Suddenly, her face flashed a perplexed look how my mother and her family came up with such goofy ass names. I'm glad I've been subsituting Courtney Diane's adverbs for the other words because she sure is using it a lot.

She went from complaing about rhyming names to unusual nick names. Like how do you get Ronnie from Sharon? They call my Aunt Sharon; Ronnie is that some crazy shift. I agreed and said that sounds like some crazy doggie booboo. Courtney Diane smiles and Robin laughs harder as they sip their wine and agreed by both saying that is some crazy ass doggie booboo. I just wondered to myself was her brother as cute as Courtney Diane. She takes my cup of tea holding it up really naming my sister Latte, who names their child after a foam coffee hmmmph?? With her corner smile she says now that is some crazy doggie booboo. Just like my Aunt Ronnie her daughters Olivia Tomay, aka Oli. Okay I can get with that her sister matching name is Onna Tehee and no they are not twins. Now, that sounds like you are getting ready to laugh when you say or hear her name, Teehee. We all agreed and laughed, with Courtney Diane saying thank God she goes by OT instead of tee-hee. Their brothers matched too again they are not twins, Armond Kevon and Armen Kevin. Now that is just too close in names. That must have been strong ass coffee on that day and more than a taste of wine.

They stopped at four, but if they had that extra one you know the friend of the family they would pair with the other sister or brother. Who thinks up that crazy dumb ass pack? What did my aunts and my mother do; just sit around kitchen table sipping coffee with a dash of spices and a cup of wine tripping. I'm laughing because I'm thinking of the Malcolm David's holiday sisters Hannika and Kwanza. For that moment I reflected on Shanta and Sheree's cousins that had backward and forward names Edward Shannon and Shannon Edward you thought of that combination, humph did those coffee fumes travel or became airborne. I guess those coffee fumes from Courtney Diane's aunts traveled. My other Aunt Veretta they called her Etta and her daughter Nakia DeLynn, aka Kia that's okay match. We both say not twins Courtney Diane glances at us with a smile adding her match Nikia Derell was Nikki ok that works too. I thought it's funny because I hadn't heard that name Veretta in years. I remember being told by Veretta's brother Floyd that she was up to seven kids wow. I could only imagine that Miss Clovis and Reggie Coy were enjoying them on Reggieville homefront or was it Clovisville. Funny you don't hear that name often. As I tune back to Courtney Diane, she had an expression of puzzling concern. Ok ok now Aunt Alberta or Aunt Al now that sounds cuckoo is, she an aunt or uncle. My family came up with some whack nick names. Oh, hell crazy first names with attached middle names. We all said in sync that is something wrong up in here.

Her matches were cuckoo had us cracking up. Made me flashed back of my great- grandmother Mommy how did she feel having the name Douglas Thomas, was that some back then confusion?? While her sisters Mattie, Sadie, Saferia had girl names and she was stuck being named after her uncle. I guess that was the luck of the draw. She wasn't the oldest or the youngest again her name by chance and not position. Mommy couldn't read or write but she sure knew how to fight. Yep, she dealt with being named Douglas Thomas and there were no short cuts on her name. Mommy had a strong heart, strong legs and she slept with a big gun, razor strap, and switch blade along with a heavy hammer underneath her pillow. It was funny when she chased my sister Emma Jean out the door for sassing her. Wow, that woman could run surprisingly at her age. I still laugh at my brother breaking away from a fight and Mommy locking the door as she pushed him out, saying we don't do that. She was raising fighters and not trying to have us fearful or looking over our shoulders. My brother Charles probably didn't look at it that way. Still didn't know that I would be calling on that ancestral strength. I'm thankful that she was my great-grandmother. As we listened to Courtney Diane, I still picture us sitting around being so relaxed. It was the one time I was able to spend time before Bill came over and ceased us from talking. It felt like I had to go home because my mother called me home or one of my siblings came over to my friends and said mom says its time to come home.

I still pictured Courtney Diane sitting in a large comfortable light brown leather chair with her wine glass on the end table, Robin and I was sitting on each end of a nice soft kind of dark tan leather comfortable couch with the television on low looking at us entertain it. Courtney Diane says hold up hold up now listen guys I'm having a moment here and I just got to share this shift. Robin looks at her with a smile and said you are being a little sensitive. I looked at Robin, she has a gentle spirit I just think she doesn't advertise about her bark and bite are the same. Only time I saw her upset and showed the look to support it was when she was talking about that trixie. Courtney Diane looks at her smiles calling her a heifer. Robin crosses her eyes and responds with cow and makes a moo sound. Robin laughs as she tries to generate a tear for her, as she wipes the corner of her eye looking at her. Lookey look as she chuckles at Courney Diane to look before the tear evaporates. She responded back with I do have feelings. Robin laughs you still trying to convince us uh. She laughs I know I have at least one feeling. Robin laughs you have feelings. Courtney Diane laughs feeling no "s" on the end.

So, if you get emotional understand that I am saving that feeling without the "s" for a special occasion. We responded at the same time saying ooh ah, okay. She looks in my direction and says now I'm gonna quote my girl here Rita, I smiled just to hear my name said and it so felt good. She continues, walk with me don't drop my hand. Now Aunt Al names her girls Elisia Joann we called her Eli there goes that generation of confusion. As Robin and I laughed and commentated, we paused saying in sync, "we know that they match but, they are not twins. Courtney Diane looks at us smiles and continued with saying Elayer Jane and called her Layer.

I had a thought within a thought about my friend Joann back home. I heard she joined the army and taught hand to hand combat. I'm sure she stayed 4"7 and quick if not quicker. She took on one of the rookies and he ended up in infirmary. Then another taller, bigger, stronger rookie thought he could take her on too. Only if he knew what I saw he wouldn't have chanced it. He ended up in the bed next to the other rookie she put in prior. I laughed at what was said that the bad rookie stated man I think she held back because nothing is broken. One thing they both agreed on was it happened so fast and that they were both in a lot of pain and, she was quick and good. I see she held up to her reputation and became quicker. Armed forces sawed off secret weapon, humph. I'm trying to hold in my laughter on this bus, but these thoughts are killing me as I pictured the characters, and this puts me in a place of happy and relaxed.

Then my thoughts faded into looking at Courtney Diane and the armed forces were the right fit for her. Her bark and bite are the same as she had said about her mom. I come back in to hear her say now I love my cousins and they love their names. They love it I like it. Sierra is enjoying the scenery and being away from home. Funny and delayed later Courtney Diane's cousin Layer, if you do say it slow it sounds like lay her, (tee-hee-hee). We took Courtney Diane advice and said it slow and at the same time our eyes enlarged and in sync we said ooh. Now humph, she held true to that name, something like a scant. Courtney Diane said that Layer and her sister JJ ran well together in the day. They both dated old men at their young age and they taught them well. I thought about that of some of the girls I went to school with that dated older men and were all advanced beyond our imaginations, like Violynn, Terri, Roxanne, Vendeese, and who could forget Penny with biggy smalls. Wow what are they doing now? If you had a lot of enjoyment at an early age what is there to look forward to, and what profession did they choose, or did it choose them hmm?? Courtney Diane went on with her; Aunt Al had another set of names. Katya Ann, (now get this I heard shift again), they called her Mittens because part of her name starts with Kat. What the flick is this kinda dit. Robin and I said again in sync, 'family match' again and we smiled saying we know they are not twins. Courtney Diane totally ignored us adding more family members such as Kyler Annette and get this they call her Leler. Was that a far reach Leler where did they fly that name in from? Leler's brother came in flying solo, no twin name; they called him Xente Gene or Tee. Ladies help be understanding how do you get Tee from a name that starts with an X?? Talk to me don't hum or run help me with this thought. Matter of fact why use an "X" you don't pronounce. What they just had to try an un-used alphabet huh or what??

She throws her hands up in the air as if she just gives up with whatever!! How do they make this dit up what in the hell is wrong with my family with these crazy cuckoo ass names? Who has that kind of creativity? Robin and I laughed saying 'your family'. We laughed as she was trying to get her point across, (she added a little chuckle in there herself). As I reflected, people on the bus probably thought that I am just totally cuckoo as I chuckled to myself. Courtney Diane with, her mother's Uncle Encin O, and the O is just a letter no name attached just an empty ass letter "O". What happened did his mom pass out from the annesia before completing saying his whole name and just said oh well and the day ended on that small minor thought?? What happened to the follow up? He has one son name after him, but the "O" stands for Other, not other who names their kid after an adjective?? Their daughter little Jacqueline missed the name game. Their family stayed away from our family nonsense. They only see us on special occasions. As I looked back the sisters must have made a.... pack; that they would share names, had some fascination with twins, there is not one set of twins in our family and that they would have five kids a piece because their parents had four or five kids. Courtney Diane goes on with I just figured out that dumb ass shift, today. What about Uncle G O. I made a mistake by saying ooh 'Gio' is a nice name. See looked at me as if I really didn't understand. Rita, she says out the corner of her mouth no not Gio the initial "G" and 'O' together GO. I guess his momma got stuck on the middle name with being "O". No name no meaning just sounded of what the hell just put the "O" there and I will get back to it later and later faded away into the abyss. Courtney Diane insists on having us listen to her couch therapy. She softly called us ladies and insisted on having us listen. She said someone please hold the door open. Now I'm not beaching, (haven't heard that word in a while replaced beaches with an i-n-g, or bee itching, hmmm). I'm just venting on some outdated thoughts. They had to have had something more than coffee, wine or something to come up with these crazy combination names. Maybe too much inhalation of the amora of spices while cooking. Yep, they encountered some type of toxic fumes.

Think this out you don't usually hear your first and middle name unless you are in trouble or filling out some paperwork. Why they got to say the whole mother of friend's name. Now get this forgot about this far distant cousin practiculy overseas but the fumes from my mother's kitchen carried along with aroma of that strong coffee and taste of wine. Anyway, her cousin Roberta Racine did the same name game too. Now that I am getting the hang of this I gonna take a courage sip and throw a dart in the dark. See I am gonna take a shot in the dark on her nickname and I would say they call her Tay, because of the ending of her first name. I am just as crazy because said that I was right on that crazy shift. Her name is Richelle Jean and Rouchelle Joy now RJ would work right. I briefly thought about that mean Nurse Rochelle she is probably still working at that clinic still with very little conversation or feeling with no "s". Now, Richelle Jean aka is Reggie or sometimes Wanda don't ask, and Rouchelle Joy is Randi or Wilma again don't rattle your brain this is some family blue skies. Listening to her I had to work hard substituting some choice words she likes to say. Hmm I really didn't hear her say dumb ass or with your dumb ass, hmmm. Wow Courtney Diane was getting deep into her family names.

Hello, she says as she leaned forward in her chair. This is not normal whats wrong with my family?? Tell me this isn't crazy. She looked at us as if she wanted an answer. Come on stay focus as she crosses her eyes and Robin looked at me and crossed her eyes mouthing watch this. What about the other cousins that names rhymes like Shulene Corrine? We looked back at her and continued laughing. She laughed saying watch her maybe her other alter ego Sonya might show up. Maybe not today but give it time Sonya will make an apprearance.

Courtney Diane isn't a laughing type of person, but she does crack a side smile occassionaly with a tee-hee-hee and ha-ha-ha. She was looking at us while we were saying that your family is funny. Help us spell funny is it with an "E" on the end? Robin laughed saying so you're adding another vowel "e". Courtney Diane glances at both of us, then looks back at Robin saying I know my vowels "a- e- i -o- u" and I will see your ass later outside heffa, cuz you got jokes. Robin says, (laughing), ooh I'm sorr-wee with a "wee". Or should I be trembling now or later as I go outside, (while putting her fingers up to her mouth as if she was chewing on her nails show- ing fear), saying ooh I'm scared help me Rita help me, (in a little girl's voice), adding we know no "s" right? She puts her arm up to her forhead looking with one eye open and the other one closed saying I am so confused help me. We laughed through it all as Courtney Diane crack a smile through that hardness.

She is beautiful with or without make up with smooth skin, with one deep dimple that she passed on to her son Henry Luis. We are laughing maybe through our own silent pain but need each other for just a laugh and sisterhood bonding. It's one of those things or situations just go with the flow and walk with me and just don't drop my hand or you will get lost, especially if you skip around. Hey, we can skip together if your want to. My mother's cousin went with the letter "R" theme. Every child she has names begins with an "R". We paused for air and started back laughing so hard that Courtney Diane joins in, (which was rare), as she sipped on her wine and uncrossed her legs to cross her legs again and saying what is wrong with my family? She said it out of the corner of her mouth shaking her head from side to side and that was the end of that, and we never revisited that topic again.

Courtney Diane just needed her moment and she got it. Until now for me I needed that flashback laugh. Robin glanced at me with her brown/blue eyes widen just a little with a corner smile and saying hey you forgot about your freaky cousin Fergie, you know the one they name Gladys. Courtney Diane looked over at Robin with her brownish eyes that closed slightly with a response of damn my family got some 'uck' up when it comes to names. What is wrong with my peoples as she sipped slowly from her wine glass looking over at Robin saying Robin Denise and starts to laugh. Robin's eyes widen with a quick cross of her eyes and postion her lips in a pucker up with ut oh oops, so sorry, Courtney Diane, my pookie!!!

Chapter 22
Rhona's Loves Flour

Courtney Diane smiled through her infrequent laughs and Robin asked her about her crazy cousin Rhona. Is she still cooking with flour, or is she still baking, or should I say frying uh tee-hee-hee, ha-ha-ha?

Robin laughed saying why you going there with that?? Now you know it's been some years ago or you flashing or what Miss Courtney Diane. I can still see Robin's expression as she bought me up to speed on her cousin Rhona. Rhona grew up chasing boys... But she is doing better now. No children, no husband, no dating boys. Courtney Diane smiles oh now its dumb ass men uh. Robin, (smiled through her laughter), oh now you are having some flashback about my family. Why you got to go there with me, and why my family??? Inquiring thoughts want to know, what have they done to you??? You know they love you, tee-hee-hee. They both are laughing and I'm just looking at both with an ah of wondering what they are talking about. That wine gave them both the giggles, as you enjoy seeing their sisterly bond. I was just happy hanging out with them and laughing. Courtney Diane was laughing and crying while trying to tell the story. Robin was laughing hard too as she listened, occasionally crossing her eyes at both of us.

Robin continued with Rhona was boy crazy. Courtney Diane interrupts now she is dumb ass for thupid men. Robin glanced at her crossing her eyes and picks up where she left off. Rhona was not any different from any other girls are at that young age, but she did take boy crazy to some crazy extremes. Before she knew what freaky weird was, she was chasing boys under the bleachers, back seats, parks any where she could? The girl was just nasty, trifling and didn't have a clue she was. Her academic study course was Scant 101. I flashed back on my classmates Vendeese and Terri. They were high school scants and I wondered what profession did they persue, or what profession chose them, because hmm they were good at one thing. I can't remember who said this, that Vendeese and Terri may have not been around the block, but they weren't new to the neighborhood.

I turn back into Robin saying that Rhona's mother, Aunt Brandi worked late and was a single parent. Aunt Brandi constantly told Rhona that she didn't want any boys over their house, no form of company. Everyone grew up with that rule no company when your parents are not home. I remembered that rule so well. When we did violate that rule, something always happened that those words would echo louder with a slap into reality, because we had to deal with the consequences of our own actions. As adults we understand it better. But our young minds can't fathom any form of exercising self discipline. Then again at that age you simply don't care because you think nothing will happen. Right!!! Something always happens.

Rhona's brother, Carter and her sister Yaana both worked and were in college and few years older. You know how it is the baby of the family is always busy, neglected and sometimes spoiled. So, you figure by time her siblings finally came home, (if they came home), they were bone ass tired. Rhona was still in high school and all she had to do was school, homework, house work, and might as well add an extra curriculum, chasing after boys. That extra curriculum called pre- scant 101. Didn't we just discuss her scanty 101 training? Yea we did, but you didn't say she had a prerequisite.

Courtney Diane adds, really was she trying to become a scholar. Courtney Diane glanced at Robin adding Rhona also played catch. She would let them boys catch her, or she caught them, (she gives a wink). Courtney Diane moves like she is running pretending to be Rhona saying, ooh ooh don't catch me, tee-hee-hee. Then she added, ooh, ouch girl I got another one a track star in training or would that be cross country chasing over the hills or rolling down the hills and around the corners.

Robin inserts that her Aunt Brandi put flour outside the front door. Simple easy and would tell the story if Rhona listened or just said the hell with it. Her brother and sister were probably sleep or might not be at home. Aunt Brandi worked long hours and, hmmph work far far away. So, to Rhona surprise, one bright early morning good old Aunt Brandi told sleeping Rhona, (at least she acted as if she was to stall), that she had someone over probably some hard knuckle head boy. Rhona insisted, girl that she was studying all night until she fell asleep. Yell, (as Rhona stuttered), that's it I fell asleep on my books. That's it yeah that's it, as Courtney Diane adds I bet she was studying all night with her dumb ass. Her mother insisted that she had someone over. Of course, Rhona insisted that she didn't know what she was talking about as she rubbed the sleep from her eyes. She told Rhona to get up and take a little walk with her.

Get up walk, talk and get ta moving. I had to add that my mom Sheryl only had to say it once. Don't let my dad Eddie hear her tell you to do something and you moved slow or acted as if you didn't hear requests. That was when you felt the thunder coming from his mouth. Don't forget about that hypnotizing mole in his eye. Courtney Diane said my papa Cleve Jr.; his voice had thunder with lightening. He practiced that same rule don't let mother Florrie tell you twice to do something.

If he didn't hear any foot movement, you would still be looking for your face, (in sync we all said amen). I shared with them my childhood experience. I told them I remembered when my mom told us to clean up our rooms. When we came home, she was burning all our toys in a fifty-five-gallon barrel. All she had to say, with a straight face and didn't stutter as she repeated that she told us to clean up your room, now they're cleaned. When we heard clean, we went running to our bedroom looking under the bed and in the closets. Yep, she was clear and right. She cleans up and everything was poof gone and left in form of ashes. I laughed now but you know that was cold. Robin and Coutney Diane looked at me with amazement and they both said ooh girl your momma doesn't live out here right, does she? I laughed saying no, but she does visit. Robin picks up where she left off with, all she knew was that Rhona was the last child and you know the last child; gets the better treatment, little punishment at that point the parents are older and tired.

Courtney Diane chimes in we get our parents in their prime when they are young and experimenting and shift. Robin slowly knods as she continued. Rhona rub her eyes again asking why you can't just tell me from here. Aunt Brandi tone changes as she tells her to get her ass up out of the bed, more than ample ass, now she knows she was not playing. Courtney Diane says see why you got to go there didn't she tell her to get her ass oops more than ample ass up the first time. Why was there a time delay, just get your ass up? Sleep left running, and Rhona had my aunt's full attention. I can only imagine that her insides were trembling, and her mind was rattling trying to form thoughts together on what was really going on. I think her mind said play posseum when mom arrived, you know just pretend you are brain numb which is short for duh attack. Come on you know she wasn't pretending she is numb and the duh attacks happens often. I can still hear Courtney Dianes' interjecting with facial expression that still lingers in my mind. Just keep repeating the questions until they just get annoyed and give up. She, Aunt Brandi tells her to look down on the floor and just humor me and tell me what you see ma'am. Rhona is not getting what she is supposed to be looking for. She hunched her shoulders and sighed with I don't know I don't see anything, and that she was oh so tired from studying, (Courtney Diane and Robin winked at each other followed with a tee-hee-hee).

Aunt Brandi smiled while telling her to look again, just a little harder scholar. Robin and Courtney Diane in sync adding, girl I would have been trying to find something as they toast their glasses. Rhona still was not getting it, even when her mom called her a scholar, or genius. Sherlock Holmes didn't show up either to assist her tired butt. Those duh attacks were tearing her ass up. Damn the girl just couldn't figure the dit out. Her response was I guess that the floor needs to be vaccumed, huh. I guess, as Rhona looked around the room as if the room would whisper in her ears the answers to what in the hell is Aunt Brandi talking about. Inside her thoughts were probaby hoping that the room would just whisper to her the answer.

Rhona was probably thinking how in the hell am I supposed to know Brandy/ Mom. Rhona finally responded in an annoying/ whining voice, (that we hate to hear), couldn't you show me this later? I 'm so tired from reading all night while trying to throw in a fake yawn just for good measure and distraction as she stretches her arms out to accompanied, the fake yawn, moving her eyes all around. Was this fool really performing or what? Any way Aunt Brandi was not impressed. She responds with nope try again Rhona Louise. Now her eyes grow larger, as she looks at the floor again trying to see or just find the answer. This girl, still not getting it and her mind was working hard. She knew one thing not to ask or volunteer any information or ask any more questions, as her brain silently tells to her ssshh. Adding don't talk and try not to look directly into her eyes, yelling please, Rhona shoosh.

Rhona whines again with I don't see it my eyes are... Then her moms' responds with I know you were up all-night studying... Her brain is probably saying I told you to shoosh and no eye contact. Aunt Brandi calmly responded with since you don't see what I see because your eyes are ooh so so tired from reading; that they crossed looking at one another and you fell off into a sound sleep, and into your books. So of course, you didn't prepare for this course.

Let's try a simple home economics course. You know about frying and baking so let's test your knowledge. So, Miss Rhona simple questions, what does frying and baking have in common? Again, a simple multiple-choice question what they have in common, a) it depends, b) nothing in common, c) don't care, d) they both use flour. Now Rhona was more confused and just like a posseum in the head light look and thought. She blinks several times displaying that duh attack look. Yep that the duh attack flew in and had landed inside her head. She finsally responded with, I guess (d) mom, they both use flour. Bingo, Aunt Brandi shouts out, you finally got a right answer, so my tax dollars are still at work!!! Rhona is perplexed, and she really isn't getting this. I pictured My Aunt Brandi looking over her signature gold glasses with raised eyebrows with a slight corner smile. Only thing Rhona was good at was chasing those knuckle head boys behind bleachers, back seats, parks, anywhere her back could be supported, girl she was just ratched. No, you meant scant. Now people don't get me wrong here I love her she's family, but she was trying to find love in too many of the wrong places.

We know the worst kind of scant is the high school one. Aunt Brandi could only sigh, while she looks over her signature gold glasses disgusted by Rhona's dummy attacks. Aunt Brandi was tired from a long night, long morning and long conversations her with a yawning dummy. Aunt Brady said just one more question for Rhona especially since she had been studying all night. These are day questions that you could easily be heard in class, and I know you don't sleep in class, right not my precious baby no, no, no! So, let me see we had a home economic question and now since you have been studying let's try a simple math problem. Hmm as she smiled asking her do you think you can handle this question? I have some good visuals for you. With her hand on her hip and finger against her lip my aunt slowly glanced around the room. Let just look around to see what we can use for a visual measurement.

She shook Rhona while whispering; now you need to wake up and focus just a tad bit. We need to talk, and you need to pay attention. You know how she/Aunt Brandi sometimes talks out the corner of her mouth, while adding a smile. For that quick instance Robin and I look over at Courtney Diane with her looking back at us crossing her eyes saying as you were saying. Well Aunt Brandi said softly to Rhona that we need some binding time don't you think my little tired puppy?? Okay Miss Rhona here is the test question, what is the distance from the front door to your room? As she looked around the room saying, now let me see what I can use to measure the distance. Then her eyes look down as if she found her answer. Courtney Diane inserts that; Rhona's dumb ass should have been looking for a door to run out of!! Robin looks over at Courtney Diane as Courtney Diane saying that she just couldn't resist, I would have run my ass out that front door, just saying. They paused and smiled. Aunt Brandi looked over those gold frame glasses again, saying looka here, looka here.

Hmm, guess what I've found??? Aunt Brandi clapped her hands together saying we have something close that we can use for measurements, right here in this room. Wow what a pleasant surprise, hmm imagine that, magical footprints, just like in the movies huh. Let's count these powered foot prints. I know this white stuff couldn't have blown in here through the locked doors or windows?? I just know my little pudding didn't let anyone in the house because she listened to her mom, huh. And I just know little pumkin slept all through the night after studying and all. Mommy's little schlor as Aunt Brandi changes her voice as if she is talking to a baby. She looks over her glasses saying I just know that my baby wouldn't lie to her mommy about having company would she, no, no, no, unt un.

Mommy is just tripping let's get back to our math problem before you fall asleep from air brain studying. Do you think you should be sitting behind a desk to help you get into the groove and the feeling of being in a classroom? Nah, nervermind lets do this, let's keep it moving. Girls aren't you happy we can measure in feet and not all that centimeter's conversions crap. Because I know you are tired from study- ing all night as Aunt Brandi bats her eyes as Rhona continues her random blinking. What a mom to do but help her baby girl out and smiles saying I love my baby girl. Rhona never you mind that mommy's not tired; after working all night and making the long drive home from working extra hours. I don't need any sleep do I mommy's baby girl? Rhona don't you be concerned; these bags under my eyes they will even- tually go away. I just love you as she grabs her chin in her hand as if she going to give a kiss on the cheeks, but not. Saying I just love my baby girl, I really do. Rhona, through all this still wasn't getting this, nope not at all. Fume vapors from the ink in the book clogged her brain, I'm just saying. Hmm Aunt Brandi look down at the white stuff on the floor, hmm there is one foot. Rhona was looking at her smiling and the girl still not getting it. Aunt Brandi stood along side of the powdered prints, stopping occasionally looking at Rhona's expressions. She told Rhona to be careful and watch your steps, because we didn't want to mess those footprints up and must start all over again.

Courtney Diane responded with damn when does that heffa go to class, she still ain't catching on to this dit is her ass that mother of friends dumb??? Damn dumb ass she got her own kind of dumb, huh. Courtney Diane asked Robin was there cricket noise echoing up in her empty ass head?? Was the girl's a brain cable just wasn't connecting? I was thinking more of fire flies circling like they did in Oakwood at night but this time they were in the darkness of Rhona's head flickering light and still couldn't see. Robin laughed saying Aunt Brandi that she was asking her to walk with her this time calling her Miss Ma'am. So, Aunt Brandi counts as she walks, she motioned Rhona to follow her as she counts out loud. Humph Aunt Brandi was looking at the same time smiling and telling her not to mess her up while she kept counting. Aunt Brandi continued smiling at Rhona telling her that she could help with the counting. Now she was very considerate and keeping that in mind that Rhona was tired from studying all night (sigh). Adding that I know you are probably still sleeply and I know your head hurts from all that late-night studying.

Courtney Diane chimes in saying that her head is hurting with her dumb ass, it still is and presently as we speak throbbing from thinking with her dumb ass. So, Aunt Brandi throws in another confusing question saying; let's get it right the first time what you think? I deeply understand if you can't think or count with me because you are tired from studying all night. Rhona response was huh, with fear. Come on now walk with me don't drop my hand and please don't skip around this question. Courtney Diane inserts her thoughts with; if I was that close enough to for her to hold my hand that would have been to close for her to slap the shift out of me. Unt un I would have stayed at the end of the hallway a good clear striking distance, saying keep going I can see it from here, mom!! Just like I would be having my ass sitting in the back of the classroom. No Rhona dumb ass wanted to be upfront and personal.

Courtney Diane sips her drink with adding I'm just saying. Rhona responded I'm not holding your hand. Courtney Diane smiled let me just add that Rhona was too close to Aunt Brandi's slapping hand and she was too old to be acting this dumb. Aunt Brandi tells her that I really hope that you are sleepy or pretending because you are scaring your mom. Looka here these footprints have giving us a straight path of travel. Well kinda the feet are not too straight these feet kind of separate so we gonna do slue foot count, don't worry it's the same as feet, no conversion needed, (woo as she wipes pretend sweat off her forehead). She laughed come walk with me come on Rhona we can do this. She counts one, two three, (Courtney Diane inserts saying see three would have scared me isn't that when you get that surprise knock out), smiling and chuckling like a little girl. Courtney Diane inserts saying again see now that chuckling would have had me running. If it was me, just saying, I would be looking at Aunt Brandi like she was some type of chucky doll, while the warning music was playing. Courtney Diane and I in sync were singing the jaws theme music, dum dum dum. Robin paused adding her own chuckle. Now Rhona thought that her mom had gone crazy and she must be tired and need some serious sleep. Aunt Brandy comes up saying that the traveling distance hmm let me see was far enough to enter the house and go directly to your room look hmm with no detours.

Aunt Brandi smiles saying, I count about ten to twelve feet give or take a few feet/inches. What number did you come up with Columbo? This is the scary part Rhona still not getting it, (Courtney Diane inserts again calling Rhona, Eiestein huh). Courtney Diane look at both of us now we know she is not the brightess light, but can she get a flicker of some type of light, damn with her dumb ass. Where do you think the white stuff came from and what did she think it was? See at that point I would be feeling flight, faked passing out move, or drop down as if my knees were becoming weak, or just quick drop to the knees and plead for mercy or something… Wow add why start saying I'm sorry, I'm so so sorry now let me go back to bed please, please as I would plead for mercy. Okay I was wrong I did it now stop with the crash courses they are scaring me! Dumb won't work for Rhona, she's proven she that.

Aunt Brandi sighed with a oh well, let me help you because I know you were up studying, and you didn't get a chance to prep for this open book exam. This course was a common street sense course that you didn't pass. In your case, Rhona, the only pass you received was when you passed the classroom and went into the cafeteria and took a seat. She broke it down on how simple the need to know happened. She said that she poured flour on the front porch and that boy track all that flour throughout my house with his size twelve feet directly to your room. Now we know the distance from the porch to your bedroom by your little boyfriend's size twelve feet or give or take a few feet. Did you get ten to twelve feet Rhona? At that point she is numb and playing real dumb girl. Robin is still laughing, and I had joined in and Courtney Diane is laughing too, (which was rare). Didn't we conclude that she wasn't playing dumb, because she wasn't that good of an actress?

Aunt Brandi bought us into her TMI, (too much information). She said that Rhona's dad used to make her head hurt with almost every conversation. She said that she had to question her own interlect. Only thing Aunt Brandi could say that Rhona's dad's damn DNA circulating that dummy dit. I know it had to be him, because the other two have the same daddy and they have some type of sense. His family is on the duh side, but he was good at what he did...., along with being cute and funny. Not to mention the muscles that man had, oh yea the smooth skin and those bedroom eyes with long eyelashes and beautiful white teeth, not to forget the innocence side with a touch of bad boy. Come on Robin don't look at me like you don't like those bad boys. I don't know too many ladies or girls that don't. Who could walk away from strange /freaky turn on, not me? For that moment we all paused to reflect on why we fell in love with our mates. Robin said not only was Ramon smart and focused; but his voice just turned my inside on and other things as, (she smiled and wink), and he just made me feel good not like the other men I dated. Robin looked over at Courtney Diane to say something, since she had toned down her commentating. Courtney Diane look at both of us what okay, okay I liked the way Malcom did that Denzel bowlegged walk, ouch nice and smooth with a tight ass butt and when he turned around every thang matched the front girl. He made my heart skip, run and flip everytime we hmmm, humph and humph. I still love that man, he could rock it and pop it and just wear it out. Now look at that punk ass beach skipping in my heels and probably walking better than me that little switch beach.

Ooh I thought maybe Courtney Diane is using that one emotion that she had been saving. I was hearing but wasn't listening and I didn't realize I was smiling with my own thoughts. As she talks about Macolm David being in her clothes and shoes I continued with my thoughts. She said that she/ he left as she pictured him danc-ing and treating each outfit as a fashion show while mix and matching accessories and stuff. Malcom David acted like a little girl playing grown-up in her mother's clothes. I kinda smile to myself as I snap back to hearing my name mentioned. What about you Rita you are sitting over there smiling sipping on that Chai tea share with us. What did Bill do for you as we pause for a memory lane break? Come on and chime in and join us Rita D prey tale and tell us where your thoughts are taking you, (as she spreads her fingers on one hand across her lips). Well I like the fact that he was from Chicago and not from Oakwood. A Chicago bad boy; no one knew him, and with a touch a fine, fine and changing the spelling of fine to phine. Humph his smile with deep dimples and they showed when he talked, hmmm those almond shaped eyes, with bowlegs just made me feel special that he picked me to marry. We still share the same heart beat and my head still has the exact spot embedded when I lay on his chest. I thought about Bill and the fun we had as we learned about each other and how we still were growing. I just pray that we aren't growing apart. In my heart I just wanted him to share with me how he wanted his family to grow and how he wanted me as a wife. I was doing the best I knew how.

Also, not thinking that what attracted me to Bill was the same thing that other girls or ladies were attracted to also. When other women came around, they never bothered to acknowledge my presence. It was as if I interrupted their conversation and they paused enough to see who interrupted them making a connection. I paused and reflected and when I was asked to leave Bill's place as I was escorted to the door by Bill. Even now thinking about it I felt embarrassed all over again. The two women that could stay still have a lasting memeory, just the act and not their faces. I just remembered I felt invisible to them. No, I wasn't invisible because I remembered how they laughed as Bill told me to leave. I couldn't believe how Bill could dismiss me that fast and easily, humph. I wondered if they thought in their selfish ways I just a woman that hung out at his grandmother's house and visited from time to time. I was asked to leave Bill leaving me feeling all emotional and I was disappointed in myself for not standing my grounds. Only to add insult to emotional injury to encounter the smiling face of Joel. Good grief again, does he ever go in the house or does he peek out window waiting for that moment to look at me again with the same expression and the same words as a ground hog day experience. Maybe he was trying to be a friend and would have been there if I knew then what I know now, but that was something that I wasn't mentally ready for or mature enough to understand. I said to myself briefly why Bill, but somehow, I stopped talking and started mentally reflecting on my pain. When I came back into our conversation, I enjoyed hanging out and talking with the girls as we reminisced about our husbands' current or ex. We all in some way have encountered women trying to push up on what we thought was a secured relationship. Robin encountered and addressed her pain immediately. I think she moved on because she very seldom talks about Ramon, as for me, I'm still in love with Bill. I didn't know that I would have to fight and defend my home and family. When I think about it then and now Bill still should have been my protection. He should have introduced his pregnant girlfriend and not treat me as a friend of the family. I didn't know any better; I should have introduced myself and left on my own. I didn't know how to protect my own feelings.

Courtney Diane didn't really encounter another woman. Well in a way she did Malom David was I guess her other woman, if you want to count that hmm. I don't know how to call it. All I know is that he liked dressing in her clothes. Well at least she knew the other woman, hmm. I know she dated from time to time. She would always say I'm single until I'm married. I think she still had hidden fear of dating someone too long and that they might end up wearing her good suit and stilettos. She had s nice shape minus the flat butt, tee-hee-hee but she had boobs that clapped, mine hmm just one good applause no "s" and then the curtain closes.

As they look at me probably wondering where I drifted off to, for some reason I did that often. Courtney Diane whispered to me hey Rita D or RD. I liked the nickname that made me feel like one of them. She says I'm becoming a little sensitive you aren't sharing our me time and our moments. As she puts her hand to one eye as if she is trying a forced tear, while laughing in her own way, (with her tee-hee-hee and la-la-ha-ha). Robin says unt oh Courtney D is showing us that feeling without an "s" prey tell she has emotion no "s" right. She says "KMA" means kiss my ass. Robin says L-O-L, laugh out loud and you have to have an ass to kiss, (while she puckers her lips). Robin said in other words you have no ass so, and who will stand in for you Rita D. Courtney Diane says no I meant "K-M-E-A". Robin laughs oh you are adding another vowel uh an "e", so this is "Jeopardy" and how much for a vowel. Courtney Diane squints her eyes saying yep an "e" for free Miss Vankia or Pat Sayjeck. As I listened, in the back of my mind I'm wondering if that is the correct name. Courtney Diane snaps back with, oh really Miss Vanika, and no you didn't as she raised her eyebrows smiling. So, I 'm going to save your ass a spin, Courtney Diane chuckled as she toasts her glass. Robin jumps in saying hey hey hum, (and Courtney Diane doesn't skip a beat with), the phrase is kissing my entire ass, Vanika. Robin chuckles ooh oh hmm again who will stand in for your flat entire ass, Rita. Because your 'K-M-E-A' Miss Courtney Diane is so not working for you, and that Sayjack or whatever that guy's name is. Courtney Diane snaps with my name is Miss Vanika thank you ma'am and his name is Alex Trebeck. She glanced at me with a slight corner smile and cross her eyes at Robin oh you and him buddies now Rowbin. I was ut oh not me.

I reflected on the butt jokes and the boys throwing rocks at my butt and I didn't feel it. My curiousty had me asking and I slowly turned my head for the answer and they boldly told me that they been and continued laughing. Robin and Courtney Diane just didn't know how long it took me to accept the size of my butt. Robin says, no girl that is your heritage and here it is. Robin stands up and slaps her butt saying to Courtney Diane if I slapped your butt my hand would just slide on off. While she looked look over at Courtney Diane saying she could stand against a wall and there will be no kind or any kind of space, no air, just your flat butt blended into the wall like you are some form of wallpaper. Courtney Diane snaps with, I don't have a problem with my men slapping my ass and holding on for the long hall. Robin laugh they have to hold their hands together because their hands would just slide on off. Courtney Diane cross her eyes at both of us and raised her glass as a toast saying touché. Now let's get back to your family, tee-hee-hee and hee-hee heffa with no "s". She sips looking at us with her eyes still slightly open saying again tee-hee-hee and la-de-da-da-ha. Robin smiles, with tee-hee-hee and hee -hee to you heffa with no "s", smiling looking at me to let me know that was to Courtney Diane.

So, we all picked up where we left off. Aunt Brandi and all of us shared too much information but it was fun and interesting. We shared because we were girls, family and we were friends. I laughed but inside I was feeling that I really didn't know what being happy was about anymore. The sun is trying to come out after hiding behind the clouds today as I enjoyed this coffee. The day was clearing up and it's a new day. Plus, I was too embarrassed to tell them that this was how it was in the beginning and not the present. Although, I enjoyed the time with them, sometimes I stayed too late. The laughter and smile would slowly leave as I went home, because I didn't know what emotions I had to deal with once I opened the door. Sometimes I would stand otside the door afraid to turn the knob. I would stare at the door knob, trembling with fear as I opened the door and walked into a ball of fury or a fist of anger. I didn't know what mood he might be in, if he was home. I didn't know if I was going to be jumped on or verbally abused. What a roller coaster of emotions??

People might have thought I was special because I listened more than I talked. My father always taught me that you learn more about a person if you just listen to them for about twenty mintues and you would know who they are. In my reality I was capturing the moments and the laughter and put it into my reserve for a special time. I never knew when I might need my special time, for my just in case. While we talked, we didn't man bash. We knew our self worth and enjoyed our time. Many families and the village interested in their stock meaning us, they knew our value and enforced it. My mother wasn't much on words, but she did get her point across on how to value and represent your family and yourself. She showed us how to be different and special in our actions of intergrity, self respect and in our clothing attire.

She went out of her way to make sure our outfits were different and expensive. She taught us to have class/sophistication and many other people in the village helped her. My village also included aunts, uncles and family, friends, that reminded me of my self worth. They took the time to show so much love and support that we didn't understand but returned respect in form of appreciation. Now we appreciate it more when you are around others that a village didn't support. I plan on passing that embrace of love and support on to my daughters as well. Back to my Aunt Johanna she was so beautiful and still lives in the same house and to this day she only knows me by runaway. She said I had vaule and everyday my stock is going up words that echoed from Aisalle Evanlica and Arterrias, (Terri), adding my stock is going up and the trading is high. That's the type of value I have in myself, and the stock that has some type of trading options that fits my needs. Now we can negogiate about mutual funds but that depends on the communication options. We called her Eva she was a good close family friend and took her stock options very serious because she said that him/her were investment potentials. Every now and then when I saw Eva, she would ask how my investment was because she wanted to make sure her dividends were paying off. At first, I had a duh attack until I realized she was referring to me. What was I doing to invest in myself to increase my dividends and have some type of stock options in myself? Woo, I didn't know those words still followed me before I knew anything about any type of stock. I would reflect and picture the laughter and smiles on their faces and the words that would just crack me up at the right time. Sometimes I didn't know what to say or how to say it because sometimes I would stumble with my words as I tried to gather my thoughts. Inside I was still hurting, bruised, scared and still trying to hide my pain and marks.

I was trying hard to hide from the world the story my eyes could tell. So, for the time I laughed and listened it was worth anything that Bill might dish out to me. I would walk in talking about what I did as a distracter or just come in as quiet as possible. My thoughts are negotiating my next move. Inside sometimes I would be trembling especially if he saw me talking to Clarence or Keith. He didn't really trip about Darryl because he was out performing and seldom home. As I drifted back to Courtney Diane and Robin, I come into them laughing and sipping slowly from their wine glasses occasionally refilling them. Rhona was interesting, and Aunt Brandi did need something strong after that type of scare tee-hee-hee, according to Courtney Diane's ha-ha. I hope Aunt Brandi made it through Rhona antics and enjoyed her cup of coffee without cream. As for me this Chai tea will do me fine. Ooh Robin said that is just too much information ah, ug, from Aunt Brandi. Actually, Aunt Brandi and I talked about a lot of different things no special topics just rolling with the flow.

Aunt Brandi continued fussing about Ellis, Rhona's dad rambling on going on to say I should have rolled left Robin instead of right into Ellis. I should have left that morning and went to breakfast. I was almost done with having babies, and then here comes my baby Rhona. Wow I love my baby daughter, but I should have stayed sleep or at least pretended. Robin laughed, and she is still living at home, my aunt said she would probably move out before Rhona would, damn. Those words still holding true, Rhona is still at home. Aunt Brandi tried to hook her up with her best friend, Melody's son Gerald. Aunt Brandi had to laugh when Melody blurted out, oh hell no, oh oops sorry Brandy but really Rhona?? She added with a corner smile asking, you were playing right? Hmm she lost her grammar for that moment. You really want her to reproduce with who my son? I thought we were friends why you want to do this to me and have some dumb ass grandkids sorry unt um humph hmm. I am not sacrificing my son for that humph, (as that corner smile accompanies her now raised eyebrows). We ani't trying to have that kinda party Brandi, oh hell to the no. Damn you got me swearing and dit. I'm here to play cards not have my son play house. Ouch I thought we were cool, now play your hand. Aunt Brandi smiles as she looks over her glasses, we are cool and takes a card. Melody saying while huffing, mix Rhona's DNA with my boy, hmmm ooh couldn't have Gerald go out like that. Aunt Brandi said that after that card game she tried calling Meoldy. I was serious Gerald and Rhona hooking up. I kept calling and I knew she was checking that caller ID, some friend, scardy cat. Why should I be the only one with dumb grandkids or maybe they might not be?

The word must have gotten out, because when Aunt Brandi was playing her weekly card games with Melody, Miss Amanita Miss Janice and her Cousin Tonya's watched Aunt Brandi as she watched Cousin Tonya's son Admiral. They watched him, and they watched Aunt Brandi watching him. Admiral was very nice looking with perfect white teeth that accent his laugh lines. Our mouths almost dropped open as he greeted with that deep sounding voice and big brown eyes. Aunt Brandi said that it wasn't just her watching him walk back and forth from his room to the kitchen. They laughed as they watched Aunt Brandi watch Admiral like he was prime rib, or filet migion, and she had a knife and fork ready to carve. She was hungry in the quest of finding a good male meal for Rhona because an appeitizer will not work in any way. Aunt Brandi wanted an entree for Rhona. In a slow voice, Aunt Brandi asked Gayla was her fine well-mannered son, Tone dating anyone. Gayla responded without looking up said nope and don't even think about him for Rhona. Before Aunt Brandi could respond to Gayla, she glanced over at Miss Janice. Miss Janice looked at her cards humph saying I sure enjoy playing our weekly card game. She kept talking about the card game and avoiding looking right into the waiting eyes of Aunt Brandi. Melody snickered as she responded with a big grin. Aunt Brandi was stuck on duh and had to laugh herself saying well I tried she is on her own, gin. They all responded in sync thank God, now let's keep it moving, please....

Robin said when she was looking at Aunt Brandi as she was telling the story she remembered that she couldn't keep a straight face either and avoided eye contact too. Robin started laughing harder saying wait a minute let me just interject this. I just had another flashback of a funny. Now listen no, no really listen. You got to hear, this one ladies! I just remembered sitting with my favorite Aunt Brandi telling me another story. Aunt Brandi said that she had to pause with a wondering thought about Rhona. She said that she just had to test a theory on Rhona and see how her tax dollars were working. You know, just see how Rhona's brain really works. What is her thought process, or does it process or is there a sign inside her brain that reads, out of order still, try again but not today?

She said one day while eating breakfast she was just looking through the sales ads and looked over at Rhona eating and said hey Rhona they have common sense on sale. Rhona paused as if she was serious and excited. The girl responded with on sale where at, what store??? She frightened me so bad I could only raise my eyebrows. I needed something strong to drink like a strong black cup of coffee. Something strong enough to drink that would make me shake my head. I had to close my eyes, and hope when I opened them, I was really sitting with Alice in Wonderland's table laughing with the Mad Hatter. Aunt Brandi had me laughing but she wasn't laughing as she was telling me that she had an out of body, out of brain experience, (I wanted to do Courtney Diane's laugh of tee-hee-hee and hee or la-de-da-ha-ha then whatever). As Aunt Brandi listened to Rhona; during that leave of her brain absence she said she heard her grandmother Ardine's crackling voice saying Rhona, (sometimes she called her RL), going to have a special talent with emphasis on special. Really couldn't understand what she meant.

You know how our elders say short sentences with long meanings. Grunny Ardine, (that's what Rhona called her she couldn't say granny). Rhona had a habit when she was young of putting her pacifier in upside down in her mouth. You could take it out and Rhona would put it back in her mouth upside down, right and she would pull it out like you didn't know how this worked with much tude. Hey, I knew that wasn't normal but hey it kept her quiet, humph. Grunny said slowly as she focused when she first saw her with an upside pacifier, with open wide eyes slightly opened mouth, hand over her throat and a face expression of surprise, (looking over her reading glasses). Grunny just looked with amazement saying even slower, oh my Lord, ooh, hmmm, humph, yes, she has a special talent a special gift, my, my, my just keep a watch over her she is very special child very yes, yes special gifts. That's when it hit me what she meant. As my brain came back into my body, I paused still looking at Rhona and the reality was I wasn't in Wonderland sitting with the Mad Hatter I was sitting across the kitchen table looking at Rhona. Aunt Brandi tuned back into her reality while Rhona goes on to say I can't pass up a good sale. She said she had to get up just before her brain resistance broke down. Aunt Brandi had to ask herself was Rhona just a good performer? Rhona was so convincing that she had look at the sales ads to see if common sense was on sale. She had me scared girl because I thought that thought might be contagious.

Aunt Brandi did have a concern, because for that moment Rhona was very convincing. I blinked a few times to get my focus. I glanced back at her to see if she was playing and she wasn't. She was sure glad she didn't send Rhona to that private school. I had to shake my head again, to rattle my brain so I wouldn't be tempted just to glance at the ads again. I should have hunted that boy down and had him do right by Rhona. That boy might have been just right for her. His dumb ass didn't see all that flour on the porch? Nah he was to busy coming for the booty. I should have set a bounty on his head.

Aunt Brandi said that she should have shotgun his young ass into being with Rhona. That girl had me pleading with my friends for their sons. I guess that boy didn't know anything about flour either. Robin smiled adding, hmmph using flour to tell a story... flour. Aunt Brandi laughed saying now that was funny and Rhona couldn't recover with a lie fast enough and her brain cells were still running scared. Sometimes we forget that our parents were once our age. They have been there done that and they have seen and/or heard it all before. As I listened, I briefly reflected on the funny of Charlotte's mother and grandmother guarding the dusty sanitary napkin box and exposing her pregnancy and blowing the dust off the box causing her to cough. Old fashion ways with very little thought but the actions came with good results.

Robin refocused saying, getting back to what Aunt Brandi was talking about Miss Rhona. I guessed they didn't have a curriculum on how to lie while waking up. So, Rhona stood there and took the punishment. Aunt Brandi didn't kill her but I'm sure she was hoping that death was better than the punishment that Aunt Brandi dished out. Wasn't much flour left but Aunt Brandi went and purchased more flour and when that ran out, she went and purchases some more. Aunt Brandi had Rhona doing a whole lot of baking and a whole lot of frying and cleaned up all the residual from the flour. She told her now you understand the many uses of what flour is used for. I think when Rhona coughed flour came out.

I had to ask when did the baking and frying stop. Robin laughed girl I don't know and can't even remember. I just remembered that cookies, cakes, pies, chicken dinners were given to family, friends and neighbors. Rhona had cooked and fried so much there was no room in the refrigerators. When I did see her during that minor ordeal, she had flour all on her face, arms, legs everywhere ladies. I had to ask just out of shear curiosty did she see the flour on the porch. As she spoke, I remembered my mouth staying open in hearing her response. Yell, she said that she saw that white stuff all over the porch and thought her mom had drop or spilled something. She strongly felt why she should pick up something she didn't drop or spill. Rhona was dead serious saying that she was tired from studying all the time. She insisted that was her job to go to school and study, (at that point I had to put my hand over my mouth to keep from laughing). I laughed so hard I started coughing. She said she told that fool, not to worry about that white stuff on the ground. Just go head and step or jump over it. Get this confirmation of this fool in training, this knucklehead boy stepped right into the flour because he said he wasn't jumping for no one. I could have popped him on the back of his wide head. Wow two idiots or ignorance reproduced. I hoped they used protection. Courtney Diane chimes in again saying con and dum. So, the condoms were for both of their dumb asses, huh? At that point all I could do was shake my head and allow the thought to fade away please let it fade away. This is a visual I didn't want lingering.

Robin smiled continuing with, they must have merged the words con and dum together, because I didn't hear anything about her being pregnant. I'm so glad she didn't reproduce. Robin smiled adding you know Rhona asked me since I love buying perfume and familiar with various fragrances asked me about common sense fragrance. She said she had missed the sale that her mom told her about and had a hard time finding that fragrance. Rhona insisted that she wanted to try that popular new fragrance. First, I had to pause like some type of station identification, except it was my brain taking a break. I could see how Aunt Brandi jumped up thinking this stuff or thoughts might be contagious. It does throw you off where your thoughts are just ooh, and then hmm, making you stutters with your answers. I said ooh no um Rhona you did say common sense right. She said nah "common scent" as if she was proudly correcting me. Saying you know when those new fragrances come out, they sometimes have them on sale. There is a new one out called common sense. My mom said that it was on sale. I came back as best as I could with a straight face and with a very slow response it's not a fragrance it's a thought process.

I watched her trying to process her thoughts. The look on her face was scaring me. I then had to accept the fact that we had the same bloodline, oh damn. Then I snapped back with fright mixed with a little shock. Rhona should infinity never, ever reproduce and if she does, she needs some co-parenting. Never ever should she be left alone to hold a conversation with her child nope and nope, (and a slight sigh of nope again). Ooh thank God, that we missed that I might be pregnant bullet amen. Girlfriends I had to get away from her those words or thought process before it became airborne. I didn't in any way want those nummy cells connecting to my brain cells. I had to take a deep breath. I was scared to let my breath out. So, I went around the corner to exhale just in case. Just in case her brain cells were trying to find a path of travel to my brain cells, ooh no and no not to this mind or body. I had to check all senses, by saying words and placing my hands on my lips to feel the vibration as my ears heard me speak. Girlfriends brain cells just don't reproduce but I felt them trying to escape from Rhona. Just in case this was contagious I stayed away from folks for at least twenty-four to forty-eight hours, for just in case.

We both looked at her with our mouths open as Courtney Diane says damn, she is beyond dumb ass and just ran right into thu-pid. We all just started back laughing about the flour, using our "common sense" with no aroma other than the smell of flour.

I just couldn't imagine all that cooking and baking with all that flour. You would think Rhona would want her food baked; no form of frying or baking desserts. That would be the last thing on my mind. Nope ate fried chicken like she never had it before. See that is confirmation that the cables are not connecting, and the fire flies are flying, and the crickets are making noises in her empty head. When you do see the light coming from her its not her it's the fire flies spreading their wings. I hope that someone else would help the girl find the light switch. Funny, but not so ha-ha, Rhona ended up working at a bakery. You would think that would be the last thing she wanted to be around or come near. Again, I bet she still didn't get it, probably felt working with flour gave her experience. Ironic, and yet funny in a strange way to be introduced to flour, uh. I bet she knows a lot more ways how flour can be used now. The best lesson earned is the one you learn. And she learned from that open book test/class. Don't forget about when she graduated, she was the only one that ran across the stage to get her diploma. You would have thought she was running track.

Before Aunt Brandi looked over her signature gold glasses with an open mouth in disbelief, Rhona was sitting back in her seat, sweating. The audience mouths were already open from laughing. On that day Aunt Brandi had the stiff neck she didn't even bother to look around at the crowd because her ears were already opened to the sound of their laughter. I could only imagine Aunt Brandi reinterating in her mind that she should had rolled right out of bed and left her daddy alone damn. Courtney Diane inserted Aunt Brandi should have put on those glasses, so she could see clearly and got her ass out of bed instead of rolling over. She smiles looking around the room until she makes eye contact with Robin. Robin responds back looking around the room and made eye contact with Courtney Diane smiling as she sips her wine in a whisper, with you want to go there with asses.... Courtney Diane touche with a smile requesting to please continue. Robin takes another sip and said, with that entire extra curricular that Rhona was participating in, she really wasn't supposed to graduate. The office made a mistake and they couldn't reverse the wrong. Now Aunt Brandi realized why Miss Rhona ran across the stage before her diploma disintegrated. I guess she used common sense that time and not the fragrance...

Chapter 23
Now It's Robin's Turn

I had to ask was that the fresh smell of baking flour or smell of flowers hey just asking. Courtney Diane added, speaking of flour do your Uncle Boris and his dog Chico still have that trifling habit of crop dusting? I love your Uncle Boris, but he didn't give any courtesy warning and kept it moving. Chico would look back at you as he walked away. Uncle Boris walked, smiled, laughed and kept walking slowly as if to make the smell linger longer. That old fart (no pun meant), would have the dust from his butt following right behind his ass. That made the dust of aroma linger after Uncle Boris and Chico passed, and no pun meant. Robin looked over at Courtney Diane saying that you are just on a roll. She smiled and responded with I don't know haven't seen him or Chico in about a year. I asked Robin, you have an Uncle that flies a plane, wow that's alright? Courtney Diane laughs as Robin says nah, unt, um, nope, nah, no, nada unt um. She pointed to Courtney Diane saying, Miss Sonya over there is just being messy.

Uncle Boris and his dog had a habit of walking and passing gas. Their puff and pass are like a silent killer, no notice, no warning, just when you take that deep breath then bam, damn he got your nose again. It's like your nose went into a siren, with noise and red strobes. Robin and Courtney Diane both laughed as they fan their noses. Uncle Boris puff/pass is almost like a drive/walk by but using his own gas. No pun meant. Uncle Boris would always say that there was more air out than in. He said the sound is a sign of good healthy cleansing. He laughed as he passed giving us a quick good bye. Courtney Diane inserts he needs to cleanse his healthy crop-dusting ass. Robin smiled saying are we really going to go there. He got gas so just let the man pass. After all Uncle Boris meant no harm in helping the ozone, with his force field. You must admit he had a sense of humor. He would smile through his missing dentures and chuckled as he passed by. Now in his hay day he passed gas with speed. It happened so quick your nose questioned where that smell came from. Uncle Boris now moves just a tab bit slower, so the puffs have the tendency to linger. We have gotten used to him, Chico and their puff pass.

At first the puff would through us off, because we thought that he was too old to be doing that rude crap. We would just hold our breath as he passed, again no pun meant. Our noses had to learn the hard way. Not thinking he would be that rude, but we noticed the smell only when he was around. Sometimes he would catch us by surprise and really sent the nose into a running scare. We all had to ask what in the hell did him and Chico eat. There was that one time he moved slightly faster when he said he had an enemy at the gate. Uncle Boris being older we thought maybe he was tripping about a real enemy at the gate. You know someone trying to enter his yard and hurt him. With his fast moves and crop dusting we all laughed when we figured it out. It meant he had to make a quick bathroom run, before the enemy escaped. At that point we all laughed as we finished sipping our drinks.

Chapter 24

Courtney Diane on No Baby
Boos and Family Woos

While Courtney Diane was closing her eyes, Robin motioned to me and mouthed watch this and she acts like she is poking something. More than likely she is just going to mess with Courtney Diane again. Robin asked, have you seen that hickey placing, box shaped, future daughter in law, since we are talking about scant in training and school extra curriculum. Courtney Diane look at Robin with a corner smile and just rolled her eyes at her and responds with oh really. Uh um Robin smiled and said I haven't seen her in a while. She used to vulture around your place looking for Henray, you know her future baby's boo. Now what did she call you Mama Courtney just left off the Diane and added Mama, huh. Courtney Diane snaps back with, she can't stand when people forget the Diane. My name is Courtney Diane, I am not her damn mama, she is someone elses headache. I already have my butt ache called Henray with his dumb ass bringing that road ho around me. What happened to her calling me, Miss CD.? That stant heffa lucky Shelly didn't come out. Unt oh not Shelly, she doesn't come out often. When Shelly comes out its way too late to run....

Miss Shelly has been waiting a long time to make another cameo. Don't worry, Shelly or Miss Courtney didn't hurt the little heffa that was trying to become your protégé through your baby Henry Luis. So, Robin looks at Courtney Diane raising her eyebrows with a slight smile what did you do? Courtney Diane glanced back at her with her eyes slightly close, I didn't do anything to that scant... She is not worth the energy, effort or thought I would have to put into that boxed shape scant. I really can't stand her trifling ass. She like a fly that you just want to shew away, but it just keeps on coming around buzzing in your ear. That boxed shaped scant was that nasty fly calling me Mama Courtney. Just for one moment she wished she could produce a pie and find a good spot on her face just to smash it. That thang almost had me repeating my online anger management course. I had to woosa and breathe.

I had to walk away. Because the other me knew and I know me, and I would have put my sawed-off feet into that heffa, sending her orbiting somewhere and that somewhere wouldn't be a nice place.

Now the new me, knew that I couldn't put my foot up her ass. So, I exercised my training and regrouped, and I walked. Then I thought maybe I could put my foot in the middle of her back, hmm nah might leave my size eight footprint. Yep, I walked away and looked straight ahead. Yep. Courtney Diane said that she was proud of herself and had to give own self a dap. She smiled going on with saying she was thankful for those online anger mangagement classes, and shift. Hmm, she had me surprised that she didn't use the "f" word, humph. I watched Courtney Diane shaking her head as she enjoyed the sip of her wine. She smiled out the corner of her mouth saying that, Henry was thinking with the wrong brain. That day Mr. Henry thought with the wrong dumb ass brain. So, I knew I really didn't want her trash ass coming around me or my place. Especially couldn't stand her, after she tried to mark my boy up with hickies. I blame Henry dumb ass too for allowing her to brand him, so no good young lady would talk to my boy. That was confirmation that she was a gold-digging nasty ass huzzy. Just showed you how nasty trifling and desperate she was. I could have punched Henry Luis in his throat. That was when I knew I didn't want her coming around.

Now Henry Luis wasn't innocent he claimed he didn't feel it. I said oh really and I popped him right in the middle of his big ass forehead. My finger went right between his eyebrows separated just enough to allow my fingers to fit in. I asked him did you feel that, dit?? Henry looked at me as if I was crazy. I looked at him saying so you do have feelings with your dumb ass. He looks at me like I'm crazy and I looked back at him as if he still was a dumb ass. Robin and I give a look at each other without words waiting for Courtney Diane to say dumb ass or either with your dumb ass. We were on key here it comes as Robin and I glanced at each other, laughing saying with your dumb ass. Courtney Diane wasn't paying too much attention as we commentated. She told Henry, you felt that dit right, with your dumb ass, and then you felt that boxed shaped huzzy sucking on your nasty narrow neck. I keep trying to tell his ass that you are not the only car driving up that scant ramp, roll your dumb ass back and back away from that gold digging scant in train-ing. Miss Courtney Diane did not like her one bit, tee-hee. Well that thought, and memory helped keep my mind off arriving home. As we are getting closer to our stop, it's good seeing more familiar neighborhood landmarks. I hope my joy won't go away. Right now, I am feeling pretty good. Right as I see the familiar strip mall, I reflect on another conversation with just the girls. Courtney Diane tripping on her family names as she sipped her wine.

Robin mouths again smiling showing her beautiful dimples, saying to me watch this and acting like she poking Courtney Diane again and asked what about your second-generation family twins like Jessica and Jasnie or like this one is rhyming names, Royel and Noell?? Come on Courtney Diane the creative combination of rhyming, creativity plus the different spelling of names. You know, and she spells the names slowly T-i-p-h-a-n-e-e and B-e-t-h-e-n-e-e. I thought on hmm that is a different way of spelling the name I always thought it was spelled with two "f". Courtney Diane just goes with Robin's flow on her family. Robin adds (as she sips her drink with), hmmm this next generation way of thinking. Nice way to use phonics under the guise of not knowing how to spell. Courney Diane responded with funny, (while crossing her eyes).

Robin says see you're rhyming Tiphanee, Bethenee and that's funny, it's in the blood line, tee-hee-hee. Now riddle me this, is your funny creatively spelled f-u-n-n-e-e or is it spelled the normal f-u-n-n-y? Please Miss Courtney Diane educate us on why your family likes to move vowels around. I watched Robin lean forward as if she was really interested in the answer, as for me I went along for the ride occasionly looking out the window. I wanted to hear the response on this one. Robin kindly chuckled with, we didn't mind your family creativity it's very interesting uh, what you think Rita?? Before I could respond I just smiled as Courtney Diane responded with no anger calmly, pointing at each of us adding ug you cow, you heffer. She looks at me with a corner smile calling us both clowns adding give me a reason to stretch my leg and foot directly, (then she stops mid sentence as her eyes squint again with that laser look of death with love).

I had a silent thought hmm maybe those online anger management classes were helping her redirect, refocus, and re-think. Maybe there was no remedial classroom needed. Courtney Diane had to remember a lot of "re's", or should I say wee oops no it's "re". She comments on Jessica and Janie. With a little frustration she said that they are ten years apart, so you know they are not twins. That's my second generation of cousins Tyrona and Tyreena with their crazy asses. When you say or call them "Ty" they both answer with "what" in sync everytime. You say Ty the cables just don't connect enough for them to ask which one you want. Now if that's not a confirmation of crazy with borderline thup-id. This is a shot in the air, and me being a thinking woman, I asked why not call them Rona or Reena. At least that way it doesn't appear that they share the same thought process.

Noell and Royell, hell Royell just a baby can't walk and Noell stuck on thup-id with the rest of the bloodline cousins. Courtney Diane adds how can I talk it's in the bloodline you know the next generation cow. Robin laughs cow aren't you part of that bloodline?? She paused squinting her eyes as if she "zoop zoop" with laser vision and returning to enjoying her drink as she slowly munches on a snack while slowly bobbing her head. Looking at her bob her head put a vision of how my dad would bob his head as he ate no music just bobbing his head slowly just like Courtney Diane. I can only imagine that she was just chilling to the tunes in her head. While tuning us out as she listened to the calm tunes playing softly in her mind. My dad had a familiar expression of calm showing just like the calm on Courtney Diane's face. Maybe that expression meant they were content and in their own mental relaxed zone. Looking over at Robin my thoughts came back with a quick, ooh don't poke her again. I mouth to her no, no don't do it....

Chapter 25
We Made It Home

Those mini flashbacks helped me weather my mini storms. The hours seemed late I guess because the day was long. We passed many scenic areas and we walked and ate and now it's time to go home. Our stop was two stops away and my heart feels as if it has skipped a beat. For some reason I feel a little nervous and uncertain what waits on the other side. Sierra starts to stand for she knows where the bus will stop. On this route we didn't have our familiar faces of our bus drivers. They usually drop us off very close to our place. It didn't matter we only had a few blocks to walk. Sierra's little sister is still moving and letting me know time is getting closer for her debut. As we walked toward our place, I didn't see our car. I say to myself all this worrying for nothing. My heart kind of saddens at the thought that he might not care about us being gone. Did he even wonder if we were okay?

Little Tim is playing outside with Momo's boys and Tim's cousin. I still can't understand him, but Sierra communicates with him very well. The innocence in both allows them to talk to each other regardless of their cultural differences. They called for Sierra to play and she looks at me for the okay. I tell her let's put your stuff in the house and you can come back out and play for a little bit. I go into the apartment and it seems so quiet and empty… No sign of Bill or life. Was he gone all day and where could he have been?? He didn't leave a note or any signs that he might be returning. My heart saddens, and my thoughts just wondered why. I put the leftovers in the fridge and go outside with Sierra and sit down on the stairs and watched her play with the other children. She looked so happy as I just set there wondering. Clarence comes out and joins me with a plate of fresh smelling cookies that Keith had baked. The aroma was in the air and my little unborn daughter allowed some space just for them. I can tell that she was ready for the yum yum too. Clarence and Keith both knew I enjoyed his cooking.

I try to smile and give very little eye contact to Clarence, so he didn't see my pain. I didn't know what to think or what to say or how to act. For some reason Clarence and I started a conversation which was random thoughts. We talked about how big Sierra was getting he added that the baby was growing too, via me. I didn't know if he thought that he was giving me a compliment or what. I guess coming from him it was good. I chuckled and said it was from those big cookies Keith loves to bake. We both laughed, and my heart and thoughts relax.

He talked a little about his pain. He said that he was married to his wife Mayala for three years, and he had two kids, Clarence Jr, and Laniece. Since they were older, he didn't see them as much as he would like to. Their mother was his high school sweetheart. When he saw her walk down the hall way, he knew she was the one. I thought to myself was that the same way Bill thought about me when I sat down in the library? Was I the one? I surely didn't think that when I sat down with him in the library. All I wanted to do was study for my exam. How many times did we pass each other as I was entering, and he was leaving class? He must have noticed me more than I noticed him. I guess I did notice him, but it wasn't in that way of going out with him. Funny how I didn't know he was looking at me? I guess it was flattering to hear Clarence say that because it confirmed again that Bill sought me out of many other women that could have been in this situation. Great, did I win or what, humph?? I guess I showed them.

Well, getting back to sharing Clarences's story, he said that he went away to school and their relationship just drifted away. He chuckled about being married to someone else before Malaya but didn't last. They stayed together in a bogus with benefits marriage for two years. We just weren't a good fit. While he is talking, I was looking at Sierra playing and wondering where this conversation is going. With no emotions showing he said during his divorce Malaya was still on his mind. That was when he realized how much he missed and really loved her. He didn't know how or remembered how I detoured to my first wife Bridgette. She was a high school friend, with a sad story. Bridgette story was that her mother tried to get her to prostitute, bring in the money and she wasn't going that route. But Bridgette ends up getting pregnant. She was my friend and I was working and had medical benefits so said let's get married.

I asked did you love her. His response was no she was my friend. Sometimes we slept together but I was young, and I had other girlfriends. This wasn't a marriage of love because, I told her that I wanted to be with Malaya and have children with her. My girlfriends would come over and hang out with both of us. When she had her baby, I don't know why she tried to include me in as the father. She wanted me to be the father and step up, so we could be a family. I made it clear that I wasn't the daddy and I married her, so she could use my insurance and love was not included in this package deal. I was trying to do the noble thing by putting her on my insurance. Then the living conditions got old and Bridgette got on my nerves.

She worked, looked good and had a shape and mind hmm, but I realized she wasn't the one for me. So, I really didn't count her as my first marriage. It was better to have a hurt now than many little hurts later. She didn't deserve that, and I wasn't that kind of dog. I watched him smile as he looks as if he is picturing her as he talks about Bridgette. She was a friend I was trying to rescue from having her mother pimp her out. I was a noble dog. He tried to joke, I only howled when necessary. Clarence raised his eyebrows with, nothing, but a little bow wow in me, (and he howls). I laughed and said you're just nasty as he shook his head yes. The children glanced at him while he was making the howling noise. We both laughed as the laughing children went back to playing. I looked at him that is just too much information. Inside it wasn't helping me, considering my shaped left more than nine months ago. Anyway, Clarence story is helping a little in taking my mind off Bill. He said his brother, Steve kept him up on the 4-1-1 on her and that she still was single, no kids and still got that shape and looking fine. Malaya stayed in contact with my mom Gilda and my dad Jerry could careless. Moms did always like her. Moms didn't like many of the girls me or my brother Steve brought home. And we could drag in some howlers. Actually, my brother and I had our share of ladies and never really thought about settling down.

Back in the day I ran track and Steve played football so the honies were coming out of the woodwork after us. I looked at Clarence and he is slim that confirms and in shape and able to survive Keith's cooking without picking up weight. Clarence winks with saying, we were hot and knew it and took full advantage of our looks and our athletic physique. I just looked at him with an expression of really. And he raised his eyebrows and smiled, oh yeah. Steve is still single and collecting honies and spending their money. I laughed saying he sounds like a pimp. Clarence pauses in response and says hmm maybe… I thought about Malaya and at this point in my life I wanted to marry her and have children with only her. Although Bridgette was fine, and I loved Malaya. As time went on, I knew Brigette wasn't the one. Our lives had become routine and we just faded away in our marriage and knew it was time for us to go our separate ways. No hard feelings just part as loving friends. I never heard from her or looked for her. This was a done deal and we both knew it and moved on to share lives with someone else.

When I came back home, I found Laya and told her I made a mistake and that it has always been her. We married and moved out here to sunny California from the Midwest. We both worked, she worked the naval base, as an inventory supply clerk. I worked across town at different location as a warehouse manager until I scored my job at Lockheed. We had our boy and girl and I thought everything was going well. I married the girl of my dreams and had the children I wanted to have with her. We were making good money and life was what I pictured, until hmm… I looked at him and his expression change. It was strange that I for some reason felt his pain he is getting ready to release. I never really thought that men felt pain. They are always showing nothing but strength. I guess they are as human as we are.

He said that he noticed that she started changing. Suddenly Mayala started working out before going to work. She would leave about 5:00 in the morning with me cheering her on. I worked the swing night shift from 7:30 to 3:00. This scheduled helped with the expense of childcare. She was coming home late which threw my schedule off. I had to be on the road by 6:00 and she would come in around 6:30 or so. See Rita I worked at night so when I came home, she would be going to work right, (as he displays a question mark look on his face). Again, Laya would say that sometimes her schedule would change so if she was late that made me late for work. I started getting this gut feeling that something wasn't right...

So, I asked my daughter's godmother Brenda what was going on since she was her supervisor. She gave me the whole run down. I had to take it rather I wanted to or not. Don't ask any type of question if you are not ready for the answer or look for something you really don't want to see. Brenda said that it was a guy she met during deliveries. See Laya did inventory for the base. I guess he delivered more than conversation. Brenda said that Laya was not working out. She had been coming in late for work and from her breaks. Brenda had to write her up and she was border line of possibly more discipline. I sat there with my mouth open and watched him talk about his betrayal. I asked him did it hurt to hear that. He looked at me and said hell yes. Pain is pain, any type of pain hurts. Clarence said that he was blown away and wasn't expecting that hit. Laya was my all and my queen. All I wanted was to marry her and have children with her.

I decided I had to see it for myself. So, I didn't go to work one day. I could go onto the base, because the gym was for military and civilian. I went to the place she said she worked out. Didn't see her I even waited for some time to see if she was going to show up. Nope didn't happen. I should have figured it out all that working out and her ass was still flabby. Tell me Rita how can you wear draws and your ass still wobble?? I didn't care I loved her. I didn't care what she looked like. I saw her the same way I saw her when I first layed eyes on her and fell in love. I knew something was up, but I didn't want to think that she would do something like that to us or our family. So, when she came home from work, she had a little pep in her step and that all familiar glow. I knew I didn't put it there we haven't been together that way in awhile. I remembered we used to have fun, (and he winks); everyday at least three times a day for years. Even after the children were born, we were still having fun. I looked at him and asked do I really need to hear this part?? I felt those words like an arrow piercing my heart. Bill hadn't touch me in awhile and I just wondered how Bill looked at me. Not like we could do anything as big as I was, but a hug and pat on the butt or something anything that showed some type of hey babe expression. I silently asked myself, did Bill still have the same eyes and love from the time we sat in the library. Does Bill remember our first date? He asked, and I answered did his love for me changed.

As I sat and listened looking at Sierra play with the other children, I still wondered where was Bill? I looked at Clarence asking did you ask her about her workouts. I wondered if I would have the nerve to ask that question and really be prepared for the answer. He said hell yes, she is my wife and I wanted our marriage, but I didn't sign up to share her. As I listened, I am still in ah about men showing such emotions and actually hurting. For some reason it always seems as if women were on the receiveing end of that kind of of pain/hurt and disappointment. I really felt his pain, but still curious so I ask again so I could understand...

Clarence went on to say that we tried to attend counseling, she didn't want to go. I wanted to have date night, nah from her. I talked to our Pastor and her close friends. Laya just wasn't feeling us and just wanted me out of our place and her heart wanted some serious Clarence gone. She went as far to say I hit her and called the police. I couldn't believe she would go through such extremes. Who was this person I married and just couldn't live without? She was the only one I wanted to marry and have children with. He kept repeating what he wanted, and it may sound simple he just wanted his family. This was just what I wanted with Bill. It just sounded funny but not ha-ha just strange hearing it from a man.

Police did show up and she tried to convince them that I hit her. She didn't have a mark or bruise on her not even any dried-up fake ass tears. I watched her lie on me and it just pierced my soul and heart. I told the police I didn't touch her, and she kept trying to convince them, and again I just stood there. She showed no love and no emotions while she told her lies. The officers listened as they both looked at us. Trying to figure out what was the real situation and who was lying and who will be leaving. The one thing that helped was that she had just got her hair and nails done and everything was still in place. Thank God for her getting her hair done, because if I didn't know any better, I would have believed her too...

Chapter 26
Clarence Had to Look Forward

Officer Windell asked me if there was anywhere, I could go. I told him no, but I knew by their expressions and words I had to leave the home/family I really cherished. This wasn't the same woman I married. I knew it was over then and I had to go. I went to my second job at a club where I deejayed. It was a good outlet looking at people dance and enjoy my music. At least someone was enjoying something that I was good at. It was a good distractor but sometimes my mind drifted back to Laya her lies and betrayal. It put me back in a sad place I didn't want to be and where was I going to go after the music stops and people going home. Pretty much after the party was over and everyone is gone, I'm now alone with no home.

I hadn't been away from my family, not like this. After leaving the club and that night I was feeling a little down. I tried to play my music and smile, so no one could see or feel my pain. Funny how you don't think anybody is paying attention to you or notice any type of change in your character. The bartender Coco asked me what was up. I didn't have the pep that I usually had. I guess she saw through my pretense. I told her that I was put out of my house and I didn't have a place to stay and was just trying to figure out my next step/move. She opened her heart and said that I could come and crash on her couch. Coco was dating, so there wasn't any kind of concern about sharing a couch at a friend's place. So, I had all my stuff packed in my trunk and took her up on her offer. It beat sleeping in my small car. As I listened, I looked around to see if Bill might be pulling up at any moment and didn't want to be caught talking with Clarence.

He said we had that arrangement for a while, and I went through with my divorce from Laya. It wasn't easy, and I did feel some pain, but in time the pain faded away and my life went on. Clarence made it sound so easy, could I get over Bill like that and move on without him. This was a scary thought, but people do it all the time. Some love last and some pass through and eventually fade away and sometimes the memories that come with it. How sad because other people are affected by the separation. Will Bill and I stay together or be one of those statistics and just fade away. I really hope not, I still loved Bill and just like Clarence I wanted my husband and family. Both people really must want the relationship not fair to be one sided and unbalanced. Marriage is working together with a little give and take. When one is off the other should be able to pick up the weight and when the other is off, they should be willing able to back them up.

Clarence said the arrangements worked for a while until one day she came home and said she needed to be put to sleep. She sadly said, (as he paused to make his eyes look puppy dog sad with raised eyebrows), that her and her boyfriend had broken up and she needed to be put to sleep. At first, I didn't quite understand until he said it again with a corner smile. Then I had a duh moment again and I laughed, and he chuckled with me. We both were laughing through our pain. He didn't know how much he helped me and maybe I helped him too. At least it felt like it and it was an eye opening for me on the feeling's men have. He laughed and said after that he put her to sleep often.

Clarence said that they ended up moving to a two-bedroom apartment, because we had only a sleeping arrangement every now and then. She was nothing other than a friend I would rock to sleep. She had a boyfriend but still wanted us to do this and it became more and more of this. I hadn't heard that term in years. The last time I heard it was from Reva when she said that she and Maurice did this. I had to ask what he meant. He said a drive by hit it and leave. Then he went into detail about this... I felt like I was back in school, but ths time adding a sex education class. I learned the hard way. By thinking it was indigestion and all the time someone was growing inside of me. Mom never talked to me about sex. I guess it was hard to accept that I might be having sex, or she just didn't know how. I didn't receive the short version that Reva's mom gave her' just don't get your ass pregnant'. My mother did show attention in a way that I would have felt better if she did say don't get your ass pregnant at least it wouldn't be humor at my expense. She did know how to laugh at me along with my younger sister. I remember one time I thought birth control pills were vitamins. That would have been a good opportunity to share with me instead of making a joke out of it. In her world she should have noticed that I really needed for her to talk to me or share something, look what it cost me, my innocence.

Clarence was breaking down the friendship verses sex, said there are different categories; hit it and leave is you just do it like the spur of the moment, satisfy the moment no meaning just self gratification, now having sex alot but and there is a but, don't want any type of attachment, still a form a gratification no true meaning. It's like you are just hanging out you know just kicking it and you both just feel it and it happens and tomorrow is another day. You like spending time together but you know it's not going anywhere. Making love, (he kind of closes his eyes briefly as he if he was remembering), means you are involved with the person, intimacy looking forward to the intensity a feeling of remembering with high expections not just physically attractive but emotional attachment too. I looked at him and the only thing I could say was hmmm, okay.

Coco wanted to be rocked often, before I went to work; if we went to the store, she wanted in do it in the bathroom or while driving didn't care anywhere any place. I asked her what's up with your guy and she said he didn't do it like I did. Coco would smile and add he didn't quite put me to sleep the way you do. When I heard do it, I knew from my brief Clarence sex class that there were no emotions and was a spur of the moment no love, no nothing. How do you feel after doing it and the person makes it clear that you are nothing? I thought that was sad and some form of abuse. He said that she wanted it everyday and everywhere. By then it really got old and boring for me her nah but me yep. By then my divorce was final and I was ready to start dating and Coco was not included in that process. No way did I ever give her the impression that it was nothing but a booty call, no love, no kissing, no hugging, no happy we are together. She acted like it was okay until I started talking to Barbera Lynne and started bringing her over to our apartment.

Coco would give Barbera Lynne a look that made me feel uncomfortable, but she didn't trip. She kept her poise and set her ass down on the couch right next to me. I was impressed with her style and kinda liked her. Coco started acting funny after that she was moody and wasn't too pleasant to be around. I knew it was a matter of time and I needed to start looking for me another place and I told her I was looking. The atmosphere had changed, and my welcome was worn out. She wanted more than her mouth could say, and I could see it in her actions and feel it in her thoughts. She was having feelings that I just didn't have for her. I had stop putting her to sleep and I was enjoying my rest. Coco asked a question she that she wasn't prepared for the answer. She asked was I putting Lynne to sleep. Clarence laughed and said no because I really cared about her and I didn't sleep around. Opportunity had presented itself with Coco and like any man hey she asked and I obliged. It was my duty to help put her to sleep. He smiled, and she slept well. After all she asked, and I did and that was then, and this is now. I was up front about our relationship; I didn't try to hide anything from her.

I smiled and said she thought she could change your mind since you were putting her to sleep. He said I never lead her on and I made it very clear on my position with her, (no pun meant). I said I know but it doesn't change her thought process. Yep, but I didn't change my mind. One thing I have learned then and now that once a man has made his mind up there really is no changing. Then Clarence expressions change as he said something happened that I never would have fathomed. He had my attention and I could have heard theme music with drums. I could tell he was uneasy but sharing his experience. Clarence said one night he came home tired from working all day getting ready for inspections. He said she didn't say too much to him and he went to bed exhausted.

Next thing he knows the door opened and Coco jumped on him and pinned him down trying to have sex with him. I asked how could she over power you like that? He said she a larger woman and very horny. I looked at Clarence and he was a slim man, but I didn't see any weakness. I could see her taking advantage of knowing that he was exhausted. Clarence said he was sleeping on his side and she flipped him over and put him into her. I asked how could that happen if you didn't want it and how did she get your clothes off? He said that he slept in the nude and men sometime wake up with a… I stopped him there, ooh too much visual yuck. I smiled as he continued. Clarence gave a play by blow reenactment. We struggled and fought hard. She was holding her own and I wasn't giving up either and I grabbed some scissors and cut her braids. Now that pissed her off and she jumped up off me cussing and swearing. I got up and put on my clothes and call the police. She looked at me like I was crazy, and I felt violated. I thought this was some reversal of him feeling violated. I guess this can happen to men they are just like everyone else again an eye opener.

Clarence smiled with do you believe the police finally came and I told them what happened. They looked at her and she looked alright. They smile as they gazed upon her figure. Then they looked at me as if I was crazy. One of the officers says she could rape me. They looked at each other and thought dit was funny. Coco and I agreed on one thing without talking just facial expressions and with tempers flaring. This situation was not funny in no way a ha-ha, especially not to me. They were no help and I knew it was time to get out of there before someone really got hurt.

After that situation we just stopped talking and I slept with the door locked and pajamas on. I listened as he tried to correct the problem within himself. He didn't encourage her or mislead her. She had made up in her mind she wanted to be put to sleep indefinitely. Wow was this indeed was a true twist. The girl raped my ass and thought we were going to be okay, ain't that some dit. Hard to believe he was raped and hard for men to tell because other men would probably think it was funny. There is no funny ha-ha when someone is raped or violated. Clarence didn't have to share but there must have been a need and I felt good that he trusted me enough to share something so deep rooted and personal.

I asked him did he date a lot when he was younger and after his divorce. I didn't date much. I really didn't have any conversation about dating from my parents, other than have some mad money for just in case. My parents seem to assume you should know, without talking to you. Clarence said he didn't date until he became a senior and hadn't touched a girl. He was afraid of getting someone pregnant…

But there was sexy Lexie the high school cheerleader fine and fast. Lexie teased me about being a virgin. My ego kicks in and I told her that I get it all the time, but inside I knew it was a lie, but I was trying to convince her. She looked at me as if she knew I was lying, because I kept stuttering. Lexie said she didn't see me with any girls, then added insult with I probably didn't even have a girlfriend. She gave me an open invitation. Lexie told me that after the game we're going for a ride. I had my mother's car and I thought I was cool. Inside Rita I didn't know what the hell to do with her suggestion. All the time we were driving after the game I was wondering how to get started and what to do. I knew where to insert but what about before and during. Shoot I was almost ready to pass out from anxiety.

We got something to drink. In that time and era, it wasn't hard to get something to drink or have someone buy it for you. We both enjoyed that bottle of Courvoiser. We all hung out in the same area with other cars doing the same thing. So, we drove to an area where the security didn't drive around. When we did stop Lexie became sexy and she pop those draws off put her one leg on the dashboard and the other one I don't remember but she was ready, and that mellow from the Courvoiser kicked in. Well we did it I guess she like it, I don't know been so long can't really remember. All I do remember was that it was hard for me to really get into it, because I was afraid that the security would come and flash their lights on us. So, it was hard to concentrate, and the pressure was on. He laughs and that it was done, no more a virgin and I moved to Texas.

While living in Texas, I worked as a security guard at a bank where I met Miss Zia; she was the president of the bank and a local madame. I guess you could call her Madame President. She helped me get over the fear of girls and ladies. I had such mistrust in women, because the ones I knew wanted to get pregnant. I wasn't having that nope, one woman and one family. Miss Zia convinced me and told me that she had some friends she wanted me to meet, and that they were willing to pay very well for young man such as you. I looked at him and he looked okay, he was handsome. I didn't stare because I didn't want the wrong impression to happen and I belong to someone else and thought it would be disrespectful. He said she taught me a whole lot and I learned more from the ladies I met. I could hear the bell ringing because school was in session. When I escorted a lady and saw my first $2500 check for an hour worth of time or a little more time in some cases hmm, I had a different thought. I quit my security job and worked full time for Madame President.

She had many professional women I took care of, lawyers, doctors, CEOs' They would pick me up in a limo and take me to a location and bring me back home. I asked did he have sex with them. He said some I did, some just wanted company, and some wanted some strange things done, like spank them. I spanked one so hard and scared the woman and she didn't ask me to do that again. One wanted to make love in a coffin nope drew the line on that one, others wanted a golden shower. He said he dranked a lot of water obliged her too to assist with the golden shower request. I thought all of this is yuck. Its funny ha-ha then like now my imagination couldn't fathom what sexual acts could happen for $2500.

When we were in the long social hours at Melba's birthday party and talking with Robin and Courtney Diane, they said that they would take from the dirty movies and what others partners you have had and incorporate.... That would make your man very happy. Even then I wasn't sexually active, nor did I really look or like those types of movies. Maybe Bill had gotten bored with his Midwestern home-town wife. Maybe I should have listened to them and just tried because something or someone might be taken care of him for free. Oh well when I drop my weight after delivering our daughter, maybe I will try to spark up the bedroom. I hope that works, any way back to Clarence antics that I really enjoy listening to. His class on sex terminology was impressive. I continued to eagerly listen as he tried to convince me on the difference between, a prostitute, ho and a kept man.

Everytime I said either one he corrected me with he was a kept man. Okay I guess either way you supply the same function. Rather kept or strolling you still end up in the bedroom. Clarence talked about how some of the clients would send their family out for the day or hours, so he could come and take care their business, and some were some real cougars and just needed escorts and after dinner dessert, (he smiled and winked and kept going) ...

The cougar part made me think back to when we were laughing about hooking up with Keoni's fine boyfriend. How did it go hurt me, love me, make me write bad checks, give me a reason to be overdrawn with insufficient funds? I knew our check-ing account couldn't afford Clarence. I wondered and asked if he had girlfriends during that time. He said yeah four. I asked were all four at different time? Yep he laughed they were all at the same time. Sometimes they would be there when the person/benefactor arrived. We would go up to my room and I would go to work and when done they left. I asked how the women felt about that. He said I told them up front that I was a kept man. So, they knew, and I left it at that. If they wanted to stay cool if not still cool, replacements were not hard to find. I asked why he stopped, he said just like anything it just got old and my mama Gilda found out.

I laughed under my breath and he smiled at me with a puzzle look on his face. Gilda asked what jobs you work that affords you a condo, different new cars, food in fridge and new clothes with more suits than a Pastor. I broke down and told her I was a kept man. Inside I knew I was called a kept ho, pimp but I knew that I was getting paid $2500 an hour, because I was that good. I wore $1,000 gators, had walk in closet with jewelry, shoes, clothes arranged in order. Had cars that I tore up racing or gave away, didn't care I knew I was going to get another one, don't know to this day where all my stuff went. I was well kept man, well kept. Didn't think about the money ending I was having too much fun spending. Well yeah, I gave up an apartment and just left everything there and within a week had another place all furnished with another car. I asked him did he save any money. Nope young and wasn't thinking like that. I was doing drugs, weed in bulk and with that comes many friends and many ladies, yeah. I could have purchased a house but thought why I lived in a nice condo, money was rolling in and I was spending it as fast as it hit my hand. Now moms she opened my eyes to some serious reality. She said you don't know about these husbands. They could circle around and come back or could come in and kill or shoot you while your guard is down. There are too many diseases out there just too much of nothing the route you are taking, just trouble with disappointment. When she put it that way it was time? I asked how much time did you put in? Clarence said about four years. So, I had a lot of coochie so that's why I didn't trip if I'm not with anyone. So, when these hoochies try to get me, because they think that I have money, that's nah. What they think they have gold coochies? Don't need the headache or trouble from a hoochie's couchie. All coochies are all the same just with different faces.

We talked about marriage and I asked if he missed being married. He said he wanted to stay married to Laya. She was the only woman he wanted to marry and have children with. She hurt me a lot after the separation, and she dated the guy that broke us up for a bit maybe hmm about two years. During that time, I end up getting a one-bedroom apartment and one day she came over to bring my children by and wanted to know where I stayed. She laughed at my place because I only had a mattress that sat on milk cartons and another crate used for a table. I was content and her laughing at my place that didn't even bother me either. She liked the area and ended up getting a place upstairs right above me. It worked because now I could see my children more because they were still young, and I wanted to be in every part of their lives. I didn't have a car and when I would walk to the bus stop, she would hunk with the finger and laughed. The only thing that bothered me was hearing my kids say they wanted their daddy. Now that hurt but I knew this situation to would pass. She started dating the guy upstairs across from her apartment. That guy had someone, so he would creep over to her place. On purpose she would yell out while she was getting busy just, so I could hear.

Really, I didn't like all that noise it's a turn off. You have three sounds some people make during intimacy. Here we go again with a class on sex noise; the animal that growls, the sirens that shrieks, and the one that wants, you to talk or she talks. All up in my ear hearing the woman yell in my ear saying you like this or is this the best coochie or what. In my mind I was thinking would you shut up or just be quiet. They didn't know that I have had many and this was a turn off and I didn't return their calls, nor did they make a return visit. See Rita you have that one good woman that is your queen. She goes around momma, family and friends she is the keeper, okay. Now you have the one now we talked about categories now here is another class; you see this second one she's cool you take her around a few friends that you know won't get you busted you know they know how to keep their mouths shut about the insert and not let the queen know, because she's a keeper, and the third one is just a fun buddy indoor pet. Happy to see ya, but I don't live with you, not planning on living with you and you don't sleep over, ever ever, infinity ever!! I looked at him with my eyebrows raised you say your not calling her ass. He raises his eyebrows like hey. But there is sometimes a but, not often. We as men can have the best thing that ever happen to us and some how funk it up. We have a woman that will wash our dirty draws and cook but we will find a way to uck it up. That's just what we do as men and we are good at it. I agreed my brother, Charles was the same way had many queens and settled for bargain basement love, excluding his ex-wife. She did put up with a lot, so I had to agree with Clarence on that one. Funny I heard the same comment from my old work friend Daimen; humph must be a silent men anthem. But the one you want to be with sometimes space happens and you somehow grow apart. It was hard getting over Laya because I loved her, but now she is just a convenient gap that's open like seven eleven. Her legs are always open. Talking with Clarence opened my eyes to the fact that men do hurt, and pain is pain. It doesn't matter where it comes from it still hurts. I felt his pain but saw in his face that pain has long faded away into a memory and only stored for a reminder of not to ever return to the gap.

I kind of chuckled and Clarence laughs with me. I asked him what happened to.... He started to say there is something I want to tell you about the mall. At that point Sierra comes over with Tim and gang and they want to go in and play hide and seek and look at some movies. I thought why not it is not too late. I told Clarence bathroom is calling as I slowly try to rise from the steps. He jumps up to assist and says girl when are you going to pop out this child? I laughed as I took his hand telling him less than six weeks and I am so ready. He laughs with you look like it. I'm glad he didn't call me big like Bill would. That wasn't flattering; it was rather painful and very hurtful.

As Clarence said pain was pain no matter at what level it still hurts. It felt good to know that chilvary was not dead, because I needed some assistance with standing to my feet. Thinking back on the boyfriends I had kind of for a second boost my ego when they would pursue me. Now I wondered with the way I look would they try again. Bill had me feeling like crap sometimes I hated looking at myself. I tried so hard to hide the pain from Bill because that would only encourage him more to be mean and angry. I didn't want Sierra to see my pain or my unborn daughter to feel the hurt. Just as I am going into the apartment with the kids Bill pulls up. I looked at him with no expression and just turned my head as if I didn't see him and I kept it moving right to the bathroom. While washing my hands I just look in the mirror at my reflections and I just started to see if there was enough in me to cry.

I didn't know why and at that time, but I just wanted to cry. It didn't last long because if I am able to cry it is only for a short period. I took a big breath and wondered what I would open the door to. I didn't know why I just took a big breath to release myself from that temporary frustration of what? I was feeling myself and my ancestral strength. I washed my face to refresh my thoughts and hoping it would fresh my spirits. That temporary cry attempt did produce some tears, it helped I guess it did refresh my face and soul.

I went into our bedroom opened the patio door. I felt the breeze on my fresh washed face and closed the door with strength and ready for anything that might come out of his mouth or any action he might act on. I didn't care and wasn't going to argue either. Today was not the day and my joy will not be removed or taken away. Bill opened the door to hearing kids playing. I didn't know how long he had been gone. I am glad that he didn't see me talking to Clarence that was one headache argument I didn't want or need, but one thing I was ready. He asked where I have been with a smile. I replied gone and how about you. I turn my head away from him and continued to go to the back rooms. He followed me and tried to hold a conversation my answers were short and to the point. Bill insisted that he had to go into work again. I looked at him and responded with okay and walked away. Inside I wondered what the heck you wanted, leave me alone. What did you really do today? I walked away and said just hung out. I went to work. What job do you have he asked? Oh just; raising our daughter and carrying the other one and cleaning up the apartment, and refrigerator, playing with Sierra and making sure she stays busy, doing laundry, making beds and get exercise so when I deliver our next daughter that is less, I had to worry about with my shape coming back. Bill couldn't respond back to what shape and I walked over to the couch and sat my fat ass down and turned the television on and channel surf, hey hang ten. He just looked at me and went back into the back bedroom. I thought yep if you worked all day your ass should be tired......

There were times when Bill would clean up and you could eat off the floor and the smell of pinesol would linger throughout the apartment, but that was so far and in between. Sierra didn't say too much to him either. She glanced at him said hi and kept playing. I heard water, so he was either taking a shower or getting ready to go back out. The way I was feeling, and the long day I had, I really didn't care. I wanted my family but right now Bill was getting on my nerves. I think this came from the daughter I was carrying because I felt we were sharing the same feelings. Get to going if you are going and you don't even have to say good bye just go. See you when I see you and maybe this time I will really be gone. Especially if you stay out all night don't count on me being up. This is not your bed and breakfast inn. I was full and tired. Bill didn't know what to do. For once the tables were turned no one in the house cared. For once we had a life too it may have been in this apartment, but this was our domain and our place.

Chapter 27
Today Was a Good Day to Grow

Today was a good day for learning and growing in the right way at the right time. Bill left, and I didn't ask or look in his direction, just didn't care today wasn't the day. I watched Sierra and her company play and they always hide underneath the cabinets and I laughed because they always looked everywhere but there. I have always loved looking at children's innocence being played and the joy of just having fun. I continued channel surfing because everything on me was exhausted and my daughter was kicking and letting me know the time is coming soon. Right when I was getting ready for Sierra's company to go home Tim's Aunt Natalia came over looking for him and the gang. I liked that because I really didn't want to move from this comfortable position. My feet felt like a pair of hearts throbbing and my legs felt the relief of being stretched out on top of the coffee table. Sierra came in and kind of curled around me and we both were feeling the long day catching up with us.

By that time sleep was getting ready to set in we heard keys at the door. He couldn't have been gone that long and why was he coming back. We were ready to take an early nap or just call it a night. Either way sleep was going to hang out with us. Bill opens the door with a smile and says let's get out and go to the movies. I thought wow right now that was the last thing on my mind. Sierra and I were both fighting sleep. I looked at him with his twinkling almond shaped eyes with the deep dimples showing through his smile. I never could resist, and I didn't, and I said why not. He grabs my arm to help get up and reach for Sierra also. She gains that last residual of strength and says sure dad let's go. Inside I wished he would have kept going. I really didn't want to go somewhere else and sit to just end up following asleep. He was trying to reach out and I wanted to be on the receiving end. I thought about Clarence and how he tried everything to keep or save his marriage. He showed me another side to how some men really do have emotions and hurt like we do. Was this a reach out moment for Bill? With us not responding did this scare him or was this just wishful thinking on my side. Well we loaded up as is and got in the car.

Before getting in I looked around to see if someone else might have been in the car. So far, I didn't notice anything different, so I told myself let's go and have fun with our family. I asked myself did I really want the answer with my wondering hormones? Enjoy the flowers and the moments you wanted, no crumbs today. Like Mama Sadie said he had to ask, and he did ask if we wanted to go out for a movie and I said I do, and I did. It was getting dark and the apartment was full. I saw; Robin and Courtney Diane who gave me a heads up, Momo and Amos chasing after their younger boys like always, Little Tim speaking up a storm in Danish with his family. I remembered one day I looked at Tim and his apartment and saw a glance of his grandfather. His grandfather reminded me of my grandfather Yank, and he would just sit there and watch television while reading his TV guide. Not much on conversation unless it was his brother Hank or my dad. Then the conversation was endless as we watched television in the other room eating candy and drinking soda pop or go with my grandmother Hazel on a pool hall run. We tag team my grandmother's and great-grandmother's house. We either walked or stayed at my great- grandmother's Mommy place. At mommy's apartment we had a playground with slides, merry-go-round, swings and plenty of room to play.

My mother would take us over to our grandparents/great-grandmothers' almost every Sunday or sometimes we would spend the weekend. Mommy spoiled us big time. She would cook some juicy hamburgers, bake a mean peach cobbler from scratch and soft scramble eggs for breakfast. Sometimes she would heat up milk in a bottle when we were younger and had the nerve to laugh as we drank milk from the bottle like little babies. I missed her love and energy. She didn't go to school and couldn't read or write but she knew how to live from her life experiences, and she passed it on. I still laugh when I remember how Bill was yelling at her as if she was hard of hearing and the expression on her face of why is this fool yelling?? I had to tell him she can hear it's your grandmother that can't. Although I was older, I still felt like Mommy's little great- granddaughter. To this day I can still picture her place, remember her phone number and the side of her cheek that held chewing tobacco and how we would always kiss her on that side.

Mommy would always smile as we kissed that side and I remember the warmth from her. She was beautiful inside and gorgeous, and I still have her in my heart. It's been over thirty years, but it seems like yesterday I was playing the piano as a little girl for her to hear and be proud of me. I wished I would have kept up with the lessons. Anyway, we are on our way to the movies. Don't know what movie he has in mind but if Sierra doesn't like it, we will never hear the end of it, unless she falls asleep because of her long day. In which I'm kind of hoping she does because I am feeling a little tired too. I tried to hold the yawn in and fight the tears that want to accompany my yawn. While trying to fight the tears and yawn Sierra lets out a big noisy yawn that had me look back and Bill looks in the rear-view mirror to see her. She looks at us with her glassy almond eyes as if what's up daddy and Rita, ooh I can't stand when she calls me Rita….one day……one day. We both asked at the same time are you yawning. She responds with nope just stretching loudly. We both look at each other and our smiles meant as we turn our heads. We weren't expecting that type of response from Sierra.

For that instance, Bill melted my heart and the heat warmed my soul and body. Wow that felt so good at that point he grabs my hand, and only thing I could do was smile, and sigh because it felt so good. Just that touch reminded me I was still human and the love for me was still there. Today was a long day and I wasn't expecting this at all. Actually, I didn't know what to expect. I just knew I was hurting and wanted to run away from the person inflicting the pain and hoping he would come looking for me like I saw my dad do so many times when my mother left him. I kind of feel now that she really didn't want to leave, she just wanted him to respect and appreciate her.

Then I think back to my Aunt Johanna who used to always call me runaway. I still don't think she knows my real name. I just know that I don't want to continue this cycle of running away just so Bill can appreciate what he has in his family. I left everything in Oakwood for him and I still want to be married I glanced over at him and smile because I didn't know his thoughts and he smiled at me and he didn't know my thoughts either. Even if I tried to share it with him, he wouldn't understand my thought process. Right now, I am enjoying this special family spontaneous time just like I remembered as a child my parents used to do with us. I enjoyed it then and just like I enjoy it now. We look back at Sierra thinking she might be sleep and she looks back at us with the expression with a small smile, I'm not sleepy yet, nice try. Right at that moment she smiles and as we turned our heads and look at each other and just that quick she fell asleep.

Bill says since we are out let's just go with the flow and enjoy each other's company. For once let's be spontaneous!! Then that dreaded question came up what did you and Sierra do today??? I had a mind freeze and a duh attack all at the same time should I go into details or just give the short version. Hmm the short version, because I didn't get a chance to rehearsh what I would say if ask??? So, I became spontaneous. Well is was think quick or slow but respond. My response was, yeah well Sierra and I took a different route and came across a new bus route and just went exploring. I thought why ruin the moment but in the back of my mind was telling me to tell him because he needed to know…

I told him that we found a new restaurant that's like a breakfast/ lunch place called PataRee's Pancakes and Sierra just loved it. A nice young couple Pat and Ree owned it and it had a child's theme, but adult calmness. Sierra fell in love with their daughter Mackey or MacKenzie and that little girl was so polite and well mannered it just tickled me. She stood right by her parent's side greeting customers in a child professional way it was so cute. Her and Sierra played and enjoyed the birthday party that was there. Oh yeah, I ran into Catrice and would you believe she is pregnant with twins. Bill responded with what, you're kidding me aren't they at eighty children now! We both laughed in sync saying nah ninety. She is having twin boys so that would put her at eleven. We both said at the same time wooa, wow, better them than us. I laughed you don't want a house full of kids. Again, we agreed I said no, and Bill says oh hell no. Then we laughed even harder and kept laughing as we passed many exits. We laughed so hard that our unborn daughter moved as if we were waking her up. I rub my stomach to try and calm her down and Bill placed his hand on my stomach as if to assist in calming our daughter. He got so used to rubbing my stomach that he didn't jerk back like he did at the beginning.

I told him I saw many of Greekums's sisters, nieces, nephews, and the kids just kept coming out, like clowns out of a small car. It seemed endless on the children coming in for a birthday party. Oh, yea Ree's sister Shanta and her husband Joel have an evening restaurant called ShaRoberts it is really nice, and they invited us back for their birthday celebration for her and her best friend Chantell. Bill and I smiled at each other as we agreed. I added maybe next time or just go there just to have a nice dinner. He agreed that didn't sound too bad. Oh, I forgot their parents Gordon Maurice and Robin Denise own a bowling alley and skating rink that would be nice to go to also. I asked him did he ever go skating or bowling? He said bowling okay skating, nope all I did when I did go one time was mop their floor with my body, came home bruised and dusty. I laughed guess what the name of the place is called. He looks perplexed at the question. I laughed "Mop the Floor". I guess they had the same experience that many shared. I told him I mopped the floor skating and tried ice skating and fell so much I came home soak and wet ooh and add cold. I felt like a walking ice sickle. He laughed I came home so dusty, sore and moms said the same thing boy what did you do clean those people's floor.

I laughed picturing Bill's mom, Naomi's face with those deep dimples smiling and laughing while dusting Bill off. I pictured Bill as a little boy using his old school pictures smiling and helping her by dusting himself off as they both laughed. I always admired their relationship because it was very loving and caring, yet Naomi wasn't overbearing. I liked the way he treated his mother and the deep respect he had for his dad Richard. Who still to this day scares me and at the same time I have no fear of Naomi just a lot of love and respect for both. Bill's baby sister Rita looked just like her mother and I enjoyed talking to her and loved her energy and she was very smart. I would tease Bill sometimes saying why did I get the dummy. He would laugh saying, I guess you were just lucky. Then we both laughed and kept it moving. We still would say funny things to each other. I missed how he would just come up behind me holding me close or hitting me on my butt. I sometimes didn't like it and didn't understand it was a form of affection Bill's style. Now I miss what at the time I couldn't stand.

When his sister started getting serious about her boyfriend Ben, Bill was a little concerned. They were very close, but she had her life and Bill was married with a family. She went off to college and fell in love. Bill had to learn how to share his sister with her husband, which wasn't easy.

Looks like the rain is trying to clear up and the sun is fighting the clouds to come on out. So many things were clearing up that night and the conversation was flowing. Then I asked what my heart was holding back. I asked him what you would do if Sierra and I left. His smile went away, and he pulled his hand back and ask why you would say that Rita. I don't know just felt that we were becoming distant. Sometimes I feel and think that you hate me more than you love me. He responds with first don't play. I love you now just like I fell in love with you when I first saw you when I was leaving our psychology class. I noticed your smile that small ass waist and your bad shape. I watched you walk and how you carried yourself. You were always smiling or laughing and energetic. I listened, and his words were very pleasant to hear. I felt like a school girl smiling as my heart warmed with the thoughts of, he remembered. His words sounded good and boosted my ego some-what, but the waist is gone and replaced with our second daughter. Bill says that you seemed very smart and was different from the women he was used to dealing with.

His Uncle Cully knew your family and only had nice things to say about you and them. Then when you came into the cafeteria, I acted like I was reading but all the time I was checking you out. I thought how funny you never know who is re-ally watching you. He said that he wanted to talk to me when I looked over at him and smiled. I just couldn't put the words together, next thing I knew you were gone and laughing with Katrina. I laughed saying she was my partner in crime, only if he really knew, woo. Then opportunity came when you came into the library alone, no Katrina, no other girls with you. I tried to act as if I didn't notice you when you glanced around the library looking for somewhere to sit. In the back of my mind I was hoping that you would sit with me and not the other guy at the next table. Then you came over to me and ask if I mind if you set here. Bill said insides he wanted to say out loud hell yes, sit your fine ass down. You sounded just like I thought nice polite and different. I'm in ah as I listened but wondering what is his meaning of different. I had to get my questions out before you jump up before I could get your digits. Then we talked, and I knew then you were the one. I told my moms about you actually that was all I talked about, and when I went home to Chicago you were all I could think of.

Some old girlfriends came by and I just wasn't feeling them because I could only think about you and what you might be doing. Then I find myself calling you more than I ever called any girl. I listened, and I'm just overwhelmed. I don't want to lose you or our family. I know it hasn't been easy, but we never had problems talking to each other. I agreed that is something we never ever had a problem with even until this day we still can communicate. It felt good to hear the thoughts Bill had and shared them with me. He told me before but this time his words sounded different. Because now I am no longer that sixteen-year-old girl he meant, now we are sharing our twenties together. These overdue thoughts he held in were much needed for me to hear.

I looked out the window and replay some of my clumsy moments with him. It was only because I was excited seeing him. I felt so embarrassed and Bill would just smile at my clumsy oops. Just with a quick photo moment, I remembered one time running up to him and my toe hit the phone just right and disconnected his call. Bill smiled, and he just looked at me like no you didn't, but he didn't yell or anything, he just smiled. I chuckled at when he had a couple of drawers opened on his tall dresser and I tripped trying to grab myself and my fingers land inside the open drawers but in catching myself I close the drawers on fingers and smash them inside the drawer. Not to mention how I hit myself in the head with the car door. Funny, how things pop in at the right time and at the right moment. Inside I am so glad I did talk to him about leaving and he opened and said what I needed for my heart, mind and soul, this was much needed.

The breeze felt good and I hope Sierra holds the thought of staying sleep for the rest of the night. We are driving with no destination in mind just enjoying the evening breeze and the calmness of the atmosphere. I slowly glanced at the cars passing and the scenery changing. I look back and realized how much Bill and I have changed faster than we really wanted to. I know I am not like some of the women here and probably becoming boring to Bill. I hope he understands that he needs to help me, so we can continue to grow. I don't know what he wants unless he tells me. All I know is that I am trying as hard as I can to be everything to him plus more just to keep him happy and keep my family together.

Sometimes I feel as if my energy is slowly fading and my spirit is confused. I lost myself and I didn't know where to look. I love the fact that we are riding, smiling, talking and just being with each other. I didn't know he still remembered where and how we meant and when we started seriously dating. He remembered more than I thought he did. Now look at us a child and half away. I never thought I would have left Oakwood and would be living in California. I turn around and look at Sierra and she is sound asleep and snoring slightly. Her baby sister must be sleep too because normally she is up in the middle of the night with high energy. I chuckled as we pass a chicken and waffle place thinking back on what Bill's Uncle Jim, said about Aunt Chris eating chicken.

He smiled as he said that the way she eats and cleans the meat off chicken bones she could make an archaeologist think that dinosaur bones were still around. I remembered Uncle Jim laughing about dry bones and Bill was doing the same thing laughing as he was telling the story too. I guess you had to be there to understand the depth of their laughter. His Aunt Chris would leave nothing for her dog to work with. I tried and pictured their dog; Sheba Coo looking at Chris saying now Christine what am I supposed to do with these dry out chicken bones you sucked all, the grisum, calcium and any type of taste or juices. Now I have to dip these dried-out bones into my water bowl just, so they don't stick to my teeth, and so people won't be looking at me as if I am smiling puppy/dog, Christine. I guess I'm supposed to bury these dry bones and allow the dirt to moisture them Christine. Now Christine if I jump up and bite your ass one day just remembers it's because of them dried bones. I kind of chuckle a little and Bill looks over at me as if what is wrong with you and what are you laughing at. Bill really didn't laugh much, but he did have a sense of humor. Hmm neither did Sierra and other members in his family. His mother Naomi laughed a lot, but she pretty much was the only one I can think of.

That is what I like about Bill his smile, with dimples, sexy bow legs, almond shaped eyes that he passed on to Sierra, his miniature twin. Hmmm I guess I sound a little like Catrice talking about Greekum and co-signing our girl time with Robin and Courtney Diane. Now a funny ha-ha of you understand when you have eyes just for the one you love, and no one else matters anymore. I guess love can blind you sometimes just like the rain hitting the windows or the perspiration forming on the windows and the soothing taste of the coffee slowly fading away. Bill and I talked while enjoying our drive. The converation was random with no real meaning other than it felt good to talk and not be yelled at or belittled. It had been a long day and I wanted to just go home and lay it down, but I wanted to continue to enjoy nothing and do nothing but just enjoy the ride with my husband and my daughter. I just wanted to let the breeze just take my thoughts away and let me just be mindless for one minute. Night is coming slowly, and the breeze now has a little warmth in it. Kind of reminds me of the summer in Oakwood and in the late night sitting on the porch watching fireflies, listening to crickets and fighting those nagging mosquitoes. Sometimes we would sit on the porch just enjoying nothing. You might have small conversations or just look at the stars, cars passing by, neighbors doing whatever and sipping lemonade in form of Kool-Aid in a mason jar full of ice. Then when the mosquitos start bitting and, that was the clue for time to go inside. I do miss those days I guess that's why I am just enjoying staring at the rain while sipping on nice cup of coffee with my me time and thoughts. Since Sierra 's asleep we turn around and head home, as we listened to Sierra snoring from her full day and I am feeling just a little tired myself. I am so glad that we didn't go to the movies I really wasn't feeling it.

Chapter 28
Momo is Different and So Am I

As we pulled up, I see Momo walking slow with the assistance of her husband Amos. The weird thing is she is not yelling at her boys, Bert, Chris, Craig or Ryan wasn't fighting each other, Ryan wasn't crying, and the boys weren't bouncing balls and she seems quiet which was not normal. This complex was an eerie quiet. How could such a beautiful adventurous day come to this? I watched Momo as she drags one of her legs and as I spoke to her, she motions very slowly. Her left side seems as if it can't move. Something is wrong I felt it, see it and I look at her with concern as Bill carries the sleeping Sierra into our apartment. This was not like Momo. She's normally yelling, laughing, cooking, talking loud with so much energy and working some type of sex antics into whatever she was doing. Her boys rallied around her to assist their dad and she smiles as she receives the attention that sometimes she hated. Right now, all I see is the love they have for their mother and the deep love Amos has for his wife. He never said much but it showed all in his eyes. Whatever they might have been through you can still see the love they both share. I want to go over and ask if I could help but I don't want to interfere with the family moment that looks very delicate. I will pray for her and Sierra and I will check on her in the morning. Well let me check first I didn't want to expose Sierra to something that she might not understand, but I know how crazy Momo is about her. Maybe Sierra would put a smile on Momo's face.

Momo did teach me how to cook some real nice dishes now this will be my time to return the favor and show her what she showed me. Maybe she will fuss at me like she always does, and I looked forward to it every time. I think I lived for that and the hidden sex antics she woud throw in there just because. She would say it with such humor, yet she didn't laugh as she fussed. I remembered how she laughed at me when I tried to fry chicken. She smiled through her laughter that chicken tastes better when it's not burned. It was so frustrating trying to cut up a chicken, it almost made me pass out. She laughed at the chicken parts that didn't resemble any parts of the chicken after my crazy chopping. I remember my dad telling me that I should keep turning the chicken, so it can cook evenly, but somehow, I drew frustrated after cutting and just rushed cooking. Momo was right the chicken parts were sort of cut different. I was hoping that she wouldn't notice that the drumsticks didn't have legs. I just remembered that I stood in silence as if I was invisible practicing again not being in the room. I didn't know if I was more afraid of rejection from poorly dissected chicken or being laughed at. Another fear was Bill noticing the burnt dissected chicken and that would add to the list of something else for Bill to belittle me about. Momo laughed but didn't come down hard on me.

She got me again on her sexual antics. I remembered her telling me to flip the chicken continually just like Bill flips me in making those babies sweet heart (she chuckles to herself). I shyly laugh because talking about sex always made me blush and felt a little uncomfortable. We just were kind of private about that in Oakwood. Now we had some classmates that were advanced sexually in years and we would listen to them like a child listening to a bedtime story. I laughed and told her Bill has never flipped me. She laughed and said Amos and I flip and flop like a fish out of water, humph, hmmm. She puts a smile on her face, closed her eyes, and shakes her head and hips as if she was remembering. I laughed saying that I'm too young to flip or flop. Oh, I'm too old and she shakes her butt, which seems to be her signature dance. The same dance she did with her chant dance. I had a sudden thought Momo puts sex with almost everything. I look at her shaking and wiggling saying Amos and I still get our freak on, and we still get some flipping and flopping in too. Then she would wink with adding that I am not talking about flipping the mattresses on the bed over, no sir-ree. Although we are overdue for a new mattress, (and she smiles at me raising her eyebrows to get clarity on what see meant).

Momo broke it down with there was a big dent or should I say imprint in their mattress. She added that spot in the mattress that you don't have to feel around, and you can find in the dark. Amos hearing his name peeks in saying you frying fish?? Momo yells back nah fool frying burgers. Amos you are delirious go take a nap and I will call you when dinner is ready hun. He laughed with repeating you cooking chicken, while saying yes dear. As he walks slowly saying I like the flipping and flopping, he winks as he leaves the kitchen saying I still smell fish, (chuckling). I couldn't believe that Amos had a little swag as he moved slowly with an added jig. His voice fades away as he heads toward the bedroom turning back to give a heads up with a smile and Momo blows him a kiss and plants her hand back on the side of her butt. I guess he is really going to take a nap with no fussing maybe that bed holds some good memories. With a quick glance she winks and goes back to what she was doing, not skipping a beat. Singing and humming saying I like to flip and flop and show Amos what I still got hmmm, and he got a lot we both flip and flop. I'm still thinking ew and I don't want to even vision the flipping of them just the delicious flipping of burgers she was frying…

With a glance from the hamburger patties Momo looks at me and says what we're too young or you saying we are too old?? With a slight sigh she said don't be hating I gots to get mine. In my thoughts that was too much of a visual, ew. Girly you are never too old to scream his name at the right time; humph you know what I mean!! There are still things we haven't tried yet. On this one I would just have to guess and place no visuals with Momo was talking about. My mom always wanted me to dress sexy. I would change my outfit if I thought it showed too much skin. In my mind I wanted the imagination to be used maybe I should have listened to my mom. Inside I wanted to scream and take off running saying ew get that vision out of my mind, help me somebody help me ew!! Momo and Courtney Diane I guess are freaky in the bedroom just like Clarence. As Courtney Diane said I can do freaky just can't do weird. I can't really imagine sexually how to please Bill, sometimes I wonder if he was bored with me. In the back of my mind did I fit in? Was I too conservative and was the mid-western values fit in with sexual freedom?

I enjoyed the conversation it just makes me reflect on Bill and our relationship. After all we are still young, and I have time to learn. I just want to keep my husband happy and not have him detour. I have seen or heard of so many other relationships that faded away and went away. Bill knew I wasn't sexually active this is a whole new world for me. I thought it would be nice knowing that I wasn't out there like that. I listened to Momo and Courtney Diane talk about sex and sex wasn't there problem. Momo still flipping and flopping with Amos, Courtney Diane would probably be with Malcolm David flipping him while wearing her flip flops if he didn't like wearing her clothes and dancing in her stilletos.

I wondered since I have been pregnant, will Bill miss our closeness and want to be with me after the baby is born. I reflect quickly on the pain I had experienced when I tried to talk nasty to Bill. I tried calling his name and just saying words I had heard in a sex movie he had taken me to. As I called his name and said what I thought was words that fit the moment he made me get off him during sex. I just remembered feeling the rejection, humiliation and so small and unwanted. I try hard to hold up my smile, so he couldn't hear or feel the pain and hear the tears flowing inside. I still hold on to that pain and the scare just has a scab because it still hasn't fully healed properly.

Robin talked about how she loved the rain it reminded her of the excuse to sometimes skip work or class to hang out or cuddle up with Ramon. We were young and dumb without a care. We just wanted only to spend time with each other. I could tell she still loved him, but I could also tell she moved on and wanted to marry again.

Now on the other hand Courtney Diane loved the rain at one time that was when she and Malcom David got their nasty on. I remember how she started a little chant while shaking her head from side to side as if she is listening to music. Saying oh yea back it up and hit the front place it in then try it again, then jump up jump down then you're ready for another round, hit that butt and say my name then let the games begin, ooh. Robin looks at her with expression of really, you trying to be a rapper. She responds with what and goes on. Robin softly says Courtney Diane you know that we are in the room, while you're dreaming about what, ooh doing the…. Really do we want to know??? Her response was with the cool breeze and working up a sweat kept the bodies real busy and moving. Yep, with eyes closed, she was thinking about her bedroom boo. I was thinking, ew vision again. She missed Malcom David in her own way and would probably be with him if he didn't look better in her clothes…

Now the rain is just rain to me. Hey now Rita knows something, Courtney Diane adds, the girl is on her second child. Robin responded with T-M-I. Courtney Diane responded back with, what the hell is that? "Too Much Information" Courtney Diane get with the times. She responded with K-M-A heffa. What does that mean? Oh, you don't know Robin? I thought you knew those current terms; you need to get with it. It means, (Robin braces with a smile for the answer). Here it comes…. "kiss my ass". Robin again says oh, but Courtney Diane you don't have an ass just assests, l-o-l.

I told them that I liked the rain because it makes everything look beautiful and fresh. Nature getting its thirst fulfilled. They both looked at me as if where did she grab that from, and we were talking about love making and freaky memories of good fulfilling sex and making real love. They grab my hand and tried to walk or skip with me, so I didn't feel out of place. Robin responded slowly smiling while crossing her eyes saying that everything does look clearer and the air smells so fresh from the earthly cleansing, I agree. Yep I see clearly on a rainy day and the sun comes out later. Courtney Diane chimes in with yep, yep and blah, blah, blah and all that other and she catches herself before she says the finale, (last word) ….

I love it when I can sit here and enjoy the rain with a good cup of coffee and feel the cool breeze that comes with it. I guess when I was younger, and my bed was right by the window I would crack it just enough to feel the breeze on my face and the coolness that my body and sheets felt. I guess that is why I enjoy the rain and the breeze that accompained it so much. The rain allowed me to escape and relax at the same time.

Robin looks over at Courtney Diane to amen what she just said. But Courtney Diane's eyes are still closed. She probably was thinking about Malcom David in his birthday suit and not her pant suit, ha-ha. She must feel us looking at her because suddenly, she opened her eyes slightly not wide and says yea, yea I see clearly when both eyes are open. Yea ooh the sun shining and everything looking fresh yep, yep rain is good, got it. After her response she takes a sip and closed her eyes and her expression shows she went back to the thoughts or day dreaming, before we interrupted her.

Hmm I must agree you do see clearly when both eyes are open. For some reason I couldn't share what I wanted to say and still save face. I was still trying to get used to all this openness about antics in the bedroom. I felt it should be left there. But inside was I so embarrassed because of what I lack. This openness could have been my opportunity to ask for suggestions. Fear set in and I couldn't ask for advice. Inside it saddened my heart of the thoughts of thinking that Bill might be out there with who ditty getting his nasty on.

Anyway, I still liked the rain for many reasons. It was my friend it helped me hide my secrets because it allowed me to cry. That would have been a good day for rain, so I could cry, and no one would know. I sometimes wore my glasses, so no one would see the window to my weeping hurting soul. I learned not to cry due to the beatings and Bill telling me I cried too much. To this day I have learned to suppress my tears and not show the pain on my face. I guess I learned how to have a poker face even though I didn't play poker. Although I learned not to cry it didn't mean I didn't hurt or feel pain. I just learned how not to show it. People might think that nothing moves me, or I just don't care. Which is far from the truth I just learned how to adapt and live. It was at that point that when Courtney Diane had said she didn't want any crumbs of affection or to split a heart.

Funny but not ha-ha that was what I was settling for. The one Courtney Diane saying is, I don't think that much of you because I don't think of you at all. Maybe I should hold on to that philosophy, so I don't mentally get overwhelmed. Bill could be so distant sometimes with the emotions that I had to ask for permission to touch him. He would give me such a look as if I was violating his space. Then I started looking at myself and thinking, maybe I'm not what he wants anymore in a woman. Sometimes I would look at other women and wondered if that was what he was interested in since there was very little interest in me. I often wondered if he was talking to someone and when he would jump on me. Was the beating because Bill and the other woman were mad at each other and he came home and took his frustration out on me. I couldn't never really understand my random beatings or the belittlements. Should I pay attention to the phone hang ups, the late hours, the hanging out with friends that seem to not come over as much? Should I mark on the calendars, so I can see a pattern?

Listening to the women talk it was kind of obvious I was just in denial again and just didn't want to hurt at least not that day. I put on my big girl panties and muster up enough energy, so no one would know how much I hurt. Was I patiently waiting quietly for some crumbs of affection to fall so I could gather them up? Hopefully gather enough crumbs so I could feel some affection from him, and not be reminded of how much he seems to hate me. My thoughts move all over and around, but seldom settle down. Sometimes my thoughts at anytime can just start, then switch, between conversations with the girls to being entertained by Momo.

I think about listening to Momo learning new recipes and absorbing her words, thoughts and family atmosphere was healthy to see. So, I smile while keeping quiet not really saying a word like I normally did. I continued to listen as I had always done with her and everyone else. I loved her strength, life experiences and her energy she unselfishly shared. Momo would say sweetie see how I pat it and winks with a corner smile and mold this hamburger as she moved her fingers slowly, gently around, while looking at my reaction as she continued to flipping and flopping. Then adding see how I'm holding it in my hand you are getting this sweetie. You got to take it slow, no rushing, just take your time and enjoy the feeling. Then she would smile with adding; now that is what I am talking about. I try not to focus on that image in a sexual nature, because I did like her burgers. Her burgers tasted just as good as my great-grandmother Mommy used to cook. It's funny as I think about how mommy mixed and flipped and flopped her hamburgers too. Wow was this some type of old nasty thing or was my imagination trying to work a crazy. Oh no, heck no not my sweet Mommy... Ooh and yuck please don't let my mind go in that direction I want to enjoy Momo's burgers, without thinking of what she and Amos did with that meat. Yuck meat ew vision, vision, stop, stop. My thought was ew with the visual really didn't want my mind to go there, ew again. I couldn't imagine it then or with Clarence when he was a kept man for $2500 an hour. My imagination couldn't or wouldn't stretch that far, ew didn't want to see that visual either, yuck.

Momo could multi-task while talking mess at the same time and keep her dance beat going. She laughed saying go girl and let Bill flip and flop you just like I am doing with this hamburger patty sweetie. She could take any food or subject and turn it into some type of sexual antic. Did she like it that much or was she just horny all the time? She reminded me of Catrice and how she talked about Greekum. I didn't want my mind to stretch that far with them either, but something was deeply there 11 kids, woo. You could see after all these years they still have love for each other. A love that was only for them to understand. We both laughed as I watched her cook and she does it with such ease. While she was talking, and I could feel her her looking at me out the corner of her eyes with a side smile as she flips and flops the burgers in her hands.

I laughed enough to make noise for the both of us. She had control over her house but at the same time not letting her husband feel any less. One day her son Ryan came in wondering what was for dinner she responded with, whatever I'm cooking. And take your little five-pound ass in there and tell your brothers to wash up for dinner and tell your daddy that dinner is ready. It was good to see that they still all ate dinner together. We did it at my parent's house until we all turned into teenagers and the appetite changed, along with everyone being home at the same time. I gonna try and make it a practice with my daughters and husband to eat at our table. Family time and keeping up with their daily activities.

I always liked talking with Momo. Her conversations were never boring. She was the only one Bill really allowed me to talk to without having a curfew. In his world he probably felt that she wasn't a threat only if he knew what she can talk about, flip, flip, flop, flop and a tee-hee-hee. I sometimes wondered if she would hear Bill yelling at me or any of the fights we might have had. Even if she did, she allowed me to save face and not feel embarrassed. I didn't share too much with her, even though I did want to talk and ask her opinion. I missed my family and friends, sometimes I just needed someone to talk to, so I wouldn't have to pinch myself to make sure that I was still alive.

Bill and I had good times and good conversations but sometimes I didn't know when. Plus, I wanted someone/anyone to talk to every now and then, like I did with Robin and Courtney Diane. I had a good day and enjoyable night, but I am concerned about Momo. The only time I didn't want to hear her yelling was when I went out with Robin and came home pass my curfew and didn't want to wake the hopefully sleeping giant called Bill. I just remember making it home and out of nowhere here comes Momo, Amos and their energetic sons. I just wanted them to hush so I could sneak in. This time I missed hearing her yelling voice and her sons being energetic. Her sons had a routine of the sound of two bouncing balls and the other two picking at each other in which ended with one of the little ones crying.

I smiled as I reflected on when we all attended Melba's going away and her daughter Michele's birthday party. Remembering Momo hula hooping while her sister laughs, at her not being able to hula hoop like she used too. Her sister Minana, (but they call her Miss Minnie, hmm they had a lot of "M's"). Momo, Miss Minnie and her little niece Melina or Melony, (reminds me of the issue Courtney Diane had with her family), a lot of "M's" Miss Minnie responded with didn't you have more room, (with the biggest smile I ever seen). Momo glanced at her laughing that she was able to get into the hula hoop. Her sister laughed and said I think this is one of those cases where one size doesn't fit all; Momo looked at her laughing along with everyone else. This wasn't any type of jab just everyone having fun and no one getting upset. Momo re-adjusted her energy as to make a point. She started dancing taking it down again with her signature dance shaking her butt, with her known wiggle at the same time. That day I saw in her eyes no one could control her emotions. She sang, laughed and sung a tune with words no one could repeat. Momo had her special style moving in a way no one could copy her dance steps. Her age didn't mean anything because her body had the moves and she was very flexible. I can still see Amos with the gleem in his eyes as he watched his wife dancing. Funny it just seemed like yesterday that this all happened.

I still have Momo's tune in my head. Some were yelling how low will you go, while she is really dropping it and twisting. Wow she was going down low. I could tell she was something in her day because she still has some type of crazy residual. As they are chanting how low will you go Momo, how low will you go? Her response just went back chanting I don't know, I don't know let's see, cuz I don't know not yet. While others were saying go Momo, go Momo, go, go, go Momo, others saying how low will you go, and she's says I don't know, I don't know!! I just remember the tune and rhythm were both in sync.

She kept chanting and laughing saying let me see, let me see, look-a- here ya look-a- here. I guess she was really feeling herself while the chanting crowd got caught up in a Momo's moment. Well she made it down, ooh, yep she was flexible and then her chant changed to help me up somebody, come over and help me up, come on y'all, anyone help me up. I'm serious y'all come help me up. When they realized that she was serious, they stopped and rushed over and helped her up while everyone is laughing because she was still chanting with the same tune, just chanting different words. She was chanting, laughing and trying to twist and shake her butt and shoulders as much as she could all the way to the chair. While the guys were trying to balance her and themselves as they lifted her up. She must like that tune because she adds more words as they take her to the chair. Momo added another chant saying, now take me to the chair over there, and now take me to my chair. Sit me down slowly; now sit me down, ah. Momo now using the same tune with another set of words was ah yea I like this, ah yea I like this. We all looked over at her with concerned eyes. She smiled and kept chanting, humming and we realized that this was her way of letting us know that she was alright. She was still chanting I'm okay ya, I'm okay as the chant goes into a hum, she rocks from side to side in her chair still feeling and humming her tune.

I still had concern about her moving slow, as she was assisted by her sons and husband. Amos glanced at her with a smile making sure she was okay. I hope she doesn't lose her zest, energy or her heavy voice that I love to hear yell or fuss at me. She was beautiful inside and out. Everyone in the complex loved her and her family. She was a bright and positive fixture there. I found myself smiling thinking about Momo and pray that she will be better in the morning. As I walk, I didn't realize that I was humming the chant along with shaking like Momo into the house. Bill looked at me with a strange expression. I looked back at him with, 'a what's up'. I still wasn't paying any attention to the fact that I was dancing, moving and humming that chant. Bill looks and smiled and said you are shaking like Momo. Inside that felt good, because that was a huge complement about someone I held dearly to my heart. I responded so slow that he thought something was wrong with me. I didn't realize how much of a deep thought I was in. Bill asked again this time with concern in his voice if I was okay. I just said that I noticed Momo was moving kind of slow and hope she will be okay. Bill asked if she was fussing or yelling. I told him no not this time and I am really concerned that is not like her. Rain or shine she is just like the mailman never stopped fussing or cussing or yelling or laughing. While sometimes humming Momo singing voice was beautiful. I could sit all day and listen to her. One thing if anything she was consistent. This was not routine and her boys weren't making any noise either. I could see the genuine concern in Amos voice and the boys face. When Amos or the voice spoke, it was no louder than a whisper.

Bill saw the sadness in my eyes and felt the crackling of my heart hurting for her. I felt a hug with the gentlest kiss on my forehead. To my surprise it was real, and it was from Bill. My heart felt his warmth and melted right into his arms and merged again with his heart beat. Bill wasn't all that bad he had and still has a heart. Just something was just irritating him, and he just didn't know how to express it. He asks if I would be okay, because he knew how I felt about Momo and her family. I told him that I'm okay just concerned about Momo. He smiled and embraced me as much as he could because my stomach was out there, and our unborn daughter wasn't going to allow you cramping her space. I play over and over the embrace I received from Bill. I could feel the warmth from his body and the spirit of love from his heart. It felt as if our heart skipped a beat while I felt our baby sigh with movement, like alright mom and dad.

I chuckle about Momo talking about flipping and flopping. Bill pulls me back and glances at me and I see the concern in his eyes too. Without words we communicate with the warmth and eyes of I'm okay really. I loved holding his hands, smelling his cologne and lingering onto the embrace that just felt like so much love coming from him and transferring to me. He had put tired Sierra into her bed and she was knocked out. I was feeling a little tired myself. As I go into the room Bill helps me take my clothes off and my shoes. He takes off my shoes while massaging my feet and ooh that felt so so good. Bill never massages my feet, and I didn't want him to stop. It felt sexual now that was a new form of intimacy for me. As I put on my gown with his assistance, I just look at him with so much love and grateful that we are together. He is still the handsome man I met in college and no regrets. He chose me out of all those ladies, Bill chose me. I had something in me that Bill liked enough to bring me home to his mother and show me off to his dad. Unlike those scants that they had talked about that never make it home or out of the bedroom. They just get recycled/regenerated with the same name and that is scant. The looks fade away and the memories never linger.

I think back on a good friend I went to school with that bought me lunch because he thought I saw him. I knew he was married but didn't know what his wife looked like. I just remember the waitress telling me that my bill was paid for. Of course, I was curious of who would pay my bill. I didn't really see anyone I knew, nor did I look around to see if there were any familiar faces as I set down to eat. So, I looked over and see a person I knew from a rival high school by the name of Juan Paul. I smiled as to say thank you. At that time, I noticed he was with someone but this particular person I knew too, and I knew she wasn't his wife. She fell into that category of high school scant. Surprisingly she had no husband but many many men. Like Courtney Diane said many cars have been up that ramp, yuck. He responded with a shock look of you're welcome but don't say anything. I had heard that he married Alesia but that was all I knew. The ironic part was if he didn't say or do anything, I wouldn't have known he was even there. I came there to eat and chill alone. I chuckle in silence with guilt must have tore his butt up.

Anyway, I like the way Bill was making me feel and it felt great. As I lay down, he lays next to me with the smell of his cologne lingering into my nostrils and seeping into my memories and spirit. Tonight, we are one again. The end of a perfect day for us but I still have concerns for Momo. She was like a mother to me, especially since my mother didn't talk to me often and let me add she didn't like me. I now had my own family and it was growing. I lay on his chest and my spot is still there as he puts his arm around me, kissing me on my forehead. I wondered if he thought about us leaving him. But only if he knew that we would be moving into a shelter. I realized that shelters were not for me. I needed to grow up and make this work; after all, like Mama Sadie said he had to ask. Those words still linger in my mind and I can hear her voice so clearly. He did ask, and I said yes. I know there are trying times and there are also good times too. Actually, better than bad and I must keep that in mind. It's just when the bad happens it's bad. Maybe I need to ask more about his day. Every time I was around Momo, she would always say to Amos, daddy how was your day. She would listen, and he would tell her. Then she would tell him what time dinner would be ready and that his bath water was waiting for him. Now that was something, I never saw my parents do. I guess because they were so busy raising us, they forgot about themselves.

I am slowly learning how to be a better wife, cook and mother. I smile as I reflected on burgers and flip, flop, that Momo displayed with her signature dance. I fall off to sleep into Bills arms peacefully. The night was ours. I wake up to flowers and breakfast in bed. What a nice pleasant surprise and everything looked and smelled good. Sierra was still sound asleep. Bill asked what you guys do that she was so tired? I thought should I tell him, nah just had a good adventure and reminded him that I told him about it yesterday. His response was oh yell. I knew he only listened to about 25% of what I said and remembered 10%. I told him that one day we need to go to PataRee's Pancake house or ShaRoberts for dinner and maybe go bowling and it is all in the same complex. I smile saying this would be something new, different and exciting, something spontaneous. He smiled and said that's a do. Uh I never heard him say that before. I repeat that's a do. That's different. He looks at me as if my mouth didn't move and I didn't utter any words. This time it wasn't worth changing the mood we both were in. Our daughter is almost ready to come into this world and Bill is coming straight home. After eating breakfast, I tell Bill

I am going over to Momo's to make sure she is alright. He smiles reassuring me that she will be okay. He said that he would take care of Sierra just take your time. I slowly get up and go into wobbling walk. Today I'm feeling good and in love with my husband again. Sometimes he surprises me when the little things he does mean big things to me. I am glad we are together.

As I go to the bathroom to get ready, I noticed Bill doing the dishes while Sierra has finished eating her breakfast. When she finished that last morsel of food she jumps and starts helping Bill wash the dishes. They look cute together as father and daughter binding sometimes in silence or small talk. I loved seeing them together. Bill did in all ways give Sierra quality time. They worked well together especially when they do study time. We both educate her in preparation for pre-kindergarten. She is smart and well spoken. No fear in her unless she gets in trouble by her dad which is very rare. His voice has depth and looks stops any actions Sierra might do that would send her on time out or to her room. She didn't stay in time out long. Once she got her act together, she would come out and they would pick up where they left off. She would come back after her time out more loving, laughing, and back to cuddling under dad. There were no hard feelings they just keep it moving. Now, when it comes to me, I can't get Sierra to call me mom. We still to this day have that same conversation. Sometimes when her friends are around, and she says she was talking to Rita they are in ah when she tells them that I am her mother, and that she has been calling me Rita since she was two years old. One day I will hear the words I always wanted to hear "Mom" or something that sounds close other than Rita. It's funny she knew enough to call her dad or daddy and not Bill.

I know I'm getting closer to delivery just looking at water makes me run to the bathroom. I can't wait I'm bloated and tired and when she is born, I will be just tired and not bloated, (I hope). But it is all worth it to have another little one that will love me, and I can love her and Sierra. I have so much love to share with them. I hope Bill is not sharing his love with someone else. Today he is giving me some crumbs, or does he have me nibbling at a carrot just to satisfy his guilt for how he has been treating me??? No one knew that I had difficulty with trying to hold on to my family. Some days I just wanted to cry but couldn't because my crying made me weak in Bill's eyes. I learned early in our marriage especially after Bill hit me in my eye, not to cry. I learned also how to administer my own first aid. My pop/dad would always say put a cold towel on your eyes to help with the swelling, (for just in case). He would say that if someone died and he knew your eyes would be swollen. My dad didn't know I had another use for it. That was my secret and I was still performing. Acting as if I was loved by Bill and we were happy. I knew I still loved him and always will.

Chapter 29
Clarence Stories Continued

Hmm looking out at the rain I wonder does it look back at you. It comes in handy in so many ways if you are crying the rain hides your tears, giving you a good excuse. Now that I think about it, the rain offers so many excuses that people believe and not question. Which allows no one to see your pain or just be lazy and no one will question your answers or actions. It put Robin and Courtney Diane into a place where they were happy with their spouses. Bill and I didn't need changes in weather for us to be intimate. We were young, and we just did it. I guess you can say Bill was like Clarence he put me to sleep. Funny how Clarence started putting people to sleep at an early age and sometimes was paid well. I guess sexy Lexie taught him some good sleeping moves. I loved talking with him he always had me sitting on the edge of my chair with his life antics and his brother Steve stories. They both love the honies regardless.

If Bill saw or knew what we were talking about I would either be in the hospital or the morgue. Just thinking about the 'what if' with Bill, makes me shake. But Clarence's stories were funny and yet true. Just when I thought he was done he would say no not done yet. So, I evented my imaginary bowl of popcorn that I would eat when he told his stories. Actually, I used that bowl of popcorn often. Of course, I re- freshed my bowl of popcorn every now and then. We talked about his second wife Malaya. The one he wanted to have children with and always loved. Clarence talked about high school he played football and ran track and she was a cheerleader and when they dated. But her mother Miss Kinyette was strict as hell and Malaya couldn't do anything. He spoke calmly where sometimes I would just chuckle or smile as I listened to his childhood antics.

He said that he worked at McDonalds, and it seems as if everyone at sometime worked there. I know I enjoyed working there and enjoyed what it taught me about people and patience. Malaya's mom wouldn't let her eat fast food, so she never tasted McDonald's. This was my opportunity to introduce her to my wares and practice what sexy Lexie taught me. I laughed because I remembered what he said about his introduction to sex. He said oh yea sexie Lexie and Miss Zia taught me about variety. I had a smorgasboard of women; all this is making me hungry. I say variety his responds with a smile of rememberance of sure your right variety. Hey man got to do and I got to bring my Laya some McDonalds when I got off. I rode my bike over to her house and we had a code. I would put the food on the window sill of her bedroom, because her brother Levi would bust into the room every chance he could especially if he thought I was there. He was just being a bratty brother and that little ass just couldn't leave us alone. So, she would let me in through the window and when I heard her brother I would just get under the bed. When he left, I practiced putting her to sleep, then I rode on home. We did this for a while, but I just got tired of her not being able to do anything. So, we went our separate ways for about six years. She was always on my mind, so I came back to her and we dated and end up getting married.

Our marriage lasted long enough for us to have my son Clarence Jr. and my daughter Laniece. I smiled saying, a kept man at the going rate of $2500.00, an hour not a day or a week. He smiles sure your right as he closes his eyes as if he was having flashbacks. I forgot about Clarence said that his brother was running track and little thicker than he was. He said that was how he got the honies him and his brother Steve. His physique shows that he stayed in shape. He said that he had received a track scholarship and that the college couldn't give him a four full year run. So, he went into the Navy. Clarence moves around with his stories just like my thoughts.

Clarence said that he had taken this one girl Chanin, (the track Captain), and he was the captain on his team and thought that would be a good dating combination. He steps back saying nah a one-night prom date. Chanin sister Monaye was a freak, given it up in all kinds of ways. But Chanin was straight lace and I thought hey, what the hell maybe I might get a little something, something after all it was prom night. We had a track qualifier for state the next day and I had to get the edge off, (he smiles raising his eyebrows, my thought ew again). Clarence said proudly that he was dressed in a tux carrying a cane and knew he was looking good. I laughed and said really a cane. Oh yeah, I knew I looked good actually fine. I looked at him and said fine stop. My father's cousin Otho Corneilus or cousin Corney was given gas money to take us and pick us up. I asked was this your dad's first cousin. Yep Jerry's first cousin never seen him before and didn't see his sorry ass again. We get to the prom and Chanin forgot to bring her prom ticket.

So, Cousin Otho Corneil had to take her back to her house and get the ticket. I was just as mad as my cousin Corney. I wondered and asked did they make the prom with all that traveling. He said laughing no but probably wasn't laughing then. He said that they missed about two thirds of the prom and didn't get a chance to eat. My ass paid for all that money for a couple of dance moves. I just knew when this was over it would be all worth it. An after party then another kinda of party he adds a smile). Me dancing and smacking and tapping that track captain's ass. What little time we had it was over and no cousin Otho around. Tried calling cousin Corney, nope no answer. At that time, we didn't have cell phones. Since my dad only gave him $50.00 that went on that round trip thanks to Chanin. I laughed saying I guess he did his part he told your dad that he would take you and bring you back and that trip for the ticket fulfilled his gas money deal with your dad. He hunches his shoulders eyebrows raised and said I guess so and we were left there as we watched everyone leaving, smiling, kissing, holding hands all that stuff (ooh substitute time) before getting some stuff if you know what I mean. I did know that answer and just looked at him.

Of course, my date didn't do none of that. I just remember looking over at her thinking it better be worth all this because right now I just wasn't feeling any part of her until tonight when I'm holding on and riding that ass. I laughed did the ass have a face. He said yeah, she was fine, but the ass was tight, a track type firm round boo-tey. So, we were left there, and my partner Quinn had a limo and didn't want us hanging out because we were the last ones left. What happened to cousin Otho Corneilus? His ass never showed up. Quinn asked if we wanted a ride to the after party and I said oh hell yes. I looked at Chanin saying let's go and come on!! He said that he had a room at the hotel if I wanted to come and crash there.

Before I could answer, Chanin finally opened her mouth didn't talk all night but now she can talk, and said oh no, no and no, I'm going home take me home!!! The voiceless girl added my name, Clarence we have a track meet tomorrow!!! I just looked at her and felt like calling her names I wouldn't say out loud. I could only imagine what they probably were. Ooh I am so glad he didn't. He said the after party ended around 2:30 or 3:00 and we went to White Castle for burgers. I had to ask you went to White Castle's in the limo?? Yeah, we were hungry we didn't get to eat because we got there so late the food was gone because someone forgot their prom ticket. So White Castles' was on the way to the hotel where "Q" was staying. Again, he asked if we wanted to come with him to the hotel. Chanin speaks up again louder saying no, no and no take me home!! So, the limo takes us to Chanin place and "Q" says you can come and stay with me at the hotel. I just knew something was going to happen, so I told him to go on.

No sooner than I turned around she runs up the steps to her house and closed the door no hug, no quick feel, only kiss my ass. I had to think that what she said as she turned her ass around and ran into her house. I ran behind her knocking on the door she peeks through the curtain of the front door saying go home Clarence you have a track meet in the morning!! I wanted to call her so many names that I wouldn't say out loud.

This was around 4:00, 4:15, bus didn't run around that time in that area and the track team bus was leaving for the track meet at 6:00. Then it hit me oh my goodness I had to run four miles home in this tux, holding this cane in these hard-tight ass shoes. Rita these shoes were not made for running. Understand Chicago blocks are long blocks I ran for four miles in about fifty minutes. When I made it home, I was in a puddle from my sweat and all messy. When I made it to my room, I was taking clothes off throwing them down and trying to get my uniform together. Steve asked did you get the draws man?? All I could do was say take your ass back to bed. Clarence went on to say his brother Steve, broke out laughing so hard he was crying, rolling, talking mess and passing gas. All I could say was uck you at the same I'm still throwing my shift together.

I told him that I had to get my track gear together because the bus leaves at 6:00, (and I didn't make it home until around 5:30). Steve usually held my blocks, so he said I am going with you. l tells him let's get some gone. So, we get to the bus stop and wait for 1 to 2 minutes and realized that the bus isn't coming so we take off running. It was 3 mile run to the school. I asked if Steve was fast and he said yeah, he was a running back. He was ahead of me when we took off. I kept saying we aren't going to make it. We saw the bus take off and I felt my heart drop. Steve kept saying we are gonna make it. I could only shake my head and Steve said funk that let's hit it.

We took off just like in the movies. Funny that is just how I felt as I am listening to him sitting in the front row of the movies. He said they were running through backyards, jumping fences while dogs were nipping at us just like in the movies. While listening I asked were you laughing while you were running. Ooh nah we were serious about catching that bus, this was qualifying for state. Steve knew that the bus had to stop and had to hit this certain area, and we had a chance and all we had to do was to meet the bus at that location. Steve was still ahead of me and with his quick thinking picked up some rocks and threw them at the bus. Those rocks made a loud ass noise and the bus braked. We ran our asses to the door and the coach said he knew us. The driver opened the door and we made it in and headed to the back of the bus. Everyone on the bus was saying how you could almost miss state qualifying? I heard them as I felt the sweat dripping off me and sleep was on my mind. Voices and faces were all a blur.

Didn't really hear them but I saw the look on Coach Jerry's face it was a blur. I was sweating like someone just poured a whole bucket of water on me. I was tired and sleepy from running seven miles just to get to the bus for the track meet, all I knew was exhaustion. Only thing I could say was hey sorry Coach Scott/Coach Jerry. Coach Jerry followed me back to the bus. He came back to the back and chewed my ass out. I heard about 1 to 2 minutes of much of nothing. I was sweating like crazy and fell off to sleep while he was chewing my ass out, I guess. I think I might have given him 3 minutes at the most. I just knew he was talking to a snoring sweat drench-tired runner. When we made it to the stadium they had to come and wake me up. I asked how long was the ride? He said long enough that we had to wake your tired ass up.

I didn't care I had broken so many records, but this time I was running against guys I had never beat throughout the year. I saw Spaulding or was it Sterling he was one I never beat, and his name matched his ability. Coach Jerry had me down for about seven running events. He asked me which one I could run. I knew I could do the 200 and the relay for sure. Coach was okay with that, so I did those events. It took two races for you to qualify for the third race. The first one for 200 run against people I knew I could beat. I was about twenty feet ahead of them and that's when I clowned by turning around and running backwards while listening to the crowd roar from the bleachers. I'm feeling good and laughing, then I turn around to win that first heat, same thing for the second qualifier. I again did the same thing except I was 15 yards ahead of them still turning around running backyards listening to the crowd roaring and yelling again.

Now we are at the third and last qualifier, with all the runners I didn't beat at all during the year including Spaulding. Doing all that clowning took some of my energy. My brother was holding my blocks and I told him man I don't think I could do this; I'm not feeling this one. Steve said funk this shift we didn't do all this for your punk ass to punk out. We are going to state and party. All you have to do is make third place, that's all you need. You don't have to win bro just place. Listening to him I realized how much love they had and still do for each other a brotherly bond.

I enjoyed hearing him talk about him and his brother, Steve. They balanced each other out. Well I took my block the gun went off and I took off. Spaulding, the other runner Karner and I were neck and neck one two three. After the run I was bent over holding on to my uniform feeling that seven-mile run, and all my heats. I heard someone yelling across the field you mother of friends you made it, we are going to state. Before I could catch my breath, Steve runs a football play and tackles me knocking me down. He 's slapping me all in my face and head saying mother of friends you did it you made it to state. Before I could catch on to all his excitement, I told him to get the funk off me! As I listened it was Steve's way of saying how proud he was of his brother. Just when I threw him off, Coach Jerry comes and pats me on the back and told me to go look at the board for my times. I saw my time it was 23 seconds with PB next to it. I had to ask, what does PB mean? It meant personal best. So, I said let me understand you done your personal best as tired as you were. Yep and the coach knew I was feeling it but still tired, just wanted to get some needed sleep.

Then one of the runners from Howard high that was known for their fine ass girls came over to congratulate me. My mouth drops open as I stared at this fine ass girl walking toward me smiling. My eyes were focused enough to start from head and end at her tight ass butt. I knew she was smiling at me there was no need for me to look around. You are so right I was feeling myself even tho I was bone ass tired. Now she had every thang, looks, smile, long hair, white teeth with deep dimples, small mole on her cheek and body with a track butt, she had much booty. She introduced herself as Tangee, (the girls track captain), known as Captain Glitter. I see why she sparkled, very classy different from the girls I went to school with. When he said I thought about how Bill thought I was different from the girls he dated at his school must have some form of truth. The girl had me cheesing and shift. She had looks that could drop anyone to their knees.

She asked, didn't your school have your prom last night? I told her that I wished I would have taken someone else it didn't work out. She smiled and said if you would have taken me, we would have had a good time.!! She smiles out the corner of her mouth and winks, we both knew what she meant; damn was all I could think for that second. She kept saying a real good time with emphasis on real and good time saying my name Clarence, (she sounded so sexy, damn). She said that her parents were out of town, and her sister was watching her, hmmmph what a waste, that's all she could say! Calling me Clarence while looking my ass up and down. She made my name sound so sexy and parts on me got pissed off. As she turns to walk away, she smiles and says nice race Clarence, personal best hmmm. Miss Glitter said again a real good time and I could have showed you my personal best…

My mouth dropped open and my mind going all places and hoping not in the wrong place, because I had only my track shorts on and didn't want to be exposing to where she was taking all parts of me. He looks at me with an eyebrow raised. At first, I didn't get it then oops oh okay ooh. As I watched her leave, cadence is playing in my heart and mind of left, right, left, right and then the left, hmmmph. Then she turns around to see if I was looking. Yep I was looking right at her and I was looking right at her ass. I had to ask this silly question were you counting her steps. Uh humm, I was looking at her ass go left, right, left, right and a stutter right, and when the left chick hit. She turned around to notice that hell yell I was staring at every thang, (tight and petite and she could be my spinner).

Just being the naive person that I was I asked about the spinner statement? Clarence smiled raising his eyebrows with that the imagination went into an ew state. I forgot that Clarence's dad Jerry was in the service, so he would have some idea about candence, but I didn't fall for that same trap of assuming he could dance. I thought Bill could dance coming from Chicago. He had steps that you should just go show and tell or show no one. His looks helped people to ignore his steps but looking at Clarence move he is a little stiff but has rhythm. I guess he must have had plenty of practice because he had to be doing something for $2500.00 an hour. Again, I can't let my mind or thoughts even go there.

As I drift back, Clarence said that, Tangee smiles while whispering and mouthing a real good time Clarence puckering her lips. And then she did a slow lick with her tongue around her sexy thick lips humph… As my heart started to beat faster the cadence got stronger left, left, left, right, left you got get on her left and got to on her right, because all she kept saying was, we would have had a real good night. You don't know how long those words echoed in my mind and lingered in my thoughts. All I could think of was damn and all the vision of her left. Then flashes of that whole night; Chanin and cousin Otho Cornelius, the long run, eating at White Castles instead of the meal I paid a lot of money for just to go through a drive through for an ungrateful ass holding out scant, hanging out at the prom watching everyone leave, running in my tux with those tight ass shoes with a cane, drenched and stressing about making it on time before the track bus leaves, all that shift came hit my ass all at the same time.

Once Captain Glitter got out of my sight, I picked up a trash can and threw it banging everything around me. Smashing the lid putting dents in all sides of that can went into a whirlpool and built up rage and took it out on that trash can. No one could understand why I was mad. Mad that I could have had this fine ass girl but instead I went with old sorry ass Chanin. I was laughing so hard Clarence looks at me with a pause when I said so you trashed the trash can. He raised his eyebrows like he normally does saying you're right, I trashed the shift out of it.

At that point I felt the closeness. It was as if I was talking to my baby brother, in which I didn't have but Clarence was a good placement. I was slowly putting my extended family together. I asked if Chanin made the track meet. He said no her sorry ass didn't even show up. Clarence started all over again about the prom to watching the sparkle in Miss Glitter fade away. He said, everything flashed back from that night, that morning, from my dad's cousin Otho Cornelius driving us because Jerry had paid him to take us but didn't pay him to bring us home. Now help me understand what happened to the round-trip run. Hey, he hunches his shoulders, not enough gas money oh hell it wasn't his prom and Jerry just gave him just enough. We end up getting a ride home from Quinn's older brother Crandel, we sometimes called him Buttons who acted as his chauffer and took all of us to White Castle because Chanin left her prom ticket and we missed about 2/3 of the prom including the meal that was paid for too was all gone."Q" had a room at the hotel and offered it up again. I told my partner to drop us off and I will make it home giving him the eyebrow raise, Quinn and Crandel took the hint and drove off.

I just knew I was going to be putting Chanin to sleep, while holding that track butt. Come on we were all dressed up partied and didn't want it to end, you know what I mean at least end the right way. With his smile I knew what he meant. While I knew my partner "Q" was getting it on with Monaye her sister. Chanin kept telling me she was saving herself and we both had a track meet in the morning, and this was qualifying for state. I didn't care I just wanted to get busy and whack that ass. Whack it hard and long because she had a track booty. I looked at him really do I need to hear or know this Clarence. He said yep. She wouldn't let me in or through her front door, hell I would have went in the back door. He raises his eyebrows you know what I mean. Again Clarence, TMI, too much information. I was mad as hell and she kept on saying no and that we both had a track meet and the bus will be leaving early in the morning about 6:00 and Clarence you know both of us need our rest. He said that I wanted to get rest after being with her. He said she looked at him like he was crazy, no Clarence go home I'll see you in a few hours the bus is leaving early. That scant ran up the stairs and didn't even give me a kiss, nothing, not even a quick feel of the booty.

All that flashback hit my ass, and I know I'm repeating but ... I could have been with Tangee instead of tight ass Chanin scanty ass. I knew I didn't or wouldn't have any problem tomorrow about qualifying he says with confidence but not cocky. Looking at his physique you knew the girls chased after him or he chased after them and that he was an all around althlete. He reminded me of what Maurice might have been to Reva. How could she get away with Chris yacking her ears? I remembered how Reva smiled saying that Chris talked her into going to the prom and she got more than a dance and a corsage. Let me see how her mom said it, what was done in the night got you nine months to life. Funny, how I tried to convince Reva that I had indigestion, because I had convinced myself. I remember her saying with a corner smile in nine months that indigestion will need a name.

As I chuckle Clarence didn't have a clue of what I was chuckling about. I always enjoyed listening to him and he always said something that just made me either smile or laugh. He had been a good friend to me since I have been living here. If Bill knew, ooh I would just hate to think about the consequences I would face. We have always had good timing because Bill has never really seen us talk. He missed us sitting on the stairs just making random conversation.

So, I took a shot in the dark and asked did you make it through the front door. Oh hell, Rita here we go again. I just wanted to keep the story and conversation going. No, I had to run home because my ride was gone, and I had the track meet. My parents didn't have a car, so I had to run to school, so I wouldn't miss the bus for the meet. When I made it home Steve was up asking did, I get the draws, did you get the panites bro. I just put my head down and said she wouldn't give it up. He laughs and said no you took the one saving herself, when you should have taken her sister the easy freak that was given it up. You had a 50/50 chance and came up short uh. I really didn't need to hear that, to this day he still reminds me. I didn't get any sleep by time I got home I had enough time to change into my track uniform and Steve wanted to come so he could party. Hey, hey so he ran with me to meet the bus. We were hoofing it almost missed the bus Coach Jerry just gave me that look, and I look back as I know. Coach Jerry pulled me to the side and said don't be running backwards when you are way ahead. I would do that because I was that fast. The only school I had concerned was our rivals Elgin and Howard high. We ran I qualified for state and Steve and I partied, too much. I didn't go past state oh well stuff happens and, move on. I found myself laughing for the second and third time hearing the story I was still amused.

The next school day my boys were asking about Chanin and did I get the panties or what?? I couldn't come up with a reason other than that she liked girls. I was shocked on that one and said no you didn't do that to her. He nods his head yes and said he felt bad, but he had to save face with his boys. When she saw me and said how could I do that to her? I kept trying to call or talk to her, but she didn't want anything to do with me. The school talked about her bad with stares and whispers. I did feel bad, but we made it to graduation because it was just around the corner. I heard she end up marrying a preacher. She knew early what it took us a long time to learn. Keep it right to get the right person. I had to admire her strength when many were trying to have her alter her morals and beliefs.

I could only imagine how Reva felt as Chris and peers pressured her into getting with Maurice while they lived their lives. Guys give into pressure but in different ways, through anger, laughter, or tears. Only difference is sometimes it seems as if the feelings don't last long and they move on. I often wondered if Bill felt anything after the words were said that couldn't be retrieved. Do they care about the pain that follows with the bruises and the tears that can't go back once they come out? How do they feel and why can't they stop the pain that they were inflicting on you?

Chapter 30
The Mall Trip or Just a Trip

Clarence and I would sit and talk long it would be minutes but felt like hours. This time I was able to enjoy our conversations while Bill and Sierra were hanging out at the mall and park. The expression Clarence gave me was why I didn't go with them to the mall. I said all that walking would wear me out and since I was so close to delivery, we would have to make too many pits stops. He insisted that there was something he needed to talk to me about. The urge for the bathroom came again so we couldn't finish. Still to this day I wondered what Clarence wanted to talk about pertaining to the mall. It was a nice break for me and much needed me time with a dash of adult conversation.

As time moved on, I wobble back to the apartment to just put my feet up. I do miss my family and wished I could have gone with them, but I would only slow them down. I'm okay with being entertained by the television. I enjoyed sitting and relaxing while channel surfing until I find something, anything that will relax me and baby girl, so we could sleep during the night.

One thing I know about this one she will be very active. I look around the apartment and gaze at the blessings of furniture, food and family. A big difference from when we first moved out here with no furniture, no food, and no clue on how to survive without our family being just a phone call or blocks away. Bill and I had to grow up and communicate. Our parents came out, but we still missed them and had to accept the life we were trying to make out here in Oceanview. We had beaches, sun, palm trees, and some rain, but not our immediate family or childhood friends. I tried to stay in touch as much as possible when the phone was turned on. So, I had to learn how to substitute my family. I loved listening and feeling a sense of belonging to a new community. From apartment to apartment we made families through others. Now our family will be increasing soon by one more daughter. She will be coming soon, and I couldn't wait. I hope Bill is as excited as I am. This is the first child we had together married. Married me/us, wow??? Mama Sadie words still echo, he had to ask, and I said I do tee-hee and so did he. Bill didn't want anyone else raising his daughter and neither did I but, I was ready if I had to.

After the way he treated me during my pregnancy I was ready to move on without him. Sierra was depending on me and I had to put on my big girl panties. She made me grow up quicker than I wanted to. Bill needed his big boy draws and I couldn't hold them. We both didn't have a clue on how to raise a child. We were still trying to raise ourselves and support a growing family. Playing house had left before we entered California. All I knew that someone was depending on me and I didn't have anyone to depend on. I couldn't wait for Bill he didn't show me any signs of wanting to be a father let alone a dad. It sometimes felt like a slow movie. No more playing house and our happy was slowing fading away. I wanted a new script with a better starring role. I just didn't know how to bring it back so we both could be in sync again with each other, just like it was before…

Seeing someone hold his daughter many years ago was an eye opener for Bill. Karma finally came around and now he knew what it felt like. I was kinder I did introduce him. Inside I knew he was hurt and wasn't expecting his pregnant friend of the family, (meaning me), to have someone else interested in her. The circle came around quick without any energy effort or thought. After that we were married and moving out here away from our family and friends, our lives merged and changed. I really didn't have any regrets, because if I stayed at home, I do believe we wouldn't be together, too many people involved in our business and Bill's playing grounds would have become a field with people I probably knew or went to school with. No thank you I rather not know the name or what their faces look like. Really hope that I would not be put in that position at all. Being pregnant has my emotions with an "s" going in all different directions. Before one emotion is trying to become stable another comes in and confusion and crazy is traveling all through my veins, blood, mind and soul. Bill doesn't have a clue of how I really, really feel. He just thinks I'm tripping.

I wonder how Momo is doing and tomorrow I'm going back over and try to help in any way that I can. Now I'm hungry for anything and everything and I feel like I have the munchies without getting high. Ooh it is so hot in here and this fan is just not getting it and the television is heck of boring. All these channels and nothing worth looking at, wow. Where is my family, I should have gone with them? Even though I would have to make many stops to the bathroom, but it would have been fun just hanging out and looking at future clothes I will be wearing after I deliver, (tee-hee-hee). Now I just wanted to rest and not eat because later I will be feeling heartburn. Hmm see there goes those emotions with a "s". Courtney Diane always correct you on there was no "s" attached to my emotion.

I needed to talk to my mother or mother- in- law or friends or someone, somebody. I knew I needed to refrain from making those desperate calls. Because I knew me once I started talking, I would just run that phone bill up again and I would have to hear Bill's mouth. I didn't need to have another phone turned off. We had the phones turned off so many times, because of me and my loneliness or just because. It's not like I have something else to do to fill that void.

I know Bill still loves me in his own way. I just pray he will love me better and more. After all we are all in this together. He asked, and we moved out here to be together and became a family. Why do I keep trying to convince myself? I still miss home, but I have been substituting my family with other people. What's up with that Rita D.? "Rita D" I like that nickname Courtney Diane gave to me. Like Courtney Diane would say tee-hee-hee and hee, with an added ha-ha, la-de-da, minus the heffa part. This chuckle had my unborn daughter laughing with me and giving me a contraction in the process. I now know what they are. When I was pregnant with Sierra I was living at home and right in the middle of the night I start feeling like I had a bad cramp with the need of a bowel movement. This was my first pregnancy, and I just thought I had to use the bathroom. I told my mother that I was cramping. She jumps up out of bed and I go to the bathroom to take a shower. This was routine for me. I was told when you're pregnant don't get caught with holely draws or dirty feet. So, I didn't want to get caught with dirty feet. As I go into the bathroom, I locked the door in my normal fashion and I heard my mother fussing for me to have my fat butt get ready and unlock the door. Now I understand her anixiety but why my butt got to be involved in her excitement.

I called Bill and he met us at the hospital which surprised me since he was absent during most of my pregnancy. They rushed me in putting me in a wheel chair and loaded me onto a gurney. Everything was confusing and happening so fast that they pushed my parents out of the way and rushed Bill into scrubs and pushed him into the delivery room with me. All I could think of was the pain that I was in. I rememeber looking into Bill's almond shaped beautiful smiling eyes and I had to put on my big girl panties while telling myself don't scream like I've seen on television. With each push I smiled as I concentrated on his eyes and smiled back all I knew was don't scream. I pushed and pushed, and it felt like hours with a bad bowel movement as Sierra traveling down the birth canal. It felt like a bad cramp and all I wanted to do was straighten my back for comfort, which didn't come. In my mind just like now I would wonder what my child would look like after carrying her all these months. The time is approaching but all I remember was I pushed until Sierra came out, with such a relief. With what felt like much exhaustion I proudly look into Sierra's eyes and she shows expression of being mad or highly pissed. My small seven-pound version of Bill was a beautiful version of him.

When I think about childbirth, I realized how much I must have loved Bill to take my body through this again. I just remember saying all that work and she looks just like him. Wow a lot of work then just like it is now. I wouldn't trade anything in the world for that experience. To have life in you and watch lives come into our world and hear that cry and feel the warmth of her body on your body. What a blessing.

To this day I may not know what is bothering my daughters, but I do know when something is wrong. You don't carry a child for nine months where you are sharing food, blood and thoughts and not to know something is bothering them. I still look at my daughter and reflect on when she was born and remember how she played and the words she couldn't say sometimes. Like invistheble which she was trying to say the pledge of in the visible, and could sing a song all the way through, but could barely talk or form her sentences. There she was in that memory bank I kept on reserve just for that. This is something that I have and its mine and is just for me. That is something I earned and cherish dearly. I love my daughter Sierra and thankful for her. While I watched her grow, she unknowingly helped Bill and I to grow too. New parents with a newborn we had no choice but to grow up. We tried and are still trying. With all those parenting books no child is the same and you really can't group them all together, but many try. The time is approaching for me to see my next bundle of joy will she look like Bill, me or a combination of us both. I could feel her movements and ready for her to see her family. Clothes, blankets, baby bed were all ready for her arrival.

I heard the keys in the door. Bill smiles as Sierra runs up to me right when her sister is kicking. Sierra smiles as she feels the rumble and movement of my stomach. Bill glances at me and he has stopped smiling. Inside I'm trembling, and wondering did he see me talking to Clarence, was I over at Robin's or Courtney Diane's house too long, was I smiling and laughing too hard?? I tried to show no fear and nervously smile so Sierra doesn't pick up on my emotions. All I knew was get in the kitchen and fix some snacks maybe that will help be a distraction. I haven't seen him all day so what could I have done?? Sometimes it didn't take much but it would be nice to know what I was doing, that would help me out, so I could stop. I ask Bill if he wanted a snack and he snaps and says what difference does it make it's going to be the same old 'ucking' thing. Inside I'm trembling more because for that quick second I couldn't think of anything to whip up while nursing my feelings and being hurt at the same time. It wasn't like I was the best cook. I learned by watching and asking people for their recipes or watching them cook. Even tho Momo could turn any meal she was prepping into something sexual, she still had skills. Hmm, no wonder Amos wouldn't talk much, because maybe he was still in his sexual ecstasy. As for me all I wanted to be the best; wife, sexual partner, mother, cook, friend to Bill so he wouldn't have to find it somewhere else.

I'm trying to control my pregnancy emotions, but I want to yell back and tell Bill how I really feel up in here!! After gaining some strength and after hanging out with Robin and Courtney Diane the roar in me was debating on when to roar. Sierra runs to her room as if she knows what is about to happen. Does she hear some theme music that I didn't hear, did the wind shift and I didn't feel the breeze? My eyes showed the thoughts I had that my mouth was to afraid to say. The roar I was trying to surface reverted into a purr. Before I knew it, Bill yells some obsenities and before I could respond to why was he talking to me like that? I felt his hand go across my face and all feelings shivered inside my soul. I stood there and felt my eyes fill up with water and roll down my cheeks. I didn't make a sound because I learned not to cry, not to whimper, not to ask or say anything back. I just stood there and slowly walked away and went into the bathroom. As I looked in the mirror at the sadness and the aging in my face, I just knew this too shall pass. I heard the door open and slam close and thought if he wanted to go out just go like you normally do. I'm used to being at home with just Sierra.

Sometimes I didn't remember the last time he made me feel like I was doing something right. Sometimes Bill would look at me with looks of disgust with a quick glance, making my insides tremble and my spirit shrink inside. I got confused on how to please him, what am I doing wrong and what do I need to do? Sometimes I couldn't believe that I am afraid to look at him for fear of what the spirit is in his soul. Sometimes his spirit seems at if they both surfaced together sending my spirit out the room screaming leaving me there to just tremble. Nervously I try to make conversation which isn't too much since I didn't get out often. So, I test the wind to see if it is favorable and if not, he will cut me down to the size, just like the baby I am carrying.

I look at myself and wonder why? I then add more abuse to myself by thinking Bill is bored with me. I'm not that energetic, funny, or an attractive woman and is he looking for a replacement? I hide within myself in my thoughts in my spirits, so he doesn't see or sense my pain. I seemed to be doing a pretty good job without him. Funny but not ha-ha that when you get abused you learn how to abuse yourself, by adding more pain to the pain that already exsited. For my thoughts kept me company when I just needed something to hold on to. I don't want to share my pain or be judged and if I did share would I see the pity in their eyes. Did I want to look into their eyes as I told my story. I didn't want to share the empty loneliness that I feel with the constant mental and physical abuse I continually suffer. So, I wear my glasses, so no one could see the pain my soul is in. Now I know why Toni wore her big glasses it was to hide from the viewing of her soul.

I feel like Bill's servant more than a wife. I feel like the other woman minus the scant title. The appeal I once had I feel has faded with the high energy that has become only a memory of my past. The only joys I have and had been seeing Sierra grow. Feeling the movement of my unborn daughter and the joy in knowing she soon will be here. As I feel my spirit and soul continue hurting, I start humming to my unborn daughter to ease her mind and left her know that daddy is nice, and we love her. I'm trying so hard to protect my daughters and where would I go if I left, back to Haven's mission and have three sleeping in an unfamiliar bed, no money, no job, just no. I wipe my face, but the tears continue to flow with no sound. I look and stare into the mirror looking at my reflections. It seems as if the reflections ask me well Rita what are we going to do?? I force a smile and wipe my face again, so I can go and check on Sierra. She has fallen off to sleep looking so innocent and sweet. I change her clothes moving her very carefully, so she wouldn't wake up. I tuck her in like I had done so many nights; stroking her hair and rubbing her back or sometimes I just rock her. Comforting her is a comfort for me, because I want her to be at peace. As I watch her, a smile comes to my heart and joy is returning. I'm glad she is sleep because right now I need some me time.

Bill did put Sierra to sleep reading or telling bedtime stories we both took turns, but Bill's stories were random all thrown into one. I think what made Sierra fall off to sleep, because she was trying to sort the three bears away from the three little pigs. He had a way of telling bedtimes stories and as I listened, I would laugh, and a smile was placed gently on my heart. Well where is he now? I know Bill will either come home late or not come home. It seems to be a pattern. I wouldn't stop him from going out. It just would feel better if he would offer for us to go out more often. Although I am pregnant, I'm still human and want to spend time with my husband. I didn't want the crumbs I wanted the whole meal. As I leave sleeping Sierra I go and get a cold towel for my eyes. I still remember my dad's words. A cold towel will help the swelling. I was still talking to my unborn daughter and reassuring her and calming her spirit down. She feels what I feel as we share the same body, but I want to spare her from my feelings right now. I go to my empty bed and allow my body to warm the coldness that was trying to take over. Only thing I could do was continue to pray and know tomorrow will be better.

I go into my archives of memories for laughter and reflect on my childhood. My parent's old house basement used to flood. We were always told not to go down there when it flooded. Didn't realize how bad we were until I reflected on how hard it was for our parents to find babysitters. Well this was the time when Mama Sadie was supposed to be watching us. While she was watching one of her soap operas, we snuck downstairs to the flooded basement. I can still hear the laughter of my sisters and brother. Sonny and I were always close, and Emma Jean and Bonnie were closer. So, we had to jump from the stairs to the bar to avoid falling into the flooded basement sewer water. We made it over to the bar but coming back we had to get back without falling into the water, so Mama Sadie wouldn't know, (ooh wow just thinking still makes me chuckle). Sonny had me on his back and we made it back to the stairs.

Then we heard the cries for help from Emma Jean and Bonnie. Sonny and I were rolling back and forth laughing. We looked over at Emma Jean stretched out with Bonnie on her back holding on to the bar and the window. Just thinking about the vision still makes my eyes water and soul laugh. Through our laughter we heard help Sonny help, Rita help. During that time, we're still rolling back and forth on the ground laughing, and then we heard a pluck, pluck and they fell into that sewer water. Well Mama Sadie found out about them. EJ and Bonnie had the smell to go with their wet clothes; Sonny and I were in the clear, tee-hee, hmmm. My parent's piping system was shot didn't know then what I know now.

We had six people using one bathroom and if someone was taking a shower no other water could be running. If someone was showering not thinking and out of habit, we flushed and/or washed our hands to hear the person in the shower screaming because the water temperature changed. We would leave out laughing boy were we bad? We did have a toilet in the basement, but as bad as we were, we were scared to use the bathroom in the basement at night. I was afraid to go down to the basements at Druid Hill, (elementary), and the library, nope and uh-uh too big and it echoed. The thoughts ease my mind as I laughed and smiled myself to sleep just reflecting.

Just what I needed a picture of us running in and out of the house getting yelled at by our parents and not to let the door slam and what happen the door slams oops. I think that was for every household, don't let the door slam, don't let in the heat out/in and be home before the street lights came on. Those were the days of fun and laughter and not a care, nope just enjoying being a kid. I laugh at how my mother was embarrassed by my smile. I often wondered what else she might have been embarrassed of by me. I had the most raggedy rotten two front teeth she hated for me to smile. The funny part about my rotten teeth was I didn't eat a lot of candy; my younger sister Bonnie did. Well my brother helped her with the dental bill. The one time of many we were running through the house, my brother was chasing me, and I ran into an open door that took the one tooth. The other time my brother and I were throwing things at each other and he hit me in the mouth with a small hard yellow bowl. Wow were we wild and bad, no wonder no one wanted to babysit us hmmmph. Not a bad dental plan saved our parents some money.

Those thoughts helped me slowly close my eyes to fall off into a deep peaceful sleep. I found myself laughing but not a crazy laugh, because a smile was place in my heart. Life is confusing but don't have to be so hard. Elders use to always say you have the rest of your life to be an adult. I didn't understand then all I knew was I just wanted to grow up. Now knowing what I know I would have enjoyed every precious minutes/moment as if it were my last breath. I see things with a little magic, but I know now I was preparing for a new magic prescription. So now I'm trying to see clearer and the magic will slowly fade away. Some might say innocence, others might say naïve or maybe gullable, but in my way its just me using my vivid imagination to help me get through and keep it moving. I know it has worked for me since I was a child and as an adult, I need it more than I have ever needed. Yes, Lord thank you for rocking me to sleep. The tears I shed tonight will be dried by tomorrow. I hug myself and smile and with a big breath I finally fall off to sleep....

Chapter 31

It's Morning

Morning came and no Bill lying next to me. This time I really didn't care. I have another child that I been blessed to have, and the time is coming soon. The contractions are coming little more frequent. She is ready and probably thinking I better get out of here before he hurts both of us. I can feel her moving more. She is becoming a little more restless. I can feel her smiles and chuckling with me as we both fell off to sleep last night. I wake up to some severe cramps I know this feeling it's time. Now I need to start keeping track of the contractions. I hope Robin or Courtney Diane are home in Robin's words "just in case". As I move slower the cramping stops to give me a breather. Ooh that was a strong one but, they are not close enough for me to be concerned at least not yet. They are far apart, and I don't know where Bill is. Right now, it's Sierra and me. We are going to have a hot breakfast and do what we do hang out. We are going to check on Momo and see if she needs anything. Clean up around the house and watch Sierra play and maybe Clarence might be around, so I can hear another story. I wouldn't ask him to take me to the hospital because Bill would not understand.

I'm just trying to give birth to our second child and I just might need a ride. He was there for the first one and hopefully he will be there for the second one too. Ooh that one hurts, that one got me too. She is kicking harder and often, she is literally kicking my wide ass. Like Courtney Diane would say K-M-E-A adding a vowel, kiss my entire wide ass and Robin's response would be you don't have an ass who's going fill in for you Rita? That was always the response. When does Sierra baby sister sleep? Sierra was no where near this active inside of me. This one has high energy. I'm grateful the Lord allowed stories, thoughts and vision to take me to my quiet place. Where a smile comes on my heart and my soul feels the warmth from the blood flowing through my body. One promise I made to my daughters they will not ever see or feel my pain. I might not be able to save myself, but I will try to save them. I thought I had no where to go, so I allow my imagination to work and take me mentally away again.

I talk to myself and take Courtney Diane's suggestion from her online anger management class on how to redirect, regroup, and reconstruct my thought process. I can't remember the other "re's" to not concentrate on, but I will refocus my happiness and redirect my energy. I couldn't cry anymore, and people probably thought I only had an emotion, no feeling without the "s", but pain is pain and it hurts, and it shows up in many different ways. I learned how to have an invisible mental first aid kit and would take it out when needed just like a prescription. I had band aids for cuts to the soul, I had a needle and thread for cracks in my heart that just needed a little stitching, make-up to cover up bruises, along with my invisible cream, cold pack or cold towel for any type of swelling. An emergency hug for just in case and memories of an old flame to make me feel needed and wanted in a special way.

Thinking of an old flame my imagination thinks of intimacy of holding hands and passionate kisses and not the fly by pecks I get from Bill or the occassional accommodation affection. I guess I am eating crumbs again with no flavor. I picture myself dancing slowly with him as our eyes meet just like in the movies. I reflect as a child looking at the television watching the actors pretend with each other and I imagine what their lives are like after their marriage. These thoughts just make me laugh as I feel the sun coming through warming my body and it feels so good. I stop and remember that Bill can't dance or sing. So that romantic dance while singing in my ears is shot and laughed away. I picture his face as he makes all the effort to try to dance and sing. Then the sound of Courtney Diane's special laugh of tee-hee-hee, la-la, ha-ha echos in my mind. A calm spirit comes in and convinces me that I am okay! I had to keep in mind that after all Bill is taking care of us. Well not really us some how I have been left out, but we are still together working on it or working it out. Bill will come home, and our daughter will be born into our family. We were giving another chance to embrace our family with a new addition. Maybe he will realize what he has, and we are his family. We are his family and he shouldn't forget that we belong to him, I belong to him. Maybe Bill wanted both worlds freedom at the cost of putting fear in me and our marriage. This was Bill's way of controlling me through fear and intimdation, and it was slowly working. Either way it was Bill's way and Rita lost her voice.

I didn't know enough how to really fight back but I was learning a lot through the many conversations I had encountered. That was the reason I moved out here was to be one. I wanted to live out some type of childhood fantasy of being married with a picket fence, without twelve kids acourse. Catrice made it almost with her eleven children. Now she knows what her mother- in- law, Anuna meant when she said Greekum was potent. Humph she should have asked for some type of clarity. What is that old saying if you don't know you better ask someone?

Twelve or eleven kids later she surely knows what that word means now. I wondered how she and Melba were doing and if they get together from time to time.

I do miss being around them and often think about the last party we attended. It was so great seeing the blessings in Toni and Jovan relationship, and how they had the adhesive to stick it out and stay together. It warmed my heart seeing their girls laughing and talking without fear. I can only try and imagine the life during and after they realized how much they did love each other after the toxic anger left and love became stronger than ever. They looked and sounded as if they were always on their first date. Maybe that was what Bill and I needed. We need to start planning date time even if it's after the girls go to sleep. We wouldn't have to worry about a babysitter just some candles, movies or soft music and romance like we used to do before we married…

I long to relive those feelings with Bill and not continue to feel as if I am a burden to him or feel that he just can't stand being with me or looking at me. When he gives me that look it just makes my insides shrink and my emotions shiver and leaves my mind confused and empty. Maybe when our daughter is born, this will bring more life into our family and appreciation into our marriage.

I reflect on my brother Charles and asked him again about what happened when Mommy wouldn't let him in after he broke away from a fight. Although this happened, (wow many years ago my brother is now in his sixties). He said that he ran to mommy's house after breaking away from a fight he was losing. He made it to Mommy's back door, and she pushed him back out, locked the door and told him to finish it, or pick up where he left off. He said she said with a straight face that either you fight until you win or until exhaustion sets in. Mommy told Sonny in a calm voice we don't do that. She taught us not to run away. I laughed because Mommy told him to get his ass back out there. It's strange when you hear your great-grandmother swear because you place them in no bad words, category.

Charles inside response was that was why my ass was running because it was getting beat. But we both learned from that you don't give up; finish what you started, no running away. Just like EJ learned when she forgot to turn into the gate while fleeing from a group of girls. She didn't make the first go around and was running so fast she missed the gate again, while my mother stood in the front door watching the dust kick up from EJ short fast running feet that were seriously trying to get away. Mommy words, we don't do that probably echoed back to my mother as she stood there being entertained. Sounds familiar just like when my brother Charles tried running away from a fight, a woo moment and Mommy pushed him back out saying we don't do that, maybe that was the same philosophy that was passed onto my mother from her grandmother, Mommy. She told him he only had two options one fight until you win, or you just get too tired to finish. That was something that we still remember generations later. Mom didn't open the gate or door to assist EJ. Mom just stood in the front door and watched her mouth get her in trouble. That day came when she couldn't out run her mouth; yep it was finished that day. They

— 351 —

caught EJ at the corner I guess when all was done, she made her way back to the gate and opened it herself. Wonder what thoughts were going through her mind when she saw our mother standing in the door?? I'm sure her mind had a many of thoughts for our mom, but she knew better to say the words or show them in her eyes or expressions. I try to fathom her thoughts but laughter clouds them because I'm picturing EJ short legs moving as fast as they could go.

Where are my thoughts running away to that I can't make any type of moves? Funny but not ha-ha I have run away from so many things, thoughts not knowing how to really finish. I pictured my beautiful Mommy standing in the doorway with the same expression and strength that triumph through depression, husband abandonment to raise my aunt, grandmother and uncle along with my mother with limited education and financial support. She didn't run away or abandon her responsibilities or give up to self pity. She had a good talk and told herself that she had to get her ass in gear. Because we don't do that, finish what was started, a life with no husband. I never heard her complain or say anything about her regrets. In the end she had a place to stay and the husband that left her with three kids struggling, in death he left her his pension. Ironic how things turned around it's God's way of giving you double for your trouble as He did for Job. My brother and I used to say that we felt sorry for anyone that ever broke into Mommy's house. I remembered the switch blade, razor strap, utility knife, long gun, butcher knife and hammer that all manage to fit just right underneath her pillow. She was ready to finish anything that anyone started. Her strength I will in all ways need and rely on. I'm thankful for her bloodline and all that she represented then and now. I still miss her, and it's been over thirty years. Mommy's mind was in all ways intact. I remembered when she told me that she was converting back to her childhood. Wow what a woman and what a brilliant stable mind she had. I have and will continue to share her strength with my children and anyone else that might need to tap into that ancesterial strength. Hearing Mommy swear would sometimes throw me off because I held her at a high level, but she said what she felt. One day I will have that type of courage but for now I will shiver in my thoughts and spirit. I'm just trying to understand why Bill is so mean to me and what have I done that he can't tell me, so I can correct it.

Let me see what could be wrong in the eyes of Bill?? I had his first born now his second daughter, cool okay, occasionally burning some meals, making sure the bathroom tissue was face down instead of up, I kept the house clean, but it is always not up to his standards, but I continue to try. I try to be there when he arrives home, so he can come in smelling his dinner when he does come home around dinner time. Sex is out he looks at me with hatred so how can you make love with those types of feelings. Anyway, he really doesn't touch me. I get the crumbs of emotions that drop on the ground. Is it the crumbs and my heart that starves and wants to beat? Crumbs and cameo I had to think about again and I look at others and wondered how they could, settle for crumbs of affections and cameo appearances. Then when I turned my head back, surprisingly I was looking at my own reflections and realized that I too was desperate for crumbs and cameos. It wasn't just the trixies singing that anthem and convincing themselves its okay. We at some point compete for crumbs of affections. The names maybe different but the need for the crumbs do exsist out there for us lonely women. Well maybe not Robin she will just cut him loose, Courtney Diane ooh she would just cut him. I wonder maybe she should really take that on-line anger management to a real classroom.

I wonder how I got pregnant this time. Communication wasn't ever one of our problems but lately he really hasn't been talking too much to me. Inside and outside I know I am no longer that energetic shapely beauty hanging out in the Caboose in college. What would I do over if I could and what my life would be like if I wasn't out in in Oceanview? I lost that zeal/zest and I'm slowly losing my feelings and just becoming numb. I look around the room and see the pictures that Robin finally took of our family. That was a fun day I was just hoping that her camera lens would not pick up the dried tear stains. She did a good job, perfect capture of our family. Bill acted right that day we laughed like we used to, and we cuddled. Accomodating affections made a cameo in a form of Bill hitting me on my butt. Wow!! Robin laughs and saying enough of that's how you got the second one coming. Although I used to hate when he did that, but now I miss that crumbs of affection. Only if she knew this was a surprise to me too. That was the day Robin captured a happy loving family.

As the cramps increased, I make it to the bedroom as I hear Sierra snoring in her room. I sit on the edge the bed looking at the pictures of us on the dresser and hope that no other woman will see the smiling faces as she disrespects my home. I think back on what Robin said about the Trixie in her bed waking up to her and the family pictures on their dresser and realized that is a crazy type of feeling. No one should have to feel that type of pain. Your home is your home, and this is your family, such a violation. Bill is still my husband and Sierra is his first and only daughter right now until our second daughter arrives and that might be soon. And the way that I am cramping she might be coming soon. I flashback to Courtney Diane and Robin pretending that Courtney Diane was on the runway sash shaying as Robin was taking the pictures. We laughed and sang and chanted like we did with Momo.

I got involved let me see how, did that song go. Miss Hottie, Miss Hottie she's working that body, as Courtney Diane's alter ego called Sonya, was working the poses and the body. Funny how she stopped when we said pause, then pose/ pause then pause again. Robin made the click sound while Sonya moved again walking fast and swinging like the models and posing, then again Robin would say click. Then it went to work that body work that body show them that you are the hottie corney as it may have sound, we were having fun. While saying Miss Hottie work that body do the pose pause, you know!! Wow we heard so many clicks until we just clicked out and laughed until we cried. Our imaginary camera ran out of film, oh well we were done anyway. Even Courtney Diane got in a little tee-hee-hee and la-de-da and ha-ha then followed up with a whatever. I love them, and I love the way they talk about their kids and family members and I love the way they accept me into their sister circle. I didn't know if the neighbors knew what was going on in my apartment. And if they did, they didn't make me feel bad or judge me. The pictures do help capture the moments that sometimes your brain won't replay.

Although Sierra looks just like her dad, she does have my smile that was passed down to me from my mother, Sheryl. You had to test the wind to see which character would make a cameo appreance. She could be so kind. Then the sweetish granny could transform into something not normal. She could take flight at any time on her broom. Funny it is the same way that Reva spoke of her mother calling her Glenda and testing the wind and day of the week for her flight schedule. Dad, old pops on the other hand was funny and I missed the talks we used to have and the laughter. He helped me understand when to fight and when to take flight. Ooh if mommy knew I'm sure she would make me find that person, so we could finish the situation. He was there through the boyfriend pains, baseball wins and losses, telling stories about his past and sharing too much about my teachers. Old pop talking about a train was pulled on her. Now being young and sometimes the cables didn't connect but I knew enough that a train had more cars than a caboose. Other than gagging that was totally T-M-I, just too much information. How could I look at my teacher the next day and not want to make a train or whistle sound, landing me again in the principal's office. I told him that makes me really want to respect my teacher and keep a straight face in her classroom. It didn't matter I didn't tell anyone that was her business and that was many many years ago.

I had to deal with my teachers, school adminstration because they too knew my dad and his whole family. I used to hate when Aunt Jo, (Uncle Danny's wife), would come to Druid Hill. It seems like everytime she came to my school I was sitting outside the principal's office again. She probably wondered when I went to class or when did I stay in class and my young thoughts were when you did go to work, tee-hee because we seem to be looking at each other.

I love this Chai tea and the warmth it provides to my body. Maybe I better hold off don't want to be up all night using the bathroom. Sierra is so tired and where is Bill he should be here he knows that time is getting close for the arrival of our baby girl. I love her and can't wait to see and hold her for the first time. I wonder if she will look like Bill or me or combination of us both, either way she's ours. She was made from love and God and no one can take that joy away. No Trixie, no scant just no this is our joy, our family that I am so thankful to have, and Bill chose me. I need to practice like Miss Dorothy said a many of times go for what you know, and

I know I am married to Bill and we are family and will be until… So, all I know is Bill, our marriage and our increasing beautiful family.

Miss Dorothy had me thinking back when she started that phrase. She said she was pregnant and hanging out with some girlfriends. Okay think Rita make your mind work on these names. There was two tank Terri because she was tall, and thick, Aggie, or was it, Abby and Shehe Sheila because in her younger years she, was a tomboy until Booker straighten her out, as she winks at me you know what I mean! In the back of my mind I was thinking yuck is she related to Momo everything about Momo was sexual even her cooking. Nah Miss Dorothy said she liked boys she was just as rough and tough as they were. The girl had some hang time. She could play football and not touch, ran fast and was good at the hurdles. I remember how Miss Dorothy still had her beautiful shape/ figure and energetic personality. She was another one I enjoyed talking to. She lived just around the corner from me and every now and then I would stop by and just say hi. She welcomed me into her home just like Momo, Courtney Diane and Robin. So many people and families have adopted me into their hearts, and I have adopted them too. They have helped me in so many ways to get through so many things. They help ease some of the pain I felt being away from my family. I still miss my family and learned to adopt others and make them my family. I sometimes miss hearing my family voices especially my parents and brother and sisters. When I do call home, I find myself talking as if I'm next door. I want to keep up with what's happening with my family, friends and Oakwood. I just want to reassure my family and friends that I am fine, so they wouldn't worry so much about me.

I was the only family member that moved away and stayed. My brother left only to return and forever regrets that move. I guess I did a lot of first; to graduate early, to go to college, and leave Oakwood. That was where faith and courage helped me through such a big move. Didn't realize I had it when I decided to follow Bill to Oceanview. I just knew my place was by the side of my husband and for both of us to raise our daughter and grow old together like many older couples I grew up watching. I wanted the picket fence with us just trying to keep our family and the bills together and continue to grow and go. I know there would be some types of ups and downs that's part of growth, but we must keep that line of communication open and for some reason that is what has been fading away from our life.

I miss the the laughter, the smiles and the cracking up on our relatives and the friendship I felt with Bill. Bill was my best friend and I hope I'm still his? All I have is what's in our apartment, my family. I'm not working but I would love to. It is so boring staying at home. I wanted some adult stimulating conversation and work my brain and release my bottled-up energy too. I need some type of release and some type of different fresh air. I want to smell the leather seats, feel my hands grip the steering wheel and let my butt feel the comforts of the drivers' seat. I want to breathe again the air of freedom. Exhale and see the flowers and a change of scenery. Man, I used to do so much in Oakwood. Now I've become confined to this apartment and I'm bored. Bill's absence is getting old. Now don't get me wrong, I love being at home with Sierra, but I do need some mental serious stimulation. Tomorrow will be another day with the same situation. I know I don't need to be driving and I haven't driven in some time. The way I'm feeling, I'm going to the store and I will be going by myself!! I know this is a bold move, but I need some air before my ourt daughter is born. I don't know when Bill came home that morning and I didn't care.

I woke up no cramps feeling better this morning for some reason better than I felt last night. I get up out the bed easing up not caring if I woke Bill up. I'm going to run to the grocery store and not the corner store. I'm not taking the bus or walking to that high price corner store that is around the corner. It has been a long time since I have been to the store without Bill and Sierra. The keys are on the counter and they are encouraging me. I get into the car looking around to see if I see any signs of another woman leaving her presence or absence just for me. Good no souvenirs so far so good with ease and big breath of sigh. I start the car enroute to the store and the sound of the engine is music to my ears. Matter of fact let the music blast and let the music ease my soul. Funny part about this moment of liberation I didn't know what I am going to the store for with very little money. Once I arrived, I take my time getting out the car and walk with no rush. There was no need to hurry. Bill will figure it out that I'm gone when he wakes up.

I look around as I go down different aisles with no thoughts of what I want to buy. I see a lady pushing a cart full of kids and wonder where was she going to put the groceries. Wow she sure does have a lot of them. She seems to be very patient as each one puts in their special request. When we went grocery shopping with my mother requests were not allowed and if you put your hand on any item, her response was are you going to buy it, if not put it back. That cut that entire special request out accompanied with a look that you knew not to go there ever again. When I hear the voice of the lady for some reason, she sounds familiar...

If she is who I think it is it has been a long time. As she approaches, we both make eye contact with the expression of you look familiar. I try not to stare but she looks at me without a care if she was staring as her expression shows that she is trying to focus and recall who I might be. When she opens her mouth and I hear that southern drawl with girly I knew instantly it was Charlotte from the clinic. Her face looks the same just a little more weight than I remembered, but we were both younger and smaller during our clinic days. She yells out Rita girly what you are doing out here, a long way from Oakwood. Looka here I'm a long way from home too girly. Look at you pregnant again the last time I saw you were pregnant look at history. No indigestion this time huh?? I smile and laugh saying you have been a bit busy, as I look at the cart of smiling curious faces. I loved her energy then and God knew I needed it now. She was my ram in the bush and, age and time has been nice to her. She laughs with yep Johnny Lee and I been a bit busy.

She starts pointing to them as she names them. We didn't know we went from baby to babies. I smiled babies meaning more than one. Yep the good Lord threw me a curve and that ball landed smack dab in a bucket of fresh milk. That milk spattered all on me and by time I wiped my eyes three little look a likes pop on out, and we were counting them one, two, and a three good Lord and I said that is the last one, right?? Talking about a workout, ooh that was a job harder than milking that heffa on a good day Rita. I laughed but inside heffa was the only word we could say without sounding like we were cussing and now it seems strange to hear it in a different content. I told you I was popping them out you thought I was funning huh, Miss Rita. The first one came out was boy, so we named him Johnny Lee Jr. We call him JR, so people know which one we talking to or about, but sometime, I forget when I'm fussing and call his daddy JR which confuses little JR. First boy first pop, Johnny Lee, second pop Monroe Joe laughed that he had miniature replacements for his grown sons. Johnny Lee's momma InaJoy wanted more youngings running around to spoil and recapture her sons' youth again and she got em. Now his brothers, Frank Matthew, named this one Reed Edward, we call him Reedy or RE and Johnny Lee other brother Turner you know the one we called Truck name this one here Munson Jace, we call him MJ. Tammijune was my first born, girl came out looking smack dab just like her dad. Tammijune was named after Johnny Lee's mother's sister that everyone loved, and she didn't have no kids, so we named her after his aunt and her other sister. His great- Aunt Elana spoils the heck out of them when they go to her farm. They go from farm to farm raising havoc and being themselves. Just being youngins and all. Baby factory is closed no more names for loved relatives. They can just need to pick one and call them their favorite.

Tammijune is around here somewhere with her daddy. She's helping Johnny Lee with the grocery list. They are like two kids together, I bet they over there scoping out those zingers. That probably was the first asile they went to. They like cocount raspberry ones, mostly. This little one right here that looks like me is Linda Sue and she has a little puppy called. Before Charlotte can say the name, Linda Sue smiles and says it with her mom Miss Coco, because I like hot coco, with mushmellows hmmm yum yum. Charlottle laughs saying she dresses that puppy like it a baby dall. Miss Coco doesn't do no outside she is strictly an indoor dog. Oh, excuse me as Linda Sue says mom, she is a puppy. Miss Coco goes outside only for a bit of fresh air and that is it. Her paws will not get any type of dirty. They all respond so politely saying it was nice to meet me. I smile and tell her I had a daughter name Sierra that keeps me busy with her high energy and she came out looking dab like Bill too. So, I know how you feel and now I am expecting another daughter anytime now and she is very active.

She laughs and you out here girly isn't you fretting about flooding these floors if your water bag breaks. For that moment I didn't think much of it. I just needed some air and a taste of freedom. I just had the need to feel the comfort of the driver's seat. I really had to get behind the wheel and go. Just feel the breeze and go where I wanted to go and listen to the music and just sing off key and laugh and drive feeling the air hit my face. She asked me how long I've been living here. I told her right after I had Sierra. She said that they lived on Johnny Lee's parents farm and things just got a little slow and we were having these youngings. Rita I was popping them out like an ear of hot corn being heated up just pop, pop and pop again. Only thing I could say was woo. She added that her grandma Ruby said I had some child bearing hips and I lived up to her words. I asked how they were doing.

She said her mother Sybil doing fine she got a boyfriend and don't see her much. Grandma Ruby just got married to her so called robbing the cradle husband, that is seventy- five and she's eighty- five. That Granna Ruby smiles and says I still know how to rock his world and I'm not talking about a rocking chair either girly. My thought was is that like the flipping and flopping, that Momo and Amos do that keeps them investing in Sealy mattresses. Charlotte is cracking up laughing as she's telling, me that Granna Ruby said that she is a young eighty- five years old, and she got some serious experience, (she winks). Some things you just don't forget, time does work with you and, last time I checked breath was still coming from me and him. Sometimes the breathing gets a little harder, (winking), but no oxygen needed just deep breaths. Don't you want a new grandpa, darling? I thought eew does she know Momo and her gang, really! Charlotte went on to say that Granna Ruby, you know about breaking in new mattress huh girly. In my mind that was too much on the visuals, ew. Granna Ruby laughs saying that she didn't want to deprive us of a granddad, and then she blows me a kiss. Granna buried a many of grandpas that were caught in compromising positions. I guess she does have a good strong beating heart.

She growls when she says it to remind me that she is a happy purring cougar. Those youngins got hitched in Las Vegas went through that drive thru chapel and ordered a plain burger with fries had to watch their diet and all. They said they went thru the drive thru because they move too slow, and by time they would make it to the alter bells would go from ding to ting. Granna Ruby said that they needed to save their enegy for the honeymoon, as she winks this one might last. I thought to myself shouldn't they be enjoyning retirement and grandchilddren, but I guess you had to look at they are still human and breathing and doing what they want to enjoy their lives.

I drift off thinking that I hope Bill and I will grow old and still have that kind of fun love and still getting busy. My thoughts refocus, and I find myself laughing with Charlotte. We both are laughing, and Charlotte is adding, ain't no heffer mooing at my granna. Granna would always say I am not waiting for the cows or heffa to come home or moo. Heard enough of mooing now I want to hear some other sounds and you know what I mean. I got needs too girly. She's eighty-five but looks and act as if she is in her fifties. I can't keep up with her. Charlotte gets more excited saying that her Granna skates, ride horses, swims, and walks daily. I rather chase after my children than try to keep up with her and my mama.

We both agreed that we have been here for a bit trying to play catch up. Charlotte tells me that Johnny Lee joined the service when farming wasn't paying the bills and they had to do something. Youngins were popping out of me like cherry blossoms in the spring. We are getting ready to go over to Italy imagine that girly. Yeah Rita giving up farm land for an island. Being around all that water and none of us really know how to swim imagined that huh. Now we jump in the lakes where he can stand in, but heck we can't stand up in all that water and we can't take our puppies. Charlotte's, (look alike), daughter Linda Sue says momma the boys they have dogs, Miss Coco my puppy. They all start naming the dogs Tommy, Hammer and Nala. Now those are outdoor dogs and they will be staying with Johnny Lee's parents Robert Joe and Inajoy.

His parents are still farming with Johnny Lee's brothers and uncles. Everybody is just doing the same thing, and nothing change other than us not there. Heck it's probably quiet now with our youngings not running around yelling and playing jumping and getting into everything. These boys get into stuff I couldn't imagine. Good thing they came when they did cuz they love to russel and tussel all the time. Tammijune hangs tough with them and Linda Sue brings up the rear. Nope they don't give me any problems or concerns, they fight and wrestle, but they watch out for each other. As we talk I look at the freshness that is still in Charlotte. At a glance I see a sparkle in her eyes as she turns toward a rather handsome slim man approaching her with a little girl in the basket. Johnny Lee and the little girl are smiling at her, holding boxes of zingers. Charlotte smiles at him saying I knew it you been hanging out in the zinger section again didn't we talk about that Johnny Lee!! As he opens his mouth showing some deep, deep dimples and deep blue eyes that look like a fresh blue lake of water and that those deep blue eyes seem to be just for Charlotte.

She shakes her head as he says; now Char don't be doing that. Tammijune kept eyeing them and I just caved in. Tammijune looks at him as if she is in shock and opens her mouth without words as she looks at him and then Charlotte. Like what do I have to do with this? I just had a feeling that Johnny Lee placed them in her lap just a minor distractor. Now Char and his voice sounds very soothing he is not what I pictured. When Charlotte said he picked her up and squeezed her, I just pictured a bigger man. He pleads his case and sounds just like a little boy. I love their conversation about those boxes of zingers. He says now Char, honeybun I only got one of each I didn't go crazy. I just, well we couldn't resist, and again the little girl looks at him with her mouth open again, as if how did we come into this I can't read. Charlotte's voice softens with Johnny Lee now we talked about this at home and in the car and again once we got into this here place. His voice lowers adding, I know honeybun, but you know how I like these. I don't eat them often come on Char please, pretty, pretty, please, with that the whole cart of kids harmonizing in saying pretty, please, mom!! Johnny Lee smile gleams as he looks at her with deep love and puppy eyes. He takes her hand and calls her Charla; pretty, pretty, please Charly as he kisses her on the cheek. You can see it kinda makes her blush, but she likes it. She looks at him with the same love and enjoys holding his hand still showing love as if they were high school sweethearts.

My heart warms and my eyes water as I look at the genuine love, they have for each other. The cart full of kids chant for the zingers. Charlotte is happy to hear ding dongs will be an additional treat. You see Johnny Lee's looks and smile is in all their children. Linda Sue resembles both but, in that instance, she looks like her dad. Charlotte gives in with okay Johnny Lee but if you gonna get those boxes of zingers, I'm getting my boxes of ding dongs. The kids and Johnny Lee yell yeah as if they were at a game or rodeo. She introduces us as a friend she liked and met at the clinic some time ago. Johnny Lee yells out, I remember the one that thought she had indigestion! We all laugh, and I said I just needed a big burp and it came out some nine months later with a name. We all laugh as Charlotte tells me they had to be going as she turns that cart around. I had to chuckle asking myself when Charlotte asked, where was the that asile with the ding dongs?? I need something to snack on later as she winks at me with her signature smile.

They all chant ding dongs here we come; they kept saying until the vision and sounds both faded away. She still walks the same way she did when we were in the clinic with a bounce as if she been asked to dance. They both laugh, and you can see he is happy that his wife said okay on the zingers and you see the happiness in their family. I was refreshing to see a young relationship handle a situation so calmly and seeing a happy family and at the same time showing their children how to love. No yelling, no fussing just smiles and laughter. As I think about getting some raspberry zingers and maybe a box of ding dongs. Johnny Lee, Charlotte and their family looked so happy and perfect. It kinda gave me an inspiration to just try it another way with Bill.

My angry thoughts were gone but it felt good to see Charlotte after all these years. Who could have imagined running into to her and her family? Wow and what a big family, well they had that heap of kids she talked about at the clinic. People glance at me as I chuckle to myself thinking back on the clinic, Charlotte counting those babies as they popped out. I imagine with joy the arguments if any and the fun they have at home. I needed to be here at the time I needed to be here.

Now what am I here for? Bill won't be that understanding if I come home empty handed.

My cart is as empty and my billfold which has not magically increased in dollars or change. Whatever I get it won't be much, but the visiual I witnessed with Charlotte and Johnny Lee was priceless and precious. Oh Lord you knew I needed to see Charlotte because you know I am a visual person. I want to try a different way regardless of how I think Bill feels about me. There must be love there, for Bill to always come home. While driving home I have a different game plan with Bill, my marriage and my family. Like Mommy said we don't do that, you must finish what you started, and I am starting to understand I want my husband, and my family. I started to feel some type of confidence and just started humming. I realized with my off key singing I needed to hear some real singers. I blast the radio and the song that played when we first came into California was the song joy and pain with sunshine. We have had rain quite a bit and sunshine too, now I'm waiting to see our rainbow.

Chapter 32
Now Keith has a Story

The breeze is blowing fresh air into my nostrils and the brain lets out a big sigh. I feel fresh and giddy. As I pull up, I see Keith looking out the window and Robin pulling up with her daughters. They all wave with their beautiful smiles and I agree that is another sign that everything is going to be okay. Oh yeah and alright my soul is flying and not shivering, and my daughter is just relaxing in her temporary home, called my stomach. I have a small bag of groceries and floating in my walk. Keith comes to let me know that Bill and Sierra left with Clarence. His cousin Loren had come into town and wanted to see us. I haven't seen or heard from Loren in years. He was into traveling and women, wow this is what we really needed. Oh well what the heck now its time to practice my thoughts on turning our relationship around. Maybe we need to have Loren here to show Bill that he should appreciate having a family. Before I go in Keith wanted me to try a coconut oatmeal cake. Hmmm the combination sounds crazy but if he baked it, I know it will taste good and I can smell the freshness. I go into the apartment put up the small amount of groceries and return outside to sit and talk with Keith, while enjoying his fresh baked creation. I sit on the steps as Keith brings a nice piece of cake. As I take a bite the moisture is great, and the taste reminds me of the fresh lemonade and sandwich I had with Robin when we went on my freedom run.

For that moment I didn't fear Bill seeing me talking to Keith and the feeling of a lot of strength. Not cocky just confident. We talk small talk as I continued to enjoy the cake, conversation, fresh air as the sun provides warmth to my body. We watch the neighborhood children ride up and down the street laughing and smiling while just being kids. I tell Keith that we did that a lot in Oakwood. We treated our bikes like they were cars. We rode all over the town and made sure we made it home before the street lights came on. Keith agrees they had the same rule too.

He reflects on one time he had let Kinney from the family they called "up to no good" just a family that bullied the neighborhood and when they ran out of victims, they would turn on each other. They loved to fight and that wasn't just for their past time. The Uptonogoods were centurions of the neighborhood grid. I had to know if that was their real last name. He said we called their family that for so long that we forgot their real last name. Now that we are older the last name fades away and their actions become part of our memories. Kinney and his brother Ron would always circle around the neighborhood terriozing folks. They had a habit of throwing rocks too. I laugh, but not at that. I remember when I was a younger the boys threw rocks at my butt and I didn't feel them. I just heard them laughing and they told me what they were doing. Clarence didn't respond and went on with his story saying that when they would play baseball in the local vacant lot they would play, and they would stop because they thought they heard rock sounds. Then we would go back playing ball then pause to hear the thump thump of more rocks. Then they realized it was the Uptonogoods giving us a warning that they were coming...

We grab everything and what was left was left and we all took off running. What was ever left considered it a donation. We weren't about fighting it was about surviving. We took off so fast no one's feet were hitting the ground, because we were all airborne. Hey Rita, we all felt like the road runner running with a zoop and flee. We left in a cloud of smoke. I laughed is that how you got those track trophies? Keith smiles through his laughter saying oh hell yes, all we knew was to just run. The last thing you wanted was to get caught by Kinney or Ron or any member of their family. The girls were fine and just as bad. They looked good but don't touch and you hope they don't think you were fine. Dating them was a short period of time and went right into wees getting married.

I had to laugh at that one, because that reminded me of Courtney Diane's brother fine Corey Davon hooked into wees married and pregnant again, again and one more again then again. I 'm laughing so hard my baby is giggling too. Maybe they might need a fifth of something strong. Keith laughed looking at the neighborhood kids ride their bikes weaving in and out and chasing each other. He said that he had got a new bike for his birthday and was riding and enjoying it just like you see those kids. Not bragging just enjoying being a kid with the innocence still present. Then I see a family member from the Uptonogood, Kinney or just Upto. My thought was aw man was my timing off, shoot. Kinney comes over talking not being nice just being his bully self. He liked my bike and asked could he ride it. I knew better, and my parents told me not to let anyone ride my bike. I agree because that's what my parents told us too. Different states still universal in parental rules no one rides your bike, no company when your parents are not home, and better be home before the street lights come on.

I set there on the steps of my house just like we are doing now, couldn't go in because Kinney still had my bike. He bullied me into letting him ride to the end of the block, only thing his block was no where in my sight and I couldn't go inside unless I had my bike. I watched him ride to the end of the block feeling okay. He's doing what he said then he speeds up and turns the corner out of my sight. All I could only think about was how much trouble I will be in. I hear my parent's voices ehco in my mind and as my soul shivers in the corner of my brain. Convincing me from afar that was a dumb move. My mouth drops open and I just set down like I lost my dog. The street lights came on and no Kinney, no one around because the neighborhood knew the rules with the lights. I wasn't thinking about dinner just thinking about what is going to happen to me when I go inside without my bike.

If I stayed outside, they wouldn't know I violated that bike rule. I look up and down the street while sitting on the steps waiting anxiously for Kinney to come riding down the street. Hopefully Kinney will be turning the corner soon. I saw him speed around, finally with my bike. Right when I was ready to suck it up and deal with my punishment. Here comes Kinney riding my bike like it was his and he just didn't care how he rode it. Zig zagging doing wheelies and doughnuts. I watched him just destroying my new bike. He looks at me while it is moving and just jumps off and says here is your old bike. Hey, I didn't care it was new to me and I took that bike in and didn't ride it for a long time. My parents didn't understand why I wasn't on it as much as they thought I would be. Only if they knew what I didn't want them to know, and I knew enough at that young age not to let them know.

We laugh about the Uptonogoods and the ones I knew in my neighborhood. Certain families you just didn't touch or bother. If you got into a fight you will be still fighting their next generation. Wasn't worth the fight just the flight mold and live to keep it moving. Majority of the bad families have died off, regenerated, or just changed from that life of bullying. In today's age it's just too dangerous. We lived to fight, but we fought to live, and the key word was we lived and either to be the best of friends or acquaintances. But you had a special kind of respect and kept it alive and moving. We laugh at our childhood antics and realized we have a lot in common.

I just wanted to know if he was going to ever get married again. He said no because he was still married and made a mistake with his wife and ego played the lead role. Pride, stupidity and stubbornness had some hang time with him. Keith shook his head and said that he was so secured and gradually turned into being insecured and didn't realize what happened until it happened. He thought everyone wanted his wife Kiante. She was and still is gorgeous. But I was young and dumb and didn't know how to appreciate what she was trying to do. All she was trying to do was be apart of me, doing the right thing in being my lady. I'm not interested in anyone but her, those ladies you see coming around here are for Clarence or Darryl, nope not for me. My heart belongs to Kiante, with her she is my favorite candy bar. When I unwrapped that package, I knew just what I am getting. There is no surprise same flavor that I know and love. With each moment I was with her it felt like that first and last bite of my favorite candy, hmmm. I chuckle through my smile of what a compliment Keith had for Kiante. His description is different but understandable. I respected his perception, his thought he put into that emotion and his love, for his wife.

He had to put much thought into that feeling, because it came so naturally and smooth. That thought was straight from the heart no detour at all with any stuttering thoughts. I haven't set down with Keith in a long time and miss and enjoyed the entertainment and attention. Between him and Clarence they both had stories that I set anxiously listening to, as I tried to put faces with their family members' stories. As he talked about her my creative curiousty questions sets in. How did you meet Kiante and when did sparks fly, were they there when you first saw her?

He pauses and stares at me as he slowly pulls out his wallet and looks at it with a big sigh. While he was going through the motions of pulling out his wallet, I watched each facial expression with inside passion that surfaces through his eyes. I could see the love that I heard with the analogy of his favorite candy bar. He gazes at a small picture that he is fixated on. I only feel that this must be his favorite candy bar. He handed me a picture of a beautiful exotic woman that had a smile that you could feel coming through the picture. She not slim but looks comfortable. She reminds me of a humble wife that cared and loved her husband but had no time for Keith's foolishness. Amazing that old cliché a picture says a thousand words, it did, and it showed through her smile. I looked at her picture so hard that I felt her staring back at me. Not with anger but love in her eyes that match her beautiful smile.

After seeing her picture now more questions are trying to form in my mind. Wow why is Keith baking cookies and not keeping it heated with Kiante? A lady that name is as beautiful as her smile. He slowly takes the picture away and looks at her showing the face of how much he misses her as he places her back into his wallet. Although, I had questions from Keith's expression now was not the time. He tells me that he made a mistake and just didn't know how to correct it and time just lingered on until we are years apart.

She worked hard at a bank and would try to talk to me about her manager. I was too busy or tired to really listen and when I did, she didn't get a good percentage. Rita with some men we listen to about fifty percent and hear about ten to fifthteen. Nothing personal that's just us, no harm but reality. She tried, and I didn't, and I paid the consequences. All she wanted was my time not a lot just a little and I gave her less. There was no reason just me being a jerk then just like now. He pauses as if he is forcing the words as he reflects what happened with their relationship...

I was going to surprise her one day for lunch. No reason just because of me not listening to her, or just because the sun was out, I don't know I just wanted an injection of her, my Kiante. I had a good day at work. I was just appointed to lead supervisor. Funny that I wanted her to hear about my job, but I didn't want to hear about hers. Only time I listened was when she had a sentence with my name included. I took a break from eating my cake and said to Keith must everything be about you? He looks and responded with I guess so. But I didn't think is about... He pauses about her job it was what her manager was trying to do, and he was doing too much. One thing I said in the wrong way just transfer or look for another job, shift. I felt helpless in trying to help her and another added problem. I couldn't do anything, and she liked where she worked and invested long years. She was working there before I met her. I didn't want her to lose her job. She worked too hard to get her promotion. I watched her burning late night candles studying and preparing for her promotion. At the same time making sure dinner was ready and kept me pleased as he winks.

In my mind this man that bakes and shares sound heck of selfish. Keith went on to say it was about me and boohoos feelings. As I look at him, I could see the pain through his selfishness he suffered. She had been overlooked and re-evaluated and reinvented herself and knew she needed a higher education and knew in detail what the promotion entailed. I watched her network and work and work for this promotion. Not one time did she complain. She just wanted me to just listen and I couldn't hear her? That was something she wanted that part of me. You know that something that you couldn't buy at the store. She just wanted that special part of me, my ears.

As I approached her building for lunch, I watched her get into the passenger side of her bosses' car. As he buckled her in, he leans over her and kisses her on the lips. I walk up and just stared at her and him and just cussed them both out. The strange part was I was so numb I couldn't tell you what I said but I'm sure my eyes said it all as I turned away, not hearing her trying to call out my name. Her boss tried to approach me, and he needed to step back before another character came out of me and jail time was not an option. Nah man I would have hurt them both had to step because I wanted to funk him up. I knew what I saw. Words didn't need to try to convince me that it didn't happen; no words or excuse could erase that visual. Those were my lips, my wife, and my boobs. They should only know my touch at that point I felt violated. I had that visual while driving home and that was not part of my program. My ego set in and I just booked. I wasn't home when she arrived and didn't want to talk to her. There wasn't anything she could have said to change my mind. She can have that entire shift, the house everythang. Then her girlfriend/co worker came to my job and bought something strong to me. I looked at her as if you must be fool coming here where I work, talking about nothing and its definitely none of your damn business. Her co-worker Latha tried to tell me that her boss Morton was the reason that she didn't get promoted the first and second time. He had been bothering her for years. I looked at her as if she was lying just being a girlfriend, but inside I knew this must be what Kiante was trying to talk to me about. Again ego, stubborn and me just formed a brotherhood and refuse to listen. I responded back with to Keith with that percentage again, huh. In the back of my mind I wondered if Bill had the same percentage or did, he blah blah my voice like I did his.

Kiante tried to tell me that they had to go to a training class with the district manager of Erika. Erika was new and didn't know about this bank history. She was there to audit and leave. I really didn't want to hear what Latha was talking about. I just wanted to get back to work to keep my mind occupied and not think about what happened. My co-workers were wondering what was going on and jammed me later in form of some type of shop humor. All Latha did was piss me off more. I had to ask why he kissed her. Latha pauses saying he took her by surprise. I told her that pause said a lot. Looking at Keith she probably was thrown off by his facial expression, because this expression he just showed would have through me off into a stutter moment too. I said to Latha, your ass didn't know either, and you came all the way over to my job for what? I could tell by her slow response and her mouth open with no words forming. She really didn't have any type of response. Asking Keith did you give her a chance to explain? And do you think that your actions didn't throw her off also. He hesitated to ponder that thought with the response of I didn't know. Did my ego react to quick?? Her words made me think harder on if I made the right decision to leave, but my gut had a different feeling.

I just shook my head at Latha and said now you can leave. I didn't have anything to say nor did it change my mind. Just wasn't any room for forgiven and I wanted to break Morton's narrow ass neck. In her absence and defense, I said slowly while looking at him, Keith only if you could see your expression you probably surprised her, and scared that poor lady. I've known you for a bit and that look made me tremble. I did a Courtney Diane and Robin move of ooh and put my hand up to my mouth as if I was trembling and scared. Although, he had a slight chuckle I could see that he had to think about that. I shared with him we as women marry for love and are deeply devoted. Kiante may have been preparing hard for her promotion but understand it wasn't all about her it was about the "us "theme. She wanted to support you so you both could have more.

I told him that I knew a couple Jovan and Toni that were married for years. She wanted to better herself, but his ego didn't allow it and it went to some serious extremes. After many trials and pain the one thing they really needed to do was to communicate. Not with a fifty percent listening but hearing each other. Come on now what did you gain by leaving Kiante and not listening to her. And look at you now Keith, living in an apartment with a bunch of men baking. Wow that was something to look forward to when I grow up. You were okay with giving up a beautiful wife God created just for you. She picked up your dirty draws off the floor, cooked and supported your ego, hmmm. Let me recap and understand you gave up your beautiful wife, to stay with your cousin and friend, nice trade. Humph, for some other man to gain at your expense. Now, let me ask you this, if I didn't rave and hmm about your baking would your feelings would or could be hurt Keith, because it's about you right. Did you get your feelings hurt when Clarence or Darryl shows no type of appreciation? I could see it in his face he was absorbing what I was saying this time I had him listening at least more than 10-20 %.

I didn't tell him all about Jovan and Toni. Only that they missed out on many years they could had enjoyed by just communicating. They both wanted an "us" theme, but Jovan's ego, stubborn thoughts, and other issues formed their brother-hood, as I wink but this time, I had a slight smile. He paid the consequences of losing his family, but he regained them by growing up. He gained knowledge and embraced his wife and family, but it was at a cost.

Morton/Melvin/Marlan right, I glance at him as he corrects me by saying Belvin. My response was does it really matter Morton or Melvin/Belvin really whatever just that name along should make you laugh. Where's the threat he had to laugh when I said that. Don't you think Morton/Melvin or excuse me Belvin threw your wife off by his actions? Kiante didn't have time to react to that surprise being confined to a buckled seat and was surprised by your surprise huh. With that conversation I noticed that Keith's expression showed that he was thinking. We both looked at each other raising our eyebrows at the same time. Keith places his finger on his nar-row chin as I look at him and mimic his actions. He had to rub his chin on that one again. I laughed saying you need to rub your head and separate that inside brother-hood group you had formed. Really, I saw that picture of your wife Kiante, and she was smiling for you and you only. Now come on Keith is this where you want to live the rest of your life. Really with no women coming around for you because you have a wife, but you don't live together. It's like being pregnant, either you is or you isn't pregnant. Ooh did Charlotte just pop into that familiar phrase she would say. If you ever started dating a good woman, she doesn't want to hear you are still married.

What woman would want to carry your many problems and thoughts that would require too much energy and emotions? Trust me she wouldn't care what you look like and what you could do. Why should she help or support your indecisive-ness of I'm married or I'm not? Trust me she is not going to allow you to waste any part of her time. Courtney Diane would say I can get a dill pickle from anywhere. Unless it's just a one-night stand then leave the money on the stand. He laughs so you are calling me a ho. I laughed I didn't call you that, but that one-night role did. You wake up alone and, in the end, lonely, baking cookies. Don't get me wrong I'm blessed to have you share your bakings. I do appreciate you and the love you have always shown to me and Sierra. I look at him as I take the last bite saying don't play or stop sharing, because this cake is to smile for, yummy.

He couldn't help trying not to laugh, but his face showed that he was truly lis-tening. I didn't know the percentage, but some percent did show that it stayed. If you love her has time healed? Is she with someone? He hesitated to say nope still in the same place with the same furniture working and attending school. A thought came to mind and I shared it with him. Hmm so she left everything the same way waiting for you to return, to no surprises, no uncomfortable feelings back to the home you two made together.

Hmmm that does sound like a bad, selfish lady huh, with no consideration. Why should you go back to her because she understands you, bad lady huh? At first, he wanted to snap, and he caught himself. We both smiled at each other. So, you are still protective of her huh. That means you still love her. Why are you still here, go home to your wife? Stop punching yourself in the stomach. He laughs at saying what!! Really why are you beating yourself over something that might have been a big misunderstanding and both of you need to talk and straighten it out. Someone must make the move. Kiante did make a move when she sent Latha. Because she knew you didn't want to talk to her. Now is that not special? She involved someone else in her pain and her problems to take the chance of coming to your job to talk to you. Then you send the friend back trembling because of your brotherhood response, hmmmph, call Kiante. If she kept everything the same, she should have the same telephone number. So, you have no excuse if that is what your heart desires and you get permission from the brotherhood that you created or formed to make that call.

We both laughed as I said you have a three to one vote, (with your brotherhood of thoughts). I couldn't tell you really what to do that is your decision either way I support you. Just think about it. In the back of my mind I didn't know why I went there with those words of encouragement or gave my thoughts airtime. I just know I watched Keith's expressions and he was into our conversation. It felt good talking with Keith, as I excused myself giving him a hug which was rare. I took a big chance of Bill and his cousin pulling up. In this case Bill wouldn't try to understand what had transpired earlier. Nope his ego and other emotions wouldn't allow his brotherhood to veto.

I told Keith I enjoyed our conversation, but I better go the bathroom is calling me. I didn't know if he knew the real reason. Fear was still lingering and, I just didn't want to take that chance. We both smiled at each other with knowing we both knew what that smile meant. I left knowing and feeling good that he was going to call Kiante. This time he will listen giving her a higher percentage. Rushing to the bathroom I glanced at the place to make sure it looks presentable for Bill's cousin Loren. It has been some time and I wondered if this unexpected visit was behind one of his many women. That's all we need at this time. I love Loren he is funny, entertaining and really will make someone a good husband when he slows his role and grows up. The apartment looks fine so now its time to throw something together because I know everyone will be hungry. I wouldn't mind serving some of that oatmeal coconut cake that Keith baked. An unusal combination but the outcome was delicious and yummy to Sabrina. I think I heard her stretch with a long burp…

Chapter 33
Welcome Back Cousin Loren

I straighten up the third bedroom even tho it looks like a baby room. Loren needs his privacy and we didn't need to see another man walking around in boxers, eew. Actually, Bill didn't wear boxers; warm up bottom was his form of pajamas. So, ooh no visuals on the boxers.

Right when lunch was almost finished, I hear the noise of keys in the lock and Sierra laughing as if she was being tickled. I could only imagine that it is Loren carrying her and tickling her at the same time. I don't know if she remembers how he would spoil her by carrying her everywhere and buying almost everything she laid her eyes on. He didn't have any children, but he would make a good father again when he grows up, but then again that playful side is what makes him different and fun to be around. I didn't know if he really wants to settle down. He might be enjoying life the way he's living it now, just him and no added responsibilies or added drama. As door opens just what I thought Loren holding onto Sierra and Bill smiling at me in which I am happy to receive with a smile and hug from him. That embrace from Bill felt so good and his body felt so warm. Loren takes his other arm still holding Sierra saying enough of all that kissy and huggy; that's why you have another one on the way.

He reaches for me to give me a hug as well. While letting me know that I still look good. Now that felt good to my ears and my soul. I look at him saying put Sierra's butt down she is too big for you to be carrying her. He laughs as he lowers Sierra and she takes off to her room like she had wanted to walk all this time. It's amazing watching her establish her independence. As the elders would say she is making room for the next one. Her sister will be here soon, and she will officially be a big sister.

Loren compliments me on the aroma in the kitchen and reflects on the days I didn't know how to cook and was burning everything. He had the nerve to ask if I was still making crunchy potato salad? We all laughed because Bill knows that I'm still burning food. In that case nothing has really changed other than my crunchy potato salad. Cooking was not my forte. I had to do on the job training. Bill and Sierra may be slim, but they do not look like they are starving. I went to check on Sierra and she had crashed on the floor. She was so tired she didn't make it to her bed. I whisper to Bill and Loren to come see this. They laugh, and Bill gently puts her in her bed giving her a kiss as he pulls the cover over her just like he does to me. Yep his girls and that move just for us. As I turned around, I put my hand on his shoulder to motion him that lunch is ready. As I looked at Loren and his slim body frame, he rubs his flat stomach saying thank you and how hungry he was. They gathered their plates and head for the kitchen table, and I join them as we all just play catch up. He laughs at Bill saying I didn't think you would never ever infinity get married let alone have a baby and now you have another popping out.

No, I take that back Rita's popping them out you just having fun with the popping that heater that needs to be unplugged. I silently laugh at the thought of Shukeeya Catrice's sister- in- law running out of names and named the tenth one Tenyah. Wow you stop because you ran out of names. I wait for Bill's response wondering what he would say if I popped out that many. Bill smiles man I got the best when I saw Rita in the library. I knew she was the one. Loren laughed everyone in the family knew Rita was the one. You told every and anyone that you found the one. When your ass should have been studying in that library you were too busy studying Rita. Inside I felt giddy and thankful I heard this and that we both were sharing the same feelings we had for each other with our families.

They talked about family and that his brother Akil was married with four children same baby momma, Alice, with little drama. You know my momma, Miss Rosie Josey wondering when will I l be having any children sharing my last name. I keep telling her when I get one you will see her right after me. Her response is stop getting those bargain basements, "save a scants", deals and please stay your butt away from the clearance section mister. I told her I've been listening. I moved up to the first floor, floozies and huzzies. What's wrong with trying every floor until I get to the top, hmm? Now see I have improved. Eventually I will end up at the top floor momma just be patient with the elevator journey. They glanced at me as I chuckled and in doing that they start laughing too. They didn't know I was thinking about what Robin had said about her bargain basement men and remembered she didn't know she had gotten one from the clearance rack because the tag fell out of his forehead. Of course, Courtney Diane would say, with his dumb ass.

As I gathered the dishes, they move to the front room laughing and talking while taking their sodas with them. Loren laughs do you have anything stronger. I laughed back saying ice. He laughs you got jokes Rita, and that's why I love you cuz. Bill turns the television on asking man why are you here, and what really happened cuz? What's really up? Loren stops to pause laughing while asking for some ice cubes to make his drink stronger. He said I was living with this beach Fifi, with that name I should have known she was a beach. As I listened, I hope Fifi was her pet name no pun meant.

I can't stand when moms right. I went to the lower floor and picked up fleas in form of Fifi. I wasn't looking for a beach she raised her leg and found my ass and she knew how to mark the spot. Bill laughs so you were saving a ho and not a scant. Yeah man somebody got to show them some love. I listened and smiled as Bill said if he is a save a ho then who is going to save him. I bet he didn't look at himself as being a man-made ho. Hell naw, didn't know she was one but found out later. I should have known when I saw her squat man. I went back to Oakwood to you know visit the family and the old neighborhood. My home boy Holland was getting married and I was in the wedding. Partied, played got laid and went home early thinking about my Fifi. The married thing just got to me and I knew I needed to slow down and think about getting married. Mom's words kinda played in my mind. Being apart of that wedding had me in serious thoughts. Do you believe that Claudey and Aniteah finally called it and got married? Don't know why after they lived together forever just trying to make it right. Hell, they had enough children in their wedding party there was little to none to add. Don't know and don't care.

So, my boy Virgil / Studs picks me up and I'm all happy and shift ready to see my Fifi, my woman, yeah baby raise that leg, my little spinner. Fifi marks her spot everything to make sure other women know her ass exist, just leaving bracelets in my jackets, or her big ass shoes in my back seat or tool box, but she can't get to the area in my car where I carry the honies numbers. Bill said stuttering Virgil the one we called "Studs", yeah because he stuttered here's still around. That was not what I was thinking of when he said studs, but this I knew would be interesting story to hear. Yep he is still in Chicago anyway. I get out the car walking up to the apartment feeling mighty fine. Cuz, can you believe I had a little thump in my heart thinking about this thang, marriage and all and maybe its time. Now get this my key did work but top locks were locked from the inside and I had no key to unlock them. I know we need locks in Chicago, but we weren't in New York. I yell at her, Fifi come unlock the door!! She yells back that she doesn't have on any clothes. My response was like I haven't seen your fat ass before. I shout back and, open this damn door now!! I tell Virgil; hey Studs take your ass around the back and anything or anyone come out that back door beat the funk out of them. He didn't need to talk just beat his ass. If he did man he'll be-be-be still beat, beat beating his ass da-da, damn ma-ma-ma, man. Bill chimes in with remember that Studs couldn't get the' f' out and end up being uck you ma- ma, man. Then Holland would chime in saying I got you funk you and you and he would point to everyone and dapping Studs saying I got you man. Then Studs responds back with saying than, thank, yo- yo- you. Then everyone would say in sync you're welcome with all us laughing.

Loren laughs he hasn't changed we still support him with his words but all out of love. So eventually my puppy, Fifi opens the door half dressed as if she dressed in a hurry, right beach. I asked her what the funk is going on as I speak, looking at her as she tries to adjust her clothes, calling me by my pet name Lorenzo. She was stuttering with her clothes like Virgil/Studs talks. Virgil brings someone from around the back that he beat the funk out of, and he did mess his ass up. I guess my little puppy, my little reach around wanted the kiss and the cake, what the?? Now Miss Fifi knew how to pull the chain and let the dog come out. I laughed thinking about how he sounds like Momo with her sex antics. Loren takes a sigh break in his laughter as I hear Bill chuckling. Loren said that he looked at Studs and did he handle our business. Studs did, his stuttering ass said I be-be, da- da beat the uck, started to sound out the "F" then changed it to dit out of him per your instructions. I looked at Studs with a nod of let his punk ass go. I looked at her and, in a blink, I left her at the door, telling Studs lets get the funk out of here. I turn around and look at her telling her you can have all this shift beach, I'm audi duces. She was yelling out calling me Lorenzo. I wasn't having it. I go and crash at Studs and Zetta pad.

Studs tries to clown me, stuttering saying Lor- Lor- zo. I look at his stuttering ass saying don't Zetta call you Veggie or the other name duct tape or was it, duckie. I don't want to take my imagination to what's that's about. Now bring your veggie ass on and let's get some gone. Studs being him said yo yo pa-pa-pa point. What you are sleeping, wa-wa with tonight to- to- to with those pa-pa-pillows. Hug on Lolozow, (while laughing). Before he could close the door, he said it's Virgie, lo-lo-lo- zo, Lorenzow. I threw one of the pillows at the door and get this shift when his ass blew me a kiss, the kiss even stuttered, asshole. Then I realized too that I had only two pillows no Fifi. I had one on the floor and if I didn't pick it up the other pa-pa-pillow pillow would be lonely. I got my tired ass out the bed and proudly hugged my pa-pa-pa pillows. He had my ass on that shift Bill. I was crashing soundly at my boys' place, and his ass was right. I was sleeping with the pa-pa-pa pillows tonight, but I'm resting away from that crazy ass puppy. I needed somewhere to crash hard knowing I am not going back to that beach or near my pad. I didn't know where that stalking ass puppy might be hiding.

So, I go to work trying to keep my business my business. Then I look up to see, no I heard, the clopping feet of Fifi and her side kick beach Lucee. Both showing up trying to front bad in front of my boys and my business. I heard their yepping a mile away. They looked like two dogs running the streets. I should have known, just like two little muts yapping, barking, and walking toward me wagging their tails with no kinda of bite. Bill I wouldn't mind both, climbing all over me, but another time and this definitely wasn't the time and sure was not the place. It would have been funny if I wasn't at my business working. My boys/partners and the public were, in front row view of this laughing and shift. Inside I was boiling I wanted to snap their necks but don't do hitting women. These beaches had the nerve to come to my job brandishing a big ass knife, shouting Lorenzo. I guess I was at some point supposed to be concerned uh. Calling me mother of friends and that I'm not leaving her, and I need to bring my ass back home. Who was the funk I think I really was, and she wasn't sorry? Now, these puppies were trying to grow up and run with the big dogs. For a quick second I had to pause and look around to see who the funk she was talking to or was I being punked and being filmed. Cuz someone had to be taping or videoing this shift. This shift couldn't have been really happening. Something had to be going on for her to make this bold ass move.

I guess she had time to think of some sorry ass reason for not coming to the door. She insulted me. Listen and please get this, she said that she couldn't come to the door, because she was getting her hair ready for me. She boldly said that she didn't do anything he was her stylist or some shift like that. What was he curling her scalp, because her ass is damn near bald and she sports a wig or a weave. Even that wig was as twisted as her clothes; her hair showed fright I guess that curling iron put a little friz in that piece of hair.

This thang tried blowing smoke up my ass and try to convince me that it should tiggle, no that shift irritated my ass. She called me so many adverbs that I lost count of the mother of friends, and something needs bleaching. I told her that the "L" train derailed. You know what she said during this entire shift. Who is training derail and Lucee wants to know if he was cute? Let's pause Fifi responds girl not now shut the up, I'll get his number later I got this. I got you girl and we all can do this tonight Cece. I tried to understand hmm Cece and we're going out? Loren added in the midst of clarity where we/us going out to? I'm trying to get my ass, her ass all asses away from my ass.

Lucee/Cece lost all her sentence structure. Cece yelling, like I'm just saying here if he be cute no body calling me uh why not get with Derail?? Loren still laughing saying he had to pause and inside he wanted to laugh at this fool and her side kick. Lucee looked smart until she opened her mouth and the words flowed thru her big ass gap. Bill oh it was hard, but I was trying to keep a straight face had to cuz. Man, I had to put on some restraints. Shut the up and get you and your paw pal out of here. The more I listened increased to her foolishness the more I wanted her ass out. What the hell she talking/yacking about training what the?? She had me pause to think what the funk she heard me say. Did she listen to the full sentence and the contents?

What the funk did they both share the same brain and ears. We are in the middle of a heated but calm discussion and she is talking about some type of crazy training with derail. Why and how could she come up with training derail and Lucee asking if he's cute? Not with that big ass gap in the middle of her teeth. How does she hold the food in her mouth? Look like it took effort to keep the gap concealed by keeping her mouth closed which looked like it was hard as hell. Were they both sharing the same brain? As I listened, I had to think about how did she get, train derailed to train derail? I guess she didn't hear the "ed" on the end, but I guess if you say it slow enough hmm that's scary, but funny. I continued listening in amusement about Fifi laughing that was a good one, train derail, humph.

Now this chick is at my job putting my business on display for the public front seat amusement and oh hell yea the boys were laughing, and walking like her. Patting their heads switching and shift saying I thought his name was Loren. They took turns completing the sentences saying nah girl his name be Lorenzo grrrrr. My boys were laughing at Fifi and Lucee's dumb ass. Bill they were performing acting like they were waiting for the "L" train, or a bus or something. They just stood there looking both ways as if they were looking for the train or bus to arrive. Did they forget that they work for my ass? They were playing and pointing at the two guys mocking Fifi and Lucee saying they were looking for the train derail was on, because they didn't see Derail get on the train. What train did he get on, the train that derailed? Saying is Derail cute motioning tell him call me girl. In the midst Cece asking you think he's gonna call me, make sure you give him my number. My boys are yepping with their mouths open laughing with no more words coming out because they were too busy laughing and mocking them. Now they looked cute, but this had to end before it got too hilarious and not at my expense. Actually, their walk was better than Fifi and Lucee's switching. Their walk looked like some type of limb swing off a tree.

I looked at her and calmly smoothly walked away as she followed me calling me mother of friends as the laughter faded away. Man, I didn't say a word just walk, no talk and moving, with just enough swag. You know that Chicago calm. I calmly go to my car. Fifi might have thought I was going to my car to grab a rag to wipe stupid off my forehead and maybe ask her to wipe the dump off the back of my head. Bill if she was a man, I would have beat her ass, but reality set in that I had a riding partner. Slowly I pulled out my little buddy that hangs out with me occasionally" little Loman", give him some airtime. Maybe Miss Fifi thought that I would be shivering in a corner holding my ass and shift, (he catches himself pointing to his middle area). Bill calmly laughs and adds to the story by saying do you think she left without her medication. She left without something but manage to grab that big ass knife before she left. Loren looks at Bill with this question, now a bullet if I'm correct can beat out a big ass knife huh. What you think now I could be wrong. I watched as he turns his head showing that signature smile. He said he turned first to her friend Lucee as I stretched my arm out. Lucee takes off don't know what direction. I just heard the pidder padder of her big ass feet breaking wind. She ran away with some speed and dust saying don't forget Derail's number. Her words faded into the wind. She got on the Dan Ryan express without a car. Don't know or didn't care what direction she went in my eyes were on the prize Fifi. She froze, and her ass didn't break a blink and neither did mine.

As I looked and listened, I could only imagine that those almond shaped eyes didn't have the know twinkle present. Now I told her that I had been enough mother of friends and all other adverbs she wanted to add. I look at her face she was so scared she pees, man she pisses on herself. I kept my eyes on her only to look down at the puddle not blinking just wanting her to understand what my audi means.

After I thought about it, she probably didn't know what I meant about adverbs with her stupid ass. Just like saying who trained Derail even he had to laugh as I walked away from her and her puddle. I told you man she could raise that leg, squat and all and told her to get the funk away from here. Cuz I swag back into my shop with my boys looking at me laughing, shaking, wiggling, switching all that shift. The only thing I could come up with because my mind was still on that shift that Fifi tried to pull was aren't ya asses getting paid. In sync they said yep and getting entertained too. Then they added is there something wrong? As I walked away shaking my own head their laughter faded into small conversations as my own thoughts was, I need to get some temporary distance from this place. It was at that point I knew I had to advance from the basement and try other floors. Get in the wind via American/Delta/Southwest somebody's airlines, bus or train. I had to, I needed to get out of here fast before that feline circles back with her crazy ass family.

Loren smiles slightly as he continued talking about advancing from the basement. I chime in saying what if the product is slightly damaged or that floor is closed. He pauses given a glimpse of thought saying. There's always room for improvement, but I will pass on the floor where renovation is needed or in the progress. That was when I said its, time to take a break and I decided to fly out here. I needed to get away from that drama and come to Cali to see my favorite cousin, his beautiful wifey and my favorite baby cousin Sierra. I had to get some gone and go somewhere I could mentally chill and shift. Loren apologizes for the profanity. I smiled and looked over at him saying you were upset or still recovering from that derailment. He glanced at me and said oh you got jokes too. With a smile he didn't know that I had substituted his words. I do it all the time. I had become very fluent in changing the profanity. Normally I get a headache substituting words when I am around Courtney Diane and he was an amateur compared to her. Sometimes she would create her own words. She hasn't used too many lately. I guess those online anger management classes are working. Although, she doesn't smoke she would probably want a cigeratte after hearing Loren use her favorite word "funk". Loren was no where near that headache that Courtney Diane would unknowingly give me along with being amused.

I laughed as I thought about the conversation, I had with Clarence about his brother Steve and the woman he was staying with. Their mother Gilda had busted Steve antics and sounds like she didn't give it a second thought. He was living with a nice girl and that loved his trifling butt. While visiting their mom made some observations that she bought to the attention of Karen. She told her women would come by while she was at work. Karen asked how long they stayed, and she said long enough. She really like Karen and couldn't support the wrong. Mother Gilda corrected it right into a surprise when Steve came home from work. Words were exchanged between Karen and Steve with her exiting and leaving him forever. She didn't return not even a phone call or a courtesy kiss my ass. That fool was with Karen for over twenty years. She would help with moms when she was sick, what the, as he just shakes his head. Brains will not be his legacy.

Only thing he could do was look at his mom and ask -why. Her response was simple; I didn't like it, but I liked her. Their parents were short on words but in the same breath got their point across. Thinking to myself while in my own glaze, I couldn't believe that Steve said he loved Karen, and that he was faithful because he didn't love those other women. Now I had to take a partial thought or a saying from Courtney Diane, what button did he push that shot an infray dumb ass thought, like that into his empty dumb ass skull, (and she meant skull no brain included). Steve had residual of giving that thought/belief airtime by saying it out loud into the airways with his dumb ass. I had a frozen thought of that really was a dumb ass philosophy, like is you is or is you not pregnant, (courtesy of Charlotte). Courtney Diane phrases played so much in my head as I listened, and the timing was just right. Like when she said that you give me too much credit for thinking of you that way, but it you do alter my name put Miss in front of it so we both can pretend we have, a mutual respect. With adding expression that was a woo, because she was very clear, (coming out of the corner of her mouth showing a slight dimple). It wasn't that she didn't have any feelings well minus the "s". She made it clear that her philosophy was that, she didn't have a game piece to place on a game board for blue skies games, and that no chance in hell was she going to be a game piece placed on the board game called blue skies. Can't stand the aroma of blue skies it clashes with the scent of my perfume. Courtney Diane made it clear that she paid too much for this shift to have blue skies over power her fragrance. She was always calm when mentioned if someone thought she was threating them. Her response was clear like everything she ever said since I've known her. Courtney Diane would say that threats nah that's giving up too much information and a waste of her time. If it's going to happen no warning is neither needed nor necessary.

Chapter 34

Between Loren and Clarence
There is no Boredom

Clarence had me again smiling and laughing inside about his family as I cleaned up the kitchen and phased in and out of what Bill and Loren were talking about and their words turned into a blah blah blah. When his father Jerry had surgery, they had taken out his two front teeth. When Clarence arrives to the hospital his father asks where was his two front teeth? He explains to his father that they had to remove them for a reason, come on dad he had to have a reason. He convincingly said that they didn't want them to fall out during surgery, and his father's response was oh now you some damn doctor or a dentist. Take your narrow ass and go out there and find me my two front teeth. Come on dad he said that the two front teeth were rotten. He said dad they took them out for a reason. His dad firmly/strongly repeated you a dentist/doctor go out there and find my two front teeth. He could only say I had dentures that were attached to my two front teeth. I only had five teeth now I'm minus my two front teeth. His father said it slow, with firm understanding of go and find that damn doctor and find out where they put my two front teeth.

I tried to hold it in so Bill and Loren didn't think I am losing it over here and they wouldn't find laughter in what I was thinking as I held back the tears from laughing, plus I wouldn't be busted for talking to Clarence. Clarence tries to reinforce the reason for removing his two front teeth. Jerry is not feeling the reasons for removal of his two front teeth, not amused and reinterates the reason for the need of his two front teeth, (raising his eyebrows that look so familiar). He said slowly you're not fully understanding me. When I go and collect my money, I need to have my two front teeth. I'm not having my tongue fitting snug in that space where my two front teeth belong. Apparently, what you are not hearing and what I am trying to tell you. I got to make my collections because they still owe me my money. Jerry said on Wednesdays I get on the bus and make my collections. Clarence says dad you still doing that? What the funk Clarence look at me I need my two front teeth. I see the the facial expressions on Clarence face as he quotes his father.

At the same time, I'm reflecting on Emma Jean taking Mommy's teeth and was caught playing with them as our mother tried to deny they were at her house. My mother was busted, because my sister EJ was trying to put Mommy's full set of dentures in her mouth onto her full mouth of teeth, (she had mommy's two front teeth attached to many). I'm laughing harder with tears rolling down my face as Clarence moves his head with his signature eyebrow raise continuing the task of the missing two front teeth, looking and saying what his father kept saying. Do you think they would take me seriously, when I go collect my money with me missing my two front teeth? I run a collection agency, meaning I collect my money. So just like when he had to think quick on a cheeseburger hold the cheese he went and found the doctor that performed the surgery to explain why his two front teeth were missing. I just remembered asking through my laughter did you find his two front teeth. I reflected on the expression Clarence had when he responded that no they threw his two front teeth away and, he said it as slow as he was saying the way his father said about his missing two front teeth. So silly me asked what happen to his two front teeth?? What the hell Rita, which was what Clarence, always said after my response to many questions. He sent Steve out to collect while he was waiting for his dentist to replace his two front teeth. What the funk Rita. I just laughed because I had to know what happened to his two front teeth…

I chime back in on Bill and Loren's conversation. Loren was laughing at how Fifi would carry a brick in her purse for just in case and that just in case came when she busted his car window for being in the wrong place. According to her, she pulled the brick from out of her purse and broke my damn windows. Man, I don't know if she used the same brick prior. The only window she left was the windshield and don't think her crazy ass didn't try. I saw the chip marks on the windshield. What is wrong with the brick carrying puppy? Cuz there should be some bricks missing from the back of her house, grill or something. Where is her crazy ass getting these bricks from, damn? Let me take that back she carries one brick in her purse and rocks in her smaller bag just to throw at my windows. Her house should be having some type of leaning motion, from collecting and removing bricks. Hell, her house should be ready to cave in if she keeps pulling them from the same spot. Unless it's the same recycled brick she carries in her purse for her crazy ass antics. Something wrong with their family if they don't notice the lean, don't notice something missing.

I flashback to when my mother threw a brick through my father's window. I couldn't understand that logic other than it felt good for that minute or second. But the next day someone had to pay for it and it came from the family account. Kinda reminds to of the logic of why some of my friends enjoyed getting high. There you go with that temporary feeling, because it feels good. That was always the answer or get high to avoid my mental questions or the answers I try to avoid. Couldn't understand why you would pay for something that smells and for a product that alters your brain and at the same time make you look silly. That would be a nope tried it one time on a half or a puff puff pass a joint. My world spinned all night and I didn't like that feeling. Although, I only did a few puffs with my friends, didn't matter I still got high. They were true friends and didn't try to apply any type of peer pressure. We would laugh at the names they would call me like square and there we go again with my name being altered. I would laugh adding I'm the one driving you all home. We would laugh it off, but they never stopped hanging out with me. I didn't cave into peer pressure and we are still friends, some thirty years later. Only one time, Bill tried to have me do a line of cocaine, nope I played it off and squeezed my nose like I saw on television but that wasn't me either. I can find other ways to blow what little mad money I had. Didn't do it then and later I'm glad I didn't get caught up in doing something to just be accepted. I had to learn more about myself with a sober mind not one that's all polluted.

I like watching Bill and Loren enjoy their conversation through their laughter and it was a good sound to my ears other than hearing him fuss, cuss and critizing me every chance he had. I heard Loren laugh louder through his confession while saying I had to laugh because that was me dude and it was worth it, thank God for insurance and an innocent lie. I glance over at Loren and watch him act out his words and actions as if he is reinacting the scenes from his life story. They talk about women and drama. Funny how the men have us beat, they just don't like the word drama but that's just what it is. Drama is drama they just don't like that word to label their emotions.

Loren said that he told Fifi my little puppy that I was at my boy's house passed out after playing poker all night. Luey P didn't want me to drive in my delicate condition and you wouldn't either would you. So, if you called, I didn't hear the phone or you breaking out my windows. I was drooling and knocked out on his couch. Baby why didn't you come to the door and see for yourself? You would have seen my mouth open passed out on his couch. Open door bam, right there, sound asleep, (of course I could see her weakening as Loren's eyes and dimples played their part). I had to smile he was really working that scene, humph no drama he should write a script or a song. That morning I'm afraid that you would think I was with some other woman. I was thinking of you and wanted to drive home in my delicate condition to see my Fifi. Luey P saw that I couldn't focus and, him being a good friend allowed me to crash at his pad and his wife Danette gave the go ahead. You know she normally doesn't let just anyone stay or want all our noise up in her house. Yep she was there, and no crazy would be happening in her house. Bone was there, and he offered to give me a ride home but me being the caring person I didn't want to put D-Bone out of his way. You know he moved to the northside. My little puppy

I had to remind her that D-Bone/Vince or Vincent (sounded like Marvin), but oh well it's his story; he's not Victor or Carl. As I listened looking out the window at the rain I pondered if I should ask what D-Bone mean. Will it fall into the family of Courtney Diane or something silly like when I heard Studs thinking it was maybe sexual and it was as simple as because he stuttered. I remembered how I stuttered, and my mother helped me by having me reading books out loud and speech classes at school wasn't special just needed some assistance. Teachers cared and went that extra yard to get the help you needed.

Bill chimes in with a question showing on his face I thought Bone was Victor nah you confused him with Finley. I try not to laugh to hard thinking back on I knew a Finley. My father wanted me to date and maybe marry him. Finley had no neck and I would laugh as I told my father did, he want a bunch of no neck grand-children. I vaguely remember his expression of how he kinda pondered that thought and he never mentioned it again. Loren smiles saying I did that to funk with her ass, I was feeling it. She asks who else was there I named off every name she didn't know but tried to convince her she did. I watched her expressions and I knew she was getting confused trying to remember as I kept calling out imaginary names. I had to remind her, (as he wink, winks), of Marco, Melvin's little brother. You know you wanted hook him up with your girlfriend Lucee but too late he's married, and Herman the one you thought was related to Preston they asked about you and told me to tell you what's up. Hmm they remember you.

I knew I was messing up my little Fifi's mind and game plan and my ass kept that shift up. Ty still wants to talk to your sister Skyler. He's a good guy, (wink, and wink). Your girlfriend Lucee is too much for him, he's quiet don't date much and a home body. Hey, I was surprise he made it, cuz all he does is work. If it wasn't for the poker game and not a party, he would still be hanging out at home alone, all alone, (as he puts his head down with puppy looking eyes). Every question she had I had an answer, bam, of course accompanied with a big sexy smile. Oh, an occasional puppy eye looks or when needed. Since she was a fifi, (puppy/feline), I knew that was something she could identify with. I looked at her trying to straighten out the names. And I kept throwing some that didn't even exist. I kept on throwing those balls all type of shift at her as she stutters saying I thought your buddy, Dirkey moved from the northside. My response with a straight face was babe who's Dirkey, (I look at his smiling face while he's raising his eyebrows), knowing I know Daly, hell why not I was on a roll. Her ass deserves all those curve balls, for breaking up my shift with a brick and throwing all those verbal adverbs.

I should have snatched her small purse. The one that she carries the smaller rocks that she used for throwing rocks at my windows, to see if I'm home or with someone other than her in my bed. Bill's expression through his laughter shows he knows he was more in a lie than innocent. They both say must have been Friday,

because that's the day I'll tell you anything. He laughs saying Loren was she someone I know. No man a friend I met at his card party/poker game, so you see it was
worth it. My little puppy, Fifi felt bad and confused as he raises his eyebrows showing the family signature dimples and beautiful almond shaped eyes that had just
a little twinkle. There whole family had fine cousins. His brother Akil became a
gynecologist now you can't get any closer to women than that. Again, they were fine,
and I just smile and can only imagine the number of women coming after them.

A fresh hair cut always did it for me. Hearing him talking about haircuts makes
me smile. Everyday Bill is clipping at his hair its amazing he didn't have any bald
spots showing. I tuned back into hear Loren still talking about his haircut. Teague's
place was already crowded. Then it happened again. I had just got my hair cut from
"Youngblood's place walking out with a honey trying to shout out that had been
looking at me. This hottie had a body from the neck down. She was not my type.
I need her to be from head to toe my brothern. She had back much back but the
front cuz just didn't match. He repeats laughing harder saying the front and back
just didn't match. Man, from the back I just knew this would be the next Mrs. Loren
with those child bearing hips and butt. I just knew my Mama Rosie Josey would be
mighty happy knowing grandbabies were on their way. You know cuz, my Mama
Rosie Josey can show off those grandbabies and make her proud and shift. This girl
had a butt you just had to smack and attack and just lay it on back, humph. Why
did she have to turn around? She just pops that vision, blew all thoughts away and
made me numb.

Then to make it worse loud mouth Fifi runs up barking and yepping like some
little puppy, raising her leg trying to mark her territory and shift. What she needed
to do was squat her ass down somewhere and leave me alone. I laughed, danced,
while singing and didn't know I was singing out loud. Bill and Loren glanced over
at me probably thinking I'm laughing at them, but for instance I did think that Fifi
broke up his game pieces. I was in and out of my world of thoughts. I went back to
what I was originally laughing and giggling about. I was reflecting on what Robin
and I had made up when we were chanting about Courtney Diane/Sonya when
she's on the runway. Come on Miss hottie hottie your working that body, body.
Then she would smile, and we would make click sound and then the song would go
into a hum. That vision just made my spirit dance. When I thought about Courtney
Diane's signature walk and it was a walk of woo, that I'm sure people paid attention
to. Her walk wasn't cocky but confident with that demand of respect. I think any
where she went, she would have heads turning. Imagining her walk and the runway
moves brightens up my day. That had me rocking and shaking and I didn't know
they could hear me, and they paused and glanced over and laughed as I paused
back saying what? They turned back to their men talk or temporary men room or
bonding and Loren surprised that Fifi would just happen to be driving by. With a

puzzled look Loren questioned himself with, did she have some type of GPS on my ass? Get this shift I don't think she slowed her car down she jumped out. Man, she moved so fast I don't think I heard the brakes brake. What is wrong with this fool?

Oh, damn here we go again she got the big brick purse. She gets out and starts shouting those famous adverbs again holding her purse. Man, I looked at that purse and its looking heavy cuz. It looks brick heavy oh damn again, shift rocks. That crazy lady would throw rocks at my window, when she had the smaller purse. I'm thinking its hailing outside. Fifi dumb crazy ass just wanted to see if I would come to the window or if I was alone. If it wasn't for her tricks, I should have left her crazy ass then. I couldn't believe this shift is not normal, does she have another brick in her purse, or is the same recycled one from last time. Cuz come on does she carry them in a back pack in her car, or on her utility belt or store them in her trunk what the funk cuz and take out as needed and put in her purse. Who does that crazy ass shift but Fifi? I had to calm her ass down before we both would be in his and hers jail cells. I heard myself trying to explain to her crazy brick throwing ass that I wasn't trying to yell at that woman. I didn't know that lady, she was trying to shout at me. She had nothing I wanted not a thang. Who would want to talk to my ass with this brick throwing carrying beach? The funny thang I cared for her crazy ass.

Man, I should have gone to the back of her house to see if there were some bricks missing. That house should have some type of leaning going on. Man, I'm not kidding then he laughs singing a lean back while his slim body leans back with that family smile. That whole family is crazy. I just went halfway to Fifi's backyard and saw a sleeve hanging from the grill. What the funk was that about burning somebody shift. Found out it was her dad's clothes. She said it like this shift was natural/normal. Father had what she called an interlude and got busted and her mother invited him to a barbeque and burned his shift on the grill. Her crazy momma made it simple act of something had to be done and she did it and went on with her day. Her momma told the dad, now you can take your "interlude", your bag of ashes since she wants parts of you. Now she can have a barbequed ern of your clothes. Bill, I had to ask, what the hell does that family use that backyard for and where did they get those whack ass philosophies from. Burning clothes on the grill, leaning ass house what the funk. I had to laugh but I don't think they heard me this was some cuckoo drama carrying bricks and barbequing clothes.

Thinking back on the rock throwing people Clarence talked about I think it was Kinney and the Uptongood family of bullies. He's right that is not normal she is beyond crazy and cuckoo. I think Fifi had Courtney Diane beat. Pandora's family hitting husband with irons, phone or whatever was near, or handling their anger when it comes to their men, but they might run neck and neck with Fifi's family. Ooh bricks that is worse than carrying a bat. Fifi must have a good throwing arm. She needed more than an embrace; she needed an anger management class or just go straight embraced jacket via Bellevue. Loren still talking and laughing saying, man that crazy ass Fifi my little puppy, she would go through my clothes, holding them up and sniffing and shift, holding up to her little puppy name. She would look through my phone trying to check every message and timing every place I went. I've been in this game long enough to know to have a backup phone and turn if off when I get home and hide it where I know she won't look. This beach was crazy, and I dealt with her and her drama but for her to try and trick me oh hell no. Bill asks where and they both look at me because I can feel their eyes and their unexpected silence. Loren laughs at Bill saying if I tell you cuz I got to kill you and I got nothing but love for you.

Bill asked did all those relatives show up at the wedding and reception or just the reception. What Holland had about 100 brothers and sisters? Bill, man it was a lot of them all looking the same, just in different sizes, shapes and height. Hey Bill, you remember when Holland came over for dinner and he was guarding his food eating with two forks. One fork for eating and the other fork just straight up in his hand for protection, wrapped around his plate guarding his food. I just remember moms looking at us and saying only that Rosie Josey way, boy where you been in prison or did some juvenile time? Holland politely said, no ma'am we just had so many in our family that eating was a job. We had to guard our food from each other because my brother and sisters would take each other food and you were on your own if you starved. So, I had to protect my food with an extra fork for just in case, because they would snatch your food with quickness. It wasn't safe to leave the table to use the bathroom.

This made me think about dinner time at Catrice and Greekum house or when all the families get togethers. Bill yells out snap do you remember when Holland said his dad would come home late after working long hours and loved to funk with them. He would wake all of them up and do an all clean on the bedrooms. With full military inspections room, walls, corners all had to clean. All twelve of them would line up against the walls sleepy because it was a school day. Moms tried telling him that they had to get ready for school. He looks down the whole row of them and back at moms and says I guess they better hurry up then, as he enters his bedroom and takes his nap until its time for the full room inspections. I had to think back maybe my mother burning our toys was not so bad compared to being awaken out of a dead sleep on a school day. Wow parents must be universal in issuing out whatever discipline. The one thing they did mention was they got their butt up out of bed not like the difficulty that Rhona had when Aunt Brandi insisted on her getting her more than ample ass up. Aunt Brandi repeated herself, but Holland's dad I'm sure didn't repeat himself. I don't think he ever repeated himself. Just like at my house my dad only yelled our name once. Fear is fear in any one's household. My fear was in form of Bill. I watched and listened to them laughing and talking. It felt good hearing the laughter while enjoying Loren being here.

I missed seeing my cousin Cliffy and enjoyed him making that long trip to see us. That eventually faded away but not the love we have for one another. This was good, and we are all happy and enjoying the day. Blessings come in so many ways and ours was in form of Loren and Fifi. Hmm imagine carrying a purse of bricks for just in case and keeping them in the trunk. I guess just in case has different meanings for different situations. What will be my, just in case? As I finish the kitchen Bill turns his head toward me saying come on in here and join us. I welcome that offer and tell him let me go in and check on our daughter. I glance in there and she was as tired as she was when Bill's parents visit and wore her out.

As I walked pass Bill, he grabs me and pulls me to fall on his lap. Now that was a twist and that attention was a big surprise and I loved it. In the back of my mind I was laughing like a little girl do it again again please, so I don't forget the feeling. Loren laughs see that's what I want, that love and laughter and the way you support each other. In the back of my mind I was wondering who and what was he talking about. Were we beamed up somewhere and returned to our humble apartment, more loving? Was this a front, was I awake or was Bill really trying to change and bring life back into our marriage. Either way I enjoyed the moment, the minute, the hours as I embraced the attention to hold on to. I laugh it off through my confusion, while my insides are telling me to just enjoy and don't go cuckoo.

I shook my butt on his lap as I move and set next to him. Bill puts his hand on my thigh and the warmth penetrates my body into my soul and every part of me is feeling this. It felt as if my body, soul and spirit formed their own sisterhood and said ah. Just like a cool tall glass of fresh squeezed lemonade. Sabrina was feeling the extended warmth and starts moving. I place Bill's hand on my stomach, so he could feel her movement. Loren was observing us and smiles as his expression showing that he was pleased at what's happening while being in deep thought. I let him feel her kicking and he snaps his hand back just like Bill did the first time he felt his daughters' movements.

Sabrina must love sweets when I eat them it seems as if she is jumping for joy then calms down to peaceful rest. It feels funny but at the same time she is developing her own personality, because Sierra did not like sweets in any form. This was a picture moment I needed to capture. Only if Loren knew what was sometimes happening in our household, but he doesn't need to know, ever. Let him keep his captured picture with him. I will have plenty of pictures just like I have of Sierra. Just takes some time and money to get them developed but their pictures will be balance. Unlike my baby picture, well you can't call me a baby. I'm about three or four years old, sitting on one leg and that is the only sign to show I was born. Here I go again an insert and the friend of the family that just happened to drop in on picture day.

Loren looks around with the calm energy with questions showing all over his face. He asked what was on the agenda tonight or while he was here. I/we got to do something other than chill. Bill responded with your ass just got here what do think you might or like want to do. He smiles, and he cuddles me you know I'm married. I smile yeah Loren you know he is married. Loren looks at us saying you know that I am right here I can see you both, and remember I was in the wedding. We both say yeah, and you left with one of the bridemaids. Loren smiles and looks so busted but still wanted to meet and greet some new friends. I like this family laughter time. Bill is feeling family too I can see and feel his spirit. I place my hand on his thigh and feel the warmth penetrating from his thigh and the gentle rhythm from his heart beat and the beat was strong and for me. I melt inside and shiver at the warmth that we are sitting together with family and feeling the moment.

I am really loving this and love seeing Loren again and listening to his antics with women. Fifi was the best story, actually better than the one that talked so loud, that she had you questioning your own hearing. Then everyone around her started talking loudly and they sounded like they were trying to talk at a concert or were mad at each other. Then there was the the one he said had more hair on her chest than his or the one that bit him. Not to mention when he chose Cecelia over Suzette in which she responded with trying to sharpen her knife on his arm. Then Cecelia left him for a younger man, so he went back to Suzette who welcomed him back. Then Loren traded her in for a younger model name Chinwe. Fresh off the plane from Florida and didn't know about his wee bit of history but she found out through Regina, Sareena and Suzette. They really didn't know about how his dating seasons work. In the spring he looks for his ladies and if that didn't happen, he waits until next spring to try again and enjoy the summers being foot loose and fancy free. Loren winks while smiling saying he will be making some new friends. He must have felt something for her, becasue Fifi last past spring, summer and made it to winter. She made it through all the seasons. At a glance I can still see the residual in form of scars she left with Loren. Hard to believe he could be wounded. I wondered if Bill has any wounds or capable of being emotionly wounded. Many women, many tales like Clarence's smorgaboard of women, did feelings ever come into play. Clarence said he had many cultures all in one state and he loved putting them to sleep.

They reminisce tales of the good ones that got away and years later he reflects with some regrets. I'm enjoying the affection that changed from crumbs to a full piece of something that I could taste and enjoy the flavor. But what will be the flavor of the day or during Loren's brief stay. I love Bill and maybe it's just because and I just need to be patience with just because. Like Mama Sadie said he did ask but sometimes I wonder what I answered to by innocently saying yes? We hear Sierra wake up and she comes and jumps in Bill's lap and you can feel the proudness of having his family right there next to him. I ask if she was hungry and she just wants to feel the warmth of her dad just like I was feeling. Loren smiles as he starts speaking to Sierra just changing the direction of the previous adult only conversation.

Sierra responds but you can tell some of the sentences he just didn't understand. We laugh because you just go with the flow of her words. Sierra is always so serious as she tries to hold a conversation, such a big mind for such a small body. Sierra snuggles more into Bill as if she is trying to find her spot on his chest. He squeezes my leg to confirm that he was feeling us. That gives me a jilt that penetrates my heart placing a smile on my soul, and with that rush I let out a sigh as if it was from my spirit. Both Sabrina and I were both in agreeance on that emotion. I don't know what Bill was thinking but I do know what I am feeling. This time I'm not confused and no fear of what might happen when the door closes when we are left alone. Many things have happened on this couch from intimacy to me sitting here alone channel surfing to balancing myself after being knocked to the floor. So, the pleasure, pain and comfort have an added more memories to hold. Today the memories will be placed in the archives for just in case, and this quality time will not be wasted on nonsense. Loren changes the mood and suggests that we go out to eat his treat. Bill laughs at who could turn that down free 99 and Sierra smiles but doesn't move from the comfort of her dad's embrace or her spot on his chest. In sync Bill and I asked where he wanted to go or what did he have the taste for? Loren laughs I still and see that you both are in sync, just food and the night life in Cali. You know cuz this is my first time to California.

In my mind I know what that means family time, then lonely time for me. He wants to hit the streets. In which was understandable he's young and needs to erase Fifi raising her legs. This time I didn't mind because he would keep Bill out of trouble and Bill would be busy keeping him out of trouble. With that combination my sisterhood was at peace. This was like a drive through, go out and eat then drive us home and drop us off and keep it moving, minus two passengers. I didn't have the taste for anything, just hoping that I could eat and enjoy whatever they decided on and the aroma wouldn't make me earl. Sabrina is very picky about her food and will let me know immediately if she doesn't like the smell or taste. We ponder together what or where we wanted to go. With so many appetites Applegees or IHop or any other place will work. I look at the time and it's too late for PataRees and I don't feel comfortable enough to suggest ShaRoberts, might be too expensive.

Sierra still looking so tired and the day it almost up, I suggest that we try tomorrow. In that instance Bill and Loren agree and suggest that they just go and get take out. In the back of my mind they just want to get out and spend some talk time that they couldn't do here. Their mobile man cave, I guess. I do a Courtney Diane and smile out the corner of my mouth saying you two just need to get in the streets. They both busted showing their dimples as if I caught them in their opportunity to get away. Sierra says that she wants to go with her daddy. I smile and say well the air is fresh and you can spend some time with Cousin Loren. She giggles and runs over to him giving him such a big hug and he caves into her affection asking her where she wanted to go for her surprise. In her small voice and innocence says surprise me Cousin Loren, while squeezing his hand and pulling him at the same time saying your funny and I just love you. That really got him, and he melts even more into her small hand that's pulling him. They both look at me as if they were saying you got us, and my look was yep, good. I recommend that maybe tomorrow we can ride over to PataRee's, at hearing that Sierra lights ups saying I can play with Mackey again. Bill looks at me with ah what was this place. I respond to his expression saying that remember I told you about the sisters and their husbands own restaurants at this strip mall and parents own the business in that same area. Remember I told you they had invited us to Shanta and Chantell's birthday party and that Sierra was invited to Chantell sister Carrisa's god-son Ryan's birthday party and we couldn't stay. I look at him as he tries to refresh his memories and just says right just for me to stop at trying to remind him.

I found myself getting excited just as if I was Sierra looking forward to seeing them again. Kinda of what Loren did to Fifi minus the just messing with you name game. I didn't mind making a sacrifice today for going back to PataRees and seeing Sheree and her husband Pat and maybe Shanta and Joel might be there and their brother Curtis Alan or Alan. Oh yes and maybe meeting their parents Gordon Maurice and Robin Denise hmm that rhymes might be there.

Are they related to Courtney Diane's family, funny with a "y." wow can't believe how excited I'm getting just seeing them and the place again? The route we take I hope it doesn't go pass Haven's Place. That's all I need for Sierra to blurt out that was going to be our new home and there were twins, I was playing with and what were their names again Rita acourse not mommy. That was a silent moment I didn't want Bill to know or must explain to him with Loren being ear shy away. Any other time Sierra doesn't really talk around people. I hope if we pass by Haven's Place this will be one of her times where she holds true to her words. Sierra had a habit that when she didn't want to speak and when the person would leave, she would say with a straight face that she didn't feel like it. I want Bill to see how a family works together and how young they are making it work as a couple and that I'm developing connections too.

They load up and this is my opportunity to check on Momo. I haven't seen her all week and I must do my daily hey. As I walk over to her apartment little Tim talking and playing with another little boy. I thought I heard him call him Vris which I think he was saying Chris. His English is sounding better and just love looking at his energy and very giving innocent nature. His Aunt Natalia or maybe his mother Eula/Helen glances out the window as I smell the aroma of stew or something with beef. It's so strong I don't know if it's coming from Momo which was good that means she is up to cooking. Amos answers the door with a towel hanging off his belt. I can only assume that he was the one trying to cook. Is he now flipping and flopping burgers or trying to fry chicken? He motions me in the only way he has done since I've known him of hi and looks over at Momo who is sitting in the recyliner in a sort of daze. Although she seems dazed the pleasant facial features still exist. Amos was a man of very little words, but it showed in his eyes the love he has for Momo. When she hears my voice, her expression lightens up maybe she might be thinking I have Sierra with me, but that's a nope I have her sister riding shotgun. I return a smile and rush over to give her a kiss and hug. I missed her, and she shows the same reflections in her face. She talks better but still a little slower and I must be patient in trying to understand what she is saying. All I know was now that I am here, she finds the energy to fuss at Amos as he makes every attempt to struggle and try to cook. He had more flour on him and the floor than on the food he was slowly burning; at least I know the smell wasn't coming from here. I set down telling her about Bill's cousin Loren was visiting and the baby was doing fine, and Sierra will come over tomorrow and bug her. I look at her and I feel so much love for her, but it makes it hard to see her like this. I missed seeing; all the energy she had and making sexual antics with the food while she's cooking with her little body moving and shaking as she hums while preparing her food and fussing at her boys.

How would she say it, you hungry boys and they would say yep, ready to eat yep then hold that thought and eat don't matter what it is its food. She never skipped a beat it was always the same rountine and now it's changed just temporary. She will bounce back her eyes and spirit were telling me it will happen just don't know when. At anytime she will be back to her Momo self, loud, laughing and dancing to any tune she has placed in her heart and mind. I think back when I first met her, and she was trying to talk to me. Her energy threw me off at first because it was different for me sex, food, yelling all that was who she was and is. She still has life just for now in a different way. Her way her time and she will pull out of this; she is too much of a fighter. I loved looking at her cook with so much love and passion as she measured or just threw stuff together without a sweat and laughed at me when I asked for details on how to prepare a meal.

My mom Sheryl laughed too because I didn't spend too much time in the kitchen. I was out having fun while Bonnie was helping and learning how to cook from stratch. I'm paying for it now but had a lot of fun then. EJ ran the streets so much, then just like that one day she didn't bother to come home. We talk about much of nothing and I leave when I smell the burnt dinner Amos worked so hard to finish was completed. The food did have a different look. It was kinda of difficult to tell what food group it belonged to. The only thing I knew it required flour to cook and little imagination no, nope a lot of imagination to turn food into a mystery. As the boys' rush in saying their quick hi's to me as I watched them smile through their disappointment as they glance over at the plates of food and the extra for seconds. Their face shows he tried again and oohs with extras, yummy with a hidden yuck on their faces. The questions they used to always ask was what was for dinner this time I didn't hear it because no one knew. I looked at Momo's face and she smiles raising her eyebrows saying slowly that she loved Amos and it was a good thing she didn't marry him for his cooking, and she winks at me.

Amos smiles back through his floured face and the mystery dinner that awaits them with many extras. I see she still has it everything was sexual, so she was slowly coming back. They rush over to help her to the table, as I leave, I hear her laughing saying that you guys are just stalling, come on let's eat our mystery dinner that your dad work hard to prepare. The oldest son Craig tries to convince them to close their eyes and pretend. His deep voice sounds just his mothers. She passed on the deep depth in voice gene. Momo probably had fun with pretending to be a man with her voice. If you close your eyes you wouldn't think it was Momo talking. I silently chuckle as I listen to the youngest son Ryan say his prayers. I hope I get it right "Dear Lord we thank you for the mystery food we eat but can you give us something that we remember what it's suppose to be, or a taste, help us remember cuz I forgot what we used to eat familiar food please, thank you Lord, amen. Oh yeah thank my dad for trying really, really hard in making our mystery dinner, breakfast and sometimes lunch please help us Lord we need you soon!! I try to hold in my laughter as I look at the little hands folded in prayer. I felt the love coming from everyone around the kitchen table, then just like now on that heart felt prayer I remembered. It left everyone with little smirks on their faces even Amos and Momo worked up a chuckle too but not too loud. You hear the ahs, but Amos says just use your imagination that's what I do. Then they all start laughing as one big happy family. Their laughter merges into one sound that represents unity. Closing their eyes as they take bites of whatever Amos had cooked the prayers had work. Smiles came back to their faces and they laugh, talk and enjoyed the taste of their mystery meal. I leave with joy in my heart knowing that I saw Momo coming back in her own way.

Today the sun was trying to come out and the rain was not happy, but life keeps moving just like the rain it stops when it's ready in its own way. The reward was the smile in the form of a rainbow. Being pregnant made me feel good and needed just like this nice cup of coffee and the rain reflecting off nature and today was a beautiful sunshine day in Cali. I pretty much waddle back home and try and make Loren's room comfortable. There was a bed in the room that Melba had given us since she didn't have the space. We turned the third bedroom into a baby room slash guest room. Good thing I kept a lot of Sierra's clothes and baby bed wasn't expecting, the oops few years and nine months later. Just a little more time and my bundle will be delivered. I'm closer to delivery than further away from just finding out I'm pregnant.

Doctor Upesi and Doctor Deck were pleased with the rate my daughter was developing and no more looks of concerns from her or any indication she knew I had gone to Haven's Place. I would say the time is flying ah but nah sometimes it seems to just place itself on hold long enough to catch your breath. When they finally make it home Loren was carrying Sierra again like she couldn't walk. Not only can she walk she can run and that's what she does as she runs to me with the toys that her cousin Loren had purchased. Her little arms can barely carry her gifts. I just look over at both of them, and Bill motioned with his finger pointing to Loren as he says wasn't me it was him. I laugh really either way she got both of you. They bring back a smorgasboard of food, Mexican, Chinese, Carribean, with fries. Now the fries I can enjoy the other items hmm my body partner, hmm she might enjoy. After all that Sierra wants a quesadilla that they didn't purchase as she looks at the take the food out. I see the disappointment in her face and I jump up saying I will make one especially for you. With that she smiles as she goes into the front room to play with her toys. Loren feels bad and I tell him don't worry about it you got her more than enough and she will get over it and she did.

We look at a DVD, Shrek and commetate on almost each scene laughing and just going down memory lane. Sierra wasn't feeling too much laughter for she was really into Shrek and after that she wanted to look at Kung Fu Panda. We smile at each other feeling the same passion of we hope that she is sleep by then, ooh Panda. Bill reminds Loren when he was living in Chicago of his girlfriend Yohannes, you remember Yoyo that went crazy when you called it off dating her and you were wishing you knew kung fu then. Loren stutters saying wow cuz now I still look over my shoulder. You know, she still lives in Chicago with her crazy ah butt. I look over at him and he knows the look, oh my bad Sierra don't use those words cousin Loren did an oopsey. He smiles with an okay nod from Sierra as she stays in tune to Shrek. Yoyo and I had some classes together and hey I thought she was cool and all until she started getting too serious for me. Her timing was off, and I was moving on to the next honey, um what was her name hmm Jondra/Johnnie?? Only thing Johnnie was more focused on her education and wasn't feeling me but hey we just hung out.

One day Johnnie had come over and we were just chilling doing much of nothing and I heard noise at the back door as if someone was trying to break in. I went to the door opened it no one there no problem set back down. Now someone was at the front door trying to open it. This is some crazy, (pause ooh), I look out the through the peek hole nothing. Then I hear the window moving as if someone was trying to break in. Now you know this was some tripping oops. So, I open the door and it's Yohannes stomping hard down the steps. Okay, okay when she hears the door open, she runs back up the steps looking all type of crazy and scared me. Only thing I didn't do was scream as I ran back into the apartment. I think my voice and my scream left running in front of me. The look I saw had been straight out of a psycho movie. I didn't hear any running music, but I heard my voice say just run. I set down inside I had the shivers and telling Johnnie as calm and cool at the same time trying to control my breathing, but inside I was scared but couldn't show punk, oops.

Johnnie looked at me as if this was some crazy stuff going on. I want to say heck this was crazy to me too you ain't solo in this. Yoyo left, and I should have cut that yoyo string along time ago. I slept alone thanks to her and had flashbacks of her running up the stairs looking all types of crazy. Man, I had visions and he act like he is still shivering, (Loren is so dramatic). I had to let out laugh and so did Bill. He looks at us and he had to laugh with us. Later that week I ran into her at the school bookstore and I asked her what was up, and she apologized for her behavior. She just wanted our relationship and went crazy with knowing I had someone in there other than her. Only if she knew it wasn't that kinda party, but I knew there was a reason we weren't talking, and she confirmed that reason.

All the time Loren was talking I kinda chuckle thinking back on when Henry Luis, Floyd and his boys were talking about one of them being chased with knives by the girl he left at the party. On this one I would have been mad too. I hope Bill appreciates me and knowing that I'm not that type of crazy, but men can make you do things that will bring an unknown or known character out. We may tolerate certain issues, but we do have a tad bit of residual that can trigger at anytime and make us snap crazy. With my performance how much out of character am I. I know I adjusted myself to my husband but how much of Rita did I lose. I been called meathead, beach and those are the good names I remember, but when was the last time he called my name with passion of being his wife and the mother of his daughters. It's funny but not ha-ha on how you learn to perform and audition without knowing you applied for the part. I've been married for some time but does Bill share the same years???

Chapter 35
I Love to Hear Their Laughter

I listen and observe Bill and Loren laughing and sharing old stories. I look at Loren and he was who he was, and marriage was not around his corner. I wondered if he enjoys his life going from pillow to post with different women or does, he wants to someday make it to the top floor and settle down. Does he like or live for the dramas and the crazies? That seems like a lot of work just in remembering their names. Who wants quantity and not quality? How long will his charm and looks last? At one point an oonee is an oonee; love should have something to do with it. He was not in college anymore and the high school years are far gone. I smile at Bill as I form my thoughts about Loren. Have they or Clarence ever thought about how greedy that sounds. It's like a glutton but dealing with lust and women. As they finish from one of many, they are gazing at another one to top off their glutton appetites. I could be wrong but my opinion, just self-serving gluttons or another form of just being lustfully greedy. Who or what will ever satisfy Loren's or many other people like him no emotions just a lust appetite.

When he does settles down, he will make a good husband and father because all the chasing has or will come to an end. What's left after you've tried everything and anything? He loves children and they just gravitate to him. He has a degree and owns his business, no children but want to have a house full for his mother Rosey Josie. I want the same so Sierra will have plenty of cousins to play with. With Bill being here I'm safe from getting into any unknown trouble. As the night grows long, I prepare Sierra for bed. Loren puts her in her bed, and holding a child looks good on him. She tried to have hang time their wish came true no Kung Fu Panda, and their family lived up to their reputation of wearing Sierra out. I give Bill a kiss on the lips and ooh and hmm his lips felt so soft and tasty. I taste the combination meal he had, and it tasted better on his lips. I melt as I feel the love and warmth again that this time will help me fade away into an intimate dream. I love Bill and that kiss felt as if he still loves me. I feel Loren's eyes on us and as I go to give him a hug. I see the smile that surfaced from seeing his cousins still together. Maybe this will assist with him making it to the top floor and stop chasing tail. I leave them to themselves as I lay it down waiting for my husband to lie next to me. So, I could feel the warmth of his body or maybe he might just kiss me on the back of my shoulder. I miss that, and I continue to remember how good his lips felt.

The covers felt soft and my thoughts are just putting my head on that spot that has been reserved for my head. I don't know how long they stayed up I just remember drifting off hearing them laugh through their talking. I gently was feeling the warmth of Bill's body press up against mine. Bill felt that kiss just like I did, and his body motion and touch shows it. I don't know what they stayed up talking about but I'm enjoying this. He kisses my shoulder the way I have always liked. Yeah, my wish came true. I tell myself to not open my eyes, so this dream doesn't fade away. He holds me in ways I remember and we both didn't forget. This is a night for both of us as we finally fall off to sleep in each other's embrace snoring away. Tonight, is our night and just adds to the rest of our life. Bill and I look at each other in the morning to the smell of breakfast smells and pots banging. We embrace one more again and laugh at each other as he gently helps me out of our bed. We walk in holding one another as Loren glances at us laughing, as Sierra stirs the pancake batter. Loren cooks the bacon and sausage and burns the pancakes. Some of the food I smell cooking I didn't know we had, Loren must have gone to the store with Sierra. She knows her way around and no telling what else Loren purchased for Sierra. I laugh at their singing off key making up words together communicating through eyes and laughter. Yep he would make a good father but first he needs to become a good husband. But before all that it's time to eat! We laugh as we scrape off the burned parts to taste Loren and Sierra's hard work.

I think about Amos' mystery meals and Momo telling them to use their imagination on what they were eating. They seem to be used to those mystery meals. I don't think they really mind just the fact that they are eating at the table as a family and allowed to use their imagination as they savor each morsel of food. Even in her sickness they still work together not skipping a beat. We gather at the table not with mystery breakfast just well cooked. Talking about what the day may consist of and much of nothing. I go and make a bathroom run as I hear a knock on the door with muffled brief conversations. I look into the mirror and this morning a smile is greeting me as I wipe my face off.

No tears or mental first aide kit, this was going to be a good day no time for any Oscar performances. When I finally came out feeling fresh with my soul rejubilated there is no one there. I hear Loren talking about how fine she was. I could only think that it was either Robin or Courtney Diane checking up on me. It's been a while since I've talked to them. For some reason I have been busy trying get ready for Sabrina and checking and helping with Momo. I asked who was at the door and it was Courtney Diane. Bill said she just came by to check on you and your boy Loren fell in love. I laugh you sure it wasn't lust. Nah cuz this might be the one at least while I'm here. He sings while dancing moving on up to the top floor, the elevator finally moved. I look at him saying she's not like that and she is like a sister to me. I look at him saying she would make Fifi look tamed. She's not the one to mess with; her bark and bite are the same. Loren growls saying I would bark for her. Maybe she could be the one to tame the dog in me. As he makes the woof sounds, we all laugh, but in the back of my mind Courtney Diane will hurt him in more ways than one.

I showered and got dressed as they cleaned up the kitchen and Bill vaccums the floors. I blew a kiss to Bill and told him that I will be right back. I'm going over to Courtney Diane's place to say hi. He smiles as Loren tells me to have her come back over. I glance at him saying Loren are we really going to travel that road with no car. He smiles laughing we can go the slow scenic route just don't let her shade me. Come on cuz I wouldn't do that to you. Come on invite her back don't blow my cool. I will play fair if she comes out and play with me. I look at him saying that's the reason why you can't play at the park you don't play fair. He smiles I will this time, promise come on as he sounds like he was whinning. How could I resist. It's really up to Courtney Diane she 's grown, and it will be either yes or no or with your dumb ass. Haven't heard those words in a while and I kinda miss her words.

I haven't seen too many of the neighbors lately everyone must be doing their own thing. Robin is probably out working, filming and working somewhere enjoy-ing herself. Courtney Diane looks nice in her fatigues, and she could easily become a model. I just wonder was she like Joann beating the men up with words and looks. Courtney Diane was taller than Joann's 5"2' or so in height. The difference was Joann put them in the hospital and one of the men said I think she held back. I had to chuckle on that one because I can only imagine them lying in hospital bed bandaged up comparing injuries.

Miss Courtney Diane calmness is just her distractor. And don't let her corner smile fool you she is Mother Flo's daughter, and probably her favorite. If she looks at me and then her watch I know what that silent thought meant, was it time to care about Loren leaving for Chicago. Hooking Loren up with her hmmm for now that's a not. But if she comes back I will only on the if. Sometimes I look at Bill and Loren and wonder if Loren's heart is open for love or crowded with lust. And Bill was there someone else filling his heart and pushing me out because it was just too crowded. Lust is a powerful emotion sometimes it's hard to compete with. On the other hand, why should you have to compete when your mate should be protecting you? They are supposed to be your shield. When you get pushed out do you go and look for an open heart somewhere else? Just like the crumbs of affection it does leave you starving and hungry for affection in any form.

Sometimes, Bill's lack of affection has left me emotionly starving. Where a short kiss is appreciated. Just feeling his lips temporarily feeds my starvation but that was only a temporary fix. How many other people are affected by the crumbs of affection? As I pondered those thoughts gazing into just air, I hear a light knock on the door. Bill and Loren pause enough through their laughter of conversation to see who might be at the door. To their surprise it's Courtney Diane. Loren's eyes light up as if he made it to the top floor, penthouse! Only if he knew Courtney Diane was way beyond the penthouse. She was just letting me know that she was going to see Henry and just stopped by to check on me since Robin was visiting her parents. I introduced her to Loren, so he could mentally close his mouth. She shows her signature corner smile and dimples and was dressed in jeans and a loose-fitting shirt. She could wear a bag and make it look designed just for her. She should have been a model but now she's wearing designer fatigues. Loren hops up to greet her as Bill silently laughs at his mannerism. I ask if she wanted to go with us to PataRee's and just hang out. She hesitates as Loren anxiously waits for her response. She smiles and says I 'll take a raincheck, but maybe later tonight I could come back by. Loren smiles and asks are you sure we can't change your mind? Then Sierra chimes in on please Auntie Courtney Diane. What an attack team move by Sierra and Loren. For that moment they reminded me of Johnny Lee using their daughter Linda Sue to convince Charlotte about purchasing zingers. Sierra being on cue with Loren, shows their signature smile gene. Now I can see Courtney Diane's smile as if she might change her mind as Sierra almond eyes twinkle with the signature smile, she inherited from both parents.

Sierra and Loren are working their magic ganging up on her at any cost. She smiles and leans toward Sierra and says Auntie will be back and I will see you and your cousin Loren, while she slowly looks up at him with her signature corner smile. I guess she was saying through her expressions that I too know that game all so well. She always seems to be in control with no emotion. How does she say it, "I don't have time for emotions it's too much of a distractor. Emotions can take over and you just lose it and it's hard to regain control. Then she would add that she would get pissed off because she knew better. Now Loren just lost it when she included his name with Sierra. Inside I could feel him giving Sierra a high five on backing him up, smart move Sierra. At her young age Sierra was a quick thinker. Loren shows his signature smile with dimples slightly closing his eyes with hope she might return. Looking just like Bill when he was or used to try to woo me. All I knew was it didn't work for her, inside I had to laugh Loren had met his match on this one.

She was not moved, and he didn't know her like I do. I'm sure she was flattered but not impressed. Courtney Diane was tall slim and gorgeous but not conceited just confident. I was entertained and amused this was really funny. Loren just couldn't let it go. He smiles at her careful not to touch her saying, I'm going to hold you to that. I'm from Chicago and I will hope that I will see you before I leave or before you go. She smiles, inside I knew he was getting on all her nerves as she tried to save that emotion without the "s" on something special and Loren was not the something special. In her words with his dumb ass tee-hee la-da-la-ha-ha, whatever dude or what was your name Lawrence. Her expression said it all, but neither Loren nor Bill picked it up. I did because I knew Miss Courtney Diane. She's not coming back I knew for sure that this was her cougar night out with the girls. I haven't known her to ever miss a night.

We all get ready to prepare to go. I fumble around my closet looking for something to wear that wouldn't make me look like a flowered covered couch. Warmups no, just add to the wideness and a dress nah, look like a walking bell again. Maybe just a nice pair of stretch pants and nice top might work with just a dash of lipstick or Vaseline, with my hair pulled back. In sync my thoughts and heart let out with a huge sigh. I splash on perfume I haven't worn in a while and I think I am ready. As I walk out Loren smiles at me saying how nice I look and Bill joins in. I can't believe he agreed. Kinda shocks me that he was not making wave motions or rolling motions as I walk down the hallway. And he didn't make the wee noise or earthquake move like he normally does. Yep today is a good day. Sierra runs to me saying how nice I smell. Bill just couldn't resist and comes over to sniff slowly and kisses me on my neck. This took me by surprise again, another form of unexpected affection, (inside I laugh at him marking his spot by raising his leg). Well we are ready to go, and I am so excited. Feeling the fresh air and just getting out and having family time. It's been awhile since all of us have been out together. Sierra needs exposure to family time, so she can pass it on to her family someday. Loren picks Sierra up as if she can't walk and I don't think she minds. But sometimes I could see in her expression she wants to walk. Sierra likes walking because she is a big girl now and soon will be a big sister. I look at my family and we look portrait pretty, click, click...

I will store this for later just like the rain as it slowly comes down carefully feeding nature in its own way. Sipping and absorbing as just like I like slowly sipping this coffee and letting it warm my body and spirit. Today was a nice day and the night looks moonlight bright. The day was a California day, sun shining, and the air was crisp. Sierra looks out the window as if this was her first time, riding and sight seeing. She and Loren are quiet as they both look out the window with very little conversation. I just hope we don't pass Haven's Place. I kinda sit on edge with the anticipation on our scenic route. This place was more beautiful than I remembered. There is a difference from bus route and car scenery. As we pull up Sierra's excitements is showing as I look at an almost filled parking lot.

As we enter the servers Ofa and Britney remembers us to my surprise saying our names. Sierra and I felt not only like family but important and not like the word potent that Catrice got confused with. Sheree and Mackey greet us as Sierra and Mackey hug one another as if they were best friends. Sheree gives us an embrace as she welcomes us sharing that she is expecting too. She motions for Ellis to seat us and take our drink order as we exchange possible baby names. Sheree said since they know it's a boy her hubby Pat favors the name Jaxson Eddie, not sure because she still thinking about other names, but Eddie will be the middle name, so Pat can carry on his fathers' name. Mackey not being too shy says we're calling my baby brother, "Blue". Sheree smiles yep she gave him the nickname "Blue. I look with an ah as she explains that is her grandmother, Robins' favorite color. I giggle with her saying we are having a girl and we are naming her Sabrina. For some imaginary reason Sierra liked it and after considering different names we decided on that name. Loren and Bill stand there with their mouths open wondering how I know them. Funny but not ha-ha the same questions I wanted to know about the staring scants at the restaurant and other places, but now was not the time. I introduced Bill and Loren, and everyone smiles looks familiar. Mackey wants Sierra to tag along with her and Bill gives the okay as they run to the play room. Mackey and Sierra look more like sisters than new friends. I enjoy hearing their innocent laughter and looking at their bonding as they skip off to the playroom.

We have a new server by the name Joniah, and Loren can't help himself from flirting with her. I think when it comes to him flirting is like breathing, he just always needs that breath of fresh air. I can tell she was being polite and irritated at the same time. To distract her I had to research my archives and asked what happened to Cache and Jasmine. She lightened up saying they went off to college and Erin comes in later. I just smiled saying when do you graduate? As her smile widens her response was that she was just a junior. She adds that Cache and Jasmine were replaced with Shelby and Blake and we have a new cook name Herman or Sherman. I smiled saying nice, but in the back of my mind that should eliminate all that flirting from Loren. Now that she updated us, we can now place our orders. Silently I'm saying Loren leave this obvious young lady alone, so she can do her job!! A slim young man and young lady approach our table and I try to focus on their face and smile. He reaches his hand out to me as everyone at the table paused to see what was happening. He says that I know you probably don't remember me. I was here with my family for Shanta and Chantells' birthday party. I'm Edward Shannon and this is my older sister Vanetta. We were just passing through and giving Sheree and Pat a shout out before we leave. Inside I'm laughing because I remember him and his cousin having names that were backwards Shannon Edward and Edward Shannon. I introduced them to my husband Bill and his cousin Loren. Everyone smiles as they express the pleasure of meeting each other as they parted laughing. They place an order and enjoy some talk time with Shanta and Sheree. With that statement Loren sighs saying let's order. Bill and I look at each other just knowing each other thoughts and they are directed at Loren. Both their eyes widen as they look intensely at the menu. We must have looked at the barbeque at the same time because we laugh talking about hmm barbeque. We wanted barbeque but wondered would our tastebuds go numb??

I told them that when I tasted Uncle Duckies' barbeque for the first time it burned my lips. I lost all sensation and the inside was so inflamed that steam came out in form of an inflamed burp. Bill said his lips became numb and the sides of his tongue had no feeling after eating his barbeque too. Loren agrees and adds not only did my lips feel numb, taste buds numb, inside burning later that night ooh all came into one burning sensation. With that, all of us said on cue, it's time to order. Loren asked me how many times have you been here? They seem to know you very well. Bill waits and wants to hear the answer on this one. It's nice to know that I do have a life outside the doors of our apartment. I could tell by their silence they are impressed the same way I was when Sierra and I first came here. Ellis brings the drinks as Joniah/JoJo brings the goodies for Sierra and crossword puzzles for us. No one will ever be bored at PataRee's. I told them that this would be a good location for Sierra to have a birthday party, and that next door was the bowling alley with a skating ring. Did anyone want to go bowling after lunch? They both hunch their shoulders at the same time as if they were twin brothers. I loved looking at the relationship they were able to keep after all these years. They both decide on steak which didn't surprise me, and I will go with a familiar turkey sandwich with cranberries with extra napkins for just in case and for busy Sierra the pancakes with the smiling face.

My first introduction to that delicious turkey sandwich with cranberries and extra napkins. That was an entertaining day with with Robin, with an added bowl of imaginary popcorn. Right after placing our order Aletha and Ofa run over to our table almost out of breath. We look at them like what's up or what's going on?? Identical twin girls, Danielle and Dayna giggling running with them as they catch their breaths in between innocent smiles. At a glance they looked like the twins Anita and Annette that I grew up with and lost contact with. In the back of my mind I am wondering if Ofa and Aletha are the bus driver Hector's daughters. A small world if they are his daughters and giggle at the fact that I know their dad. They smile as they catch their breath asking where was Sierra? Before fright could enter our minds, we tell them in sync that she was playing with Mackey. They both glanced, over at the play room and ask was it okay to go say hi to them? Once we gather our senses from going into possible shock, we just nod our heads with our mouths open, yes. Bill and Loren look at me what was that all about and how many times have you been here. I told them just once with a little corner smile as I hide my little secret. That thought faded away into their conversation occassionally including me. That didn't bother me too much because I had my own entertainment and plus feeling good to just get out and as a family.

They talked about the summer vacations in Oakwood at Grandad and Mama

Helen's house. Loren said he had run into Joel when he went over to Grandads'. Joel had moved out of Oakwood and was living in Denver. For my entertainment I just remember going to grade school with him and seeing his smiling white teeth greet me as I was thrown out by Bill at his grandparent's house or when Bill made me feel invisible. I just fade away and come back into focus when I see Joel. That was one memory that I want to fade away because I'm here and those scants aren't. I look and smile at Bill, but my thoughts are I wish I could reach over there and choke the mess out of him and pop his head. He smiles back at me just because. It's funny that we smile at each other with different thoughts. Only if he knew and probably don't remember and probably don't care. Why should I give it any energy that was so many years ago and I don't remember what their faces look like nor should I care after all he asked me.

Shanta comes in letting Sheree know that the caterer from "Personnally Yours" is here. Chef Harris needs to know the locations to set up everything. Shanta spots us and comes over to greet our table. She remembered us and smiles at everyone as she greets us, and still I have seen that smile before not only on her sister Sheree, but it looks so familiar. I can't believe she remembered Sierra. Shanta calls my name smiling, while asking if I want to come over to her place and see the new layout? I jump at the opportunity well at least as fast as I could while in ah about being part of such an honorable request. I look at Bill and Loren and tell them I will be right back, and you know what to order for Sierra and myself. I give Bill a smile, and a quick kiss as I eagerly leave to see ShaRobert's. I'm excited as I see Chef Harris and her helper Apprentices Jordan and Tanisha/ Nisha. At least that's what the name tags displayed, but I heard Chef Harris calling her Nisha. They look like they are related and so professional in their chef attire.

Chef Harris greets Shanta with a warm embrace and tells her she bought some extra samples for her. As Shanta's smiles with that familiar smile that makes me ask myself where have I seen that smile? Shanta asks Chef Harris, how was the wedding reception in Paris for her nephew James and Jessica? I lean in because I want to hear too, a place I would love to someday visit. In her haste to prepare and prep, she whispers I will have to talk to you later, and it was an experience. Only thing I could see was her big smile as Chef Harris hands her a sampler plate. The display plate is colorful and looks delicious with different aromas. I can only imagine the flavors. Shanta offers me a seat and ask me to assist with the sample tray. Chef Harris always spoils her by supplying this display of Chef's eye pleasing delights. I kinda hesitate because I know I have that turkey cranberry sandwich Bill ordered, but everything looks so inviting. Just like not knowing about avocados the sampler plate looks foreign to me as well. Inside I feel a little embarrassed because I couldn't begin on how to identify such a fancy display of appetizers. I give into Sabrina's craving, ignore my lack of cuisine knowlege and as I sample the food it slowly melts into my mouth. The only thing I felt was my eyes closing. I look over at Shanta and her almond shaped eyes are closed too. Her smile and eyes look so familiar, hmm. She smiles in agreeance looking at Chef Harris and they leave me with the sample plate as they look at various areas for setting up.

I could tell that there are at least two to three parties going on. When she returns to a few missing samples I ask was she expecting a crowd. Her hubby, Joel, with Sheree's hubby Pat enters with DJ Magic and Phil ready to set up as they glance at me with such a big smile that looks familiar too. They both pause enough to embrace me as if we have known each other for years. This is such a family and they remembered me. Wow I look around and everything looks so perfect. She said that DP Securities is celebrating fifty years of service. This was a combination of employee appreciation and birthday party Mike the owner. Shanta smiles at Joel saying, make sure you call Davenport or his wife Avis to make sure his party doesn't go past capacity. That's all we need is to have the Fire Marshal write us up again. The other room is reseved for Robert and Deborah anniversary and the last two rooms' younger crowd Rachel's 25th birthday. Mr. Woodson's what seem to be normal fussing says Rachel's sister Brandi just added a few more guest that wasn't calculated. He walks away shaking his head saying don't want the Fire Marshal coming back again. He adds I guess tomorrow I will tell you about the booking request for Grant and Doe and how many people that will be attending on the same day of the 50th anniversary.

Did you add the number of people scheduled the same time for your Aunt Lillian and Uncle Carroll, but since I'm off humph and the fussing fades into the kitchen with I'm just saying? There was another younger crowd Rosezette's 30th birthday party that seems to have a smaller party maybe that will balance both parties. I look at Shanta and Sheree and admire how professional they are. Then their brother Alan Curtis, (or was it, Curtis Alan) is a DJ on the local station and performs wow, they are young and busy. I bump into a smiling photographer wearing my favorite navy-blue polo shirt with the name "Blue Optics" bringing in equipment. She apologizes about the bump and introduces herself as Becki the owner and hands me a card with a big smile saying my first setting is on her. I'm like ah with the kindess that I always received when I come here. This is such a family, oriented business. I thank Shanta as I excuse myself to go back to PataRee's to tell Bill and Loren about what was going on next door.

Of course, Loren wants to see what the new flavor of the night might be or his late dessert. He just loves hanging out in the basement. Oh, how could I forget he moved from the basement to the first floor with floozies and huzzies? I guess he forgot about falling in love with Courtney Diane. That was a quick romance. She would break his heart and make it in time for her" Cougar" night out with Robin. I see a nice-looking couple walking towards Shanta, Sheree, and Alan Curtis. From their features they must be their parents. They look familiar and their smile and laugh are in sync. She brings them over and introduces them as her parents Gordon Maurice and Robin Denise and they make a beautiful couple with a pleasant demeanor. The whole family seems to blend into one in their resemblance. Gordon Maurice says he is going over next door to check out what's going on. To my surprise he asked Bill and Loren did they want to accompany him. Robin Denise smiles at me and offers me to go with them. Her smile and facial expressions look so eerie like we could all almost be related. I smile back and told them thank you and that I was just over there and had a chance to sample Chef Harris sampler plate. Robin Denise laughs now she is an outstanding chef that is requested all over the world we are very fortunate that she is family. Every chance we get we use her because she is not always readily available. Bill and Loren look back at me like little boys as if they were asking permission to go next door. I thought that was a first asking permission well okay then. I told them go ahead, the food will be coming, and I want to be here whenever Sierra breaks away from Mackey. Mackey's grandparents laugh good luck on that one. If they are playing in the game room, she will only come out to get something to drink or a quick snack.

Right then I heard familiar sounds of restaurant dates confusion. Coleman is fussing again about mini cakes for each celebration, Mr. Woodson is now fussing about no one told him that this extra party room was being used by Charles and Veronica for their first anniversary and did we get the 10th wedding anniversary reception for Brian and Asha. Wow I reflect and remember our first anniversary dinner and stares by unknown waitress. Wow will Bill and I make it pass ten years and someday enjoy our 50th anniversary? Sheree responds on behalf of her sister saying Mr. Woodson you were scheduled to be off you need some rest. She probably meant we need the rest because she smiled as she was saying the words, but her eyes said something entirely different. Her almond familiar shaped eyes said it all. His response was quick with oh in a rough sounding voice and you said that to say what, but I forgot to tell you that and CJ the DJ will be setting up and will be coming later, oops. While slowly walking away fussing until the rough sounding voice faded away into hearing the fussing continue faintly with Coleman. That was an ooooh and aaaah moment.

He returns smiling and slowly walking saying well I'm here and what about the room for the newlyweds. Wow was that a delayed response. Beth Lauren fussing about no structure, no order since Trevor left for FBI training didn't you give his responsibilities to Randal and she needed Darica and Delana to come out of hiding and help. I just laugh silently because that was the same thing happening with just different guest names. Before I could say anything, Bill must have remembered that I told them about the bowling and skating rink, because he asked could they see that as well. I talked so much about going bowling or maybe skating, Bill had to see it. When Bill and Loren stand next to Gordon Maurice, they look so familiar kinda creepy they look like they could really be related. The resemblance is so strong they could be brothers are first cousins. Bill doesn't act like he knows Gordon Maurice, but they seem to have bonded. This is just what we needed a pause time from the routine that we had fallen into. Loren was an introduction to the fresh air we needed in our relationship. He reminded us that we were still young and breathing and that fresh air feels good. For now, I'm sitting in the passenger's seat enjoying the view, tall palm trees and the smell of fresh flowers. I admire the beauty and the aroma they represent.

Today the rain has faded away and the perspiration on my window has faded into a rainbow. JoJo brings our food with the assistance of Ellis and the aroma makes me want to sample Bill's plate, since trying Chef Harris sampler plate. That turkey cranberry sandwich seems to be larger than before or maybe being awe-stricken I didn't notice and had a larger appetite. Right when I reach over to grab one of Bill's fries, I hear them coming toward the table. They are laughing, talking about basketball and returning for the bowling alley or the parties happening tonight. They both just seem happy and been added to this new family. Bill smiles and kisses me as he sits down grabbing a fry and feeding a fry to me. Wow this has not happened in a while, that fry represented more than just yummy. Bill is feeling this now, but what is Loren feeling? I hope this break away will help him get over Fifi and ready to skip more floors. Hmm, maybe he should take the stairs and have deep thoughts as he travels to each landing. Maybe this is a time for healing for all of us; God knew just what we all needed including Sierra and Sabrina. With each bite we nodded and smile. Funny just like my father would do while he was eating. Time has showed me just what that meant, enjoying the meal, the environment and his family. When Bill comes home his wife and daughters in all ways will be there waiting. Sometimes the time would be late, but we will always be there waiting.

Sierra finally comes to the table to do just what Gordon Maurice says get something to drink and a take a bite out of her smiling pancake face. Smiling as she catches her breath saying I'm going back to see Mackey okay daddy and mom. Before we could respond in a puff she's gone. We can see her from our table and at the same time continue enjoying our feast. Loren talks about how big the bowling alley and skating rink are and wants to come back to the invite at ShaRoberts'. I listen to see how Bill is going to respond because Melba moved and Momo is not in a position to babysit. So, what is hubby thinking he is going to do with Sir Loren? On this one time I wasn't going to trip not worth the frustration. I would love to come back but there will be other times since we know how to get here. Loren is good time, just like Bill's good time Smitty friend there is one in every group. They are that person that brings life to the party and keeps it moving. Loren was that person and tonight Bill will be too. I just want him to bring back my husband.

Sheree comes over to the table just to make sure everything is okay, and the steaks were prepared to their satisfaction while introducing her new manager in training Jonathan C and his twin sister Janae was in training until she went back to school for her masters. Plus add that Janae finished her masters and now is married with a beautiful son. Bill and Loren reassure Sheree, that they will be returning. With that she says good to see you and please come back again, now that Mackey has a new best friend and we appreciate your business. When Bill smiles at her Sheree seems to do a double take as if his face and smile looks familiar too. Hmm it wasn't just me.

Today this was the place to be. I gaze around the room as I did last time looking at the many conversations and family enjoyment. Everyone's into their table settings of conversations, and just laughing, smiling and not interfering with or paying any attention to what's happening around them. Everyone was in their own world just like we are sitting here doing the same thing laughing and reminiscing. I hope this joy doesn't go away. Bill and Loren talk about the touch downs and the winning three -point shots. The school or outdated trophies have tarnished. Yet, they continue to bring them out and polish them with their memories and resurrect them back into the air through conversations with egos and bragging rights. In reality, they are still boys with mustaches. It's really time to pass on that running touch down or that three- point shot to the next generations. Pass the balls on and keep it moving. Same thing with cheerleaders, they need to put their pompoms down or pass them on. I did and now I know that I am married with daughters. I continue to smile while they go through almost each triumphet play. Seems like they are playing imaginary ping pong and they had to match each youthful hay day talents. Yep close the door to the barn and let someone else graze off it, because someone must cheer from the sidelines.

As usual I will not add anything to change this feeling. Sierra makes it back this time with Mackey saying we just came for a break as she sips her drink but avoiding her pancakes and they both skip back to the room. Bill smiles at them as Sierra finishes her drink while giving her dad a hug. Yep she is still a daddy's girl. I look over at Loren staring at them with not a look of envy but maybe a touch in his heart that he is ready to try and settle down and have a family. I had to ask so Loren what are you thinking about Fifi? He snaps back out of his day dream saying oh hell no that's a done deal. So, are you ready to move from the bargain basement clearance rack? Well cuz you do get a bargain for a small fee. I laugh saying you ought to stop. No, no Rita hear me out those bargains need to be picked up and checked out. Now look at me as the checker or product manager making sure the products are useable. Bill and I both want to see where this is going. Loren probably doesn't know where he is going either. If he did, he would get out from that basement and go to the top floor. Does he have a picture of him next to the word dog or does he share the word dog in the dictionary with Courtney Diane's son Henry Luis. Maybe Loren has lived this life so long it's natural for him to act like a woof woof. Loren opened the door to our life and looked in and looked around. Now it's up to him to use whatever he needs whenever it's the right time. He will know and so will the one he falls in love with…

Loren had a nice high school sweetheart Arlee, but she was more advanced and wanted more out of life when she graduated. Arlee wanted a career, opportunites to travel and own her own business and hopefully become an enterprenuer. Last I heard she completed her master's and went into partnership with her sister Patricia Ann and opened a chic boutique and created her own clothing line. Hmm maybe I should look her up when my shape decides to come out of hiding. As I think to myself her clothes might be out of my price range. I just remembered how hurt Loren was when she left and never came back. He should have followed her, but he didn't do too bad he owns his own auto shop and photography business. He probably was over there talking to Becki the owner of Blue Optics and knowing Bill he was probably talking basketball with Gordon Maurice about his high winning shots.

Bill was a high school basketball player that proudly competed in All State and played every chance he could and found out later so did Gordon Maurice. With them having so much in common I hope that would be a reason for us to return. For once everyone was happy and Bill for once was not flirting and not making me feel invisible. We are all laughing talking and really enjoying trying to solve the word puzzles. Loren and Bill are trying to cheat by looking at the answers at the bottom. I had to laugh when I would play with my sisters and brother, we would always cheat that was the fun in it trying not to get caught. I guess that's the excitement in not being faithful, and the excitement in cheating without getting caught, hmmph sad. When were kids playing games and sneaking or cheating and laughing at the same time, seem so innocent? Because you are the only one that knows, unless someone saw you and both of you just held on to that secret. Remembering the thrill of just knowing that you were getting away with it was the excitement. I guess they both mean the same with cheating, living for the thrill/excitement. Only thing is dark can't hide from the light at least not for long. The sadness in this is the innocence are affected more, the unknowing casualties of a selfish war. How can you allow the storm to come in and leave you stupid? That's a lot of turmoil. Looking is okay but come on now sometimes you need to exercise some type of discipline that needs to come into play. It's okay to look but love needs to come in to prevent lust filled games. Some line of demarcation should be drawn into the sand, with a mental note don't cross this line or you will lose everything for a thang. Is it worth sacrificing your wife/husband family for a cheap moment or in some cases seconds?

Sierra finally comes back ready to eat her cold pancakes and endless drinks. We are still playing with our food knowing that we really can't take another bite. I only had room for half of my giant sandwich because the other half was being shared by

Sabrina and she informed me that we are full so stop eating mom. She said in her own way keep going and, in her way, informed me of indigestion don't even think about it. If you do it, we will both be up all night. How could you argue with that? There will be room later after one good burp. Bill and Loren are so stuffed they look ready for bed. I suggest that we leave while we can walk out of here. comes back as she periodically did and without hesitation from the looks on our faces brings containers for us to take our food home with the ticket. The meal was very reasonable which really impressed Bill and Loren. Loren gladly paid the bill leaving JoJo with a nice smile in form of a nice tip. He wasn't short on spending money yet at the same time he could be frugal. He spares no expense when it comes to Sierra. With our money crunch he doesn't know how much he has helped us. Financially, yes and just by his presence has been another blessing.

The door Loren looked into considering getting married, I just hope that he opens it all the way and finds his happiness. We tell Sierra to say good bye to Mackey as we say our good byes to everyone with warm embraces. They welcome us back and we look forward to returning. Mackey and Sierra hug each other just like they were best friends. Sierra needs some friends her age and for once it's not boys. We walk slowly to the car and I can't wait to get in and close my eyes. My timing was off because in napping we went a different way and what I tried or wanted to avoid was passing Haven's Place. Sierra yells out daddy I've been there too can I go there and play with Anyiah and Anise. I wouldn't mind saying hi to Minister Tamara or seeing the beautiful Miss Demtria. They were very kind and pleasant to me at the time I really needed it, but for now I will pretend that I'm in a deep sleep, maybe I should open my mouth and make some snoring noise. Without hesitation he said that we need to get home and how do you know about that place. Thank God from the outside it just looks like a large house. Loren is sleep and now I'm really pretending to be in a deeper sleep and Sierra distraction went to the other children playing in the park. She asks can we go there. Bill said you want to go everywhere even places you don't know. Ooh I dodge that bullet, just didn't want to ruin this day and end up in an unnecessary fight especially with Loren here. I can feel Bill wondering about that house. There were no signs to indicate this was a type refuge. I snug more into the seat as if I was lying in our bed trying to get as comfortable as possible at the same time keeping my eyes closed. I'm pretending again and place my hand on his leg to distract his thoughts and possible questions, all while pretending being sleep. I hear Loren and Sierra in the back snoring and for my mental fear can rest for now as Bill takes his sleepy family back home. I pretend we are happier than we really are while hoping people don't see the visions that are deep inside trying to come out into the light.

I wonder does Bill pretend with me and we both are competing for the Oscar like Robin and Ramon. Somedays I would like to put the Oscars I have won away and enjoy the rain that hides my tears. My thoughts of today pass into my memory as I pretend to continue to be in a deep sleep. I wonder right now what Bill was thinking, what thoughts are floating or just hanging around or was he just numb. When I look at him sometimes his eyes seem so blank, but I know there must be some type of thought process going on. He couldn't be in the duh mold twenty-four seven. Does he still love me the way he did before we married and has it grown stronger or with each day or year or is it fading away? How often should I hear the words I love you. I guess I don't need to hear as much as I need to feel the love, and I don't need the attention at the end of a slap. At some point I need to stop wiping the tears he helps me generate. I still love Bill and my love for him has increased every time my heart beats for him. I see him as trying to provide for his family the best way he could and love us the way he knows how.

Today was a good day and we all enjoyed it. I just have a feeling when we get home Loren will want to come back and enjoy the scernery. I just hope Loren doesn't end up like Uncle Glooley having women fighting over him in the nursing home yet died alone. I'm sure Rosie Josey would like to see at least one grandchild from her eldest son's wife. For me I just want to enjoy my daughters and hope that Bill and I will grow old together and have fun playing with our grandchildren and watching the sun set. I feel the car slowing down so we must be coming closer to home. I open my eyes slowly; you know you have to after coming out of a deep pretend sleep. I stretch and go through the whole motion. I start my Oscar performance by saying that was a nice ride as 1 motion to him to look at the two sleeping with their heads touching each other. There we go another captured memory moment. Bill opens the door for me as he goes to open the door to get Sierra out her car seat. She slowly wakes up enough to see where she was and falls back to sleep placing her head back on her dad's shoulder. He liked that feeling as much as I liked looking at them share that intimate moment. That motion causes Loren to wake up and stretch saying that after that meal he needs to lay it down for a bit before going back out. I think that must have been a oops because he caught himself as Bill gave him a look of oops, I didn't talk to her yet.

That's right he didn't talk to me yet, that's a nope/not. I glance over at Bill with a look of what's up. I raise my eyebrows saying with boldness, so Bill are we going or is it just the boys. He smiles saying I didn't think about it until we went to ShaRoberts' and they invited all of us back. Loren wanted to get out and I didn't really know where we could go babe. I smile so now its babe and my come back was really honey. Amazing how they come up with pet names they normally they don't use. Babe uh I guess he forgot my real name, because Rita is seldom used. As we walk and talk Loren is silent looking at his surroundings and wondering where this will go. Right now, I don't care. Loren has been so helpful by being here and just a little sacrifice won't hurt. Bill has been coming straight home no strange smell of cheap perfume or late-night calls. Loren needs to be around women that don't come from the clearance section. Not only does Loren need to stay away from the clearance area but, he needs a break from the brick throwing Fifi. I'm curious of what she looks like and does she have a utility belt with bricks or a box full of bricks and pebbles in the back seat? I had to admit that was different. Where does Loren go from here? What was he getting from this visit and have we really helped him like he has helped us? I don't think he realized how much it has meant him being here. I know it has refreshed Bill and I don't think he realized he had a fresh breeze come into our life and created some type of spark that was fizzing out. I look over at Bill as he walks down the hallway to put Sierra in her bed and ask so you are going out? He turns slightly with his boyish smile saying only if its okay babe with you. There goes that babe phrase again, does he really know who he is talking to??

Kinda reminds me of how Johnny Lee was begging Charlottle for zingers. His deep blue eyes just faded into Charlotte's heart and she caved in. That's just how I am feeling now as I look into Bill's brown almond shaped eyes that is showing the twinkle that I fell in love with and his deep dimple smile. It still exists, and he still loves me, so I guess the answer will be yes because he asked. In the back of my mind I really didn't want him to go but I didn't want to block his cousin time with Loren.

Chapter 36
Loren Keeps Trying and I Just Keep

My insecurities and flying hormones are going to have to come to some type of agreement. Why not let him go why I should be the bad guy? What can happen Loren needs someone to be there to keep him out of trouble and make sure Bill comes straight home, no detours just straight home to his sleeping family. This wasn't worth the time, thought or effort to put into past pain and just for once let go and let him go. I rather have him ask with some respect than start an argument which might result in additional pain for me. Mama Sadie and Mommy would be proud of me and it felt good to me too. I really wanted to go but there are other things I can do while they are gone. Watch the television look at me or watch Sierra sleep through the night or what about rearranging the bathroom, humph and whoopie.

Wow I have so much to pick from. Bill and Loren both take naps as if they are resting to be ready for being out all night. This is not what I agreed to, but I did say yes. Loren was looking nice yet comfortable. Bill was looking like our college professor Mr. Hanif, in his sweater vest and that was Bill's nick name the "Professor". Loren teases Bill calling him by a new nickname "Professor". While adding that he stayed so long in the shower singing you actually came out the shower thinking you could really sing, oh hell no. It seems to not faze Bill that even his high school music teacher told him he was tone death. Loren still laughing saying that, the Temptations didn't have to worry about you being a replacement singer. I smile saying he sings only for me. His singing was for my ears and I hear only harmony. Loren pauses looking at me saying so you are tone deaf too. I just remember turning my head to the side saying hmmm I guess we are both in tune then. With that support Bill smiles at me as I look at how handsome he is. They both look like cousins and very eye catching. The aroma of their cologne lingers in the air and I just wonder in the back of my mind who will be that close to smell it. I like the smell and remember how I used to sleep with that same scent that lingered on his t-shirt. Now he was wearing that cologne out to have someone else compliment him on his scent. Maybe Loren's charm will have the women gravitate toward him and not

Bill. I watched them both as they act like little boys going out without their parents, splashing on cologne and talking and saying much of nothing. Loren laughs at Bill saying you look like a professor with that sweater on. I agreed he did look like Professor Hanif, but Professor Hanif was no joke, education was the key.

Professor Hanif had the look to match his gentle but tough demeanor. Bill was not moved by our agreeance and motions to Loren lets go as he grabs the keys. Bill shows a quick flashback of let's go with an expression that he was forgetting something. Then he snaps back smiling as he comes and hugs me. I smell that cologne on his neck and feel the warmth of his cheek against mine. His lips melt into mine with such softness and moistness. Wow what a heart throb this was giving me, just great. My heart skips a beat and the twin cousins skip out to have a good time. Please, please don't let my imagination work overtime while my hormones are trying to compete with my thoughts.

After all Bill is married and Loren will remind him, or they might be so busy enjoying themselves that they might night notice the cladly dressed women shaking and moving on the dance floor or walking around them. Refresh your own memories Rita remember when you were hanging out you weren't really looking for any particular person either. You were just hanging out with your girlfriends and dancing with no thoughts of I will take you home with me tonight. Because you knew that it wasn't that kinda of party. Maybe this will be the same kinda thought. Just not that kinda of party right Rita. Wow I can't believe I am debating with myself. Now I know what Leeler/Lene meant when she said her family would talk to themselves then get into an argument with themselves because of their own answers. Well look at me, here I am doing the same thing, but in silence. How do you play ping pong by yourself? Bill situation has changed he is married with one daughter and another one on the way.

When will he have time to play catch up with someone else, he needs to be catching and playing with our family? Thinking back on Loren's innocent lies, he could smile and talk himself out of anything or any situaiton. Or depending on if it is Friday and he's liable to tell them anything. Must have been a Friday, Loren had put himself in a situation with someones' woman. He was always trying to holler at someone that had the front and back that did match. I know he had to be talking to or trying at least to holler at what was her name Tynee. I think that's what he was bragging about talking to her sisters Kaleta/Kinna or hmmm Cayco. Funny the light came on sooner before he could do anymore of his damage that was trying to find light.

Tynee's boyfriend confronted Loren and Tynee at the mall humph of all places seems to be a popular meeting spot. With a look of what is the 'unk' up? He strongly confronted both, good thing one had bags and the other stood there empty handed engaged in a deep no sound of mouth movement in conversation. When the angry boyfriend approached them, it had to throw them both off. Loren thought quickly on this one and I had to entertain the thought or wonder what floor this one called Tynee came from. He had to ask what's up with a few choice adverbs as Loren would call them. What's up with always using my name in abverbs? Can anybody remember a brother's name? He came to the defense of hey, hey, hey man I am not interested in her like that wo, wo oh hell no!! I'm not saying anything about your taste in ladies as he smiles while glancing at her. I've known Ty for some years. Bill this dude looked at me when I said Ty. I didn't know if that was too close for comfort for this man towering over my ass. Again, no offense man but she is not my flavor, not my type, not nowhere near my type of hell no! Excuse me Tynee nice seeing you but you are your man's here flavor. I have different tastebuds. He smiles as says man step over here. I had to show this tower that I got game because I got his game piece hmm. Now game was over and its time to move and find another game piece. Loren then whispers to the towering upset man that hey, I was trying to get with her sister. Would you call that a family affair and he sings a few lines? Then the beast calmed down asking him was it Chayta. I asked who was Chayta, like I didn't know?? I did dumb to numb to his giant ass. We looked at each other knowing what we meant. Loren says hey man maybe I need to re-think Chayta. The angry man smiles saying now Cayo not too bad on the eyes either, and what about Kaleta. Do you believe this man was trying to help me out? I didn't need his assistance with no booty hook up. Now I felt a little slighted that I needed to show dude what I work with and how I roll.

I showed him my own personal entourage. I didn't need any sympathy help. So, I show him my private viewings and allow him to look at my harem. I gathered his eyes widened as he looks at Loren's pictures. Those women probably were very cladly dressed or no dress, ew vision. I never could figure out why women would lower themselves but that's me and only my opinion. Loren watched the boyfriend eyebrow rise with a smile as he glances over at Tynee and gives her a quick wink that the boyfriend didn't see. He was so in such a ah with the sexy scenery of ladies. Tynee stood there trying to develop some type of tude getting mad and telling the giant lets go! Inside she probably was sweating from getting caught and knowing later they will be talking. Yep the light came on. After the boyfriend shakes his hands saying man my bad, someone was sending her messages that she was responding to meet up at the mall. I just well hell man as he shakes his hand followed by a dap asking him to accept his apology. The boyfriend then glances over at Tynee telling her let's go. We have to do some talking with your shopping ass, spending up my money and meeting folks. She smiles slightly at me mouthing call me, and I respond to her hell, no! Then I add her to my don't call/hell no list, or ever hook up ever again, just too dangerous. I don't need or want that type of drama in my life.

Life has that invisible ticker tape flowing saying for "entertainment purposes only" with the microwave ding for the fresh batch of fresh imaginary popcorn and I just heard the ding. I had to laugh on that one he's walking script of drama acts.

Although I know he could handle himself, but why does he put himself in those situations? Loren avoided a beat down. The way he described the angry man this person could probably embed Loren into a wall with one hit. Hmm Loren is slim and tall, but size doesn't really matter. When I think back on Andrew and his cousin Joann knocking people out with their slim physique and quick moves, good example on size don't matter. Loren wasn't cocky just not afraid of the walking "Tower". He practiced what Mommy embedded in us we don't do that. We don't run, we finish whatever started or happened. This philosophy will allow you to move on and not have any parts of the past looking for you because it wasn't settled. I would also hear about Bill and Loren's bouts they encountered in the streets of Chicago. Bill was struck with some brass knuckles, but the scar left on his lips that I love feeling enhanced his smile. Bill chimes in on asking so which sister did you switch over to? Which one you think Chayta the one that came highly recommended freak, as Loren displays that signature smile accompanied with a wink. I didn't know about her being freaky, but curiosity had me tossing, (he winks with you know what I mean). Now she is on my list to contact when, then he stops which I thought was good I really didn't want to hear about her speciality.

Loren laughs turning his head to see if I was listening. Man, I heard Ty scream and it wasn't from a dream. She was like some type of siren in my ear, man I'm not into breaking an eardrum. Bill now get this I don't mind saying my name, but siren makes a brother want to get up and run you know what I mean. I left her dreaming with thoughts of her screaming. Little did he know that I heard him and thought about how Clarence did a quick ettiquette bedroom class on how not to scream or show certain emotions while being intimate? In his own way I guess he did what Clarence famous statement he put her to sleep. I really didn't want to vision or entertain that thought, yuck, vision ew. Do I need instructions? Bill needs to tell me because, I wasn't active he was the only one I knew I thought he would like that. I was hoping as Bill listened, he wasn't getting any ideas of missing out on that type of excitement, especially since we will be expecting Sabrina and he will be becoming a more stable family man at a young age.

One thing Bill forgot that I was three years younger than him. I'm still young but I know what I want and want to try and hold on to. I'm trying to keep those scants from falling all on him with their specialities. I'm just trying to keep my family together while Bill is trying to figure out his role. I hope with Loren's tales of tails don't fog Bill's mind and he can start seeing clearly. After all he is the head of our household. I depend on him in so many ways that I lost my first name and gained a new last name. Not to mention the other altered names he calls me. Bill wasn't the only one that gave up a life. Actually, I didn't give up my life but formed one with Bill to have a better life for us and our family. I was doing well before he came into my life. I was enjoying the freedom of exploring the world of good times and learning more about myself. I lived with my parents, had a car that was paid for, money in the bank, managing my bills and at the same time respecting my parents clock called curfew. If Bill passed through and kept it moving and I had not met him, I don't think I would have missed what I didn't know existed. After all I was in my hometown playing and living on familiar turf. Now the reality of all this is, that I'm not at home, nor in the comfort of familiar turf and sailing on the boat ride called my life.

After all he did ask, and I said yes. I could have turned around and kept it moving, but I wanted to give it my best because to me Bill was the best thing that happened to me. I still loved him and wanted our family. Growing up I seen many happy elderly couples and whatever their past was they managed to keep it together. I'm not naïve; I know some had some bumps and thumps, but they mended and molded and supported each other with minor or major sacrifices. Bottom line they made it work. I'm a big girl and I have to put on my big girl panties and walk it out. I can't hold Bill's big boy draws and help him step into them, because I'm holding and helping Sierra with her panties and soon Sabrina's diapers. I can't stand up if I'm constantly bending over helping people step into their underwear. This will become a big backache for me and an easy way out for Bill.

At some point in life I hope that Loren will step up and accelerate the elavator ride to the top floor and give Aunt Rosie Josey those grandchildren she has been longing for. I think she says that just to get Loren out of the basement and from the clearance area and find a good respectable woman. She just wants one lady that she could show off at church and listen to without substituting adverbs. I think I heard Loren say that Mama Rosie Josey would add don't wear yourself out trying to make it to the top son. In simpler terms don't wear a good thing out. He smiled at Bill saying that I don't mind wearing things out. With that statement they both raise their eyebrows with those twinkling almond eyes.

I really would like someone to talk to. I need to release my thoughts and the anxiety and not be judged. Mommy is gone, and all my mother tells me to do is pray. My patience or lack of, wants immediate answers, a quick fix. My mother and I weren't ever close, but I need her now. Now in so many ways I don't want to come across as a failure. I need my mother, my parents and my family to be proud of me. I want to go and talk to Momo and I know she would listen, but she trying to heal herself. If I told Courtney Diane her response would be why not drop his dumb ass and keep it moving with no detour, no rolling back, I don't believe in useless time. Then there is Robin she would smile and ask if you do what is your action plan. Plan on your act and act on your plan. Inside I was hoping that I didn't fall or slip into those accomdating affections.

I thought my plan was simply get married raise our children and grow old to-gether; I guess I thought it was simple. What would be my action plan? My dad always said if you leave, don't have your mail looking for you or you looking for your mail, and always have some mad money available. That wasn't my answer leaving but how do I make it work so we can stay together. Well I have very little mad money because my mad money went on temporary insanity bus rides and meals. So, leaving and setting up another home was not part of my equation or a part I wanted to add to my life. I really can't talk to my friends they would only try to talk me into coming back home to Oakwood. My heart knew but that wasn't the answer I wanted to hear. I know they only had my best interest and that's why we are still friends some thirty years later. My mother would be added to the list of wanting me to come back home too. I can't leave I need to see this through. I just need someone one to talk to for just a release. If I go over to anyones house Bill will come looking for me. He keeps me so isolated from developing any type of friendship. I just want one close friend other than myself.

On rainy days like this I just want to run outside. Just let the rain hit my face and erase the tears that left some residual or invisible stains on my face. Just allow the water to hit my face and scrub off the stains with my praying hands. I heard Courtney Diane say that if she shed one tear that's one too much and someone must pay for that. I wondered how many she shed for Malcom David during her transition of thoughts of leaving him. Did her tears evaporate before they could become erased or fade into her smooth complextion?

I need to start to see clearer and open my eyes. Let my spirit get fresh air and at the same time cleanse my thoughts. I just want to release the thoughts that I can't say and stop the stuttering on how to form my words into thoughts. Keeping your business your business is how we were raised, and mentally and physically I can't afford the consequences of the unknown. For now, I will continue to sit inside with my Chai tea and enjoy the view of the rain outside. Yep right, a foggy vision is alright I guess for now. Today I will relax my mind and see clearer tomorrow or maybe sooner. Any way I'm here while they are enjoying the events at ShaRoberts'. The many events that they have I will be ready for the next one and keep them coming. After all I'm three years younger I want to pop my fingers and twist/shake my butt too. Let some heads ooh and ah me and see how Bill likes that. Look at Rita like they did in high school and college. Hmmm I caught Bill's eyes and didn't know it. How many other admirers did I unknowingly know existed? Thinking back did I block other potentials that wouldn't have given me this type of drama? I wondered how long I would have stayed in Oakwood or would I be so comfortable that leaving wouldn't be an option that I would have ever considered. Like Mommy said we don't do that, finish what you started, because we don't run or like Mama Sadie said he had to ask. Yep and I answered maybe that should have been a Cory Davon special of yeah with a slow okay to focus on my answer and allow thoughts to form and evaluate before blurting out yes. Such a small word has made a huge impact on my life. One impact was by just leaving the comfort of my hometown Oakwood.

I really didn't have any regrets just ongoing concerns. Concerns that I really don't know how to understand or know of how-to bring clarity to my concerns. How do I explain or talk about something I don't know how to put into words? Momo is like a mother to me. I just want to sometimes just lay my head in her lap like a little girl and have her tell me I'm okay and everything will get better. Hang out with Robin and Courtney Diane and laugh away my pain and loose myself in their conversations while being entertained. In between thoughts Clarence's words laugh through me in silence saying I left my fool card in the safe because today I don't want to deal with the consequences. Today the fool card is in the safe because I don't want to deal with the consequences of my action or forget to test the wind direction for Bill's mood swings or attitude adjustments with me on the receiving end.

I want to run back home to Oakwood, but that is not the answer and failure is not my option. My feet want to move in some type of direction, but they feel like they are inside cinder blocks. I'm leaning in different directions, but my feet can't move or simply won't move. I'm stuck, or we stuck in trying to help each other grow up. We are both confused and need to work out our confusion and make this work. We came to California together and we need to see this through, together. Just like Mommy taught us we don't do that. Those words still echo in my brain and spirit years later. Her words lived longer than her life. I miss her so much and wish I could call just to hear her voice. But I know I have to grow up and realize that she is not coming back.

Sierra wakes up and slowly comes and lays her head in my lap to join me and her sister, and I needed that. Yep that is just what I needed. My thoughts wander to a place where I think about Bert's prayer over the mystery dinner and how he struggled to say innocently the right words. This made Momo chuckle but not too hard because you could see that she wanted to support Amos. She loved him enough and appreciated the hard work he had put into dinner and that he was trying his best. It was good seeing her improving and that family time still exist at the dinner table. One thing I wasn't used to their place being so quiet. While Sierra cuddles, she wants to look at Shrek again followed with Kung Fu Panda, great. I hope she falls back to sleep. Two nights in a row with the monkey and donkey is more than enough. I look at how much she looks like Bill in a small version. I'm thankful that she has both parents. At the same time, I wondered what Bill and Loren were getting into. Sabrina is waking up and Sierra jumps because she felt the movement of her sister. She smiles asking can her sister see and hear the movies. I tell her no, but she can hear and feel whats going on. Sierra turns her head and starts with the questions what is the best part she likes in Shrek. I have to tell her I don't know she was sleep, and she felt you against her and she likes it. She was trying to get your attention to let you know she feels you. With her mouth wide open Sierra is amused by my statement. Only if she knew I had to say something quick before all the questions started flowing out. I watched her smile turn away as she tunes back into Shrek.

I think about daddy and daughter time when they are playing or washing dishes together. Bill sits patiently with Sierra as he helps her get through the words in her books and work math problems. I like how she says daddy with so much love and I get called Rita. One day mom will come out of her mouth. School will be starting soon for her and I will miss our time together as she explores a new environment. I guess our bus rides will slow down but not go away. Now Bill will have a riding partner called Sierra and let's see which direction he will travel home. Sierra sees all and tells everything only at her time in her way. No more secrets for daddy ha-ha-la-la and tee-hee. I like the feeling of her lying in my lap and her sister gently sleeping with an occasional kick and they are both at peace. Just maybe I will get a peaceful rest and pass the time away into slumber. I need to do something with my thoughts so that I'm not staring at the clock wondering what time Bill and Loren will come home. Right when I doze off, I hear Sierra getting into her sleep by a slight snoring noise. I nudge her to get up because right now she is too heavy to carry, but this time I take her to our bed, so all the girls can sleep together. We used to let her sleep with us until she starts sleeping all over the bed and we would wake up tired and she would be well rested. Just like we had to come together on putting her into a stroller the bed offered some challenges, but we pulled it off and she now enjoys her big bed. Tonight, the girls are going to enjoy this big bed. Daddy can come in and see his girls sleeping peacefully.

Shrek is not on and the sounds from the television fade away as we all fade into deep comfortable sleep. We slept so hard I didn't hear them come in, no rattle of the keys, slamming of the door or laughing through conversations. When I had to make my bathroom run, they both were crashed on the couch not making much noise. They looked as peaceful as little boys resting after a long playful day. I stared at them and a smile comes on my face that generated from my heart. I felt so much love for them. I try to focus as I glanced at the clock and realized what my parents would say they respected the clock. I guess they didn't have too much hang time, must be getting older or maybe they just realize that there is really nothing out there, but trouble and Bill is now a married family man. No time for chasing mini skirts and mini memories of last night. Maybe I might surprise everyone with a big breakfast for my family. I lay it down for another two hours and wake up to start breakfast. We have plenty of food this time thanks to Loren and now I will show our appreciation. Pancakes, hashbrowns, bacon and soft scrambled eggs is what they will wake up to. Yes, a new day, with the pleasant aroma of a hot big breakfast made just for my family. I find myself dancing and switching picturing Momo as she would prepare her meals. I feel my body doing her little sexy dance and humming with no words in mind.

Today the only care I have is when Sabrina will be ready for her debut. She's moving more, and the visits are always filled with a praise report. Dr. Deck and Dr. Dailey are happy and Dr. Upesi continues to look at me with her angelic smile. I don't look bruised or mentally frustrated and afraid to answer her with a straight face as I tried so hard to hold in my shame. I know or at least I feel that she could feel or see the pain I had been hiding from myself. I knew something was there just didn't want it to surface into the light. Sometimes Momo would look at me with sincere eyes and love felt through her embrace. It was as if she had a magnifying glass studying my tears that the rain didn't wash away. After all Bill has been on his best behavior and I haven't shuttered from the fear that sometimes come out his voice. Sometimes his looks make me feel as if I'm younger than Sierra and I am being reprimanded for not listening. I can hear but when he yells, I just tune out the words and the depth of his voice. Everything tremors my sprirt, my soul and confidence all find a spot to hide. Again, they packed up their bags and took off and will return when they feel all is calm. Just great I did need some type of back up, cowards. Everyone is waking up with moans and groans as they stretched and smell the aroma of a fresh breakfast.

I hear the mumbles of Bill and Loren discussing last night and the honeys Loren was talking to and the name they called Bill aka Professor. Bill loves wearing his sweater vest and with the added glasses he could resemble a professor. I laughed at thinking when I went with Bill to get his eyes checked the doctor unknowingly said out loud that I know you don't drive without your glasses. Only if he knew how vain Bill was, he wore his glasses but not all the time. Those glasses turned his almond shaped eyes to a small pupil with a cover. Either way I still had the same eyes for him nothing but love. He was perfect to me. His height, build, wavey black hair, deep dimples, chiseled physique and bowlegs, yep that's what turned me on. I like seeing him walk toward me and walk away. Yep I like that cadence of left, right, left and right. Now that's makes me want to get some hamburger meat and flip and flop it like Momo says she does with Amos and her patties.

I smile as I glance over at them and Bill looks handsome while sleeping. I smile as I tell them breakfast is ready and just needed some swaggers. They start laughing as Sierra runs to her daddy for a high jump and hugs. Loren smiles as he looks as if he is taking a mental snap shot of Bill and Sierra. Bill grabs me by the waist and kisses me on the back of my neck and again those lips feel so good and moist. Loren comes behind him and gives me a kiss on the cheek thanking me for breakfast while saying that he might have to make another trip or just pack up shop and move on out here. We both laugh but Loren might be serious on this one. Bill smiles but I can see that he was just a little pissed with Loren. He says in calm voice that's one thing Bill and I had in commom we didn't believe in yelling especially when trying to get our point across. Well there was an exception to that rule…

Loren looks at an expression of what?? Bill takes a breath asking what was up with you going up to that woman sitting with her husband telling her how fine she was and complementing her husband. The confused husband hesitates but agreed and his ass was pissed, and we could have gotten our hmm. Loren's calm response was that could have been his sister, girlfriend or humph. All I was doing was setting it up for if she was single or married and if things weren't working out humph. But if I return and she's by herself and wasn't limited my future opportunites. You see how he looked at you and kept looking over at our table. That's why we had to get the hell out of there because of Loren's roaming ass. With all that it still would be nice having him out here but living and visiting is two different things. When I visited, California it was fun but living here, is different. I'm still trying to get used to my surroundings and at the same time trying to survive without being around family and friends.

I miss seeing my parents and family and talking with Melody Lynn, Debbie Ann, Claudia and Sharon Denise and the strength that I admired in them. I wanted to have my children grow up with my family and friends just like I did. As time goes on some parts of Oakwood fade away as I continue to become more familiar with Oceanview. My home is where my family is and for now that's here. They yum, yum the food and Sierra wants to sit in Bill's lap as he tries to eat his breakfast. I guess she is feeling her daddy moments and missing him right now. I looked at them both as he feeds her as if she was very young. She is enjoying it and smiling as she looks around the room enjoying being or acting like a very little girl. Daddy's little pampered spoiled daughter. It really doesn't matter, that's his right to pamper and spoil his daughter. Loren talks about the food that was catered by Chef Harris and all the parties were off the scale. I had a smorgasborg of women in all sizes and comfortable ages. Here we go again Loren really needs to slow his role. I pictured him, and Clarence's brother Steve would roam the streets for treats and never have that appetite fulfilled. They will end up lonely with a deep decay of loneliness like Uncle Glooey. I don't wish that on anyone, and I could be wrong and don't mind if I am.

Loren seems to be happy but on the other hand people think that Bill and I appear to be happy all the time, just like Robin and Ramon and Courtney Diane and Malcolm David. They all said the same thing appearances are just that a starring role that sometimes you have the front seat and people unknowingly know you are performing. In their case both ending in a contract called divorce. So, I know looks and actions can all be deceiving. Bill and I have our moments, but we are family and he seem to be happy.

I just want Bill to treat me a little better, so I don't have to guess sometimes on how I should act. I want to be myself but through all the changes I don't remember who I am. I have so many names mom, wife, and so many other as Loren would say adverbs thrown at me. It makes me question on how Bill looks at me when I walk away or walk towards him. Does he want to flip and flop or just flop down and snore the night away and wake up to his own beginning. How do I get that flopping feeling back in Bill where we touch, love and embrace one another? What happened to the names that had love on the end not the insults I've been trying not respond to? My inner response is filled with pain but no tears and hurt that Bill can no longer see or feel what he is inflicting on me. I have become numb to my pain but haven't master numbing to the words yet. The words have such penetration that it lingers like a small pinch. Eventually it fades away but somehow it leaves a temporary mark but mentally reminds you why the mark existed.

Breakfast was greatly appreciated then here comes the silent blow the hit that throws you off and makes you stagger your walk and mind. Loren smiles as he says to me you look like you are ready to go and hope I'm here to see my little cousin come on in. Bill's response without a filter says I sure will be glad too, so all the floors will balance back, because it can't support her weight. Before I could respond Loren comes quickly to my defense with hey cuz that weight is your daughter and Rita is willing to put her life on the line to give birth to another child, your child. You can't do or say that Bill. Bill smiles turns into anger for being corrected on site. He gets up holding Sierra and takes her into the bedroom. I look at Loren with a smile and mouthed thank you the tears are filling up in my eyes and I try hard to make them dry or control them, so they don't come out. I hope and pray saying silently please let the numbness come in. I don't know what's going to happen when Bill comes back. I fear for Loren I'm used to the blows rather it's verbal or physical. I know they are cousins, but Bill probably feels that Loren stepped over the line. This was a surprise to both of us because; Bill never said anything like that in the presence of anyone. Loren needed a break and I hope he got what he needed, and we got what we needed from him. His visit was pleasant and feeled with family love, but he is Bill's blood line and blood is thicker than water. Bill comes back and kisses me on the forehead saying that he was sorry and thanked Loren for representing. It may sound sincere but somehow, I feel I will pay for his embarrassment. I quietly excuse myself to the bathroom. I look into the mirror and just stare, no reason just stares as I turn my head from side to side, as if I was examing my face for bruises. I look to see the tear stains faded so I don't have to replace them. That was the small pinch that I have to try and let it fade away, so I can go out and perform before the crowd. I smile as if nothing happened and everything is okay, and the Oscar belongs to Rita. Not beach, not any other name he wants to call me. I think back when I was young when they didn't call me by my name. It was either EJ's younger sister or Bonnie's older sister. No one seemed to know my name. I felt invisible no name, no presence and here I am again in the same situation. Bill had forgotten my name and somehow, we lost our connection.

I love feeling my daughter move and cuddle inside me. I love it when I hear her loud heartbeat through the monitor. With every beat I'm thankful that I am the vessel carrying another daughter. Bill will not take that joy from me. This is the only thing he can't take. He doesn't know how it feels to feel her movements and touch my stomach and feel her body parts growing. I'm not that woman he looks at that has this perfect figure while pregnant. I'm who I am big or small I do have feelings with an "s". Bill will not take my joy and when I walk out my joy will still be in my heart, soul and spirit. Man didn't give it and man can't take it away. I look into the mirror and smile for I'm still alive. That kiss on the forehead was for show but my smile is for stay. This was out of character of Bill. Insults he would throw at my soul to penetrate my spirits were always done in the comfort of our conversations. There was never an audience. I can only gather that when they went out yesterday that Bill was in clear view of many women that Loren innocently critique as they passed by or as he made attempted to talk to them. Maybe then was when Bill realized he was shackled to a pregnant wife and reality set in that he was a married family man. I figured one or a few got his attention and he came home and compared me to them. Here I go again in an imaginary competion that I thought I had made it to the finish line called "the altar".

I slowly open the bathroom door and what catches my attention, the faded blue stain on the wall that seems to linger and not totally fade away and at the same time remind me of the consequences of my actions. Well here I go deep cleaning distractor. Pinesol, Comet time for cleaning so I can meditate on refreshing my spirit and not bust out any form of anger or tears. I open the fridge and start removing and moving items around and managing not to say a word. Nope, no words just a light hum to myself, this will be my distractor. Now I kinda understand why Momo hummed sometimes you need a little distractor. Bill and Loren watch me as I gather and move without making any eye contact or conversation. They ease up and go back into the front room and continue with their casual conversations. Loren notices my movement throughout the kitchen and smiles saying that when his mother, Rosie Josey is upset she gets into that type of deep cleaning humming and not saying a word that's when we all leave. Because during the process we don't know the out come of her anger, spirit or mind thought as she finishes and usually, we don't want to be around. No one should be around if they knew what was best for them, and that would be to leave or run. There are some severe consequences to her action if the wind shifts cuz. That part was not funny and not good to be around when the house is clean and the attitude should be well adjusted at least the person who made her mad. That person should be ready for anything and everything. Or just funk it and get the hell out until her ass is calmed down and the house is clean. While Loren was talking, I could feel Bill" s eyes on me. He had me wondering where his thought process was probably going. I have done this ritual a many of times and Bill never noticed until it was brought to the light in form of Loren. I could see the concern in his face, (maybe Bill was feeling more embarrass since he got busted). He really didn't understand me or what was happening with us. It took someone from the outside to help what was going on in the inside, amazing.

Chapter 37
Time to Clean and a Time to Move

Cleaning and laughter got us through the days and hopefully the last visit to see Doctor Deck or Doctor Dailey will end with good news. Loren welcomes the invite to go with us to our appointment. The relationship between Bill and Loren didn't change. I think it might had grown stronger with respect for each other as adults. We were greeted with the angelic smile from Doctor Upesi and Nurse Evelyn looked at us as if she was counting heads to a larger exam room. I was glad that Doctor Upsei saw the family support I had and that we were doing better. Sabrina is moving as if she is hoping that this would be her last visit. Loren is in ah as he listens to the heartbeat as he views the sonogram of his little cousin. Sierra sits on Bill's lap looking and listening with the joy of knowing that her sister is on her way. I glance over at Loren and smile saying she will be here soon. As he pulls his eyes away, I can tell he is thinking about something. His slow response was wow that's what's growing inside of you? You're eating walking and living for two people. We should be waiting on you hand and foot. He looks over at Bill with amazement saying, cuz, wow man I didn't know this is some deep shift. I guess better you than me, because I'm not ready but you never know. I'm getting deep signals from Rosie Josey stressing me hard on some grandbabies. Not to add my brother Dr. Akil or sometimes calling his ass Doctor Doug saying my brothren how is that working for you trying each floor. Now if your elevator is out of order, I can prescribe something for that elevator rising. Oh, Doctor Doug got jokes. I don't know about the babies maybe a baby and my shift do work. But dude I need to get married first if I'm going to do this, I got to do it right. I don't want to be like Aniteah and Claudey, or Holland, didn't need to add any to their wedding party, or Studs who lives with his baby mama who keep popping out but he ani't pop no question.

Now if I do this, I want one shot no divorce, no counseling just us keeping real and getting it together. I've watched you two work well together and I know that is straight up not easy pretty much a full-time job. But you stayed together no one is leaving, you two just staying in tune with each other. You both seem to communicate sometimes without words just looks and actions. Inside I'm wondering what apartment he stayed at, because it couldn't have seen all this at our place. What tune was Loren listening to? Funny how people don't know when you are performing, I guess Bill and I were very convincing. I had to close my eyes and open them to make sure I was not hanging out with Robin's Aunt Brandi in Alice and Wonderland or sitting at the round table with the Mad Hatter!

Doctor Deck reassured us that time is very soon as he finished the exam smiling while leaving the room. Loren response was I hope to be here, but I need to get back home. Momma missing her baby boy and I need to be cuddled. Bill busts him out saying are you going back to Fifi? Loren response was oh hell no, oops. I reached for Bill to assist me up from the table as Sierra jumps off his lap and Loren leaps toward me to assist as well. I think this was an eye opener for him. Maybe he might just go to the penthouse and stay away from the basement bargains he has been getting. He said he wants to try every floor but that sounds like that thought is getting old. One thing I had to give him credit for he is living his life and not trying to destroy anyone elses. He is who he is and the women he hooks up with know that. But for some odd reason we always feel the need to try and change the person. You get what you get, and you work with it. Loren wants to settle down but not just settle. I can respect that, and I hope the one he does choose will realize that she was the one. After all he has chased almost every skirt, there is not too much left that he hasn't had or experienced. I guess he should be ready to settle down after he has traveled on the elevator to each floor.

Time seems to fly and I am awakened by severe cramping and back pain. I know this feeling all so well. Now I just need to look at the clock and time the contractions. I don't want to alarm Bill and make Loren nervous. If he is like Bill, I don't need them both looking at me like paint drying on the wall. I move and try to get more comfortable. Bill is not feeling the movement he is sound asleep. He looks so peaceful but if they start coming sooner that peace will go away with my slight scream with a nudge to wake him up. A little chuckle and smile come into my heart as I picture Courtney Diane, Cory Davon looking at their Mother Florrie look at her watch and look at them and look at them looking at her looking at her watch saying is it time to care? Well this time this will be the time to care. Let me concentrate checklist; feet are clean yep, other areas clean yep, underwear right yep, hair straight well yep. Well you might be going, and the checklist is a go. Courtney Diane and Robin are both in Florida visiting Henry Luis and seeing where her new post was located. Courtney Diane reminded me and Robin that she was not a Florida fan, but her boy was there. We would laugh at her saying I thought you cut the apron string and let him run and stretch his legs in life. You are always talking about stretching your legs now you have a break. Her response with that corner smile was you both right. I've cut the apron string and I neatly placed them in the kitchen drawer. So, in other words when needed, it's available, neatly folded now kiss my ass. I smile as Robin laughs saying here, we go again. She would add again that you don't have an ass who gonna fill in for you Rita. Then I would look at them with how I got involved and Courtney Diane would add do we need to play "Wheel of Fortune". Oh, here we go add a vowel "e" right for entire ass and again who will fill in for you and your entire ass that in your imagination exist as she winks at me. Bottom line she did cut the apron string she just didn't throw it away. She placed it nice/neatly in her drawer.

I don't know if I could cut the strings from Sierra. I can't even fathom that thought. Right now, I just have to wait to see if her sister is ready to join her new world and breathe in the fresh California air. I was hoping in the back of my mind that Loren would hook up with Courtney Diane, but she will be moving to Florida and he will be leaving for Chicago. That's more than a two-hour drive, nope not going to happen. If she is fussing about Florida weather, I can't see Chicago being a second choice. Loren was in love with her on first sight, but the sight faded into the next skirt that passed by.

One day he will settle down but today is not the day, maybe not tomorrow and next year hmmm ouch that was a good contraction longer and harder this time. They are coming and lingering okay let me start back timing them again. Funny when I fall off to sleep awaken by a contraction and thoughts as if they are working some type of combination of pain and joy. Just like that song and my sunshine will be here soon. Last run with Sierra it was thirteen hours before she decided to embrace her new world. On this run I'm not looking for that type of marathon with this one. I just have a feeling it will be soon. My mother will have to hear about it and that was what I will miss her being there and helping. I guess I have to grow up a little more because my family and responsibility will be increasing as the thoughts pass and the contraction continue to put me on alert. In the back of my mind should I put Bill, Loren and Sierra on alert and have them stare at me waiting on my every move will have them jumping out of their seats and raising my anxiety level up. Funny how I thought my first pregnancy was indigestion and year's later Charlotte reminded me of my naive belief. Indigestion funny but in that process my mind was in deep denial and just couldn't believe that happened. Yep I needed that talk that Reva said the reason for her and others in the clinic needed. Majority of them needed that talk that all parent(s) avoid the "s" word. I could not only raise my hand, but this would be an anthem to others. Have that sex talk with your children educate them in the house, so they don't find out the way many of us have and left raising ourselves as we raise our children.

I still wondered if Reva made her dream come true in the entertainment industry or had any more children. The last time I saw her was in passing after I had Sierra. She was the same size with the corner smile showing a slight dimple but tired eyes still entertaining about her mother Miss Aberlynda aka Glenda the witch. She displays a corner smile as she said that her broom was temporary grounded. I thought by now my niece customized motorized broom would have been temporary grounded. But I looked outside on a clear day and saw the motorized broom with red tassels flying with ease with a crooked smile. I realized as I glanced up yep that's her, my niece. Reva didn't know how just saying that took me to a place that was a hmmm. I looked at her as she talks about her mother and I realized how much love and respect she has for her with a forgiven heart. Reva laughs at least that day saying that her mother still calls her Miss Dorothy. Still talking about Maurice, the dog bow wowed out, and yep I was in Oz with the total dog that had many characters, the cowardly lion, because he doesn't come around, the tin man proved that he couldn't stand up because he had no spine and as the strawman no kinda brain process.

Reva said she had to agree in my mind that her mother was right and in between her cigarettes and drink in hand I had to grudgingly give confirmation to her drunken theory. She fessed up saying that she had a front row seat to the consequences of her actions but believed an innocent lie. I thought that must be a popular phrase because that was the same weak excuse that Loren used, hmm must be a man's thing. I had forgotten that I had run into Reva in my favorite food craving for Bronco's. I loved the homemade fries and double cheeseburger and a large coke ooh yummy. Really love that combination then and now I'm paying for those large fries' cravings while pregnant with Sierra. Bill and I hung out there a lot eating the same combo.

I can only laugh at what Reva said that her son, Benji I heard a slight chuckle when she said she started at a young age calling him Budgy. Because Budgy was bugging her, in a loving way. Plus, she wasn't used to hearing someone calling her mama. She knew that she didn't like it when her mother called her Dorothy. Reva shook her head saying she caught herself doing the same thing with Budgy/ Benji. She added, just like I got used to being called Dorothy, Benji got used to being called Budgy. One thing I do know that she will instill in him and there will be an on-going conversation of more than don't go out there and get someone pregnant. Won't give him nightmares but she will pop those wet dreams. Reva would remind him that if you can't take care of yourself you don't need to have someone involuntary depending on you. Don't play the starring role of "thu-pid" and don't be out there audtioning either. I remember with concern in her voice saying that she will give him more than don't go out there and get some dumb ass silly girl pregnant. That similar one liner that was given to her and her sisters will not happen to her son. We deserved better and my son will not learn the hard way.

Maybe one day I will try and call the number Reva gave me. I need to check on her and her mother. In the back of my mind my parents will be there, and I will be

NOW I SEE CLEARLY

there for them, but I know because of the kinda love they have for Bonnie she will be the one they will probably want to take care of them. I guess that's the price you pay for being the favorite. I can only right now imagine what this might feel like taking care of your mother. Reva's corner smile slowly goes away until I can only see her light deep dimple. Her eyes were tired because her mom had taken ill to cancer and sclerosis of the liver but wouldn't give up drinking or smoking and she stayed at her mom's house when her siblings got themselves together and bailed out. Ungrateful heathens she murmured out the corner of her mouth. Reva said that her mother had called her Dorothy for so long that she thought she was losing her mind then. At first it pissed me off in my silence and she knew it but let me get away with that thought, that I learned to accept her fun at my expense and just stopped reacting. Now she's not hurting anyone with her harsh words. I seemed to always be the target but, in her laughter, and pain. Funny with no ha, that all this time I thought she couldn't stand me. But out of all my siblings I reminded her of her. She left me the house and there we stayed as I continued to take care of her and my son Benji. It's hard seeing my mom fade away and she won't work with you to help her and I have to help her, she's my mom. Now I'm the momma and at the same time trying to take care of Benji as I put my career on hold.

I sing to an audience of two Benji and my mom and they smile as I try to soothe their hearts and spirits. One thing through it all, I never stopped loving my mother. Now let me back it up there were times where I couldn't stand her even when she would call me Dorothy which irritated the hell out of me. I learned to smile and take it, because it was my mother being herself. She always said she lived her life the way she wanted to and too late for regrets and she would drink to that. Then Reva went back to talking about Benji as I watched the tired eyes water and she talked about her mom and she switch more to a pleasant thought saying that her son was book smart and, she wanted to keep him focused and away from the fast tail girls. I had to think back on Courtney Diane and the talk she had with Henry Luis on you are not the only car driving up that scants ramp and the other akas names she assigned to those girls; like trixie in training, rachected scant, or highway ho, ooh those are the ones I remembered. For some reason I think she went passed the one liner and kept the conversation going rather he wanted to hear it or not and tagged team him with his Aunt Robin, so he knew that a village was surrounding him.

That's what we had grown up with and it dwindled down almost drying up, as we grew older, maybe because we would listen but not hear and understand until later in life. You learned to appreciate the time you have with your family. I appreciated the time, energy and investment of my parents. Didn't know how much I needed them then and now and the future showed me all they instilled in me helped developed me into a good person and the strength to see anything and everything through. Like mommy said we don't do that.

As I walked to the back-room eyes are following me wondering what is really going on. As I waddle to just lie down, I glanced at the blue marks that are still on the wall that just seem not to go or fade away. Inside I still do remember that night but try to force it out of my head as I mentally try to keep count of how far the contractions are apart. I tell everyone that I'm just going to lie down. I hear Loren say hey cuz I think she is getting close. Bill duh attack didn't notice but he will when its time, our parents are not here and this time it's on us. I try lying down and get as comfortable as I can, but the contractions are coming harder and longer. I feel that Sabrina is getting ready and giving me her warning in her way. I start trying to doze off during the break of contraction and hear a knock on the door with faint conversation. Either it's Robin or maybe Courtney Diane made it back from Florida. It couldn't be Momo she comes out for fresh air but doesn't stay out long and plus it's late. I try to recognize the voice, but sleep has me fading in and out just like being in a daze as the voices sound so muffled. Whoever it was I kinda heard laughing as I heard that I was tired and trying to get some rest. I must give Bill credit he was always nice to our friends, guest and welcomed them in. It was just the otherside that others missed and sometimes I wouldn't mind if that part faded away, so I could have the man I married back.

Charlotte and Johnnie Lee looked happy after having a cart full of children, Catrice and Greekum had team of children and Micheal and Michelle had three, Veretta with the number of children increasing everytime she returned to the states three girls and twin boys. Floyd said she said that was it before the twin boys popped out what a surprise, so with two, Bill and I can be happy too. Will I want more only time will tell? I had a front row seat to seeing how happy they are, were and still hanging tough and through it all they are stronger. The Tarvers, Sheppherds, Hollingsworths, Cormiers and Walkers and many other couples that have slipped my mind but not my heart that have stood the test of time. They had an understanding for each other and showed and demonstrated that love doesn't end but continues to grow. It's amazing how they made time for each other. I watched for sickness and in health vows with Momo and Amos as they laughed through his mystery meals with their family. While the sons prayed for the food to some how have a different flavor. I enjoyed the family meals and the holiday times where we all were in the kitchen preparing many entrees. That was the only time when we had a lot of foods prepared from scratch. Never knew what an avocado was until I moved out here and didn't want to embarrass myself in front of Robin. I wasn't aware of how to eat them or not adventureous enough to taste them. Living out here I learned how much of a country girl I was moving from Oakwood to the big city. I never thought about Oakwood being a small city. Then my thoughts wandered off in between sleep and reality that Robin, Courtney Diane held it together as single parents, and didn't seem to be bored or emotional or financially struggling.

I sometimes wondered if they miss being in a relationship or just right now this wasn't the time for them. They followed a philosophy of leaving prepared and saving your mad money for when that madness may occur. I don't want to think about not being with Bill, Sierra and Sabrina not being with both parents or to struggle emotionally and financially. Although my parents fussed and fought, they hung in there and provided for our family and we really didn't want for anything we played and ate as we blended into our neighborhood.

Every household had both parents working and providing. There were a few single families on the block, but we were kids playing didn't think much of it. The one thing that they didn't have to hear was that old phrase wait til your dad gets home which was not good to be on the receiving end. As kids we thought wow you don't have a dad, so you don't get the same type of punishment, now that sounds nice. Until this day my parents are still together and love and support still present where they can still complete each other sentences and that's what I want for Bill and me. Ooh this contraction lasted longer falling off to sleep and thoughts I forgot to keep track I need to start counting again. When they start coming a little stronger, I will give Bill the time is now look. This is so strange, years ago when I had Sierra, I had to admit that I was scared. My mother wasn't here to drive me, my father wasn't here to paint the room for me or paint the wall that still shows the blue stain, nor did I have to call Bill to tell him I'm on the way to the hospital. This is all new for the both of us and I can only imagine how Bill might feel becoming a dad again at a young age.

I know it's too late to think about if we can afford another mouth. I want to work and be among the working environment; I loved it then and miss it now. I do want my own money and help Bill out with our family. I do like being at home with Sierra, but she soon will be starting school. We will not be taking our bus rides or long walks. This go around I'm raising another daughter this time no mom, dad, EJ, Bonnie or Sonny to help. No visits to Mommy's house to show off my daughters, no Mama Sadie to share wisdom, no Hazel to just say hi to. I miss seeing Sharon, Debbie and Melody Lynn coming to the hospital or house to see how I was doing or me going to their place doing the same. So many things I took for granted that I really miss. I can see their faces but can't touch their hands too far away. I want to go home but I'm no longer daddy's little girl but a married woman with a family. I still can see my parents' faces with tears of hope as we drove away so many years ago. My parents tried hard to share in my joy and hoping that the man I married they trusted to take good care of me. In some ways Bill has provided for us, but sometimes his split behavior has me confused, scared and wondering in the back of my mind did I put too much trust in him. All these what ifs and thoughts are riding my emotions. I have to keep in mind he asked and I'm here, we are here. I need to stay focused while Sabrina is working her way down my back. Time and thoughts had me lose count and I need to start counting and timing my contractions again. Just as my eyes close again I focus on Bill smiling at me with a tray of food and just checking on me. His almond shaped eyes still have that twinkle as he looks at me accompanied with his smile and deep dimples. I told him that the contractions are coming, and I think we are getting close. His eyes glazed over, and I could see the fright in his eyes as the smile tries to nervously stay. Only if he could view my soul and spirit and knew I was shivering in the corner. This time my soul/spirit didn't back up and leave they stayed to see this through. I need my ancestral strength to help me out. Bill nervously asks how far are your contractions? I say they haven't made it to ten minutes, but I will let you know before it gets to that point.

I asked who was at the door and it was Natilia looking for little Tim. He was hiding again. I laughed because the only place he knows to hide is under the cabinets and he for some reason he likes the bathroom. Bill mentioned that Robin checked in on me and that Courtney Diane is still in Florida and sends her love. Henry Luis and Floyd were in Florida enjoying a good time in Daytona Beach. Courtney Diane needed to check on them to make sure no scants noticed the neon sign in the middle of his forehead. Only she could say it, with your dumb ass. In the back of my mind I think Henry Luis scant pregnancy scare and thinking about how many cars have rammed up her ramps detoured his vehicle. If he remembers they both said, go into neutral and reverse back out and keep it moving, the right lady will come but not under those circumstances.

What would have happened if I didn't go into the library that day what turn would my life had made. Can't go back but I can look forward to sharing my future with Bill as we raise our children. Here it comes this was a big one well I guess it's getting closer to Sabrina's debut. I tried breathing deeply while closing my eyes just hoping this will go away, because I have at least a week before my due date. But as active as Sabrina has been, I think she is ready to sprint on out of me and see what her family looks like. I tried calling out to Bill, but my voice volume can't go any higher. I tried sitting up with each grunt and sound to help me move better like that helps. They are coming stronger and I take a deeper breath and yell out for Bill and this time he hears me! He rushes back to our bedroom with Loren as they show fright on their faces. My thoughts were get over it and get over here, so we can get out and get gone!! They take each arm as they gently try to lift me up. It seems like everyone was in sync as they lift, Sierra rushes in with my shoes and Bill says let's go! We have gas and the bag is in the car.

Bill holds me up as Loren as usual carries Sierra as if she just learned how to walk. Bill straps me in and the fragrance and kiss ease my mind but doesn't take the cramps away and the discomfort feeling in my back. Loren shows so many emotions that I really want to laugh at him, but I don't think the way he is feeling he might just pass out. I keep my breathing going as Bill makes me nervous with his

NOW I SEE CLEARLY

driving. I know we need to get there but all in one piece please. I tried to breathe, smile and get as comfortable as I could but Bill's driving ooh. Sure, do wish I had set in the back, so I wouldn't have a front row view. Only thing to remember is protecting the face and breathe, you will be there in no time. I hope that either Doctor Deck or Doctor Upesi and Nurse Evelyn are on duty that will ease the visions of my parents not being there. Doctor Dailey would work too. I just want to see a familiar face. I'm glad that Loren is here that way he can keep Sierra company, while Bill cuts the cord to his daughter named Sabrina. As we arrived at the base, they are familiar with us and they send word ahead. As we pulled in, they rush out with wheelchair and gurney ready for me and Bill. They are moving so fast I hope the delivery will go fast too. They take me into a room for examination to tell me that I'm not ready yet, but I will be ready before the day ends. This puts Bill's mind at ease. Loren brings in Sierra and they do just what I didn't want them to do was just watch me as I tried to adjust to the pain and the stares. The food smells good and I'm so hungry but can't have anything to eat. When they tell you that you can't eat, then you feel like you're starving. These ice chips are not making it as soon as they enter, they dissolve before I could use my imagination on what type of food I might taste. The cramps and back pain were increasing as Bill tries hard to comfort me by holding my hand and gently rubbing my back as Loren's tries to entertain Sierra.

At this point we are at a wait and see stance. I close my eyes and try to focus on good thoughts. Like picturing Momo dancing in the hoola hoop and her sister Miss Minnie saying weren't you smaller? Then Momo breaks out into a dance/chant of go Momo go Momo and the rest are saying; how low can you go, and she shouts (while dancing), I don't know this went on for a while. Until she couldn't make it back up and that was in form of a song as she was directing them to sit her down. She was still singing while giving them directions. The song and tune were the way she would talk about flipping and flopping hamburgers and turned it around into a sexual act. Like she did with almost every meal I was around to watch her prepare, while dancing and twisting, with Amos responding and snickering. He would smile and in a low voice saying, I liked to be flipped and flopped, (followed with a skip). I didn't know what Amos meant when he asked if she was frying chicken, his response to her is I liked to be plucked. Momo told me what it meant and laughed at me when I would look at her with my normal don't get it look???

Amos didn't say much he kinda of reminded me of my grandparents Yank and Hazel. Not much on words but in some way always seemed amusing. Thinking of food and fried chicken and Aunt Chris ate so much chicken, that her husband said people might think an archaeologist lives here as her dog was pissed for getting some dry bones. Then I chuckle about the questions relating to fried chicken from Aunt Brandy. I reflected on Robin's cousin Rhona who she didn't get the flour footsteps on the carpet or confusing common sense with common scent ooh that was dangerous. I can feel my smile enlarging as I thought about Uncle Boris and his crop-dusting antics with his dog, Coco following in his master's dust creating his own wind flurries. I could go for those raspberry zingers and beg for them like Johnnie Lee did to Charlotte. His deep blue eyes looked so ocean blue and showing nothing but love for her as he deeply pleaded for the zingers. I was amused as he added their daughter, Tammijune when they were busted coming from the zinger aisle. Food is the only thing right now I seem to think about, as I glance over at the monitor for the heartbeat of Sabrina and the rate of my contractions just as I did with Sierra. I didn't know I would be looking at it again. The line doesn't need to show how strong they are. I can tell them through my grunts and movements. Sierra is getting restless, so Loren offers to take her out for something to eat. Knowing Loren as I do that's short for food and presents. She has him so wrapped around her finger I feel for his wife, daughter or son. I know he will spoil them with love and affection with gifts tagging along. I think this is an eye opener for Loren and maybe he really might think about making his mother, Rosie Josey happy by bringing home the whole package a wifey and some childrens. Finally leaving the basement and after sampling each floor, finally making it to the top floor and meeting the next Mrs. Loren and she gotsta be right. That would be billboard news on who she may be.

Chapter 38
It's That Time for Real

This time the hospital is so different maybe because I was younger and so much was happening then. The next thing I knew, I'm pushing Sierra out as I looked into Bill's almond shaped twinkling eyes and his smile with deep dimples that added to warming my heart and lifting my spirits. The time is lingering, and night is coming and almost going into another day. This room is white and pure, and many nurses are coming in and checking on me. One nurse stood out by the name of Nurse Lauretta. Her smile added warmth to the pure white bright room. The doctor that welcomed me in was new to me Doctor Amanita. She was pleasant and informative smiling as she says we have a room reserved for you. I looked at her with confusion in my eyes slowly blinking while she's prepping me for surgery. She describes what was happening and telling us that I will be delivering before the night is over. I looked over at the clock and time is ticking. After glancing at the clock and watching Bill munching, I was becoming hungrier. The ice chips are just not helping my thought right. I just want to hurry and stop waiting. I close my eyes gently as I try to relax through the contractions. I hear someone calling my name and its Doctor Deck. So, nice to see a familiar friendly face and Doctor Upesi angelic smile checks in on me. She heard I was in the room. Now I'm more relaxed and Sabrina decides she is through waiting and wanted one of the two doctors to bring her on in. Nurse Kibbie came in smiling and prepping me for surgery. She was short with a smile that made her look younger than she probably was. I'm thankful for another angelic smile. Two men came into the room to roll me down and in passing I vaguely saw Nurse Evelyn looking. She is smiling at me saying that she will be here when I come back from surgery. I just remembered nodding my head and feeling very tired and so sleeply, but the contractions wouldn't let me sleep.

I guess its time and the night isn't over yet, but the day is surely gone. In passing thoughts I'm remembering my checklist; that yes, my feet are clean that was a first and must on my underwear. Bill is by my side dressed in scrubs and mask. I'm glad that I can still see his twinkling eyes and feel the smile behind his mask. His eyes are telling and saying that he loves me, and I squeeze his hand saying I love you too. The emotions reacted, he didn't squeeze my hand back or make me feel he loved me or mouth the words. I needed more than his twinkling eyes I needed to hear the words. Maybe he did in between the doctors telling me to push. With so much going on I just needed to concentrate on pushing so we can bring our daughter into the world. Bill was hoping for a son but not this time. After all that pushing and the way I'm feeling, not anytime at least not soon. This was not the time, just too much and too far away, to even think about adding another baby. I heard and knew of people that tried for a girl and ended up with a lot of boys. I don't know if I want to play that type of "keep trying until I get what I want" game.

One thing I didn't think that they realize how much your body goes through as you are popping out those babies. In the back of my mind I still think about Bill's mother Naomi, and how she was afraid of having twins and I had that same feeling. So many people like Veretta, Catrice and Charlotte that were surprised by either twins or triplets. Ooh I don't know if I could really handle twins at the same time, while trying to take care of my other children, and give Bill the attention that he still wants and needs. We make it into the delivery room and its lights, action and push, then stop, push and this goes on as Sabrina is making her way down my back. I just want to scream as loud as I can, but my voice wouldn't make a sound. This goes on and on as I push and push until they tell me just one more. And I pushed like it was my last bowel movement, and with relief I hear my daughter crying as they allow Bill to do the honor of cutting his daughters' cord. They place our beautiful deep dimple, coal black hair daughter onto my chest. My heart fills with so much love that tears fill my eyes as I see our daughter; I had been talking to for nine months. Bill is smiling and kissing me with those soft lips as I look into his almond eyes that are now twinkling for us. Nurse Kibbie takes her away from me to make sure everything is okay as they roll me into the recovery room before taking me back to my room. Bill's eyes watered up as he held her before they removed Sabrina from his arms. Sabrina holds Bill's finger with her little hand and his eyes well up again just like they did when Sierra was born.

As I look at Bill my insides are hoping that we can be a family again with love, laughter and finding my spot again on Bill's chest. I hope and dream that I will be comforted and no longer will have to settle for crumbs of affection. I smell the aroma of love. Why can't that aroma absorb into my skin my and spirit? I missed Bill so much I want to feel his hand caress my face and not strike it in anger. I don't want to be his sparring partner anymore. I should be getting blows from kisses and embraces for just because. As I watched Bill eyes follow Sabrina, I see the love he has for her. It's the same look he gives Sierra as they talk, play and fall asleep together. It's been so long I don't remember how Bill looks at me anymore. For some reason it feels like a faded memory. I smile as my headaches from searching and trying to remember that look of love that Bill once had for me.

His beautiful almond shaped eyes still twinkle but I just can't see the brightness. Hmm emotions flaring up again as I try to let go and enjoy the birth of our second daughter. I fight back the tears in remembering how his hands were placed on my throat, or the hit to my face as I laid there trying not to sniff and just let the tears and snot meet each other in fear of getting hit again. I think about the blue faded marks that's still on the wall where my body was thrown. The most humlimating moment was trying to make love to him and trying to be different and was asked to get off him right in the middle of being intimate. So, with those thoughts how did I get here giving birth to another child that had to require some type of intimacy? I laugh inside asking the silly question how did I get pregnant, was it because he asked?

Loren brings Sierra into the room before I fade into my thoughts that will take our joy away. Here I am thinking about everyone's feelings with no regard for my own. I force a smile through the pain of just giving birth. Sierra wants to jump on the bed which will send the pain running out the room with me following it. Bill's timing is right as he kisses me on my forehead, and I melt into feeling his soft lips on my forehead and I feel myself settling for crumbs again. Loren reaches and gives me a hug and kiss. He was the first to ask how I feel. I guess Bill missed his performance for the camera. Sierra gives me such a big hug at the same time being careful that she doesn't hurt me. Only if she knew I have almost become immune to pain that I have received for many years. This will change, and it must start with me...

What have I accomplished with my life? I look at the freedom that Robin, Courtney Diane freely enjoyed. I see and hear the freedom of laughter and smiles in the relationships of Momo with Amos, Charlotte with Johnny Lee, Debbie Ann with Froggy (Brian). There are so many more that I see and hear and wonder if my marriage will sustain the test of time and as we age together and as our hair turns gray. Will I look at him the same way I looked at him at the altar or as I used to watch him sleep so soundly? I have a feeling or just a thought that people think I don't have any feelings. My feelings with an "s" have become numb. I search to feel alive and be with the man I married many years ago. Then I lay down and place my head on his chest so gently hoping that my timing was right, and I wouldn't feel any immediate rejection as I hear his heart beat and breath with him, so we can be in sync.

I know my head print on his chest was right where I left it, at the same time not letting my thoughts drift off into wondering if there was another head imprint with the fragrance that I had smelled years ago. Just want the intimacy of just feeling his skin again and see the twinkle in his almond shaped eyes and those deep dimples showing as he smiles gently at me. Sometimes those almond shaped eyes changed when he was fussing, cussing, yelling or hitting me. They conform to a look that makes me shiver inside hoping my fears wouldn't surface. I had to take my mind to a safe place where my face or eyes wouldn't change the mood. I have so many Oscars for my performances I might have to get larger imaginary closet/cabinet.

I know if I wait the time will happen where I can sleep gently in my husband's arms and be as peaceful as our daughters sleep innocently in their beds. I shouldn't have to beg for crumbs, but some little taste is better than nothing at all. At least he comes home every night and I feel his body in the bed along with his scent of cologne mixed with a scent that's not mine, and he thinks I don't have sense with that common scent that Rhona thought was on sale.

Now that was funny, what was that new fragrance called "common sense"? She just knew it was on sale. I ponder the thought of how you could confuse common sense with "common scent". Hmm makes you wonder if the crickets and fireflies are still floating or flying around in her head, humph. I wondered if she ever figured that the echo noise, she was hearing was the cricket noise and the flashing lights were the fireflies. For some reason I look over at Loren as he says he going to run Sierra to get something to eat again. I know that's code for another gift for her. I laugh as I tell him that you are spoiling her. Loren and Sierra smile at each other as Loren asks Sierra, do I spoil you and she proudly respond with, no. Then Sierra whispers out loud putting her mouth to his ears trying to cover them, saying that I didn't tell our secret that you spoil me. We all laughed as Sierra puzzle looks trying to figure out why we were laughing, and she gives in and starts laughing too.

I smile saying no road rage. He smiles showing that familiar family smile saying hey cuz that only happened one time when I was fooling with Fifi dumb oops butt. Fifi has put him through some changes. He was telling both of us well he was telling Bill and I heard some of it and when I came in the room, he bought me up to speed. Saying that Fifi was driving and he was on the passenger side just chilling trying to avoid hearing Fifi yapping all the damn time. Man, when does she shut up, even when she sleeps her mouth is open? She never seems to close her mouth. This dude cuts her off and gives her the finger and she so adverbally lets me know. I give out a huff and damn, and o-kay! Then I look over at him saying what's up and my dumb ass move was I gave him back the finger. I guess I had to act like I was defending her honor. That probably was a surprise to her, you know the honor part.

We pull up to White Castle and this guy follows us. I wasn't looking for trouble didn't really want to be bothered. I just wanted some White Castle cheeseburgers and not this drama Fifi created. The dude walks up to me again here we go with the adverbs calling me all mother of friends and something needs bleaching. I turned to go in, and that right foot and my mind came into sync saying, oh hell no drop this mother of friends. I turn around and I think it shocked him that I did turn around and I asked did he have something to say? Now he's calling my Fifi all kinds of beaches and nope here I am again defending her, ha-ha, honor. I wait to see what his courage will do since he had so many words. He tries to grab me, and I try knocking his head off. I pushed him back and he grabs me and as he pulls away scratching the hell out of both my arms. I hit him dead in the middle of his chest and watch my fist cave in around it. That knocked the wind out of his mother of friends, and he jumped in the car and took off. After all that, I didn't have any type of appetite for burgers and now I just want to get out of there. I look over at Fifi and her mouth was poked out with much tude which was a first, her mouth was closed. She doesn't even close her mouth while shes eating. Fifi has food flying out of her mouth, everywhere with her saying a soft excuse me. I looked over at her I'm all scared up, pissed and knuckles bleeding and shift and her jaws all and shift tight. I had to ask this question just had to wonder what this puppy was pissed off about. She finally opens her mouth as we hit the freeway saying that I didn't have to do all that. I had to catch myself. I told her that I was defending her honor and that's all you have to say? Why didn't you say that shift before I got my ass out of the car? Any other time her mouth was running why numb up now. That defending her, ha-ha ass honor will not happen again. I'm sure that was a first for her ass. I had to look at her twice and glance in the mirror to make sure I didn't look as crazy as she sounded what the hell! Now my ass was pissed, and I told her drop me off and Luey P's, I'll get a way home. I knew I had to get away from her crazy ungrateful ass.

Bill and I both remembered that story at the same time. We start laughing harder as Loren's laugh turns into a smile because his facial expression shows that he knew too what we were laughing at. Then he gives in again and starts laughing as Sierra continues to laugh harder not knowing what the inside joke was. This was more of a inside joke. When I think back on Clarence taking his prom date there and not getting a chance to put her to sleep or his dad Jerry asking for a cheeseburger and hold the cheese at White Castles. That must be a popular location, must be like Bronco's in Oakwood. Now that was a hang out for Bill and me in the day and during my pregnancy. For that instance, I just loved looking around the hospital room at the white walls I remembered so many years ago. I remembered the dull colors on the wall at the clinic where I first found out that I didn't have indigestion but was actually like the other girls in the clinic very pregnant. In my innocence and naive thinking reality left my brain or thought process. Just like Reva said make sure you give your indigestion a name in about nine months. I didn't really understand what she meant then. I still was in la-la land licking a lollipop. It seemed then just like now that she had it all together. I admired her strength and the energy she put into unselfishly taking care of her mother and son while placing her career on hold.

Then there was Charlotte that had a cart half full of small heads and just as happy. I never heard any complaints from either of them. Whatever life threw to them they caught it with ease then sat down calmly, no sweat, and no tears and enjoyed a nice cup of tea. Just like this relaxing Chai tea that Robin and Courtney

Diane turned me on to.

The rain and tea are just right. Now when the rain stops the sun seems to be coming back into my life and I can smell the freshness of the flowers. I remembered Minister Williams told us a story about an older woman that brought soup to a funeral and gently placed the bowl of soup next to the beautiful arrays of flowers. Everyone was puzzled about how calmy she walked to the front of the church and placed a bowl or could have been a pot of soup. Inquiring minds, and puzzled looks had and wanted to know. Minister Williams politely asked the older woman why she brought a pot or bowl of soup to the funeral. She calmy, gently and respectfully responded that if he can smell the flowers then he can wake up and eat this soup. She said that to let people know you should give the flowers and the soup while they can enjoy the aroma and the beauty of the flowers and eat the soup while they are alive. Short story with much meaning and has a long-lasting impact that still there to this day.

I want us, me and Bill, and our family to enjoy the flowers and the big pot of soup, especially, while we are still young, and as we gracefully grow old together. But for now, we need to live for each other and raise our daughters together. Tomorrow we should be going home not like that three day stay that we used to have so we could sleep in. What a kill joy, but this time my husband will be bringing us home and not my dad. I miss my dad and our conversations but now I have daughters. I hope that Bill, Sierra and Sabrina with have that type of close relationship. Wow this means that my mom won't be there to help me with Sabrina. I watched her so many times come into the room before she went to work to sneak a kiss while Sierra slept. As I watched her, she was so happy and enjoyed the presence of Sierra being there. I wondered if it allowed her to make up for some things, she wanted to but couldn't because she always had to be a working parent. Now she's different, she is a loving grandmother and I hope to someday be one too. That was so far off. I now have one in diapers and another on her way to preschool. Never thought I would have ever left Oakwood or the comforts of my home or move away and be married with two daughters. Wow I really hope this is it. I just can't see myself like Charlotte with a basket full of bobbing baby heads. Don't have anything against it. I didn't really imagine myself being married with children living in another state either. I don't know if I scared of growing old or just scared that Bill might leave me.

Throughout my life I have seen happy couples that you know weathered some storms. Just like my life sometimes the rain comes and goes but I'm still waiting for that promised rainbow and another fresh cup of Chai tea. I have become so numb to so many things but not to living alone. Just the thought seems so lonely. How do the older women do it being by themselves and, just living alone? Right this minute I'm now married and right now that's all I know. That's all I want to feel is loved, married and wanted. I gave up the employment world to raise our family while Bill has the luxury of moving amongst the adult world. I look at my world and now I've added formula, changing diapers and washing dirty clothes weepie. My life has become so rountine, with a little yawning/boring. Now that Sierra will be attending preschool and riding with her dad. I guess that I will start back on the bus route again or just pushing the stroller to the park and various other unseen adventures. At least I know of some spots to hit and wait for the weekend dad to show us light, and fresh air and take us some where that doesn't require me to have a bus transfer. Don't get me wrong I love my daughters and California sunshine, but I still miss my family from time to time. I just want to see them and hang out with my friends and their kids. I would love to see customers again and be on the other end greeting them in the form of employment.

I need a break before I just totally lose my first name. Growing up friends of my silbings couldn't remember. I was either EJ's younger sister or Bonnie's older sister. I felt like an insert or like I was just the friend of the family because no one could really remember my name. Sometimes I felt that my name just faded away and I became whatever name that popped up in their mind to call me. I sometimes was referred as her or she, or just no name. Well at least they knew my sex. I guess that should be some type of minor compliment, ugh. When my parents would add shift in front, or the end of my name just depended on which parent was calling me. Funny with no ha-ha but didn't know then that my name would continue to be altered in some form or fashion. Sometimes when Bill, does call me Rita, I think that I'm in trouble for something. There were other times that I had to admit that it scared me when he does say my name especially, when in comes in form of yelling! I should one day get bold and quote Courtney Diane by saying if you are going to alter my name, put a "Miss" in front of it, so we both can pretend that we have respect for each other.

I do respect Courtney Diane's calmness and straight forward response, but some of them quotes could get my ass kicked by Bill. I rather have him put his hand on my ass and not his foot. I fought in my school days but nope, not with Bill nope. I will keep those thoughts to myself and not let him see the expression surface through my eyes or facial features. I will continue to stay numb. If I said something like that, I better have the car running or the bus pulling up so, I can quickly hop onto it and have them floor it and don't look back. Now Robin on the other hand had her style of calmness, and chill style. Not short on words but classy in her deliverance. She would confess that she has not always been like that. Depending on your actions people will question your emotions. But just sometimes you just didn't want to answer all the questions of what's wrong. You learn to say little and people will ask less. If I'm trying to adjust to my emotions the last thing, I need was someone asking me questions about something I myself was trying to digest, didn't need any additional distractions. She added with her slightly dimple smile that this didn't happen over night and the next day sometimes wasn't promising and flurries would circle sometimes not allowing her to see clearly. But you learn to open both eyes, so you can see clearer. I had to practice my mind and thoughts to stay focus. I pondered Robin's philosophy on her life style. I welcomed both her and Courtney Diane's outlook that has helped them cope or deal with life turn of events. With the words of wisdom from Momo in a Momo way, I hold them dear and very close. Ew I still invision her dancing and prancing talking about her and Amos flipping/ flopping and it wasn't turning over the mattress. Occassionally she said they had to ew vision please go away and it's okay to stay away yuck. I didn't know then that what they taught me will aid in my life later.

This tea is delicious, and the rain is trying to take a break just like the brief break I have been having lately and it feels so good. Loren's visit was a blessing for both of us. I know he will have to leave soon but for the present we are enjoying the laughing, remberance growing up in Chicago and updates on family and friends. Just listening allows me to understand Bill little better. This break again allows me to get my thoughts together and keep my family moving into the wholesome heathly loving family with the picket fence. I dream and hope that someday we would live in a house like the magazines I used to look at when I went to the clinic. Loren's visit helped us appreciate what we have, and I hope that appreciation stays but only time will tell. As I think about him when he returns to Chicago will he have appreciation for leaving the basement and aiming higher than a quick bargain? Fifi might not be the one for Loren, but I hope to meet that special someone for him. For now, Loren is enjoying the sights and the tours of his life with ease and a smile laughing all the way. I didn't get much rest in the hospital with the shortage of staff; your baby stays in the room with you. So that did it for some much-wanted rest and as I lay there looking at my bundle of joy wrapped so peacefully sleeping. I see Bill again and Sabrina as she slumbers in nursery rhyme dreams. I wondered what she dreams and what her voice will sound like and will she call me mom? The words I long to hear since Sierra has some difficulty with calling me mom. This time as we leave the hospital, we will leave as a family and not riding in the car with my dad wondering why Bill couldn't pick us up from the hospital. I guess then I knew that I would be on my own and had to grow up and put on my get girl panties.

I still wondered in so many ways how I got here and what happened to Rita? What happened to my dreams, my interest and my goals? I lost myself in the words and names that Bill called me that I became numb when someone actually called me Rita. I need to refocus my thoughts and know this time it will be different. The situation has changed our family. We are growing and hopefully together and not apart. If we keep the line of communication open, we should be okay. Communication was never our problem even between the name callings or as Loren would say I'm tired of being all those adverbs, or quotes. Courtney Diane if you are going to alter my name, add a "Miss" in front of it so we both can pretend we have a mutal respect for each other. I respect Bill and his decisions he makes as being head of household but at what point or measure does, he still respects me. How can you switch so quick to showing me love, to making me think you hate me? I guess there is a thin line between love and hate, but hate is such a strong word. Mommy used to say when you said you hate a person you rather see them dead than alive. I hope on this one that Mommy was wrong, or would I find out later how true those words would hold . some type of truth...

Looking so proudly at Sabrina and wondering, what will her voice sound like as I hold her so dearly to my heart. I study her features while waiting for Bill, Loren and Sierra to arrive, so we can all go home. This will be my reality that I'm sitting next to my husband and we are going home together.

Loren comes in behind Bill smiling and both seem nervous. Sierra is holding her dad's hand trying to look and see what her sister was doing with her smile that matches her dad. Nurse Ellee gently holds Sabrina as Bill assists me into the wheelchair to our waiting car. It's funny how memories can fade. I didn't remember being wheeled out when I had Sierra. I just remembered all the thoughts floating in my head as I rode home with my dad looking out the window wondering what was ahead, what did I get myself into and where was Bill. That became an unknown pattern Bill was missing a lot but, in his absence, it made me grow up faster than I wanted to. I had grown up for the sake of my daughter that didn't ask permission to be born to such young confused parents. If Loren wasn't here how often would Bill be with us? Loren was our blessing in healing our relationship and I guess we were his refuge from brick carrying Fifi.

Once seated and loaded ready to go I looked around the room and as we walk down the corridor. I pictured how Reva and Charlotte pranced down the corridor with their own style of walk that felt like a long death walk for me. This time the décor has improved, and the nurses were nicer. Bill eyes twinkled as he kisses me on the top of my head as Loren and Sierra walk down the halls looking around as if this was their first time being there. After the goodbyes we load up and I find myself again looking out the window smiling and wondering what road we are traveling, or will we change lanes and travel down different roads. Right now, I must get my mind set on the positive. Bill is here, and we are a family. Why do I continually try to convince myself of what we have? Fear sets in and controls but in other areas my emotions have somehow stayed numb.

The fresh air and beautiful California scernery have not lost its beauty. I enjoy the ride as I listened to Loren and Sierra talk as if they were seeing everything for the first time. I looked over at Bill and he picks up my glance and smiles briefly and takes my hand. The warmth from his body feels as if he was reassuring both of us that we are going to be okay. Every now and then Loren and Sierra are fussing over the sleeping Sabrina. For some reason Bill takes a didfferent route home. I glanced at him with the look of what's up. He smiles as he squeezes my hand and we stop at a drug store. He runs in saying that he will be right back. He comes out with a beautiful bouquet of flowers that just added to the beauty that was surrounding us. His lips felt good as I was presented with flowers. Sierra says those are pretty flowers for, then she stops before saying mom. One day she will call me mom if not I still have Sabrina. The ride became more pleasant as we arrived at our apartment, our home. The neighborhood is calm as I see Clarence and Keith walking into their apartment. I don't think they saw us, or they would have come over or maybe not. Sometimes Bill would give them a certain look that said it all without words. I just knew and still remembered that I couldn't have any male company over when Bill was not home. Even if it was for an innocent cup of flour or sugar to support Keith's baking. I just had that feeling that Keith would be moving out and joining his wife Kiante. I always love happy endings and see the good in any relationship. I still see the good in our relationship...

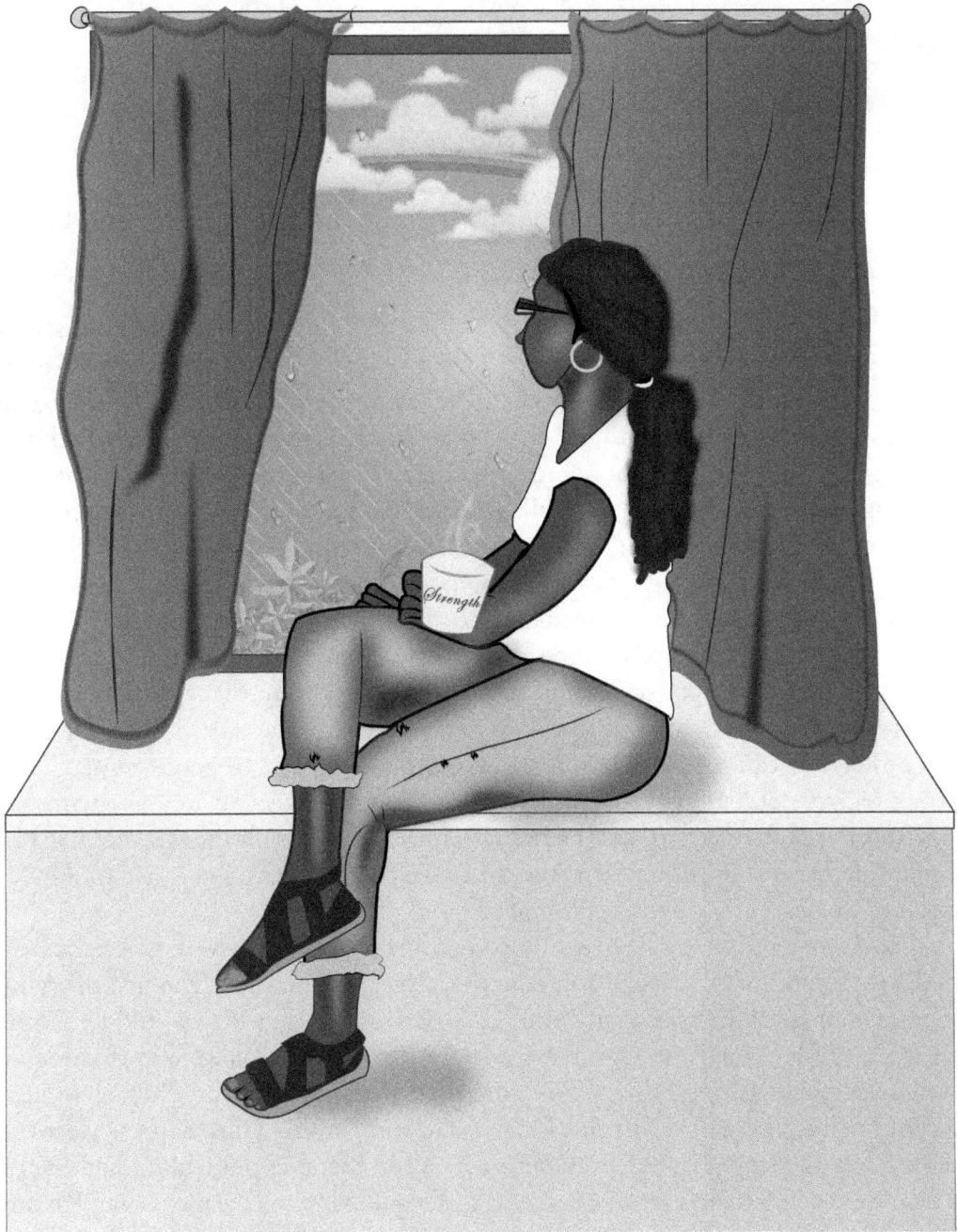

SECTION 3

Will the Rain Ever Clear?

Chapter 39
We Made it Home Again

I still sometimes can't believe that we have a new addition to our family. We are still growing, and I love it just like I still have love for Bill. The house is clean and quiet as we bring in Sabrina to her new home. We had put Sabrina's baby bed into our bedroom. Bill wants to put her in the bed, but he has always been afraid to hold his daughters when they are so small. The only time he held both was when they came into this world holding his finger. Just like history it happened with Sabrina too. My movement is not too fast and Loren leaps over to assist me in any way that he can. He fumbles a little, but his heart has always been in the right place. Laying Sabrina in her bed for the first time was a sign of welcome home and welcome to our family. I loved looking at her and smelling the baby scent that absorb our room. Sierra comes in trying to sneak a peak of her sister as she starts her role as big sister and protector. I can see the determination in her eyes she will be good at taking care of her baby sister. I'm glad that Bill will have an a few days off to assist with our new addition. Loren is here, and he helps so much. It seems like he is more than our family. He has only been here for weeks that felt like months. Loren is not annoying, and we desperately don't want him to go.

Bill, Loren and Sierra were eating something that didn't have a familiar smell. Did Amos mystery meal make it over to our place? I laugh silently to myself trying to remember Bert's prayer, that the food be something that they would be familiar with, so they could eat. One thing I did notice was that no one in that family complained about being hungry. I'm more tired than not hungry. I didn't get much rest in the hospital with them checking on me and Sabrina. Plus, Sabrina wasn't in the nursery she stayed in the room with me. A big change from when I had Sierra. There were going to be a lot of changes that I would have to face more than I wanted to, but I knew I wasn't alone in this. I had Bill and he had me for life. Sabrina was sleeping so long I had to check on her in between my nods. Bill smiles as he brings me my lunch in bed. There were a variety of colors unfamiliar to me. I know prayer will help me eat and digest this colorful food. I asked for pepper. Bill response was you don't know if it needs seasoning. I just know pepper helps anything that resembles food. Should I start my diet now? After all coming home in the same maturnity clothes. That didn't make me feel like model of the month. I need to wear something because wearing designer sheets in form of clothes won't work. I refuse to be part of Bill's jokes in criticizing my size. I need to dig deep inside myself and call on my inner strength and prayer to get my mind, body and soul into a real good understanding with each other. I don't want to go back to that type of pain. I want to move forward being a better wife, mother with a healthier mind that is and will be focused on keeping my marriage alive. No new entries trying to violate our vows and disrupt my family, my environment, or our world.

I try to take a quick nap to avoid the mystery meal. Before I could close my eyes, the food and aroma are filling my nostrils and my brain has just shut down all senses. As colorful as it was there was some type of flavor trying to come through just didn't know what. As they looked at me for a what do I think? I force a smile as I feel my stomach cramping and my mind silently upset with me for forcing the meal into my stomach. I hear a whimpering that sounded so soft. It was Sabrina telling the world she is waking up and ready to make her cameo. As I rise to attend to her, reality set in that my mom wasn't here to help me like she did before. My dad wasn't there to get the bottle for me. I had to be mom without my mom. I needed her more than she will ever know. Well I got to answer the call of my crying hungry daughter. Bill, Loren, and Sierra rush in to answer the sound of her crying. Sabrina's almond shaped eyes blink at me as she makes it clear that she is hungry and wet. No one rushes to change the diaper that went a little more than wet. Once their sniff alarm triggered the smell, they all ran out the room. Someone barely seven pounds and seventeen inches long ran men that were 6" feet plus out the room! As my dad would say there was more room out than in and she filled that end up.

As I changed her diaper Bill sends Sierra in with Sabrina's bottle. What cowards now what if it was Sabrina's own form of crop dusting like Uncle Boris? The bottle was just right as Sabrina enjoys her liquid meal. I watched her rest and look at how everything on her is so small and she looks so peaceful as she falls back to sleep. This time I won't miss the opportunity to join her in a peaceful slumber. Bill comes in and checks on us removing the tray of unfinished meal, I just couldn't stomach. I wait to see if he might just kiss me for a just because and the just because doesn't happen. The beautiful flowers he went out of his way to give me bloomed with joy, but I was feeling and anticipating some form of affection. The flowers and emotions just didn't match. I don't know what to say or how to say it. I still love him but have his words of saying I love you just become empty words just to fill a void when I say I love you. I learned over the time not to say those words for fear of the response or no response at all. For some reason I thought coming home with our daughter would make him happier. I watched how happy he was with Sierra and the joy of having two daughters on his lap and calling him daddy. Rita don't trip you lay next to him and he comes home to you. In the back of my mind how much of him comes home to me. There are days I feel I'm fading away in his heart and memories. I'm not going to let this effect me anymore and I need to step up to the plate.

I don't hear any talking or noise as I doze in and out of a restless sleep. For some reason I jump up looking at Sabrina looking and sounding peacefully asleep. As I walked down the hall my eyes glance at the blue marks that still slightly stains the hallway walls. That stain continues to remind me of the event that caused the stain. The cause is still fuzzy to this day. I never knew when events like that will occur again. Somehow, I became the scapegoat for whatever happens in or outside our apartment doors. The room has a still quiet. Ashtrays are empty, and the kitchen is clean, not even an empty glass in the sink. It's not an eeire feeling of where is everyone. My pace is slow as I continued observing our apartment. Right before I decided to take a seat on the couch, I hear a slight knock on the door. To my surprise which was a very pleasant site Momo made her way over with Amos holding her arm. In the normal fashion fussing about she was able to walk and stand. Opening the door my mouth was open as wide as my eyes. I rush to her as I welcomed them both into my home. Amos smiles telling her to call him when she is ready to come home, and he will come back. In the Momo way she says yes daddy I will call you when I'm ready to come home and you get your rest because the season has changed and its time to flip the mattreses. With that Amos does a little skip as Momo looks at me smiling as I remembered her flipping and flopping burgers and mattresses, ew vision again really Momo. I laughed as I vision her talking about the flipping again and yuck really. She smiles which is slightly crooked and I guess she is back.

Before she takes her seat, I welcome her back to sleeping Sabrina. I watched her eyes water as she looks at her with love. I picked sleeping Sabrina up and we walk into the front room where I assist Momo with holding Sabrina that makes a cooing sound with her toothless smile. This was a clear sign that Sabrina is okay with Momo and her spirit was right. We make small talk about the delivery and our health. We laughed and talked just like I used to do with my girlfriends back in Oakwood. We laughed as I asked what time her curfew starts or if you don't call will Amos automatically come looking for you. This was something I was familiar with. If I was gone too long Bill would come looking for me, so this felt right at home if Amos came over for Momo. I must have sounded like a little girl asking will you get in trouble because her expression was one of hesitation, with a question with the response I don't think Amos wants this on good day let along a bad day. We both laughed as she does her signature move while sitting down and holding Sabrina. Her embrace is good and steady the way I remembered her. I'm happy that she is coming back.

Momo slowly tells me, don't let Amos' demeanor fool you he can handle his own. She said that when they first met, he was in the service and I was dating a guy called AB short for Aven Blue. I had been dating AB for about two years. AB was who I knew, and we had talked about getting married. The thought of becoming his wife blinded me to who he really was. Don't leave out ego he was a lady's man, but I caught his eyes. He was tall, stout with a smile that could melt an ice cube. He wore flashy clothes with a smooth complexion and had real talk and had a different type of game than I was used too. He drove a nice big clean Cadillac and had his own place. He was about ten years older, but he didn't look like or sound like an older person, so our conversations seemed to blend in. AB looked at me with that smile and I smiled back and gave him one of my famous rack hugs. I could see how Momo could catch a lot of eyes at her age. She still has body and beauty, but at the same time I'm mentally trying to figure out what is a rack hug. Here I go again wondering what a spice rack has to do with a rack hug, hmmm. Momo's legs are shapely and strong like Mommy's, accompanied with special walk that turns heads especially Amos.

Momo says that she met Amos at one of those Officers' Clubs. She went with her cousins Lori and Leah. She was looking for an officer and I wasn't. I didn't want that type of structure in my life all proper and crap. But I caught the eye of this fine shy looking officer hiding behind his wire frame glasses, gorgeous dimpled smile and with a smooth complexion. I had to act like I didn't see him looking at me with his fine ass. You know play it off by laughing dancing in that one spot and that occasional smile with no eye contact. I knew I had the package, but I also knew I was somewhat engaged to AB. Rita, Amos was different from all the clowns I dated, yep clowns they were amusing and were for entertainment only. I got bored and was looking for something different but didn't know if I was ready. I've been with AB for a while, but I liked Amos' conversation and how smart he sounded. Oh, yea don't forget the look and that proud walk with those bow legs looking mighty fine in that fitting uniform. I didn't have to work at holding conversation with him. I was talking to someone that was on my intellectual level. Very simulating and relaxing.

Talking to AB would give me a headache trying to understand his simple screwed up logic, which only made sense in his world. When Amos made his way over to me, I turned my back, so he could see the whole package. Yeah that's what I'm talking about it was a me moment. I had on the right outfit that I was saving for a special night and this was the night. I wore very well the "looky look outfit" and I added the walk of confidence showing that I could hold my own. Leah was laughing with me, while she was telling step by step what he was doing as he made his way towards me. Inside my heart was pounding because I was feeling him but didn't want to come off like some desperate high school crush. His approach was at officer level not of that babe or honey or street junk talk. He gently took my hand and introduces himself not by rank but saying his name was Amos. My cousin Lori, who was only paying attention to an Officer that had been checking her out while she was instructing me on Amos moves. This was a good night at the Officers club for all of us. Lori left me when her Captain Levi came over and before I could blink at Amos. She was gone onto the dance floor and that was it. Amos being a gentleman stayed with me but didn't offer to dance until a slow song came on.

At first, I was like officer right just a little bump and grind because you like my outfit. He did complement me as he gently escorted me to the floor. This was a smooth move that matched his fine ass walk. I listened to her as if I'm at the movies looking at two people romantically attracted to each other. He brought me to him that had me melting that I had to catch my thoughts, so he couldn't feel me becoming liquified in his arms. He had on light dap of cologne, fresh haircut and his body felt as if it melted into mine and we became one. That slow song was slow enough for me to feel in heart beat as he spoke words into my ears. He softly and respectfully asks if he was holding me too tight. I was thinking Rita tighter wouldn't hurt, and let this be a long slow song…

I felt he was the one and AB was the one I needed to let go. When the lights came on, he didn't disappoint me he was finer in the light. Lori was a little disappointed when her Captain eyes looked at each her. She had every excuse of why he couldn't call her until one excuse was that she was married. He threw a curve and asked are you happy. Her slow response was an indicator and he said I'll wait. She couldn't believe how persistent he was, and he started looking good and sounding better. She gave in as Leah chuckled saying she got a man and that she had to go. Lori and Levi went out and he put on his glasses and that corrected his eyes. With that minor adjustment his eyes were no longer trying to greet one another or saying did you see that. Surprisingly, they ended up getting married and moved to Georgia.

Amos walked me to my car and opened the door for me. Unlike AB we would fight on who would get through the door first. Now if I made it to my side, he would look over the car and say what you wating on get in, lets go. I got in and we sometimes went to the liquor store for his forty ounce, or friend's house for card games or dominos or to the juke joint. The juke joints we went too were always crowded as you inhaled the aroma of stale smoke. Some of the women acted like somebody's lonely dog looking for someone to pet their lonely ass. They were just waiting for you to go to the bathroom, so they could jump in your seat and sit next to your man. While you were gone, they would try to talk to any available man that looked like they could afford a drink for them or be their spare tire in your absence. Just wasn't into those musical chairs anymore. Hey this is the same tired ass game with men too. They come there looking for someone to take home for that one no name event.

As I listened, I reflect on that scant Veren/Vernale something doesn't really remember her name or face. I just remembered the rachet scant took my seat next to Bill. She looked nasty then and still probably has developed a stronger foul odor in chasing other married men. Funny I don't remember her name or face. I guess its true why bother they are not worth it because they just get recycled or regenerated. Now how did Sister Tarver and Robin say it, I don't look at you as being a woman because I don't look at you as being human, ooh? How those words still echo and the statements that were said in the past has strength still in the present and will probably linger into the future. I pause for a moment to change Sabrina who is waking up for her next meal and there still is no sign of my family. Where could they have gone without leaving a note? But for now, I'm enjoying my time with Momo and this tea and the rain while remembering our conversations. Momo smiles saying that when Amos called her the next day, his voice sounded so sexy, especially when he said my name, humph. I wanted to howler say my name again, but slower this time. I really couldn't picture him giving out orders and why wasn't he married. What was the catch to this sexy, nicely built, calm officer? He had no kids and no woman. What was up with this situation or did he have a man?

Leah talked me out of tripping with the what's up and take my inquisitive ass out. Just go somewhere people are sober, not slurring or inhaling second hand smoke of different calivers. I stop questioning and went out with Amos. Rita I was nervous because he was different and how should I act. Being with AB was a toxic relationship that I didn't realize how so much poison we were to each other. We were infecting each other with what had developed into a norm for us. The voice inside said do you want to continue to be toxic or smell the aroma of fresh cologne, clean haircut, and don't forget he is fine. Just go and be yourself that's all you know.

Now I had to do a fashion show on what to wear, dress nah too dressy, skirt hmm maybe to show off my legs, hmmm already did. Amos told me to dress comfortably. So, what does that mean I'm comfortable in my raggedy pajamas? I go through my closest fussing and throwing clothes everywhere, trying to make it right just for that night. I didn't realize how nervous and anxious at the same time trying to make this a perfect outfit with my soldier man. What outfit would cover every asset? I had to be comfortable at the same time and I needed to wear some sit-down shoes, nah walking shoes flat or with a little heal. Didn't want to look taller than him, but I didn't think that mattered to him he didn't come across as insecure. I wore a nice pair of jeans with short top to show off my assets with slight heels and soft scent. She smiles at me meaning my ass. I laughed saying I gathered that when you said assets. I wasn't going to debate like Robin and Courtney Diane did about her butt being flat and to do the wall test. Courtney Diane assets did blend into the wall, tee-hee-hee. Amos picks me up in a nice black on black clean new Audi. He knocks on the door with a bouquet of roses. AB would be outside blowing the horn, honking, yelling from the window and telling me to hurry my ass up, what a gentle jerk.

Amos car smells of his cologne but not over powering and no where near being a cheap brand like AB. I seat in his car listening to his soft jazz which was soothing. I was relaxed, and my seat felt like I belong here. I glanced over at Amos, without staring, and thinking he was finer than what he was when we left the club. What's up with him and what's the catch? We go to an outdoor concert with wine and not forties ounces out of the bottle, music and no stale second hand smoke or people yelling, shouting or cussing or bumping or stepping on your foot like your foot was in their way. I was dressed just right, and he let me know in a nice polite gentleman manner. His smile said it all and my eyes said yea baby I know I got this. He had on some nice fitting humm jeans and white shirt. We were both dressed as if we appeared to be a couple. You would have thought that we both had advance notice on what we would be wearing. Unlike AB with shirt opened, colorful clothes, like a crayon box, heavy jewelry, rings as if his fingers were afraid of being lonely. He had to have at least three rings on each hand. I was impressed when I first met AB, now nah. I felt comfortable sitting in the front seat of Amos' car and my insides believed that I belong there. I had to remind myself that I do. Inside I was boiling over of why this man is so nice and no one has snatched him up and why he is with me, whats up, really come on. This is too right, and it feels too good. I smiled at him didn't want to spoil the moment, but I had to know.

Leah wasn't here sitting next to me. So, she couldn't kick me from underneath the table which was her way of saying shut the hell up. He smiled as his light brown eyes looked at me through his wired frame glasses that fit his face perfect. When he took his glasses off, I had to hold this thought inside of damn he's fine. His deameanor was calm as he said go ahead and ask if I can't answer it I won't, fair. I agree fair but what would be the reason why you wouldn't answer. His response was there is a time for everything and if I tell you all, then we can't get to know each other, need to leave room for growth and conversation. Pretty good answer I liked that answer, but my patience couldn't wait. I rushed out saying do you have a girlfriend back in where are you from again? I'm from Oakwell and no there is no girlfriend, no engagement, no ex, no baby momma with drama, there is no one I want to be with other than you. I'm in the present and the future includes seeing you again. Hmm he said the right answer at the right time in an ooh humph sexy voice. He didn't see me pinch my self, but I pinched myself hella hard just to make sure I wasn't dreaming.

I had to take a big breath to smell the aroma of his cologne and hold back the scream from the pinch or the voice saying girl damn don't mess this up. How about you? Wow that hit me. I thought that I could ask but didn't think about him asking me the same questions. Without hesitation and said that, I'm solo none of that minus the baby momma drama. I nervously laugh no babies, no daddies, and no nothing. I turned my head toward the window for just a quick mental breath. Then the mind said quick duplicate of what Amos just said dummy. I thought of AB for just a second as my sugar daddy that has been giving me a toothache. Time to get rid of that pain if this is as real as I think. My toothache was going. I guess I was just waiting for the right person to pull that tooth.

In the back of my mind I was wondering if AB was looking for me since I wasn't available for him. I came to the realization that there would be no future, but this toothache had lingered too long, and it was time for it to go. I made the decision that it was time to pull the tooth out. I hadn't talked to AB in a while and when I did the conversation was very short. I came up with excuses of why I couldn't see or go out with him. I knew he would be looking for me, and I knew that I could only stall for so long. AB wasn't smart but dumb didn't hang out with him either. I knew that Leah wouldn't tell AB about me dealing with Amos. After all she was the one telling and convincing me that I needed to go out. She laughed but was serious that I needed to hook up with a different caliber of men. I knew my parents didn't like AB and Mother Quincy couldn't stand him either. She thought he was too old. Every chance she had her looks and the words reminded both of us we were not a good match. He probably thought she was playing but she was of great sound mind and mouth. So, I was covered as far as the family not telling AB about Amos. I should have told Amos about AB, but this was not the time. So, I lied about AB, because he had faded away and was not in my view. I was into Amos and AB was the furthest thought from my mind. After all I had the excuse of, he is a lady's man he will replace me in no time if not already.

Not one time did Amos try and kiss me. I wondered was this real and too good to be true or was the hidden fault that he couldn't kiss. Well Miss Rita I found out that night what his lips could do. That magical kiss made me want to flip and flop him right there. I knew that there would be no flipping and no flopping. But Rita just that kiss took me to a place, humph. A place that I wanted to be like that little kid that wanted more and just throw his ass down and shake him with my special smile, ew. I listened as I watched Sabrina stretched out on the blanket on the couch as I rubbed her back to sleep. I think about how the kiss from Bill felt and I for that moment agreed with her that was what Bill did to me, and I was like a puppy I wanted to follow him home. Momo smiled and winked as she said that night lead to days, nights and months that we were dating. AB was a thought that just faded so far away that I stopped taking his phone calls and that fresh air I was inhaling was Amos. Sister girl don't think I didn't want to wrap my legs around Amos, but he stayed a gentleman and respected me.

Then that one day came when I was feeling confident and when I pulled my mirror down, I saw in the rear a familiar car. Rita my heart dropped, and stomach ached, and my thoughts were if that's him this was not good. I knew that Aven didn't leave home without his little soldier. I asked myself to tell me it wasn't AB. Momo said that she blinked and refocused thinking that would change the vision.

She hoped not to ever see. Yep I had clear vision it was Aven Blue in his Cadillac following us.

Amos didn't notice how nervous I was getting. My insides were ready to jump ship and leave me. Following was a past action, today's verbage you would call it stalking. Why couldn't he just fade away and accept that I faded away from us into Amos. I never told Amos about AB didn't think there was a need; we didn't travel in the same direction or circles so what was the chance of us running into each other. I took Amos's hand with a nervous smile I had to tell him. The warmth of his hand was soothing and soft, not like the rough hands of AB reminding me of his construction work. His demeanor didn't change, and he knew that someone as fine as I was had to have an ex somewhere and that nothing changed. Well had to tell him that change was following us, and he was crazy, and borderline could act stupid. He smiles saying calmly okay and pulls over. AB pulls up behind us and jumps out with those heavy gold-plated chains dangling. We both exit the car and being with Amos, Rita, I felt secured. I knew that AB carried his special/soldier and I have never seen a special on or around Amos, but he didn't seem afraid.

I stand by Amos as AB walk strongly toward us. Amos didn't move, didn't blink and didn't reach for anything that might have been hidden inside his car. Inside I was feeling him and knew right then and there he was my choice. AB could leave and hang out at the juke joints and get one of those honies looking for that empty seat and free drink. AB shouts at Amos and he listens. Aven Blue voices that I not only was his lady but, his fiancé too. Oops I forgot to add that shift busted. That's when AB pulls out his special and Amos didn't blink or stutter. This man was looking finer by the minute and I wanted to flip/ flop him right there. I laugh as I told Momo visuals again, ew. She smiled and kept on talking about AB pointing his special at Amos. My officer responded only once to what AB thought in his world was a threat. Amos asks in a smooth, cool, calm, and clear voice, "How are you going to explain? This threw AB off. He wasn't used to someone calmy talking to him or not trying to run away. I was curious too and I wanted to know the answer with Amos fine ass.

At that point I wanted to spank his ass and say get him. Amos said clearly again how you are going to explain? Hey inquiring minds wanted to know, especially me. The pricelss look on AB was, "what the hell was wrong with this little man" (because people usually ran away or hide from Aven Blue). He stated as he looks directly into the eyes and body of AB, since he was much taller than Amos. Amos didn't move me out the way; he didn't step back from AB. Amos stood calm and kept his eyes directly on AB. I was more afraid for Amos because I knew what AB was capable of. I looked at how AB towered over Amos and I didn't want anything to happen to this man I truly fell in love with.

AB and our relationship had expired a long time ago. I just didn't have the nerve to give our out dated relationship an official good bye. I should have womaned up and said something. Amos was an officer and very much a gentleman. Then I finally heard Amos say something after AB paused through his threats and swearing. That didn't mean anything, and Amos ask again, how you are going to explain how I beat your ass with your own gun. Then Amos camly told AB that he's leaving, with his special friend to have some alone time. Oh, adding that have a good evening. It's getting late and I got to take my lady home.

Amos stood there as if he was waiting for an answer or ready for combat. His stance didn't change nor did he back up or move forward. I would put my money on Amos. He stood there while I watched Aven Blue try to dissect what just happened. When Amos stood up to AB, I knew this was our relationship. I guess he was right when Amos said he was waiting for the right woman and that would be me. Amos grabs my hand calmly and gently and we walk back to his car. Amos opens the door for me and walks around the car looking at Aven Blue for our last time. For some reason the man that I thought was so tall fell short in so many ways. For the instance when I look into the rear-view mirror AB looked larger. But after the whole ordeal AB look smaller as we drove away.

This was simple equation I fell out of love with Aven and realized that I was falling in love with a man that to me seems like he will show and give me his world. With that no reason to look back on love that didn't exist, just made a cameo with Aven Blue. I don't know how long AB stood there and the care I had was left standing with him. We took off and we never looked back or talked about what happened and why I didn't tell him. I had to get real with myself. AB and I was playing house. We didn't live together. I would go over to his house or he would hang out at mine. Funny, without the ha-ha that we acted as if we were engaged, with no proposal. We said we were married with no ceremony or rings. We were in a place that really wasn't real just pretend, just like you do when you were kids. I'll be your boyfriend if you be my girlfriend, then kissy, kissy and what now. My eyes opened, and I wanted to scream at myself that I wasted all this time with Aven Blue. He wasn't husband material and I was impressed with him, but the thrill was slowly fading away as I began to grow bored with our relationship. We got caught up in a rountine realationship that was so predictable you had to yawn. I would look at him and there was nothing there, no heart, no feelings just going through the motions of pretending we are still playing house. One of us had to grow up and I stepped up to the plate and had to look into my future and realized when I open both eyes, I saw clearer that this was not how I wanted my life to end.

When AB left there were no feelings of loss just an empty numb feeling that he was not the one. I didn't sigh I just humph and smiled and looked over at Amos and I knew he was for me. I knew he was the one that we would say until death do us part. I didn't want to get married to divorce. Amos told me that his parents were still alive and had been married for over sixty years and was still happy. That was what I wanted, and Amos talked briefly that was how he was raised, and he was only going to get married one time. That opened my eyes and warmed my heart. Because AB and I never talked in that manner and I was just in ah of fantasy of what married life would be with Amos. No need to think about AB because I was with my future husband and the father of our sons and my own babies' daddies.

I left with my officer and left an insecure man and toothache. The man that I thought was all that and was all that I didn't need in my life. After that little encounter Amos and I couldn't get enough of each other. When he did put it on me, I woke up to the sounds of me snoring and drooling. When I woke up with a ring on my finger, marriage certificate on the night stand and with a smile on both our faces as I glanced over to my smiling husband. Now this was love and a complete package. Amos had more on me than I thought I had on him. Humph that man is still fine with that swang in his walk and can still make me drool and go into a deep knock out snore.

Chapter 40
Loren is Free to Leave

I laughed with Momo, but I reflect on Clarence on how he would say how he put his clients to sleep, putting emphasis on putting them down. I didn't want that image lingering ew. I say to Momo visuals again Momo I got to sleep. She laughs there was one night you didn't as she glances at the sleeping Sabrina. I had to laugh as she laughs back ew visuals I'm going to have night mares. Momo laughs saying that I guess I need Amos to rock me to sleep again. She shakes her body and for some reason I join her in the shake. This conversation was much needed, and I couldn't have had this type of conversation if Bill and Sierra were around. Momo and I talked like mother and daughter. I didn't know that she was going to share with me a side I didn't know about her. She glances at her watch saying its time for me to go home and cook, the boys are tired of Amos's mystery meals. Amos and I are going to cook dinner together and bang some pots later. She said that he was fine, and she didn't marry him for cooking. We get our banging of the pots/pans in the bed, ting. I love those pan sounds. I look as she walks slow but independent of her cane or walker. She looks back at me saying that she got to go and bang some pots and shakes as she put her hand on the door knob. She was evidence of a walking blessing. I jump up to see her out and the embrace she gave me was her way of saying thank you for helping me. She didn't know how much she had helped me grow in so many ways and how much I appreciated our relationship. Nope Amos didn't come looking for her like Bill would have covered the complex looking for me. I know he missed her you could hear the door open and the sound of his voice excited about seeing his wife as if they just met at the Officer's club. Only thing she said that confirmed what I have heard for years, that a man that need many women to make him a man, is a man chasing his tail and others that only amount to quanity and no where near quality.

Big difference kind of like Robin said about recycled scants why bother knowing their names or faces they get recycled, regenerated, and replaced. Courtney Diane would insert that they are roving refurbished hohohos. All the time they are thinking they got something in what they didn't know that this man was more in-secure than they were. They needed to be validated by the number of conquest and they never grow up. Many of the sitcoms you see make a mockery of not wanting to grow up. Married with Children, Peter Pan the list goes on just like they do. They have little friends and can only brag or show off their latest tarnished trophies. Now they are good in bed, very good at that talent, that comes with charm. And they might have looks, but the charm outshines the looks but all that gets old too. Oh, and when its time to recycle or regenerate to another scant batch the other scants don't know that they have been replaced. Their love for lust is as temporary as the memory they have for their last quest. Not caring or concerned about the emotional damage they left behind.

I think about how Bill and Loren might have one time fell into that category. I hope and pray that Loren will find a good woman and give his mama Miss Rosie Josey those grandkids she is expecting from him. I sit next to the still sleeping Sabrina glancing around the front room. For just in case I straighten up the front room, not that it needed cleaning but just in case Bill's mood might be altered. I hear the noise of my family returning and the sound is so welcomed to my heart. Loren smiles waving a ticket saying I'm free I can go back home. Dancing and sing-ing, ding dong the witch is gone! Gone you hear me gone gone! I'm confused as I looked over at Bill for the answer as Sierra eases the mystery saying cousin Loren is flying back home and said he didn't need Fifi's broom. Cousin Loren is so funny. Loren high fives Sierra's little hand co-signing yea cousins, Fifi is married and I can go back home. Now don't get me wrong I love you guys, but my life is back waiting for me to join it. Ding dong she gone ya didn't hear me. Yes, we did in song and in statements. Bill takes the seat next to the sleeping Sabrina rubbing her back and leaning down to give her a kiss. Sierra kisses her and rubs her back with her little hand, and you can hear Sabrina cooing to their touches. Loren sits down with his soda drink saying that Fifi is married. It's done; she's gone and got married. He added laughing it was not quick enough.

I asked who she married at that Bill and Loren laughs. She married Juan Joaquin Jr. We called him Three J's because he didn't like to be called Jr., that was his grand-mother's mothers crazy doing. Bill chimes in that crazy TJ stayed in and out of trouble in school and the law. I asked who is TJ? Loren said that's Juan Joaquin Jr. We started out calling him three J's then the T for three and the J equals TJ and he like that better. We some how narrowed his name down, that's what we do. Anyway, he hooked his crazy ass up with Fifi crazy ass and they had a crazy ass relationship that ended up with them getting married. It almost didn't happen the judge reco-nigized him from other court cases and found out that he had a warrant issued for him and had him arrested. For me that would have been the second sign the first one is Fifi is crazy. I guess TJ, didn't know about that brick carrying with pause she crazy. Her crazy desperate ass oops, bails him out and they get married.

He married her after being bailed, nah humph that would have been a heck no. TJ can have her crazy brick throwing ass. Bill laughs with Loren reminding Loren that he had a few of his girlfriends. Loren laughs nodding his head yea he did and a few of them I liked but TJ blew that. Bill reminds him didn't he hook up with Thursday on your Tuesday, and Wednesdays he acted like nothing happened until you went to visit your Thursday and she had much too much tude. Bill that shift was not funny ha-ha our ass we, us had a deal. Bill comes in we had deal. Then he changes with, I was not a part of your dream team. No, he winks at me nah. The dream team consisted of just a few of us Nippy (always cold), Funnel (Neal or real name Funneal) and TJ. And we would date our women according to the days of the week. Monday was rest, Tuesday was this one, Wednesday was the other one and we had it down packed that way no one would screw it up. No pun meant but it was fool proof until TJ's greedy ass decided he wanted my Tuesday, Wednesday and Thursday. So that only left Friday and some other odd days and rest on Mondays. He threw everyone off so the women we used to put into dream land was awakened by TJ's crazy antics. I laughed not only did this dream team sound cuckoo where is the love and I can't believe that someone or ones got away from Loren. His eyes twinkle it was more than a few that got away from me. So, he's not the complete dog I thought he might be. There are some feelings with an "s" inside that body.

He says they had been at the airport getting a ticket for him to leave in a few days. That explains why they were gone for such a long time. Nice break but I did miss my family. Glad they made it back home safely but sad that Loren will be leaving. Now what will happen with Bill and me? We will no longer have that buffer. I'm going to miss him and his antics. The stories he could tell and the fun we had with him being here. It was very refreshing to Bill and I could see that Loren, was going to miss his cousins. Loren busted out with a stronger laugh Fifi my little puppy is now married. Yea baby I can go home, and he rocks his shoulders back and forth. I'm flying on a natural high. No more rocks being thrown at my window and no more bricks through my windshield, no looking over my shoulder or her and her side kick Lucee yepping at my business. Don't you know that Fifi tried worring me about Derail's number. There was no time for her or the person I don't know who. Who trained Derail because the train has deralied?

We all burst out on that one and all Loren could do was shake his head while he joined us in the laughter. Sierra was in her room and glanced out to see what we were laughing about but, it didn't interest her, and she went back to doing what she was doing. Sometimes you had to check on her when she was quiet. One time she was drawing on the wall and just blinked when we asked her why. From now on, (Loren says clearly), no more bargain basement clearances. I'm done with the bottom floor maybe baby steps and try the first floor. Its time to move up and get real with my life. Like you cuz you have a good wife, mother and two beautiful girls. He nods his head yep cuz I'm feeling this. I didn't think that I would see you married and with kids. I need to step up my life and take mama words to heart. I'm getting too old to remember all those women's names.

I guess Courtney Diane saw early what Loren was about and as a common courtesy, she just amused us, but she knew about Loren's type. One thing her and Robin had they were not desperate or dying that they should just settle to just say they have. I got to give them their props. Bill and Loren got so relaxed that they started to light up a cigarette and I had to clear my voice before they started. I had a talk with Bill about that if you can smoke outside for my mother, Sheryl you definitely should be outside smoking for your daughters' tiny lungs that are trying to develop. He agreed and when I cleared my throat, they both caught themselves and took the conversation to the rear patio. I felt good on that one rule. Not too many moves or rules I would make because I again never knew what will set Bill off. Loren will be leaving soon, and I didn't know which Bill would return. Which emotional Bill would surface? Would it be the nice loving husband, father and my friend or this one that personality has just split in front of my eyes?

I did like seeing Loren happy to go home I know he missed his brother and mom. I pick up Sabrina and put her back in the bed. Bill wants to hold her but still struggles with holding his tiny daughter. I had to remember that I stayed with my parents and Bill held her when she was older. No, no he did when she was born but I felt he got caught up in the moment with doctors and nurses around to help him hold his daughter for the first time. Loren goes to the room he called temporary home singing ding dong the witch is gone, she gone, and Sierra chimes in bye, bye as they both dance with their signature smiles. They both dap each other I think they are going to miss each other more than Bill and I will miss Loren. Loren looks at us saying I'm packing up my suitcase and getting ready for a life free of Fifi! My little puppy has left the room! I don't know if he's ready for an empty house, but I don't think it will be empty for long. Loren's heart might miss her for a tad bit, but he will get over her. I don't think as my father would say no grass will grow under Loren's feet. Will Bill sprout little weeds and slow up and spend more time with his wife and daughters?

Maybe Bill will stay out less because hanging out in clubs can grow old. Let's grow together so we can view our lives through the same pair of glasses. I still hide behind my glasses, but our view should be merged into one, so we can finish each others' thoughts and sentences. Oh, how I would love that. I've seen that happen with my parents, many couples that I had encountered. My friends, Debbie Ann and Froggy, I still must correct myself Brian and they are in my age group. So, I know it can happen and I want it to happen with me and Bill. I love this man so much. I pretty much gave my life for him when I went into birth for both our daughters.

For Bill to show up to cut the cords after my groaning and pushing. While enjoying Bill's time off and Loren leaving, I will be mother again and a stay at home mom. I love my daughters, but I want to be back amongst the working, living and earning my own money other than the monthly stepend I get from Bill.

It seems like it was so long ago when I worked at the bank feeling free and making my own money and enjoying driving my blue Vega. I had a life while I was still living at my parent's house, money and I had Sierra. I still had it going on with freedom I took for granted and surrendered it to being shackeled to this apartment. I get furlough days of riding around on the bus site seeing. Bill enjoys his freedom of not being committed to being at home. He gets away by working, two weeks yearly training and this office hours that I'm still trying to figure out what that means. But the ha-ha-ha will be coming his way, when he has to take Sierra to preschool, and she can talk and will tell what she sees and hears. In the meanwhile, I'm here which seems like dejavu home with another daughter. I love my daughters dearly I just want my first name back. Something back in my life to say I did exist before becoming a wife and mother. Not talking about partying and hanging out just some me time and not become invisible.

Sometimes I feel like I'm losing my presence, my name and me. I had experienced not knowing my name so much as a child I was either; Charles or Sonny who we still call Sonnyboy from time to time as old as he is too old to have the boy on the end married with kids, or sister, Emma Jean, EJ younger sister or Bonnie's older sister no one seem to know my name. So here I am a wife with many what Loren would say adverbs added to my name by Bill. Then I have my daughter calling me Rita because Sierra refuses to call me mom. But that's not how I want to hear my name I earned that title. Some way and somehow, I lost me. I want to work but Bill won't have it. He wants me home waiting for him to come home with dinner ready. While he enjoys the California sun and fun meeting more people and maybe a joint every now and then like I didn't know. So glad I don't have to roll them and have Bill get mad at me for rolling them wrong. A feeling comes over saying that I need to get ready for what I don't know but I do know that I need a change.

Time flies and moves even when you are standing still. It's getting time for Loren to leave which he will be missed, and Bill will be returning to work in a few days after Loren returns to Chicago. I wonder slightly how married was Fifi and will she try to see Loren. Only time will tell with Fifi, but she just sounds like a person that just don't walk away that easy. It sures sounds like it to me that she was on the rebound but really wanted to marry Loren. That was something that he wasn't feeling, no babies with Fifi for Mama Rosie Josey. I wondered if she realized how close Loren was thinking about marrying her when he came back from his boys wedding and Fifi had her beautician over. Funny Loren told Virgil to take care of whatever comes out that back door and Studs did. What a nickname when you think of studs you think of so many other meanings other than stuttering just like Juan Joaquin Jr. went from Three J's to TJ. They knew how to dissect some names and come up with nicknames that made sense only when they were explained. Then you would find yourself in a "oh ok" moment because for some strange reason you understand the fit. With all this remembering does Bill miss the life or fun he felt he left behind? Am I boring to him and that's why his late nights sometimes are the reason for him to miss dinners? Here I go again tripping and fading off into whatever land. The land with no name to add to the area, where my brain and memories come together to help me get through.

Rita calm and redirect yourself and just enjoy the time with Loren as Bill spends some last-minute moments with his cousin. With Loren being here it did feel good having bloodline family here. I miss seeing Cliff driving down to see us and my mother coming out. Although she criticized me, I miss that, miss seeing her and hearing her voice. Phone calls help when the phone was on. I had to learn to use the phone for just in case, unless I received a call. Then the time was limited because Bill didn't like me on the phone too long. I learned that the hard way and I only need one oops for me to remember. He didn't hit me with the phone just the look the almond shaped eyes turned into. The look was enough to put fear in and scared ran away with courage. I limited my calls unless Bill was gone, and time allowed me to have a comfortable conversation with family and friends. I think they kinda detected when I could talk by the way I would rush them off the phone. They didn't know what was happening on my end and I did all that I could to not let them know. So far this was my secret and I didn't plan on telling anyone. I learned how to master my disguises in looks and bruises.

Time seems to go slow in some cases and fast in others. Sierra will be starting pre-school and Sabrina and I will be exploring new territory. Sabrina smiles a lot in her sleep the angels are playing with her. Time is coming for my family to go back to reality of work and Loren leaving for Chicago. This time we promised to stay in touch. It was nice being included in an adult conversation. Bill and I used to communicate to each other now and then. Sometimes I would find myself shivering and stuttering when he asked a question. I felt like I was getting reprimanded for something I didn't do. One time he asks why you cleaned the kitchen and didn't sweep the floor. I would jump up and pull the broom out and start sweeping. His voice gets stronger saying I just asked why, and my answer wouldn't surface just the movement went into action. I wondered does Bill notice that I try to do every and anything to not have him mad at me? I couldn't hear his voice when he started yelling. The only form of adult communication in the house and it came sometimes in form of yelling.

It was good to see Momo coming by and able to get her thoughts out and move better than the last time I saw her. She laughed at me saying now she had another daughter to spoil. She was tired of being spoiled by her boys she needed some air and space. She loves them but didn't like being smothered unless it's Amos and you know what I mean. Again, I tell her visions, ew and then she would respond with at least it wasn't flipping or flopping or the banging of pots and pans hmmm. Rita, girl you need some imagination. I didn't know how right she was. I didn't want to lose Bill to some freaky floozy because I didn't know. Momo had a point but still the visions were ew. She would laugh but she knew in time and conversations I would consider what she always shared with me. In her own way she was trying to keep the fire in our young marriage.

When I was younger Debbie Ann, Sharon Denise, Melody Lynn or even with my sisters, sex was never discussed. I would listen to Robin and Courtney Diane talk about it, but it would only make me blush. I should have listened more to the California experience and show Bill a little something something. Then he would probably think I had an affair and have me revisit the shameful time. That, (sigh) one and only time that I tried saying words, and to have him shame me and ask me to get up. Now that was hurtful. I didn't want to experience that rejection again because it was and still painful. Sex was not discussed or viewd on television or movies. Acting out anything sexual was unheard of in my conservative city of Oakwood. That was taboo, and you were considered fast and stay away from him or her. Your reputation would follow you.

Just like Reva said how many of us was told don't get your ass pregnant. No one discussed how you could get pregnant or prevent it from happening. Once it happened you were considered loose or tainted. So many names went with being pregnant out of wedlock. I remembered how I felt and how I was treated and that wasn't a nice feeling. Made you feel ashamed instead of supporting you in a situation that was frightening and made you grow up faster than your mind could catch up. The looks, the stares, whispers and comments were way over the top with the lack of considerations that you could hear and had feelings. It was all about their disappointment that we didn't live out their dreams or the short comings of themselves. They missed their opportunities in form of their dreams that they tried to pass on to us. We needed that talk... We were sent out without that protection and all they had to do was talk to us and not assume we know or knew. That was not the answer to a very sensitive situation. They should have taken the time to talk to their children regardless if it was a boy or girl. We/they both needed to know how to respect themselves, their bodies and other people. That old cliché don't get caught with your pants down or what happens in the dark will come to life and it did.

I had a head start graduating at the age of 16 but didn't know anything about that sensitive subject. I do regret leaving my friends and growing up too fast, but if I didn't graduate early, I wouldn't have met Bill. Hmm what luck right and chance of meeting him in the library with having limited choices between him or the nerd.

Hmmm wonder what ever happened to that nerd. Get focused like Mama Sadie said he had to ask, and he did, and I said yes. No regrets I had fun with Bill while we were in college and we are both learning about each other. He was raised a certain way and I was too. We are trying to combine our family styles into one and we need to keep the communication open. We actively need to listen to one another with that midwestern respect that we both knew and were raised in. That was what we had in common and our families were familiar with each other. Yep didn't know Bill's name just saw him in passing. I would see him come out as I went into our Psychology class or see him reading a magazine in the cafeteria still really didn't pay any attention to him. I was too busy hanging out with Trina and having fun and watching other men on campus. We did occasionally go to class. I guess that's where the lack of maturity was when it came to discipline.

James educated me on discipline when he chose studying over spending time with me. That shocked me into another mind frame because I thought I was all that and a bag of chips with a soda pop added. He popped that thought and that thought never resurfaced. James stayed focused and I went on to be with Bill and James on to pledge with a fraternity and graduated. Nice wonder if he still looks as fine as he did when we were in college. Now Rita get that thought out of your mind remember what happened last time, not cool.

Sabrina sometimes slept during the night, but morning came early along with Sierra and Bill. Getting up was hard since I was still sore and moving slowly. I couldn't sleep due to the alarm sound of Sabrina's feeding time. Yep, I sure did miss my mother and how much she helped me through Sierra's baby life and toddler's tantrums. I had to learn to adjust to my new schedule on a full-time basis with no relief from family or friends. I hope Bill understands why sometimes I'm tired and not think that I'm just lazy. So, I force myself into everything I can think of. The day arrives to take Loren to the airport he leaves early in the morning so Bill and Sierra ride with him for it's too soon to take Sabrina outside. Soon I will be exposing her to fresh California sunshine and fresh blue skies and warm weather. Loren thanks both of us and appreciated the time he spent with us and Bill and I both say stay away from Fifi. He laughs saying she is so married, and I am so free from my little puppy. She was my headache now she's TJ's headache! I just wanted Loren to know how much we loved and appreciated him and want only happiness and some grandbabies for Mama Rosie Josey, and to stay away from the bargain basement clearance area.

Loren laughs I still got to try each floor he dances singing moving on up making ding sound as pushes in the air next floor saying lingerie and yes you can help me. I chime in what if the front and back don't match. Bill joins in with from the head to the toe. That felt good Bill and I working as a team. I liked and missed how we used to laugh and hang out just having fun. He turns slowly saying oh damn

I guess ding next floor and then she won't be the catch, or the sale of the day got to keep it moving. Then he goes back into his own little slide dance smiling while singing. Yeah, she gone oh I got to face it she gone now I can go home. I look at him saying don't crack the door because Fifi might just try and open it wider. With a quick pause as he absorbs what I just mentioned. I could tell he was listening and surprisingly Bill too. Maybe a small percentage but I think he understood what I was trying to express in a loving and not prying way. Bill looks at me also like where did that come, while showing a slight smile of approval. I look at him with an expression of what. We all laugh as he dances showing that signature smile and his almond shaped eyes grow smaller with a little twinkle coming thru. Family feels so good to be around didn't know how much you miss them until their gone. So many things we take for granted. Now its time for Loren to return home and see if he can find a mother for Mama Rosie Josey's grandbabies. Before leaving, Sierra's a little upset that her favorite cousin is leaving but he reassures her that he will be back. My eyes watered as he comes toward me for the good bye and thank you. Loren reassures me in his cute smiling way saying I may be difficult at times maybe, but while the twinkles glitter through his almond shaped eyes on the other hand I'm worth it, (as he slaps Bills hand for approval). I couldn't help but to smile showing what dimples I might have and just said to him no you didn't go there while glancing over at my husband. Bill supports me with no you didn't just oh well what my wife said. Loren's eyes twinkle as he looks at us like he is caputuring a picture. He pauses and keeps a tear from falling saying how good we look as a happy couple. Inside it shocked me for that instant. I didn't have on my glasses that I sometimes hide behind, and he called me cute/beautiful, wow and scary because, I lost the visions of what my features once were.

For that moment I like hearing we made a cute couple and we were noticed. For that instant Bill and I held hands. Surprisingly, he grabs me by my waist supporting me and the warmth from his hand penetrated my soul, his arm around my waist gave a kick to my heart letting me know it still beats for him. I reflect on what Mama Sadie said he had to ask. Bill called me his wife and those words meant so much to me it was like hearing I love you in which I haven't heard those words in a long time. Loren and Bill make their way out as Bill kisses me, making me feel all giddy, like a high school crush. That old school girl crush inside had me thinking he noticed me. I do have concern with Loren, but I know he will do find, and I just hope he stays away from Miss Fifi. He seems ready for whatever he may encounter including Miss Fifi. I try and picture what she might look like but only cuckoo comes to my vision, but no face appears at all. I would ask for him to describe her but didn't want him going down memory lane. I wasn't going to give him any reason to try and pry to see her. Turning back should not be an option for him he has so much to look forward to, like giving Rosie Josey those grandbabies.

I talk to Sabrina she smiles and listens without a clue of what I'm talking about. Heck sometimes I don't know where my thoughts fade off into either. Just know I love holding her and watching her eat, smile and hearing her cooing. She reminds me of Sierra, yet Sabrina shows early that she is not Sierra. I see a little of me there establishing her identity early, that's my girl and my princess in training. Here I go again home alone with my thoughts, formula and time. It's sad that now that Sierra is starting school, she now has a life outside the doors of our apartment. One good thing about it Bill will have to come straight home no detours and no office hours whatever that means. Many years later, still not knowing what office hours mean still bugs me. While Sabrina sleeps, I clean up while keeping an eye on her and trying to take little naps. Sabrina is too young to go outside but soon we will be taking our walks and riding the bus around town looking out for other places to venture off to. For now, work is here for me and no more Loren stories just another day.

I want to be as fresh as I can when Bill and Sierra come home, so he won't be mad thinking I didn't do anything all day. I want to hear about their day. Momo is doing better so I don't have to check on her as often as I did before. Robin and Courtney Diane are out of town, Clarence is at work, Keith is busy working and hasn't seen him lately and Darryl Alan is performing on stage out of town. So, it's pretty quiet around here lately. Not too many visitors I guess they are waiting for Sabrina to get a little older in which I appreciate, so we both can get rest and she can build up her immune system. Right when my spirits are feeling good and thoughts of what to do.

My eyes for some reason catch the slightly faded blue spot on the wall. Now my thoughts focus on that spot that won't go away maybe we should, hmmm. I don't think paint or thoughts can remove that stain that has been there for years. How do I approach Bill about wanting to move but inside, I didn't want to leave our apartment complex where we learned to love and feel like a family. It was hard leaving the complex where Melba and Mike and the rest of the gang, but now it would be harder leaving Momo, Robin, and Courtney Diane along with Clarence's stories and Keith's baking, hmmm yummy. I don't know what monies we have saved and for what reason could I tell him why or maybe just say that we need to add another color to the wall. Getting a job is out now that I have my little beautiful daughters Sabrina and Sierra. I want to live more outside these doors and be back amongst the working living. I want to work and have my own mad money and contributing something to our family. I have some money stashed but not enough to go on the run with my daughters in tote. If I had enough money would I really run that was a question I would sometimes ask myself. Then look around and think about younger and older couples that worked together and seem so happy with just being together. Maybe on the outside Bill and I looked happy and for the most part I like to think and feel that we are. Bill doesn't tell me as often as I would like to hear that he loves me or show affection as much as I would like for him to. I guess that would ease my insecurities. I can't tell Bill about feeling insecure that would be one more thing I feel he would hold against me and use it when he needs something to fire at me. I want the burning love he had or hopefully still has for me to wrap me up, so I can feel secure again in his arms and heart. Feel complete with the addition we have added to our family. I love Bill and that I know and feel for real. I don't want to think that he might be supplying accommodating affections with someone else. If we are missing something or if I'm just not getting it let me know. Communication has not ever been a problem with us and it shouldn't start now. How can I fight for something that penetrates in the air and dissipates?

Chapter 41
How Many Diguises Do I Need

I don't want our relationship to fade before we get a good grip on this as we grow young or old together. I just wish sometimes I could go deep from my stomach and just yell out the things that are bothering me. I want someone to hear me. But they would just look at me like I was crazy, and I probably would sound like Charlie Brown's teacher blah blah blah and blah. What would I say and how would I say it and what would be the resolution? I can't even come from behind my glasses or my own masquerade or my disguise, so no one could accidently see the pain in my soul that surfaces every now and then. I don't know myself when my strength will occur. Maybe it occurs around Bill and I'm not aware of it. Maybe he sees it trying to surface and tries to strip me of sexual confidence and strength. I thought he would be happy getting someone designed just for him. I guess it goes back to the regenerated scants that always multiply and go on the prowl for whatever piece of your man or any man they can get. No conscious and never closed including their legs, nasty scants. Nasty probably would respond with yup I was with your man and my reply with yep maybe, but he cleaned up and came home. Oh, let me add did he leave you any money on the nightstand. With a tee-hee-hee oh you did what I didn't want to do, fool. On the other hand, you are left with your own funk, waiting for the next time he wants to see you and not the other way around now who is the smarter.

Because a known fact is, I see my husband everyday and you are just a small night crawler with no fresh air and no day light. You're just a one-minute pleasure because he doesn't have the time. He leaves because he had to get home tee-hee to wake up to his wife. Hmm that felt good having that thought. Yep, he comes home and rolls over looking into my face and my smile.

Just like Courtney Diane's Papa Cleve Jr. said when her brother Cory Davon ran out the house running from their dad because he knew what was coming. Her father started to run after him and stopped in mid running stance and stood there in the doorway saying he'll be back he got to come home. At the age of eight flight was always surfacing but when he took off home wasn't on his mind. What was on his mind was fear to his rear, which exists at any age. I did get in trouble for playing with my dolls in the water, making a mess in the bathroom. I knew what was coming by the thunder sound in my father's voice. I ran and took flight too. I hid under the bed, I didn't have too much imagination or was I smart enough what I saw and learned from my siblings. As kids we knew that we would have to return home.

Funny how fear takes off and your body is bringing up the rear. This was a slow day Sabrina is sleeping and I'm not too tired, just still sore.

I want to call home and talk to my family or friends, but I don't want to run the phone bill up. I wanted to talk to my mom about so many things, but I knew all she would say was pray and my response would be I am praying everyday. Just when I decided to sit down to watch a few channels to my surprise I hear the phone ring. I'm so anxious that I catch on the first bell sound like hitting the buzzer on a game question bamm, but in this case pick up the phone it rung. To my surprise on the receiving end a familiar voice saying whats up cuz. Loren called just checking on us and seeing how his newest cousin was doing. His voice was a breath of fresh air to a boring moment. We talked about the fun we all had when he was here and that he looks forward to more visits. We both agree we need to stay in touch with family. I had to ask after we got the how everyone is doing routine and was up to speed on our family members. I slowly asked how Fifi was doing. With a hearty laugh, Loren replies with, I guess alright. She is still crazy but not with Three J or TJ that was a brief marriage the flight to Vegas probably lasted longer than their marriage. I ran into TJ at White Castle laughing at his ass for marrying Fifi. I bet that will be the last time you go get my current meal or left overs. TJ response was you still mad about Mariann and getting our women days mixed up. Now don't you think I got pay back when I married Fifi crazy ass??? I had to dap his ass on that one. TJ's payback eased off from the antics of me losing a few ladies to him.

She tried calling I just ignorned her calls and tried coming by the house. I had to do the peekaboo through the blinds just to have eye to eye contact, when I looked through my blinds. At first that shift trip me out when I blinked through the blinds, and she blinked with me! What the hell?! Rita, I heard myself scream like a little girl then snapped back. I knew then oh hell no! She screamed, "I see your ass!" I listened as I walked away saying I've seen your ass for the last time and your side kick Lucee. Cousin Rita at first, I wanted to run through my own house trying to find a place to hide. I had said to Loren you had to spine up. He was still saying that I won't see her ass in here either, hit the wind with your crazy ass and take that broom flying friend Cece with you. Tell Lucee that Derail is not interested in her leaching gap tooth ass. Yeah and get those yepping noises off my porch. He pauses saying I like that oh hell yes, I had to spine up. I had to do something that thang is crazy as hell. Get this she had her side kick Lucee still asking about Derail and why he didn't call her. I went upstairs and laid it down and left her and Lucee both banging on my door like they were police on a raid or something. I knew that door was not opening at all and eventually they would tire out and take their yepping asses on home. I left them both banging on the door as I went to my room and laid it down. I turned their bangs into a beat and was like a lullaby to my ears putting me to sleep saying over and over she's just not getting in. With all that I had to fess up Joaquin did do me a favor oh yea he came through at his own expense. I end up talking to TJ comparing stories and he had me beat on that too in that case oh well okay we're even.

TJ thought maybe she was slightly crazy because her family trait of crazy stayed in the bloodline. He tried getting her away from her family and they only increased when they came by to visit. He almost had her whole crazy ass family visiting them on 24/7 basis. And let's not forget her sidekick Lucee. She thought she had her own room and board free of rent and open my fridge like she bought in some groceries. In school Fifi yea she did some cuckoo, but she was crazier as adult than she she was in school. I thought with age she would have mellowed out somehow but not her. We were talking about some shift trying to talk like adults and she hit me with one of those long ass skinny candles. She pulled this shift from out of her purse, didn't see that shift coming. I wanted to wear her ass out but I don't hit women but that don't give her a free card to hit. What's that old saying keep your hands to yourself because if you hit me it will be you that will need the help? Loren laughs never heard the ending to keep your hands to yourself. Nah that humph broke my shift with a brick. We agreed we both got off easy. She popped me on the head and that shift hurt. I had to laugh at him saying that was better than the bricks and rocks she used on me and my shift. At that point cuz we just started comparing notes. I stayed longer with her because I really cared for her crazy ass. She was funny, exciting and willing to try anything and I could work with that. Now when it came to babies, which was a whole different thang. She didn't represent well in being a mother I would want to raise my children. Too much energy and I couldn't have a bunch of little ones throwing rocks at me. Especially the first time I come home late or have them following me oh hell no.

TJ said he was so desperate to get away from her that he knew he had a warrant and called the police asking begging them to come and get him. He would be the one sitting on the curb smoking a cigarette waiting and doing the Chicago calm. I had to correct myself cuz this is what I wanted to say to the police and try to convince them through their laughter. There was no need to panic cuz I called you. I repeated myself slowly for clarity allowing them time to trace my location. This is not, I repeated, this is not a crank call! I called you come and get me! I have traffic tickets; failure to appear there is a warrant in my name. Can you get with this she put me on hold for what to laugh or trace this call? Because I did hear some dumb ass giggling as they put my ass on hold. Hell, I gave her the number I was calling from just in case we got a disconnect, damn. Get this I described myself, so they wouldn't pass my ass up. No confusion on picking up the wrong caller. I stated very clearly so they wouldn't be picking up someone that looks like me 5"4 with a beard, brown eyes. I describe myself in detail all my shift is tight no beard just nice cut goldtee. So, let me break me down, so I won't miss my ride. I'm 5'11 short hair cut, hazel eyes wearing green/blue striped shirt that will be open, so you can see I have no weapons. My blue jeans will have the pockets turned inside out showing no concealed weapon, so we have good communication clarity. There will be a neon light flashing on my big ass forehead saying with your dumb ass "you married her". The neon lights flashing "you're kidding" in Vegas or getting arrested before the wedding wasn't clear enough sign. But you manage to bring the dumb ass sign home with you. For that instance, I thought he might have borrowed oh Henray's sign his mother Courtney Diane said he had on his forehead, "blinking with your dumb ass", as she was talking about his crazy girlfriend too. Much in common and much distances away.

TJ laughs saying he really wanted to smoke a joint but just wanted to get away not go away. Get this cuz TJ recommended or highly suggested that the officer (s) to slow up with the back door open and he would just jump in, place handcuffs on the back seat and he would cuff himself, because again he stressed that he was the one that called and wasn't going to run. He kept trying to convince them that he called them guys to come and get his ass away from this crazy ass lady. TJ tried telling the dispatcher he had a warrant come and get him, with emphasis on he called them. Loren laugh with they/dispatch listened and was acting like TJ was talking crazy drunk.

This was not a crank call it was a come get my ass call! Oh, hell straight sober, no booze, no liquor. He told them or suggested that they shouldn't slow the car up too slow, because she will be right behind us running. She is a crazy ass lady and I don't think you want her on a Friday night. Because, she would make a short custody stay real long and an entertaining weekend. Just hit the gas and please don't break at all sirs just slow up enough for me to hop in the backseat. See all politeness and shift comes out when you're scared or need some serious assistance. In this case it was both go, don't brake and don't look back those eyes will get you. I want you to come and get me, remember that I called you. This way I knew that I would have a secured place to stay and I don't have to worry about her finding my ass or coming by breaking my windows or hitting me with those long ass candles.

While he's telling me his version, I'm laughing so hard tears are rolling down my face. He's laughing too as he is telling me with a pause to catch his own breath. Bottom line you say this to say what Loren are you solo now or still trying each floor. With a pause I think I'm ready to stop shopping right now and take it slow and take a break. I laugh telling him you forgot who you were talking to, you want me to believe that?? He had to laugh and agree that he is leaving the basement and moving to the upper levels effective immediately. Then we just switch as he asked about Sierra and how he missed her. I told him she missed him too for a minute out of sight out of mind. She's back to being a daddys girl and in school. So, it's just me here with Sabrina watching her snore. How's Aunt Rosie Josey? That was a slow oh well she thought I was going to bring back a report that I met her grandbabies future momma. She had to admit in her Christian way she didn't care for Fifi's character. She smiled and said she felt that if we had children right after birth the first thang to do is bring in a priest or pastor which ever one was immediately available.

I love my mom, but I told her I had auditions but nah on any leading role maybe next floor. She popped me in the head, but it wasn't with one of those long ass candles TJ ass was getting popped with. Because of the time difference Bill hadn't made it home from work yet. We laughed so much and talked about everything I forgot to ask what happened to TJ. Through his laughter he had me laughing before I could listen to what happened when the police came. TJ said when show their slow asses up, that they were puzzled as he kept telling them we really needed to go. He again put emphasis on I called you saying it as slow as he could. Nah they wanted to talk and ask some dumb ass questions. I kept trying to explain to them as they frisk my ass that I called you saying that shift slower than before. What part did they not get about my phone call? He said when they finally showed up, he stood up open arms and assume the position by himself didn't need any assistance and kept eye contact and open arms so all parties participating, (including me) had communication clarity. No bruh. No oops, no nothing.

They started laughing until one of the officers stopped/paused in mid sentence, as I tried to plead with them, we need to go I called you. Again, I said that I had warrants officers. Can we go now? I have no weapons, no resistance I just wanted or just needed to go please. I called you they had my ass pleading like James Brown and shift. Fifi came from wherever she was no sounds of walking just the sound of her using her favorite adverbs. Now get this Rita, one of the cops recognized her and said oh hell no I dated her sister Kenna. She was cool, but her family...that's another story. The other officer said I've responded to her house and she and her family are crazy as hell. He motions to the other officer lets get the hell out of here before she reaches the car. Hell, they were moving so fast they almost forgot my ass. I had to yell hey, hey and hey I called you open the back door. Inside he said he was rolling tried to put emphasis on I told you we needed to go. Fifi was on the move didn't think she could move that fast. I'm laughing non-stop inside because I tried to tell them about that crazy lady. What they thought he wanted to do was spend the weekend in county jail just because!!

They started talking about the family as I listened trying to keep my composure. He said now her other sister Skyler and cousin Shyra is alright, but she still comes from that crazy ass family. TJ said as they pulled up to the station, he asked the officers if they could please keep this on the down low officers, or if they mention it please don't give up my name. Those assholes couldn't wait to bust me out as I was getting finger printed everyone was looking and laughing at my ass. Inside I was pissed but on the other hand I was safe away from Fifi crazy ass. It made it through my hotel check-in process, ready for my cell and a cot. Those jail fools tried laughing and I did the jailhouse what's up and shift. I looked at them and said this will not be your funny day and don't be your fool. They got my message of hell no, not today or tonight. Hell, they knew of Fifi and Skylar there too, what the…

That was the funny part, but TJ didn't think it was funny. When he went to court everyone was looking at him laughing, smiling or putting their hands over their mouths to muffle the sound of laughter. People in custody were laughing and the audience laughed when my case was read. The judge had a sense of humor saying I'm releasing you on time served. TJ shouts for only a weekend are you serious?! I can't get longer; did you look and review all my charges?? Sir I have a failure to appear that should deserve some type of time consideration. I don't want to go home. The judge smiled saying yes on the release for the traffic tickets and you're not a threat just a bad parker. And for the failure to appear, you are here, no failure! With tears in his eyes that judge couldn't hold back the tears of laughter. Loren said that I was listening how he pleaded with the judge to let him serve his time send him back to his cell. What kinda of justice was that shift, courtside courtesy? They let me go immediately and I had my mother's car running with the passenger side door open. While I'm looking around just in case Fifi and her side kick Lucee might be lurking around. I told her to take me over to Stud's place and don't slow the car down.

I got in the back seat and laid low. I laid my ass down in that back seat thanking God we made it. I knew Fifi didn't know where Studs lived and his wife Zanetta wouldn't have any signs of crazy at their place. She has her hands filled with Studs/ Virgil crazy stuttering ass and Zanetta can go crazy. So, my option was that I put myself on house arrest and I created my own safe house. What kinda of judicial system was I a part of, where they work with you when you don't need their help?

So, I crashed at Stud's place with Zetta's permission and stares. He said that he told the judge that he was so desperate in trying to stay in jail, he couldn't pay and didn't have the money. So what ya gonna do? I'm broke!! They weren't feeling or hearing me. I pleaded like James Brown with a cape on. Loren laughs saying he wanted to bust into a Temptation move, while performing as James Brown with sayings "please don't release me!" while doing the "tempting" Temptatation walk back to my cell. That didn't work either just amused the audience. I wasn't too proud to beg or plead to his honor. The courts said he had fees that were workable with an agency assigned to the courts and that they gave him an extension. He told them again he couldnt pay it because he didn't have no money! They said that we have an agency that would work with you on payment arrangements and they are very reasonable. Did they not hear me, or did it just fall on deaf ears? Why in the hell he couldn't extend my stay instead of extended some sorry ass payments? I said I couldn't pay with an attitude and that shift didn't move him just amused his ass. He probably knew or dated Fifi's crazy ass mama Rosetta. They needed to put my ass in the comfort of my comfy cell. What now?? I get courtside courtesy when did all this shift happen and got to pay too.

For some reason I could visualize the whole story and that was a Loren special. We laughed so hard that when our laughter calmed down, we went into small talk. Loren said Fifi made a man want to become a fugitive. I escape to Cali and TJ escaped to Studs place, hugging those pa-pa-pillows and putting himself on house arrest until the coast was clear. For a few days that was his safe home. He eventully divorced her and that was when she tried to resurface and look my ass up and I was gone. When she finally came back to my house mentally, I was so gone from her crazy ass. I needed that break thank you cuz and extend that to Bill. We talk small talk a little more and I told him I would tell Bill and Sierra that he had called. As we said our good byes Loren was what I needed.

What's for dinner my meal making is very limited should have hung out more in the kitchen with my mother. By time I was ready she wasn't interested in train-ing me and Bonnie had the cooking down pack. My mother didn't have to give her step by step instructions. I guess I missed that class. Momo has been helpful but that's only when I catch her cooking and didn't want her to think I only came by to sample her food, didn't want to wear out my welcome. My parents already said that you didn't want people to be happy seeing you going rather than coming. Momo never complained about me coming over. I think she enjoyed teasing me about sex and cooking. The more I blushed the more she gave me those unsightly ooh visions. Humph flipping and flopping burgers, needing new mattresses, ooh vision again or the pot and pans in the bedroom yuck. Too much information but maybe I should be taking notes. After all Amos is still talking about flipping and flopping and sees only his Momo after so many years later. Is that what keeps the realationship go-ing. I enjoy the intimacy of holding hands laying on Bill's chest while listening to his heartbeat and feel the warmth and softness of his lips. Making love is good and should be enjoyed. But Bill hasn't had too much interest in me. I don't know how Sabrina happened but I'm glad she is here. This time she looks like both of us and Sierra finally has her little sissor. I go in and check on Sabrina and try to get dinner ready. Humph don't know what I will cook might be one of those Amos mystery dinners, hmmm. Not much to work with in the fridge or cabinets. We are kinda low there is a need for a grocery run. The groceries that my mom bought when she was here lasted a long time just like the food Loren helped us purchase. And now, its store time. Time flies now it's cooing time with Sabrina. Bill and Sierra walk in with a bag of honey buns but that wasn't the kicker right behind him is two of his marine buddies.

I had a hard time picking out something to cook for three and here we have un-expected guests. The last time I got my butt kicked for compliments from his bud-dies. I hope history will not repeat itself. I put together a stew using hamburger and tomato paste and soup with some biscuits. Hearty and plenty wasn't expecting company. It sure would have been nice for Bill to give me the heads up. Sierra is happy about school and spending time with daddy she is such a daddy's girl. He introduces Newport and Ash the first thing that comes to my mind is cigarettes. I asked do they smoke because I didn't want smoke around Sierra or Sabrina. They laughed saying that Ashton/Ashvin is Ash, and my other buddy Ashby and Newport were from Newport Beach, and he introduces himself as Alvin / McKoy who looks like he could pick up a car. I smile as their smiles brighten up the room and here, we go again in good physical shape and cute. I don't remember their names just their kind military nature. I glanced at them, but inside what a fresh view!

In some type of military sync, they compliment Bill on his beautiful wholesome wife. I didn't really know what they meant by that and I played if off as if I didn't hear them. But they kept on going saying man how blessed you are to have children and just being a family man. Inside I'm shivering because I forgot to put on my glasses. Oops and oh no I didn't want them to see my eyes, this is not good! I had to think quickly again, show off that accommodating affection hmm nice convenient term. I humbly tell them that we have a light dinner and that they are more than welcomed to stay. I perform the act of accommodating affections, and I give a gentle kiss on Bill's soft lips. His lips had that a taste of honey bun special. Although Bill had already invited them, I was just co-signing Bill's surprised dinner invitation. I looked into the freezer for a quick form of dessert with a surprise apple pie. I'm glad that I get them when they're on sale, those sales come in handy. I heat up the oven and by time dinner is done the pie should be ready. When we were younger my mother always had dessert for us after dinner. I'm just passing on our family tradition. I didn't know later that I would be exposed to more family tradition than I wanted to. I'm glad that I had time to clean up and the scent of Pine-sol that Bill loves to smell was fresh in the air as they opened the door. When we were younger, we learned that trick. The house could be in disarray all day but when we knew our mother was coming home, she smelled the scent she loved to smell was Lysol, and we didn't disappoint her. There was nothing she could complain about and we looked like perfect children. When she arrived home, we would be our rooms either listening to music or doing our home work. We gave her the picture she wanted and needed to see after her long day at work. We did the same for dad, but mom was different, and we learned at an early age how to do what with each parent. I guess we were studying parents 101.

Sierra sets the table while Bill and his friends are in the front room talking about the office, sargeants and parts of their past. I wanted to ask so bad what does office hours mean, but my gut feeling informs me silently don't do it. I continued doing what I was doing as I hear Sabrina crying. She must know that her dad is home too. I bring her out for Bill to hold her while I'm getting the dinner and table ready with Sierra. I know Bill has a hard time holding Sabrina because she is so small. He puts up the front, in front of his boys and he seems to be doing a good job. Sabrina feels the comfort of her dad's heart beat and her cryings turns into calm cooing. I watch him as he looks with so much love in his eyes down at his sleeping daughter. She doesn't seem hungry just wants to be cuddled aka another known action called spoiling her, why not Sabrina is a daddy's girl too, the tradition is just being passed on. As the aroma of dinner feels the air, I welcome everyone to come to the table because dinner is ready. Bill looks at me as if he needs assistance with Sabrina. I gently take her and place her back into her crib. While walking back to her room I look at how peaceful she looks, and it was just like looking at Bill sleep. She has so much of his features with a little dab of me in there. As I put her in the bed, I want to hold her a little longer because I just love her so much. I hear the noise of the clatter of plates which was the cue for me to return.

I join in so we all can sit and enjoy dinner together. Sierra says the prayer and our guests are impressed as her parents smile proudly. Conversations are coming in many directions which is a good sign that they feel like they are at home. I'm sure this is much needed since they are separated from their own families. I didn't mind our family being their substitute it was an honor. The aroma of apple pie fills the room while we enjoy our humble dinner and they seem to like my minor creation. I excuse myself to take the fresh baked apple pie from the oven. They all turn to see what I was doing. In my mind I'm hoping it was for the pie, but my eyes caught Bill looking at them looking at me. It feels good to know that I can still turn heads. Inside I hope that Bill takes this as a bold compliment from them and not any of my doing to draw their attention. I nervously smile because I didn't want that type attention although inside it made me feel visible. While they are excusing themselves from the table, Sierra helps collect the dishes, so she can run back to the room to check on her sister.

They sit back in the front room finishing up and adding to the conversation they had at the kitchen table. While the pie is cooling, I peak in on Sabrina watching Sierra trying to read her a story while she sleeps. That is a picture moment that still stays with me. I start preparing for a warm bath for both Sierra and Sabrina. Sierra breaks away from Sabrina long enough to help serve her dad and his friends' pieces of that fresh baked apple pie. I think it was McKoy or Ash saying that you have it all, the girl next door, family and to top it off with the apple pie. How could you give this up? That phrase threw me off guard, because I didn't know what they meant how you could give this all up? Is there something going on or this was just a figure or speech and meant nothing? Maybe it was just me tripping but it didn't sound good to me. I ask what they would like to drink with their dessert and shouted out just a few items. Water was fine for all of them and they didn't want to mix the flavor. They just wanted to enjoy and savor each morsel of their fresh baked apple pie and a small taste of home.

Chapter 42
Courage Is Making Cameos

I go and wake Sabrina, so I can bathe her again and give her a warm bottle and keep her up for a little bit, so she can enjoy her family. I have always loved the smell of babies and watch them learning how to explore their new world. Bill noticed me moving around actually kept his eyes on me. I don't know what that was about, but it felt good. Sierra watches while I bathe her sister and asks question after question as she includes her day at her new school. She tries and remembers their names and her facial expression shows her trying to work her memory. I remembered enough from last time to stay away from Bill's friends, especially when they leave. I don't know if Bill will need to give them a ride home or will this be his excuse to leave. No new tricks, just a different day. No worries we will probably be asleep whenever he returns. Sierra and I laugh and play with Sabrina until she falls asleep as Sierra starts to yawn. I asked her are you getting sleepy Sierra's response is always I'm just stretching then in a few minutes she is sound asleep. So, I must hurry to put her in bed too. School seems to be wearing her out and gives me a little break. I place sleeping Sabrina in her bed as I rush to give Sierra her bath before she falls off to sleep. I read her a bedtime story different from the ones her dad tells her that confuses her and tires her out. Nice strategy and it works everytime he tells her a story. I love listening to them as they laugh and talk and play right before bedtime.

Sometimes he comes in and we sit and talk as I lay my head on his shoulder. He doesn't mind if he did, he would tell me. Sometimes I don't know what upsets him but wish I knew so we could work together. I get myself ready for bed because I know I will sleep alone and wake up and he will just be there. I do my regular routine and watch television until it watches me while listening for the soft cries from Sabrina. I would cry softly but forgot how to cry. Inside I want to know what Bill is doing, communication was not ever our problem, but we don't talk or laugh as much as I would like for us to. I miss him so much. I miss us being us, I miss us acting like a couple, and I miss us acting like a married couple. He had to ask but sometimes I wonder if he was forced. Nah that's one thing I know about Bill he will not be forced. When I got pregnant, I remembered that argument so well. He didn't come here to get married and my bold response was I didn't know you were going to come here and get me pregnant. From that day I went on with my life adding one more person called Sierra. She made a big difference in my life. Sierra made me put on my big girl panties and grow up.

If I had to do it all again, I would do the same, because I would still want to be Sierra and Sabrina's mother and proudly being Bill's wife. I can't change what already exists, I can only change the direction starting with me. I had a good start finishing school at the age of 16, not bad in college and managed to stay in some of my classes so I have some since of direction. My life is not over but I have convinced myself that I couldn't do more because Bill wants me here safe where the world only sees me on his terms. This marriage was a contract between the both of us, and I must keep my focus and stand up. We merge into one but who is Bill trying to merge with tonight? I asked myself, Rita do you really want to take your mind there? Then I answer myself with no I'm going to relax and think about where do I go from here? As for now, I'm going channel surfing until I fall off to sleep in my empty bed. Maybe I should bring the girls in with me, so we can all be together. How many times will I ask this question over and over? I guess until I get the answer that satisfies me, but until then I will visit this issue later. I fall asleep in a bed filled with my daughters sleeping soundly. I woke up to just see if Bill might be sleeping on the couch or in the girl's room. To my surprise he's not there what excuse will he have this time? I sit at the table waiting for the door to open just how my father would sit on that short wooden stool waiting for us to come home. Now I can only imagine why he was upset not only did we break into his sleep but broke his rules and straight up form of disrespect.

When Bill unlocks the door, I can see the surprise in his eyes as he looks at the disgust in my eyes. I didn't ask where he was, I asked a simple quick question and said it slowly for clarity. I asked him how I go about getting a gun. His eyes widen with such a request because this was way out of character for his wholesome wife. He gathers himself and asks why you are going to shoot me. I think my great-grandmother, Mommy came out. My direct and stern response was, with no I'm not going to shoot you. Since we are here by ourselves if I hear someone jiggling the lock on the front door, I'm shooting the knob off. For the person on the other side I hope whoever it may be that they don't have their head near the lock or any other body parts. With that boost of courage, I get up and attend to our daughters. At that point I didn't want anything from him no hug, no conversation, and no nothing just get away from me. Bill asks you don't want to know what happen. My response was I know you needs a shower. I didn't look back when I responded I wanted to see what I wanted him to kiss. Today just wasn't the day, it wasn't fair, and I didn't deserve it. If you didn't want this, I can take my daughters and go back home. All I need is a job. I still have skills and still young, someone will hire me. I wanted to add the way your friends looked at me; I won't be single long here or back in Oakwood. Bill used to say when I went back to Oakwood, I got some courage. He didn't know I didn't need to go to Oakwood to get the courage that is slowly growing inside and developing.

Bill thinks he knows me. What he doesn't know we as women, wear many hats that comes with many characters in form of; mother, wife, girlfriend, confident, lover and nurse to make their booboos feel better. So sometimes they all come to a mutal agreement that they are sick of your ass too. Right now, there was a release of I'm tired of your ass and weak ass antics. I'm putting my mother role back on, because I have two daughters to attend to and today, I will not be his babysitter. He comes in trying to soothe me with touches I missed. But today I'm not in the mood for his weak ass accommodating affections. His touch and words will not work this morning let him think about respecting his wife, his family and the clock. Last time I checked the phone did work. I wake up Sierra, so she could eat and get ready for school. Bill goes in and checks on Sabrina. In the back of my mind, I'm hoping that he envisions Sabrina and Sierra not there to call him daddy. He had a brief visiual when Mickey was holding Sierra at a young age. Yep, another man holding your daughters and I'm sure he remembered that visual. Humph, that quick visual wasn't a good feeling for Mr. Bill was it? Who was holding you last night or this morning?

Would I get a gun nah the last time I had a gun in my hand was in ROTC class in high school. I was a good shooter in that class, actually "made marksman" (a little something I kept to myself) ... Although my great- grandmother slept with a big gun under her pillow along with other weapons that was in my heritage, circulating in my bloodline. I didn't carry on the weapons legacy, but Bill didn't know that. I surprised him with that action and that simple request. He may think he knows me but not all of me. Sierra being herself asked Bill why he didn't tuck her in bed. I replied with her why didn't you daddy?? She said and kinda scolded him for sleeping in his clothes. He tries and laugh it off saying daddy was tired. I just glance at him shaking my head while still trying to get her ready. Good answer but was it the truth. I didn't care he should have been home with his family. The excitement I had earlier about the conversation I had with Loren and just missing Bill was all gone in an instant. I found myself looking no actually staring at him trying to really figure out who I had married, and who and why am I putting up with him possibly sleeping with someone else. The man I fell in love with is he still in the room and in my heart. Bill glances at me as if he is reading my thoughts and confused by the glare directed at him. He knows that my mind and thoughts are moving as he tries to make small talk with myself and Sierra. I don't really answer I just continue to look at this man I called my husband and best friend. I'm in awe of the gall this man has coming in the next day, as if he was only gone fore a few hours.

I asked if he will be taking Sierra to school and is work on his agenda. He tries to smile at me but the smile for him is meant with a look of well what do you really want to happen? He tries to tell me what happened. I really didn't want to hear it and I really didn't care. The only answer I wanted to know will Sierra be going to school. Don't want to hear his imagination. In a few months it will be time for his two weeks away with training. I do believe that because his boys come and pick him up for their two weeks training every year. The break would do us fine. Maybe while he is away from his family that song that plays inside both our heads of everytime you go away you take the biggest part of me. If we were to leave, would he lose the biggest part of him, or us? Bill takes the much-needed shower as I get Sierra dressed and her breakfast ready. As far as for Bill nope, not today, breakfast for one will be served. Wherever he laid his head he should have had breakfast there, this will not be his drive thru resturant. He rushes around the apartment trying to get ready without my assistance. Normally I would wake up and help him with his pleats in the back of his shirt and have breakfast and lunch ready for him. This morning the routine changed, to his surprise he looks around the kitchen wondering where's his breakfast, and the assistance with his shirt. I act as if I'm not in the room. That old trick I felt when I was younger being invisible that trick comes in handy. This was a new one I learned was the "doctor's office". This is where I sit there reading a boring magazine, and maybe answer the receptionist or just ignored her/him and if I answer the answers would be short and direct. That's what he's getting today until my more than ample butt feels like getting up out of this chair in the doctor's office. I'm sure you will get breakfast and lunch somehow after all you do have the car. He leans toward to kiss me good bye. This time I'm not in the mood for his soft lips, or his embrace or the aroma of his cologne. Bill tries to thank me for dinner yesterday and making his boys feel welcomed. I gave him of look of do you really want to go there. If so pull up a chair this is going to be a long conversation…

Inside I feel good about this courage that seems to fade in and out. That ancestral strength has not left me. I guess I occasionly ignored the tap on the shoulder when they are trying to get my attention. Now they are slowly getting it. Bill seems stuned by my lack of affection. Humph I guess he forgot about the stories I told him about my family. We loved each other but we weren't huggers or very affectionate. Good grief my great-grandmother slept with a knife, hammer, switch blade, big gun, razor strap all under her pillow, my grandmother only threatened to kill me with a butcher knife and hung out at the pool all with us in tote. While Hazel gave us candy, she would socialize with her friend by the name of Lightening. I just remember she would show us off as we heard the pool balls hitting on the pool table, the many conversations and the smell of stale smoke and liquor with dim lighting. The ironic part to this day when Hazel looks at me, she has a puzzled look on her face as she tries to figure out who I am. I was only three years younger than Emma

Jean/EJ and she thought I was EJ's daughter. I think what she really saw was the transformation happening in front of her eyes, as my looks form into looking like her and my mother.

Humph I guess that would be shocking to anyone. Humph it's shocking to me to see a change happen with age and time. I'm the only one in my family that has that strong resemblance; I guess good grief, humph. The two people that love me but can't stand me, I now strongly resemble what kind of crap is that. My grandmother Hazel don't know who I am, and my mother Sheryl may love me, but she doesn't like me maybe I remind her of her past, present and what her future could have been. Getting back to my unaffectionate family, we love but just don't hug. So, does that sound like I come from a family of kissey, huggy and blooming flowers come on really? We loved each other now that I think about it our whole neighborhood was kind of the same philosophy. We came home from school changed our school clothes, did house work, homework and went outside until we were called in for dinner. We all ate at the table and that's where conversation would begin. Weekends parents rested as we stayed out of their way. Humph sometimes you don't have to always embrace to show a special type of love. I'm trying hard to be affectionate, a good wife and mother. Come on Bill work with me just like I'm working hard to be all these roles, wife, lover, friend, nurse, mother, and counselor, whatever the need may be for that moment or day. The roles that I didn't know I was signing up for are subject to change. I should have read the fine print in our marriage license. Let me calm down because this has gotten old and boring, your routine has gotten redundant.

As I give Sierra a kiss good bye Bill again is stunned as if I had forgotten to kiss him. Not this time Bill no accomodating affections. I watched them as they pulled off with Sierra waving at me. This day is my day still enjoying this cup of Chai tea and just thinking about how accommodating I have been. Sabrina cries letting me know that it's her time for attention. I look at her almond eyes slowly blinking at me with that familiar Bill smile, and with that emotion it warms my heart and I'm back to being her mother. Well actually I never stopped being her mother just pissed off at her dad. We laugh and smile at each other as I feed her and change her diapers and clothes. I walk with her through the apartment talking about the items she is seeing. Then I sit down with her and read a book as she lays so comfortably and secured in the cradle of my arm. I hear a gentle knock on the door. I'm glad that we are awake. I open the door to see a smiling face with a plate of warm cookies filling Sabrina and my nostrils.

He asks is it okay to come in? He knows the rules but today it's okay because I didn't want Sabrina outside yet. He comes in sitting the plate of cookies on the counter, while admiring Sabrina. He can't believe all the curly hair she has and how beautiful she is. I just smile with saying you know where she got her looks from. He chuckles with me and sits down saying he wasn't going to stay long, but he wanted to hear it from him and not from someone else. Inside I shiver because I don't know what he is going to tell me. For the longest him or Clarence were trying to tell me something and every time we always had some type of interruption. I brace myself and in the back of my mind I now kinda know how Robin felt when Ramon said he wasn't happy and wanted to talk. My eyes widen with suspense of what could he possibly have to say. What did Bill do this time? I still wonder what this term office hours mean. I brace myself as I hold Sabrina. Inside my heart is racing my brain is trying to go numb and my lungs are afraid to exhale. So, I hold my breath for the sigh to be released. Right now, I hold Sabrina and take a whiff of her baby scent laying her gently against by breast for now she is my security blanket.

Keith notices my expression and reassures me it's okay not what you think. All senses that ran away came back with courage. I smile as I exhale, and it seems Sabriana is relaxed with me. She makes a little sigh noise as if we were sharing the same heart and feelings again. A big smile comes on his face when he tells me I have good news and bad news. Right when I had just had that big sigh of relief my mind says oh now here, we go, and you wasted that big exhale. I said okay start with the bad news, so we can end with something good. Well Miss Rita I can't bake for you and Sierra anymore or Bill. I looked at him with saddened eyes wondering what any of us could had done to him for him to feel this way. I searched my heart and mind trying to figure out if Bill saw him bringing desserts or borrowing food. If that was the case, I know for sure I'm in trouble and thank you for the heads up. My mind raced for what seemed like minutes when it was just seconds. Keith laughs no it wasn't Bill it was because of you. Now what did I say I normally listen more than I talk now what dumb thing did I say. See that's why I need to keep my thoughts to myself. Here my thoughts are racing causing my heart to beat faster again. This time, I cradled Sabrina before I laid her little body on the blanket on couch. I asked if Keith would like something to drink maybe this will distract any anger, he might have towards me. Here I go again accomodating affections. Well Rita take a deep breath and take the punch. Keith kindly said he didn't have much time, but he wanted to talk to me. He said are you ready for the good news? Keith can see by my actions that I'm anxious and sitting on edge? He said he took my advice. Now I'm searching in my archives of what did I say to him? I haven't seen Keith in a long time. I just figured he was working overtime with Clarence.

He reminded me about his wife Kiante. Now my heart and mind smiled when he said his wife. I tried to remember but I don't need to because Keith reminds me of our conversation. He said we were sitting outside nice day calm weather and you reminded me that I was an idiot in your own way of believing my eyes and not my wife. Melvin /Marvin as you said laughing really. I had a moment and I had to laugh at myself and let my ego land and called my wife and see if we could talk.

We've been separated for years but we never talked about divorce. I didn't want to think about it, but I didn't want to come to some type of realization that we might not grow old together. I've dated, and I realized it was a waste of time because they didn't measure up to Kiante. She was the one I had memory flashbacks on and that shift messed with my mind and I could only see her. I cleaned up and headed back to her place to see about starting over again and making the love we still had for each other stronger than a cup of black coffee. We both laughed because that's strong. I looked at him and he wasn't wearing his normal wrinkled pants and shirt. He actually did clean up and very well and had a nice aroma. Not that he had bad body odor. I just never have seen him in pressed to impress clothes. Then it hit me without saying anything, I wondered if Bill might come home for lunch and see clean shaven Keith sitting in the front room with his daughter, dejavu again. Inside I panic because I know the rules no man in the apartment when Bill is not here. Although right now I might have the upper hand I don't want to lose it to getting my butt beat for something that is so innocent. I never knew when Bill will explode but I don't want to be the one supplying the dynamite. I was trying to share Keith's joy at the same time hoping he would hurry up with the story. He said that they were taking a honeymoon that they never had time to take and would be going to Paris. I get giddy saying wow now that's a romantic honeymoon. Inside I envy them that's one place I would love to see and be with Bill under the Eiffel Tower with fireworks. Wow that would be so nice. Keith is talking as I fade away into visions of Paris and Bill.

He said that Kiante wanted to personally thank you for talking to me. I gave you the credit for showing that much love and concern about someone that you didn't know. Some women wouldn't have done that. They would have tried to convince me to leave and hook up with them. There are some trifling women out there and I don't have time or money to sponsor them. While the trifling looks for my next paycheck and continued sponsorship. I agreed with him saying I look forward to seeing his wife again. He laughs yea my wife and I'm married. I remind him just like Mama Sadie said remember you had to ask, and she said yes. Communication is the key don't go to bed angry that way you appreciate looking at the smile in the morning. It's been a few years and you both have changed talk about the changes so neither one of you will be surprised. Sometimes surprises are not good. He agreed saying that he had to get moving because they were going house hunting. I tell him how blessed he is getting back with his wife Kiante and going to Paris and now house hunting.

Wow you should renew your vows. I can see the hesitation in his pause, and he touches his face with his hand, saying that is not a bad idea. I can show her that I can be and had gotten more romantic, huh. Hey Rita, you are the best I hope that Bill continues to realize that. You are a beautiful woman inside and out and don't let him mistreat you deserve better. Inside I'm crying he noticed that I am a good person and I still have looks. Didn't look at myself like that in a long time. Beauty left with some of my other emotions. Crying has left me somewhat numb. But somehow, I had to bring life back into our life and marriage, but what is Bill doing he needs to step up his game too. Keith says he is going, and I walked him to the door hoping that Bill has not changed his mind and circled back to check on his family or to check to see what mood I am still in. It's still the same but I'm still at the doctor's office and I haven't changed my thoughts other than maybe I should have listened to his entertaining excuse. I just wasn't in the amusement stage.

Keith gives me a hug thanking me again and nervously I respond with you and Kiante are more than welcome and I'm going to miss your baking and borrowing. With that we both laughed as I closed the door to a friend that is happy being married and knowing no other women will mess up their marriage. My mind is still stuck on Paris and the Eiffel Tower, what nice place to spend a honeymoon. My honeymoon was in form of moving out of Oakwood to sunny California. Throughout the morning I think about the happiness with Keith and Kiante reuniting. Then I come back to my reality of what will Sabrina and our morning consists of. In the back of my thoughts of Bill kinda linger and I wonder will we last. I have a feeling that Bill might come home for lunch, so I'll prepare a meal for him. I sit the sandwich on the counter just in case he comes home while I'm in the back. Last time I had that feeling was when my mother talked me into going to the movies with her. I remembered telling her I should be packing because I told Bill I had been packing and just had a strange feeling that he would be coming home. That same feeling is circulating now. I hear keys in the door as I act like I'm surprised. But he is the one that will be surprised this time when he sees his sandwich on the kitchen counter. He comes back into the room as I'm changing sleeping Sabrina eating his sandwich.

I guess he had sometime to think and my prayers were answered. He tries to kiss me and I'm still at the doctor's office just not feeling it, but I do still love my husband and want our marriage. He sits on the bed looking at me with his almond shaped eyes with a boyish look of I'm really sorry. He told me that he was getting high with his friends and time got away and he was in no condition to drive. He said that he didn't want to get busted on base. He knows he should have called. I just looked at him saying you still doing that. I knew he probably was, but I put my head in the sand. He said I did but I wasn't doing it here. I wanted to ask who all was there, but my courage wasn't ready for the answer. Did he conveniently use Loren's innocent lie he used on Fifi, because that line sure sounded familiar? Although I didn't hear all the details, I know I heard enough and that it did sound familiar. I challenged myself of if I should say it sounds familiar or just let it go. He came home so you both are still on the same page. He came home, and you knew he would. I agree with myself or convince myself he came home to see how we were doing. He came home to see if he still has a wife and family? I look at him and see the almond shaped eyes looking at me with that twinkle I love seeing as he embraces me. I laugh saying as I looked at Sabrina that's what got us here the second time. Bill holds me tighter saying you want to make three. I laughed saying I want to work. He smiled and said not now you need to be here with the girls. Inside my voice was saying I need one of those Fifi bricks since the same story is being used. But why would I break something that belongs to both of us, kind of silly. Am I being silly with Bill he should have called or just came home? He should have called or something and just don't leave us hanging or thinking something happened.

I didn't want to end up like the women that would come to the bank and couldn't balance or write a check. I'm losing a lot of my independence. I need my first name back and I need my own account other than my mad money. Sierra needs more clothes and we need more food. If I worked, I could help our family out so much. I do know where Bill is coming from as far as me staying home but if I found a good babysitter that would be the best for both of us. I want to support Bill and not constantly asking him for money and his constant reply being what's the reason for the need. The first time it threw me off I've never been in that situation before. I've always worked and had my own money with the freedom to spend on what I wanted when I wanted to. My parents taught us early about saving and financial responsibility. I used to look forward to paying my bills. Until Bill came and he would tell me you don't give up your last dollar to pay bills. I did and now humph.

He does take care of the bills. The phone is still on, but I just want more for our family. Now I had to ask for lunch money what if I wanted a snack. That would be out and just lead into Bill talking about my weight. I want a house where Sierra and Sabrina can run in the backyard and we can put a swing set back there and bar-beque, just like we did so often in Oakwood. Here I go again missing my family add my girlfriends too. Why did Bill come home? I'm glad he did but why do we have to keep revisiting these actions. The other question is why I continue to put up with it. I guess the gun question did raise an eyebrow. Would I shoot maybe that would depend on which heritage surfaced?

Chapter 43
Welcome to the Neighbor I Guess

I haven't seen Courtney Diane and wondered if she is back home. I call her while holding Sabrina and behold she is home. She said she had been busy and sick and didn't want to get Sabrina sick and where did I get that name Sabrina. I laughed saying the same place you got the name Henray Luis. Her response was touche heffa. I moo back to her and she tee-hee-hee's, with you've been around me too long and I like it. We talk about her transferring to Fort Marshal and that she knew it was coming now the time has arrived. Inside I didn't want her to go because she had become family to me. So many families in this complex have been my subsitiute immediate family and sad to see part of my adopted family leave. She reassures me that she will be returning time to time because she is letting her sister JJ/ Juanita Jalise and her cousin Jazelle Jalese with a pause don't go there you know the issues with my family and those twin names. You know the family rountine that both are called JJ.

Now get this shift the next generation Jazelle Jalese will be living here with her bad ass kids Nekia Nay and Nakaya Nya, nope not twins next generation with no imagination. Their nick names are Nay, and Kay there goes that rhyming crap again. Don't let their smiles and cuteness throw you off and their mother is lazy and loud as hell. Just giving you the heads up when you see a mouth that is constantly open and limping lady, yelling momma and kids running like they just escaped from school and every minute is recess. They don't tire, they don't sleep, and they are extremely loud and like souvenirs so watch your shift. One good thing about this she admits my family is not in the streets. In my mind okay let's do this, because I really don't have a choice.

They will be upstairs away from you and you won't hear their momma yelling and them yelling back. Robin and her girls Denise and Nicole might be pissed from all that noise. Robin is working and earning her money okay, between work and her girls are wearing her butt out. Between track practice, music and Robin's busy schedule they won't trip on noise when they are not here to hear. It is just when they

── 482 ──

are home trying to rest. Courtney Diane leans forward with direct eye contact Rita remember JJ my sister's secret, she likes married men, keep her away. I wish I could put a neon sign on her forehead and the back of her head, so people can see the sign when she is leaving or coming, saying stay away from her dumb ass. I love her, but she has some issues, and has had them for some time. She did it with other people boyfriends until she perfected to how to get husbands at any expense. That's why she has that limp and alone, that's what happens when you do ugly.

God don't like ugly and He's not fond of cute either. I told JJ if I hear any name in form of Bill, I will tear up my anger management certificate and propel her with my right foot. Karma makes many circles and hers came around in form of a bus. I smile back thinking Bill and I can hold up to any aka's another known actions. I think back on what Robin said about not sharing a heart and that she had moved out of his heart long before he noticed that she was gone. Have I moved over slightly in Bill's heart to make room for someone else? Bill is my all and all and my heart beat belongs to him and our family. I can't picture our family minus Bill. Why does this JJ have to land her trifling limping ass here? I know of her and what I know just makes me uncomfortable. I'm not giving Bill and our marriage too much credit, by adding JJ to something that doesn't exsist. Maybe it will not happen. After all I'm here, he asked, and we have been married for a long time and we are going to make it. I haven't had these types of thoughts since my school years and I made it through, and I will make it through this. There was that one time that scant set next to Bill and took my seat, but that will not happen ever again. My guard will not be compromised, and I will stand my ground this time and any other time. My focus is on my family just like I've seen many couples stand the many tests of time. I didn't come this far to go back to Oakwood, unless we go visiting as a family. I wouldn't give my mother the pleasure of blaming me for not fulfilling my marriage obligations. It would be my fault in their eyes before they would place any blame on Bill, because in her eyes Bill can do no wrong. Yep it would be my entire fault and I would feel like I failed my marriage, my family and myself. The same feeling, I had to endure when I was pregnant with Sierra. That was such a rough time.

I'm glad my friend Melody Lynn was first to become pregnant, and I was too young to understand how she felt and too busy to be there for her. To this day I regret missing out on being her friend and the battles she went through by herself. Her mother Agnes, who when the wind shifted became Abagail, was too busy tearing her down instead balancing her support. Then Debbie Ann was the second to become pregnant and we were there. Her mother Miss Evelyn had a sense of humor and energy silimar to Charlotte's mother Sybil and Grandma Ruby. This time I was a little more mature but not enough to still understand. But history came around again and there I was just a little busy and not hanging out with Sharon or Debbie. I was busy hanging out with Bill and enjoying the college life. Then that indigestion happened to me. I didn't know enough to realize I was pregnant. I really thought I was having some bad indigestion. Until Reva told me in nine months to have a boy or girl name and add a social security number for my indigestion. Then good old Nurse Rochelle confirmed my fears and sent me out the room wondering what directions I was going in. Not sure, numb and totally confused and scared. I was blessed to talk with Charlotte who made being pregnant a joy. Especially, how she had me laughing about a dusty tampon box and a calendar full of dots to keep track of her period. Simple and easy, just like unplugging the clock to have proof of what time you came in, way past your curfew.

With my mother, Sheryl or Shellee when the wind shifts, conducting her investigations and lurking around every corner. I couldn't hide pregnancy too long because she was on a mission. That seemed like it was such a long long time of hiding from her. Then Sharon Denise came next with a mild case of nine-month indigestion, hmmm. This time I was able to be there for her. Her mother Miss Rebecca had energy like Reva's mom. I guess in a sense I had my friends in other people inside the clinic sitting spiritually with me. It still didn't take away the fear I had inside, while I was still trying to convince myself that I had indigestion. This time I made time to talk because now I was coming from a place of experience and pain. I didn't share all the pain with my good friends, but this time I made myself available for all my friends rather in laughter, love, pain just sharing our experiences with childhood memories. Although, I didn't physically see their children as much as I would like to see them growing up. We still manage so many years later to still stay in touch. Sometimes I have too much time on my hands. I'm sitting here looking out the window watching the sun and the rain compete. I never knew why mommy would sit in that high chair just looking out the window. As I stare out thinking I have a feeling she was doing the same thing. Just her thoughts, her me time and God.

Momo talked about her great aunts Gretchen and Zabeth and I try to picture what they might look like. Momo seems to have strong genes and weight fluctuates so they might be my height or a little taller with racks. It took me awhile to realize what racks were. I guess my rack is in the back. As Loren would say the front of the back did match and gave Bill two beautiful babies. Now his mama Naomi and Papa Richard can enjoy wearing out their grandkids every time they come. I guess I passed the Bill/Loren test. Sometimes things do land on my rack and stick. Not to mention in grade school the boys throwing rocks at my butt and watching the rocks bounce off. I didn't feel it only heard them laughing at my expense.

I've admired the strength that the elders in all ways demonstrate without hesitation. Momo said troubles don't worry them and when troubles do come their way they just needed to talk. They would look up to the heavens to keep that relationship going. Gretchen would say I need to talk to Him and Zabeth would always follow with well what did He say. Her response was as she looked up to the heavens and back to her saying He was talking to me. In other words, don't utter words that were a private prayer and conversation. Now Beth when you talk to Him you just keep it to yourself, don't need to know. They very seldom were separated and are still alive walking, talking and moving very well. Women of strength and much character their philosophy is that it's easier to repeat what you said than to back out, but on the other hand I don't like to repeat because you should be listening. Hmm I guess that's a nice way of saying mind your own business.

Aunt Gretchen smiles at Zabeth after making that statement and they continue doing whatever they needed to do that day. She drives and Aunt Zabeth rides as they look around still enjoying each other living as if they don't have a care or concern in the world not bad uh. Momo talks very highly about their travels and adventures, saying that no grass will ever grow under their feet. Funny my dad says the same thing when I was waiting for Bill to come around. Am I letting grass grow under my feet waiting for Bill to to come around? How can I wait for someone I'm married to and he had to ask that's what Mama Saide said? A simple line to a confused thought. He always comes home so how am I waiting. Humph I guess I'm waiting for him to be more affectionate and kinder to me, treat me better and not take me for granted. I need to look at myself because it's me that is allowing this to happen.

I can flip this scene or script and be my own leading lady with my husband being the leading man. Too much time Rita too much energy, effort and thought for something you might just be imagining. I wondered why Momo brought up her great aunts. Aunt Gretchen was married for thirty years to her Uncle Spencer who shared each others heartbeat until his heart beat for the last time while they both embraced each other. She said that was and will be the only man that she will ever embrace and didn't want to replace that embrace with some knuckle head. It was time for her to live. As for Aunt Beth her husband was from the old school trying to beat her into submission. One night he came home one too many times drunk, smelling of perfume at the same time complaining about his cold dinner. She had it all, a nice big house, didn't have to work but did work a part time job when she wanted to just get out the house but had to be home to have dinner ready before Uncle Spencer came home on his routine of being drunk. He was a functional dysfunctional drunk. They had money, and everything you could want but he wasn't faithful to her or their marriage vows. She finally took one big breath as she gazed at herself in the mirror, and she didn't like the reflection she was looking at. Momo said the family didn't know she was going through this. If we did, we would have yanked her out with no regards. We would pull her out as she was kicking or screaming, she wanted to stay. Our family didn't do that and wasn't raised to participate in such bizzare antics. Because one time we didn't get involved we lost the aunt that Beth is named after.

Auntie Zabeth Nanette she married Uncle Sid and they appeared to be happy. I just remember watching and listening to Momo as she struggles to tell this story for a reason that I'm not sure but with all the respect I have for her, I listened. He was in the service and they married and moved out here to California. Uncle Sid promised her daddy Leek that he would take care of her. He promised, and daddy Leek believed him and took him for his word. See your word was your respect and reputation. We tried to stay in contact with Nanny but long-distance calls with short money made it hard. So that old saying no news is good news works but not with every situation. Years passed, and the conversations faded away and the last time we saw her was when she left us to start her family with Uncle Sid. We just hoped and prayed that she was doing well. Didn't hear about her having any kids so we figured since they were so lovey dovey when they were here the love and honeymoon kept on going. When we heard about how and what they were doing it didn't come from Uncle Sid's sorry ass it came from his cousin Date. Didn't know who he was just knew he was Uncle Sid's cousin.

He spoke with Papa Leek; Mother Nettie didn't want to hear what her heart was feeling. He said that Nanny had passed away she had been sick. Papa Leek couldn't understand why the man that gave his word to protect his baby didn't have the respect enough to call. Date went on to tell them a little about Nanny and the good she had done working for the church and helping him raise his children when his wife, Eleen took ill and stayed until she fully recovered. He talked about how much she missed her family and talked so much about her parents and siblings. He felt that he could identify them as he called out their names. Date didn't go into too much detail, but Papa Leek had to know about his child. Date said I owe it to Nanny's family with the respect and love he had for her. Daddy Leek could hear the crackling in his voice as he's telling what happened. Mama Nettie tries to hold on as she watches the expressions of her husband. Date said that Sid had been abusive to Nanny before they married and moved to California. I was surprised she married him, but Sid swore that he loved her enough to change and stop the tears flowing from her eyes and seeing the bruises on her face. Sid, he did stop for a bit and talked about bringing her back home to see her family. Time and money got in the way and she kept on him about his promise to take care of her and let her see her family again. I think in the back of Sid's mind he knew if she went home, she wouldn't come back. Your family was very tight, and her family would have saw through her pain and talked her into staying at the same time looking for Sid. Nanny wouldn't tell you guys about the nonsense he was putting her through, but you would have felt her spirit screaming for help through her eyes.

I think the affair was the last straw. They got into an arugment and he beat her bad. I could only imagine that there was a pause on both ends of the phone line. The beating put her into a stroke that she didn't recover from. Papa Leek asked with deep breaths can we bring our baby home. When was the funeral and where is she buried? Date said that's another reason why I'm calling you, Nanny was creamated and Sid took her ashes and transferred, and he is out of the country. That's when they both broke down, we can't see our baby again. Date responded with hesitiation please remember the smile she had for you guys when she left. That was the smile that Nanny had and kept the last time I saw her. They couldn't fix the problem or the situation, but we can work harder in staying in contact with family. So that's why you see us still eat, talk and show the next geneneration what families do and need to keep on doing. By God's grace we need to value life and family.

I listened and wondered what happened with Beth. Well with time, complaining nagging husband she had to act. His routine played out and the cold dinner temperature extended to the bedroom. At that point nothing to lose but much to gain, in another form of heat called freedom. She needed some circulating body heat not the vapors of his cold heart that beats to the rhythm of a glass and bottle tapping together as they form a union in his body. Beth was hanging in there until her children were at least heading off to college age. Her oldest son Mooney worked for her husband and didn't know how he was going to feel about my move to act. He was old enough to know what was going on but that was his paycheck that might affect his plans to move out on his own. Rita, she tossed and turned until she rolled over and set up got up washed her face saying its time...

She didn't want her life to end up like her Aunt Nanny. Nanny was a good person and so Beth put her plan into action. How did Robin say work your plan and plan your work something like that? Aunt Beth had some money saved but not enough to fully run away but she knew it was time and she had to get away. Mooney was her oldest son and Spencer's stepson. Beth didn't have any contact with his father. Eventually Mooney's dad Dominic moved back to his country and that was the end of the connection with his son. So, one day she just woke up and a voice said its time. Mooney, to her blessings, had saved money for a house and was going to surprise her when he moved in. Nice surprise and timing was right. Beth packed few bags for her girls and other son. Told them we are moving and take just what you want. Don't ask no questions just move and don't look back. While they loaded up in her car she went back in, just to leave a parting gift for Spencer. She left a cold dinner on the table to match his heart and he could heat it up with the heat from his liquor. Her son, Mooney took her to the house that he purchased. Beth stayed there until she got on her feet and her parents helped with the down payment and that's where to this day that she and Aunt Gretchen live.

Spence tried looking Beth up and pleaded with her to come back home with their children. With family support there was no need and her son Mooney found a better career opportunity and left Spence's Company. Beth received child support and saved the money for her children to pursue careers and attend trade schools.

She laughs Aunt Beth says she lost two hundred pounds that day in form of Spence. She didn't go back or pondered the thought if she did the right thing. We didn't force her but stood by her decision on whatever she decided. We as family joined together to not let what happened with Nanny to ever happen with any member of our family. To this day we have kept that promise. I listen and still wonder why Momo told me that story. Did she know, or did she hear the noises coming from our apartment? Momo said the only ring she wanted was the wedding ring from Amos and not being in a boxing ring sparing with a person that confessed an undying love and promised never to hurt me. How do you respond from that I just smiled and listened? Inside I wanted to yell out do you know because I don't know when or why Bill acts the way he does toward me. It's been times where I didn't say or do anything to warrant being yelled at or be his sparring partner. In the Momo way somehow, she found a way to bring sex into the conversation. She said I don't serve Amos cold food. We keep our food heated and the oven is always warm, but the temperature setting will rise. With that she raised her eyebrows along with her signature shake. My typical response was visuals eew, yuck. Her come back well since you have the visual there was that one cold meal we had when the power went out, but we were able to power up and get that generator working. Humph humph hmmm then the power came on that day. Eek, Momo really another visual?

I appreciate her and the love she in all ways shows me and my family. She had me think back on some of my friends that suffered severely by the hands of someone that said the words "I love you". I haven't heard Bill say those words to me in awhile, maybe the fact that he comes home, and we are still married is his form of love? I still would like to hear those words. As I watched Sabrina grow learning how to crawl sooner than I thought she was just trying to keep up with her sister and friends. I would feel for her not understanding when they would run past her. She had a unique way of crawling that looked like a combat crawl. Then once she catches up with them, they not knowing, run right past her again as they ran back outside.

I realized that Bill's two-week training will be coming up soon. That will be a form of fresh freedom for both of us. Maybe the break will reveal that we miss one another and we both are willing to bring our hearts back together so that we can beat as one again. My heart still beats for him and I don't like when it skips a beat, because it throws my rhythm off. Courtney Diane will be leaving for Fort Marshal and I'm really going to miss her. Robin is on assignment and I miss her and her girls coming around when they are around to play with Sierra. They were her big sisters although Robin's youngest daughter Nicole is not that much taller than Sierra. Sierra has always been tall for her age. There was one time when she was at school, she said the kids were teasing her about her stomach. I had to think about how to handle this without any form of violence. We laughed as we sang because I eat good, because I eat good as she rubbed her stomach. She laughed, and she said her friends laughed and I figured they did what children do. They played and never looked back. Innocence still existed in the hearts of youngster. Time moves on Sabrina starting to cut teeth and everything that comes with it. Even the part her practicing her teeth on biting into your skin. Keith comes by for what might seem the last time I will see him and his wife, Kiante. As she embraced me, she whispered thank you. I just remembered how this threw me off and I smiled mouthing your welcome. All I did was what I would have wanted someone to do for me. That's what we should do is support one another and not tear up relationships. Not be a Trixie under the disguise of a padded shoulder, but to support with honesty from the outside looking in with respect and timing. Kiante was beautiful as she was inside as she was outside. Her pleasant demeanor explains why Keith didn't date and was waiting for that opportunity to set his ego aside and refocus on the whats, whys and his contribution into their seperation. Well I take that back he did refocus by baking as his distractor. Sierra is going to miss laughing with him and those big oatmeal cookies with frosting, hmmm, me too.

I haven't seen Robin in a while or her daughters Denise and Nicole. I know she has been busy, but I hope she is okay. Wait a minute if something was wrong Courtney Diane would be in the news or she would let me know. I miss seeing her and the girls. I'm thankful that she stopped by to see us and can't wait to take another family picture that she promised us. Hmm, family picture maybe that would remind everyone, including Bill that we are a happy family. Who am I trying to convince, me? I keep telling myself everything will work itself out. Only if I knew what the problem, then I could work on solutions. Bill comes home but sometimes his mind is somewhere else. He spends time helping Sierra with her homework, reading and playing with Sabrina, but when it comes to me it seems like it's a chore. I ask permission to hold his hand or touch him and that's met with a look that was familiar with me for my affectionate request. Sometimes he makes me feel like the other woman and I'm available only when he wants me to be. At some point I guess I am. When he smiles, I smile back when I do get an embrace which is seldom I carress it as if this is my last embrace. I tried to talk to him about Keith and Kiante and he could careless about the details of their life. He took the excitement I had for them. So, I go back into my routine of caring for our daughters and at the same time trying to keep the apartment clean.

That same day as I sigh for Keith moving, I see new movers coming in with boxes one walking with a limp and the other one yelling. Okay from the sounds and the looks I know who this is the twins that are not twins the JJ's. Really their timing is so off as I watched kids running all around and up and down the stairs yelling and shouting at each other. Courtney Diane opens the door slowly, yelling back do not bring all that noise up in here. I know ya act and may look crazy, but must you always give confirmation, damn. Really although her yelling wasn't too loud, I can hear her say get your pint size asses up here and glue yourselves to the couch. I can imagine her look with pursed lips while talking and her eyes going smaller as she uses her imaginary laser eyes to zap them. It worked, the yelling JJ stopped, the children noises stopped, and the only thing that kept going was JJ's limp. Wow that bus hit her hard, that limp is very pronounced. Well, she can't chase a man, but she could walk fast. Now Rita stop, this woman is nor will be a threat to you but keep your eyes open she did bring a twin. They glance at me without speaking just a glare as they move in items quietly. I smile as they glare, and I continue on with my life in my apartement. Courtney Diane comes over saying the day arrived and she is glad as a happy flower blooming in the spring that she will be leaving this week. She just wanted to see me before she leaves and to make sure that the JJ's move in with Nay and Kay. They may be loud, but they are good people just not too friendly.

You can tell that Nay and Kay are sisters but just in different sizes short and talkative. The other sister is tall and seems sneaky while looking laughing with their innocence showing as they glanced around at their new enviroment. The mother and JJ look straight ahead occasionally looking around at their new enviroment as if they were sizing up the area. They glanced at Clarence smiling and whispering just great not even in the door yet. Their looks seem so familiar inside I kinda gathered that just how Courtney Diane carries herself a little different from what I am used to. She may sometimes seem not approachable, but she is being herself, but I haven't ever seen her hurt or say anthing to intentionally hurt anyone. I'm not one to say anything my family is friendly, or we are known to be social anti social funny by not ha-ha. That's just the way we are no worries and not snobs just being us and not very affectionate. Bill doesn't know how hard it is sometimes to be affectionate only to be rejected. Bill doesn't have a clue on how that hurts nor does he even care. I don't know each day the emotions change, and this is another thing I have to surpress, along with the tears. Pretty soon I will be a walking robot, feeling numb but moving. Occassionaly Bill reminds me by calling me my pet name meathead. I guess babe and all those other names dissipated into the air and bypassed my ears. I do sometimes get rattled when he starts yelling and when he gives me that certain look. I don't know what is going to happen, but it does scare me and from that it becomes a domino effect just rolling and falling. This effect has me mentally and physcially falling, tripping and stumbling with my own words, while looking for a corner to hide in. I guess with that adding to another character flaw to my long list. This is just great in giving confirmation to my pet name meathead. There I go again another name other than my birth name. In which my parents didn't help sometimes. It was either shift Robin or Robin Shift just depended on which parent was talking to me.

Funny how Robin used to say how they teased her with her name Robin Hood, robin bird or robin's been eating her worms look at her red breast. She would laugh about that because we both didn't have racks. Courtney Diane did but the rack she had made up for the flat she didn't have. Robin would tease her saying that if you stood against the wall you would blend right into the paint/wallpaper. No butt little guts showing just very flat. I look at her sister and cousin and they have racks, hmmm and not shy in showing them off. Courtney Diane tries to hide them every chance she gets unless it's cougar night. Come to think of it I haven't heard her talk too much about her and Robin going out "girrling". I guess it would be more of purring. I think about how I miss them very much and as I stare out window with thoughts going blank. I wouldn't have imagined how they would be such a strong part in my life. Bill comes in sometimes expecting dinner to be ready and the house spic and span with the smell of fresh pinesol. Similar to the expectation of my mom when she came home from work, they both feel so eerie. Similar punishment not allowed to go anywhere just stay in the house.

During the weekends Sierra was excited that she's not the only girl anymore when she sees Nay and Kay. I get a strange vibe with them as they try to tag team her on her toys and what little snacks that is in the house. My mother always taught us its okay to share but you don't give away everything, then when you want something it's not there and they go home and eat what they have at their home. We didn't have a lot of money only the few dollars of mad money stashed. If I didn't have that or that allotment that I must use for the house, we probably would have less. Every time I ask Bill for something extra his response was always what do you need it for? I just remember when I worked how good it felt to have my own money and to do what I wanted to without strings attached or twenty questions drill. He would drill me so much I would find myself apologizing for just wanting minor things. Oh, I hope that I'm not turning into those ladies I worked with or saw coming into the bank. That couldn't balance a check book or know how to manage their money because their husband handled all the finances. Then when they left them, they were left in awe state.

Nay and Kay aren't too friendly, and they seem to want to fight a lot. Just the short time they have been here I had to remind them of that when they were playing with Sierra. This is so foreign to Sierra the loudness the rough playing along with the foul language. I had to draw the straw with them coming over. This also prevented the JJ's from coming over to look at Bill as their possible next conquest. I don't think Bill has seen them and if he did, he probably didn't pay too much attention because he hasn't bought them up in our mini week conversations. One day the sisters came over while I was dealing with Sabrina. I observed one sister touching Sierra that was sexual in nature. I pulled them away from Sierra and wondered what have such young eyes seen that they had to immitate those moves? I told them that they had to go home, with hesitations they left but with much tude. I had to stop them from coming around Sierra they were not a good influence. One day while changing Sabrina's diaper I heard a nosie followed by Sierra saying ow. As I go to the door, I see the sisters running toward the stairs. I asked what happened and Sierra said that Nay had hit her. I told her to hit her back. Sierra followed her up the stairs and I heard a familiar sound followed by an ow. Sierra yells back to me from the top of the stairs that I hit her momma. I tell her to come on back home. I'm trying to raise Sierra right, but not to be somebody's punching bag. Now they know how it felt and to this day they never raised their hands to hit her. I guess they all had a good understanding if you hit me, I will hit you back. Their Mother or JJ never did come to the apartment about that situation, but if they did, I was ready for them. Funny not ha-ha how can I be ready for them and not Bill.

I never know what upsets him and I'm still his wife and best friend. I tell Bill what happened with those little girls and Sierra. He didn't know their mother or see their aunt which was good to hear. This conversation breaks the ice as we are talking about our daughters and parenting and just good to have a refreshing conversation. He talks a little about work but gets mad when I get the names wrong. This is something that I have been trying and practicing at remembering names and faces. Actually, this is the only adult thing I can do to keep my mind on tact that the world still exists outside these apartment doors. I look at him and the love is still there.

Chapter 44
Why Do We Have New Shiny Keys?

I miss Bill so much and just want us to have to good quality time. Bill spends his time with Sierra by helping her with her homework as he holds Sabrina. He is a good father and my blessings that we are still a family. I fought in school, but I don't know what or how to fight for Bill. While cleaning up for the night, Bill gives me a break by playing and reading to our daughters. I noticed some new shining keys look fresh cut and one has a designer like diamond on it. They look like an apartment or house keys unfamiliar to me. Last time I checked the locks weren't changed so who belongs to these new keys. Does someone have a space in his heart and well as he has a key to their place? How do I ask without being snapped at or felt like his so-called meathead or sounding insecure? Am I tripping this could all be innocence and displaying all my insecurities? That's all I need for him to pick up on that and hold it against me when I least expect it, but those keys are new, and I've never seen them before. Plus, there is a red diamond shape and red is Bill's favor color. I wear red although navy blue is my favorite color, but I do all this altering for Bill. I want to ask about; office hours, mall visits and other questions. I will someday find the answers to or brave enough to ask. Just like the smelly food with two receipts same mystery of the appearing new designer keys. I just can't see the Marines issuing out designer keys to Corporals. Time is coming for his two-week training as Sierra finishes school. Wow she's growing up and sees more. She knows when to say and when not to say because her dad taught her well. Not that I would drill her. I remember the last time she innocently said something, and Bill just knew I had asked what Sierra had innocently volunteered. I looked over at him laughing playing and reading to the girls then I glance back at those new keys.

I have to rest my thoughts, so this doesn't consume me, and I destroy a good evening. Bill will be leaving for two weeks and I know we will miss him. I miss him when he leaves for work and just long to hear his voice. He occasionaly calls throughout the day but that has slowed down for some reason must be busy at work. I look forward to his calls during the day it's kinda good to hear an adult voice and his voice is so soothing. His kiss on my neck felt so good but I love the softness of his lips when they touch mine. Lately it's been accomodating affections for now something is better than nothing and he always came home. Weekends he spends with us so when does he have the time for anything extra other than his family. As he laughs with the girls, he passes Sabrina off to me with her open arms reaching for me and Sierra laughs as they tickle one another going into her room. Bill passed Sabrina at the right time she had a smelly surprise in her diapers that was ripping. This aroma might be like what Robin's Uncle Boris might smell like on his walk bys. Sabrina crawling like a combat crawl and would have done the same thing with the nose hitting aroma. Funny when Sierra was creating her dirty diaper she would move to an area as if she wanted privacy in not knowing what the act meant. She wouldn't let anyone come near her while you smelled her actions. After that she would then get her diaper, wipes and lay down to be changed. That was when Bill and I knew it was time for her to be potty trained. But in training her we would un-knowingly put fear into her when we would see her ready and rush her to the bath-room and she lost that sensation. So, we would watch her like we were looking at a clock waiting for the right time. Now that I look back on it the look of excitement would scare anyone. We were new parents without a guide book and tried to do it in a sense of on the job training. The second one makes it so much easier. I don't know if more will come. When I was younger, I thought about having a bunch of children since I came from a family of four, but life changes as you see the world and your thoughts and visions continue to change as you mature or change. I enjoyed playing with children with the same joy of returning them back to their parents.

As I grew older, I enjoyed my independence and the freedom to come and go. Having Sierra at a young age expedited my maturity level because I now had some-one depending on me, and Bill's mind frame was enjoying his freedom until he saw Mickey holding his daughter. I wondered when he saw Sierra bouncing on Mickey's lap and seeing his family laughing and going on without him was that his slap of reality that life was moving and going on without him. Just like the two scants that were at his house that looked at me as if I didn't belong there or interrupting their time with the father of my baby. We both had reality slaps and had to move regard-less if we wanted to or not. I often wondered how long I would have waited for Bill. I was in my hometown and ex-boyfriends and men were available. The only pause in acting was my heart was still beating for Bill and I didn't want to waste anyone's time especially not mine nor did I want to hurt anyone either. "Billmania" still ex-isted and no one could break through. I didn't give anyone a chance. In doing so I probably passed up opportunities that would have been an altering life change. Like what would it have been like if I married James or Mickey? They have both moved on but that doesn't stop the thoughts then or the thoughts I'm having about them now. I've seen pictures of them or heard about what they are doing through mutual friends and they still look good and doing very well, with their families. So, life goes on I wondered if they felt the same way. My mother told me one did come by and she had a talk with him and I missed that opportunity. Where would I be career wise if I stayed on Oakwood? Just staring out the window and sipping this Chai tea just takes me back to so many places and thoughts. I kinda know how Mommy felt when she would just sit there looking out the window with no conversations just sipping coffee and just looking out the window. Sometimes all you need is a blank thought until the one you want to think about pops into your tranquility. Watching her when I was young didn't understand it then but respect and appreciate it now.

Sierra's school is having a last day of school program. I look forward to attending to see her classroom and her friends whose names she stutters as she tries to remember. I would watch her as if she was researching in her mind the names as her eyes wondered around saying her classmates' names. I only attended one conference but look forward to the return. I just remember looking through my closet trying to piece something together that fit and resembled an updated wardrobe. That act was depressing and tiresome because nothing really fit either too tight or looked like a moomoo. I looked like a walking floral couch. I imagine the Marine wives looking fit and picture perfect, as I look at them looking at me making me feel like a huge spot light beaming down on me. All this anxiety just to go to last day program, but I had to stay focused the event was for our daughter's graduation. Bill plays it off like it is no big deal, but it is our daughter's graduation ceremony and we will be there supporting her. I believe if you support them when they are young, they will practice until it's made permanent and embedded into their mind and life.

My parents used to put us in summer school every year. I think it was their way of keeping us busy and we didn't have to be bored doing nothing. As I got older, I found myself going to summer school and reading because my parents put a practice in me that helped me graduate early at the age of sixteen. I want to instill those same practices to Sierra and Sabrina. Robin instills strength in her daughters. She would have them carrying bags and not allowing them to stop or complain. I watched Denise and Nicole develop into beautiful educated young ladies that have and will probably practice on staying focused and busy. The few times I talked to my mother about what to wear she would make fun of my different sizes. Through her ice vapors she surprised me with a beautiful dress that wasn't too small or too large. This time she smiled gracefully in her present that didn't hide a punch shot at me. The box from FedEx also had some pretty outfits for the girls so we all would be ready and dressed for this joyous occasion. The day arrived, and I put on this beautiful navy-blue dress that even Bill did a double take and complimented me. Inside I'm screaming alright mom your taste continues to flow, but the fact that Bill noticed made me feel like I smelled fresh flowers as I blush in their beauty. I take a pause and phrase of what Momo might say. I took a chance and said that it looks better on and even better when you take it off. Then I throw in one of those Courtney Diane's corner smile with a wink. Bill pauses looking at me because I never really said anything like that. What seemed like minutes waiting for his response, was really long seconds. When he did finally respond, it was a slow okay and he just smiled. Inside I really didn't know how to take that, but I just turned it into a compliment in Bill's own way.

We leave, and I visualize us showing up as a happy well-dressed family with everyone to see. Once we get there Sierra takes off with her friends as Bill carries Sabrina. While I look around the room at the students' creativity and thinking that I couldn't believe at one point in life Bill and I were once this small. Miss Sammy, Sierra teacher approaches us greeting Bill and looking at me as if I was a friend of the family. I reach out my hand to her saying I'm Sierra's mother and it is finally nice to meet you. She tries to gather herself and recover from whatever shock she was in by meeting me. She slowly says its nice meeting Mrs and I smile Bill's wife. I try to play the stuttering and shock off. But inside whom did she think I was standing next to him, and who was picking up my daughter that she thought someone another person would come. I asked Bill, what was Bill this teacher, Miss Sammy? Why did she stutter and mentally skipped around me and looked back and recovered? It was so hard to keep my composure of wondering who Miss Sammy confused me with. Sierra runs to a smiling teacher by the name of Miss Myka who out of the staff did acknowlege me. I had to do a quick recovery smiling yes, I am and over there is her baby sister with her dad and my husband. Her reactions were one of okay and my insides and thoughts are now everyone here should get this right. I don't know who comes in here, but I am married to Bill and yes, I am Sierra's mother, mom and all that. My mind is racing on why they are so confused on my status with Bill and Sierra. Plus, what business is it of theirs. There are twenty plus kids in here worry about them as well. I smiled and try to look calm as I did the beauty queen smile and wave, looking at Bill and trying to find a spot on his face to smash my imaginary pie for putting me under the spot light.

I'm glad I didn't wear a dress with flowers that would have really increased the whispers. My reflection to their stares is a look of how can I help you. How would Courtney Diane say it with your dumb asses? Robin would turn it around by saying wow I look that good and that important that they are adding me to their boring life well thank you. Because I don't see you like that and oh by the way my dress is imported from my momma. I start to look around the room at the attractive women in various shapes and sizes. Somehow, I switch my anger that I had toward Bill unto myself. Now I'm comparing myself to them and wondered which woman Bill would be interested in. For some reason I feel like the other woman again. Which one of them own or do they know the owner of those new shiny designer keys. I started a practice that I didn't know then that this would become a practice that I'm making permanent. What happened and how did I put myself mentally in this situaiton. I become so paranoid I had to remove the visions of being married to Bill and turn myself into the other woman? The smile I was so gladly displaying like a beauty queen contestant has now left my face and heart. I became quiet, as I listened to the program and force myself to try to enjoy the laughter of the audience as they enjoy the graduation.

Sierra looks as proud and happy as she stands giving her valedictorian speech. That would be a proud moment for any parent. She was not afraid to speak up and out. Bill holds Sabrina on his lap as he grabs my hand as confirmation for the proudness, he is feeling. I wasn't feeling him and for that instance I don't really respond. I can feel him glancing at me as I continued to look straight ahead. So, he wouldn't see the pain that my heart is forcing my eyes to show. My glasses sure did come in handy at hiding my eyes. Now what am I going to do about this pain? That's right get out your imaginary first aid kit to mend your heart and aspirin for your headache and heartache and a cold towel for the swollen for your eyes from crying. Then I had to remind myself you're numb to tears, so you don't need the towel. Oh, silly me how could I forget. When the program was over, I can still feel the eyes on me, staring while whispering. Why can't I force myself to think that they are looking at me, us because we make a nice-looking family or admiring Sierra fussing over her little sister. I can't I grasp that thought and move onto a happy place the weekend is coming and Bill will be leaving. I try talking to myself as if I'm cheering myself to just make it work Rita. This might not be what you think although you do have a funny feeling lurking around in your heart.

Bill takes my hand as he carries the sleepy Sabrina and Sierra holds onto my hand while the looky loos observed Bill, and his wife and family leave together holding hands. Yep he comes home to his family. Now they are left with a visual to calm their whispers. Regardless of who comes in here yes Bill is married with a family. Bill tries to hold a conversation, but my thoughts are so many miles away. They are focused on the whispers, the stares, the hesitation on who I was and those new shiney keys. What does all this add up to? Why bring sand to the beach each gradual is all the same and you can't hold on to it for long. Why bring a woman to the beach when there will be plenty of women there? Clarence broke that meaning down to me during his sex class. Momo would add sand is also used to tell the time and remember time in the hour glass can run out. Just like sand slipping through your fingers grab a handful and you lose what you had guaranteed in your hand. But if you think about it if you turn the glass over you start all over again and the key word you start all over again. How many agains do I want to go through? If Bill wanted to date these California women why bring me here. I had a life in Oakwood and was enjoying my life. For the first time in a long time I wanted to click my heels and go back home. I wanted to go back and start my life all over, but I didn't want my daughters to grow up with Bill not being there.

We started this together and we will grow old together just like I saw in so many older couples. I'm sure their marriages have withstood the test of time and they made it. The ride seems longer home since silence was in the air. Although we lived in what was considered the valley the hills looked higher as the sun set. I wondered what I should make for dinner to change my thoughts. I take a deep silent breath and ask Bill how we were going to celebrate Sierra's graduation. He smiles and said we already did. I half chuckle I know you are not going to count that as the celebration. He stops me in mid sentence, with we can stop and get something for dinner. Sabrina is sound asleep as Sierra says she wants to go to Del Taco her favorite place for a bun taco and her favorite strawberry shake. That sounds good as my thoughts on how to ask about those shiny new keys. My thoughts were on the designer new keys and why were those women staring at me. For some reason I get this familiar stare from them as if they are dissecting my every look and motion or they considering me as being the other woman. Ironic because sometimes that's how I was feeling. I felt it was just like being at the resturant and those waitresses seemed to know Bill and wondered who I was. I guess the big diamond ring wasn't clue enough for them. Bill tries to ease my expression of disgust. Bill asked if anything was wrong and this was my opportunity to respond but I didn't want Sierra to hear what I wanted to say. I numbed up and missed the opportunity and responded with the typical oh nothing just thinking. The voice inside yells out liar my response to that was and your point is. Mind, you know this is not the time! My mind asks then when would be the time?? Maybe that's why he doesn't talk too much to you because you don't stand up to him. I respond back to myself saying when I did, I got my ass kicked and where were you?? It ended with my bad that's what I thought coward. Now here I go again sounding like Leler/Lene family aruging with myself.

We make it home and Bill gets the sleeping Sabrina as Sierra sips on her shake and I carry the food in. Bill put Sabrina into her bed as I set the table up for dinner. Sierra is excited about the program and tries to talk about what her mind could remember, and her thoughts are all over the place, hmm does that sound familiar. I listen but not hearing her stumbling words for my focus has not left the stares and the new set of designer shiny new keys. When our quick dinner is up, I look at the keys and say to Bill those keys look new what are they for. Bill acts as if he didn't hear me but my little back up is listening. Sierra says daddy those keys are shiny and pretty are they ours. Bill plays it off no just holding them. She continues holding for whom? I look at him because we both want to know the answer. He grabs her saying for you and he tickles her as he picks her up. Great there goes that answer. I pause as I tried to ask the many other questions that are racing in my mind. I know now is not the time while Sierra is still up. I will wait for her to be sound asleep for just in case. Bill's routine of reading her a bedtime story until she falls off to sleep worked again.

I'm immediately confronted by Bill of asking why I said something about the keys and was acting funny at the program. Now I can't get with this, he's trying to blame this all on me?? He is the one that has the keys and the women were looking and staring at me not him, with their whispers. So how was I acting? I was just noticing my enviroment and this felt strange and the looks/stares became annoying, (I sigh with a real deep breath of courage). I asked Bill what he saw in me that warranted him saying that. I enjoyed seeing and hearing our daughter speeches and had the lead role in the play. What part did he pick up on where did pride play a role in place of proud? They tried talking to you and you ignored them. While he was covering the room, he didn't notice that I tried saying something to them with a smile and they walked away from me. The attention I received was with stares, whispers and giggles. My response was they didn't know who I was, or maybe they did and didn't care. His looks start to change with a response with they didn't know you, because they were all new replacements. Ooh hmm never thought about that one?? Think quick was that why they kept staring at me with their whispers. I tried to explain that talking to them and he kept looking at me as if I should go into the corner on time out. Bill's responded with anger and treated me as if I was being reprimanded again. He added what makes you think they were thinking about you? Well Bill because as they whispered, they were looking right at me and women know women. I wasn't the only married woman there. Bill comes back was probably because you looked nice in that blue dress maybe that's why. Oh, you noticed you were too busy laughing with your admiriers. Then it slipped too much courage does one of them belong to the new designer shiny keys? Oops practice made a permanent statement. His angry response was what the funk you are talking about beach. Oh, here comes my other pet name haven't heard that in a while. My response was maybe you need to go with the owner of the keys. Bill didn't give me a response. But I had to ask myself, "Rita are you ready for that answer?"

Before I could say what, I wanted to say, I found myself flipping over the bed and a pain in my left eye and cheek. I just stayed on the floor as I listened to the routine sound of the slamming of the door. He was right I didn't have the answer to the reason for being stuck on a question. I felt the swelling happening immediately no tears just pain as I gathered my thoughts, strength and body to get up and go into the bathroom for a cold towel. I tried not looking in the mirror because I've seen that look before. I noticed that my neck is red. I don't remember him putting his hands around my throat it happened so fast. Did I lose consciousness or was it the shock of what happened that Bill got that mad? What now Rita you gave some unknown woman that had no respect for you or your marriage power over you. My heart skips a beat as I try to understand why I went there. Bill was right they could have been looking at me because they didn't know me and the dress my mom sent did tuck and hold my bumps in well. But the keys he didn't answer the questions about the new designer keys. What happened he forgot or couldn't come up with an answer then to get tag team by me and Sierra. That just threw his thought game all off. So now that he's gone is, he going to the person that gave him the keys? Here we are in the weekend before he leaves. What am I going to do about next month's rent and transportation? Calling home is an option I really don't want to use.

Back home girlfriends like Sharon, Debbie or Melody would help but they have their own family and lives to deal with they don't need my added tears. My mother would send for me, but I'm just not ready to go home as a failure with two kids, no husband, humiliation and the silent laughter of returning from California to Oakwood. I had to face the fact that Bill might not return, and I need to make some decisions. To say what was on my mind wasn't easy. I just took a fun day and turned it into a nightmare. The bible says weeping may endure for the night, but joy comes in the morning. What happens when you can no longer feel enough to cry will joy still come? I lay on top of the covers with my robe covering me rememebering Bill lying next to me. His scent fades into my nostrils trying to remember the last time I laid on his chest. I recall where one time he had to open his eyes as if he was trying to recognize me. Who else would he be waking up to, that he had to focus? Do I go back to Haven's Place that's a nope? Do I have time to get a job and car and try staying out here and making it work with my daughters? Could I go back and pick up where I left off in Oakwood? I'm not quite the same and I'm sure Oakwood has changed. My parents helped me out more than I realized, and I miss them so and so grateful for them. My mother always told me to pray and I wanted instant response. I prayed but I feel that maybe God is mad at me too. Somehow, I need to reflect and look at my life that is now shared with Sierra and Sabrina. Could I do this really by myself? Bill being in the service with a steady check, paying the bills I depended on him. The last time we went to the base divorce lawyer the amount of money wouldn't cover diapers let alone food. What was it fifty dollars a week for a baby what would it be now seventy-five for two? Wow for transportation we only had the one car and Bill had it most of the time, how convenient for him. He had a life outside these doors and my life somehow just stayed within the confines of this apartment complex. When I did try and use the car, I was on a time frame. I couldn't enjoy the freedom of fresh air and the feeling of my hands gripping a steerling wheel. The small things I missed. I had to explain to Bill where or what I needed the car like I was asking my parents to use their car. He would argue with me on the sheer fact of asking for something I thought was ours. So, Sierra and I caught the bus or walked and made friends with various bus drivers as we learned and enjoyed the sights and freedom.

Occasionlly we celebrated anniversaries or birthdays, but always ended in that precious time turned into night not to remember. I toss and turn trying to sleep with wondering what tonight and tomorrow will bring and the days to follow. I asked myself at what point did he decide to hate me and trade me in for a new set of shiny designer keys. What happened to our love that we left Oakwood with did it change as we crossed the states? I want to know at what point did I become not good enough. Bill took so much from me. Sometimes I didn't know how to act or who to be, when Bill came home. So many disguises and performances I had to remember. What hat shall I wear today or what expression should I display? I would be happy to see him, and he would just take the smile away. If I didn't smile for fear, he would ask what's wrong with you now. I was just happy to be married and being his wife. I didn't know what to do anymore each day of our married life was confusing.

Bill didn't realize that this was new for me too. I didn't read a book. I'm trying my best because I don't know any other way. When he asked, I said yes because I believed in both of us and wanted our family. I was hoping that he wanted this marriage and our family as much as I did. He asked, and I said yes, but I didn't know what my yes included. How did the communication break down that we couldn't laugh or talk with each other anymore? I miss my Bill, I miss my husband and my best friend. But I don't want anymore confusion and I really need to think this out. Looking over at the spot where Bill would be laying is empty and this time, I'm not expecting him to come home at least not tonight. I'm not expecting to see his almond shaped eyes twinkle as he smiles at me. Tonight, I won't feel the embrace that I haven't felt in months that seems like years. Tonight, his lips will be somewhere else. Why should I take my mind their and inflict pain onto myself? No change in his actions or excuse for leaving now just his routine.

I tossed and turn re-enacting what I should have said and shouldn't have said and the what ifs, all night until frustation and thoughts just mentally drained me. My face and neck were sore, and this pain put me to sleep for a few hours. Night seemed so long as I occassionaly glanced at the spot where my husband should be. This was lonier than I ever felt. I miss him more and wondered what the days to come will be like. What lies ahead for Sierra and Sabrina? I want to talk to someone but who and where would I start. Who would listen and how could they help me with my dilemna? Then I shiver of thinking if it gets back to Bill what would happen. He hates when I talk about our affairs and somehow, I know the word would get back to him. But what do I have to lose he hates me anyway at least that's my perception? The people I could talk to would be in the comfort of their homes as I wondered the out come of my fate from Bill.

Robin and Courtney Diane are away and plus Courtney Diane would want to put some type of hurt on him. So that won't work, and Robin would make me think about my action and act on my plan. In which I don't know what my plan of action would be. In my short life I never had to think this hard. They once said in sync that no one in a marriage should have to work at being faithful and that is something that had no option and not open for negotiation. If I went over to Momo's she would know. She probably already knows from the stories she seems to tell me. Amos might say something to Bill like how would you explain? Of course, Bill would be confused but the kicker answer would be Amos saying how are you going to explain how an old man kicked your ass, or what about the uncles that took a trip to correct their brother, Uncle Eudell. They really did kick his ass. Then after the ass kicking, they sit down and ate dinner. They hugged talked maybe laughed and went back home.

I wake up before the sun and look in on the girls while glancing back at my empty bed and a clock that confirmed morning has arrived. I miss Bill and wondering if he is missing me or us. How did we end up here and should I start making plans for returning to Oakwood? I think I can deal with the morning and many questions that would come at me at the same time wondering what Bill is doing and who he was doing it with. Maybe not but in time someone or something would replace that frustration. My dad would remind me about grass growing under my feet and this time I'm feeling the roots trying to come in and tickle my feet to let me know that something was sprouting. My dad, Eddie was good at keeping me grounded and not wasting time on thinking about time. He always reminded me to make the best of every second and enjoy everyday. I look at how sound the girls look, and I kiss Sierra. I go and pick up Sabrina and just look at her peacefully sleeping. Then glance at the couch thinking he might have fell asleep on the couch. His body is not there stretched out. No signs that he came home and left. I need and want to talk to someone, but I didn't know who. I hug and smell Sabrina with the fresh baby smell and put her back in the bed and go into the bathroom. I stand there looking at the woman in the mirror. I look and blink and realize this is me looking at me, and this is what I am really seeing. Just in that moment I think and laugh as I visualize Loren looking through his blinds and seeing Fifi and they both are blinking at the same time. He laughed at hearing him screaming and probably running through the house making sure everything was locked. Funny thoughts were confirmed when he said, I found my crazy ass almost running in my own place securing windows and doors. Hell, I didn't know what her crazy ass was going to do, and she had her damn side kick Lucee with her. That would scare me too, but Loren has a way of telling stories that makes you feel like you are sitting right there when it happens. Then you wait for the ding from the microwave for your imaginary bowl of popcorn, as I pictured him running through the house. Similar like they do in the movies and I'm in the audience with an imaginary bowl of popcorn watching and laughing while enjoying his theme music.

Chapter 45
Loren's Back Home

When I heard the phone ring all anxiety surfaced. Inside I get nervous thinking its Bill calling to check on us and say he was sorry or that he loved me or just anything to let me know we are okay. I can go with okay. I pick up the phone for some reason taking a deep breath as I embrace the voice on the other end. To my surprise it was Loren just calling to check in on us like he had been doing since he left. Loren must have felt me thinking about him. His voice was soothing and the answer to my prayers of not telling him what happened just to talk and hear a calm friendly voice. I asked him the normal routine questions about Fifi. Not thinking about maybe he is trying to get over her in a man type way. Since Loren didn't show a lot of emotions, I just figured that he was okay. He seemed to laugh and maybe that was his way of laughing through his pain of getting over her. He laughed about trying to advance to different floors not necessary in any order all he knew was that the basement was out. He said he was trying to date went out with a few honies but just wasn't feeling them. I asked through my own pain, what were you feeling. His easy answer without stuttering Loren said love. After being around you and Bill I'm thinking about making that move into becoming a family man. I listened to his excitement as I tried and deal with what will our family become. I laughed with Loren trying to diguise my sadness in laughter and questions to keep my mind moving, and not idling on the what ifs and where was Bill. How do I answer that question when Sierra asks for her daddy as Sabrina looks around for that familiar daddy's voice and laughter?

Loren talked about a cutie that he met. He laughed saying that you can consider her the second floor. Name was Patience, but she did not live up to her name and had a wee bit of a temper and mouth, which threw looks and body all out the door. If I'm going to deal with that, I might as well go back to the heachache I know called Fifi. But that's a hell no and keep it moving hell no keep it running!!

Mylene was my first floor cool and all but too many babies. Hey not a put down just not for me. That would drive my momma, Rosie Josey crazy as hell with all that yelling and shift. My mind had to ask because I might be in that same situation if I decide to date. She had eight and all knee-high popping out of every area in her place and seven different daddies. Her bod didn't show no eight children had exited. I went over to her place early, you know see her in the natural. Rita that was always the best way to see what she looks like before make-up and what the family was doing when they are caught off guard. Surprised me I thought I had advanced maybe to the second or third floor. No, my ass hit the childrens floor. Her looks and mind were tight. She was well mannered had ambitions to open her own day care. Now that they were talking, she would be a good care provider with eight kids. She had practice and patience and not the Patience that I met. She reminded me of a car accident and not paying attention you hit the last car now it's all your fault. This was a collison course and I didn't want to be on the receiving end of raising eight kids, seven daddies and wanting to have one or two on my own was out. Which each child, I counted and heard register tapes, ding noises, register tape non-stop noise, long reciepts running like some type of ticker tape popped up on each one of her kids. That was too much per child. Plus, I would have to buy a larger house. While I'm working, they are enjoying our place and only time I would enjoy what I'm working for is on the weekend, as I try to watch a game. Now if my baby's momma, called Mylene, my "Mymy", decides she wants to go out, after all I met her at a nice club and she now has a live-in babysitter. Had my mind and thoughts going into too many directions on changing my lifestyle. Nope that would make me a stay home daddy while Mymy is laughing because she struck it rich. While I turn into someone's punk ass babysitter known as Mister "PAB". That was why her ass was out because she finally found a babysistter for that night. That was too much weight that I wasn't ready to carry.

Mama Rosie Josey said boy you are standing on thin ice and keep this up you will fall through. This was a hole I didn't want to fall through with kids landing on top of me. Mama said get you some ready before you go blind and I almost did. I'm laughing with him and thinking about how my head turned with counting Catrice and Greekum's many many young heads. After the laughter your Mama Rosie Josey, would get those grandbabies she wanted. His response, while laughing was that would over whelm her, with filling up a whole row of seats at church. Not that she would have a problem, but don't think she met a bunch of grandbabies all in an I do sweep. Once we say the I do's I have a whole basketball team with some bench play-ers. With my mama being retired and all I don't think she would want to have every Sunday family get together. That would wear my mama out and that is something I will not do. You know Rita I love my mama and I want her to be proud. It's not like I'm not trying. I just love having my fun when I want to and the only responsiblities I have other than me is my shop. The building is paid for and I'm not feeling taking out a second mortgage right after first day of marriage.

I shared with him how I long and having our own home someday too. Wow listen to me I don't know if I will be still married. Jovan and Toni made it work through their sometime toxic relationship why can't we do the same, (acourse minus the toxic relationship). Bill just needs to get his head together and needed some head space. He asked where was his big head cousin? Hmm he asked the question before Sierra which caught my laughter by surprise. Only response I could think of that he was out doing Bill. When he comes in, I will have him call you and you know how he is about returning calls. Loren tone changed when he added that Bill needs to act right, he has a good woman and wife in you, cuz. He should appreciate the loyalty you have for him and your family. Any man would kill to be in his place and fit into his shoes. I bet not find out my cuz acting stupid again. You don't deserve to be abused in any way and you can tell him I said it, or I will remind his ass. I thank him. Inside I was wondering if he's picking up on some sound of sadness in my voice or laughter. Suck it up Rita and change the conversation tone. I laughed slightly saying you know your cousin. We both are new at this marriage, and parenting, and we are merging two different family lifestyles. We are making it come together making it work. Loren interjects don't let it be you doing all the work let him get some blisters on his hands. I laughed blisters on Bills hands right. I smile a smile that Loren can't see or feel but here I go performing for that Oscar again. That response seemed to work he responded with a yell your right. Loren said that he has that bad habit too. His honies would chew him out about not returning their calls. To his defense he said I'm gonna call them, but on my time. My time is different from the honies' time. If I call them back in two days, I did call them back. I couldn't hold back saying and you think that's okay. My dad always has a saying a courtesy kiss my butt is better than nothing at all. Do you think it's fair to have them hanging around waiting for a call? His response was quick and cute if they are waiting for me to call then I don't need to be with them. Because that means they don't have any type of life and don't put all their lack of no entertainment in their lives on me. It's not that type of party at least not for me. With that touche I had to agree with him. That was his perception and I respect his view, might not agree with it but that's on him and the consequences that come with it. I'm glad Bill didn't call me days later. We were always together and didn't need to talk on the phone much because we were together. My thoughts fade away briefly from Loren and think about the time we spent together and the phone calls and just the many years we had invested into each other. Especially our younger years, not that we are so old, but I felt that I was the one turning and looking old.

When I come back from my day dreaming thoughts, I heard an unfamiliar name and heard bacon and eggs. This threw me off, so I had to convince Loren to repeat what he just said. He laughs with paused saying I couldn't believe it myself either on this lastest shift Fifi pulled off. This one honey was nice, had some looks, nice bod. I had to interrupt him is that everything? His response was yep as he continued. I meant Diamond as she was well polished, worked at a jewerly store. I was looking for a nice watch to match my attire. She represented the store very well. We talked, meant for lunch and she took me and our talking slow. No children, no boyfriend, going to school to become a Bio-Chemist. She had brains, beauty and a lot of booty. Didn't mean to cut him off but I have to say too much vision just like talking to Momo. Yep beauty and booty he repeated without hesitation. She had a sense of direction and it wasn't to your local liquor store. I don't mind an occassional drink but don't want a drunk that's so not cool. I pictured Loren showing that dimpled smile with the twinking in his almond shaped inherited eyes. There is hope that Aunt Rosie Josey will get those grandbabies. How could Diamond resist his sexy charms and she sounded special and he finally moved to the top floor. So in between him laughing as he talked about sometimes pausing to check on me to see if I was still listening. I just asked so where are you guys at now are you two dating exclusively? Well that's when I heard a pause. I, we made it to the point where she felt comfortable to come over to my house.

I was hesitant myself because of Fifi crazy ass lurking around. I would go to her place and respectfully leave, and she would come over and leave. I didn't have too much of a choice. Diamond made it clear if you want to stay late your ass need to come over earlier not that vampire shift. She made it clear early in our relationship that spending a night was not an option, take your tired ass home and you can get all the rest you need. I started feeling comfortable, no Fifi so one night I bolded up asking her to take this further and spend a night. I still will respect her in the morning, (with that I could feel Loren's wink coming through the phone). In my mind this was not a one-night stand but maybe a possibility of moving this to a more serious stage. Hey Rita, she might be the one. The one to give my mama Miss Rosie Josey some grandbabies. She had those child bearing hips yes, she sure did. As I listen it seemed to be in the past tense. I let him continue for now he had my full or partial attention because I'm still listening out for the girls to wake up. Don't get me wrong it felt good looking at her sexy fine ass and I could continue to wake up to her. Really cuz this might be the one. When we woke up that morning it felt good looking at her in my bed. I could do this. I watched her every move with proudness not for conquering but, because I was feeling her and the family thing. She was getting ready for work and my part was to have breakfast ready for my Diamond. Thinking back that's how Bill got me. He was good at cooking breakfast, as for other meals, (hmmm), he tried. How would Momo say it I didn't marry him for his cooking. Perception on the cooking is slightly different from hers but the same. Loren goes on as I go in and out on our conversation. He said I go out to get something out of my car. Can't remember what but had to get something out of the car could have been my phone.

My car! I couldn't believe this childish shift was not only egged but raw bacon layed out like they were in a skillet and toast on the hood, and the back all crumbled up, and grits over each window saying hi, with a note wrapped with a bow, saying here's your breakfast. I hope you and that beach enjoy because I did, deuces beaches. She picked a hot Chicago morning, oh well and damn. Now my ass is pissed. I just had my car detailed and had my Diamond was inside. My thoughts were how was I'm going to explain this shift to Diamond. She comes to the front door just to check on me and all I saw was her mouth drop open with no words. Deep stare and her eyes rolled with a slight cut throat look in my direction. Hell, that shift left my ass speechless too. I could explain slash tires any sex could have done that angry shift. But only a woman, no only crazy ass Fifi would do some shift like this and she probably had her sorry ass side kick Lucee throwing the grits, that beach. I had to ask were they hot grits. Oh, damn oh got joke huh. When I glanced at her and then at my car I funked up. I see my Diamond come out with her over night bag, saying I don't need, nor want drama in my life. I'm focused on my life and career don't have, no I will not make time for some sorry ass ex-girlfriend lerking around you or my ass. In my grown ass life, I don't play house or with little boys or little girls' games. You need to grow up Loren. I listened to Loren and it seems at if he was still riding the elevator and trying each floor until he makes it to the top. This time he made it to the top and the door closed on him right when he was stepping out with that big dimple smile. Filonia aka Fifi took that joy. She shut the power off to that floor, or did she recall the floor back to the basement. I wanted to say so bad why not just go to the top floor and call it a life and stop shopping on each floor. I think maybe when he was trying to exit but the elevator closed before he could exit. I don't know who recalled the door, but I do know in this case it closed and said try again like a game board card.

Maybe Loren is trying to focus as he continues talking about Diamond. I heard the concern in his voice saying his Diamond added, she thought that I was better than that and I should have told her. Especially if we were moving in some type of serious talk or straight direction and didn't need these curves. I tried pulling her back to try and explain she wasn't hearing or having it. The only kiss I got was the one that said kiss her ass goodbye. This woman had natural beauty. I saw what she looked like first dawn rising. My momma, Miss Rosie Josey would have been proud with knowing grandbabies might be coming or possibly arriving sooner than later. Diamond wouldn't return my calls and quit the store where I met her, and the owner gave me a note from her saying don't bother looking for me. This was a long ass note Diamond put in bold print that not every woman falls for your smile or charm it's what's in the inside. She left me a message via phone like the note wasn't enough. She said that situation was too dangerous for her. She thought this was going somewhere but couldn't believe I would deal with someone of that type of calibur. This was too much and not worth my sanity or health. Then to add insult to pain she had already inflicted, I was really digging into you and ready to move a serious forward. Then as concludes with a last "PS" take care and leave me the hell alone. I know Rita don't say it; I know what you are thinking. I should have trusted her and where I wanted to take our relationship, yep I should have told her. You don't know how many times I rehearsed that line of I should have. Now I heard the pain in his voice and tried to come up with something to bring the tempo back up.

I can feel his pain and I get overwhelmed because I still have my own issues going on and the combining both emotions were mentally over whelming. I tried hard not to let Loren know what happened. I know how he feels about Bill and love the family thing we have or had going on. I asked him, (while trying to bring a smile through the phone), do you think that Fifi left without her medication?? He coughs with oh snap let me tell you about Miss Filonia, medication and shift. This tired scant had me believing she was on medication. She had a clear large plastic bag full of medication. I knew about the brick in her purse and would hear some rattling noise. At first, I thought it was the rocks she used to throw at my window, but I remembered she carried a smaller purse for the small ass rocks. So, I asked what that rattling noise in her purse couldn't all be medication??? Come on now, medication shouldn't be making all that noise. She showed me the clear bag full of brown medication bottles and some large white ones. I snapped back thinking this scant is crazy and she got medication to prove this shift.

One day I asked her to show me her pill bag. You know just out of sheer curiosity. Some of the labels were removed from the familiar brown prescription bottles. Different sizes, different uses and some were labeled look like from some type of label maker. Remember cuz my brother Akil hip me to certain medications. So, I was kinda familiar with some medications and knew about placebos and sugar pills. I opened one container that said ibuprofen on the label, wrong spearmint mentos, and the aroma of spearmint hit my nose. I asked were these so-called prescriptions are they all just candy. Fifi smiles saying, yep they are better than placebos. Don't you know she busted out in a laugh telling me to hand her the big bottle she needs her M&M's to calm her ass down. Then the girl pours a handful in her hand and throws them all in her big ass mouth. Smiling as I heard crunching sounds coming out of her loud ass jaws. Rita, she gave me all confirmation of crazy, straight up ass cuckoo. This girl actually had a bag full of candy in her purse with her famous brick.

Now that was when we both seem to need a laughing moment at the expense of Miss Filonia/Fifi with her aka's another known antic. Well I had to admit to Loren that Filonia aka Fifi wasn't crazy but rather cunning and clever. After all that wow was the only thing I could think of as I tried closing my mouth. I had to ask so where is Fifi now. Hell, I don't know she keeps up with me more than my own mama. I might have to make a fugitive move back to Cali again. I let it go on asking anymore questions about Fifi. He sounds like he is over her. He didn't respond with his usual, my little puppy and her raising her leg. I think that must be similar with what Robin said about her trixie. I don't look at her at being a woman because I don't look at her as being human. Hmmm I think that about means the same thing. He didn't disrespect her, he just didn't put flowers with her name. I learned slowly that when a man says he done he's done, interesting. What's Bill's philosophy on ending a relationship or marriage? As my father would add a courtesy kiss my butt is better than nothing at all. Was that a kiss Bill's butt move?

Through our laughter I heard Sierra talking to Sabrina and Sabrina trying to respond. They really sound cute, but I tell Loren that his cousins are awake. What seems like hours into our conversation was less than thirty minutes. The timing was right and just the answer to a prayer my heart was holding onto. His response as always, tell them I said hi and might see them soon. Oh, and tell my big head cousin he needs to keep his ass home. Inside those were my thoughts, but first I have to get him home. I recovered and told him I sure will.

We both hung up as I wondered what we shall try and do today. I know I will practice my dads' philosophy, don't let any grass grow under my feet and today we won't. I take a big breath with my normal sigh in this case and go in laughing with a smile looking at the miniature Bills. They keep me going and my heart from being totally from feeling any crushing sensation. Today I must keep it moving. As Courtney Diane would say walk with me don't drop my hand or try to skip around me and run and get your ass hit. I had a little mad money, so we are going on a ride to PataRee's for breakfast and entertainment. This will get us out of the house and show off Sabrina. If he does come home, he will see that we weren't waiting around looking sad and all broken up. I may be broken up on the inside, but my daughters will not see it and the world didn't need to know.

I start looking for clothes for us to wear and the next bus route. I look forward to seeing some friendly familiar faces. This will be fresh air for all of us. I think back on Fifi putting eggs, raw bacon, hot grits and toast on Loren's car. Hmmm, ooh that was different, creative, and the bag full of candy and pass the big bottle she needed her M&M's to calm her nerves. I sure wish I could meet her or been the fly on the wall when she does her "AKA's". I do feel for Loren missing out of having a nice relationship with someone special. Surprisingly the girls don't ask about daddy or look around for him. Maybe they might know or feel he's not here for his reason and not us. We load up and ready to go and we see little Tim looking out the window waving as Sierra waves back saying his name as if he could hear her. The day is early and fresh, and we start making our move. No one in sight everyone is probably sleep or just enjoying a Saturday morning just like we will. This is a familiar ride and look forward to being around family atmosphere. I gathered up my mad money and bus pass and we are on the move and it's the girls' day out.

Sierra greets a new bus driver by the name of Jimmy we greet him asking about the ususal drivers on this route. He says this is normally not his route, but he was just filling in for Ethan Tim/ET. He was polite, looked young but sounded old, and had very little conversation. We smiled as we looked for a window seat on a slightly empty bus. Sierra looks out the window and starts to describe what we are seeing, as I try to keep Sabrina stable in her stroller, so she doesn't roll away. I still wondered where Bill was and if he's coming back and how long has, he known this trixie. I need to decide if I want this marriage after he has been with this mystery trick. Courage is coming in from somewhere must be that ancestral strength coming in and trying to get my attention. My life will not end, actually it would be a beginning maybe rough at first, but I made it without Bill before. My struggles will bring strength. Like mommy said we don't do that, finish what you started whether it's married or as a single parent raising two beautiful daughters. My parents may not be here physically, but they are here in spirit after all they raised me. This puts a smile so big in my heart that out of no where I take a big breath and smile. I looked at Sabrina as she tries to look around at her new enviroment. I know if she could talk, she would ask where are we going? Sierra just enjoys the bus ride and the mystery of where we will arrive. Maybe after we leave PataRee's we will walk the mall and make a day out of our Saturday.

This is the girls' day out `no rush and no clock ticking. I like that sound we are out without a care, hmmm. I've gotten used to not having a car but wouldn't mind if or when I get my own transportation, so we can be in the wind. Let Bill make a car happen and he will wonder where me and his girls go and why he couldn't ride with us. I don't have a Mr. Trixie, but I do have a trick, now you see us and now were gone, poof. I look at the smiles on my girls and now I feel even better. The sun is out, and my life might just change, and I hope I'm ready. Funny how you look back and what seemed like your life was over now that doesn't seem as difficult as it was then. Now I'm enjoying my tea as I keep the thoughts of how I made it. I think I was enjoying the bus ride more than the girls. As we approached our transfer point Jimmy helps me with the stroller as some of the riders politely move out the way. Sierra takes my hand as I tell her we are going on our next adventure and I had a surprise for her.

I hope that Mackey is there, because they play so well together. The next bus driver by the name of Darrell had such a gentle demeanor and his smile showed the warmth of his heart. He jumps up and assists with the stroller and greets everyone with his gentle smile. The bus again is not too crowed and again we have beaten the mad Saturday rush. Just some minor changes but the bus route is still the same. I didn't realize how good I was feeling until Sierra says your humming like a bird. Funny I didn't realize that I was humming since I haven't done it in a while. Normally I hum to block off the mean names, the snide remarks or the belittling. My normal, "AKA's", were a verbal ass kicking from Bill. Humming would block the pain preventing my heart from shredding. Words do hurt and sometimes the pain lingers longer than I would want to. I guess my heart is feeling better too. I'm not too focused on Bill or his antics. At least not today or right now or how did Henray and his boys' say it ret now. Sierra gets excited as she starts to see familiar signs and Sabrina sees her excitement and joins in with her laughter. We have arrived at PataRee's and we are greeted by Ofa and Britney. They rush over to Sierra and want to grab the excited Sabrina. I'm kinda hesitant right when I was about to say no, Sheree comes toward us still pregnant with Jaxson. She makes pregnancy look so good. She still has a beautiful shape and nicely dressed. I wish I could look like her maybe Bill would keep his eyes on me. I watch how her husband Pat looks at her with so much love. I hope or thought Bill looked at me that way, but I guess not, because he's not here with me or with us. Bill may be with someone else that turned his head and many other things. Communication was never our problem why now?? If there was something, I wasn't doing just talk to me, so we can make us work. I don't have a crystal ball, nor can I read his mind. I can only see how you feel toward me when you are snapping at me and it seems to be more often. His almond shaped eyes change into a shape that makes my insides shiver while avoiding any eye contact. His eyes have somehow lost the twinkle I once loved to see. Lately I only see the twinkle when the girls are with him. If Bill has lost his love for me just say so. Of course, that would hurt, but care enough to allow me to move on, love me enough to let me go. If you don't want me someone else will or am I just your selfish convenience. For some reason I'm not hurting I guess because I'm still sometimes, emotionally numb.

I look around and the place is booming as usual. Mackey runs out yelling for Sierra. They laugh as they give each other a strong embrace. I smile as Sheree looks at Sabrina and reaches for her. Sabrina stretches her arms out for Sheree, as Sabrina tries to free from herself from her stroller. She seems to say through her expression's freedom is freedom!! What I noticed about my girls developing personalities is that Sierra seems to be serious with paying close attention to her surroundings and Sabrina is more playful and happier. Sheree couldn't resist Sabrina's out stretched arms. I smile as I looked at Sheree holding Sabrina, as she escorts us to what seems like the same booth, we set in everytime or the times we have been here. She calls her sister Shanta to tell her we are here with our newest addtion Sabrina. She arrives reaching for Sabrina and starts bouncing her as she holds her. Sabrina is loving all this attention. Right as I'm looking at the smiles, I feel the joy that is finding me. Robin's daughters Denise and Nicole come in with must be their dad Ramon. He was nice looking kinda resembled Gordon just like Bill and Loren, small world. They see us, and I can't believe how much older they are. While standing next to Shanta they look like they could be Shanta and Sheree's sisters. They introduced Ramon and he seems very nice and not the bow wow dog Robin made him sound like. Looks can really be deceiving look at Bill and me. Inside I want to go and see the infamous "Mertruck" that the girls had talked about. They were telling me that their mom was out of town on an assignment and, laughed as they said that their Aunt Courtney Diane left early to go and check out Henry's new girlfriend, I think her name is Bernadette.

We might go down there this summer and hang out for a few weeks. Looking at their father Ramon's expression I don't think he was in agreeance with that, or this might be the first time he was hearing their summer plans that didn't include him or his decision. Before I could introduce Shanta and Sheree, they seem to know Denise and Nicole. They embrace and look at each other as if they have known them for quite some time. Found out later that they had known their Aunt Robin before they were born. When you put them together, they all could pass for sisters. When I look at them and think about them now Denise and Nicole would be what Shanta and Sheree would be once they are older. They seem to have very similar backgrounds. The feeling was good on my decision to get out of the apartment and glad we loaded up and took the long ride. Denise and Nicole offrered us a ride home but I wasn't feeling Ramon and didn't want to sit in the front seat with him. Plus, we were going to the mall to hang out making our day long and enjoyable. What reason did we have to rush home to an empty apartment? Nope there is no reason at all to rush. I'm sure Bill is doing Bill and we are doing us.

Just in true fashion Mr. Woodson comes over but this time Shanta did a reversal. Asking him did he have the room ready for Marietta and Greg? Today we are having a double anniversary party for young age group Eric and Elizabeth and Eric and Biana. Mr. Woodson pauses because he was just stunned by the look on his face and his response was now, we have twins' parties Eric and Eric. Doing his normal walking and fussing in a low voice made me feel like home. He almost looks as if he's talking to himself. He and Coleman must be getting along, because I didn't hear the routine of complaining about Coleman. I wondered if they were the Erics are the sons of Gina, Maria or Bruce and Wayne. It's been along time since I've seen them, and they could be around that age. Our meal seems to be larger than my money, but Sheree made a family plate special just for us. Although she is busy, she still had the time to make us feel like family. Shanta gives me a hug as she follows Mr. Woodson and decide with Chef Harris, of Personnelly Yours, for the upcoming events. Mr. Woodson turns toward her as they walk out together isn't, she in Europe. Shanta smiles I hope not. Mr. Woodson for some reason must have the last growl. He grunts saying did you see that note for Dale and Annie or was it for Anna and Henry. Hmm I know an Ann was in there somewhere. He seems to chuckle as Shanta just smiles shaking her head while walking away. Mackey and Sierra runs to the table prayers are said as they run off with fries laughing. Sabrina looks as she smells the aroma of food and not feeling the bottle. I give her a french fry for her to suck on. I see the dimple showing through her smile that she is like that new taste.

I love my daughters and I still love their dad regardless of what happens. This platter is so so good, and I know I won't be able to eat all this neither will Sierra. Watching everyone working together was warming. Before we get too comfortable, I ask Ofa to bring Sierra over with permission from Sheree if Mackey can join us. Wow looking at this plater we had more than enough food plus some to take home. They jump for the opportunity for more fries, then take off again. Time is still young, and we still have more stops to make. I needed this more than they could ever know. Passing by Haven's Place reminded me of where or what I needed to do. I think about the angelic smiles of Demitria and Tamara. Now I won't go there unless I have to, but I think I would rather move back to Oakwood and pick up and live again. Britney comes over and checks on us while Sierra and Mackey dip their fries into ketchup. I don't want to break up the fun they're having, but they don't understand how the bus rides work on Saturdays. I break the news that it's time for us to go. This place seems to be a popular place and we are never disappointed when we come here because we are family.

I look for Sheree because the next time that I see her she will be holding Jaxson Eddie. We receive hugs with much love as we leave for the mall. The day is still young as we go on to our next venture. You can call this the girls only tour, tee-hee-hee. I keep trying to convince myself that we will be okay I just have to keep it moving. I can't lose myself into Bill. I had to hold up and not let Sierra or Sabrina see me break down. Funny not ha-ha but I've become so numb. Do I know how to break down? I can't cry but I seem to can't get mad either. Who am I becoming? I had to get my name back with no attachments. The day is as beautiful and for once I'm feeling the day. The bus to the mall pulls up with the same gentle smile we left with. Darrell was bus driver again and he assisted us with the stroller again. The bus is not as full, but you can tell that people are waking up and maybe in route to the mall with us. Sierra talks about playing with Mackey and her fun time, while all the excitement puts Sabrina to sleep. Sierra is hanging tough and I don't want to push her, but we didn't need to stay around the apartment being bored.

My great-grand mother, mommy walked around downtown and walked to almost everywhere she needed to go. Her legs showed strength and years of much walking. I watched her as a little girl, and I wanted to inherit her beautiful shaped legs. Mama Sadie went everyday to the Mother of Veterans hall, and where ever she traveled, she went to the nearest Senior Center and just hung out. I remembered Mama Sadie said when she turned one hundred plus that she just didn't feel like getting up and going to the center. She told my dad one time that she was just tired, and God called her home to rest at the age of one hundred and eight. Mommy we didn't know her age because she didn't have a birth certificate and we assumed maybe she could have lived to be either late eighties or early/late ninties. Her friend

Miss Reed would walk everyday to the bar holding her pocket book as Mommy would call it. She would say that Miss Reed could get hit by a bus and get up and keep walking. Miss Reed lived to be one hundred and three. My grandmother Hazel took more care of her than she did her own mother, but maybe this was her way of giving back and making up for past deeds. We walk the mall as I look at the beautiful outfits, that I could see myself someday wearing, only if I could afford them. My wardrobe is so limited. When I get some money and the madness goes away, I will make sure my daughters and myself will have many clothes to choose from.

Chapter 46
What Will Today and the Night Bring

Just give me time and thought for now I have to figure out what the next day will bring. I don't know what tonight will bring or if it will bring Bill home. I might have to prepare myself for another night in an empty bed. Nope tonight will be our own little slumber party and we will all sleep in one bed. Tonight, just like our day was for girls only. The joy will stay and not fade away. I'm with my girls and enjoying the sounds of their laughter, joy and conversations. I'm not missing out on the lengthy sentences and questions that Sierra generates. I love the sounds from Sabrina as she tries to communicate in her own way. This is a joy that's hard to put into words you just have to be present. I'm so glad I get to see the twinkle in their almond shaped eyes and the dimples thast accompanied their smiles. Sierra hanging tough, in keeping up with the stroller, while Sabrina is in between naps and viewing her new enviroment. I look in the store windows seeing so many items/things I wish I could purchase for everyone and the apartment. I see families with both parents pushing strollers, and just mothers out with their children. Saturday seems just like a Sunday family day. Somethings I just take for granted. I remember how my parents used to take us everywhere with them. Then we were old enough to or bold enough to say we didn't want to go. I felt then much like now that this probably must have been a mutual agreement. They really wanted their own quiet time too. Amos and Momo's family go everywhere with their very active boys. Their entrance would be noticed and when they leave maybe grateful.

Maybe tomorrow we can go to the park and hang out again. After all this is a "Girls weekend Out Tour". Plus, school is out so no Monday rushing and the skies are blue. This time will help me make a clearer decision I need to make about our family. I don't need to think about what other people are saying as we stroll through the mall. I can't believe occasionally some male attention looks my way, which makes me nervous. We are enjoying the day of walking, looking and just minding our own business. Menatally I'm so trying to hold it together. My insides are just jumping around. My mind and eyes are trying to adjust to this ping pong act happening inside me and my brain, heck add the heart too. I just hope we don't run into Bill or I see him out with someone else. In a way that will give me the visual I need to step away and begin a new chapter.

We need to head back home before Sierra tires out. It's time to head back home and face what is or is not there. I don't know what awaits me but I'm glad that I didn't sit around waiting and nursing my internal wounds. We have just enough time to make the transfer point. I see a familiar face this time it's Fred and he still recognizes us and smiles at our new addition while assisting us onto the bus. Where we sit is too far to hold a conversation, but it was good just seeing him again. Sierra smiles and greets him I guess she remembers him too. All this amusement and rides has just knocked Sabrina out. I guess one day she will share in the visuals as we ride home. Hmmm where will our home be?? I don't know if I can afford this apartment. I can always down size to one bedroom or studio. After all we need is one bed that we all can share and no need for plenty of room. Although I'm excited about the girls sleeping in my bed, I wish it could be all of us. Sometimes Bill and I would look at each other smiling because, he was with his girls and I was with my family. It was rare when we snuggled together while sleeping in our bed. If I'm feeling this way does Bill have any of the thoughts about his family or what or how we need him. On our way home anixety sets in and Fred being kind drops us off in front of our complex. He assists us again and Sierra politely thanks him. Before I go to our apartment I glanced at our window and the place seems to be dark, no change from when we left. That doesn't mean he didn't come home. Bill could have stopped by the apartment and noticed we weren't there and just left. Hmm in that case I'm okay with that scenario. I swing by Momo's, so she can see the girls. Inside my emotions and thoughts are just stalling going home, because I'm not ready for what is behind that locked door. I kept myself pepped up and had many destractions but now they're all gone, and the reality is I'm home. Momo might pick up on something might be wrong, inside I am hoping that the girls will distract her. Yep if I do that, she will not look into my eyes trying to figure out what is wrong. She notices my laughter and it must sound a certain way for her to believe it's from the soul. She seems to know me just like my mother. Maybe she does know me more than my mom. I miss my mother but Momo is a good replacement for now.

The noise from her boys, Bert, Craig, Manly, Chris and Ryan will work well if Sierra has the energy, and sometimes she does. Ryan is not whining I guess he is growing up too and keeping up with his brothers. When I approach the door smelling a familiar smell, the aroma is the scent and sign that Momo is cooking. No mystery dinner tonight. I knock on the door with gathering my thoughts, so I can force a smile. We're greeted by a welcomed smile from Momo as she reaches for the sleeping Sabrina as Sierra takes off with Ryan. Amos is sitting in his chair just chilling looking at the television, while glancing at the newspaper, enjoying the aroma of his dinner. Momo's strength has returned enough for her not to only cook but she has that little shake dance back. So that lets me know that some type of sexual antic will be coming, and my response will be the same visiual, yuck/ew. Here we go again!! She's making big juicy onion burgers and of course here she goes with the flipping and the flopping. This time she observed my reaction when she asked how was the flipping and flopping with you and Bill.?? I look at her saying my usual yuck and really Momo. But inside I knew she asked this time for a reason. Did she pick up on something or was it that intuition that was working?? Was it in my smile, my reaction, demeaner or did she hear the arguments or the routine of Bill yelling at me?? Something happened did my disguise or performance didn't work this time am I losing my oscar performances. I need to rehearse more and be on cue. I smile giving her back her answer of oh yes how do you think we got Sabrina here. She smiles with that response, as she reaches and takes Sabrina back to hold her, while the burgers are simmering. She looks at me with eyes of concern asking me if I was okay. I didn't have my glasses on and I look at her and try to sound as convincing as I could. I responded with the same tone I used for myself when I try to convince myself I'm okay. Momo smiles and offers us to stay for dinner. It seems as if she was stalling too. For some reason she didn't want us to leave at least not now. My insides agreed, this was just what I needed. Why should I rush home to what an empty apartment, with empty feelings and not knowing where my husband is laying his head?

The boys set the table and Sierra assist. This felt good sitting around the table with a family that does everything together. Sierra asks if she can say the prayer and Ryan gives in. There was much of anything/ everything in the conversations going on. Except for this one time, Momo says or ask Bert or was it Ryan a question and the answer didn't come out right. She excused her and Bert or Ryan from the table. All we could hear was muffled sounds coming from the bedroom. One sound was very clear and distinctive and that was the sound of a thump and body dropped, (like the sound of a book dropping to the floor). I could only imagine it was the sound of Bert or Ryan hitting the floor. They return to the table as if we didn't hear a thing. Everyone kept eating as if they didn't leave the table including me and the girls. Inside I knew what happened and I doubt if it would happen again. Thinking back on it makes me chuckle just like now. That was just what I needed. Funny that this seems familiar to Uncle Eudell and his brothers sitting around the dinner table conversating, while Uncle Eudell sits there with black eyes and banages, while enjoying the dinner conversation with them.

We are fuller than we were before we ventured over to Momo's. As the hour gets late it's time for us to go home and unlock our door. I have succeeded in staying away but we had to go home. I had to face whatever is behind my door. God didn't bring me this far to leave me. I want to call home but what will that do but cause more confusion, and that's not an option I need. We load up as Momo loads us up with more onion burgers and fries. Sierra loves the attention and burgers but too tired to show appreciation. Sabrina beats Sierra in falling asleep. Momo fed her a special burger just minus onions and were baked in the oven. Momo watches us move slow and offers a night of looking at movies with their family. Every Saturday is family movie night and we were invited. I smile but decline again missing out on an opportunity to continue to be around family and enjoy their atmosphere. She seems to want me to stay by her expressions and encouraging me to just stay a little longer. I tell her reluctantly that I need to get them ready for bed and I know that they are tired. Now Momo has flipped the script of distraction on me. I thanked her again, as we walked toward a dark apartment.

Inside I know he hasn't been home, but I was hoping that he might have stopped by just to check on us. After all he knows that I don't have any family out here. I open the door slowly knowing that my thoughts were confirmed. Sierra rushes in and turns on the lights while I push the stroller looking around the room. I take a few steps and I don't hear Sierra, because she has passed out in her bed. I guess that onion burger and fries and our long day out was more than enough. The phone rings and my heart jumps thinking while hoping it was Bill. Maybe he's been calling all day and was wondering where we were. I pick up and it's Robin checking on me and wondering why I was out pushing a stroller on a Saturday. Only answer I could come up with, and quick enough was that Bill was at work and we needed some fresh air. She seems to accept that with no more added questions. Robin told me that the girls saw us out at PataRee's and how big your girls were getting. She laughs saying they got my butt and that she was out of town on an assignment that took longer than she thought.

Courtney Diane wasn't available to assist because she had to fly out early to Fort Marshal. Now you know that she flew out early because Henry is dating a new girl and he talked a lot about her and she had to check her out. Robin adds Courtney Diane saying she had to go early, right early my butt and she laughs adding you know she doesn't have a butt. Henry latest lady seems to be nice enough for Courtney Diane to fly out early and not calling her a boxed shaped scant. I asked what was the verdict.? Well she seems to like her if she didn't you know. She would have called her every thang in the book. Courtney Diane remembered her name she called her Bernadette with no attachments. Wow that's different. I guess those online anger management classes are working. You know how over protective she is over her baby boy. Henry has a promising basketball career and don't need no gold digger trying to audition for a leading role. Not that type of party and too many tricks from recycled/regenerated trixies. I can't blame her. They don't go away they just keep on recycling.

Right in the middle of the conversation she asks how I am doing. I don't know if it's my pyranoia or she just asking?? Inside I get nervous did she pick up that something was wrong like Momo did?? I stumble in saying that I'm fine, Sierra is sleep and I'm getting Sabrina ready for bed. Then out of no where she asked about Bill?? Which was a first, because she normally or barely included him in any conversation or concerns. I said like a pro he's alright just being Bill. I don't know if she was okay with that, but it seemed to work for now. I tell her that I need to go. Robin tells me that you need your own car, so you and the girls can get out more often and not be busing it with strollers and a toddler in tote. I laughed saying that we are working on it. Bill feels the same way. I don't know if Robin fell for that but for now it worked again. She told me that she had to get back to work and that she would get back to me and hope to see us soon with love. She didn't know that I felt the love when she called fussing. Her expressions of concerns were different from the fussing coming from Bill. Actually, it was very refreshing she cared enough to fuss because she was concerned and not pissed off. Love was there and that's what I needed. Again, timing was good because I needed to hear her love come thorugh the phone. Especially because I was disappointed that it wasn't Bill voice I was hearing on the other end. I don't see the two JJ's, so I know he's not with them; thank God that their reputation has not reached our home.

I get the girls out of their adventure clothes and put on their PJ's as I look for some comfortable PJ's for me. This bed feels so warm and fresh. Before I get too comfortable, I jump up because I forgot to put the food up. But mainly I just wanted to check the phone to see if it works and wondered if that was the reason for Bill not calling. Although I have the girls, this apartment still feels lonely and dark. I miss Bill and I had to get real with myself and realize that he's not missing me. Maybe it was me and an opportunity presented itself for him to leave in his own coward way. Kinda selfish I'm here away from my family to be with our family to be back where I was in the beginning, returning with my family of girls. What would happen if I moved back hmm? I did turn some heads maybe I still have it.

This place is so dark, but I can still see the faded blue marks on the wall. Why did my eyes and mind go directly to that location? Why does that stain seem to glow just for me, or is it me tripping? Why now does it glow, why now? How did my eyes make it right to that spot? Do I need to be reminded of that day or is this what I need to help me move on? All I know is that I'm tired mentally and physically. I need my rest too because I don't know what the tomorrows will bring. Today was just a day and again I must get prepared for my tomorrows. Looking around and I think about how far we have come from that big blanket we used for a table, iron board and just to rest. Now we have an apartment full of furniture. One day our closet will be full of clothes and places to wear our outfits. Soon Bill will be going away for his two-week job requirement training. Humph no car, no money and no hubby, I didn't enlist for this. Night came fast yet it seemed to to be a slow day. The girls were knocked out snoring in sync which sounds cute and funny. I smile as I remembered when Sabrina was born, and Bill kneeling down to Sierra saying that you are a big sister now and you have to show your sister how to be brave and be there for her. Just like Mom and Dad are there for you, you have to show her. Sierra listened and seemed to understand every word that he was saying. When Bill said to the sleeping Sabrina when she was born, that your sister is here. She has been waiting a long time to hold you. That was the one quick time after delivering Sabrina that she opended her eyes just for her sister Sierra.

My thoughts fade into thinking of Bill's smile and twinkling almond shaped eyes. My heart smiles on the times he spends with his daughters and the love he shows them with laughter. I miss hearing him trying to tell them bedtime stories only in his unique way. His way exhausted Sierra as she tried to keep up with the characters that seemed to not fit the story. Bill and Sierra showed love and understanding in their own way for each other. I'm missing Bill for he is the only man I know and want to be with. Somehow, I had to keep it moving. I don't know if the move will be fast or slow. I just had to really give this some type of serious thought. I lay down with my sleeping girls watching the television watch me. This action sounds familiar, but I don't want to get used to the familiar thoughts or feelings. What joy will come in the morning, for tonight tears fade into my pillows if only I could cry? As for myself, tossing and turning actions rocked me to sleep. I think mentally I was extremly tired/exhausted. The girls were just as tired and I'm thankful that they turned in early. Surprisingly, we were out longer than I had expected. After all those concerns, what was there to rush back to? The aparment is quiet, clean and calm. No signs that he came home or made a cameo. There were no outside noise coming from Momo's sons or the JJ's and family. Come to think of it I haven't seen or heard from them in a while. Well at least I know Bill is not talking to one of them. It's funny but not ha-ha that I'm becoming immune to his actions and seem to know what his taste in women and they don't meet his criteria. Now I need to detour my thoughts and allow the toss and turn to rock me asleep again. The warmth from the tossing will warm this cold bed again. I remember how the morning came early and I was more tired than I was the day before.

No smell of bacon and eggs, no sleeping husband on the couch. I was hoping but in reality, not surprised. This was a day that I had to contemplate making that dreaded phone call asking my parents to bring us back home. I wanted more for my daughters and knew that they could get it here in Oceanview, but I didn't want them to feel the hardship of our future struggles. Haven's Place was not an option for me with now two daughters. So, what will be on our agenda today? I don't want to wear out my welcome at Momo's. They wouldn't mind us coming over, but I don't want them to get to the point where they rather see us going than coming. This will not be a day we sit around idling our minds at least not me. The girls will play and keep it moving and enjoying what they knew as life. I check in on the girls and they are still sound asleep. I had to use my mad money sparingly for just in case. I want to take them to the park, but it would be hard to watch Sierra and take care of Sabrina at the same time. Well we just had to make our home a fun hour or hours. I jump in the shower thinking that Bill and I only took one together. Funny when we did try, he fell out of the shower. We laughed as my eyes watered. I do miss him and being us, laughing and talking. I miss how we used to get upset with each other and apologize by saying your mama or your crip leg dad. Then we would just bust out laughing and that was it. Communication was never our problem but the ironic part I didn't know or understand what the other problems could be. I was willing to try if I knew what and how to change for our family. This is overwhelming, but I had to figure this all out. Those happy endings that I saw in the Hollingworths, Walkers, Tarvers, Shepherds and Reeds did they have to go through any of this to have peace in their later years. Woo this is hard work. Maybe they should write a book on how they made it work.

I remember telling Bill one time that if they read the book, (him being the book), before judging it by the cover he would be a lonely book. Now look at me I'm a lonely book on the shelf. Breakfast needed to be started this morning for three. Looking out and looking back didn't know I would have further to go in learning. I go check on Sabrina to check her diaper and it's a little wet. I'm glad I took a much relaxing shower, now its time to get the girls ready. The park is out but we can have fun here. I will make some panecakes, sausage and that should hold them. They wake up and didn't ask where their dad was. I don't know if they were feeling part of my pain or anixiety or just thought he was at work. After all it was morning and they really didn't understand the days of the week. So, with that thought we will keep it moving. Sierra sets the table as usual while Sabrina tries holding the napkins as Sierra moves and appreciates telling or instructing her what to do. Sabrina seems to understand because she looks as if she listening to Sierra's every word. I glance at the window hoping to see Bill walking toward the door or hear the keys works its way through the locks. I quickly pick up the phone yep its still working just not working from Bill's end. What could he be up to and what was he trying to prove, or did he already prove it? Has he moved on and we are now on our own, kind of a cold way to express it, wow? Sierra does the honor of saying the prayer adding to my surprise that where ever my dad is, please bless him too. How did she know to say that? I haven't talked to anyone nor did I say my thoughts out loud…

I guess it's that sense that they have without knowning what it really means. I do believe that her dad is on her heart and mind, just like he's been on mine for

ROBIN REED-POINDEXTER

some time. I wish I could shake these thoughts and keep everything light in my head. I'm trying so hard not let my thoughts surface to my face. I hope this prayer from the innocent heart will go through. I don't know what I want but I do need for Bill to be here with his family, minus the new shiny keys. Not much to clean around the apartment but let's have fun and make a mess. Yep let's express our freedom and take the museum type atmoshpere away for a day.

Chapter 47
Our Day Starts Today

Our day will start now! After we eat, I'll put the dishes in the sink and just wipe off the table to prepare for finger painting and freedom. I sit Sabrina in her high chair and Sierra joins her as I get the finger paint out and paper that was reusable. Let their fingers show expression on this used paper. They go crazy and get paint on their hands, faces, arms, the floor and the laughter show how much fun they are having. I join in and the fun begins for me too and I like this, no actually I love it. Normally, Bill is playing with them while I'm busy cleaning up and doing laundry. But today Bill is not here.

Now I get to get involved in the fun. we paint with fingers, with brushes, with laughter and I enjoy hearing their laughter. I didn't notice I was singing with their laughter because they try and sing with me in their own way. No special words just the words they know how to use with our off-key harmony. I guess we all were a family of being tone deaf. The teacher that told Bill he was tone death would probably laugh at us all knowing that she was right. Sierra sung songs when she was smaller and couldn't put sentences together or read but she manages to sing a whole song and did very well. As time went her singing voice became better. We are happy, and the sun is trying to come out through the clouds that seem to follow you. Once the clouds move away the hiding rainbow will surface. The beds are not made up, the television is blasting, and you would think there was a party in here. But that is a nope, just me and the girls having fun!! We move the the table when we hear music playing on the television and we all break out in a dance. Sierra and I are making our moves while Sabrina break out in her baby bounce on beat.

I look around the apartment and the day is still young, and the place looks a hot mess and I don't care, or should I say we don't care. My thoughts were to keep it moving as we kept it shaking. Momo would be proud and Robin and Courtney Diane would be joining us shaking to the groove. Today is better than yesterday. I'm thinking less of Bill and enjoying our freedom, but the reality comes and goes on the financial aspect of how we will survive. Well for now we are in our own me moments. Go go Rea and Brina oh yes. When the songs go off, we go back to painting. The girls shout and want to hear more music. While they are painting, I look for some music for us to dance to. I can't really find anything, but the thought they wanted to dance is a welcome form of freedom. While the paint dries, I wipe their faces as we sit down and watch a children's movie that just came on. We sit on the floor together laughing and just enjoying much of nothing. Sierra leaning against my side and, Sabrina in my lap and, we are all quiet and deep into the children movie. I'm into this movie myself this will definitely pass the quiet time away and no monies involved. Wow, all this fun in the comfort in our apartment. With so much excitement we fall to sleep in the middle of the day. Somehow, we all were stretched out on the floor and laying all over each other. I look at them as I fall off back to sleep to join them. I guess that miniature party wore us out, we are such party animals.

I don't know how it happened and, I didn't feel the change but when I went to stretch, I didn't feel any weight on my body. I jump up to see Bill lying with them on the couch. Was I that tired that I didn't hear or feel them removed from my body? I look at him sound asleep with the girls laying all over him. I want to throw water on him and ask what reason or right he had to be here? How dare you disrespect me and think this act didn't happen. Why are you here, we were having fun and bonding and and…? I was laying on the floor what happened to helping me up and placing me on the other couch or bed. I just look at him and now again I understand that thin line between love and hate. Right now, I'm on the borderline. All three look so peaceful as they slept, but what happened to the last two days of M-I-A, (missing in action). He didn't leave no money or transportation. So, all that's smoke he's trying to convince me that it tickles, but only went up in smoke like his cigarettes. This is not a puff puff pass situation. This seems so wrong? I may have said somethings, but we could have talked. We never had a problem with communication, and I don't know where the breakdown happened or when. One side is saying, "at least he came home" the other side is saying, "how many agains are you going to go through?"

I walk away and just head to the bathroom passing the blue stains that just seems not to go or fade totally away. I just look in the mirror and wash my face. The dancing and the joy have taken a lower level. The music is playing but the volume is so low you can barely hear it, but the tune is still there. I had to fight hard mentally to keep it playing. I remind myself, no pain will penetrate your joy and words will not take you to a place that you don't want to visit. I smiled nervously at my reflection and the smile came back. I go into the kitchen to clean up the painting mess we left. I look at the pan of bacon grease and I hear the words of Mama Rosie Josey saying son you are not as slick as you think, there will and trust my words there will be someone that can stand in the grease and make you feel you need another greasing. She would add, don't think all your dates are foolish. One day or days you will play a tune of being your own fool. For that instance and looking at that grease it had a reason.

My song and hum that I had in my mind and heart came back smoother. I smile as I revisit the sounds of laughter and the fun, we had just enjoying our quality time. I smile and think about the venture to PataRee's and the ride and the opportunity to get out and get away. It's been a long time since Sierra, and I took a long bus ride. This time we had an added passenger Sabrina and it felt so good. Now Bill returns like nothing happened, but it did, and I grew up. I cleaned up while listening to the snores coming to an end and to the noise of them waking up. I turn my head to smile at the girls, but I can feel myself just glaring at Bill with that borderline feeling. My eyes look at him without the twinkle without the dimple just without. I had to walk away because I can feel my insides boiling as I think about how he left. Something I could have not said or rewording them differently but it happened and we should be able to talk about it and not runaway. After all that's the name my Aunt Jo gave to me. That's my very special name and this time I didn't runaway I stayed here with our girls.

I take the same face cloth and wipe my face again and again don't remember why so many times, but I just did. By that time Bill comes into the bathroom. I try to move out of his way not looking at him or saying a word. He slows up to take my hand and puts us back to the mirror. He said this is the image I love seeing just like I still love you. I know I was crazy in leaving and I did leave you. I need for you to forgive me. I was with someone but not the whole weekend. He said he told that person that he didn't want to be with them anymore and he was going back to his family. I go to pull away I didn't want to hear this and I didn't want to ask why. I just wanted him to go back to where he was. I told him that he should go back to where his heart is because it wasn't here if you could leave that easy. I don't share a heart and I'm not going to share my husband.

He listened for once as I told him from the heart how I felt. I do feel, and you bought me out here. I didn't ask to come here, nor did I ask you to marry me. This is so unfair. I'm here taking care of our family while you are taking care of your trick. Bill stares at me as his eyes watered. I wanted to look at my watch and ask was it time to care?? He probably was surprised that I'm talking and saying words with courage. He only knew what I showed him. Bill didn't really know all of me because I'm still learning about myself. I looked at him and ask why should I forgive you?? Would you have foriven me if I left you for someone or if you found out I was see-ing someone? After all you are not home all the time and you work late hours. I add some thought with courage adding wasn't you who told be about soldier's wives fooling around while their husbands are away for two weeks of training or on tem-porary assignments or transfers?? Hmm, matter of fact you are leaving this week for your two-week training. I smiled and raised my eyebrows looking dead into his eyes. Inside I was fuming and scared at the same time verbally kicking his ass and getting into his thoughts. For once he listened and said I told her that I didn't want her, I wanted my family and my wife.

Inside I guess I should be impressed or grateful for one second, he thought about us and not his selfish needs. Should I jump in the air and hit my ass and say well what do you think about that you stayed with your wife and family!! I just looked at him with the impression of okay. I looked at him as I took a big breath and said to him holding his hand news flash kiss my ass. I walked away hoping that nothing would hit the back of my head or be snatched into the bedroom and the door closes and the striking noise echos the room. To my surprise Bill says which side. That hit my heart and just made it smile. It was our old way of communicating and that felt good. My heart was penetrated by memories and his eyes twinkled and his smile was the way I remembered. I had so many questions, but my mouth couldn't work with my brain to form the words to ask. He said let's go for a ride I have a surprise for you and the girls. Inside I was thinking wasn't, I'm going back to my wife enough surprise?? We load up and go for our ride. There are no signs of anyone being in the front seat. We strap the girls in and we're off. The ride seems unfamiliar, but it all leads up to the base and we are greeted by one of MP"s. Bill's friend Raul gives him something, and they dap and say okay/later.

Don't remember meeting him but he seems nice. But when they are in uniform and with the same haircut, they all look the same. I didn't know what or where we could be going. We go to the commensary sometimes, but it doesn't seem like this kind of a ride. Bill does a slight u-turn, but we are just outside the base. We are in a beautiful very clean residental area with large playgrounds, schools all looking uniformed and very clean. Almost like a sterile kinda clean. We turn into the drive way of a large manicured lawn house. Bill smiles and says here we are. The shiny keys belonged to this place. I don't really believe that because the shape was a lot different. This time I'm going to keep my peace. The girl's eyes open along with mine as we just look around the house. The house is huge, and many houses are on this block. I feel strange, because I don't want to leave our apartment family like I have done before and start all over again. Here we go with the agains again. What about Momo, Robin and Courtney Diane? Hmmph, this is just outside the base. Will Amos bring Momo and the boys over to come and visit us? This location just seems so far away. Would they come near this base to see me and would this push me away from everyone? I was already isolated from my family, now that I have established a new extended family and I'm leaving them again. Bill seems happy as he pulls me through the house showing me every room. He said he slept here over the weekend and that's why he was so tired, getting everything ready for his family. In the back of my mind I'm thinking right yuck, ew. I didn't land on fool then skip or stumble over to thup-id. Inside right now I'm just pissed. I'm going to hold this thought and keep it moving. While holding his hand and skipping back around pissed and for now just do the duh act. He's happy saying the rent is really low and there is daycare not too far and he can still take Sierra to school.

Sierra takes her sister hand as they look into each room. Some rooms were furnished. Bill said his friend Kegan and his family were stationed overseas and he didn't want to leave his house empty. We just had to pay utilities and small amount for rent. I look at Bill and he was just cheesing and feeling he had done right. I nervously hold Bill's hand as we gaze around each room. I had to admit that the house was larger, and I missed living in a house. Bill always lived in apartments, so this will be what we both need. I will support his decision and excitement, but I will not forget about the weekend of loneliness and abandonment. That's not one I will skip around. In the back of my mind I'm doing the packing because he will be leaving. Mama Sadie is not here to help so this will be a solo packing. Well if Robin or Courtney Diane is around I can ask them. At least I'm getting away from the JJ's before they could fish around my house and try and hook Bill. Come to think of it they don't look like his type of bait.

The yard is large more room, but I don't know anyone here. Well I didn't know anyone at the other places we have moved to either. But everything seems close yet far away. My thoughts does any type of bus service even come to this rich looking area? What has Bill gotten us into? This seems to work out for him but maybe there might be a chance for us. Since he didn't talk to us, I will keep this as what Bill calls a surprise. Does Bill think that I would have talked him out of it and was he really thinking about us? Inside my stomach, thoughts and everything is floating and moving and wondering where this is really going. What assurance do I or we have? Here I go again picking up and moving. I don't think that Bill and I would have realized that we would be moving so much. My reality wasn't a thought about ever leaving Oakwood, my comfort zone, my family and friends. Bill gave up a lot too; he left Chicago his friends and family.

I can't be selfish in my actions or thoughts. We both need to grow up but we both need to grow together. I look at him and my mind is still racing. I don't know what to say or how to act right now. I want to say no but I want Sierra and Sabrina to have room to grow and play. This will give us all room to grow and have backyard fun and maybe barbeque in the back yard if it is permitted. I picture the girls running, playing and dancing. Not like Fifi's mom burning clothes, we would be burning que meat. But if Bill does that antic again would I have such nerves. For now, do we both knew how to que, but the thought is there to try. That is just what we need to do is just try. I'm trying to convince myself as I look at Bill carrying Sabrina as he walks with Sierra looking into every room. It seems like there is no rush to move, but it sounds like with Bill the sooner the better. So, I guess if I don't want to be the odd one out, so I join in. We would move from concrete to grass to roll and play in, but what about the walks, the bus rides? Maybe this would be the opportunity to mention or wait until Bill's heart is open to purchasing another car. The house is roomy, and some furniture is here, but what happens when they return. I catch up with my family taking a breath in and exhaling.

How long do we have to stay here or how long will Kegan be stationed overseas? His eyes twinkle so I know its okay to ask about the car. While he is telling me at least three years or so and his wife Silvia went with him, so there is some time. Who would want to give up being stationed in Italy? I thought I would love to be there myself. I jump in insisting, then this would be a good reason to get a second car since we have a large driveway. Bill hesitates and with a slow response lets me know what he is thinking. I don't know his thoughts or expression at that time, but he does say calmly let's save some money and then we will see. To me that was funny not ha-ha because this was the thing I didn't know was about our finances. Hmm now how could I wait for something I didn't know. So, I don't know if that day will come, but at least it might be still in his planning stage. For now, I keep the match going with more questions. This was a bold move and I asked how much money we do have saved, since we will be saving on bills. But will our utilites increase since we have a house and where would or how would that affect our savings plan? His response was you should know you pay the bills.

Oh no dear I use that monthly check for groceries. Since we are speaking of monthly I do need a raise. Do you know how much I can help us in picking up Sierra or dropping off, and since we are so close, I can get a part-time job. I look into Bill's eyes smiling adding that we can add more to our savings account. I couldn't believe this threw him off. His response was presented with a smile that put my fears at ease. Touche I guess I'm learning something through all this. I'm learning so I will add this to my mental notes for just in case happens again. We hold hands and Sierra grabs my hand while Bill still holding onto Sabrina. For this moment we are in unity and a perfect family picture. Maybe this will work, if I keep an open mind and stay focus.

Momo told me out of the clear blue that her and Amos go sparring from time to time, and don't let his quietness fool your ass. We just pick which one is worth sparring without throwing any sucker punches. None of that physical crap there are rules ours is just keep it verbal. If he tried that I would knock his little ass out and hang him on a hook and watch his little feet dangle. I was taught you hit the person back that hit you so there will be a mutual agreement on how that felt. We take our corners chill with no heart feelings, because neither one of us is going nowhere. We do a just a calm your ass down time out. It's okay to disagree in just in how you disagree. I'm his wife, his best friend not his clone. I still have my own mind. My thoughts don't end when his begins. That's right I'm not Bill's clone or be whatever woman he's trying to make me be or disappointed in what I'm not. I'm not some trick you're trying to fix into a wife.

Momo adds only in the Momo sexual way, saying I will knock him out with her racks. I'll give him a left and a right and leaving his little ass snoring. My usual response was visual ew Momo really, but she was there right on time with the right words. She added don't let the people from the outside effect your decisions inside. I always remember with Amos and Momo no matter where she or he was they always ended up together ending with just a hug for no reason. She said Amos is her companion, Momo would give me a wink, with saying just what I had practice keep your business in the house. But I need to talk to someone before I explode. I don't want to leave Bill and the love we have for each other, but I left my mother and the relationships I had with my dad, family and friends. From time to time I try and visualize what they would be doing and as adults. What I would be doing with Sharon Denise, Debbie Ann and Melody Lynn. I still talk to them, but I don't tell them what is always going on. Maybe I didn't want to feel embarrassed or talked into coming back to Oakwood, or constantly making up excuses for the reason I returned home. At one point the many questions would exhaust my many answers. I just didn't want to answer to family, friends at the same time being silently reminder that I failed. That would be the last thing I wanted to be reminded that Bill and I are no longer together.

Bill and I still nicely spar when it comes to our family, that's what always broke the ice. How do we get back there but while still moving forward? Just like Mama Rosie Josey told Loren this is not just your world there are many other planets in the galaxy. Don't be your fool or fool yourself into believing in what your world has convinced you or convinced yourself. The world turns, and it will come back around onto you. Just keep that in mind and get some right and get me those grandbabies! Funny that was their sparring and understanding that they had. So, for now Bill and I are just sparring and taking our corners. We will move in and one thing that helps is that we don't have to hurry, and this will give us time to put in our notice and move. In my world of planets ha-ha, I mentally prepare to move again.

I rub Bill's back, so he knows that I'm in approval of his decision. At least we are together, and I will put that trick on hold. No more antics or tricks in the bed. I want to learn some tricks but the last time I got my feelings hurt and that was more than a sparring match. I barely recovered and I'm still here. My parent's strength and grandmothers Mama Sadie, Hazel, great- grandmother Mommy and throw in my aunts helped me. I didn't think their words would last this long. I heard and listened, and the words were stored until they needed to surface. I got to plan my move and move on my plan whatever that maybe. Senior Pastor Turner said some time ago that when people throw mud at you don't try to wipe it off because it will just smear/spread just let it dry and shake it right on off. So, in other words Bill your mud throwing words will not spread or penetrate my feelings or enter my soul. I will let your words dry in mid air and just shake it on off and keep it moving. For now, I will go along with moving and hopefully Bill will recognize what he almost lost.

Sierra is excited about her room and wants to share it with Sabrina. I don't think she realized what her simple request entails until clean up comes. But for now, she wants to be with her little sister and I'm okay with that. Being the middle daughter, I shared rooms with EJ until she booted me out then I shared with Bonnie. Sierra is okay with moving not realizing she will be leaving her friends. She's so young I don't think anything like that phases her at all. As far as she is concerned this is something new and fun with a backyard. With that action I had to think back about Fifi's backyard with the missing bricks and clothes hanging out of the barbeque pit. Their family must be crazy enough that cops and inmates know and remember them as a crazy ass family. I grew up with families like that you wouldn't even get into an argument because to this day you would be still fighting their next generations. We learned early how to live and walk away. Just like now I'm not going to argue just walk away with holding Bill's hand as we prepare to move again. We make it to the car as Bill opens the door to put his girls in as I look at him place them inside their car seats. He smiles at me moving so I can sit down and buckles me in too with a smile and kiss like he used to. It feels good but in the back of my mind where has his lips been. I can't feel the softness of his lips because I don't trust not knowing where they have been.

I feel his pain in trying but does he feel the pain that I feel and how it has affected our relationship. Sometimes men have the tendency to act like they don't care. I have feelings just like everyone else, its just hard for me to show them. They might show them in a different way, through anger, insecurities or silence. This is another route I will have to learn. I'm not a cold person, blood still warms my body. The girls and I will take on as another adventure and travel and learn a different bus route, yippee. All the houses are so beautiful, reminds me of the houses in Oakwood. I didn't see any children, but they could have been inside. I just look out the window at how everything looks so different to what I was used to seeing. No children or buses running every fifteen minutes. The sun is setting in beautiful Oceanview and my mind is trying hard to absorb the beauty. This area seems so foreign. No familiar faces or noises. Am I ready for this move? I guess I have to because Bill has already made our decision. I stand by him, but it would have been nice to have had some input on this surprise. We seem so far away I think that we are in another city. The sun setting is still the same, but it still feels different. Where were the stores, so many wheres and hows and whys? Somehow or somewhere I got to put on the performance and accept my role. I remember glancing at Bill wishing I had a pie just to smash it on the side of his face...

Chapter 48
Will this Home have Our Heart

When we arrive home, only Momo's sons are outside throwing footballs, then their little brother comes out and they include him in. He has a big smile on his face and happy to be on the big boy's team, even if football is almost bigger than his little hands can hold. A familiar smell is coming from Momo's kitchen and I know it's not Amos cooking. After all, how did Momo say it I didn't marry him for his cooking, but we can bang some pots and pans and I'm not talking about in the kitchen. I'm going to miss that and her yelling at her boys, and little Tim always trying to hold Sierra's hand and her big brothers Chris, Bert, Ryan, Manly and Craig, keeping her safe. She had her little protectors and will be leaving them soon. Tim didn't mean any harm in always wanting to hold Sierra's hand. Makes me think about my teacher Mr. Lee. When he came from Italy and he said that he would pinch the girls on their butts. They complained, and he told the principal that if you liked someone it was customary to pinch the girl on her butt. With a smile between the two he told him that he couldn't pinch anymore. Which was okay with him he found other ways to get the girls attention through track, and those deep blue eyes that probably remind you of Charlotte's husband Johnny Lee. Mr. Lee had so much energy as a teacher and track coach. To this day I still believed that this seventy plus man will unzip himself and the real forty-year-old man will pop out. He could teach/coach all day, conduct track practice, go home and help his son build a deck and still have time to walk with his beautiful wife each day. When I met Bill, he wanted to be track coach and physical therapist. Bill would work out each day running and keeping his fine physique that he managed to keep throughout our marriage. As for me my weight fluctuated. Maybe this move would be a beginning of someday purchasing our own home. Just like Jovan and Toni minus the toxic route. I don't know where to start in packing and telling a few people in the complex that we are moving. Bill seems so happy as he enters the apartment, he only seen long enough just to take us to our surprise.

He smiles with dimples showing saying that we need to go out tomorrow and see if Momo is up to it. Then another shocker Bill told me to go and get my hair, nails and toes done. Wow I haven't ever had my nails and toes done before. I'm so used to doing them myself with clear polish. Wow added color to my nails and toes and someone else taking care of my hair. I don't know where this is coming from, but I will check with Momo. Did he get a raise, or did we have some extra money? Bill has never offered me such a luxury. I've seen some nair/hair places but Robin or Momo might know. I couldn't believe how excited I became. I just gave him a big kiss as I felt both of his arms wrap around my waist. For that moment everything that happened last week faded as I felt his heart beat for me. His embrace and kiss were for me and I feel apart of him merging back into us. Did he realize that he had a family? Everything he could possibly want was inside this apartment. Bill's soldier buddies would love to be in his shoes to see how they fit with comfort. My insides are ready to explode from excitement and my family is back together again. This is a good ending before Bill leaves. We are embracing, talking and showing love in front of our daughters. They haven't seen that in a while, but the point is that they see affection. We are parents showing love for each other and we will be moving into a house, a spacious house with grass and a backyard. I guess it's not such a bad move and I will finally leave that blue faded stain(s) on the wall. This would be a new beginning for us and opportunity to grow in our relationship and with our daughters.

I'm going to miss Courtney Diane's family stories. The last I heard she was enjoying Fort Marshal and Henry Luis new girlfriend Bernadette, (sounds like it is becoming serious). Courtney Diane stayed firm and strong in keeping her son focused on school and his sports schlorships. A big difference from the box shaped girl she couldn't stand. Come to think of it not too many of his girlfriends she could stand. Courtney Diane viewed them as, they were always tricks in training. The best one was you weren't the only car driving up that ramp. Ew that's another unneeded visiual again, ew. Knowing Courtney Diane when she said it no part of ha-ha showed on her face. She probably added with your dumb ass. I miss her saying that but I'm sure she will make a surprise cameo on the JJ twins. But for now, she's happy with her son's choice of not choosing a girl but a woman. Bernadatte didn't know then but she helped Henry Luis make it to the pros. Hmm I can't believe that I'm getting the works done. I know what to wear that navy-blue dress my mom sent to me. I need to redirect my energy, because I'm going on a date! I kiss Bill again while he's playing with our girls. I'm so excited I tell Bill I'll be right back going to check in on Momo. He shows that dimple smile with the twinkle in his almond shaped eyes with a heads-up motion.

Courtney Diane's eyes must have been burning because I saw Robin walking with Courtney Diane in uniform. She looked very nice and thinner than I remembered. They spot me and about face with hugs and showing much love. They laugh asking where I was rushing off to?? I laugh through the many hugs I kept giving them. I proudly told them that Bill is treating me to getting my hair done, with toes and nails included. They smile at me with saying that you're getting a manicure and pedicure. Inside I knew they were right, and, in my excitement, I turned into a little girl, that was just happy to be going to get prettied up. I asked if they knew of a nail place and I smiled saying for manicure and pedicure. With laughter they say in sync our baby sister is growing up. Robin tells me about Lynel's nails and feet. With that we all laugh with me saying nails and feet? Robin laughs while saying that was Courtney Diane's first advertisment, huh, feet and nails. Courtney Diane said that, I suggested calling it "A Fresh Look", I guess it made too much sense. Courtney Diane looks at her with those laser eyes saying kiss my ass. Robin's natural response was what ass?? Courtney Diane just ignores her in away that only they could do to each other. She chimes in saying that she also has a hair boutique that's pretty good and reasonable. She's located right by that place… near PataRee's. I know that place all so well, but I only know how to get there by bus. Robin offers to watch the girls, but I know that if Bill said Momo it's Momo. I had to think quick where I wouldn't hurt anyone's feelings and not piss Bill off. I smiled and asked for a raincheck, hopefully there will be more dates to come for us. Robin's warm smile with embracing words then a raincheck it is. She nudges Courtney Diane who seems to be looking around and not paying too much attention. She respsonds with what, yeah, yeah raincheck right!! Robin looks at her with her signature okay Courtney Diane smile.

Courtney Diane looks at her with her eyes slightly squinted asking have you seen my sister JJ and my trilfing cousin JJ? I hesitate saying not lately, but I haven't really been home. She smiles saying that you and the girls have been exposed to light and air?? I smile with yep light was hard at first and we then took in a breath and breathed in the fresh air too! We did it with no coughing or turning blind!! She snaps back with her signature corner smile while Robin laughed which causes me to laugh too. Courtney Diane said that she had to come back and check on my apartment. I've been getting some reports on their trifling asses and I had to see it with my own eyes. She rubs her forehead saying I had to decide on who would be the first to meet my foot. Their asses got me making this special trip back just to check on them. They may funk over their family members, but no one will smoke a cigarette at my expense. I will puff puff pass on both their asses. In all the excitement of seeing my big sisters back I almost forgot the reason for coming out. This is a first time I excused myself without Bill looking for me to come home. Courtney Diane smiles with okay I just know I'm going to stretch out something on my body, but you go and get yourself right and enjoy. Robin co-signs with I want to hear about your evening tomorrow in details. Wow for the first time it will be me telling a story and someone will listen to me.

I knock on Momo's door to the smell of her frying chicken and the aroma takes over my nostrils. Little Bert answers the door saying it's Miss Rita as he smiles asking where is Sierra? He's such a flirt, funny years later it worked to his advantage respectfully. Momo is singing and doing her signature dancing with her style of shaking. I go into the kitchen giving her a hug and she asks what's this glow about you, are you pregnant again? I smile at her with oh no. Inside my thoughts were that Bill would have to touch me for that to happen. I remember what Momo said what happens in the house stays inside, too much space outside for it to spread with the air. I didn't feel the glow, but I guess it's because I'm feeling so giddy and for that moment, I felt happy. I'm so excited that Bill and I are going out as married young couple. I told her that Bill asked if I wanted to go out actually, he told me in a Bill way. While she was cutting fresh vegetables, you need me to watch your babies? She asked before I could get the nerve up to ask. I hurry in my answer of yes, while laughing saying that we are going out on a date!! She supports my energy saying that the girls could spend a night, so your evening doesn't have to end. She took some biscuit dough rubbing in her hands raising her eyebrows saying hmmm, a little flipping and flopping and these biscuits will rise mighty fine as she turns her head giving me a wink and a smile. This time I smile saying you never know what the evening might bring. She responds quickly it will bring you both a good night sleep huh. I smile yep good night sleep and maybe something else. She said you can bring them over for dinner. I thanked her, but I told her that I don't know what Bill has planned for dinner. Inside I knew the weekend dinner was out and Bill needed to step up.

I go home not seeing Robin or Courtney Diane they're probably in Robin's place. I didn't hear any adverbs like Loren would say coming from her dark apartment. I come home to the smell of burgers frying and Bill smiling. I guess he got his flipping and flopping in early or was he getting his exercise in for tonight?? I'm surprising myself in thinking that way, but I have to do something different in our marriage. This time I will follow Bill's lead and add just a little. I don't want to revisit that awful time and bad taste it left with the scars that were still trying to heal. I'm looking and thankful that I can take a mental picture of our family back together again. Tomorrow I'll go for my manicure and pedicure to Lynel's nails and feet with a small note treat your feet. I join in and watch Sabrina's little hand hold a burger and trying hard to follow her dad and sister. We are all laughing, and Sierra says mom which shocked me, because she usually calls me Rita asked to put the music on that we were dancing to earlier.

I pick a station and dance my way back to the kitchen taking Bill by his hand, so we can dance. Funny Bill being from Chicago still can't dance and he just kinda moves his feet. We are all dancing and laughing and this feels so real as we dance and sing to "ABC". This is not my imagination I can touch, feel and hear the laughter. I feel my legs and feet moving to the music as I hear the beats from the rhythm of the music. This is something we haven't done in a while and this time we are not going to eat at the table. We will picnic on the floor in front of the television and turn off the music and look at some Winnie the Pooh movies. Sabrina jumps with some of the music as she recognizes some of the characters. Sierra helps her although she is not a cartoon loving child. We stretch out on each other as we fill up off the fatburgers Bill cooked. I'm lying on Bill and the girls are laying on both of us. Right now, the kitchen can wait for I waited a long time to relive this moment. Bill kisses me on my forehead and his lips feel so soft and just feeling the warmth from his body merges with mine and sends a little shake in my body.

He must have felt my little tremor because he looks at me smiling and I can't wait for tonight. Not to make love just to feel the warmth of his body and hear his heart beat again as we fall off to sleep together. Bill nudges me to look at our sleeping daughters. I smile as I get up and pick up Sabrina to put her in her bed as Bill carries Sierra. I get kinda giddy and confused at the same time. Because I don't know what the next step may be. I know it sounds naïve but lately I don't know which direction the wind is blowing. After I put Sabrina in bed, I go into the kitchen to clean up the residual from the fatburgers. Bill comes up behind me grabbing my waist. I just melt inside as my soul cringes, as I feel his lips on the back my neck. He tells me to let the kitchen go for the night which is very rare. Bill loves a clean house so much that you can almost eat off the floor with the fresh smell pine-sol. Actually, that is the first thing you smelled in the morning. I tell him I'm going to jump in the shower and ask if he wants to join me. He smiles telling me to get water ready. I walk down the hall with a little shake as Bill smiles walking behind me with a smooth swag.

So far, I'm doing okay not saying anything that might upset him or change the atmosphere or attitude. I anxiously look for a nice gown and hop in the shower. He joins me and this time he didn't fall out of the shower like he did the first time we tired showing. I feel like I'm on a honeymoon again. Well not really, we never had a honeymoon. Well I guess coming to Oakview was our honeymoon move. This night was special, no words, no sex just the intimacy of us falling off to sleep wrap around one another and that's just what I needed. I feel the oneness as our warmth merges with the same beat of our hearts. Not a bad night and this is what my heart has been waiting for. This makes up for somethings but not all the things that have happened. But I'm not going to ruin our night of the best intimacy I have had in sometime.

I stretch and turn over for him to reach out for me and move behind me. We still go to bed and wake up the same way, embraced in one another. I wake up to the smell of pancakes, bacon and the aroma of pine-sol. The table is set, and breakfast is ready. They/my family are just waiting for me to wake up. I was in such a sound sleep I didn't feel the movement of Bill getting out of our bed. But one thing I do know the bed was warm and no empty spot or a lonely feeling exsisted. I look across the table and realized this is what I heard what couples look forward to, is looking across the table at their mate or Momo calls it her companion/soul mate. Bill is my companion and my best friend. We enjoy breakfast with laughter and full stomachs. Bill leaves from the table and my eyes follow him to what is he up to. He comes back with keys in his hand with money saying go get your do done, nails and feet so we can go out tonight just us. He then asked is Momo okay with watching our girls? I smile saying that she even offered to let them spend a night. Bill smiles saying that's not going to happen. I want my family all under one roof, maybe one day we might do a raincheck but for now no but tell her thank you. Go get your work done and I'll be here with the girls. Inside I'm trembling with the overwhelming of kindness that is coming from Bill. I get the car... plus money, wow what just happened? I rushed out just like when Robin came by with her raincheck. I'm heading out in a rush, before the thoughts of kindness disipates and fades into a vapor. I shower up throw on some clothes, kiss the family and dash out to the car, no our car!!

Temptation tells me to look inside the glove compartment to check to see if the trixie raised her leg trying to leave her mark by leaving signs that she was here. My thoughts wondered back to hanging out at Courtney Diane's place, and she busted Robin out about her gift she left for Trixie, (adding please do not let her smile fool your ass). In the usual manner Robin just smiled as Courtney Diane told her story. Robin left the divorce papers, debit card and bank statements, yep she did all that, but she also left a little something, something for trixie. One of Robin's many parting gifts she left was a box of dog biscuits wrapped with a dog chain, with a note you should have kept your dog, (but I'm gonna inserted beach), on her lease. See what happened when she broke the chain, and the box of dog biscuits is for you to teach her more tricks or just reward her for wagging her ass. I just remember looking at Robin with glazed eyes holding back my laugh and she was just sitting so calmly smiling. Then Courtney Diane adds don't let that calm smile fool your ass she can take a woman's wig off and be brushing it while the woman keeps walking like the wig is still on her head. Then at that point Robin did responds, I'm just brushing it off and continued sipping her glass of wine with the calmness Courtney Diane just described. Well there is no cheap perfume so it's all clear, nothing showing. With the all clear, I roll down the window and adjust the seats and my foot gas up and I'm off for Lynel's without looking back. I'm out and gone for the day can't believe a whole day away. That's something I haven't done since we 've married, maybe a quick store run but nah this is my all day excusion. I will travel the bus route that way I won't get lost and arrive early enough to get back to my husband and daughters to enjoy our magical night. The day is clear, and the wind is lightly hitting my face. The wind allows me to feel the freedom as I sing off key to the music playing on the radio. The funny part I'm driving and not on the bus. Taking the bus route without all the stops allows me to arrive sooner than I had expected.

It's not quite in the same shopping area but across the street and a few blocks down, not bad but only a few are waiting outside to get in. The ladies kinda just look at me and inside I can see why Courtney Diane was assigned to this location. They kinda have her character, tee-hee and whatever. I look back at them with a corner smile like she would or no smile with a heads-up motion and that was just enough for them to speak. Wow so that's how it works. Okay I got it. I don't know what Lynel looks like. They asked what type of service I'm here for. I told them I was referred by a friend Courtney Diane she spoke highly of Lynel's place. Inside I'm giggling because she didn't say too much Robin did all the talking. One said that, Lynel will be rushing in here in a few mintues.

I guess it wasn't Lynel because they didn't call her out by name. One of the ladies tells the unname lady to do what you do and cut a little more off on the ends. The stylist, Merdie told her why I don't just cut if all off and just line it. Your hair is almost down to dust on a jug. She responds back who head is this and am I paying you or you paying me? Her response was yep. Then she added am I tipping you? Her response was nope, your cheap ass doesn't ever tip in money just words I can't use at the bank. Then she responded ooh then never mind the tip, because I want to stay consistent. She opens her hand up looking down at it saying according to my palm pilot no tip today either, with a note because my ass is cheap, hmm palm pilot no future confirmation. This went on like a tennis match. Your head Gelena, I'm going to cut but if it doesn't grow back take this as my tip. By the way is your sister Geneva coming in to so you both can tag team my ass? Since I can't tell you two apart. I'm going to start scheduling you and her separately. Gelena snaps with, so your point is either way you won't get a tip, but I will bring you back a cobbler, and to your question yep I'm surprise I beat her here. No telling who or what she stopped to do. You know her ass is always detouring instead of getting where she needs to be on some kind of time other than her own time.

I had to assume that this was Lynel rushing in and heads toward the back before I could say a word to her. Well it didn't matter it wasn't like I talk or move fast. I just had to wait for her to return, yep just wait seems to be the story of my life. Just like I sit here looking out the window just waiting for the sun to come out. Sure, enough must be Lynel because Merdie just called her Lyn saying that you have someone waiting for you refered by your girl Courtney Diane. With her saying that made me feel a little more comfortable about using Courtney Diane's name. She's slightly taller than Courtney Diane and just tad bit thicker with short cut style, deep brown eyes and sporting that similar corner smile. Merdie is shorter and seems to be louder with no smile. Lynel approaches me with arm stretched asking what I need done. I told her well the works hair, nails and toes. As I look around the room at the styles on the wall, I get some more courage while enjoyng my freedom to cut my hair. That's something I have never done. I remember how my dad would get mad at my mother when she would cut her hair or wear wigs. I didn't understand either because she had and still has such beautiful hair. But maybe that was her way of expressing her silent style of freedom. I tell her I want my hair short. Inside I am hoping that it won't make my head look any bigger than it already looks, but what the heck go for it.

My brother and I inherited my mother's gene of fast-growing hair, so if Bill has a fit time will allow for the length to come back. My sisters and I also inherited my mother's butt. My father said, in his humorous way, that if we all bend over you couldn't tell who was who? I beg to differ Bonnie was like Courtney Diane no butt. She could easily do the wall test and blend right into the wallpaper/paint. Lynel feels my hair and ask do you really want to cut this beautiful thick hair? Inside I take a big sigh of courage with yes with a hint of color. What the courage was saying inside we didn't agree to that where did that come from pushing that strength, huh. Now when you run, I run with you. Lynel takes me to the back to wash my hair and the wash feels so good, as the smell of the shampoo and the warmth of all that water hitting my scalp. All the emotions are in ah moment and I'm glad I'm here. Gelena laughs saying I want to get my toes done too. Merdie matches back with we don't have enough polish for your big ass toes, that's connected to those big ass feet and thank you for keeping them covered with those big ass shoes. Her response with a chuckle was you're welcome. While listening I feel my hair drop on my shoulders and hit the floor and what was feeling heavy is now light. I hope I didn't jump too soon in getting my haircut. Then the courage voice just gives a grunt and I respond silently with shut up. Now the tint comes in she didn't ask what color and I didn't tell her. I guess she knows what will work. I go sit under the dryer while Gelena and Merdie go at it, like a friendly ping pong match. When I return, I thought Gelena was getting her hair cut and did her shirt get wet? Then what I thought was Gelena was actually must be her identical twin sister Geneva. Wow they are identical. They are the same size only difference is her hair is slightly longer. Gelena and Geneva remind me of Anita and Annette identical twins I grew up with and I wondered what they are up to? I heard one moved out of town. Annette was the one I was close to, and since I was close, I was able to tell them apart.

Chapter 49

The Entertainment Begins and I have a Front Row Seat

Merdie calling her Neva are you still kicking ass, tell me that story again. Now what makes you think I want to talk about my trilfing blue skies of an ex-husband Oregon? Well because it's funny and I might need some pointers just in case. You know just in case my hubby, Graham might think he can creep but if he does his ass bet not go to sleep. Neva looks in the mirror saying you know that don't hurt as much as it hurt the both. Lyn responds with after all that you came in the same day to get your hair done because you sweated it out, please tell us again! Now that Neva blast back at Lyn with why you put my business on display this will be the last replay. Okay now listen slow because I'm going to tell my version, so this will be quick. Now you know Oregon used to constantly talk about the size of my legs, hips, butt, boobs any and every thang he could to find to build himself up at my expense, but I still showed him love. I watched his six pack; wash board stomach deflated to a keg and the island that developed on top of his head had a lot of space. But I'm the one that changed?? I don't know what glasses he had on, but they sure didn't see clearly. We would get into arguments about his infidelity. Damn almost anything that had a switch and he would look down at his dill pickle saying to it "stay down boy". He would swear up and down my eyes didn't see what my ears heard. I told him one time that I had stopped caring. He said with his stupid ass I don't know no damn Karen you mean Tarin, oh damn! I had to pause on his ass to check myself on what the funk did I say and what did he hear with his dill pickle with his blue skies? I had to say fool get those beaches off your dill pickle and mind, something needs bleaching. While I'm listening, I hold in the laugh on who is Karen? I guess its similar to who's training derail with a follow up from Lucee is he cute. Neva kept going with, well it's always that one time your schedule changes and you get that funny feeling when you come home. Don't know why you get that feeling but you just do. I come home, and Oregon is home for what reason I don't know. I just felt funny didn't see anything, but the feeling was still there, and I couldn't shake it… Oregon was being the asshole that he normally is, but something felt funny. I went to the bathroom and I felt his eyes following me. I felt an energy of someone's presence.

As she was telling the story we all pause to listen except for Lyn. She's working it and listening too. Neva said I went into the bathroom and locked the door like I normally do. I just set on top of the toilet lid, wondering am I tripping because this feeling wouldn't go away. Couldn't shake this feeling and thoughts wouldn't come in. I was feeling something, and it just wasn't right. Then something told me to pull the curtain back. Oh yeah that's why that feeling wouldn't go away the beach was hiding in my shower. I yanked her ass out so quick. All you could hear was me talking and her screaming for Oregon. She's in my house calling for my husband? Boy did she have bad timing, and all it did was add fuel to pissing me off more. Oregon was banging on the door and we were in sync. When he banged, I banged her head into my tile floor. I almost wanted to do a bee-bop noise. There was a song in my head, singing I hear you knock knocking and I'm beating her ass and when I open that door there will be one more, almost had me sounding like a rapper, until a voice said stop before you kill her. I reluctantly listened and left her passed out on my floor, at least that what it looked like. She could have been playing possum and if she was, she was good performer.

Now this is where my kardio kick boxing class with Ty West came in to play. You know that fifteen-minute class went to one-hour classes and gave me energy and discipline and his wife Janice worked hard on our assests, tee-hee-hee. She turns saying my shift is tight any way. Oregon was still banging on the door trying to open it. With speed I developed from Ty's class I opened the door so fast his ass didn't know, (and she gets up to show us her front kick) … I did a one, two, punch with an upper cut and ended with a round house or snap front kick. Don't matter didn't think I would ever use it. I knocked his ass out and left his ass laying next to that beach on my floor. Oregon hit me one time before this situation which put the fear in me. I told myself that would not never ever happen again. So that's why I took those self defenses classes I heard about through that soldier girl Courtney Diane. So, this is how it went again with the combo. When I opended up the door fear came in with the one, two punch. The first punch, I'm scared, then second punch I'm pissed make sure you don't miss, then the third move was an upper cut and don't miss his gut. Then all strength set in for having that thang in my house with the upper cut straight to his gut. I felt my fist get absorb and cave in that de-flated spongy six pack. Then a combo of fear and pissed set in with the snap front kick or was it a round house? I knock his ass out make it count, so I could get my big ass out. For that moment I felt like Ali moving my feet and hands. I had the shuffle, balance, jab, jab and move your ass out the building. That kardio class paid off. I opened that door so fast, his ass didn't know what that 15 minutes could do for a body!

Lyndel smiles saying out of ther corner of her mouth ooh girl you are so violent! Neva responds, yeah while shaking her head with a slow okay. She leans back into her chair with a following up with, she should have read that imaginary note, don't screw with a married man, because you don't know when the wife will come home. Oh, when a wife comes home to her home! If that beach could read the trespassing signs, do not enter attack dog on duty, but don't know which day and in my haste forgot to post the schedule oops!! I guess she picked the day the dog was on duty. In the end Neva ended her story with a few howling and laughing sounds. Neva said that puppy, didn't know she was trying to play in the big league with real dogs and still pissing like a puppy. That beach was just a litter in the box with the other puppies. I think back to Robin leaving that box of dog biscuits with the lease wrapped around the box. So that's what she meant when she said she didn't look at the woman as being human, ooh, hmm. While we are all laughing with some of the ladies giving their support, commentating on the events it was a verbal sisterhood of love. Sisters, singing anthems that we are all too familiar with don't mess with us on a good day or a bad day.

One lady said her first boyfriend after her divorce hit her all she could hear was her mother's voice saying whoop his ass, and I did royally. I didn't have to leave his punk ass ran out the front door. As soon as I finished whooping his ass, I took a break to look at my broken nail. All I heard was the door slam. Now how quick was that from the time I looked at my nail his ass sprinted out the door, and the asshole let my door slam, now you know that was a hell no!! I calmly walked to the couch and turned the channel and crossed my legs and wondered if Kura could repair a nail? With that said, some ladies were giving out high fives. Alicia stood up saying balance me ladies as she shows motions kicking her foot out and up saying that I would kick his ass to the curve. Somehow, he would have my foot somewhere, and I would make it back in time for a pedicure. She went on to say look over here ladies surveying the room, saying I don't remember sitting down with my mate and having a conversation on me agreeing to treat me like shift and I said yes dear. I don't remember saying pass the sugar and add that abusive mind shift that you have been trying to work on my brain and emotions and shift. Oh, and add don't be putting your hands on me trying to control or scare me and shift. The last time I heard you're suppose to keep your hands to yourself, or deal with the consequences of my nervous action and she motions fight moves. It's probably unfortunate that so many women can identify with all the stories or experiences. Too bad the tricks don't stop looking for treats. Why don't they move on and find a man of their own and stop sniffing around for married men? They don't think about everytime he leaves and go back home, she is reminded that she is the other woman. Now how sad and pathetic is that case? At least the trick at Geneva's house will remember when she comes to, she will be waking up next to someone's husband. The ha-ha on her ass was at least they got to sleep together, on that cold tile, bathroom floor.

Another woman chimes in saying that they get one good boohoo moment then my ass would book. Let me add one strong ass boohoo cry. The one where you are so ugly crying the mirror is too afraid to reflect. The mirror would be saying, oh hell no, either you crack me, or I will crack under pressure. The mirror added didn't you see the sign I am closed today to your reflection make another selection, or just step away from the mirror, please. See that strong boohoo pushes out all the weak memory shift and allows strength to take over with each tear. I rather have one big cry than many installments of cries or tears behind someone that couldn't care enough to hand me a kleenex or stop my tears from flowing. Once a cheat makes you wonder, and my ass will not be looking into showers, under the bed or hiding in the closet behind some scant and a man that can't be faithful. He had to open the door, hell he was the one that had the keys, and he had to close the door behind this scant. His sorry ass welcomed the beach into his familys' home. I don't know about you? I don't have or will make any kind of time for boy that haven't passed puberty; their asses need to grow up.

See girlfriends lets take a stroll down memory lane, how would their asses act if you did the same shift to them? You know his or their ass would dump you with that double standard shift. We are quick to forgive them. As for them, they don't forget/forgive us and move it on and sometimes with a younger version of you with their old nasty ass. But one thing you can count is that circle coming back on them and they will have their boohoo moment too. We might hear about it or not, but that circle will come around, so they know how much that shift hurts. Oh, and don't leave out they might try and get back into your life that shift is up to you, but as for me once I push, I don't pull back. With that she makes a pushing and pull motion and some of the ladies push with her as they laughed. Geneva puts her hands together like she is washing her hands of the whole thing. Then it was followed up with bringing her fingers together then spreading them and rubbing them together for the finale.

I like the name Shaurice and her added comment was they need to get right so they can act right then all that shift will stop. Geneva co-signs again while washing her hands and doing the finger tips again. We had to ask what that meant. With a smile she said I washed my hands of situation and the crumbs too. I got sick of his little puppies raising their legs up trying to mark their territory. In other words, those ho hos trying to let me know they were there. Oregon stupid ass didn't see or smell where they raised their leg to leave their scent with their piss, just like a dog, those trifling ass beach. "Geneva says that's why I did that one, two and round house. I worked up a sweat using all my energy. Didn't notice or feel it until when I passed by a mirror and saw my hair was all messed up. So, I had to come to my girl Miss Mercedes and had her do my do. Get my hair done in a victory do style. I didn't realize what I had done until I heard the laughter coming from Merdie. She laughed so hard she had my ass laughing and crying too. She bought me through my tears. No charges were pressed, and I left, and the rest is history. My thoughts were no wonder Robin and Courtney Diane was called back, they fit right in. That sounds like a class I would like to take somday. This would help me get back into shape and round house Bill for that just in case. They were talking about how reasonable the prices were with the quality of service. But I don't think Bill would let me take that class knowing that one day I could round house him. Next thing I knew while I was being entertained, that my hair was tinted blow dried and curls were bumped with what little hair I had left. I know I had more than dust on a jug, I guess that's how it was said. She said that my hair was so dark that you won't really see it until the sun hits it.

I get the okays from the ladies which is nice but the only okays I want is from Bill that's the okay that counts for me. Lynel performed such a beautiful transformation on my hair into a beautiful style, I gave her a ten-dollar tip. I couldn't believe the service was so reasonable. Now I'm just waiting for the added touch for my nails/toes. Lynel told me that Kura will be in about ten minutes. Someone blurted out her ten minutes is twenty. As I sit the wait is worth it as I continue to listen to the talk and laughter as other customers come in. I'm glad I got an early start. The morning is still young, and I feel and look good. While waiting, Lynel comes out serving light drinks such as apple cider, tea, and coffee in fancy glasses. I feel like I'm in luxury, wow this is so nice! I hope to come back because this would be a me nice treat. I enjoyed being around other adults and plus it gives me a much-needed break. Gelena ask girl why you so late? Well Geneva says sipping from her straw that I told me that we needed a drink and for some reason we were all in agreeance that I should stop and get us a drink. Hmmm and it was about my me or if that will help your noisey ass a me, or I got my moment. I think back on when Geneava hand motions of washing her hands of the whole thing reminded me of Sister Tarver, she would do the same thing. Accept she would tug at the bottom of her jacket and didn't do the crumbs with the fingers, but she did spread her fingers which was her way of saying I'm done/finish. One lady had a delay response with the fingers saying sprinkles, while a few others just laugh. While I'm thinking about how much I miss Sister Tarver's strength and the beauty she had inside and out.

Lynel calls me back into her chair; I thought she might have forgotten something. I couldn't guess what it could be; I like the cut, the length and the tint that for now is not noticeable. Out of the kindness of her heart she adds to what I thought was done, she arched my eyebrows. I never had that done and it did enhance my features. Wow Bill is going to see a different wife. All that is left is for Kura to come in and give me a much-needed manicure and pedicure. They kept the conversation going on that topic. Merdie said I told Graham you hit me you die. I heard that's simple and clear cut to the point. Merdie looks over at a lady that set calmly listening. She called her Tammi and asked her, so what are you thinking about girl with that expression?? Tammi pauses saying my parents taught me that if someone hits you hit them back, so they could see how that feels. But I was raised with seven brothers and my parents held strong on boys not hitting girls. I took full advantage of that shift. I would scream out and they would just look at me. As I got older that shift wasn't funny because they got in some serious trouble. I had to apologize for that shift and then I ended up having a boy. My cousin Kentel would bring over her bad ass girls and one would always hit my son, Onnis. I would tell her daughter just because he's not allowed to hit girls doesn't give you the right to hit him. But one day and if you keep doing that Onnis is going to hit you and it's gonna hurt.

Then one day we were all at church and she decided to hit Onnis. I guess she was either trying to prove a point or embarrass him don't know, don't care. I told her little ass that if she keeps it up, he will hit her, and she will suffer the consequences. So, she hit him like my mouth didn't utter any words or made any sounds and the clock struck a ting, and he hauled off and hit her with all his years of frustration extended through his umbrella. Onnis probably hit with the same frustration that my brothers had for me. Don't know how strong the hit but I'm sure frustration was flowing through the hand he used. I guess he was saying I didn't hit her the umbrella did with a little minor assistance. Of course, little Kandance runs and tells her mother Kentel. They march over to tell me what for what? Kentel tells me that Onnis hit Kandance. I look at Kentel and down at Kandance and I repeated what I had told them earlier, that just because he's not allowed to hit girls don't give you the right to hit him. I told you that when he does hit you it will hurt. Now that hurt looking dead at her and my cousin sayng now you won't do that, again will you?? I walked away with my son and didn't look back. So that hitting works both ways and some people take advantage of that shift and can mess up someone's life. Now the other knuckle heads they need to learn how to keep their hands to themselves and that includes women. Some women need to understand that 9-1-1 is'nt your personal security guard. That's just how I feel and mine is just a small opinion, (while hunching her shoulders). I watched her slowly sip her tall glass of apple cider that resembles Courtney Diane sipping her wine at the same time, her tone and demeanor reminds me of Reva.

So far, I'm enjoying listening to adult conversation, and the debates and current issues. I can't believe that I've been so isolated from life outside our apartment. There're no put downs just everyone talking the way they can without being judged and a safe place to just unload. An older woman said out of no where that we sometimes subject ourselves to indignant circumstances and/ or humiliation all in the name of love. Not judging but to just keep a pair of pants that claim that they are men and not a little boy. But they are little boys trying to hold up their pants with both hands, instead of just growing up and showing some respect for the woman they claim they love. Their dumb ass needs to hold on to that good woman and get their ass a belt to hold up their own damn pants. Just like there is a clean up woman there is a clean up man, just waiting for that idiot to unknowningly hand her over. She then smiles that's just my opinion and who ever can use it this message was just for you. Someone else said you can't keep him if he wants to go. Then someone hollers from underneath the dryer then he should quietly take his ass on. Get to stepping with his fun pal, boy toy or playmate and they can play house, but not in my house. He needs to get some gone and leave my ass alone.

The older woman paused so they could hear the yelling and finished she didn't know who the message was for, but everyone did pause and listened. I'm enjoying this form of temporary freedom, but I will be spending the evening with my husband, with my new look and a new beginning. Kura rushes in, hmmm this place seems like everyone rushes in. I'm just glad she made it. Lynel tells her I'm here to get a manicure and pedicure. My insides giggle because I will be all made up to surprise my hubby. I'm now feeling the warm water hit my feet and the rest is history. My insides smile as they relax to the warm water massaging my feet. I can only imagine how it feels to do this often. I like this feeling of luxury. I want only clear polish because I don't know when I can return. I don't want to pick a color I can't afford to replace or the time to apply it. Once I leave all the fun I had will fade away as I return to my reality as a mommy and wife. I got to hold on to my name and remind myself that my name is still Rita, with no adverbs attached.

The morning has now gone into late afternoon and its time for me to return home. I move with hesitation because I am just enjoying listening to the many conversations. The conversations were random and sometimes loud as some yelled at each other while sitting under the dryers. Wow this shows that life is still moving. My nails, toes and head are feeling a freedom for the first time, and I'm okay. Leaving was a big difference from when I walked in the door watching people rushing in. How would Mama Florrie say it according to Courtney Diane is it time to care. They were just having fun and for once not looking at a watch. I tip Kura and I still have some mad money left. I say my good byes as some respond and others just look me as who is this? I have a skip and pep as I walk to the car with keys in my hand making me feel grown and liberated. I get in looking at myself in the rear-view mirror and we both smile at each other as I journey home. In the back of my mind how many after all that trespassing talk, which one or ones if opportunity presented itself would try to slip Bill their number if he came and picked me up? Which one would Bill be interested in? Then I hear a voice telling me to look in the mirror, that's the one he interested in. I smiled back to the mirror saying it's me and he did ask. I found a different way home by getting lost when I left the salon.

Actually, this way was faster and a co-sign to my freedom.

When I arrived home, Bill is outside throwing balls that kinda looks like a two square in a Bill, Sierra and Sabrina way. They stop to look at me with smiles and the biggest smile was from Bill. He includes the girls in saying how nice mommy looks with her hair cut and tint. Lyndel said the sun would show the tint and it did. I smiled back with a little shake I learned so well from Momo. With the twinkle showing in Bills eyes I could tell he liked that shake and my new do. He now has both worlds a new woman in the same old body. They rush over to me with kisses and hugs as if I have been returning from out of town. I guess in their own way they missed me. I missed them and the freedom I used to enjoy without consciously realizing that I gave up more freedom and myself. Somehow, I will get some more me time just like Bill. I go into the apartment and look at myself one more time raising my eyebrows and surprised that this is me. I look into the mirror, no glasses, no bruises, and no shame. This is me looking back with a smile in my soul, spirit and eyes. Weeping will endure for the night, but joy did come in the morning and this time I'm not going to ask how long it will last. I go into our bedroom and I see something wrapped in a box for me. It's a beautiful wrapped box sitting on our bed. I opened the box all giddy and excited to see a beautiful red dress for me and it's the right size. Red was always Bill's favorite color and later became Sierra's too. Sabrina was attracted to yellow and orange and for me it's always been navy blue. I hold the dress up and smile as I look into the mirror and wondering what shoes I will wear with such a beautiful dress and the box had a pair of shoes too. I didn't bother myself to wonder if or how it would fit. The size says me, and I don't care I will make this work for our date tonight. I still have some perfume and I'm feeling so giddy.

Chris and his brothers come over to see if Sierra and Sabrina are ready to come over. They were told to come over to escort the young ladies to their place. They were such gentlemen and I know little Bert wants to hold Sierra's hand, regardless that she is older and towers him. Bill smiles as he calls me to the door. He didn't know I was ear shy of hearing the young men come calling for his daughters, tee-hee-hee. I can hear the uneasiness in something that is innocent and respectful at the same time. The words he echoed many years ago saying watch us have girls and sure enough we now have two beautiful daughters and the boys are already calling, tee-hee-hee. My silent conversation with myself and my own tickle comforts me. While Bill is talking and calling me, I'm gathering things for the girls, so they can start their time early. I come to the door with bag in hand for the girls. I tell the escorts that I will walk with them and they smile saying wow you look nice Miss Rita. I smile while Bill looks at them now, you're looking at my wife but this time a smile came through. I give them a kiss on the cheek and the girls said good bye daddy as they rush off and forgetting that they didn't give him a kiss. Sierra remembers and runs back, and Sabrina watches her sister and follows her back, so they can kiss their dad good bye. I knock on the door which is a respectful habit I was taught in my early years, as Momo yells ya come on in viddles are cooking. We just need the folks to join us. Everyone laughs as we all inhale the aroma of burgers and fresh fries. Momo glances at me with a slight smile as she pats, flips and flops the burger patties. I smile back at her saying maybe and I don't mean not. She laughs as we know it's an inside joke the other faces are in ah. I finally got her! But a quick emotion comes in reminding me that soon we will be moving. Then I thought about how I would miss her and the boys. I feel that's why Bill was okay with her watching them because he knew we would be moving sooner than later. Then I added Robin and Courtney Diane too, I will have to tell them. I hope that we would stay in touch, but I havent heard from Melba or Mike since they moved back to Oakland or anyone else from the old place. Now we are moving to another new place, new adventures and learning new names and places again.

For now, it's time for me to shower and put on this red dress. As I shower Bill comes in and joins me wow, we are breaking records, not used to all this attention in a good way. We shower, and we get ready for our date as husband and wife. I put on my new dress and I hope nothing gets stuck and I don't have to stuff/tug to get into this dress. Bill watches as I dress, and I watch him get dress and splash on his cologne and the aroma sends a tingle inside that I haven't felt in sometime. He grabs me to help me zip up my dress and it goes up with ease. Bill takes my hand as we leave our apartment and he opens the door as I sit as sexy as I can instead of just hopping into the front seat. We start off to what I hope will be more dates to come. I turn the radio on and to my surprise Frankie Beverly singing "you make me happy". Bill sings this song so off key while occasionly glancing at me. His teacher was right Bill is definitely tone deaf. It really didn't matter because his singing is music to my ears. I end up joining him and now we both are happy singing off key. While watching familiar signs I have an idea where we are going ShaRoberts. I always wanted to come here and now I'm finally here with my husband in my new red dress. I can't stop telling Bill thank you and he just smiles saying all the shift you put up with me this is the least I can do. Inside I'm in agreeance with that statement, while trying to not let my thoughts surface to my face or show in my eyes.

Bill opens the door while assisting me out and we are holding hands. When we walk up to "ShaRoberts" and we are greeted by Hostess Timia and her daughter in training Precious. They both are beautiful and identical to each other. Timia shows Precious how to check the guest list and then escort them to their table. Bill covered everything he made reservations prior to us arriving. I had to ask myself is this the same man I married, hmm very impressive? Precious escorts us to our table with menus and seats us in a nice cozy corner. She was very polite in telling us that our waitress or waiter will be with us shortley. Our names must have had a special note, because the bartender came over and ask us what we would like to drink compliments of the house. Neither one of us were drinkers. I ordered a coke light ice and make it look grown with some cherries and Bill ordered a beer in which I knew that he would nurse the whole night. Wow what quick service, a lady by the name of Rhonesia bought us our drinks. She politely stated that if there was anything else, we needed from the bar she was available. So far, the service is great, and the people are so nice. I just look around at how elegant the place looks not over or under decorated. Gordon Maurice and Robin Denise, Shanta and Sheree's parents came over to our table with that familiar smile that I just can't shake and the strong resemblance to Bill. Him and Bill look like they could be twins or brothers. At that time our waitress Asia ask if we would like some appetizers before ordering our meals. Bill asked me what I woul like to order. I'm at an ah with this food list, the crab cakes sound good and coconut shrimp, hmmm! Bill agrees without looking at the price. I'm too nervous to ask what our budget is. I just look at the menu and Bill ask how about a steak and stuffed lobster?

Inside I'm trying to refrain from acting like I haven't been out before. The only time I ate steak was either when I shared with my dad or when there were steaks being cooked at my parent's house and that didn't happen until we were older. As for lobster I never had lobster but was willing to try. I look across the table smiling saying that sounds good to me too. Right when we were finishing up our order, Gordon Maurice wants to show off his vintage car to Bill. Bill smiles at me as if he was waiting for permission. Wow this must be a magical night I go with the flow and give Bill a head nod that it's okay. Robin Denise sits down I think to keep me company since her hubby took my hubby away. I look at her and her face looks familiar too. She has a smooth complexion with light dimples and laugh lines. Her eyes twinkle and close slightly when she smiles, and her eyes are both blue and brown. I ask was she wearing contacts and she smiles saying no and that she gets asked that a lot but no that's the nature color of her eyes. Her demeanor, calmness in her questions and answers, reminds me of Robin. Sheree resembles her more but has a combination of both parents and Shanta resembles more of her dad with a slight bit of Robin Denise in her, but you can tell that they both are sisters. This was the first time I set down and talked to Robin Denise. We sampled Chef Harris "Chef specials" but this was different. We had a lot in common both of us and our husbands were from the midwest. Right before I could ask where they were from Shanta and Joel come over and kiss her asking if she was staying. They greet me with a smile and kiss and welcome us to their resturant and to enjoy the food. They said that later tonight they will be having a jazz band playing for us no cost. Inside I'm thinking of yes but, I tell them that I had to be respectful and check with Bill. I ask her if Mr. Woodson was working today and Shanta slow response was oh yes, great! I ask why does he always call out the names? Shanta responds with an emotional outburst, with he loves to front with me, (but I altered the adverbs like I normally do). Her quick oops and Robin Denise response was just pretend that your mother is in the room and to my surprise Shanta said yes Robin.

I smile so she calls you Robin? Robin says yes, and Shanta has been doing this since she was two and everytime she does I correct her, and we have been having this on-going debate for over thirty years. I laugh with her I thought I was the only one going through this with my daughter Sierra. Shanta says I can tell the names and the events Mr. Woodson is going to call out, because he looks at my date event log. On cue and his ears probably were burning, Mr. Woodson comes out shouting out the event log with; Mario and Luz celebrating their daughter and son graduation, then there is Carroll and Lillian anniversary party and include the Joann and Terry's retirement dinner and there is a conflict with Brandi, Gerald, and Toni's party for their mother Melody. All this has been taken care of so that's why I smile at him and keep it moving. Then she motions to Robin with their fingers going five, four, three, two, one, countdown. Then on que we will hear Mr. Woodson start fussing with Coleman about anything he can throw at him that will stick to the wall. I ask why is he still here? She smiles again with this smile that looks so so very familiar saying we are all family here. Inside I felt the warmth, that I feel everytime I come here.

I asked Robin what she did for a living and she told me that she retired from the Fire department as a Deputy Fire Marshal and that she gets on her daughter, Shanta, about her crowd control and in the count down of five, four, three, two, one Mr. Woodson lets me know in his concerned way when we have exceeded our capacity. Matter of fact my baby brother Terry was the Fire Marshal and it's his retirement dinner and his wife Joann is retiring from "Personnly Yours". I gasp oh no she can't retire her food hmmm. Robin smiles I know but they are retiring and traveling together and spending time with their grandchildren. They can't travel together if one is still working and they want to travel while they are still young. I asked how you could work with your brother. Her response was we weren't blood brother/sister we just argued and fussed at each other just like we were sister and brother. We both spent thirty plus years of our life dedicated to the fire service and now it's time to pass the baton. Wherever he was I was there right by his side, people would look at us and wondered why we were arguing and really that's just how we communicated. But the funny part we would pause to see why people were looking at us because we did it so often. We really didn't pay attention until we noticed that other people were either smiling or laughing at us. While I look at her pleasant demeanor the yelling reminded me of Shanta's family friends not in blood but acted like sisters Carissa and Chantell. Carissa, the oldest, was always yelling about something. She always seemed preoccupied with things on her mind. Chantell, the youngest, was the calm one. Very level-headed and had a sweeter personality. I looked at them probably the same way people probably look at Robin and Terry.

Wow I can't get over how much she reminds me of Robin and Shanta reminds me of Courtney Diane and Sheree reminds me of Robin's daughter Nicole. Small world just like they say everyone has a twin. As Robin begins to excuse herself Bill comes back talking about Gordon's vintage car. I listen to him and we talk about much of nothing. I'm just enjoying the atmosphere and Bill. I want to absorb this into my memory and bring it out when needed. Bill compliments me on my new hairstyle and he never would imagine me with short hair and this time I didn't hide behind my glasses. I laugh me either, but I thought it would be a nice change, maybe add some spice to our life. He laughs with Sierra and Sabrina they are more than enough spice. You know Momo and her boys are spoiling them, and I don't think they are missing us right now. At the same time, we both ask could we stay for the jazz band. With the girls being cared for by Momo and the boys we both agree maybe staying an hour wouldn't hurt, but Bill made it very clear that they will not spend a night. I don't mind because the night should end with us all under the same roof. The music is as nice as the dinner. I remember how good the lobster was and just the whole evening. Bill smile saying that we should have been doing this lot sooner and thank you for putting up with my shift. I smile saying is the aroma going away? At first, he didn't get it then he smiled showing his deep dimples and the only thing we could do was smile at each other.

In between the dinner and jazz band the DJ played, and we danced. Funny that as fine as Bill is, he still can't dance, and he seems to have passed that gene onto his daughters. At least until my family stepped in. We danced fast, slow and I felt like I was on a first date, prom date and this time it felt so innocent. I didn't want this feeling or night to end. As we prepare to leave and cover our bill we are met by Shanta and her mother thanking us for coming. With a quick rush to us was Gordon Maurice stretching out his hand to thank Bill for coming. They took the bill from us and said this was your first time enjoying our place compliments of "ShaRoberts" and we hope to see you both again. Bill reassures them that we will be back and with that my soul and heart embrace a deep breath of that would be so nice. We hug one another and realized that it is later than what we realized, and we had to pick up the girls hoping that everyone is up. Bill has made it very clear that the girls will be coming home. Right as we leave Mr. Woodson flips the script on the waiting Shanta. She's ready and responds with the event calendar log. He just smiled at her saying you got everything right? She pauses saying its right your right. His response was its all right and dances back to the kitchen singing. She looks at her mom and they look at each other hunching their shoulders. I smiled at them because we knew the inside joke. Right in that quick of a second Shanta looks at her mom Robin Denise saying I forgot to add. Right before she finishes her sentence Mr. Woodson is standing there quietly. Shanta looks at him after glancing at her mom with both saying did you put Tonyita retirement dinner, didn't see it on the schedule!! Funny ha-ha they were both on the same page and it was very entertaining. They showed that the same blood doesn't have to flow to be family and respect exists on all levels. When we left, Bill and I were added to their family. I think we are more family than we think, that smile and looks seem so familiar?

We walk to the car like a couple in love. I grab Bill's arm as I feel his embrace of acceptance. On the way home, I just lean my head back closing my eyes and just mentally enjoying the day, the dinner and our slow dance. Glazing at the stars being as bright as the smile that Bill showed with dimples and twinkling almond shaped eyes. A song on the radio that played in my heart when I would go back home and come back seeing how happy Bill was to see his girls played on the way home "every time you go away you take the biggest part of me". When I listened this time when he left, he took a big part of me too. Unlike what Geneva said about her hand was already on the door knob his action just allowed and gave her a reason to turn the knob and leave. This time in my case I will hopefully turn the knob to a new beginning and the first stop or turn will be our apartment as we prepare to move to a house with a large yard. The ride seemed so long. I closed my eyes and enjoyed the fresh air and the breeze that made its way to my scalp since my hair is so short. While the evening is coming to an end I realized again, I'm growing up and leaving another family again. I guess this is the military life packing and moving, but emotions of leaving new friends you place in your heart is not quite as easy. But I guess you deal with it in your own way and you keep it moving. How was it said walk and talk and keep it moving don't runaway or run around me and get your ass hit and if you turn around just smile.

I feel like Cinderella and my prince is holding my hand. The complex seems so quiet. I glance up at Courtney Diane's apartment and it looks dark. Maybe she might be resting, but I don't think so. How did she say it, I don't like to be around people when I'm sick because I'm a mean sick! Funny as I think about it, she always adds" er "so should "er" be added to mean. Actually, she's not really mean, just no blue skies and straight forward thinking. Good thing the twins are not around. Funny that as I think about the JJ's I haven't seen them or heard their kids either. Robin must be out with her girls, Denise and Nicole. I can't believe how old they are getting and are still active and developing into strong young ladies with a since of direction. I hope and pray that I will do the same with my girls, Sierra and Sabrina.

Bill and I walk holding hands to Momo's and little Bert answers the door yelling that we have arrived. With Momo responding let them in and closed the door sir. I heard what I haven't heard in years was yes ma'am. Coming from Momo 's family that form of respect would be the only thing coming out her boys' mouths. We walk in smiling and Momo laughs looking at us. Then directs her eyes toward me saying that we both look good, (smiling), while asking did we make a detour before coming here? Ya young and it shouldn't take that long for a quick smile and an after glow. We both laugh because we knew just what she meant. My response was maybe before or maybe it's coming! Bill gives me a nod co-signing my response. I had to admit that it did feel good that Bill and I were on the same page again. Momo's family had many conversations going. Bill talks with Amos which was very rare but good to see and hear. Bill can be very sociable but he on the other hand Bill can appear to be very shy. I carried Sabrina and Bill carried Sierra and they both seemed worn out. I knew with all that energy the boys had and Momo's filling dinner did the job, or did Momo silently do that on purpose...

Momo being Momo was her way of just making sure the evening ends perfect. I think about her smiling saying with some flip flopping and I'm not talking about these patties. Then my response pops in visual with ew. But in this case, I'm going to use this visual and store it into my memory bank. Yes, that sounds mighty fine, for just in case. Bill smiles saying let's hurry up and get the girls in bed. I felt like we were dating again, and joy rushed through my body as Bill does a little dance while getting the sleeping girls ready for bed. All I wanted was to be intimate in a way of just lying next to him or seeing if my head still hits the spot on his chest. I just want to enjoy the quiet moments of lying there listening to our hearts beat together, until the sound fades giving me comfort to fall off to sleep and wake up to Bill snoring. That night we put each other to sleep and became one again. I woke up to looking at my husband and he was looking at his wife and that would be me...

Chapter 50
The Twins Have a Story
for Courtney Diane

The girls are still sleep and, (smile), we took advantage of the time. We decided together to pick our chores. I said I would do the laundry giving me a break from housework and Bill took on cleaning the apartment. Bill has always been better at cleaning than I was. The floors looked like you could eat off them and Pine-Sol aroma lingered all through the apartment. He slaps my butt and I do my little shake as I go to the laundry room ready for spending some time there. The same way it began was the same way it was ending. Courtney Diane comes down with a small basket of clothes, with news that she would be moving on a permanent to Florida. Henry Luis was doing good and she liked his girlfriend Bernadette and they might be having her first grandchild and she wasn't going to be a long-distance grandmother. I agreed with her because I miss my mother Cheryl and dad Eddie and the fun the girls would have with them. I envy her for being able to be there for them and she needed the change and the JJ twins helped. She went on talking about her cousin JJ wasn't getting her child support you know from the baby daddy and they he had started another family. She heard he was doing good as she struggles living here with my sister JJ. That's a problem I didn't have, Malcom David always came through with my money. I laughed saying did he have a choice? Out the corner of her mouth here we go with oh hell no! My response was a slow okay. She looks at me with slightly closed eyes for interruping her but did her tee-hee-ha-ha.

Well cousin JJ didn't know where he lived and didn't have a current phone number and none of his family members would tell how to get in touch with his trifling dead beat ass. He had put his daughters on a shelf out of reach and sight. They didn't care how trifling he was because they were just as trifling. But JJ's other side of the family is treacherous. There is always a but, his other baby momma told on his ass and she didn't have his number, but she knew where his ass was working. A scorned woman comes in handy. Now you know where this is going. She took my limp leg sister to his job and just waited for him to leave for lunch. Smart move followed him off the job site, you know the man needs to stay employed that defeats the purpose. I never could understand why go to his job and get his ass fired. That defeats the purpose, now two idiots that are not supporting their child/children. JJ knew where he would go for lunch, because she had been following his ass for a few days. A lot of things happen in the parking lot of this fast food place and JJ was going to add one more thing. JJ, Jazelle Jalese, (we just call her Jaz), I got to give her props she followed Yardley for a few days, so she knew his lunch break and where he ate everyday. She jumps out of her car calling his name and of course in true fashion he acts like he didn't hear her yelling ass. You and I know her voice does carry. She could wake a dead person up and they would tell her to be quiet. Now the way I'm telling this story was how it was told to me by my sister JJ, Juanita Janise.

Jaz had two purses one on her shoulder, one was large which she always carried, and was always flat, because the girl ass always stayed broke. There was no need for a wallet, back pocket for ID, front pocket for keys and phone placed in her rack sack. This time the purse that was flat was now looking heavy. She had some of her childrens' school books inside. Oh, hell why would the kids need to review their school books for homework, right while shaking her head and raising her eyebrows?? Then she had a smaller clutch type purse in the other hand that had rolled quarters for her laundry and when they broke, she would still have her wash money. She was saying all this with a straight face just like Courtney Diane was saying. I guess that look must run in the family. Jaz calls Yardley again like a warning!! She moves her feet like what a charging bull would do. This time he adhered to the change of her voice. She charges him as he turns around. Jaz bends forward and runs her head straight into his stomach. All you heard from him was a hard strong "oof" sound. She backs up and with the larger purse she wraps that strap around her wrist and whips it right to the right side of his head making a hollow sound and backed the left with the clutch purse and hearing those wrapped quarters break. Jaz knocked his lankey ass down that shift happened so fast, and his 6"3" height meant nothing lying down trying to block her blows. She was talking to him as she beat or just whooping his ass. Calmly talking with each blow came a soft sentence just for his ears. Get this she didn't want everyone in her business. The people were watching but Jaz had their ass scared yet entertained. JJ said I had to ask what she whispered, and I hope I get it word for word because her words were tight. She had this entire shift planned out.

Jaz told him that before the police come and arrest me remember these words and embed them somewhere. If I don't get my child support of $250.00 on the 1st and the 15th of each month. Now, if I'm available I will kick your ass, do my time and get out and wear my foot or feet out on your narrow ass again until… Yardley if I'm not available due to jail time you will get some visitors. I will recruit my crazy ass cousins on my father's side know as the CraCra's. They are well known and peolple are too afraid to call them crazy and usually when they are in route running all you hear is your cra the "zy" just fades into the wind. They are everywhere, and they don't multiply they just get paroled. Now I won't be available for few months depending on how much time they give me, but here is my deposit slip with my bank and routing number and no checks unless cashier checks, or money orders or cash. If you're not in the caring mind of the welfare of our daughters, I will help you. I need for you to listen very very carefully. Now when she was saying this, she was saying her words very slow for clear understanding. No one could hear her and yet she had a captive audience and that didn't bother her to them they all were invisible. She continued whispering that I will send associates in varous sizes and age groups from the CraCra side. The youngest CraCra was kicked out of five-day cares before he was five and the 6th one didn't count because they called his parents before they arrived. He's now in kindergarten. I will get him and his buddies to come and kick the shift out of your knee caps. Every day that my money is not in my account that I provided for you will get your ass kicked by a smorgasborg of CraCra's and their associates or cousins until the money has been deposited each month. You don't know them but they all will know you!

Now the second request is if you try to quit this here job, the ass kicking will be doubled until the only safe place for you will be in jail and I have even more CraCras' there. Jail for them is like a family reunion on the state or county and they have many reunions on a constant basic. So, when one set leaves the others are entering. JJ was very clear on how the CraCra's communicates. She said that their conversations go like this; hey I haven't seen you in years, and they proudly say ah man I just got out from doing three to five or nah man cuz I acted nice and shift I got off on good behavior in eighteen months. Again, their release dates are like a family picnics or reunions. They proudly share with you the time they served with so much honor. For them it's like taking a fresh big breath rather they are coming or going both mean the same to them. When you say time to them, they think your talking about jail time. Those fools don't wear no watch don't feel the need for one.

She looked directly into his swollen black eyes requesting signs, if Yardley understood for him to take a deep breath. Now get this funny ass shift, JJ showed compassion for his response. She clearly said flare your nostrils or take a deep breath, so she could feel or see his chest rise. Yardley could barely move, and his eyes were swollen but he could hear. One more thang sick leave or being tardy is not an option you will exercise. Today you have an excuse for sick leave, and you don't want to go back to work because of the swelling in your eyes. But once you can see clearly with both eyes your ass will be back to work and on time. Again, you will be on your best behavior at this here job. Now this was a quick history lesson don't let the history follow or find you. Because there were many pages and chapters I skipped around.

Now again what was the sign for you understanding my simple requests. She had Yardley doing all kinds of inhaling and exhaling that he understood. He understood enough because he was trying to blink through his black swollen eyes too. JJ also added that if you alter my name make sure you add Miss give me my respect, I'm the mother of your first two kids. By that time the police and ambulance arrived, Yardley was loaded onto the gurney with a collar around his neck. Jaz looked at him and took a deep breath with her eyes slightly slanted as if she was using laser to penetrate his mind with her eyes, as she was handcuffed and placed into the back of the squad car. He painfully blinked because I think she might have cracked his ribs when she was straddled on top of him. Somehow Yardley managed to show her through spreading his nostrils he fully understood. She said she might have seen a tear trying to make its way down his cheek. You would have thought she felt sorry for Yardley. Nope she said she didn't support the tear that his trifling ass genera-tated. In other words, don't put your tear on me. I had many of tears trying to take care of our kids from living from pillow to post, trying to buy food, and diapers, all that survival shift. Where was his ass when I was in a boohoo momemts struggling with no support or visitations with his dumb ass?

Jaz wasn't in the apartment because her ass was in jail and I took her children over to Aunt Gigi's. Aunt Gigi's wasn't too happy to get her grandchildren under those circumstances, because she didn't know how long they would be staying. They were altering her life style. You know she trying to be a cougar and shake those tail feathers, and she didn't want them to see that she has grand little cubs. Although, I was very impressed with Jaz actually rather proud of her standing up for her children the best way she could using all her and her family talents. In my mind I wasn't used to hearing detailed ass whipping, so I asked would that really happen? Courtney Diane smiles maybe not, but her cousins are crazy and that was a good ass bluff huh?? Jaz admitted that she could have handled it a lot different because she put her liberty on the line and add to the girls another missing parent. It was just that she grew frustrated in trying to do it the right way and her patience wore thin when she found out that he moved on. Yardley moving on was her not the problem, it was the fact that he moved on and conveniently forgot what he left behind. This wasn't packages or discarded trash, but his daughters and she had to stand up for them. It wasn't like they weren't ever together. They had been together for over ten years. Whatever you must do to get what you need, to get done, just do what you got to do, and consider it done. She got her money and to my understanding it wasn't late, and he didn't miss any work. Yardley was a very exemplary employee. He would come pick up the girls with his car running for just in case and she smiles. I can see Jaz doing that oh familiar corner smile that seems to run in their family. Jaz got her money, but I had to check on my cuz and sister that was the reason for me coming home. I looked up JJ and once I caught up with her, we had a serious sit-down talk, that beach.

JJ avoided my calls, but I finally caught her ass. I had to get, the get down on what was wrong with your ass not calling me about my damn apartment. I had to get some damn written notice and annoying phone calls about my place. Here I go again interrupting while Courtney Diane is letting it air but, this was a question I needed to know did the CraCras' work? Surprisingly she responded with her corner smile yeah, they get temporary/occasional jobs. My response was at least they're able to get jobs! That's good to hear they can work, you know get jobs. For that quick moment she showed the look Reva gave me at the clinic when I told her I had indigestion. Her look was more of a stare of that you're not getting this?? Courtney Diane says you're funny. With that I laugh saying is that with a" y" or" e" ending? She responds with I would tell you to kiss my ass, but you have back up. In the back of my mind I thought what Robin would always say you don't have an ass just a long back and can still do the wall test. But if I said that with one look or hit, she could embed me into the laundry room walls. In a typical manner she goes back to where she left off with, she shouldn't have to fly back here to handle their shift. Get this Rita JJ said that she feared me. She did all this story telling stalling from me getting into her ass. All that talking and sharing everyone else shift and put her reason on the back burner. Get this shift, even the flame from the burner dies off or goes away and then she was left with now what? I told that heffa that your crazy limp ass can take another woman's man/husband, not worrying about getting your ass kicked, knived, killed or shot and let's put possibility of going to hell, but your dumb ass was afraid to call me?? What the hell, did she think I skipped rope and fell or tripped on stupid. I could have yanked her ass right through that phone. Mama Florrie kept her ass hidden from me because she knew I was looking for her. I just had to rest and after that she was my first morning priority now that I have energy. So little sister I'm giving up this apartment and moving out and buying a place in Florida.

Henry dumb ass finally got it right. On my way home, I saw that boxed shaped heffa Melinda sitting on the bus stop. She had one child hanging off/ on each side of her neck and one sitting in her lap. They looked like they were all hers'. I guess she found someone to ride up that ramp at least three unprotected times. Not judging that was on her and whom ever. I'm just glad that wasn't on Henry 's dumb ass. That could have been him losing everything to work a couple of jobs to take caré of his family. I couldn't stand by and watch her having my son working his ass off, while Miss Thang would keep popping out those babies as his career fades away into formulas and diapers. I had a front row seat to watching my dumb ass brother Corey Davon's wife Casee popping out babies. Henry's professional basketball career is in place and I like Bernadette. She's what his ass needed, and she keeps Henry dumb ass straight and on track. Bernadette is finishing up her nursing and looking forward to working on her master's after the baby is born. Marriage is in the picture but it's on their time not mine. She said that she had actually met someone.

Then in the middle of her staring at me she paused in her thoughts...

Courtney Diane gave me a look of proudness and said that she liked my short haircut, and that it bought out my features, especially since I didn't have my glasses on. Her corner smile widens saying that, now we can see your eyes. You're prettier than you realized stop hiding behind your glasses. I knew what she was saying was out of love but I'm afraid of too much attention. I don't want to get in any trouble with Bill. I'm glad she noticed but happier that Bill paid attention to me and we can still feel each others heartbeat. I take a deep breath and tell her that we will be moving near the base. Bill's friend Kegan and his family was stationed in Italy and he wanted someone in his house. The house is partly furnished with more bedrooms than I had expected with a big backyard. She must have picked up some sadness in my voice and just smiled saying that's sound good for you and Bill. The girls need space to play and it will be good for you to get out of here. There's nothing wrong with this place but now you need to grow and let go. I will be around and now you have a place to come and visit. The girls would love to go to Disney World and if Bill comes, we would find something to keep his ass busy. I smiled but inside I couldn't fathom where we would get that type of money to travel let alone go to adventure park. As I listened thinking that the change would be nice. Plus, I would get away from that faded blue mark that remains on the hallway wall, and as I slept alone wondering where my husband was. This move would change or alter those memories.

I started thinking more about how the girls will miss playing with Momo's boys, (aka big/small brothers), and we would miss little Tim too. He would always hide in our bathroom cabinet and they always look for him everywhere but there. I would miss the wiggle wiggle shake shake giggle giggle or was it giggle giggle wiggle wiggle shake then bake, what did Momo bake to go with that giggle song? With Courtney Diane moving it will be a matter of time before Robin will be moving with her girls Denise and Nicole. What she was saying makes a lot of sense and her words removed doubt about moving. Everytime I put doubt there God sends a message through someone He knows I will listen to. Robin in her way gave me a sisterly confirmation my doubts needed. We talked about her new house and my new home. I asked her was it a new home and she said it was new to her she never lived there before. Courtney Diane said that she had a nice size yard for her grandbaby to move around and for entertaining my troops. Can you picture me being a grandmother, with all that lovey dovey shift and baking cookies? My ass stopped doing all that baking and cooking the later part of Henry Luis senior year. Henry would give me the heads up that he was hungry. My response was the same all the time, and we were cool and all but you our own for vidles. Courtney Diane being that type of person baking and all I smiled saying no, can't picture that. I was thinking as she was saying it and it just came out without my tongue, brain and courage seemed to separate from each other. She pauses with eyebrow raised saying I can't believe that shift either but I am. I will spoil my grandbaby little ass and send her/him back on home. While shaking her head she just slowly smiled saying imagine that me being part of an extended family, wow that's something, what a nice blessing. I got to work on my vocabulary and shift. I laughed you mean your special adverbs. Loren introduced me to that term. While giving her direct eye contact, smiling and open eyes I waited for her response. The corner of her mouth curls, with open eyes, she says adverbs. Hmmm, I like that because I don't want the little one using granna's special abverbs in class.

So, when are you moving and what's up with this glow? Well my little sister, if you keep that look around you might just end up with another case of indigestion. When she said indigestion, she really threw me off because, her voice and expressions reminded me of Reva, again. I hope that Reva, (aka according to her mother, Miss Aberlynda constantly calling her Dorothy) was able to pursue her career. I hope her and her son and mother Aberlynda are doing fine. If Reva is still the same her strength has only enhanced with time. I laugh pointing to myself me pregnant again? I don't see that happening not in this life time. For now, two are more than enough. I laughed how I would correct people with saying I had one now I have some not one. She smiles with saying I don't know why but you sure are glowing and that haircut definitely has you looking all sexy and shift. Damn there I go again with those special adverbs. I don't know what you and Bill are going through but maybe this would be a good change. I appreciated her not mentioning the yelling and the curfew Bill seemed to mentally enforce on me. But maybe she is right this would be a good change all the way around. We need a fresh start where no one knows our name, and a backyard with room to grow not meaning any new additions just making it a family affair. The funny thing this was the furthest thing from my mind when I was younger and living in Oakwood. I wouldn't have believed that I would be married with kids and leaving my comfort zone and family. I was pursuing a career in either Nursing or Banking and adding additional family was not an added career plan. But here I am out of Oakwood in which I thought I would never ever leave and be here smiling in sunny Cali.

Humph, just like I'm doing now looking at the rain and going back and it seems like I'm right there now. Fresh rain and coffee makes a good day. While waiting for the sun to come out, I reflect and I'm thankful for the many people I have been blessed to encounter. I'm losing another family member to Florida. I hope we stay in contact. I managed to stay in contact with Debbie Ann, Sharon Denise and Melody Lynn. Although I talk to them, it's just not the same as being there face to face contact. It's not the same as being there watching our families grow up together. I missed out on my nieces and nephew's growth, but through my mother, sisters and brother I manage to keep up with them. But here I go again it's not the same as being there. They only know me through phone calls and pictures, again it's not the same. I do miss my family, but I've learned to replace them with others. Courtney Diane is still talking not knowing that I have faded in and out of our conversation. She said her new male friend, Uchie/Barlay for right now was in the service and now he owns an auto repair business. My car needed help and he came to the rescue small world uh. This was the first time I heard her talk about a man in a pleasant tone. As I look at the one short haircut Courtney Diane sported, is now long and curly in form of a ponytail making her look even younger. It seems like we switched hair lengths and styles over night. She smiles saying that Freeman didn't have any children but wanted some. There was a hesitation, he wanted some children not one. That was a hard request to fulfill and that was request just wasn't in my lifetime or my body.

She didn't want to be raising a child and grandchild together. Chasing one and raising the other one, nah. How can I enjoy my grandchild at the same time chasing after my own kid? She wasn't too old just didn't want to settle down in that way. Uchie/Barlay was cool and all, but she wanted them to enjoy each other and not be concerned about diapers and formulas, that time had passed eons ago. She said she might have to let this one go. Courtney Diane admitted that she was a lot of things and done a lot of things but, one thing was that she wasn't one sided or selfish. You had to fine tune the entire picture his happiness was her concern. But I don't want to be on the receiving end of that little possibilty of happening, (she smiles and mouths baby). You know that oops one-night stand or many years itch. She didn't want to experience being happy in a marriage then get a knock or phone call, from some sorry ass beach saying that she is pregnant or has a two-year old child by my husband. My ass would go to jail that night! Misdemeanor, felony don't matter I would be charged with something that day that moment that night! Let that thang come to my house saying I'm pregnant or showing off a child. I'll balance this shift, he would get the same treatment. I would beat his ass making sure he needed a doctor. I would balance that bat really good and have the theme song going you know batter batter swing and knock both their asses out. However, and let me say if I accepted his child I would have to wonder if they would try to make another oops at my expense. As you refer to as indigestion with a smile, some people can do that I'm not the one. That is pain I don't want to experience and with a tee-hee-hee followed up with her corner smile I might have to contact Jaz's cousins the Cracra's. You remember they don't die they mutliply through being released or paroled.

Hey Rita as she looks at her watch what time is it. It's time for a CraCras' to be released. They probably have a calendar to keep up with their release dates. Let me remind you Rita, those are on Jaz side of the family. My family is crazy enough, but we are not in the CraCra's bloodline. My ass owns a watch. I laugh saying and they do get temporary jobs. Her response was sure you're right! Then she just jumps up singing and acting out her hottie body, (she pauses), then I act like a have camera saying click. She pretends shes on the runway as we laugh through the rinse and spin cycle. That day I was pushing the courage with her. I asked how her online anger management was working out? Her eyes slightly closed, and I knew what that meant, and I mentally closed my eyes ready for the blow. Just like Henry Luis was waiting for that blow and the sound of the wind that never came the same happened to me. She just smiled and said I'm done. At first, I thought I was going to have to sit my flat ass in somebody's classroom. I wasn't feeling that classroom shift and wasn't going to make the time. I manage to not say the "f" word. Although, I miss the sensation of how good it feels to say my favorite anger relaxing word. I guess it would be close to a cigarette after sex, but I wouldn't know I don't smoke, and she smiles. I snickered as she said now, I do have some residual for my favortie word. I'm saving my favorite word for when I get a "s" for my feeling. As you know I have a feeling without the "s". Everthing has a place and time. I look at Courtney Diane with amazememt and love. I'm really going to miss her and her special adverbs.

I look around at the various apartments and realized I will miss; Robin with her girls growing into stronger young ladies, Momo and Amos and their sons growing into polite strong energetic young men, Clarence and his stories and the support he has always given to me in a special way that he probably didn't know. I have got-ten over the goodies baked by Keith, but he is happy in their new house with his wife Kiente. When I first meant Keith, he came over to borrow a cup of flour. He probably thought I was either shy or psycho because I would open the door wide enough to see his face and just enough, so he could hear me. It meant so much when he would bring over the finish products smiling. Regardless of how at first the cakes were lopsided, but he kept trying until he perfected the yummy treats. I didn't ever get a chance to tell him how I enjoyed having adult conversations with him, Clarence and Darryl Alan. Since Bill wasn't around much, I was able to talk to more adults and not be so isolated. As for Darryl Alan I will miss that hollywood smile and the kindness he always extended when he was around.

Wow I lived next door to a celebrity. This time it was harder saying good bye here than it was from the other apartment. I guess maybe because we lived here lon-ger and there wasn't that much drama. The other place we were a lot younger and growing in our own way. We tried staying in touch but that faded away into growing older in another apartment complex. The only tears I heard was the tears that I was able to generate without sound. Then eventually I managed to not generate anymore tears, so no sound was needed. The laughter and the giggles of the girls will carry on as they run and play in our backyard or the park down the street. I will miss the laughter of Bert, Ryan, Chris, Manly and little Tim running playing either hide and seek, or basketball or football as baby Bert fusses about not having good time with the ball. Little Tim english has improved but from time to time he will throw in

Dutch words with English. Sierra and Momo's sons have come to understand in a child like way what Tim is saying.

I picture the events that caused Momo to dance, when her sister Miss Minne said weren't you smaller then as Momo tried doing the hula hoop. Momo response was nope I was just younger. Then Momo went into dancing and everyone chanting; how low will you go and she said I don't know as the crowd cheers her on with go Momo go Momo and she's just smiling feeling the crowd with I don't know how low can I go until she got down low enough and her chant changed, to help me up, no really I'm serious help me up with her making a light grunt sound and broke it down with instructions in a singing manner take me to the chair, come on now take me over there and when she made she was humming the tune as she shook in her chair with that big smile, and she didn't do that again , no more how low can you go. I always love to see her cook and change everything into sex antics. I will miss the different aromas of food cooking as the aromas fade into the air as dinner is called that it is ready. Well except for when Amos tried so hard in cooking mystery dinners that aroma was such an unfamiliar smell for many long months. The boys prayed the same daily prayer make our food taste like something we remember. As Momo would say I didn't marry him for his cooking, but we do keep the pots and pans warm in the bedroom, ooh just that thought was ew vision. Ooh I didn't need that insant visual.

While thinking about food and aromas I think about Clarence's dad and his missing two front teeth and the story as Clarence ventures to find the doctor that removed his, dad's two front teeth, because he only had five teeth. Now he was minus his two front teeth. Then a vision switches into the missing dentures that my sister EJ took from Mommy and she had them and was trying to put them on top of her teeth in her small frame mouth. While my brother and I both watched in amazement as my mother insisted that she didn't have them. They go hand in hand they both were looking for their teeth. Then EJ comes to mind even more about being a good runner because her mouth always gotten her and my brother running home together. Funny come to think of it I don't think she ever been in a fight just knew how to run. I picture her and my brother running again at the same time. I reflect on EJ running so fast and missed running into the front gate. There goes my mind again funny come to think of it I don't think my brother Charles ever been in a fight. Oh, I forgot about the fight at Mommy's house and she pushed him back outside to finish the fight. Yep he did sprint away to only be forced to return. I hear myself give a quick giggle as my thoughts wondered off as I look around the complex at one-point thinking about my neighborhood and the house with the white picked fence and gate. I didn't hear all of Courtney Diane's conversation. I was enjoying seeing her again and having conversations with her. Because I know this to will fade away once she packs and loads everything to her new home in Florida.

I came back as I heard the dryer ding and her saying that you must have gotten lost in your last uh sleepless night with your Bill hmmm. Showing her signature corner smile while raising one eyebrow. I'm sure Bill tucked you in and put you to sleep. With that sentence, I think about Clarence's story of being paid $2500 to put the smorgasborg of women to sleep for that price he probably left them snoring. All she could say was that she was talking, and I had a blank look with a smile. I just played along with her because that sounded so much better at the same time felt good because last night was worth more than a small smile. She didn't know that we had been seperated what seems like months was only a few days. I was just glad to have him back in my arms again right where he belongs. Hmmm I think that's a song, but I was happy just to hear and feel his heartbeat as I laid my head on his chest and my spot was still there. Inside I don't want to leave another family but being with my husband and daughters is where I needed and wanted to be.

Chapter 51
Everyone is Moving On

Bill will be leaving soon for his two-week training. I don't mind this break because I know where he is. He managed to pick up some boxes since he has the car most of the time. Since there is no hurry, I will slowly pack a room at a time. This time again I'm on my own. No Mama Sadie to help me and now I have two daughters instead of one. Bill didn't indicate he would contribute with his hands. I mentioned to Courtney Diane that I was going to have to get started somehow on packing too. Without me asking for any help, she volunteered and said that she had some extra boxes. Although, she was having professional movers she still offered to help. I told her I will take her up on her offer. She really didn't have much to pack because she had taken some items with her to Florida. I know that she's not afraid of hard work, knowing her she just didn't want to be bothered. Financially I don't know if we would ever be able to pay for movers or be able to go to Florida. Bill reminded me that we will have other bills like dental, utilities, savings and other miscellanous bills. It was just good to hear Bill include us as speaking about us as a family. That always sounded good to my ears and made me feel that we will grow old together. Grow old together like the many older couples that I've seen throughout my childhood and including now in my young adult life. So, I know it can happen, regardless of what they went through they still held their marriage together. In holding it together they showed their children how to pass on love and support and what it takes to be the adhesive in a marriage. Bill and I are trying to keep the marriage together, because he keeps coming back and he did ask. Part of me can't wait to pack and see what a new location will bring for us and on the other hand I don't want to leave the family/friends. The friends that I have grown to love and have shown me nothing but love. My hesitation is that with an added, I hope this will keep Bill home more. I hope that there will be no more talking down to me or fear of his looks or actions. When he does that, I feel like a little girl getting reprimanded. I feel my insides getting smaller as my world caves in around me. Then after all that he would just leave. Leave me in a mystery of what did I do this time??

The mystery lingers with me never finding the answers to what did I do?

I need to move forward because this is a new place and I have to put in my mind that this is… a new beginning. I got so lost in my thoughts that I forgot about Courtney Diane and I was still talking and folding clothes. She looked at me with compassion reassuring me again that the move will be good for me, and in the back of my mind I still wonder if she knew. If she did, she was very good at covering up. I guess we all at some time we will provide a performance when needed. I guess in my performance she notices the tears filling in my eyes. But in my reality, she didn't know why and again if she did, she didn't show or say anything to indicate that she knew. Have I become that good? I had to make this work. I don't want to go back to Oakwood. I made my commitment at the altar and Bill was there too hearing the same vows. I pictured Rev. Williams sweating as he performed the nuptials as Bill, and I watched the sweat drop into his eyes. Don't forget that my dad walked me down the aisle with sunglasses on because his eyes were red, and he was drunk. I'm sure the words his mother said, and I still hear myself he had to ask. Funny but not ha-ha, what did I ask for by saying yes or I do to? I wanted to be happy ever after just like I saw in the movies growing up. That life does exist maybe not here but with the move, the ever after will come. After all we have a big house and yard. This is a beginning for family fun and events. The laughter in the backyard will be served with a fresh glass of lemonade. The houses are close but, not Chicago close. I remember while visiting my aunt and uncle watching and saying hi to the next-door neighbor as we both walked up the stairs. That was too close for comfort but, the space that we will have at this house will be more than worth it.

Bill did his job as a husband finding a larger space and thinking about his family and wanting the best just like I want for us. I'm thankful that so far, we are still on the same page and our mental communication are in sync with each other. Courtney Diane was far from being a hugger and I knew better than to make that attempt. As we finish up the last of folding our clothes the conversation slows down as she says she had to go by and see Jaz. Not only to check on her but see about her working out some payments. My mother bailed Jaz out and payment is do. My sister JJ's about my apartment and her responsibility called money is now due! I don't wanna have to add the "zy" to the CraCra name and become an insert. We may not be related but I feel a connection. Courtney Diane actually chuckles saying slowly that I guess I am reformed. Wow, those online anger management class must be working!! With that I actually received another full smile from her as she gathered up her basket in route to her apartment. I guess that was her way of saying good bye or see you later with much love and add an invisible hug. Now I need to start breaking the news to Momo and Clarence. That's going to be a hard one and not to mention Robin and the girls. I walk pulling my wagon of folded clothes again looking and placing faces in each unit and just smiling. There are no bitter memories. This was a good place for us and it's time to move on. The memories of this place, I will hold on to and not let it fade or just die away.

I open the door to hear the laughter of my family running and chasing each other through the apartment. Another sight that my memory will capture and hold onto. I join in the chase and we are all yelling while running through the apartment. Bill catches me by surprise and the girls grab both our legs and we all look like we are in a huddle full of love. He lets me know that we are going out to grab a snack nothing fancy like PataRees or ShaRoberts. Bill smiles saying that it might be as he looks down at Sierra saying Del Taco. With that she jumps and Sabrina seeing her sister jump, jumps as Sierra smiles saying yes. Del Taco was her favorite place and she loved their strawberry shakes and their bun tacos. I smile because that's a yummy for me too. We load up into the car and we are on our away. Del Taco was too crowed, and we decided to go thru the drive thru and just take it back home. It didn't bother me because on Saturdays I had cut down cooking large meals. Sundays was for big dinners, and leftovers for Monday and the rest is a guess. Not like the mystery meals that Amos cooked, but since I wasn't a real good cook it was a guess on what I could make and look recognizable. Bill suffered through the meals and his complaining about the meals have calmed down. I managed to try a couple of Momo's recipes, and she would laugh at the end results. I had to laugh myself because it didn't look like the meal she had prepared. Instead of enjoying my youthful freedom, I should have paid more attention to my mother when she was cooking in the kitchen. I was too busy having fun! Then when I wanted to help it was too much trouble to explain how to prepare when Bonnie knew just what to do. To this day Bonnie is still a much better cook than all of us. Before we married, I tried to cook for a picnic for Bill and I. My mother watched as I added ingredients to my crunchy potato salad and burned chicken. It rained that day and Bill and I just had our picnic inside, upstairs in his grandparents' house. We ate and laughed through the rain and our first picnic meal of crunchy potato salad and burned chicken. I don't know when we fell in love, but we were always together until that indigestion happened.

We talk about moving and that we needed to put in our thirty days notice. That's good to hear because that will give me more than enough time to pack and say my good-byes. Bill said that he will be leaving in a few days to go to his two-week training. I didn't like when he left but that was part of being in the service. I will miss him and now that we are together, I will miss him even more. I do have a safeguard in knowing that he will be returning. Ooh that's two weeks out of a month and we should be in our house. Wow with that in mind that's not a lot of time!! We talk about much of nothing on our way home as I looked out the window enjoying the wind hitting my face. Sierra is talkging to Sabrina who is trying to understand and respond. The aroma of the food is pleasant, and we can't wait to get home and dive in. The neighborhood is full of neighborhood children running, playing and noise of children laughing.

I see the anxious expression on Sierra's face, and Del Taco right now is the least of her concerns and playing outside has now become her priority. We both see her expression and before she can ask Bill tells her after you eat you can go back outside and play. Bill surprised me when he gave the okay with her playing with the boys. I guess he accepted the fact that they looked at her as a sister and will watch out for her. We ate at the table just like it was lunch and not fast food. As we sat at the table with the mindset that we are always a family and will always be together. I believe that break helped us both. We did miss each other and now we are family again. Sabrina has no hang time and falls off to sleep in between fries and sips. Sierra finishes her meal and with a quick look asking for permission with her expression. With that in the wind she takes off running outside and didn't let the door slam what a girl. I don't know if she knows that she is moving away from her friends, that in her way might be considered her family too. Momo is going to miss her girls and I will add myself to being one of her girls too. I glance over at Bill and his expression is of what and I just say nothing and continue with our day. I want to touch him but that is a chance I don't want to take and ruin the day.

For some reason I had to ask permission not all the time but most of the time. One day I hope that to will change. We are together, and the years have passed, and we should be closer, and I think we are. Bill and I still laugh and talk just like we are best friends in which we should be. We should be able to say and talk to each other in ways that we wouldn't talk to anyone else but to each other. We still have that only acception to this rule is I can't say how he hurts my feelings and the hitting should stop. I'm afraid to address that or those concerns. I spoke to his mother, Naomi one time about it and she said she would talk to his dad, Phil. I just needed an ear and I insisted that wouldn't work. As soon as he would get off the phone from getting chewed out, Bill will take it out on me for telling our business. They were some thousand of miles away and my butt was local and available. That was a pain that I didn't or want to volunteer for, just for asking for help. I knew my place and I didn't want it on the end of his hand, unless that hand was slapping me on my butt. We talk about packing and just small talk. We laugh about the packing that I was supposed to have been doing while he was in boot camp. This time I was doing nothing but preparing to leave mentally but not physically. When I think back on when my mother talked me into going to the movies and I had a strong feeling that Bill was coming and surprise me but listening to my mother she convinced me that was impossible. Right!! We enjoyed the movie and that night I heard a doorbell ring and I saw the silhoutte of a familiar physique. It was Bill and I hadn't packed anything or made any attempt to look like I had any thoughts of packing. Thank God for Mama Sadie, she packed my stuff so fast I don't think she even broke a sweat. Just thinking about Mama Sadie, we didn't spend much time with her but when I think about her, she had my back. After all she told my dad that Bill had to ask and that released his frustration because he listened to his mother. I guess age means nothing when you are given instructions from your mother. I still listen to my mother. I may fuss of course when she is not around, but I showed her huh. Just like Courtney Diane knew enough at a young age not to say don't you know what time it is, when her mother Florrie would look at her watch and asked what time it was. What was her famous saying checking the time to see if it's time to care? How or what response could you give and still live. That still doesn't eliminate that Mama Sadie was not here to help and it's up to me.

Bill is expecting this place to be ready for the move when he returns from his training. I knew there was a reason for my short victory. I need to walk, talk and keep it moving in form of boxes and packing, good grief this is going to be fun. This time this is a solo act with a slow or maybe a fast pace. Wow either way I'm not up for the task but someone will have to do it since I will be the only one over 5 feet that will be here. I guess it's me because the girls don't meet the height requirements. I keep trying to pump myself up to make this move. I need some type of incentivie to make those steps into packing again. But for now, I'm going to enjoy my Del Taco and my family. While Sabrina sleeps Bill and I just lay on each other watching television. No job to run off to, no phone interruptions just us, while Sierra is playing outside. She will play until she drops and falls asleep wherever her body lands, just like her little sister. Sometimes we would have to look for her when she got quiet to find her sleep either under the kitchen table or on the other side of the living room table or couch, out of sight and snoring.

We start talking about Loren and his Fifi stories. Bill didn't know about the breakfast served on Loren's car followed up with a love note. We laughed together as I told him about her bag of medication aka candy. Bill didn't add too much to the story, he probably would if it was just him and Loren. Any way the sounds of our laughter reminded me of how we used to laugh and talk, and it felt as if we were rekindling the old us into a new beginning. During our tranquility the phone rings as we look at each other like who is going to answer the phone or who could this be? To my pleasant surprise it was Robin responding to the news she received from Courtney Diane, that I will be moving. Inside I wanted to tell her myself, but Courtney Diane telling did help release all that tension of how to say the words that we are moving. We talked about the house and since Bill was ear shy, I could see and feel the proudness that he did something good for his family. I talked about how the house was the right size for our family and that we had a large backyard and when we are settled, we will invite her and Courtney Diane over for a barbeque since we will have the space. In her way Robin supports the move but will miss her baby sister while giving me words of encouragement. She talked briefly that she was away on an assignment, and the girls were staying with Ramon and his stripper girlfriend.

I can feel her smile coming through the phone when she said that it was cheaper to have her do her private dance than continue to fork up those hustled dollars. I guess the chain broke and the dog biscuits ran out.

So, I asked through my laughter as Bill looks at me wondering what, but not involved in our converation. I asked was it trixie? Robin responds with nah he had several trixies after that trick. I told you that they don't move up, they move out in form of replacements. Well let me take that back they do move up until they are replaced. You know recycled /regenerated scants. With that I ease up from the table and move to another room for more privacy and not to annoy Bill. Bill looks at me like why you are moving? The whispers start as I enter our bedroom. In this case it's not what he may think. I'm laughing and talking loudly, and I want to talk to her before the ting of the sound that my phone curfew is up. This is not like the case like Ramon when his low talking turned into whispers and leaving the room and then turned into an affair. This is definitely not the case. I'm in love with my Bill. If I wanted someone else, I had opportunities from past boyfriends and other suitors. I smile with that as I look back at him don't think that you couldn't be re-placed. It was a good day tee-hee-hee and I just decided to marry you because you asked. Plus, Bill knows me, and he knows that I wouldn't ever think about straying. Unless his own conscience caught up with him and he starts feeling a little guilty. As for me I'm like his puppy in a sense being faithful and loyal. But in no sense am I a puppy or his dog. Robin talked about her larger projects that had her working in San Francisco and that she enjoyed being back in the bay area. While she was there, she was visiting her parents and house shopping. It's time to make that move while Denise and Nicole are still young. We both agreed that maybe this was the time for us to all make that move and that she will still stay in touch with her little sister. I tee-hee-hee because that little sister being me.

She laughed saying that she tried talking to Ramon about their daughters while they were staying with him, and his response with much tude was that I couldn't tell him what to do in his house with his daughters. Sure, enough the girls came through being themselves. Them being themselves got me a phone call with a pause saying its Ramon. He's fussing about the girls and I told him in his own words; I don't think he got this, but they are your daughters in your house, and you deal with them because, I can't tell you what to do in your house. I was so proud of them not letting me down. I told them to not be kind give your dad what you give me and don't be shy. After all Rita, why should Ramon miss out on their wonder years? He was just fortunate to have the accelerated version of Denise and Nicole. I guess our girls came through. I bet he had fun when he got to use that Mertruck he made and running the girls around to track practice, piano lessons and all that other stuff. Ooh, hmmmph don't forget to add the tude the girls showed when they had to adjust to his lifestyle. Denise said they went to the store and purchased one bag of groceries for the whole house that was so new to them, payback is something uh?? You know that felt good and I gave myself an imaginary toast with here, here I toast to that too!!

Then we went on to how Fort Marshal was working out for Courtney Diane. Down there she probably acting like Sonya doing her special walk and getting away with everythang and then we both say in sync and giving up not a thang. We tee-hee-ha-ha and whatever and don't say the "f" word because she's reformed. As we laughed, and our laughter is similar, and it was then I realized that I share more with Robin than I thought. Courtney Diane's courage I was afraid to exert just came out of me. Somehow with the many conversations going we ended back on Courtney Diane and her dates. Miss Social was on hit down there especially with the privates. They thought she was younger than she looked. She was purring, cuddling those privates with her old butt. Oops that's right and I chime in with she doesn't have no butt. Robin said, no pun meant but it worked they still were checking her out with each cadence. Robin laughs did she tell you about Eli or Uchie/Barlay. I think there might be few more. She had so many at her I couldn't remember all their names, because she talked about them and those two wanted children. She said Courtney Diane had her cracking up about them wanting babies. She said Uchie or Che wanted a few babies, meaning two, right?? Eli wanted some meaning more than one and less than a few. Courtney Diane said that all was blue skies and she said if she did have one more or a few or many slap her. If she did some mess like that, she would send out invitations to kick her ass and no repercussions, straight up your foot to her ass. You know how crazy she is. With all that said you know that she's having fun. I'm sure she's using her choice words like you call them special adverbs. Then it goes into I guess her online anger management classes paid off.

The last thing Courtney Diane wanted was her parts being all stretched out because of the few or some discharges. This exit is closed to the baby processing out of her wound. Eli didn't help he had a twin brother Trenton/Trent and you know how she feels about that twin stuff. She knew with Eli, she would have some in forms of twins and then some. So, if some was out, a few was not going to happen in any way, not with Miss Sonya. I shared with Robin the fear my mother- in- law Naomi had about having twins since her husband and all the brothers were twins and his mother was a twin. So, I could see the concern. That same concerned filtered onto me both times I became pregnant. I barely could handle one let alone two, ooh. Robin laughs with saying that she was so glad she dodged that bullet and never had concern about two growing in place of one. Her girls Denise and Nicole were enough for her and they had their own strong personalities. Her girls weren't shy in showing Ramon and his house guests their respectful strength. That's my girls! I told them to don't be shy and just be themselves. I guess this is one time they listened uh? We both laughed as I pictured her laughing and showing her deep dimples through her beautiful smile. As Bill is wondering what all the laughter is about, I know my curfew bell will be activated soon. I continued the conversation but, at the same time keeping track of the time I've been on the phone. Robin and I get back on the subject of Miss Sonya, or Courtney Diane about one private that they met, and words were unspoken or spoken. She was given a dress jacket that needed alteration and Private Date made a comment in the presence of Courtney Diane. Very bad timing, asking who owned this big ass jacket repeating who did this belong to? You know how she said it probably with a corner smile pausing fighting back the words or special adverbs she wanted to say, but her response was the nice. She firmly stated that the thing about my jacket is, that she can shop in the men's department and reach the hangers. She looked so far down at this private, Date, that her eyes almost looked closed at the petite private and she (Sonya) walks away. Funny she said she could see out and he could look up and see in and they both knew without too much conversation what time it was. Knowing her she was laughing in the inside with her tee-hee-ha-ha and finishing off with whatever while leaving the private dumb founded, (or was it with your dumb ass). Yep she used that psychological warfare that she learned from Mother Florrie. Robin laughs harder let me correct myself petite is what we were in high school and cute. Private Date was just rather slim from the way she described him. She said this little solider was not for her with his sawed-off little ass, (adding something needs bleaching). He was cute but so far away from being her type, one being vertical. I was laughing so hard and time got away from me and sure to timing I stayed on the phone longer than I should have. It's not liked the phone is ringing off the hook because I'm always afraid of the phone being turned off. The calls I used to get back home just faded as everyone went on with their busy lives. So, I can understand Bill's concerns to a point. Bill comes back to the back passing our room glancing at me and I knew that was my cue to gracefully end this much refreshing entertaining call. I tell her I need to go and check on the girls as we slow our laughter down. In the typical Robin manner, I can feel the warmth of her smile and deep dimples coming through the phone saying that she was just checking on me and will be coming hopefully back home soon.

As I get off the phone, I see Bill carrying sleeping Sabrina. Her head looked so peaceful lying on his shoulder as Bill shows a big smile while carrying her back to the couch. I join him and didn't really share with him what we were talking about because he probably wouldn't find the humor, we were indulged in for less than fifthteen minutes. I join my family on the couch and pick up where we left off laying on each other with an added half of body laying in Bill's lap. Sierra comes in for a check on us break then goes back outside not slamming the door. No plans for the rest of the night just enjoying each other before Bill leaves for his two-week training. So much has happened in a short period of time. I'm going to miss him but glad we were together before he leaves. I want us to make it and I wonder sometimes does Bill know or care about how hard I'm trying. He comes home to a clean apartment with dinner ready and his children clean and ready to greet their dad. Bill has what his friends always tell him they wanted. Fellow co-workers like Sulli, Bragg, (aka ow ooh), and just to name a few. They come around and to me they all look the same just different names that I stumble with trying to remember. I do remember one thing they all look nice in their uniforms especially my Bill. I count down the days that Bill will be leaving, and I count down the days that he will be returning. This time we will be moving into a new home that will prepare us for our home. Funny I'm missing him before he leaves, and I hope this love and missing will last. As I sit here reflecting on the comment can't even remember who made this statement, that you should enjoy your freedom when they are away. Because, sometimes they look better leaving than coming.

Just think, while Bill is gone no orders and a break from honey while adding the "can yous". You know; can you pick this up, can you cook dinner and bring it to me, can you kiss my....? Now when you're hurting or sick then they start acting like they can't move, then you ask can you please get this while you are up? Then when you get well and with a smile and a thought of can you just kiss my ass, and can you get my ass something while you're up? Then you add a laugh, with the can you use me. I can't believe I'm here and thinking who made that comment as I look out the window wondering who said that. Was it Momo nah she loves Amos too much hmm what about Courtney Diane or was it the women at Lyndel's shop it's so fresh, yet it seemed so far in time away?

All I know is I miss Bill when he goes to work and when he is away at training. Sierra comes in smelling like outdoors and much fun. With outdoor aroma she jumps on the couch opening our nostrils including the sleeping Sabrina. With that aroma it's bath time before anything else. I politiely escort Sierra to the luxury of a bubble bath for a good soak. While Sierra soaks, I hear the playful laughter of Bill and Sabrina. I love hearing Bill laugh, playing and reading to our daughters. Their playful sounds remind me of how my father, Eddie, would play with us and sometimes let Bonnie and I both hang off of his arms. I didn't realize how strong my father was and to this day still mentally and physcially moving just like his mom. Mama Sadie was of sound mind and moved with much ease and lived to be 108 years old. My mother Sheryl hanging strong just like her mother Hazel still strong and stubborn and her grandmother, Mommy lived long and walked and was able to tell me that mentally she was returning into a child. Didn't know how old Mommy was when she passed. She didn't know how to read or write, and she never had a birth certificate. I'm thankful that Mommy was alive to see Sierra. I remember how Bill would talk so loud to Mommy and her expression was why are you yelling, I can hear you. I would have to remind Bill that his grandmother Helen was hard of hearing not Mommy. That was the hardest part leaving Mommy to start a new life with my family in Oceanview. Every Sunday mom would take us over to Mommy's and she would make dinner or make a mean peach cobbler from stratch. We would play the piano, over the phone so she could hear us. I still miss hearing her voice and telling her what we are doing so she could be proud of me. Although we closed the door to her vacant apartment, we didn't close our minds or hearts to her memories. My brother Charles goes to her plot to be close to her. I'm close to her in my memories. I graduated early just so she could attend my high school graduation, but she didn't make it because by then she was just a little tired. I'm thankful that I was able to share with her my high school dipolma and the joy that I would be attending college.

I had a head start and one encounter in the library changed it all. The alteration or detour was called Bill. I remember telling Bill the one of small manies that if they read the book before judging it by its cover that he would be a lonely book. This is a book I should have read before judging the cover. All these years later Bill is still fine and in good shape and makes sure that his body and looks continue to support his healthy physique. As for me I'm trying to hold my own. I just want to turn the head that counts and for me that's Bill. This short haircut I'm now sporting was a change for both of us. Now all I had to do is get the shape back enough, so I can see my waist again. I was always athletic in school and I just had to get that energy back somehow in between raising children, cleaning, cooking while trying to keep my husband happy. If I could put all my in house activites, into some form of high energy that would help my weight concerns. Sometimes its hard trying to maintain the look you once had that seems like so many years ago. While some men may keep their slender build, or it might have changed unknowning to their Peter Pan eyes. It seems as if they want to sprinkle pixie dust on themselves and never mentally grow up seeing their own body change. They watch you age with criticism on some minor or major changes. Only if they could see clearly and open both thier eyes.

My reality is getting ready for that big move. With Bill leaving my hands will be full of two little ones and packing. Although, Courtney Diane offered she really has her hands full with trying to make her own move to Florida. She's giggling and juggling her life, while at the same time handling her sister JJ and Jaz's untimely concerns. I would love to have been the fly on the wall with that conversation. If she could help me, I would be amused by the stories and support. We would laugh and talk as we packed and shared lasting moments that I know I will cherish. I don't know if I will ever see her again and just like my friends back home the phone calls will fade away to occasional conversations.

That fresh soak bath helped refresh Sierra enough that she wants to play with Sabrina who now has as much energy. Bill is playing with our girls as I enjoy hearing the giggles between them. I look around the room thinking this would be an opportunity to start putting things together for packing. Although, I play with them for a little time Bill was more of the kid than me. My mother never played with us, and my father was more of the funny man and played with us. I guess I inherited the vision that was embedded rule of, no playing time or limited playing with my girls. My parents both raised us, but mom was the financial partner and dad was the disciplinarian. They made a good team as I look back on how their children, (meaning me the insert), turned out okay. I do then just like now appreicate their parenting, their morals, and the hard working enviroment they exposed to us. Today I'm glad that no dinner was needed, because we were still full of Del Taco and snacking. Those zingers and ding dongs came in handy too. Many nights came and went until the night before Bill would be leaving. I looked at him and he was looking sexier than normal and I was feeling him. I made the bold move of flirting without permission to touch him. I thought and acted on that feeling. I know that was a bold move, but was well received by him, (yeah). That night we put each other to sleep again. I learned that phrase from Clarence, again I don't want to envision what that entailed, but enough work was involved to put the person into the snoring and do not disturb mode. As we both wake up refreshed and with a big smile, I know I will miss him even more. How was it said it's all in deliverance and how it's received to make that imagination work. The imagination worked enough to know we had some nice dreams. Jesse picked up Bill as I waved to him and kissed my husband good bye for two weeks. We have a car, a little money saved to enjoy our two-week freedom vacation.

Now it's time for the girls' freedom vacation for two weeks. In this case seeing him go away put a tear in my heart but the "honey can yous" will be away for two weeks too, (by honey). Plus, the place doesn't have to smell like pine-sol, oh yeah this is going to be fun! The hardest thought was what to do with this new form of freedom. How should we start the day, by going to the mall, or hanging out at the park or just go for a ride with no destination or just go with the flow. While driving we will enjoy the wind as hits our faces, then we can stroll through the mall. While at the mall I will look in the windows hoping one day I will be able to purchase the display outfits. As I work my imagination to support what I would look like sporting something new and different. The buffets are reasonable and maybe this is a place to adventure. I want to go somewhere I can comfortably keep an eye on both my girls. PataRees sounds good but that is out of my mad money price range. But seeing my new extended family would be nice, but costly. I will have to pass on that venture. It would be tacky to go and let the girls play there with Mackey and see Pat and Sheree's newborn, Jaxson without eating. After all this is their business and I don't want to seem to be taking advantage of their youth and kindness. The girls are asleep, and I just don't know what to do? I did what I'm doing now, just sitting with hot cup of Chai tea and reflecting on my life and the growth with the assistance of many people that lived in the village. When it comes to it does takes a village to raise a child, but that's up for interpretation. I'm still young and so many people are supporting me in my growth as I or they, (the village), pass by or move on.

There are no sounds outside so everyone must be still sound asleep in the confinements of their apartments. No sounds of people leaving for work or the noise from children on their way to school just a sound of quietness and peace. We have two weeks of freedom. Soooo, let's drive to the mall and stroll through the stores because, there is no curfew!! I know if I wear the girls out, I can pack items slowly, while they are sleeping or playing. It was nice of Bill to leave me boxes but no thought of how we are going to leave and what to take. My guess is let's take everything and sort it out later. All I had to do is get the girls up, have a quick breakfast, wash them up and then we will be on the road. Just us girls with a full tank of gas and momma has no curfew! It seems as if I'm more excited about the day than they are. Inside I feel like a little girl that's been invited to a surprise birthday party. After all this is a day or weeks of celebration, new move, my girls are healthy, and I have a full tank of gas with some mad money. I find myself moving and shaking. Sierra and Sabrina are laughing at me, while trying to shake their little bodies too. My response was just come and join me, and we are moving and shaking together. I inform them that we have a full day of surprises. The girls finally share in my excitement as we load and go. This time we ride until I see a mall that I'm not familar with and hopefully has a buffet with reasonable prices. As I walk toward the glass door, I see a full view of me and the girls. In my mind I ask myself, so this is what people see when I approach them. I don't know if I avoided the full mirror on the dresser but had no idea of the weight I had gained. My clothes still fit the same, so I couldn't use that as a gauge. Wearing warm-ups became so comfortable and since I really didn't go anywhere there was no need.

Once we entered the mall, I hear the laughter and many conversations as they carry bags of purchases not knowing or caring if anyone was looking at them. I look in the windows at the styles that I was still capbable of wearing and somehow wasn't aware that my clothes had become outdated and sweats were now my style. The girls are laughing and happy to see all the new stores and children toys on display. I see a store that might meet my needs "Ashley Stewart". I knew that I was the only one that could change my outlook. I can question myself on the many whys and whats and open a wound or make a difference. I'm greeted by a lady by the name of Miss Derricka and she has that familiar angelic smile as she welcomes us in. I look in the jeans direction that would be a start. I look around at the many beautiful clothes I would love to buy. But I have to stay focus on the reason why I am in here. My money is short but I'm treating myself. I pick a size up from the size I remembered I wore. The dressing room is large and as I tried on the jeans, I find myself dancing in trying to get them on. My daughters are dancing with me as I twist, pull and hold my breath trying to fit into these jeans as my girls immitate me. I can't help but to laugh but inside there were many sighs happening. Miss Derricka comes and offers help and I reluctantly ask for the next size. She bought me the next size with a smile and no judgement. This time I didn't have to do a dance to get inside this pair and they felt so good and comfortable, as I looked into the full-length mirror. I smiled as the reflections smiled back at me. When I get home the tag will be removed for just in case. I don't know if she was helping but she informed me that their pants give you an extra five percent spandex and these jeans were on sale. That was a blessing, the tag will be moved, and I will give the sweats a break. I wear the jeans out and put the sweats in the bag and stroll away as we look around this new mall, wearing my new fitted jeans.

We walk, talk, look and and as we look into the display windows and enter a few of the stores. Some were pricey, and others were reasonable. Right now, I 'm in a good place mentally and I feel really good. It's just us and a form of freedom that the girls don't know that we are experincing. I had pocket room in these jeans, and they don't feel tight and I can breathe. They have a play area at this new mall, and we take advantage of that freedom too. I have a roll of quarters that I keep for laundry but this time I'm using the change for the rides for the girls. I chuckle to myself thinking about the quarters Jaz had in her purse for Yardley and in her mind that probably was a good investment. Just like Courtney Diane said it was a good ass bluff and it worked. These jeans are feeling so right, I might go back and get a black pair almost a two for one sale. The girls are having fun and I'm enjoying hearing their laughter and pondering on purchasing of another pair of jeans on the same day. So glad Bill is not here don't need the added look for my purchase and I was not in the mood to explain. I look around at some of the women trying not to compare them to be or what Bill might be interested in. I can't mentally afford to go back to that insecure moment and have those thoughts rob me of this joy I am feeling.

When Bill sees me in these jeans, I can hear him saying again why do you wait until I leave to become beautiful. The beauty was and is there, it's down deep trying to work its way up to the surface from my soul. This time is a mind break and I hope Bill is thinking about us/ me? I hope he thinks about our daughters and our family and this is a whole package with no returns or no exchanges. This is what he has been blessed with and I hope we will work together to keep it together. We need more adhesive to continue to secure this relationship. I pondered long enough and; after the girls are finished riding on the cars and quarters are exhausted, we will go to the buffet and on the way, I will pick up another pair of jeans. Time gets away and we are on our way. The buffet has a small line which is a good sign that this place must be okay. The menu has enough variety that the girls will be overwhelmed with their food choices. Actually, I'm impressed with the menu too. This is the day the girls will pick out what they want to eat or try for the first time. Some of the foods

I'm not familiar with, but the presentation is very inviting. The fun part we get small portions and the option opened for different flavors or repeat of the same dish.

I want to feel the break from the "Can Yous". My hands grip the steering wheel as we breathe the fresh air rushing in through our open windows. They are unknowingly experiencing freedom. Nothing planned for today we will just let today be today and the next days until our two weeks are up. The girls love the food as we just laugh and talk about nothing. The girls asked many questions and I had the time to listen and answer with the thought of such a blessing to hear the thoughts and brain working together as they look around at their surroundings. While Bill is at basic training, I'm training our girls to know, that there is life outside the confinements of our apartment and, the freedom to let your brain breath. My brain was confined to the thoughts on how to act or not act or what to do or what not to do so Bills' enviroment would be stress free. I lost my feelings, thoughts and my first name so in this short time, I'm going to enjoy being Rita with no adverbs attached yes, and no special adverbs today. We enjoy the food and the atmosphere. I'm glad that we eat at the table, so they will know and practice table manners when we eat out in public. We get many smiles as I just glance around the room at the different type of conversations as they enjoy the trips back and forth to the buffet table. I don't have any more room and my mom Sheryl would always say don't let your eyes be bigger than your stomach. This is our lunch and it might travel into maybe a light dinner.

I remember how my dad Eddie would take all the leftovers and combine them or take the corner left of almost empty boxes of cereal and do the same thing. All those different flavors at the same time didn't move him at all. He said he was one out of ten and lived on a farm, and you learned how to eat what's available. Kinda sounded like Clarences' friend that guarded his food so well, that they thought he might have done some time in juvenille hall. Nope that was just dinner table survival amongest nine siblings. I didn't understand like I do now how hard my parents worked to provide food and shelter. I took so much for granted but I was just a kid. I didn't know and honestly didn't care until I became an adult and had to learn how to make meals stretch at the same time desireable or eatable. Sometimes ending up either burnt or crunchy. Ooh my feelinges were hurt a many of times behind Bill strongly criticizing my food or just rudely refusing to eat or try what took a lot of effort to prepare. I still have regrets not spending time in the kitchen learning how to cook. At the time I didn't see the need. Didn't think about that I would be leaving my parents home at such a young age, but it happened, and I did leave at a young age. Bill and I didn't know what we were getting into. We were just trying to do right and raise our daughter, that's now daughters. Being away from home was hard and sometimes harder when Bill was not around. My thoughts and feelings for what the future holds for our family stays with me constantly. What goals have we set for one year, two years and what goals do we have for our daughters that we can prepare them for? Listen to me I'm growing up as I think about this. I never thought that far in advance. I guess the brain is refreshing itself. While the girls are eating and breaking from their food as I feel my soul smiling.

Just that quick I flashback and think about how Reva's mom, Berlynda calling her sons' father the" Tin Man" because he needed a brain or was it a heart. I wondered does she still call Reva, Dorothy? I would like to have hung out with Reva. At a young age she seemed to have had it all together. She stepped up taking care of her mom while raising her son. In a way Courtney Diane sometimes reminds me of her with her expressions and her words. Their characteristics seem in all ways to display no nonsense. They don't look for trouble and actually try to avoid it until the curtain calls for a performance, and they will produce a strong finale. I can't believe how much fun we are having. I haven't experience this much fun in a long time. After our last bite and burp its time to leave and walk it off and venutre back home. I mentally think about what the next few days will be. One thing I know for sure I will have to pack a little at a time. I pondered about those black jeans. So, with that thought we walk back towards Ashley Stewarts. I see the beautiful smile of Miss Dee saying that she had put the black pair of jeans up for me with a couple of shirts that were on sale, if I was interested. I thought as I returned her smile that she was good at her job of knowing what her customers style and budget. They were reasonable, and I could afford the jeans and shirts. Boy will I have a nice surprise for Bill. Maybe this will remind him of why he married me. After all he did ask and again, I need to remind him of why he asked. During my conversation with Miss Dee she asked where was Sabrina's other shoe? Now were we that relaxed while eating that she kicked off her shoe. The only place I could think of where it might be is at the resturant, because I didn't see any wiggling free toes before then. So, we get our walk on and stroll back to the resturant where they have her little pink shoe waiting to put on my little princess' foot. Everyone including staff was tickeled knowing that the owner would return as they watched her little toes wiggle as we all laughed. We secured her shoes, so we wouldn't have a repeat performance, Sabrina is still tickled. Twilley the manager brings out a set of balloons for the girls and they politely smile as they say in their tiny voices thank you. I proudly stood there looking at my girls display such mannerism with their cute smiles showing off their dimples.

Chapter 52
Two Weeks of Fun/Training and Transportation

It felt good not being forced to keep track of time. I noticed that Sierra and Sabrina are getting sleepy and the good thing about that is we don't have to stand on the bus stop. We can go directly to our car and drive on home. Home to a place where there is no anger or tension, just home. Waiting for us to come back and just chill and have fun relaxing. Come to think of it I needed some nap time myself. It was later than I realized as I take the sleepy girls into the apartment. Instead of placing them in their own beds, they will sleep with me and we will have our own two-week slumber party, no boys allowed. We all fall off to sleep in a cuddle huddle in sync with our snores. Oh, what a day that ran into to fast night. You would have thought we were on furlough. Were we acting like one of the 'CraCra's that has just been released? I cannot believe the story about the one that was in kindergarten. I think she said that the youngest one was thrown out of five-day cares and the sixth called before the parents had arrived. Wow I find that hard to believe but it was true. Did his reputation precede him or what? Then I had the nerve with my naive self to ask if the CraCra's worked. The dead give away was when Courtney Diane raised her eyebrows with her corner smile saying yeah, temporary jobs, as she slowly turned her head tilting her head slightly. That one flew right over my head and I had believed that it was all legit. I had to laugh at myself again temporary jobs huh. She then added that everytime they would bring gifts over the same questions were always asked. If I go out with this gift, will I be arrested? Or should I be politer and smile saying thank you. Adding with appreciation but asking, will I be able to make it home with your gift, (smile), without red lights and sirens? With that in mind sometimes it was hard to accept their gifts but in the same breath you didn't want to offend them either, because they were apart of the 'CraCra's. I know they have feelings minus the "s" and it sounded like you really didn't want to offend them and probably need to keep in mind, the kindness of I guess the thought given for the gift. I try to envision what they might look like, but if I did see them, I would definitely have on my glasses, doing a Clark Kent move so they wouldn't recognize me. Come to think of it I haven't had my glasses on in the last few days. For once I wasn't hiding behind them. Without them I can start to see clearly. Don't need to adjust my glasses on this situation. This time I'm really enjoying the break. Although I do miss Bill but at the same time, I'm finally having some quality mental time to myself.

When Bill is around, I feel like I must rush around the apartment responding to orders as he piles additional requests, not allowing me to finish the initial request, as if I'm on a time clock. Maybe I'm in his private military corps, with orders to hurry up and wait for the next request. Oh, and if I'm not clear because I'm in the process of completeing prior orders/requests, then that is a whole different situational change. I get confused because so much is coming at me, then I get the look from those almond shaped eyes that seem to hypotize me and my brain shuts down and my eyes goes into a deep trance. Then I come out of it by waking to the sound of his yelling and his eyes penetrating right through me. My mind freezes up, emotions bring the I'm afraid up front and center, and physically everything that would or should be working together freezes up also. I gather my strength and go into the bathroom or bedroom and take as big as a breath that I can to unfreeze everything and try to avoid any form of blows that might come in physical or verbal form. But it hasn't happened in some time and now I will be leaving those dreadful memories here in this apartment. No blue faded stain that seems to remind me of that day. Now that we are moving that will all go and fade away. A new beginning with new memeories that we will be able to cherish and be happy as we move into our new home. Just the thought warms my heart as I move away from those bitter memories.

I didn't realize how much I needed this break from Bill. Maybe while he's away he might be thinking the same way. A new beginning and being thankful that his family didn't leave him or that I'm not out roaming the streets. I'm safe and secured at home. Lights out and the morning brings in an array of sunshine as I roll over looking at little Bill's blinking at me. Their blinking didn't have me screaming like it did with Loren and Fifi. I smile looking at them as I vision Loren looking through the blinds as Fifi looks at him and they blink at the same time. That would have me screaming locking and closing windows too. I think the more he pulls away from her the more of the challenge she lives for. Of course, with her side kick Lucee accompaning her, Fifi is never alone. What shall we do today? I think this would be a good time to check on Momo, since I don't have a time line and the girls can play with her sons. I love going and being around her, she makes me feel like her daughter, and in her way, she is always entertaining. I appreciate the love and respect along with the affections that Amos shows to Momo. They have an understanding that only they need to understand. Amos and Momo show nothing but the love for each other, and for their sons. Everywhere they go it's in a family form. Rather it's Momo yelling at them or Amos gathering the boys up for that mystery dinner.

Amos calls Momo, love or Mo, but majority of the time he called her love and she responds back with "Take-me". Most of the time she called Amos honee, with a hum while saying honee. She looked at him with the same sweetness that the honee represented still at the same time with that familiar hum. The other pet name hmm don't want to vision or dissect what that "Take-me" might mean. But I noticed that when he calls her love, she just gets so giddy like a high school sweetheart waiting for the phone call to take her out on their first date. They seem so young in their love and marriage that age doesn't show on their face or actions. According to Momo they are still flipping, and flopping and she didn't mean the burgers, ew vision again. Momo laughs when she said that they still have date nights. After the boys started coming, she chuckles as a result from our date nights!! So why go out when we can have our date nights at home because the result will be the same, we'll end up in the bedroom. I think she just loves to see my reactions and just like my normal, I end up saying ew, visions again. Then she finishes off with her laugh that I still love to hear. Not a hearty laugh just a warm I'm feeling good and blessed laugh. She means no harm with any of her words or ew visions. In her own way I think she's saying that you got to feed your marriage, don't ever give your marriage a reason to starve. That opens a menu with a lot of appetizers and entrees. Too much seasoning salt can give you high blood pressure and a doctors' visit. Now darling, too much of something else will send you to the doctor too and both might require frequent visits.

Bill or any husband should get their full course meal at home anything outside the home is just greedy and selfish. I could never figure out where these sayings or random comments would come from. If Momo was making them up or someone shared them with her. I just know she keeps my attention on trying to improve my relationship with my husband and my family. I have not ever heard or seen them argue. They seem to get their point across with a certain type of smile, look or special key words. One was funny phrase was when Momo said, don't jump that rope and Amos' response was don't skip around. They would look at each other and just smile breaking off into a chuckle as they kept it moving. It seemed as if they had a verbal touch. Whatever conflict they might have they always remained civil. They showed me that it doesn't take harsh words or altercations to get your point across. Momo had the look and the size to know that she didn't play, and Amos was quiet and slim. Amos words could pierce your soul and you could feel his look of don't be fooled. I like what he said to Aven Blue. Now that was smooth yet piercing when he asks, how are you going to explain, how I beat your ass with your own gun? Then those words made an encore to his favorite nephew asking, how are you going to explain how an old man beat your young ass? If an altercation ever occurred, I can see them handling their business and going back to their business, not skipping a beat with no hard feelings with an "s"".

Today might just be a lounging day with pj's and relaxtion. I haven't done that in a while. I used to relax at my parents' home, but now I'm up before dawn cleaning before the morning blinks into either sunshine or rain. I don't want to show the girls how to be lazy. I just want to show them how to feel free when work is completed then you can relax. Our place is always clean, and the smell of pine-sol always lingers. So, when or if we leave, we return home to a clean place, so we can sit down and relax. My parents instilled that practice early in our lives. Sometimes my mother would send us downtown with a dollar and bus money just; so, she could have her me time as she cleaned and relaxed without hearing us asking questions, bugging her, or running in and out of the house. That might have been her way of her cleaning to relax, just like I'm doing now with a cup of coffee and quiet time. No 'can yous' right now. Funny, why I still can't remember who said that, but she said enjoy the freedom from the 'can yous'.

I hear an early knock and to my surpise it's Courtney Diane just checking on me with a full smile asking; if we wanted to go and ride out to her parents and there was plenty of room for the girls to play and my army of nieces will be there too. My first thought would have responded with can I get a raincheck, but since this is freedom week, I responded just like I did when Robin cashed in on her raincheck. I said give me a chance to get us ready and we will be right out. There goes that lazy day and we still have more than a few days left. Sierra is out of school and we are not on a clock. We are presented with an opportunity to venutre away from home and meet the infamous Mother Flo. I shower and give the girls a quick bath and we are dressed and ready to go! Courtney Diane seemed pleased to have us join her. She didn't know how honored I was to be asked and I didn't have a curfew. I get the car seats as Courtney Diane assist while the girls wait anxiously to jump in ready to enjoy another adventure. When they asked where they were going, I would tell them it's a surprise we are going on another adventure. I set comfortably in the front seat, refelecting the same feeling I had when I was in Robin's car. I rolled the window down to feel the fresh air making sure that there was not too much wind blowing back on the girls. The girls are looking out the window with big eyes and feeling the light breeze that is hitting their faces. The direction we travel in is the opposite of the direction that we always travel. I see land, livestock and houses. The sun doesn't leave but the many grouped houses become spaced. I can only think that wow her family must be rich? As the houses become spaced and larger, my eyes become bigger as the scenery changes. All the time that I have been living in Califiornia I have never seen or been in a house of this size, wow! My thought was were we dressed well enough to enter this type of home? We get out slowly because deep inside I didn't know what to expect. Sometimes Courtney Diane scares me especially when I first met her. The thoughts and views she shared with me as a stranger threw me off. The swearing was interesting and taught me how to alter her words. I can't believe she thought enough of us to invite us to her parent's house, again wow. We walk into a house that feels like a home. Well kept large home and the feeling of warmth filled this big house. While we feel the warmth surround us, the sound of girls running becomes audible as they call out Auntie Courtney, hmm no Diane. One thing she was right on, they did sound like a herd of something. Once they hug her, they look at us not as strangers just waiting for an introduction. Then appears, a beautiful slender older woman, wearing glasses and, a smile showing off their signature dimples. Her hair was more black than gray, and her skin was so smooth, and she was holding a baby boy. I see a gentler side of Courtney Diane as she struggles to hug her mother while the girls strongly cling to all her extremities. She actully chuckles with her mother and they sound and look identical. Same height same build there is no denying they are family. I finally have a picture to go with the stories of Mother Florrie. She looks so gentle but again my mother Sheryl is now a grandmother too and she has that gentle nature as well.

Once her arms are free, she grabs the baby hugging and kissing him calling him CD/CII. One introduction she didn't need. I figured out that was her mother. As she introduces her nieces, they smile but seems anxious to play with Sierra and Sabrina. They were in a variety of ages and height. I don't know the order but Courtnee Denise resembled her name sake Courtney Diane. Lillee and Coree Danette, resembled the picture I saw of her brother Corey Davon and Reesee, Marlee and Bailee resembled their mother Cassee. They are a large beautiful family. Courtney Diane smiles saying with a chuckle rocking her nephew saying and we have here, his parents unknowing last try, Corey Davon Jr know as CD/CII. The girls ask politely if they can go back outside and look me asking if it's okay. In sync they all said what's your name again? Before the girls could finish saying their names they were rushed outside before okay was finished. I still couldn't understand how such small feet make so much noise. By that time a real tall nice-looking older gentleman with a deep laugh and voice to match walks toward Courtney Diane as she stretches her free arm and hand out to him. His voice does have thunder gentle sound as he calls her Diane. She smiles and turns toward me mouthing don't you even think about it or tell anyone. I smiled back giving her a corner smile now raising my eyebrows. I turned my head as they embraced each other as she breaks away to introduce me to Papa Cleve Jr. His size makes my inside tremor but his gentle deep dimple smile with his mixture of salt and pepper hair extended hand calms my tremoring. Mother Flo tells Courtney Diane that she just missed her Aunt Gigi and cousin Rose Ann they had to head back to St Paul. I noticed that their backyard was as huge as the house. Her dad had been riding on a lawn mower and the smell of fresh cut grass reminds me of home. As a child I used to watch my father cutting grass through the window and when he would come in, I could smell fresh cut grass and the labor it entailed.

We go and sit outside watching the girls play as if they had been knowing each other for years. While watching the girls Mother Flo brings out a pitcher of fresh squeezed leomonade. I feel like I'm part of a movie sipping fresh lemonade with the wide-open space and the smell of fresh cut grass. Courtney Diane seems so calm and for me this is very exciting, and I tried to hold back my enthusiasm. We talk about a bunch of nothing. I saw a gentler side of her and she was not using her special adverbs. She was calm and respectful. I heard a rare chuckle without her normal tee-hee-hee- la-de-da laghter from her. I watched how secure and beautiful she looked with her family. We sipped our lemonade and mostly just set there watching the innocence of children playing while feeling the soft breeze on a sunny day. I guess we did get our lazy day just in a different location. Time just faded away until we heard the yelling voice of Mother Flo calling us for brunch or an early dinner. They had hamburgers in different sizes, thick, thin, juicy, spicy and hot dogs thin, thick or long and fresh cut french fries where you could smell the seasoning on them. The condiments were displayed as if you were sitting down at a resturant. The table was beautiflly set just needed hearty appetites. We all gathered around the table as Papa Cleve Jr. prayed. Mother Florrie told me to just sit and she would get the plates ready for the girls who were sitting at a small table just for them. After the prayer from Papa Cleve Jr, he took baby CD/CII with him to look at the games. After prepareing the plates Mother Florrie joined her husband in the family room. I could hear her yelling at the results of the moves the players were making. They reminded me of my parents, Eddie and Sheryl, they loved looking at football and it would be my mother yelling at the calls. But when it comes to just being together regardless of what was going on, they reminded me of Amos and Momo. Momo loved to sit across from Amos as they ate breakfast or any type of meal. They just really enjoyed each others company and every now and then I would see them holding hands.

Just as we finish Courtney Diane and I turned into those little girls we once were as we cleaned off the table. We washed and cleaned the kitchen just making small talk or sometimes we went into a silence mode. While the girls continued to play, we continued cleaning up the kitchen. I couldn't believe how much energy they had. This is all good because after a good bath my girls are going to sleep good as we continue our slumber party marathon. The once sound of football players coming into the house now has the sound of pidder padder of small feet. I guess they do wear out. That was my cue to head back home as I looked over at Courtney Diane without saying a word and we were on the same page. She told her parents that she had to get me back home. I wondered if she brought me, so she wouldn't have to deal with her nieces and nephews. This was just a thought but as she would say probably did but your ass ate. Then my response would be I got you back.

I thanked her parents for the meal and Mother Flo hands me a heavy bag full of burgers, hot dogs and fresh fries. She had cooked so much I looked around and there still was a lot left. I remember Courtney Diane saying that those girls could put away some food. They did have high energy. I did see Courtney Dianes' parents looking at the clock and their watches, because it was getting close to time for their parents to come and pick up their family. Their expressions were clear on them not on spending a night, tonight or any night. I guess according to Mother Florrie's watch its time for them to go and where in the hell were their parents. Funny now it's time to care according to her watch. The stories that Courtney Diane said about her parents were being played right in front of my eyes. One thing that was clear, her parents weren't a joke. They didn't play but were very enjoyable. Without a doubt, you knew when it was time to leave their beautiful home. As we load our-selves into the car, Courtney Diane gets one more hug from her parents while her nieces and nephew laid peacfully sleeping on the couch and floor. Their cozy family room looked like a sleep over that I knew wasn't going to happen.

Courtney Diane thanked me for joining her on this get away. She didn't feel like having her nieces hanging all off her ass. Today was the day she wasn't feeling their high energy little asses and wanting to play with her all day like she was their personal doll or their young playmate. First time I heard her use any adverb and it was ass. In which I know the silent comeback would be what ass? You can still do the wall test, and you still have that long back. I laughed while telling her thank you for just thinking of us. She chuckles saying my parents are a trip huh. Inside my thoughts were no, I was introduced to their actions through her. No surprise just now I have faces to put with the stories. The girls enjoyed the time away and had a chance to be introduced to home living, girls around their age and a backyard. They really enjoyed playing in that large backyard, but our backyard is not as large but there is room to move. The ride back home seemed shorter but filled with so much fun that made an enjoyable day. No curfew and we arrived to a clean apartment with plenty of food. Courtney Diane helps me put the sleepy girls into my bed. I'm so glad we cleaned up before we left. That eliminated excuses for the mess. I didn't realize how late it was, time does fly when you are having fun and fun was what us/girls did have. She embraces me giving me another telephone number and to stay in touch. I laugh telling her that you are not getting rid of me that easy. I unload the bag of goodies with more than I thought was in there. Her mother had placed fresh baked cookies on top of the many other items. Those cookies reminded me of the fresh baked goodies that Keith used to bring over.

I never told him how I looked forward to him borrowing. Keith and Clarence were my connection to adult conversation and the outside world. They probably thought something was wrong with me, one being sheltered and scared. They adopted me into their hearts as a little sister. Clarence never had a chance to tell me what he wanted to share with me. I guess the unknown should stay unknown. This is my freedom and mental break weekend and I didn't need any bad news to spoil my thoughts. I didn't realize how tired we were until we were awakened by Momo's boys outside playing with little Tim. Something made me look up at Courtney Diane's apartment and her place showed signs that she had moved. My reality was in a slow mode and I thought I had more time to spend with her, but that was her way of saying good bye. That hit my emotions so hard that it just for a second took my breath away. She really is gone. I missed her already and she is on her way to her new home. No stories about Henray or her saying with his dumb ass. No Henray Luis and his friends laughing as they show fear toward his mother. Now I have an idea of how my parents felt as I drove away with my little belongings as their waves faded.

This day will not be a down day. I'm glad that we didn't have a curfew and I didn't care about the time. Maybe this is a reminder that I need to start packing. Courtney Diane left me enough boxes and Bill picked up some so there is no excuse for not packing. After all I don't want to run into the same situation I did when I had told Bill I was packing, and it took Mama Sadie to correct my procrastination. Well I know what today will consist of starting one room at a time. The girls struggle in trying to wake up still tired from yesterday. This is good because, this will allow time for me to pack with minor distractions. The girl's room will be last. My thought process starts from front to back and don't forget the middle. I grow excited about moving and looking forward to moving into a house. The many times that I passed houses for rent, we will soon become a house renter. Wow, God has blessed us with our heart desires. The feeling was great that Bill and I was on the same page sharing the same thoughts for our family. Surprisingly I get a phone call from Bill. He must have felt our thoughts come together. He said that he had been trying to catch up with us where have we been. My inside felt that tremor again but what can he do thousand of miles away and on the phone. I play it off that we miss you too and we were trying to fill the void of you not being here. I thought to myself where did that come from? I guess I was improving and ready for my oscar. It's not like it wasn't the truth but to my ears that sounded better and maybe that would soften the blow that might come through the phone. I hear a hesitation that must have thrown him off too. His voice softens as he tells me he misses us too. He asked what we had been doing. My careful response was just getting out of the house, so they wouldn't be bored. Didn't know how much we would miss you. Bill was okay because this was all about Bill and his feelings. He was trying to have control over the phone. I convinced him and chuckled that he believed me, and it was working. But we were having fun and no conversation was going to ruin my thoughts, especially not today. I let him know about the girls as I yelled for them to come to the phone. They are excited to hear his voice and they tell him just that. They handed me the phone more less they dropped the phone as they took off and Bill thinks they are still on the phone and I have to inform him that they have left the building. With that we laugh as he tells me about the training and how hot it is there. Bill ends the call with he misses us and me a lot and can't wait to get back home. One more question I had a feeling he would ask was about the packing and I had an answer. I told him that I was boxing items and stopped to answer the phone now that was good timing. We end with love yous and that was enough for both of us. As I hung up the phone I still melt when I hear his voice and sometime cringe when the tone changes.

This break felt like a breath of fresh air as I hung up from talking with Bill. I do miss him but not the unknowing when he might snap. That just sends my emotions with an "s" on a roller coaster. The ups are high, and the downs are low with no in betweens. For now, I'm feeling too up to inflict emotions that will bring me down. The girls are playing as I pack the best way I knew how. I only pack items that we really don't use. It seems too easy but maybe because I'm not the same girl that Mama Sadie helped so many years ago. I can't believe I'm here and no longer that little girl that left Oakwood with no clue of what I was riding into. All I knew was that I had Bill's daughter and I was his wife and I'm now a woman trying to stay married and raise our daughters. Bill is my breath and my heart beat. I need them both to survive to live and with each breath and beat our love would become stronger. All I ever wanted since Bill and I first started talking was to become Bill's wife and have his child or children. We were in love and I wanted our love to become stronger and not fade away or go away. I didn't want to hear the beat stop or gasp for air. I just remember as a little girl looking at married couples and how happy they were. I watched as they would laugh holding hands and glaring into each other eyes. Just like they do on television and in the movies. That was the life I wanted and long for. The happily ever after til death do us part. I missed how we used to hang out enjoying each others company without a care in the world. I love when we went dancing. Although, Bill didn't have rhythm and couldn't dance or sing, but it didn't stop him from trying. I was always entertained as he tried to bust out different moves that looked all the same while singing off key. Outside I was smiling as we danced, and he tried to force tunes out but inside I was rolling with laughter. We were young having much fun and didn't care about the future other than we were going to be together. After all he did ask. As the days moved faster the time was coming for Bill to return. Since we didn't have a curfew, we had a chance to hang out at Momo's place. The more we hung out the more she convinced me that the place to be with was with my husband and family. We didn't ever wear out our welcome, if anything we were always in so many ways welcomed.

Boy it seemed like time did fly while we were having the girls only slumber party. The honey 'can yous' will be returning but I hope the Bill that will be returning will be the husband that wants his wife and family. Bill was always very good with his daughters and played with them a lot. He in all ways had time for them and made them feel like daddy's special daughters and his little Princesses. Every now then I felt like his queen with the feeling sometimes of being dethroned. If I was the dream of his life, why does he turn some episodes of our marriage into a nightmare? I wonder why he took me as his wife and what were Bills'expectations of what a marriage, wife and husband should be. We never did have that conversation we just went through the motions and maybe imitated what we saw in various relation-ships. We really didn't have a clue we were young and didn't have a book to read with instructions. I think I'm ready for Bill's return. I will only wear warm ups when I'm cleaning. I will look and do better for Bill and give him a reason to rush home. I have done a lot of packing and I feel rather proud of myself. Bill will be happy that boxes are packed, and the apartment is pine-sol clean. I don't know when he will be arriving. I just know I need to be ready and show something for the time he was away. I ask for very little. I want what you can't buy from the store, a part of Bill that will show me the appreciation I need and the respect I should receive. Deep down inside I don't think or feel I'm asking for too much. I give him my breath and he just takes it away. I want to feel that I'm still his heart and his wife, not to mention the mother of his girls. I don't know why I hit myself with trying to convince myself why we are still together. My reality will be coming home shortly, and we had a good time while we were on a two-week furlough.

I was able to speak freely to my high school friends during my two-week furlough. They brought me up to date; Debbie Lynn received her nursing degree and was still married to her high school sweetheart Brian, (Froggy), and their children Terrell and Brielle were attending college out of state, and her brother, Tommy was still mean looking and still married to his grade school sweetheart Aileen. Not only have they been together what seems like a real forever, they still had youthful looks. Her sister Brenda became an attorney, (and still my big sister), and is now married to her Pooh. Sharon Denise's daughter, Shaquella Denise also attended college out of state. She is still enjoying her freedom in Kansas, looking just like her mother. Sharon loves the fact that she has somewhere to travel to. She says she enjoys the ride because it allows her to meditate and it's just her and the Lord in her car. Melody Lynn was raising her beautiful daughters Toni and Brandi and now she added an addition by the name of Gerald. While at the same time pursuing her master's in medicine. Sharon and Melody both were married and worked at trying to make it work. They saw the writ-ing on the wall early and had the courage to do the one stong boohoo, and walked away from their marriages, without looking back or digging up what was now decay-ing. I admired them for many years of their courage and every now and then I did or will need to tap into their strength. We have for many years kept enough connection that we could feel when one of us needs an reach out.

As for me I tried taking a few classes but with limited transportation getting back and forth to my classes was difficult. I had a head start when I graduated at the age of sixteen, then I met Bill and fell in love. Life went on without me, but I hear through various conversations through my high school friends what is happening from time to time in Oakwood. They keep me current and abreast on the going ons in Oakwood. Funny, that when I do get a chance to talk to them, I still picture them as I remembered them in their youth. I vision their facial expression sometimes with only young faces, because I have been away so long that I haven't seen them as adults.

I'm just glad to have my family back. Bill looks a little different maybe he had an awakening and freedom break like we did. I look at him and want to gather nerves and thoughts to talk to his heart about maybe finding a job to help with our increasing family expenses. That would mean maybe buying another car. After all I gave up my Vega for a trade in that should have some type of weight for replacement consideration. I can almost say what Bill's response will be. He would probably say you must have talked to someone from home and now you have some courage. I know this would be his only way to deflect an answer. He has done this performance so many times. I can almost say to him what have you heard or felt to have that thought about my courage. I don't need to go home or make a phone call to have what's been dormant and every now and then it wants to surface for some much-needed fresh air. I guess it's just me growing up. I had no choice married with girls and no longer daddy's girl, but now I'm his daughter that moved away. I still miss home and have some regrets about moving, but I can't have my thoughts hang out there if I want to move on. I'm here and not going back unless I'm with my husband. Bill goes back and forth on if he's going to make the service a career. Either way I'm fine with his decision because it would be an "us" decision. For now, I'm glad I had something to show for his time being away. I also had a freedom break that I might share or hold on to for just me. I don't know why I hesitate with suggestions and stories I've heard or was told to me. Maybe it's just my brain trying to dissect how, when, or if I will need to hold on or let go. On the other hand, my brain could be thinking, is this for asmusement or entertainment purposes only? Some stories were touching, and heart felt....

Chapter 53
Eyes Can See the Stories that Need to be Told

It's funny and strange how I remembered Sally's story at this time. I remembered her face and actions while telling her story looking very relaxed as her hair was being curled. She said with no emotions that she gave her hubby everything. One thing she shared was the drips from her heart and when that wasn't enough, she rung her heart out to give him more. She thought in giving him more he would love her more because she gave him the beat of her heart. In return he gave our love with some of me to someone else. That was when I realized I lost my beat and needed my heart to beat again for me. A surprise will make that heart stop and beat again. I just remembered listening with everyone else about what happened. Sally went on feeling the vibes. Her husband was working that night. He was a deejay and he normally doesn't tell her where he is working. She used to ask and sometimes would hang out but drew tired of the girls flirting, dancing and boobs hanging all on her husband. Sally said that she didn't trip because her husband had it under control. She would sit next to him as the women would just up front disrespect her. I admired her thought of the women were there alone and paid money or just wanted to dance with a man and they see her hubby spinning and just want to take that chance of him saying yes. Some seemed to want more with that yes, but he had me convinced that he knew what yes meant and knew how to just say no.

Now there was that one time I said yes to going out with one of my girlfriends. Everytime she asked I would just say no. I was content staying at home while Rence was out doing his thing. He never ever indicated to me that he had said yes. He would call me during his breaks, and I would have a light dinner waiting for him with a warm bath. The calls didn't happen as much as I would like to hear how the crowd was working and, at the same time ease my thoughts and confirmed that he was thinking of me, because someone was trying to get him to say yes. So, for that one time, I went out with my girlfriend to a new club she was dying to attend. Hey,

I wasn't doing anything so why not. I tried to find something that I could wear that looked nice but not too sexy or revealing because in my husband's asbence I'm still married and unavailable.

The music was popping, and my girlfriend Pamela was dancing, walking, talking and looking around for anything just in case. Why not? She was single and unattached, and her outfit matched her thoughts. The place was crowded, and we managed to find a table and order our drinks. I just went to keep Pamela/Pummie company, but my drink was my company. Pam was dancing as I watched the ice melting in her drink. She went on to say she didn't mind if she didn't dance because, she was looking at the different styles of dance moves, which were very entertaining. While looking around the room my gut and heart dropped at the same time. I saw Kurrence, my Rence, deejaying and a woman sitting next to him where if I was there, I would be sitting. This road scant had my spot. She seemed to have known him because they were laughing as she hugged him and bought him food with a kiss. This kiss was not on the cheeks but the lips. Those were my lips and he is my husband. I watched how he watched her like he used to watch me. It was then I knew this was more than a friend. I tried to hold back the tears and emotions as I watched Pam laughing and dancing. She had been through a lot and needed this time out. I didn't want to take away her few dancing minutes of joy.

We both had become home bodies. I wanted to go up and confront them both. First, I would start with her. I would just snatch her ass then, save some energy for him, but this was not the time or place. Plus, that side of me had matured. I'm a lady now and that was not the way I wanted to handle this situation, this would take some thought. Now back in high school we had a phrase called 'snatch a scant' and for that instant I thought I heard the school bell ringing. In my thoughts I wanted to do a knock down body slam. The funny part was she took her hand across her face, as she made a wiping motion saying, I'm a lady and I got class. Sally started making ding sound as she deeply stared at that flashdance floosey. She laughed saying that it took some time to get that ringing out of her mind. She had to get control of the other thoughts that were trying to come through. One thought was to stop the sound of the bell and to hold back thinking she was Ali in the last round. She said she found herself tapping her foot and moving her body, like she was rocking in her corner. She didn't know if the boxer rocking was from her thinking, she was Ali or trying to keep her hands to herself and stay in sync with the loud music. All she heard was the ringing of the bells going off in her head and her sites were on the scant. She said that if you were to look at her, you would have thought that she was dancing in her seat. But that was a hell no she was really trying to keep from making those moves to the stage. Those bells kept ringing as my watered-down drink was cheering and chanting. I remember her acting like a cheerleader with pompoms. We looked and laughed while she says, "Big G! little O! go Sal go! go get her get her and don't let go!" Then I heard the bell fade into girl, Sally really take your ass to class, in other words take my old ass home. Then she stops saying let me tuck my pompoms under my arm for just in case. Sally laughed as we listened, continuing to be captivated as she sat there playing it off. While dancing Pam or Miss Pummie dusted off the cob webs with her unique dance moves, occassionly sipping down her watered-down drink. She said that she tried not to stare in that area so. She had to work hard talking to herself at the same time shifting her eyes and redirecting from viewing the dance floor and deejay stage. Which was hard because you just wanted to look at them hard enough that they would feel your vibes and look in your directions catching her pain of pissed off in her eyes. That look would cover everything and the only physical action that would be needed was to stretch her foot off into her ass. The desire was getting harder as her thoughts and heart raced saying that they would understand.

Sally said she wanted to dance and show off her moves as Kurrence surprisingly glanced onto the dance floor. She wanted Mr. DJ to be watching her backing it up and dropping like she was hot. This was one of those rare moments where the kids were away spending a weekend and she had a care free few days. Then get hit with this shift. I never thought my Rence would or could make a hook up with someone else. She didn't know if there was a balance between being pissed off and being surprised. Because her thoughts and emotions were all over the place. She had to gather them so Pam or no one else would see in her face or eyes something had suddenly changed. This was a private matter, yet she laughed as she was telling us. I guess that was a brief awareness of contradiction. One thing she did know was that he will be coming home, and she wasn't going to skip her routine. By that time the exhausted dancing Pam was ready to go, and I was eager to accommodate and ready to go too. She didn't notice that I was in deep thought. Pam was too busy wiping the sweat off her face at the same time trying to get her dancing partner off her ass and to leave her alone. To Pam it wasn't that type of party she was exhausted, and the miniature fun was enough to hold her inner I got to get out. Yep party animals that reached the curfew of your ass is too old to be out this late. We both were yawning and that was the ding we needed to say it was our bed time. We walked to the car slowly because girlfriend's dancing feet went to standing then walking. Her feet looked good in those high heels, but each step was painful, and she confirmed it with moans and groans while trying to talk through her pain. Sally said she had to laugh and told her that her feet may hurt but they look good. She said she tried not to laugh, and they just kept walking and talking about much of nothing.

Getting home was much of something she had to deal with. She went on to say that she just kept having those flashbacks of Rence and that road scant. Those thoughts circled back again. She said that it took her back to school hearing that ringing bell again and she felt like snatching a scant. I remember her clearing her throat and placing her hand on her chest saying; but now since shes older shaking her body, I'm a lady that ho just didn't know how much I wanted to go back to class and beat that ass. She said that she had to calmly find self control and it wasn't through her watered-down drink or hearing the crowd cheering her on. This was about her and her husband, private matter uh. Lydel chimed in saying private yell right and nobody knows as she continued.

But she kept her cool as she exits the car she laughed with Pam/Pummie saying that we should do this again. Her inside thoughts were hell no! She was just keeping the night fun and cool for her girl Pummie. Sally added that for now this should hold both of us for the next ten years. Pam laughs saying the only thing that was holding up was her girdle. Everyone in the shop laughed but Sallys' laughter was there as she cut her smile into returning back to Mister DJ. I got something for him to beat and dance to and he will be singing. She hung up her clothes she had worn and the other clothes that had been thrown around the room, (which was rare). It probably took her longer to get dressed and drive there than the time they stayed. Pam lost her curls and the feeling in her feet from wearing those 3' inch heals. As for her she had some sit down and stand up shoes on her feet were fine. She just wanted to insert one-foot ino Rence's ass.

I wasn't hungry, and I knew that Rence wouldn't be either. Don't know if he had eaten or was this just a feeling. After all, that trick did put food into his lying ass mouth. Sally smiled saying that she had to take a shower just to cool or calm her ass down. I remembered how she looked raising her eyebrows as she holds back either laughter or tears. She said she had to lather herself trying to take that vision away in foam. She worked all day and she didn't have the thought to fix him a mini meal, but she did run his bath water. I wanted him to be as fresh as I was. So, we both could be smelling fresh lying next to each other. You never knew when you will have to be ready as she smiles raising her eyebrows. She said that she watched a little televison until she nodded off to sleep. She was awakening to a slight screaming noise of ah shift.

I didn't hear the door open or the sounds of any keys, just the awakening by the sounds of screaming ah shift!! I could me mistaken?? Rence screamed is she's trying to burn/boil my balls? She knew what he meant so she did what we do all so well pretend to be sleep. Now she recaps her footsteps, she had hung up her clothes and wasn't going to say anything only if he said something. Then she would have a whole lot of shift to say and share. But how does that go don't ask don't tell or just don't tell on yourself just wait. Well hell she laughed with saying that she wasn't going to tell on her ass, let his ass do all the talking. She felt him getting in the bed saying babe what you try to do boil my balls? Sally said girls she pretended to be sound a sleep trying to keep from laughing. She looks around the room telling us that she got into her performance by adding a real deep ugly sound of snoring. The snoring that you might get a cough with or a deep ass breath trying to push that nosie out. He tried to cuddle then she acted as if she was stretching and fighting and slapped the shift out of his face all under the pretense of being sleep. She held back her chuckle because she knew she had hit him hard because, she heard the sound. All she heard from Rence, was damn babe and felt him looking at her. She pretended harder to be knocked out, and shift had to add an extra girgling sound. Sally had her bag ready to go for just in case. She said that they both woke up that morning. Nothing happened because she was sleep and someone had a tab bit of soreness. She had to go into work, and he was stretching from last night. He kisses her on the back of the neck but inside she cringes, because she didn't know where his lips had been.

So, she ignores his advancement at the same time asking what his schedule was for that day. He said that he had deejay at this new club down town but didn't know about returning. Rence went on saying the whole enviroment wasn't right. Sonika/ Sonni was flirting with some man and it got out of hand and she couldn't shake his ass. So, her crazy ass starts acting like we were something and hanging on me and around me so that guy she was trying to get away from would leave her ass alone. She was bringing me food and shift and I just thought that was her being her. I've done many parties with her. Sonni was party planner and had got me that gig, but I didn't owe her ass nothing. He said that he worked and was paid for his services. Sally said that Rence sounded pissed and said that he wasn't combined with that beach or owed her crazy ass any obligations. He was still upset when he told Sally that Sonni had kissed him. Sally said that she had to keep the performance going because she was believing him and that she couldn't alter the hold she had or mistake she might had made. Sally said she was using Rence words the same way he told her. But she said that she had to perform, so she stepped back, and he insisted no, no oh hell no, Sal would not understand this shift. He acted dumb saying that he didn't know if Sonni was trying to show this dude we were attached or just taking advantage of an opportunity. He told her ass oh hell no; if Sal saw this or knew she would take her out first and save just enough energy for finishing my ass off and then go home sleep and get ready for work the next day. I told her I love my wife, not trying to go out like that and don't roll like that. She puts both her hands together to show us what her hubby did. He said I got my own shift you need to handle yours and let me make it as clear as I can. I don't do that type of shift with or anyone else.

I don't care what you got nothing can replace the queen I have at home and I don't think I will be doing business with Sonni. I'm not trying to be part of all that noise and her crazy ass antics. Sally said she was proud of her husband and the words he uttered to that back door scant. She said that this time she didn't resist the hug from him. Sally smiled no pain showing just slight tear saying that Rence looked sincere, like a little boy that was trying to tell the truth, and that touched her heart. With the added boyish look, she didn't know if he was a better performer than her, hell. Then Sally laughed with, she didn't know if he was making this shift up because he might have saw my ass or this shift was legit. Now if he was, he is better at pretending than her and if so, she got to give him his props. Girls she looks around the room how could you resist with those pearl teeth showing through his smile girls. Okay ladies I caved in and took that kiss with that long seductive hug because I'm his queen, and don't none of ya show no hate. He said that he was trying to get close to me, but I had boiled his shift and it was burning behind that hot ass bath water and then he added that I had slap the shift out his face. She did see a slight brusing behind the small scar. He was like oh hell no I might cut his shift off because my ass was snoring and fighting in my sleep and he wasn't going to take a chance with his shift, but after the swelling go down and sensation returns its me and you. Sally laughed saying I wasn't going to bust myself out if he believed what happened last night who am I to change his beliefs or mind. Sally calmed her laughter and had to admit that she was glad she didn't snatch that scant and kept to her routine minus the boiling bath water. I thought to myself was this simliar to Loren's innocent lie. I tell you just enough of the truth to make you believe me. Funny sometimes your eyes can play trips with your thoughts and mind making you all emotional. Usually the madness does occur behind a man. Sally said she wouldn't leave Rence and start all over again with a new headache nah on that shift and some in the salon agreed, but others said hell no, and that's probably why some of them are still single.

Time is coming, and we were moving sooner than I had anticipated. I didn't really want to move but I knew that I wanted to be with my husband and keep our family together. But on the other hand, I was leaving the family I have known for years behind. Plus, I didn't want a new heacdache, (according to Sally), I wanted to make it work with my present headache, my husband Bill. I don't know why Sally's story came through maybe it was telling me you can be deceived by what you think or feel sometimes. I had to ask myself are you really going to ever leave Bill and have someone else get him after all the work you have put into him and your marriage? That's what some of the ladies were saying why they stayed in their relationships, some were just because and other were they really loved their significant others for better or for worse, and my worse or better might be different from your better or worse. The bottom line and all were in agreeance that it was your decision your choice. I agreed that was right it was my decision to stay and make it work after all he did ask, and I answered. I'm determined to see this through for better or for worse and I believe that the best is yet to come. After all we have invested time and energy into our marriage and in the up bringing of our daughters, Sierra and Sabrina. I just started thinking about Sally and some of the stories from the salon.

Then I flash to imagining Courtney Diane being younger sitting in class as student/students just kept bothering her and she made every effort to avoid them. Then the nerve of them to say we can meet after school and in the Courtney Diane's response looking at her watch just like her Mama Flo saying pretty much it's time. In other words, why wait because the result is going to be the same regardless of what time. We can meet now how did that go in the confinement of this classroom with a small audience and not many will know, or which was a sign for them to stop, but they kept going not hearing the theme music just stop as the boys would say ret now. Her response probably very calm with a corner smile direct eye contact, we can meet after school with more space, more spectators, and more time to whip your ass. Hmm that would be an I think I'm sick and I'm going home real early and avoid this crazy girl. But again, just like mommy said we don't do that. If they didn't finish it that day Courtney Diane made it very clear that she would lose sleep thinking about them. That is something I wouldn't want to have on my mind when every time I would see her, I would wonder if this might be the time. Because she could give a look that you felt like you wanted to ask permission to kick your own ass. The ironic part she doesn't carry herself like she is bad you just feel the vibes. She is usually calm and tries to avoid nonsense. However, by time you gather your thoughts of what happened, you're trying to figure out what happened to get you the corner of the room trying to regain consciousness of how you ended up on the floor. All at the same time they're trying to get their focus back and stand with some form of stability as you watch her calmly walk away. Courtney Diane does have a humble side that isn't often shown or known. I don't know what happened, but she has her defense up and it has worked for her apparently for many years. I don't know if people wanted to challenge the unknown or known with her.

When we were over Robin's place, I just remember how sometimes Robin and I would ooh and laugh at some of her thoughts. She told someone that in the typical fashion her response was I didn't know what levels of ignorance you were at until you confirmed when you opened your mouth and you hit many levels in a short time frame hmm, with your dumb ass. I'm gonna miss not seeing Robin and her girls and watching them develop their strength and achieve the goals that Robin had set for them. Robin had her own style too. She was calmer than Courtney Diane and smoother in her actions. Robin was no nonsense and you picked that up through her deep dimple smile as she closed her eyes when she smiled or laughed. Being in advertisement you must have some aggressive nature, yet convincing without them knowing you directed them into the direction you wanted them to go in. But her smile and looks would probably throw them off as she snags that contract at the same time laughing on the way to the bank. She was the top in her field, yet she never displayed any arrogance. I have in all ways admired her humble nature. Robin would always say what you do for Christ will last. Her philosophy was to live your life and show her daughters by example. Robin's daughters' Denise and Nicole were very beautiful, but she reminded them to depend on their character and content and not on their looks. Because there is always someone out that looks better so it's up to you to bring in your character. She would say grow from your regrets. Robin taught herself to re-evaulate herself daily, so the situation is not repeated.

When she was really chilling with Courtney Diane she mentioned, how she had to have one of her representatives show up. I guess then just like sometimes now I was naive in saying were they other co-workers? It had to be an inside joke because Robin and Courtney Diane smiled as they both raised their eyebrows with that, I knew then that it was more than co-workers. Courtney Diane encourages Robin to break down her representation. Robin smiles showing her dimples saying when we are young, we represent; our parents rather if you are in school, church or just around the public and when you act up you have now altered your representation and your parents, grandparents will hear or know about your mishap and tap that little ass. So, when you are out you will remember how to represent. When you date or get married your representation appears as needed on this. You learn how to somewhat control but there is always that oops. So, one-time Ramon tried to hit me and control my antics, and one of my representatives appeared before she could call out her name to have her return back.

Courtney Diane chimes in encouraging Robin to tell me the name of the mean one and don't be shy. Robin says it must be Roberta she's calling the mean one. When I was in, I think junior high a friend said I look like a Roberta. I didn't then and still don't know what a Roberta looks like. Funny how we both use that name for what they call it a "representative". Robin laughs saying that she comes out when she is ready to just kick your ass or verbally take you there with no harsh words. Ironic in a very calm manner that confuses you, that you don't know if you should smile, run or say thank you, I think. Robin smiles, saying that she doesn't have any control over Roberta. She cringes when she tries not to say her name out too loud. She acts as if she is shivering, saying nervously that, I'm scared of her myself. Now she's my representative when needed. Sometimes she might come in form of a look or words, but by time she has arrived, the damage is already done, and she wants to stay and play a little longer. Normally I have to calm her down because she doesn't come out often, again with clarity only as needed. I am getting ahead of myself, let me back up to Ramon.

Ramon tried that move I knocked, actually meaning the rushing Roberta, knocked his narrow ass out. I just pictured how Robin said looking innocent it wasn't me that was her, Roberta pushing folks out of the way while laughing through her story. Ramon got that hitting act twisted and she, not me it was her actions knocked him straight out. After it was done, we set down on the couch with a glass of wine to soothe Roberta, before she became more worked up, because sister girl doesn't get out often and she enjoys the fresh air. When Roberta abruptly appeared, she shocked Ramon back into a little boy. He stuttered asking why you did that and why are you so violent that's a side I never seen of you. Hell, I've seen a side of you I didn't think exsited and for the hit I told him, so you know how that feels. Now he knows that hit hurts in more ways than one. I like Robin's demeanor she is always calm and gentle always all at the same time. No aruging or debating and if she did you wouldn't have figured it out until you are doing what she calmly managed to have you do.

Robin calmly talks about Ramon staying around. But, by that ten-year itch they were drifting apart, and she was just wondering about all the secrets he thought that he was hiding from me. She laughs slightly saying that she would just look at him thinking how or where she should cut him, then reality hits her saying that she needed to drift back and not lose her freedom. Then Robin said that thought drifted back again the last year of their marriage. She knew something was up, but she said that she was just in denial not her Ramon, not Ro but the few representatives tried to tell me. The signs were all there, but I didn't want to give up on my marriage and especially lose him to those scants. She thought about what she would be losing and not look at what she would be gaining. She stepped back and re-evaluated the situation and had a good talk with herself saying that she got to turn a negative into a positive that's the only way to keep it moving. But her eyes saw what her heart didn't want to believe and that thought drifted back again, and we know about that again, I wanted to cut him. She just wanted to hurt him in some way and the voice said again is your freedom worth all that let her have that headache that you know. She'll learn how to take stock in aspirin for her headache. So, the hitting, excuse me the hit and the arguing, nope don't need that type of frustration. Robin said that she was raised once don't think she needed to be raised again, her parents did a good job the first time.

God allowed her a graceful way out with dignity, respect and new form of freedom. Robin just looked at Courtney Diane and all she did was return the smile saying hmm and you thought it was just me uh? Courtney Diane says that Robin has calm energy. Robin represents what she wants you to see but she still is cool, just don't make her call on Roberta or any other of her representatives. She motions the count of five, four, three, two, one Robin calmly sits down on the couch. She crossed her legs saying that it was Roberta that had to calm down not her. Courtney Diane said I don't even mess with that beach, meaning Roberta as she fakes a shiver saying ooh. As I listened, I started to realize that I had more in common with them then and more now. Sometimes deliverance and how its is received can make a big difference when it comes to communication. I hope they will come by now that I will have a large backyard for entertaining.

I pack just enough so we weren't totally living out of boxes, but the time had arrived, and it was time to make that move. Bill brought in his work buddies looking fine and smelling good with their tight physique. Not that I noticed that the aroma of their cologne and wanting to follow the aroma that was lingering. Their fresh haircuts just enhance the view of watching them walk, hmmmph in cadance. Jesse, Sulli, Buckner and a new guys O'Neal and Moore all willing and eager to assist if I prepare a home cooked meal for them. This time no ow ooh, know as Bragg he had kitchen and cooking duties. They hug me and remind me that they remembered the last meal and look forward to good home cook meal. My reality snaps back from the view of nice-looking movers. That was the night that Bill showed how much of an impression I unknowingly left in form of slaps and all that came with it. As hard as I tried to remove that night, that blue stain never did go or fade away. Now we will be moving away from that blue stain. That blue stain will not ever happen again, so good bye blue. Every time I walked down the hallway mentally, I was forcing myself to look at that location and remember the actions that resulted from that horrific night. Now it's time to leave everything, including that blue stain.

I don't want to lose the relationships I have with some of the families. I hope that we can return occassionally and not lose contact with them. When we left the last apartment complex the fun and family relationships just faded away and everyone moved out and moved on to other locations making it impossible to stay in contact. Bill and his buddies left in the truck and cars heading over to our new place. I look around one more time taking a deep breath, mentally knowing that it's too late to change my mind. Clarence is at home just chilling and listening to music as he struggles to cook. He greets me with a brotherly embrace as I tell him this is it. With the biggest smile and hug he reminds me to call him if I needed him for anything. Through the feeling of the beat of his heart I knew he was sincere. I wanted to ask what he had been trying to tell me for so many years and just feeling and the look in his eyes he said more without saying anything. I felt that he was saying you're happy and I'm not going to take your joy away and know I'm here and just you be happy. Clarence added and don't make him happy at your expense, (a lot of silence with many words). Although my family and brother Charles were back home, I had another brother and his name was Clarence.

The next stop was Momo and I knew that would be another hard-good bye. I smell the aroma of Momo cooking a big difference from Amos mystery meals. Like she would say I didn't marry him for his cooking. She's fussing at the boys saying you are not going to make me crazy. I'm going to make you crazy, now get your narrow ass somewhere and take a seat. I guess that was her form of time out, and Ryan was okay he just looks like he was chilling too. Actually, he seemed as if this was routine for him. He was growing up and no more whining just a time out chill until he chilled so much, and fell off to sleep. Ryan looked so sound and peaceful. The funny part was her place was quiet. That was due to Bert, Chris and Manly having a softball game and Ryan stayed because he's a mama's boy. Plus, her cousin Mona was passing through for just a minute with her daughter Ramona. So she was putting some vittles together so they could have a little something as they make their pit stop. Her sister Mona hadn't seen the boys in a while but at least she can see Ryan's little narrow ass. Momo said that she didn't think that Ramona remembers him or her ass, because it's been a long time.

Her cousin Mona talks and moves faster and was hornier than she was. Mona laughs saying that sometimes she makes her blush and that takes some time to get her there unless you're Amos, and she winks with a shake and smile. We call her May. Mona's mother wanted to have that "M" name going but it stopped when Mona had Ramona. Her husband Raymen didn't want that tradition going and was persistant that he contributed a little something, so he should have his name in there somewhere other than the last name and make it work. The only name that he smiled on was Ramona coming from Raymen and Mona. Momo said that Mona stated that she would be on the tale end of Ramona's name. Raymen smiled his daughter his name and he kept smiling with the next sons Raymen II, (R2) and Romen, (Ro), not twins just his little village going on. According to Mona the persistant needed a little more persuasion if you know what I mean, as she raises her eyebrows. Then one more smile brought in Richmen, (RayRay) and don't ask why he's called RayRay. At first Momo had me thinking, then a ting went off in my head and I realized that she got me again, ew and too much vision. In the back of my mind was this like Clarence putting clients to sleep, except in this case Mona woke up with a smile and with my nine-month indigestion. With that I just smile saying at least she woke up with a smile. Momo laughs yep she woke with a smile that is now nine years old her long lasting tee-hee. Momo laughted harder, with she was surprised that Mona only had four babies. Everytime Raymen moved, walked, breathed, blink she was attacking him. They were very sporty she laughed saying she threw out her hip playing dunk ball. Mona loved banging pots and pans, flipping and flopping and slamming cabinets. Here I go again not thinking and forgeting who I was talking to. I asked was she a good cook but hated being on the kitchen with the banging and the slamming. Momo just looked at me, (with that familiar Reva clinic look), and I could only respond with a sincere what? When she raised her eyebrows looking with that smile, I knew she got me again and the same reaction and thought was ew, vision. As Robin would say TMI, (too much information with my added too much vision, ew).

Momo laughs as the girls run over and wake up Ryan not knowing that he was on time out. He snaps out of his brief nap and they take off not knowing that this might be the last time that they might play together. I don't know if I will be able to see Mona, but I sure want to put a picture with the tales. I should be over at our new place, but Bill had to fix some things at the place before we made it over there.

For now, I like the fact that I have some freedom still left to spend time talking with Clarence and little more time with Momo and her antics. She moves so well you wouldn't have known she had recoverd from a stroke. You can see the blessing in her eyes, smile and her movements. She welcomed and shared her family with love and an open heart. In this complex; I have established my extended family and I enjoyed everyone and everything that happened here other than the blue stain or the kneeling sometimes by the couch or what Clarence had to tell me but held back for so many years. I know we are leaving but that doesn't stop the heart from missing the family you have placed so gently there. My husband again is working at another place that we will call home. Our new place with new beginnings, and the hope that our marriage will grow into the ones that I had observed for many years.

I leave to make my move back to a partially empty apartment. Momo offers to let the girls stay until the last box is packed and ready to go. I appreciate the thought and take her up on her offer, but one thing I know is that Bill will not allow them to spend a night. I would agree with him we need to be together the first day or night in our new place. Yes, I agree, we should all be present to represent our family. Not like the representatives that are connected to Robin. I wondered what the names of my representatives would be, (that might show up). I know fear was there but to stand up to Bill like Roberta and the other women, that brings fear right up front. I walk and look through the apartment to make sure that we are not leaving anything. The place is clean but one more trip to this empty place for a final cleaning. This will finalize that we no longer lived here, and someone will be moving in and starting with their own new beginnings. Life has beginnings and endings and I want to end like my beginning married to Bill and raising our family. I just know that if I didn't marry Bill, I would have probably stayed in Oakwood hanging out with my girls and best friends, Debbie Ann, Sharon Denise and Melody Lynn. We would be together raising children and watching each others' famlies grow up together like we did when we were young. A new batch of cousins with no blood connection just a long-standing friendship and a loving relationship.

Chapter 54
Welcome To Our New Home
and I Meet Mona

The sun is shining through the heavy rain drops in beautiful Oceanview. The rain stayed with me so long I didn't think that I would ever see clearly but, today both eyes are opened, and the sun is coming through. This new place has room for when my or Bill parents come for a visit, they will have their own bedroom. My dad won't come unless he drives because to this day, he's still afraid, (uncomfortable), of flying same with Debbie Lynn's husband Froggy/Brian. There's no age on fear and it comes in different forms. I hope that my girlfriends will come out and visit. I know their funds are low just like ours. We will make it back home to Oakwood one day and show off our new addition, plus adding to the doubters that we are still married. My timing was right again, right when I'm walking through the apartment Bill and his boys showed up ready for the last load. Last seems to be the on-going theme. This will probably be the last time we come around to this location. Everyone seems to be moving and plus with only one car, that seems to always be occupied, (and not by me). I greet my smiling husband with a kiss as the guys ooh and ah laughing. In the back of my mind I just imagine that they miss their families and the intimacy that they took for granted. I know the feeling I miss my family in the same way but substituted them with other members that reminded me so much of them.

Well it was time to go and say that hard good bye. I go and get the girls hoping to see and meet Momo's cousin Mona. I was impressed with how she said she kept life into their marriage by belly dancing; reading sex books and one was called "Kama Sutra". Like Momo said she was surprised that they only had four babies and not a house full. With a pause she grabs her mouth saying let me back up. No Mona backed it up, those books put a smile, giggle and two back to back burps called Raenelle. Then he/ they threw in Raeqell the last burp. Raymen sure did make sure his name was in there in so many ways. He didn't want the 'M'" theme but somehow the "R' theme made many appearances. Raymen made that clear to Mona he was a participant too. She was too busy smiling and burping, or was that indigestion huh? Inside I laugh everybody got my joke and it only happened one time. Momo said that she forgot about them, they came ten years later. I bet Mona remembered that giggle and put that 'Kama' book down. Raymen and Mona have always been faithful to each other. With all that smiling, Mona still had smiling energy for Raymen. So many years later she's still smiling just no burps. Those six Raymen extensions still live at home. Mona's smiles became bigger with teeth and all showing. Humph, I thought his Rayville sounds like Reggieville. Reggie Coy and Clovis are still probably enjoying Veretta's bunch of babies. I think her brother Floyd said Veretta had seven or nine. I admired them for their strength and energy.

As for me I struggle with two. I can't imagine me or us with having more, but surprises can happen. When I think back about Charlotte thinking she was having one then found out she was having twins. Then she said God threw her a curve ball that landed in a bucket of milk that splashed on her face, and when she wiped her eyes to see clearer, she was giving birth to triplets. The last time I saw her she had a shopping cart full of children. Then I get a funny reminder of Catrice and Greekum with their eleven last count and the endless sight from a van of the heads running into PataRee's for a birthday party. I flashed back on Catrice not knowing that her mother- in- law Anuna was trying whisper to her about their family history. Anuna was trying to tell Catrice that Greekum was potent. Catrice laughed saying with her accent that she couldn't understand what she was saying. She thought she was saying he was important, and he was very important to me and why did she had to whisper. She loved that walking hanger with no muscles, just looked like skin and bones. They still probably to this day still have the same love they had when they fell in love and maybe stronger. So much love and they still make time for their family and each other. The last time I saw them they didn't look tired just Catrice pregnant again. She probably knows that word all so well after at least nine agains. Greekum probably joined in with saying again oh well. To look at them you wouldn't have thought they were a family of twelve plus or was that eleven with children plus the parents. Either way two vehicles are required. Just out of shear curiosity when or if Greekrum and Catrice ever ride in the same car or van. With two car seats there's very little space in our car.

I just look around our place knowing that I might not see anyone again. Well I know I won't see our apartment again it's already ready to be occupied. The apartment is just waiting for us to get out or move out of the way. This is the same feelings that I'm so familiar with, but it doesn't make it any easier leaving another family. Bill's ready for his family and as I look around, he must feel the sadness in my heart and takes my hand as he carries Sabrina while at the same time Sierra holds mine. This was a first us leaving together to a new place that we decided kinda on together. Love makes you think and do some crazy things. Maybe that's why Courtney Diane only deals with that emotion minus the "s" and saving that emotion for just in case. While driving I look around at the places that Sierra and I traveled so many times in her wagon or on the bus. I will not see the familiar bus drivers that always looked out for us like Fred, Carl, Will, or Nick and Sierra's favorites Hector, Admiral, Darrell and Ralph. Memories flash as I remember us playing at the park and Sierra met new friends. Oh yes, the walks to the corner drug store that was many corners away. The bus stops that we knew by heart and the routes and times, were a second nature to our adventurous bus rides or wagon travels. I close my eyes and remembered the time when Robin offered us a ride and I wanted to take her up on her offer so bad, but I didn't want to disappoint Sierra on our adventure. I remembered sighing as I looked at her tail lights drive away and hoping one day, I would be able to cash in on that raincheck. That resturant hmmm that we went to was so good. I still remembered the taste of fresh lemonade and the turkey cran-berry sandwich, hmmm. Robn's story was very entertaining. I never got a chance to tell her how nice is was just being out of the apartment and talking to an adult.

Only if Bill really knew how this was affecting us or me. I sometimes wish he could understand my feelings of being lonely. We didn't have a second car just a bus ticket and transfers. Sometimes those long rides were so peacefull just looking out the window as Sierra describes through her eyes what was exciting to her. As her scenery changed and the pictures, she drew from looking was my peace. Her excitement was refreshing, but there were times that I was tired. While I looked out the window, I had appreciation for much of nothing. I looked out the window just staring ahead at much of nothing. I knew we had to grow, but I just wanted to stop a long enough to see the flowers grow. But in this case, I had to pick them up and take them with me. I had to let go. I had to trust Bill that this is a growth process for both of us and our family. The same trust I had to have when we married, and we moved from Oakwood to sunny California. I had to remind myself that we both left the comforts of our parents' home.

As the scene's changes, I try to spot areas that I would like to have us travel to in car or more than likely the bus. So far, I haven't seen too many bus routes. I guess since there are a lot of houses with cars, they might have not seen a need. Well for me I see a need but who am I. We pull up to the soldiers' boys, looking mighty fine unloading the truck into our new home. Sierra yells out and while I turn to see what the commotion was about? I turn my head to see the beautiful smile of Loren! I can't believe he's back. I give him a big smile from my heart at the same time won-dering if he is on the run because of Fifi. I don't know how far her craziness went this time. Everytime I thought she made the finale; she pulls another antic which is usually crazier than the one before. We get out to stretch our arms out to Loren, as the soldiers smile as they keep it moving. Now I understand why Bill wanted us to stay at the apartment. Everything was in place and ready for us to move in and for me to cook that promised meal. The only boxes left for me to unpack were placed in the various rooms. Some of the boxes were in the garage and the others were placed in the corner of the room nice and neat. I know Bill had something to do with that. He was and still likes to have everything clean and in order, no exceptions to that rule. Loren was telling me how good I look after birth. Bill co-signs with a smile no word, just a smile. That did bother me, but I wasn't going to let him get to me, especially not today. He probably didn't realize what he did or didn't say. There were hamburgers and a bag of potatoes ready for their requested dinner. So fat burgers and fresh cut french fries were about as close as they were going to get for a home-cook meal. The dessert that we normally try to at least have with each dinner will be frozen apple pie. My mother started that dessert with meals in which has been passed down to myself and my siblings. I just know after every meal when we were younger, we always had some form of dessert. I didn't want to break that tradition but there is nothing that at the time I could think to possibility put together, (other than this frozen apple pie).

While the girls pull their cousin Loren through the house looking into each room, I will break away to prepare dinner. Bill and his friends take a break as they smell the aroma of french fries and burgers. As I pat them down and prepare to flip and flop, Momo's words echos. I pictured her laughing and asking do I know about flipping and flopping. I thought to myself, I'm looking at you how hard was that visuals. Then she flips no pun meant saying that I'm not talking about that type of flipping. I think she was just testing the water and that splash of cold water startled me. While Momo was shaking and singing she gently broke it down for me about the terms flipping and flopping. She just said Amos and her flip and flop all the time and she wasn't talking about the mattress or burgers. Then she would laugh adding with much love and reaction from me with they need a new one, and maybe should invest in the mattress company. I would respond after the shock with my usual, ew, and too much vision. I sometimes couldn't understand how she would be cooking burgers, then she switches it to bedroom antics. But that was something she always managed to slip in and would totally throw me off. Right before we left, she got me again with her cousin Mona with the pots, pans and the slamming of the cabinets. With a new place maybe, I might try new ideas. Hmmm that book 'Kama Sutra' added two more babies to her cousin Mona. Hmmm, do I want to add two more or a cart full of bobbin heads? I remember pretending and laughing in school that I would have twelve and name them after each month. Wow thank God that was childhood talk and not my reality. We had silly thoughts with childish laughter and no clue of what we laughed about.

As I flipped the last of the burgers, we began to sit in various locations. Some sat at the kitchen table and others in the front room. Sierra and Sabrina sat at their kiddie table that was just right, as they giggled while eating fries and tearing the buns off their burgers. The guys talked and laughed as they made the noise of enjoying a home enviroment with a warm cooked meal. I just remember enjoying hearing the laughter and appreciating the family atmosphere. It's good that Loren is here, because the last time I received compliments I was putting a cold towel on my face. That can't happen with Loren being here. So, I'm safe as I get back to enjoying my family and guests in our new home. I'm trying to settle the butterflies in my stomach that are nervously trying to take off. Today there will be no blue stains and no reminders and I'm making sure that I behaved myself. Funny thing was I thought I behaved and kept a very low profile. Bill's buddies had very little conversation and I had very little eye contact with them. I felt or tried to be as invisible as possible. Today I didn't want no drama just wanted my family. Loren is my saving grace and I was looking forward to hearing about Fifi. He was another connection to the outside world, and I was glad he flew in. Laughter fills the room with various conversations. I observed and again appreciated the freedom and calmess that existed. Loren excuses himself and goes and sits his tall statue at the tiny table where the girls are eating. His knees were almost hitting his face as the girls looked and laughed with him. The laughter and conversations faded into the backyard with the girls running around the back as their cousin Loren chases them as they run laughing and screaming. I watch from the patio door as I cleaned up from the conversation and laughter. I embraced the feeling that this feels like home as I watched and laughed from the inside where no one can hear a sound from me.

This place had a dishwasher now I'm not the only dishwasher in the house. Clean up was quick and nice. As I walked through the house my mind and heart are in ah! This place is nice and huge, and our furniture fits in just right and nothing is out of place other than the boxes neatly organized in the corner. There was plenty of shade and room to run in the backyard. I pictured the last time I was in this type of friendly warm setting was at Courtney Diane's parents' home. There I had a front row seat to the gentle side of her. That was a rare moment that she reminded me that she is human. She showed feelings with an "s", at least feelings that stretched out to her parents and what she calls the herd sounding nieces. I take a break and go and kiss Bill on the cheek as his friends stared and smiled. I politely take a seat next to by husband. I can tell he liked seeing the envy in his friends' eyes as he smiled at me as I took my seat. For that quick kiss of a second all eyes were on me, then they went back to their conversations. Their conversations they were having slowly faded away as they prepared to leave. I didn't get up as they shook my hands thanking me for the home cooked meal and in return, I thanked them for helping us move. I watched Bill laughing with them as he escorted them to the door. They said their good-byes to Loren and the girls who paid very little attention but did respond with a good bye.

The girls run into the house and Loren sees his opportunity and grabs a seat in the shade catching his breath. Funny, (with a ha-ha) how vivid the thoughts flash as I sit here enjoying the view. I look at Loren with his beautiful dimple smile and eyes twinkling and he responds with what? I return the smile showing my dimples saying you know what, why? He smiles responding with what why I'm here? I laugh saying a quick yep and how's Miss Fionila, you know her, (saying her name quickly), FiFi? He takes a pause with no, surprise saying I guess she's around. Her crazy ass might be around here somewhere, (while turning his head looking around). I look at him come on give it up she didn't leave that easy. Right when he was responding, Bill comes back to his seat hearing her name, and saying you still dealing with that crazy ass beach? Loren jumped back into his what was gentle now harsh tone. Saying no I cut that crazy ass beach and her antics on a permanent.

Fifi showed up to the shop looking good. Actually, I didn't know she was standing behind me until the boys at the shop stopped talking their normal shift. Their looks went into a stare and behind me there she was slimmer smiling Fifi. She did look the part, but I knew about the other crazy as parts and that shift didn't change over night. Bill looks at me and motions and mouths watch this. So, did you take her out? Loren smiled and reluctantly gave up his answer, with a strong hell yeah. I took her crazy ass out. He said that he had to get confirmation of her change, (while laughing). I looked at him with my head slightly tilted asking, so all that permanent talk was just a temporary thought, uh? Bill and I gave each other a smile and a dap. We lean back waiting for the story to come as the girls run back outside to play. I guess that old rule of either you stay in or out went by the wayside. Before he tells the story, he adds I'm getting tired of ya asses laughing at me especially when it comes to Fifi crazy ass antics. He laughs saying this shift is funny as hell uh. She should have made that shift work with TJ trifling ass. I still owe his ass my foot. Surprisingly she didn't have her side kick Lucee. He laughed I guess she got over derail. With that we all started laughing.

Loren insisted that one place he knew he wasn't taking her crazy rude ass was back to his place. So, Loren added with check this shift out, we went to the movies and she set there not talking or commentating on the movie all loud and shift. She didn't act stupid and she put her head on my shoulder acting all gentle and with some sense. But get this I'm still suspect, she did too much of crazy and her bloodline has the same crazy. I laughed asking is she related to the CraCra's? Loren paused saying yeah something like that. Fifi wasn't smacking on gum or yelling or spitting out popcorn while talking through the movies. Now she wants to act like a lady. Nope I wasn't buying it or standing in some long ass line to purchase her blue skies. I took her home then tried the dating a few more times checking the water. You know the water could be deep, shallow or just too damn hot or cold. Bill and I sit on the edge waiting for the catch, at the same time eating our imaginary bowl of popcorn. He went to say that they had walked the park and strolled through Evergreen plaza. He said that he had to pick up some sneakers and she asked could she ride with him. He thought no harm and no damage. So far, the water is calm no waves and no side effects from Fifi. Sierra and Sabrina finally came in the house because they were getting tired, and Bill and I looked at Loren to hurry up and get to the end of this entertaining story. Loren responds with okay, okay adding that it was his birthday and she suggested that we go to this nice resturant downtown. I thought what the hell and why not. This resturant had a nice atmosphere and Fifi was looking tight.

I ran into you remember Nikya Nicole, (he raises his eyebrows) and her sister MyNeisha. He tries to refresh Bill's memory by saying that Nini she was that fine ass junior that teased us when we were freshman. Bill expressions shows that he really didn't remember her or her sister. Inside I'm glad that they didn't leave that type of impression. Unlike Markay, Brian, Markus and his brothers all fine singing "Didn't I Blow your Mind"? To this day I still remember their moves and yes, they did blow my mind and all the other junior high school girls at McMillian. Humph to this day I still picture them singing in their tight polyester pants harmonizing. Ooh yep but that's my thought and secret that will not ever be exposed. I chuckle inside with I can't tell Bill everything I need my me memory moments. Loren's tone changed saying that before the Matre 'D' seats us he runs into Nini, and she embraces me with a warm big hug that brought my boyish fantasy back and I didn't want to let go of that high school dream. I embraced her, and her ass felt good. But oh no, my ass had this so call date called Fifi and I couldn't continue with my imagination. Fifi trifling ass was staring and making grunting noises taking that dream away and it went up like a puff a smoke. Bill, Nini was still as fine as she was back in high school just parts filled in with age and time that formed humph. I smile saying you know I'm still here and I can hear you right? Loren laughs saying hey we're family and Bill didn't remember her or much of anything especially after he met you. Rita don't be silly you were all his ass talked about. But anyway, once she let go of the grunts sounds Fifi's corner mouth is all twisted. The only thing I could come up with was what? Loren toned changed saying Bill, (and looks at me) and Rita, that he was pissed because Fifi had snatched his high school fantasy away, damn. Fifi's face said it all and Loren didn't care. He said it wasn't that kinda party. This wasn't a date she was just a happen that joined him in a meal. All I could think of was how I'm gonna slip my number to Nini.

Fifi was the furthest thing from his mind and it must have showed. He didn't hear a word she was saying until her ass tried ordering a lobster and it wasn't happening on his bill. He said that he snapped his ass back with a nah and oh hell no! He said that she had his ass stuttering and shift with, what the??? No, I'm not into lobster, but prime rib or filet mignon will work for both of us. He flashed her a smile and insisted that if you want the lobster, (saying slowly), go ahead. He said that he encouraged her with a lasting smile, (but inside he was really saying this is your last meal on my ass, order up), and bon voyage to your ass and good bye. He watched and thought to himself that he wanted Fifi to enjoy each morsel because that would be the last entree, she was getting from him. Fifi excuses herself, and he said that he didn't look at her walk away he was still focused on Nini, (as he sings her name). When Fifi returned smiling gentlly sits down placing the napkin with class in her lap. A male waiter brings appetizers to our table with no smile just being professional. Loren said he didn't think much of the waiter. He knew his entree would be coming in form of filet mignon with an added dish called Nini. Oh yes, he wanted to see her come and go, oh yes! I had to insert oh really Loren! Did she have those child bearing hips to make Mama Rosey Josie proud? He laughs, I would have fun trying, making Mama Rosey Josie proud? Yeah that's my mama, I love that lady and one day she gonna get some little ones from me. He added with sincerity that his brother Akil and Alice gave her four with one named after her Aamira Josay. Aamira Josey was the last grandchild and the one that is dearest to her heart. She loves the boys you know, that but it's something about girls. Bill smiles I know I told Rita watch us have girls and yep we got them, and I love em. Bill smiles looking at me raising his eyebrows like it was my fault.

Loren smiles saying that he was preparing to see his entre called Nini. To his disappointment it's the same waiter. He wasn't rude but strangely professional occassionally glancing over at Fifi as he set our plates on the table. Fifi smiled trying to thank him and her appreciation seems like it landed on his deaf ears. He was not feeling her in any way. I don't think he really appreciated the thank you, so I added another thank you and he slowly responded. Loren knew then that something wasn't right on this shift and he could feel that her ass had done something. Where was my extra scenery in form of Nini? He smiled hoping that he would to see her coming and going. He looked over at Bill with raised eyebrows with a quick wink. Nah they did a switch and he didn't see her the rest of the night, no good byes, no warm long hugs. Loren sadly says sounding like a little boy, all I wanted was to feel the warmth of her body and her booty. Get this shift right when I was in my fantasy world of Nini... Then I hear Fifi's nagging ass voice changed all thoughts and dreams, again, damn. Fifi nerved up saying that I wasn't paying her enough attention, just ignoring her. I didn't ignore her belching ungrateful ass. This trick, Fifi sitting with me, in front of me couldn't help but to see her head blocked all viewing. I watched him smiling while shaking his head saying I broke it down to this ungrateful thang. I gently told her that I paid for your empty ass stomach that kept growling, until the noise went to a purr after finishing off that lobster / steak and all those other entrees. I thought that sound of your ass and stomach were competing. I listened to your ass belching like you just had a six pack. Then I watched Fifi dabbed the corner of your mouth trying to muffle her belching noise. I asked her don't your ass know how to politely burp in public. He looks at me don't women or ladies dab the corner of their mouths? No, not her no class ass she took the whole napkin across her mouth. I just smiled saying well hmmm. Before I could finish my thoughts, he jumps into hell I'm glad it was from that end and not the other. If it came from the other end, her ass would have propelled out that front door.

Then the bill came, which was worth it to see Nini, at the same time get rid of Fifi crazy ass. Loren shook his head while saying that he took her ass straight home. He acted like a gentleman and walked her to the door, not looking at any body parts of her body that he would be missing. Once we made it to her front door, I heard the yelling from the inside. I knew this meant that everyone was home. That crowded ass house is always adding more to the crowd. Hell, her ass should have been full and ready for bed anyway. Especially after her ass ate all that lobster/steak. Fifi's last sound before snoring, should be a burp from either end. Anyway, she was not my problem, and this wasn't my place. To get over this night I sealed it with a good bye. I gave her a quick hug and kiss on the cheek and told her take care and thank you. This was my finale sealed with an audi. Oh, I did add a smile saying good night. My best birthday present happened, was taking my ass home to bed with no loud ass snoring coming from Fifi...

When she did stay at my place I couldn't sleep because Fifi snoring had me jumping out the bed thinking somebody was trying to start up my shift. She sounded like a car starting up, and that snoring noise had me jumping and running to the window. I like my car especially parked in my driveway, not to mention the gas from her ass burning up my legs. With that last comment, Bill looks at me and I smile knowing I haven't gassed his leg in a long time and, and it was only that one time. How long can you blame a girl for gassing your legs? Loren was so busy fussing and laughing he didn't notice the glance that Bill had giving me. Loren continues with saying; that he couldn't get no kind of sleep, because he was jumping out of the bed to either go to the window or fan his legs trying to cool them off from that burning sensation that was coming from the gas of Fifi's tight ass. Loren smiles well I did put her to sleep my fault huh, (his eyes twinkled on that remark).

We laughed as the girls finally became tired and we really didn't realize how late it was. That was our cue to go in and chill inside. This was a long day for them, actually for all of us. We get the girls ready for bed and place them into their own rooms. This time Loren doesn't have to share a room that had balloons and other signs that this room belongs to a little girl. I'm tired myself and I go to bed early saying good night as I give Bill a kiss good night while saying nite to Loren. I knew they were going to continue their conversation of what they really wanted to say now that I'm absent. Before going to bed I do my last check in on the girls that have already fallen asleep in Sierra's bed. The feeling in this room is warm and fresh. I can't wait for Bill to come in and enjoy the warmth of this bed and room. This was a good move and good to see Loren again. We don't have our family come out as much as we would like, but my mom makes her way here when she can. I love to see her but like a little girl I hate to see her go. She's my mommy and I still miss her, my dad, sisters and my brother. Not to mention the fun and laughter with Debbie Ann, Sharon Denise and Melody Lynn. I drift off into my thoughts of Bill and the blessed day we had and the joy of sharing our new home with family and friends. I feel the warm body of my husband and we both are so tired. We wrap up into each other and fall into our own deep snores. This will be the only intimacy that we will share, other than our hearts beating together again.

That morning we shared a bathroom that had a shower and bath tub wow. we wake up to stretching to hoping we would smell the aroma of Loren cooking a big breakfast for us. I can't help chuckling at how Fifi had left breakfast all over his car saying how she hoped he enjoyed the breakfast because she did. I would bring it up, but I know how much he loved his car and plus the fact that he just had it detailed. I'm not going to mention that minor incident because Bill will take it and roll with it. The girls wake up in a slow mode. All that excitememt wore their little energy down. There were no special plans for today other than enjoy the weekend and finish unpacking. Bill had to work this week, so little time will be spent with Loren. Loren made it clear that he wasn't staying long just wanted to surprise us and he had missed us and took advantage of the cheap airfares. His flight will be leaving late Monday night. Well that explained the light luggage. Sierra would be riding into base with Bill so that would leave me and Loren with no car just fun and conversation. He didn't care because now he had sometime to work on spoiling Sabrina before he leaves. That day we didn't do much of nothing. With that large backyard and a light breeze, we had the feeling of a summer day. It felt like being back home in Oakwood. It felt good with having that feeling of an old-fashioned summer day in the fall. Bill didn't wake me up for breakfast, but I felt his soft lips kiss my cheek good bye. Sierra was dressed and ready to go. She runs and jumps on the bed to kiss me good bye and with that I just get on up and start my day. Loren is still sleeping and not making a sound and Sabrina is out for the count too. This is just enough time for me to shower and get dressed, for just to hang around the house. I have that same familiar feeling of a little boredom trying to set in. In Oakwood we would get dressed to go nowhere. Maybe over to a friend's house or when Mommy was alive, we would go to South Oakwood and spend some time with her and my grandmother Hazel. This day felt something like that, ready to dance just waiting for the music.

I sit looking out the window just like I'm doing now as I enjoy the rain. My thoughts scatter in so many directions that I have no focus on anything in general. I kinda know why Mommy would just sit and look out the window that was her form of peace and her private thoughts. Half of my family is gone, and the other half is still sound asleep and it's just me. For some reason I don't have the energy to unpack the boxes. They seem to be in my view just waiting to be emptied and placed into new locations. I know that if I don't unpack those boxes, I will hear Bill's voice. If I don't hear his voice of concern, his almond shaped eyes will transform to one giant cyclop eye. Funny flashbacks of how Reva described her mother when she would fuss how her eyes would form into one giant eye, (cyclops front and center tee-hee-hee). That was funny as she said that she had to step back so she wouldn't get freezer burn or frost bite from the ice vapors coming from her heart. She added that she wanted to keep a chisel handy, so she could chip the ice away, so her heart could get some circulaton.

Now Reva is caring for her mother and son. She showed the same strength at the clinic that I remembered seeing when she talked about caring for her mother. Her mother was sick but well enough to give her the house free and clear. Her brothers and sisters refused to assist with the health of their mother but fussed about not receiving their fare share. What fair share the woman was still alive just a little sick. That might have been the only way she could repay Reva aka /Dorothy for staying with her. Reva's mother was thanking her in her own way for giving up unselfishly her life to help her. I support that decision, because Reva gave up on her career to help her mother. Her mother loved her more than she thought. They enjoyed the house and being around each other. Reva's siblings wanted the equity but didn't want to pay the taxes or for any needed repairs. Reva shook whatever off and kept her life moving despite her family antics. They fussed but didn't try to test or challenge her. Yep kinda like Courtney Diane, they have a lot in common. Funny when Courtney Diane said that her sister JJ was afraid to tell her that they lost or was losing her apartment and went into hiding. How did she say it; you take other womens' husbands, didn't think about that your dumb ass would or could be stabbed, shot, ass kicked or possibly go to hell and you were afraid to tell me I'm losing my shift? I guess that would be an eyebrow raise…

Chapter 55
Hello to My New Neighbors

I watched the cars traveling up and down our street not much traffic but enough for me to wish I was one of those drivers, driving any kinda of car. I think about the many cars we had. But, only one car and one driver at one time. I remember the various cars; one that we had to pray for it to start, and another one if it rained and you hit a puddle the car would stop, then there was the car that we had to use two feet and it wasn't a clutch. Whatever it took I would love to have my own car again. I wanted the freedom to just take off and not be stuck at home all the time, while Bill enjoys the sites of California, as I viewed my world from bus windows. Sabrina wakes up before the mentally tired Loren. He was tired and Fifi mentally wore him out. Sierra and Sabrina are okay with cereal yummy to them and okay for me. Loren wakes up and gets dressed. I asked if he wanted to go on adventure of the neighborhood. This seemed like a tradition of discovering our new surroundings. It sure did beat being at home all the time. We load up the wagon with smiles and ready for the road. Our timing was perfect, we meet our two new neighbors outside talking. We walk by the new neighbors, pausing our conversation to greet them with humble smiles. They greet us both, but their smiles and eyes are on Sabrina and Loren. Loren is paying very little attention to their glares. The older lady slightly gray piercing eyes introduces herself a Miss Mayla but call her Miss Mary, and the other neighbor just out side her yard introduces herself as Amerley, but we can call her Amer but sometimes we might hear the name Vicki. Miss Mary says in a low voice; don't ask sometimes she makes appearances. They both laughed and the funny part I did understand its' like Robin's Roberta and Courtney Diane's Sonya.

Loren just smiles as they leaned down to shake the tiny hands of Sabrina as they introduced themselves and she proudly tells them her name. Out of no where a young lady comes out must be Miss Mary's daughter. Whoever she was her eyes seemed to be stuck on the smiling Loren. One thing I know from talking with Loren she is far from his type, but he politley returns the smile but with less teeth. Miss Mary picks up on the connection that her daughter is trying to make and she introduces her as her single, college graduate daughter, Addison. Hmm an old name for a desperate sounding young lady trying to show dimples that didn't exist. Addison seems to have her eyes glued on Loren and by his smile he's holding back the laughter. I try to hold my laughter inside too. I had a hard smile, because in my own way I'm rolling inside myself. I'm able to hold my laughter by smiling saying to Loren we better keep moving your cousin is getting restless. With that statement you can see the eagerness from the need to know neighbors if Loren is my husband or brother. Addison's smile kept her tongue from falling out as Loren slender bow legged look walked away. I didn't want to break her heart or thoughts in telling her that he will be leaving tonight, hmm bummer. We walk for blocks as Sabrina enjoys the breeze and the ride. Her favorite saying with her small voice thanks for the ride lady. Don't know where she heard that, but she knows just when to say her phrase. We gracefully excuse ourselves from curious eyes. I could feel their eyes on us, but I felt good vibes from them. Not a Momo replacement but interesting.

Loren pulls the wagon not giving another thought to what just happened. The houses are nice and large with manicured lawns. Nice and quiet neighborhood, no sounds of kids playing in the streets like we used to when we were young, but the day is young, and they might be in school, or still asleep. I asked him whatever happened to Nini did they make any connection? He looks at me like do you want to know, or do you want to know? I respond as I try to hold back my laughter saying yep, and I followed up with a come on I'm not going to laugh. Mr. Loren please tell me about Miss Nikya Nicole, and I promised him that I wouldn't laugh about his Nini. He looks at me saying your lying, you can't even give me a straight face. I see and hear your loud smile coming out. Loren said that he ran into Nini at White Castles. He had to make a stop before going to meet Akil. I knew his ass would be late and my stomach said feed me I'm hungry. Then I heard a back up with growling not like the noise that came from Fifi's growling sounds, that didn't sound human. I had to step back just in case something foreign came from her stomach and slap the shift out of me for staring. I knew she carried Lucee everywhere, but this thing didn't have that big ass gap. My response was how can I not laugh when you are talking like this. He had to admit this shift was funny but it's real and my ass was in the mix. Loren started laughing himself which caused Sabrina to join in as she enjoys the ride. We see signs of clear land meaning the park is coming up. This park seems far away, and this is an adventure.

Loren went back to his Nini story saying that when his order was completed, he turned around, and there she was Miss Nini. He smiled adding she was his coming and going. This was an opportunity presented to get another bear fantasy hug, with no Fifi crazy ass interruptions. He asked her what was up that she didn't come back to his table… she said his girl stepped to her. Loren said he had to break in and end that connection. Saying oh hell no, that is not his girl she's her crazy ass mama

Rosetta's girl. Loren snapped with asking Nini that she let her step and she didn't step up, what happened? Nini said she had to step back because she didn't know what the hell this beach was tripping on. She hasn't seen me since high school and was surprised but happy at the same time. Nini said that thang of yours politely approached her smiling. Which I thought she was being cool and all, saying that she would appreciate if I would accept the tip from her. She said that she looked at this person wondering what tip? The food wasn't ready, but I listened, waiting for her line to come because, I wasn't feeling this beach. Her tip was stay away from our table. That Feline or Fifi whatever animal you want to call her.... said that she carries heavy items and useful tools and will break them off into my smiling hugging ass. Her tip was getting her another waiter. Then that thang added more insults saying she didn't want a mistress or a trick in waiting, waitress. Nini insisted that she didn't need that type of drama. She wanted to tell her dumb ass she was the hostess and was just helping. Nini smiled raising her eyebrows, asking where did I find that dumb ass beach? As far as a mistress shift, she laughed at me saying that was my trick. Nini snapped back and looking mighty fine saying, back in the day she would have bought out many heavy items and see which one weighed the most. Feline didn't scare her just wasn't worth it. Your little puppy, Fifi right, gave her too much credit from a hug.

Loren smiled saying that he told her, he was sorry about all that. Then right before he was ready to give her his number, he heard some energetic mouths come in yelling, 'Mama, mama', we want! He just looked at the many small sizes. She only had three, but they were small threes. They had my head slowly turning left, there's one right, there's another one, and a little baby/toddler in the center. To me they looked like they were close in age. So, Rita, that meant she is very fertile and with new baby daddys'. Baby daddies was not my option, and just wasn't feeling myself be added as a multiple choice. That wasn't for me and I'm sure that was a hell no from me! He laughs saying that he was too young and didn't want fresh young daddy drama, nah. Timing was good, and my order came up right after she finishes putting money together for payment. Broke and small ones, I wasn't feeling that shift either. She gives me her number, and, in this case, she looked mighty fine from the back. I left her there and combined her reciept with her number and my number and threw them both away. That would be the only time we would share something. Loren eyes twinkle as he asked the question of why he's surrounded by these crazy ass women. I laughed maybe you need to take Mama Rosie Josey's advice and stop shopping in the basement and stay away from those mark downs. With his twinkling almond shaped eyes, he laughs saying did my mama call you? I laughed, saying yeah and she wants to know how's that working out for you? Have you tired all the floors and ready to step out on the top final floor? We go back and forth as he pulls the wagon giving my arms freedom to swing and enjoy the walk and conversation as we explore new territory. This park is huge and cleaner. Loren wastes no time in taking Sabrina over to the slides and baby swings. When he eventually makes it to the top floor that woman would have been worth his wait. He has some growing and as much as he loves kids, he would be a good father and husband. Loren has almost hit everything, according to his smorgasborg of women. He loves women, but he exercised what seems like discipline when it comes to a commitment. His actions indicate that he's ready to settle down and give Mama, Miss Rosie Josey some grandbabies with the right woman. The special one he has been searching for, with those child bearing hips will happen someday. How did he word that phrase, 'that the front and back got to match!!

His presence has been a beautiful blessing. And, I love to see the joy in Bill's eyes when Loren and him reminisce and just talk. I try not to hang out too much with them, so they can have the freedom to talk, swear and do them. I had to admit I do like hearing the Fifi stories. But Loren has made it very clear in so many ways that she is not the one. The last thing he wanted was some loud ass kids acting just like their loud ass mama. Hey, our kids would be the ones you would rather see them going than coming, lock the doors and close the shades we are not home. That's probably how Courtney Diane's parents' felt when her nieces stormed through. I thought she was kidding but, I heard the sound. They sounded like a herd of something storming through. Funny ha-ha how so many little feet could make all that noise? All that noise and energy was non- stop. No wonder Courtney Diane's parents always looked at the clock when they came through. That explained why Courtney Diane has a thing for time, she was always looking at her watch or clock. I forgot she got that habit from her dad, Papa Cleve, Jr. from working with the railroad. Then with the added watch touch from her Mother Flo; looking at her watch and looking at them look at her while she looks at her watch with the question of what time is it and responding with is it time to care? I wondered how many times she said that to them. How many times did Courtney Diane want to say hell you're the one with the watch! I wondered if the crazy answer that Courtney Diane wanted to give showed at anytime in her eyes or expressions.

Being with family is what this is all about and those captured memories is something that is stored in the heart and we won't ever let go. My heart embraces the vision of Loren and Sabrina laughing and the joy of having family here again. I join in sliding throwing my hands up in the air feeling the breeze as I slide down or swing as high as I can. This brings back memories of freedom, I took so much for granted as a child. While we were laughing, we were feeling the breeze of freedom. Some of us embrace freedom more than others. I wondered which category I fell into. Lloren seems to guard his freedom in not allowing his space in relationships to become too confined. Sabrina starts fighting sleep as she tries to keep her eyes open as Loren carries her back to her wagon. I know he's leaving today but, when he is here, he doesn't know how much of a comfort he brings to our family. This is good to be in a new place, but fears try to join in with the butterflies that are trying to take flight inside my stomach as my thoughts go everywhere. On our way back home, Loren and I still have small talk and the walk back seemed faster.

I guess Addison timed it just right she was dressed and ready to show off her make-up to Loren. I noticed but Loren was mentally somewhere else, just like he was when he meant her the first time. She must have kept a good watch out of her window waiting for us to return. Just like I enjoy every me moment I get to enjoy my Chai tea, as the rain cleans my windows. Inside I wanted to kindly give her the heads up don't waste your time. Addison put time into her make- up and her very revealing outfit. She looked rather nice and, if time would have been allowed, I think Loren might have talked to her. She was attractive and funny. Loren doesn't pass up too many 'because she was there', opportnities. I wanted to ask him about his thoughts. Just had the inquisitive thought of how he processes his thoughts and how he feels and how the situations workout for him?

Loren needed to get away and we needed to see him. One thing Bill won't do while he's here is yell or belittle me. I learned to dissect Bills words just like I sub- stitute Courtney Diane's words. Courtney Diane said that she loves saying funk. She like the way it feels in her stomach as it travels with energy up to her throat and bounces off her tongue into the air. The force comes out with is very soothing to her ears. She didn't blink and just said it with strong conviction. Now when Bill says funk, now that's an action word or an act, and saying you means it is directed at me, so that's a directive and beach is a noun because he is using it as a name for me. So, if you put it that way hmm, its kind of softens the blow to the ears and for some reason dosen't hurt as bad when you break it down. I know when he uses his special adverbs, or directives, or nouns they become just words. Those words just make me feel so warm and fuzzy inside! I would ask Bill why are you talking to me like that? Then he adds the noun of beach and I again being studious ask why call me that, I'm the mother of your daughters. That seems to either soothe him or make him madder. He says he wants me to be as mad as he is, and my response is why you seem to be mad enough for both of us. Then his finale would end with that special noun. I have learned slowly what Courtney Diane said I have feeling without out the "s". I think I'm slowly getting there when the words that come from Bill are not very flattering. I guess the times that I was in class and not holding up the wall at the principal's office paid off. Didn't know years later that I would be using it in this form, but oh well my parents would be happy or proud that my education is paying off. Funny, now how I see clearly of the importance of adverbs, and nouns.

I guess Loren and I both have drifted off into our own thoughts as Sabrina drifted off to a deep snore. After we passed the new and improved Addison, (who just wanted a little conversation with Loren). I kind of wished that Loren would have had a little conversation for her. I could tell that Loren's thoughts were not on her. Addison was pretty, but she lived here, and he was going back home to Chicago. One thing I can say about him if you're not local, long will not work. Loren puts Sabrina on the couch and sits down.

I can tell he's still in a place that's reserved just for him. I asked him what was on his mind. He seemed to be somewhere in his own thoughts. He smiled saying that he did meet someone. I'm excited and it shows in my questions. My excitement startles him, but with a pause a smile appears. I asked what's her name and tell me the story. Loren smiled saying that her name is Desiree, top floor quality. No hidden clearance tags, educated, good job, just a little smaller than I like but she is fine. I laughed what about the hips. He responds they can make room for some babies for Mama Rosie Josey. With Bill not being there Loren was able to show his gentle side. I could feel inside that this might be the one. I felt like I was interviewing a willing participant. First question Mr. Loren, how did you meet Miss Desiree? Loren was leaning back on the couch and sits up playing along as the interviewee. He said, well I went to a game with my boy TJ. You remember him Joaquin Jose, Jr., known as Fifi's ex-husband that called the police on himself. I'm still in my interviewing mode and respond with, I do recall that story and it was quite entertaining sir if I must say, continue please. Well he was at a basketball game hanging out with TJ and some lady he was with that had a fine ass friend with her. But she was into the game and not looking in any direction towards me. I asked the history on Desiree and he couldn't tell me. TJ wasn't moved by my questions on Desiree because, he wasn't into her friend barely said her name. He put her into the category of night crawler. TJ would crawl late at night and not often and this would be the first and last time she would see light with his ass. With that tone Miss Interviewer, I clearly said, (excuse me in advance for my language), oh hell no you need to get me closer to her girlfriend. TJ forgot all the damage I went through saving his ungrateful ass from, crazy ass Fifi. We both raised our eyebrows as I looked at him, and he's was raising them again. TJ laughed at me with she loved-ed you. I couldn't go with that. I snapped back with; she made you get yourself arrested and then you argued, no you strongly requested to the judge, or should we say sang to go back to your cell, pleading was the song uh. You did everything but the 'James Brown' twist. So, I had to remind my boy that he owed my ass. TJ and I at the same time, laughed because we had our share of Fifi's crazy ass antics. Oh, and don't mention when you got your days of the week mixed up with my honey days. One those honies could have been my baby's mama. I laugh you know you wouldn't pull that baby mama on Rosey Josie. he smiles she would have killed me. I convince TJ to set it up including your night crawler. TJ if you need to make her holler in the day, make that shift happen. I continued with my interview asking, you are smiling when you talk about her, what are you thinking. Loren said she was a nature beauty and had a smile that just warmed your soul. She was beyond the top floor. We both enjoyed that basketball game. Desiree shouted, but with class and she wasn't paying me no type of attention. That wasn't the turn on, the turn on was her warmth and energy.

I tried to move toward her, and she stepped away from me but not a rude or don't bother me, just not now. So, Mr. Loren how did the game end? The Bulls won but for Desiree this was just my half time. TJ was gonna have to swallow the pain on this one. Miss Desiree wasn't going away my thoughts were clean, and I couldn't shake thinking about her. TJ went over and said something to the night crawler, and it had to be about me. They looked in my direction and my future queen headed over to her king in waiting. I had to show some type of I'm not desperate. I was feeling that this lady could bring happiness to my mama. The future Mrs. Loren approached me smiling. I returned the smile with eyes slighlty open, because I had to get my swag warmed up. She extends her hand as I say to her your team got to try harder. The lady smiles saying my team did win, I was just at the wrong game. That took me as she says I'm a Warriors fan and they did win. I had to mentally step back, this lady was no-nonsense with a sophistication that was as impressive as her beauty.

Loren takes a re-direct and paused adding that when you, Miss Rita set down at the table in the library Bill told me; how he just stared at you and you answered every question clearly and with class and something was different about you that's why he kept talking. I laughed inside because Bill didn't know that I was looking back at him wanting him to stop asking so many questions. Because my Psychology class was the one course that I really wanted to study and prepare for the upcoming exam. I answered the questions in hope that he would eventually shut them down, so I could study. He was cute/fine to look at but at that time my mind was elsewhere. Bill did come across as being intelligent, with a smile that did capture me with his almond shaped twinkling eyes that still warms my heart.

We walked back home as I tried to hold back the laughter of the night crawler example. Loren was laughing hard saying that the' night crawler' kept trying to hug and hold hands with TJ. But get this TJ was fighting off her advancements, but without embarrassing her. Loren said he looked at TJ's expressions, knowing that he wanted to say get the 'hmm away from me, but he held on and kept it cool. I was still in my interview mode and, asked do you think he came through? Loren smiles nodding his head with the response of, oh yes, he did. He said he walked slowly with Desiree talking about basketball and she knew the averages, strengths, and it was very impressive. So, with all that said I asked did you get her phone number Mr. Loren? He pauses with a corner smile like Courtney Diane's signature smile, yes and no. She dropped a reject saying she had a boyfriend. That meant very little I didn't want to be her boyfriend, I wanted to be her man. I respectfully accepted what she said, and I gave her my number, you know for just in case to. I knew all I had to do was wait, because she said she had a boyfriend. Loren said he politely opened Desiree's cardoor as he listened to TJ lie about going to call or hook up with 'the night crawler. Loren said that TJ lied so good and was so convincing, he would have waited for his call.

As we continued laughing through his interview I asked and noticed that he was still smiling. So, I asked, what features did she have that made you think about her. He said as he stated earlier (smiling), Miss Rita, it was her beauty and the warmth in her smile, and her sense of humor. She was funny and after talking with her she was very intelligent and had placed reachable goals. I knew she was the one after we conversed about where we wanted to go in life and that we had similar morals and family values. Mr. Loren, I asked, (leaning forward), have you heard from her? Funny you should ask yes Miss Rita I have. She got in touch with me. TJ gave her my number and one day I got the pleasant surprise of hearing her voice. I told you she would call. I laughed yell your right hmmm. How many women did you go through before she contacted you? Wow Miss Rita not many just a few, don't forget I had crazy ass Fifi and her side kick Lucee lerking around. Fifi and I talked but, it was about much of nothing. Desiree came to my shop and the guys for once didn't have any remarks or laughter. I should have paid them extra for acting like they had some sense. I showed her my dream of one day enlarging my place. I had just purchased the building next door and there was room to grow. Desiree was finishing up her degree in engineering and had offers on the table. She was very impressive and was making moves. I listened as I continued to ask questions and he continued to answer while Sabrina napped. Dejavu, Bill was sitting in the library and Loren was sitting and standing talking to the one that would make a difference.

Loren went on to say that they talked for months before they went out. Both their schedules were tight, and we made time one weekend. I picked her up and we went downtown. Not to where Nini worked or where Fifi could find us. She actually picked a nice jazz club. Get this she was buying her house, nice huh and in school and working. She's buying a house and had a car that was paid for and not a car you had to push to start. I asked what's wrong with that? I remembered when we had a car that we had to pray on before we drove and had another car that we had to use two feet and it wasn't a clutch. Loren stopped and looked at me with amazement saying that you and Bill are a unique special. I gave him a salute with a touche Mr. Loren and asked him to please continue. Loren insisted on adding another act that first caught his attention was her no nonsense with dudes who were trying to run game. I witnessed her shut a dude down, who in my eyes always had it easy with the girls. She might have shut TJ ass down too, but he wouldn't let me know he lost some of his game. It was very attractive to see that she wasn't impressed by the typical outward appearance of money, jewelry, nice clothes or smooth talk, etc. yet she was dressed conservatively, sporting that warm beautiful smile. I did watch her walk away but with respect. So, sir how did the date(s) go, and did they continue? Well, yes, they did Miss Rita. The jazz resturant was nice, no Nini, no Fifi or any other old girlfriends or fantasy ladies I remembered.

The view I had was on her only no distractions and, I was savoring every minute. She waited gently as I opened the door and she reached across to open my side. That showed that she was caring and no signs of being selfish. So, Mr. Loren were there many dates, or did you already mention that? Many dates did occur to where we weren't dating anymore but becoming something special. We decided early on to be exclusive to each other. We both had been through enough relationships. We both decided that there was no need or room for any type of extra distractions. There was no room or time to have something or someone come in and have a strong impact on our relationship. We both agree that we weren't having it. For a just in case I stayed at her place. Desiree place was all clean and check this out Fifi didn't serve us any breakfast. With that we both laugh. I smiled and placed my hands in my lap letting Loren know that I was impressed and happy about his new-found love.

Fifi did make what I hope was her last camero. I can't even really remember where we were but, Desiree and I were walking. Just walking and enjoying much of nothing. Then I felt something pop on my neck then felt it again while looking around as I thought what the funk? Dez looks at me asking, what's that green stuff on your neck? I checked my neck and I got popped with some wet peas. I could only imagine who would do this shift. I paused but history wasn't circling around like it did with Diamond. I took my favorite cousins' advice, (he smiles at me). My ex- whatever, Fifi and probably her side kick in action Lucee... Sure, enough on cue my whatever ex, drives past us with a straw hanging out her mouth and Lucee is in the back holding up a bag of peas. Des just looked at both no anger, no running pose. She mouthed something find out later she said I will kick you all up in your ass. She showed that Chicago southside look which was very impressive and scary at the same time. Fifi must have understood because she smiled as if she accepted the challenge, but she didn't circle and come back. I guess Desiree must have thrown her game or threat off. I'm so glad that I took your advice. I took the message and learned from that brief incident and told her about Fifi. She was calm and no threats. Miss Interviewee, I knew this might be the one. I wasn't dating anyone during that four-month break, but I did get rid of some extra baggage before we started really dating. Loren insisted that he wanted to be serious about this relationship. I asked, what type of extra baggage? He calmly said just special call girls, (wink, wink), not night crawlers that TJ dates. She made me grow up in many ways. My dates or friends were with special benefits, so I ended the benefits and quickly made it known to myself first and to others that I was beginning a real relationship with someone.

Akil laughed and Mama Rosie Josey said that I finally got my butt off the elevator. It was just a matter of time when the elevator would be going out of order. Desiree encouraged me to get more in touch with my feelings and to stop being so passive aggressive. I didn't feel like it was a problem, I guess that's my passiveness; but taking a step back I was able to realize how much people were walking over me. Her smile makes me smile and puts me in a place. So, let me add, clearly Loren, you touched a side that tapped into your sensitive side where you might be in love. I watched him pause bobbing his head saying I believe so. Loren was smiling as his almond shaped eyes twinkled co-signing the truth that was coming from his heart. Although, we laughed with the antics when he talked about Fifi, but as I listened, I could only smile as I enjoyed the intimate conversation or interview about a woman that unknowingly caught his heart.

I look at him and wonder if those were the similar words of affection that Bill shared with him about me. Loren said they mostly talked about family values. I had to look deep into her as we talked a lot about how we were brought up. You know Rita like, what changes we would make so our kids could benefit, even more from what we've learned from our own parents and up-bringing. So, Loren it sounds like Mama Rosie Josey is getting close to those grandbabies. Loren knods in agreement saying that the four months that they had been talking, he could see that. She triggered the light switch that made me think she might be the one. My dad Ramsey and my Uncle Erwin always instilled in me and Akil make sure you have a checklkist of what you want. If they passed your checklist and, both your hearts are in the right place, you'll know they're the right one. And with emphasis on the key word, 'the right one', and not somebody that you are trying to force what doesn't fit. Loren said that some or almost all were not that fit. But he had fun and now it's time to become more stable and have fun with just one person.

Chapter 56
It's Time

It's time to love, laugh and have some type of peace of mind. When I'm not with Desiree/Dez, I miss her and the smile she gives me freely. I miss her company and we have become lately inseparable. We have been doing everything together. She's the reason I'm only staying a few days, I want to get back to the warmth of her embrace and heart. Loren smiled as his eyes twinkled when he said that he got to see his Des and her smile. I miss that lady! Well Loren as we finish our interview, and may I say it was very informative. I was very impressed with your feelings and that you have finally rid yourself of that slow running elevator. He laughs saying I finally left the building. This was the first time that Loren and I talked face to face about him being in love. I don't think he realized how much he was in love until we started our interview. I always enjoyed talks with Loren but, the next time, (if he does come back), I have a feeling Desiree will be close.

Sabrina's timing is good as she rushes over to Loren almost knocking him back on the couch. The overwhelming of love catches him off guard, but he welcomes the affection. We look forward to the drive to the airport to see Loren off with sad eyes but joy in knowing that he has vacated the elevator and has left the building. I can make dinner, so he won't be hungry on the plane. My cooking skills haven't increased but in time maybe. I sure did learn how to flip, and flop, I had many lessons from Momo. Loren drags or carries the clinging Sabrina with him as he packed the one piece of luggage. Since we have relocated, I'm back to no neighbors to conversate with or a just because visit.

The day went fast, and I heard the running feet of Sierra and Bill grabbing me for a kiss. Surprisingly I liked that spontaneity in him. I tell him just give me a few minutes for dinner, so we can all ride to the airport. His answer was short and quick. That he was taking Loren and since his flight would leave late, that would affect Sierra for school. I very seldom went against him, so I just smiled but inside I was dissapointed that I or we wouldn't see Loren off. I'm glad I had on my glasses, so the sadness wouldn't be exposed. So, here we are in this big house just me and the girls. Loren says his good- byes as Bill tells him they will pick up something to eat on the way. In hearing that must meant that he won' t be hungry for dinner. I'm glad to know that tonight will be a light dinner. While, at the same time convincing myself that they just needed some male time to talk and, maybe Loren will tell Bill about Desiree/Dez. I look forward to meeting her and will miss the sagas of him and Fifi. Humph wet peas that is a new one! I guess Miss Fifi wanted to make sure that the wet peas stuck and that he knew it was her. Where does she get those crazy antics and acts out on them with boldness? The brick or, a slim candle in her purse and a small clutch purse for the pebbles, wow! That was funny when Loren said he thought it was hailing and it was just Fifi throwing rocks at his window. The funnier one was when Loren looked through his blinds to have eyes looking back at him and they both blinked. He played it off that he just hollered then later confessed that he screamed. Loren probably ran through the house before, he started locking all the doors and windows. I bet they both saw clearly when they blinked at each other. Wow this must be true who could have that type of vivid imagination.

Well I guess a small meal, will work for my little girls. I don't have much of an appetite, but my body doesn't show it. Bill hasn't said anything about my size which is very comforting because I don't need anymore added pressure. Right now, I miss Bill and I don't know why. I was thinking that maybe from the interview with Loren he reminded me of what or how Bill looked at me when we first meant. I wondered how he looks at me now? Does he feel that he took on too much by marrying me and moving out here and moving again and again? The only thing in that thought process was that, he didn't move by himself, this is a us and we thing. I still haven't looked at those boxes to unpack. For right now this is not a priority. That day we were tired and many more days to come we were all still tired. Bill would snug under me leaving me with wondering thoughts about him or what he might be doing? Bill surprised me and, and he came straight home from the airport. Just like he had said it was late and we were all in a deep slumber, (except for my thoughts).

I would encounter Miss Mayla and Miss Belinda Amerly today. They were in the same spot and, if they didn't change their clothes you would think that they never moved from that spot. They seemed nice and in a strange way resembled each other with the same mannerism. But they're not Momo she was unique and can't be replaced. Time moved, and I found myself sometimes keeping them company as I passed by their house to go to the park or take a long walk to the closest bus stop. So far, we know Lynel and Dugan as the drivers that drove this route. They don't seem too friendly, but we still enjoyed the ride. The bus ride seems to take a little longer because, it seems as if we are a long way from civilization in form of stores and any goods for purchase. One thing this area does have many opportunities for employment. I need to get out and back into the workforce. I'm drowning and losing who I am. I want my own money like I used to have and some form of freedom that Bill has unknowingly been experiencing. I want to greet someone with a smile while asking if they need help or a paycheck that says pay to the order of Rita. A piece of paper that acknowleges that I do have a first name and I still exsist. I still have a name that is not in a form of combination like Bill sometimes would alter. Mommy, mom, mother or mama is fine but, I'm seldom called that. Before I became mommy or Mrs, I had a first and last name of my own. I had a first name and I worked hard and had my own transportation. Here I am in this big house waiting for my life to come home in form of Bill and hear my daughter having more of a life than me.

Funny my family and friends probably think I'm living this fast life in Oceanview, only if they knew. Phone calls are limited so there goes contact back home. I need to talk to Bill when his heart is open about getting a job. I want some part of my life back. I want to feel free just like the wind in the breeze. I don't want to be away from my family, I just don't like the feeling of confinement. I like the way the wind blows without restrictions. I want to work and have the freedom to spend the way I used to without asking permission, and financially working together. Bill and I are in this together. I want to contribute more than dinner and a clean house. Bill never said anything about Loren and Desiree. I wondered if Loren did mention her and, Bill just forgot or just let that thought pass on through. Bill was good at times about forgetting somethings not all the time but when needed. I have concluded that there's no life here.

Miss Mary or Miss Mayla seems to be nice and must be good friends with Miss Vicki. She invited us in, and her home was very spacious and full. It reminded me of Grandad and Mama Helen's home filled with family and love. Miss Mary introduced her daughters Addison, Meese who was stationed in the Carolinas, her sons Rubin and Jeremy they're married and don't live here but make cameos visit, in which was okay by her. She added also included in her house was her brother Macy and his wife Lona and their daughters, Charm and Charity, they're around Sabrina's age. Her husband Jack hangs out in the backyard tinkering on cars. So, if you hear some noise, don't mind him he's just thinking. Jack seems to be mellow with occasional conversation. Her brother moved from Kansas and looking for a place and what opportunities that Califoirnia might offer. This is all supposed to be temporary living according to Miss Mayla. Which she smiles saying that this temporary is now entering its fifth or seventh year, but whose counting. She laughs that is more permanent than temporary. She loves the company and her sister Naylene trying to change her life around after escaping from an abusive husband. I dare him to come here. I have and will use and will do time for my sister. She speaks of him with much anger in which I don't blame her. His trifling ass thought it was cute pushing her outside in the rain with their daughter while she was carrying his second child, walking, bruised and wet. Naylene, took his ungrateful ass in with two kids. They were his, but she took care of them as if she given birth to them. How ungratful is that! Her house is large with antique looking furniture covered with that hard plastic. I remembered seeing that hard plastic covers at a few of my aunts and neighbors' homes. I don't know why she felt the need to tell me, maybe she was seeing where I was in my marriage I don't know? I didn't feel that she was searching noisy just sharing. She seems nice, but I don't feel the warmth I had from Momo's home, but I feel she's trying to be there. Her heart seems to be in the right place. I need to keep my mind open. I know and feel, that we will never move back to where we left.

Miss Belinda Amerly, (aka Vicki), seemed just as friendly. She's retired and raising her grandchildren. Her husband, Syrus is a salesman that travels often. So, she welcomes the joy of raising her grandchildren. She appreciates the noise and didn't mention anything about the parents. That was her business, and no one concerns but hers. I guess that was the Vicki she was talking about that makes cameos like Robin's Roberta. What would mine be called Rita, wow Rita that's orginal? Wow did I lose my imagination too. I got to get a job! My amusement and life are through my friends and extended family. I've went from moving from place to another, to just looking out the window wondering what happened to the time. Sabrina enjoyed playing with Charm and Charity and they became the best of friends. Sierra enjoyed Miss Belinda Amerly's grandchildren. When they were at home, she kept them busy and they stayed gone. Well she was home to talk with Miss Mayla. They fence talk when they need more fresh air. And Miss Mary still had her house full of guests and occassionaly I would wake up to the sounds of Jack thinking in the backyard.

Bill started back coming home late with a full stomach that matched his attitude. More days than some. I just couldn't do anything right and my clothes or attire was not to his taste. He did like the jeans I purchased so long ago. But I can't live in them forever and it's not like he's buying me clothes. Plus, why would he, where would I wear them to the kitchen or the backyard? I missed going to PataRee's. That's almost on the other side of town and a long, long bus ride. Sabrina talks very well and voices her opinion on the long bus rides. She enjoys the view but not the length of the ride and the many transfers from bus to bus. Driving what should be our car is a treat to just to be able to feel the steering wheel. I want to feel/grip the wheel, smell the leather and let the breeze hit our faces and not just Bill's. Sometimes I think that love came and went with Bill. There're days that I felt our love or his love for me was on pause. Only, if I could rewind to the place where we fell in love and we said our, I dos'. Or fast forward where we grow old together playing and hearing the trambling sounds of our grandkid's little feet with loud noises. Just like the herding sounds like Courtney Diane's nieces. They were noisey, but they had a lot of love and showed nothing but high energy.

Where was Bill's reset button to press and, put us back where we both loved and respected each other. I long for those days and believed that they will come. Miss

Belinda Amerly's son, Date came for a visit and made me very uncomfortable when he offered to help me with the small amount of groceries. I would constantly try to re-position the bags, as they fell out of the wagon. He was kind and helpful, but he made me nevous and, I didn't want Bill to pull up to the driveway and I suffer the consequences. I let Date know I appreciated his help as his mother smiled at seeing her son act in such a gentleman way. In my mind I didn't know where Bill might be mentally with that pause button. His hours varied and just the thought just made me so nervous and I'm sure it showed. I'm glad I had on my glasses so; they couldn't see the fear that was trembling inside. You would think after all these years I would either be used to Bill's pause buttons, but fear is fear. I don't think it went away just took a place inside and hid.

The store was on the other side of the park which was a good walk and easy rides for Sabrina. She loved the wind hitting her face as she looked and absorbed her surroundings. Funny on my way back I saw Date and just said my normal hi and kept it moving. This time it was strange because I saw two new little cute twin girls, and Date. I said Date are those your little cute twins? As I was standing there, they walked over to Sabrina who was eager to get out and play with some new friends. With a deep smile, he said Date was his twin brother and his name was Dutton, adding no worries because it happens all the time and the older, we get the more we look like each other, (we call it getting old). As he laughed through my embarrassment, he introduced his daughters, Semaj and Tuilokomana. I know her name is long, but we call her Tui.

One thing was nice that there were girls around the same ages as Sierra and Sabrina. Miss Amberly's grandchildren made cameos and she was very protective. But she does allow Susie and Shamir, (another set of grandchildren), to come over to our house. The funny part they said we had to be home and they would tell me the time. Them giving us time sounded so familiar to what we had to do when we could go over to someones' house. Sometimes we would get caught up in playing and the time would just get away from us. With that announcement of being late going home, we would dash out the house and as always make it in before the street lights came on. If we were late, we knew in advance not to ask anytime soon to go back over to that friends' house. Dutton girls were very polite and quiet. They were a year apart and Sierra fits right in between their ages. Their brothers or cousins, Tawfic and Mubeen were Junior high school age and very athletic, never understood their relationship to the family and I had very little communication with them. Miss Mary occasionally gave backyard get togethers, and Bill and I would attend. But it wasn't like the fun we had at the old place. There was no Momo singing how low will you go, or the ladies talking about the young man that they wanted to have, saying that they wanted him to hurt them, spank them and make them write bad checks. Looking at Date and Dutton they would be hollering about who would get spanked first, after they get over the ah of their tight physique. Date, Dutton and Naylene broke down their names and now the family referred to Date as DA and Dutton as DT. Only they knew how these nicknames developed into intials. They would fit right in with Courtney Diane's family with the nick names. I could hear her screaming now, as the twins check her out. She always turned heads but didn't seem to move her.

I could feel them watching me as Bill watched the men looking at me. I don't think they were looking at me in the way Bill thought. They probably were watching to see how Bill watched me and the minute conversation we might have. Funny, how looks can sometimes hide the hidden truth, because on the outside we looked happy, laughing and smiling at each other. They watched me as I made a plate for Bill and the girls before I sat down and enjoyed a nice plate of barbeque, potato salads and many other picnic entrees. Their backyard was large and organized. There was a section where the children played and took breaks to snack from their very full plates. I watched them play blind man's bluff, red light green light, hide and seek and so many other games I remembered playing as a child. The games they played, I thought were lost as modern technology invades their world and minds. The last time, (before we moved), I saw Sierra and Sabrina playing hide and seek and they couldn't find Tim. The last time was when we were moving, and the apartment was empty, and he was found in the same hiding place. So, there was no mystery when his visiting Aunt Jovanka, and his other Aunt Natalia were franticly looking for their missing nephew. While his mother, Eula/Helen embraced him with love while she gently scolded him with, wait until we get home, and no more hiding for you. He was in his same hiding place the now emptier bathroom cabinet.

Tim would laugh while his mom looked at him with concern and love that she found him. As I drifted back to my surroundings, Miss Mary along with cousins Gail and Iverson/Ivey bought homemade cakes, pies and cookies. I flashback on how much I missed Keith's cooking. I'm happy to know that he's now cooking for his wife Kiente. Jack wasn't thinking today. He took a break from thinking with his cars and was laughing it up with Miss Belinda Amerly's husband, Syrus. Laughter was in the air as they played dominos and cards with the twins Date (DA) and Dutton (DT). Addison was smiling and prancing around the twins. Who seemed to ignore her too, (which must be her routine to them as well)? They were attractive, tall, deep and gorgeous. But not my type, I had enough with the women staring at Bill. He still was my husband and no smiling or moving scant was going to come between us. I know Robin said at the end it's on the man and his decisions. He knows he is married, and he put himself in that position. Why is it that other married men can walk a way? Then you have the weak one that's searching or reaching for an excuse to justify their weak non-thinking acts. Yep Robin made it clear saying that too much thinking went into creeping.

I did like to see Bill laughing with the 'all mens' club they had unknowingly established as they played dominos and cards. We had our own 'women's only'club, playing cards and just eating while watching the children. For that special celebration we didn't have a care while we were sipping on lemonade. That day I was turned on to a new refreshment called 'sweet tea. I watched Naylene, trying to fit into the conversation but, you could tell her mind and thoughts were so far from what we were talking about. We had our own conversation going and wasn't as loud as we were at the complex I reluctantly left. Time has passed, and people have moved, and I still miss that complex. Robin and Courtney Diane stayed in touch, but it wasn't the same. I would always hear their concerns in their voices, but I always reassured them that everything was alright. Funny as I was convincing them I was at the same time always convincing myself. Was this one of the performances that we used to laugh about? I wondered who would receive the Oscar me, or would it go to Bill.

We tried a few backyard picnics. Robin came and loved our place. We didn't have a lot of money to have such a spread to accommodate a large amount of people. I tried talking to Bill about working and as they would say it went on deaf ears or in one side and out the other becoming airborne. Years past, some went slow yet sometimes time flew on by. Bill and I went back and forth about working, transportation, as our family enlarged. I look around at all the toys and disarray in each room. Time slowed up enough and now I'm with two additional faces. I remember talking to Momo about the book her cousin Mona showed off that book, 'Kama Sutra' added two more babies to her cousins' smile. Funny ha-ha, was only parts I remembered about the book was how can they still walk and is that humanly possible. Then I faded into thoughts of why not?? After all, this is a new place maybe I might try new ideas. I don't remember how long I smiled, as I visited the hospital again and one more again. That was a book that I need not see ever again in my life...

I'm happy that I have Shaurice and Bill Jr (Sonnyboy). Now I have a cart full of babies. Now I experienced and feel what I've seen as I load them into our car that Bill still consumes. Bus rides are more interesting as I try and keep up with all my four bobbing heads. Bill had me so isloated in this big house. I would occassionaly talk to Miss Mayla and Miss Amerly, either inside their homes or join them while they were sitting on the porch or their hook up corner of their fence. They would be watching grandkids and enjoying the fresh breeze that hit their laughing conversating faces. Only if that corner fence could talk about their conversations. My life had centered on Bill and now our four children. Bill was happy with his girls but happier now that he can pass his name on and his father Richard is equally in sharing in that joy. Back to me the only friends I have were my children. They gave me the warmth to my heart that I seemed to need an injection of daily. The love they gave me each day; in form of hugs and kisses just reminded my feelings that I was still loved and kept my insides warm giving me life with reasons for breathing. I knew Bill still loved me I just didn't know from time to time the levels of his love. Sometimes, it seemed to change from day to day, hour to hour year to years. I gave up hoping that I would get a life outside this house. I knew I meant something to my children. Sierra and I still have the discussion on calling me Rita and her siblings just look at me and just start talking. There goes the sound of hearing mom, mommy, mother or mama in any form. We went from Sierra putting puzzles to Sabrina playing in her own creative way and now we expand to drawings and learning.

They could be creative, and every piece of art was beautiful. All my kids had their own style and Bill Jr, (Sonnyboy), wasn't any different. He had a bad habit of chewing on crayons and furniture. He just loved to chew on anything. Sonnyboy's teeth marks would be on table edges, other people's sandwiches just to mention a few. I don't know where he picked up that terrible habit. Well, let me think this out my sister Shawn had a habit of eating the shag rugs and always taking a bite of hair from the top of my fathers' head. When it happened, you would hear my dad yelling 'all shift'. That was the sound we knew she had pulled his hair out with her teeth and that area did become thin and never grew back. Thank God she grew out of that habit! So, with that bit of history, maybe that little gene traveled from me, ooh, hmmm. Well I can't blame that on Bill. I would discipline Bill Jr. (Sonnyboy), and that didn't work he was as stubborn as his name sake. He took it like a young man, and he didn't cry or whine. I would watch him on his time out and he took the time with so much calm. I chuckled at his coolness. Sonnyboy sat there calmly and when time was up, he acted as if he just took a break and was refreshed. I left the room thinking he's not going to do what I think is going to do. No sooner than I left and returned he was chewing on the crayon like it was bubble gum, (and he was just chomping away). The smell didn't match the flavor of what was he getting from smacking on a crayon?

Well, hmmm I had a quick reflection of the vision of myself as a child. Wow, kind of a dejavu moment. When I was young, I would eat the white pages because, the yellow pages were horrible. Well this is not helping, the various outrageous antics seems to bring the finger pointing back to me and my crazy family, hmmm. So, I tried again to take the box crayons, and put them in my room while I put up the folded clothes. His sisters were in the room cheering their baby brother on, (or did they think that was his normal, hmmm, interesting). Here I go again with reflecting back on Shawn eating the carpet. I guess that was our familys' normal? The only difference was we weren't cheering Shawn on, because she was quiet, until you heard the pulling sounds of the carpet being consumed. The damage was already done and the normal was going to come out of one or the other end, (and it always did), hmmm. I think this might be history coming around the corner, sure seems like it.

Then I heard an alarming sound of screams coming from their play area. The girls were screaming and in a split second Sonnyboy, my baby Bill Jr. was choking!! I grab my son and started giving him back blows until Bill Jr. coughs up pieces of crayon, while spitting up blood. Each cough came with blood. Bill wasn't home, so I rushed over to Miss Mary's to take us to the hospital. With her urging I left the girls with her and Naylene took us to the hospital. She drove as I held on tight to my BJ. I held him so tight, and at the same time praying for my son's health. We arrived to the waiting arms of Doctor Alicia and her Nurse Karina. With their angelic smiles I slowly realeased my tired son into their arms, as Naylene was trying to convince me that everything will be okay. Inside I knew God had my son but, that didn't ease my fears. My fears resurfaced from the time Sierra hide in between the commisary store racks as I frantically looked for her. That same feeling of anxiety resurfaced of looking for Sierra and knowing I couldn't be late picking up Bill. Deep breaths and sighs were my comfort until Doctor Alicia returned saying that he's okay. She said that when he coughed up the blood it was from the crayon scraping the lining of his throat. I couldn't thank Naylene enough for everything. I hugged my sleeping exhausted son and thanking God for saving my boy.

Chapter 57
It's Clean Up Time (tee-hee-hee)

This was the first time I talked with Naylene or heard her talk. She was always in her own thoughts and I didn't want to intrude. I like my me time and when someone unknowingly interrupts that does throw me off and it seems as if you had to start all over again. Miss Mary greets us as the girls run up to their sleeping brother trying to grab some part of him to for their reassurance that they were there with love and concerns. I saw our car which meant that Bill was home, and my insides were saying this was not a good feeling. I open the door with fear of feeling that I might be met with some type of confirmation. The house was in a disarray and, I didn't have the time to finish cleaning up or prepare dinner, especially for a person that didn't keep a consistent schedule. I told him what happened as I walked to lay BJ in his bed. The girls must have sensed something because they were quiet. I felt like I was in a movie with theme music playing as the audience warns me don't say a word or just run. His almomd shaped eyes became smaller and darker as I had a strong feeling of what might be coming...

I spined up saying that I clean up this big house everyday and take good care of our children! I see them more than you see them. When I became your wife, this was for life in matrimony not life/prison sentence. You give me very little credit for what I gave up being here. We went back and forth until the words I become accustomed to hearing was funk you beach. As I alter them in my mind," F"is an action or act, and your directing it at me so that's a directive, and beach, which I wish he would add Miss to show me a little more respect. Now back to "beach" is a noun because he using as an additional name, hmm again that softens the blow. Before, he finishes the emphasis on the "ich", inside I'm still dissecting his words. My bold response was hmm when will that happen the "FU", because it hasn't been lately? Well, there's no mystery we both know it happened at least four times. Let's confirm we have Sierra, Sabrina, Shaurice and Bill Jr., running around this big house. I snap with, your son was bleeding and where were you working late again, right? I needed you, we needed you and we needed transportation!

I've been here waiting patiently for you to come home to your family. I've been here hoping that you would see my pain. But no, good time 'Bobbing Bill was out and about. Maybe if I went to the window and yelled out your name, where would the wind find you? Tell me Mr. Bill, where would the echoes from the wind found you? I paid for that spine up of courage. I felt the blows and the movement of my body landing in various locations. Naylene must have heard the commotion. I know it wasn't from the sounds of my cries. She was hearing the sounds from my body landing in various locations. As I laid on the floor, God's hand shielded me when Bill dropped his knee onto my chest. I could have died that day, that moment. Nothing was crushed or cracked, but my heart and body felt the pain. Naylene ran home and called the police. Date and Dutton rushed over to break up the fight. What fight??? I didn't know if I had thrown any blows?? Everything seemed to happen so fast, yet the movements were in slow motion. Bill didn't resist the twins. He looked surpised and calm. I don't know what I looked like. I just saw the fright in the eyes of Naylene who insisted on taking me to the hospital. The twins took our children next door as the the officers arrived and arrested Bill. My blurred vision of Bill faded away as I slowly looked around the room. I rode to the hospital with the insisting of Naylene and her family. The ride seemed long and I was in complete silence. No winds sound, no conversation, just the blurred vision of trying to remember what happened. While at the same time forcing my feelings to deny what has almost become a blur. My courage stood at the threshold of the door and watched fear take flight, and strength stayed but to just linger for a short time. Now what do I do and where do I go from here? Fear is now sitting looking at me and asking the same questions. My thoughts were now you return and ask questions???????

I went to the base hospital where I saw familiar walls but this time under different circumstances. I didn't see the angelic smiles of Doctor Upesi, Doctor Deck or Nurse Alicia or Nurse Evelyn or Nurse Karina. All I saw was fear in their eyes as I tried to answer the questions from the gentle patience smile of Doctor Adrian Tony. My silence made the room larger as my ears heard my heart beating. Doctor Carla comes in smiling talking as my eyes stayed glued to the floor. There were no feelings. I just acted numb as she asked the repeated questions that Doctor Adrian Tony asked. Inside I'm trying to pinch myself because this must be a nightmare… the room seems bright and very silent. As they waited for me to respond, I felt myself shaking my head as I tried to wake myself up from this tormenting dream. I woke up alright, to hear Doctor Carla talking to Officer Abbie. Although she's smiling, I don't know her or the Officer. I know I can't talk to them Bill will kill me and where is Bill. I want my Bill! The only person I wanted to talk to was Bill. So many thoughts were racing through my head and I could hear the pounding sounds. I felt myself becoming afraid and wanting to go back to the comforts of my home and be with my children. If I opened my mouth, would I stutter as I did as a child.

I learned not to talk and just look. I couldn't smile because my two front teeth were so rotten until my brother Charles knocked them out. The first tooth was when we were running through the house, (because Charles was chasing me), and I hit my tooth on the corner of an open kitchen door. And the other tooth, Charles, (again), hit me in the mouth with a yellow small hard bowl. I guess we did play hard. Inside I force a nervous silent chuckle thinking back on Clarences' father missing two front teeth.

The looks and stares didn't bother me, because I held my head down. Maybe I could find the answers on the floor. My insides and thoughts were trying to form words to answer so they would go away and let me go back home. I didn't want to answer the many questions for fear of my stuttering returning. My stuttering required me to attend special classes when I was in grade school, and I didn't want to return mentally back to that class. Where is my mother Sheryl? She gave the school permission for me to attend the obvious much needed classes. She was there and stood by me through my stuttering phase in my young life. Why am I here? I can take care of myself! I have been taking care of my bruises by myself for many years. Where is my dad, Eddie to make everything better and go away? Why do they keep asking me so many questions? I don't hear my voice responding so I know that I'm not talking. I'm just staring into my thoughts, trying to envision something or somewhere to take my thoughts and get my mind focused. If I take a deep breath will life come back to me? I retrace my day, and I shouldn't have let them have that creactivity time? Should I have checked BJ to make sure that he didn't have any hidden crayons? This was all my fault. I find myself thinking that I should not have let them draw, but no, no they need to draw? This shouldn't be happening what happens in our house stays there. I don't need all these questions. I shouldn't have left the room to put clothes up. I should have just stayed in the room.

I feel myself shrinking and becoming a child that was blamed for breaking a vase. The wind blew the vase over and I'm yelling to myself saying repeatedly, that it wasn't me, I didn't do anything wrong. I felt like a mouse being chased and cornered by a cat, with all these questions and stares ready to pounce on me. They just kept following me as I tried to find a place to hide from their stares and many questions. Officer Abbie wanted to know if I wanted to file a complaint as Doctor Carla waited for my answer. There was no answer because there was no complaint. Since when did they become my mouth piece? I just wanted to go home there was nothing broken, just bruises and the uncomfortable feeling from the stares. The bed of my eyes feeled with tears but they wouldn't flow. If they did, I was so numb I wouldn't have felt them flow down my cheeks. The rain that I looked at for many years in my life did it turn into a thunder storm and I forgot to seek shelter? I just set there and part of me wanted to tell everything. But would they not only listen, would they hear me and not judge me?? If I spoke up and roared like a lion, would they turn to listen, or would my roars convert to a purr? I sat there in silence missing out on my opportunity to tell what? This didn't happen often. We had good times with laughter and love. We had four beautiful children that must represent something? Bill asked me to marry him; he didn't ask me to leave. Right when I wanted to say something Bill walks in. I had forgotten the normal routine question is there somewhere you could go to calm down. That must have been the speech and the reason why Bill is standing there looking at me. Bill's eyes are filled with tears as the Doctors Carla and Adrian Tony looked at him with much disgust.

During my hospital room ordeal, I spoke up to say I'm okay, I just want to go home. They couldn't keep me or make me file a complaint. Naylene didn't hear but she came in a few mintues behind Bill to check on me. I saw the fright and concern all in one glance as I signed the papers to be discharged. Bill says that we will go to a marriage counselor and he would do whatever it takes to keep his family. I heard the words I love you and they didn't warm my soul just confused my thoughts. Once Naylene looked at what was happening she asked if she could take me home, but Bill insisted nervously smiling saying he will take his wife home. I smiled thanking her and letting her know that we will be alright. That night changed the whole outlook on what happened. Bill grabs my hand gently as we walk down the corridor with no sound and no conversation. I felt the eyes of many as I walked holding onto Bill. He seemded to be only concerned about us and ignored the stares and the whispers. The drive was long as Bill talked, and I acted as if I was listening. I didn't respond just turning my head toward the window glaring into the lights that blurred from staring too long. The blinding lights just matched the blurrs in my visions. No clarity just blinding. We arrive home to collect our family from Miss Mary. We didn't know how much the kids had heard or seen, but they were happy to see both of us and wanted to go home. Miss Mayla made her appearance and had pushed Miss Mary to the side. I just looked at her saying with my eyes please don't say anything at least not now. Her eyes answered but I knew we would talk again. DA and DT watched Bill as if he had attacked their sister. They walked him out with whisper to my ears but voice of hard concern. All I knew was I was here to gather my family and that felt good. But I just wanted to go home to the sound I waited to hear for so long the word mommy, being yelled from my children as they hugged while pulling me in the direction towards the door. We made it home finally to the one place I wanted to be. I wanted to be in my bed with the covers pulled over my head and hoping that when I pulled the covers down, I would wake up to this was a dream and just wasn't real.

I looked around the room and it was a huge mess from our Ali and Fraizer bout. Bill offered, or did he say, I don't know or remember? I just knew he said he was going to clean up and I should just go to bed and get some rest. He insisted that he would take care of everything and put the kids to bed. Inside my thoughts were you made this mess and they're your kids, what favor are you doing on my behalf? He tried to tell me how sorry he was, but the words didn't move me, because I've heard them all before. All he did was just re-arranged or altered his words, because they still had the same meaning. All those re-arranged words seemed to be blue skies, (Courtney Diane would say). The embrace that I longed for from him only hurt my body. We had begun moving away from each other in the bed. So, it's not like I missed him. There were so many chores and children that kept me tired, (physically and mentally drained). Maybe I was neglecting him, but that door opens both ways. If Bill would only help little more that would allow more time for us. I tried so hard not to be so tired when he comes home. When he's home we do get out and he will take the girls and BJ to the park. That does help with me getting some rest. I just want some us time. We are still young and shouldn't act like an old married nothing to do couple.

So, what is the problem? How can I answer questions that is confusing to me? If I don't have an answer, so, it must be more difficult for both of us to answer the questions to our problems. I don't think or feel that Bill know what's going on or what caused him to snap. He went to work, and little was said, and the morning breakfast was ready. The house showed no signs of the night before, but the image was still visible to me. It was Tuesday morning and I just wanted to stay in the house, while the little ones play in the backyard. Tuesday morning don't remember the month just that day of the week. I looked into the mirror and my eye was swollen. Doctor Carla told me that the swelling would go down. The results from the swelling changed my vision slightly. Then I thought oh yell I forgot my cold towel for my eye. I turned my head slowly, looking and examining my wounds. There was a small cut on my lip. I shook my head to see if the reflections were me. I felt my head move as the reflections moved with me. So, that was confirmation it was me in the mirror. I didn't see the life in me. I saw a face that was aging rapidly as the life was leaving. I looked harder seeking the answers from the mirror. What happened to the person that was innocent, happy, spontaneuous and full of so much life?

I love the rain as I reflect on the rain in my life. I knew that rainbow would someday return. As my scars faded away, the kids stop asking me if they were getting better. I was more scared inside than the outside world knew. I felt strong enough to go outside and face the world. I saw the fence corner conversation between Miss Mary and Miss Amberly. Inside I felt more embarrassed than ashamed. I didn't know how to or what to say. They spoke to me with love and were happy to see me, and the kids loaded in the wagon. They didn't question me or make me feel embarrassed. I seemed to have inflicted those emotions onto myself. Their conversation only stopped long enough to say hi and they picked up where they left off. But I felt their eyes on me but when I turned around, they were still talking and in the same position they were before I passed them. I had to have my thoughts come together and not embedded in my mind that the whole world knows.

My children are laughing so they are probably to young to know what happened with their mom and dad. I keep trying to convince myself that I need to be here with my husband and our children need their parents. I thought I was being a good wife, mother and his best friend. I'm just trying to understand why this man hates me so much? He tells me he loves me but is he trying to convince the both of us. Was I paying for an argument he had with the other woman? That's what I feel like the other woman minus the scant and no rached part, just scant. Maybe that's why I don't feel so in touch with him. I don't know where Bill's heart and mind has been. It has been a long since I felt like Bill's wife. There are times, when I don't feel special. Well, after the other day, at least not lately. We don't talk as much but since this happened, he has been trying to spend more time with us and our family. The storm is passing over maybe Bill is trying to show me the rainbow. The shocking part we were going to a marriage counselor Doctor Julia. She helped but in the back of my mind was she helping herself to my husband in front of me under the guise of she's helping? We listened and talked about where our hearts were. Bill listened, and I heard as she explained that I was a person before marriage. I gained a last name but didn't lose the name of Rita. She will need her own personal outlet for just her. Bill seemed to agree, and I hope with this agreeance we will open more. The girls were getting older and now I was left with BJ.

Now that I was having more freedom, I needed to work on my personal outlet. I've enjoyed reading and the stimulation that came with it. Maybe going back to school will be good, and to be back amongst the living. I want to re-educate my brain with combining my thoughts again. Miss Mary hadn't been on the corner fence for a while since her hubby Jack had stopped working on his cars. He had taken ill so Miss Belinda Amerly didn't have her corner fence company companion. She just watched her grandchildren and transported the boys while enjoying the days chilling on her porch. Naylene was home and I haven't seen her in awhile, especially after that minor or major episode. We smiled at each other as she walked with me. I didn't feel strange, but I didn't want any company. I've become so accustomed to being at home and keeping myself in peace with my family and the tranquility of my home. She seems as if she needed a break from her mother. I know how that feels, sometimes you just need a break. When we were trying to pass her driveway her brother DT was backing his car out. Then started pulling it forward and pulling it back smiling at her. Her response was oh you got funny happening uh? He smiles saying yep and you know why? That threw me off, hmm almost getting hit and that's funny?? He takes off throwing up deuces and she just laughs. She had such a happy laugh, and this was the first time I saw her smile and heard her laugh. I saw the beauty inside and not the sadness that I've seen in her for a few years.

Naylene is beautiful. She resembles a younger verson of her mom with a taste of her dad Jack. Naylene tries to explain through her own laughter what that was all about. Her soon to be ex-husband, Birk would do his dirt, then apologize then do his dirt again. She said that her brothers would come to her defense until they just were burned out from her routine. So, DT said why don't' I do this. I will call you out and run over you, dust you off and say I'm sorry oh, and let me help you up with a straight face. Let me add I know that you will accept my apology. Oh and, I will do a smile with a tear developing in my eyes and we go on holding hands singing la-la-la and let's skip too. Now Rita, Naylene said that she's listening wondering where this is going. Then he said he's gonna call you again. I know you will answer because you loved me, and I will tell you to meet me by the car, (tee-hee again), and run over you again. And again, this time I will help you up dust you off and try to get the tread marks off you. Then I would say because this time I really… really mean it this time, I'm sorry. Oops, my bad and I did it again huh? He had the nerve to put his hand over his mouth saying I did an oopsy to my poochie. I just had to look at DT like finish this up and where are you going with story about hitting me. He looked at me crossing his eyes saying what's the difference Birkland is running over you and dusting you off and everyone sees the skid marks on your back, but you. DT twists his head around saying what tread marks I can't see them. Then he says let me wipe them off. I got you baby girl. He had a point in his brotherly funny way. How long was I going to let this man drive over or keep hitting me? I needed to take the wheel and drive away, and I did right to my momma's house. So, your sister here, (sister girl), is trying to get it together.

Naylene did ask if she could come over. I wanted to say no but, she was just like Courtney Diane, she just walked, talked, and let's sit down. She did ask again with sincerity how was I doing, and she missed seeing us? I didn't know she was working. She seemed to have bankers' hours and found out she was a bank manager. Naylene said that she had to take a mental break. She laughed saying everyone needs a new pair of shoes and her feet were ready to try on a new pair. My insides wanted to ask if they were hiring. It's time for me to get back to work and buy a new pair of shoes. Hmm, this coffee is good, and the rain is just right. I know Bill didn't want me to work. His reasoning now was that BJ needed me. I was getting tired of taking care of our children and this house. I needed some fresh air for Rita. I need some me time from nine to five or eight to four or ten to two, and at the end a check payable to…. Rita or something. Naylene talks, while my thoughts are, I'm glad the house is clean and, it's time for Bill Jr's creativity time before lunch and nap.

Bill Jr. stopped eating crayons and I stayed in the room with him for just in case. He played very well by himself just like his sisters. They didn't give me much trouble until they started to get older. I guess they allowed me to rest for what was to come. It didn't matter I still loved my little people that are now my daughters and son. Rain flows just like life you don't know when the flow will stop. As we entered my humble home, Naylene was very impressed. The one reason that comes to mind is that my home was quiet and empty. I didn't have much to offer her other than water, or milk. I had just enough milk for their cereal. I hope that Bill doesn't come home and have his nightly big glass of milk. I politely asked if I could offer her anything and she politley responded with no thank you, which was an inside sigh of relief. We didn't have much food and Bill was taking care of everything. My allotment didn't go too far on groceries for six people. While Naylene was looking around slowly, I wondered what she thought about me as Rita. A person with a first, (that is seldom used), name that hides behind her glasses and afraid to speak up? BJ goes to his table and starts drawing his house and clouds and sun while practicing writing his abc's and numbers. I watch him concentrate as Naylene talks about her brothers. She loves them, but she had to keep quiet about Birk because if they knew what he was doing they would hurt him and call it a day. That was one of the reasons she was glad they lived in another state.

But when it was time, she said she drove her ass off with kids in tote and momma on my mind. Yep she said it, I'm going to my mama's house. I drove so fast I didn't take the time to look in the rear-view mirror. This girl was going and gone!! She says yes, I drove and as I drove, I saw the sun go down and rise. I kept driving and there was no looking behind me. My mama said that the only thing behind you is your ass. I pulled into my mother's driveway like I stole some money. I saw her and Miss Amerly sitting on the porch and not standing on the corner of the fence. I kindly get out the car as the kids jump out and run to Mama Mary. I slowly unfold my cramped body as mama, Miss Amberly, DA and DT smiled. I smiled as they were a pleasant breath of fresh air and a sight to see. Miss May smiled saying will this be an extended stay? I smiled saying hello Miss May and Miss AV, because I didn't know if I was talking to Miss Amberly or Miss Vicki. My parents raised me proper, so I politely said I reckon so. She said will you be needing your bags carried to the room down the hall on the right. Mama points saying that, This and That over there grinning can fetch and take them bags to your room down the hall right and center. Never you mind dem over there that one and the utter one. Date and Dutton looked at each other like they didn't know who she was talking about until she offered clarification. You, Date is that one and your twin Dutton is the utter one. She cracked a corner smile raising her eyebrows, asking you say this might be a probability or possibility you all will be staying on the extended stay plan? I smiled saying reckon so and we just left with what you are seeing us in ma'am. We have no bags, just as the kind of left in rush and we have nothing extra but a smile of relief. Her response was no problems, no worries, and probably will be needing to go fetch somes essentials. Naylene added response, (as we all laughed), no need to mind and no worries, we will make do.

The twins laughed saying you got that yep, you got this, (while pointing to each other)? They laughed while saying their new names saying no, I'm the utter one saying no man I'm that one and how you get a middle name utter. Listening and hearing the laughter brought tears to my eyes and overwhelmed my heart that I could come home. Before I left, I had spent the whole day preparing. I didn't know Birk had his ass hiding downstairs in the closet, all day listening to every thang that was going on. Thank God I didn't talk about much. All I had to do was wait and when the wait was over, and the sprint set in, fast dash to the car. I smiled as I listened. I didn't know where she was going, and I just didn't want to recall the day she took me to the hospital. I had enough memories in this house. Like, the table I hit my back on, the couch I grab onto trying to balance myself after being knocked down, the lamp that landed on the floor becuasue I was pushed. I forgot about the table he chased me with while holding something shiny in his hand. I see eveything but that blue stain that I left at our apartment. That memory was trying to fade away into a better opportunity will come with this move. So, inside my thoughts are scared, nervous because I don't want to recall that day or night. I see and feel that incident everytime I touched certain pieces of furniture. I make us a peanut butter and jelly sandwich. There's plenty of bread, jelly and butter, water to assist with swallowing. Surprisingly Naylene join in our peanut butter/jelly and water lunch. It's not long before BJ falls asleep and I just place him on the couch with me as we continued our conversation.

Naylene said she married Birk with two kids. She loved Ara and Birk Jr as if they were my own. I'm not going lie in saying I was happy when I gave birth to our Joshann and Brent. We became a blended family. They called me momma and there was no favoritism. I met Birk at church and figured hey how bad can he be? Heathens got to go to church just like they go get a drink. Let me correct myself everyone needs some healing. Don't get me wrong the church is a hospital and we all need healing. But Birk's walk was different. He skipped around the words he should have been practicing. As soon as I said I do the abuse started, the hits and the nagging that he called expressing his concerns, (same meaning just a different word). According to his terminolgy, nagging is expressing your concerns. Birk would move his schedule around just to keep tabs on me. I had inherited his insecurities that he had developed from his ex-wife. Naylene smiles saying I know I look good and all but damn give me some credit. I didn't marry to have him and a boyfriend. If that was the case, I could have continued dating. I didn't have any problems getting dates. I was just looking for something different and thought I found it in Deacon Birkland. DA tried to tell me he wasn't right but what do I know I was in love, and I thought they were being over protective again.

It was so hard getting dates that were brave enough to ask. Boys had to make it past the twins only to have my dad Jack towering over them with long tools in his big hand asking who they came to see. If they made it passed DA and DT, they thought hmm made it through the sweat but not past the tears. My dates had to face the investigating twins. Get this; they would take turns finishing up each others' questions, confusing my potential dates by having them look at both identical twins looking them dead in their eyes without blinking or skipping a sentence. They loved sharing. I caught the dizzies just looking and listening to their tormenting questions. I could only imagine the thought process they had was she worth all this? With a smile she looks at me asking well Lene, how did that work for you? She responded to her own question, with it got me no dates, no man, and no fun! Well one date made it past the bobwire, and he was the next-door neighbor, Stoney. They called him Stoney, because he needed bricks to bring his height up. The reason he passed the bobwire twins was he was short, and they had an on-going joke shorty is short. They would say in sync, how short is he, well he shorter than he is tall. When Stoney came over for dinner, they would set a plate on a high chair tray. After, many years passed Stoney made up for his height.

Naylene laughed adding, when she did go to the prom or something, they both were outside waiting or had their friends inside spying. Then you ask how I knew because, their brainless buddies, Cam and Roland; would come sit either next to us looking, or in front of us with their big heads in the way turning around saying that DA /DT paid for the movie and to come and spy on ya so don't mind us, but we will tell. Then follow up with he didn't get us no food money or drink ya gonna eat all that corn. Cam and Roland would always add, what they talk or what she says or he, (during the movie). Then they would ask each other questions about the movie. Cam and Roland talked as if I or we couldn't hear them or the other people trying to enjoy the movie. Then laugh with we have a bottle, we just forgot pardon us on your drinks. So never you mind on the liquids, alright. She pauses chuckling I remember his partners Andre and Allwyn came to the one prom I made an appearance. I was talking to my girl Roslyn and in slow movie motion I watched in amazement as she is demontrating for me to turn my head. I turned my head slowly with Roslyn and inside I felt like I was at a movie saying slow "oh no" …

Tell me this isn't real that can't be Andre and Allwyn dancing with Miss Lena my biology teacher, and Andre dancing with Miss Cheney, my math teacher. The only thing that helped no one knew who they were, (just me and my girl knew). We laughed as we watched our teachers become human. You know they made sure that the boys at the prom danced with us. I didn't get crowned the queen, but they made me feel like one. Her chuckle turned into a smile as she was saying that who and how could I complain about my brothers and his partners taking time out of their lives to be my personal bodyguard. I love them even more and I'm going to give them a hug and tell them. I love them and how I appreciated their unique form of love. My dad didn't play then and still holds that thought now. While all this was happening my momma either would be sitting on the porch listening or on that corner fence yacking with Miss Belinda Amerly. They were watching any suitors that were hoping they would make it past the porch to claim their prize called me! They might have been keeping score like this one might be potential, nah didn't make it, he hmm needs to keep stepping, and so forth as they laughed and continued to keep score. Probably occasionally looking and saying can we give a minus 0?

I listened to Naylene and realized that she was happy and didn't appreciate her brothers and parents' antics until now. Her son, Brent has two strong uncles to assist with his needs and the education and Joshann has the security of both worlds. Inside I admitted to myself that my brother Sonny was protected over me too. My sister EJ was busy doing her thing and somehow forgot about her sister but made time for our baby sister Bonnie. I always felt like an outsider when the two of them got together. They would gang up on me not knowing that it hurt and left me isolated. I don't think they did it intentionally and to this day we are not as close as I would like but, EJ and Bonnie maintained their closeness. I think that Sonny saw the damage early and set in as a big brother. He would or should do and that's just what DA/DT were doing to Naylene it made had cost her some dates, but she didn't end up in the clinic with digestion. I chuckle and Naylene looks at me as if I was chuckling with her story. Well if that worked why not?

She thought Birk was nice and attractive, but the main character she liked was how he would sit in church with his children. They would sit there so nice and quiet. I had to believe in my heart that if he is that caring with his children where is the mother? We had a chance to talk after church services. He made his way over to me without knocking anyone out of the way. I was pretty impressed with his move without knocking anyone down. This time I didn't have my brothers lurking around, so he didn't have to bob and weave. I took him around my parents, and they were impressed too. Birk did think a little in the backyard with my pop. I watch her calm mannerism you heard my dad like to think. I smiled saying yes it seems that he has been thinking a lot lately. Without hesitation she responds with a laugh adding, with all that thinking back there you would think that he had cars ready to roll off the assembly line. Not one thought has rolled from that backyard onto the streets. This has been his therapy for years. I know we get on all forms of my dad's nerves. He struggles to hide from us and momma, she pushes up front to the front of his nerves, (that has her name on it) but after forty plus years they still dance with each other anytime they hear music. Sometimes the music could be playing in their minds and they would just look at each other and start dancing. So, in saying that I guess his thinking allows him to hold on to that thought.

I join in with laughing with Naylene and I like her. She's not Robin or Courtney Diane but she's funny and nice. I don't want to add too much, but she seems to be able to keep the conversation moving. Plus, I want the conversation to stay focus on her, because I don't want to talk about my issues. The annoying part is that I don't know what issues Bill and I are having. Somewhere Bill and I have lost the means of communication. I know somehow, we will get it back; after all, we live in the same house. We must talk and maybe laugh again, that would be so nice to hear. Naylene said that their first date included his children to the fair and they had fun. His children held my hand and we walked like a real family. This reminded me when I was young with our family outings. I was feeling Birk, this family thing and he felt that part in me. Rita I was feeling the love and the giddiness that I missed out in high school, thanks to the twins, this and that one. My parents had love and music always playing in their hearts, and that was what I wanted. You know that magic music that only their ears could hear. You know that special kind of magic that lasts and last… I thought I heard that magic music softly playing. Birk was a deacon, active in the church and represented all good. He told me the stories about his wife and how she treated him, and he gave so much, and she gave so little. So, he hadn't dated since his divorce and just wanted to raise his children. Their mother went on to start another family and seldom had time for family she left behind. So, he said he had to fill in that void and that's why he was still single. I fell for his story. I fell for the sad eyes and the smile. My brothers were doing their thing which gave me the opportunity to explore.

We had dates with the children and dates with just us and I looked forward to both. Then when I was into him and his kids he started pulling back. I found out later that was just some mind and control game. All those years I fussed about my brothers this was a time I needed them. But by then they probably felt I was old enough to handle myself and went on with their lives. Funny ha-ha-ha, only if they knew how much I needed them to guide me with the first one that paid me some type of attention. I thought I was grown and didn't need them anymore. The funny thing I will always need them. I agreed with her, I still talk and need my brother, Sonny's advice and encouragement. We talked about our children and their goals, and not about our parent's dreams that they wanted us to fulfill. Our conversation was pleasant, and I enjoyed his company. Naylene didn't talk about her exit, or much of the in betweens of her exit with kids in tote. I was thankful that we didn't revisit that night at my house or the hospital. She mentioned that they tried church counseling and that fell on deaf ears with Birk. Our friend Thurmond stepped in and talked with us and it worked for a while until the time faded away with the words. And Birk was back to being Birk and Thurmond moved/relocated. So, there went our negotiator and our peace maker. We talked about church and I told her I had enjoyed going with her mom to Second Baptist. But when her dad started getting sick and my family grew. The church rides faded into family Sunday. Bill did say that he noticed that I prayed every night. I didn't think he noticed. Before Lene started gathering herself to leave she made a statement that I like then and still enjoy it today. What if marriages were like renewing your driver 's license, and you just decided I'm not renewing my marriage? So just suspend the license but, I still want to drive. We chuckled saying that make sure it's in writing. And if they needed a reason it would be because his ass is crazy, (end of reason period). We both laughed lightly so we wouldn't wake up Sonnyboy. When Lene left, I realxed on the couch while BJ continued napping. I did get some me time and refreshed on the conversation from the world outside this house.

Chapter 58
I'm Relaxed and Refreshed

I hadn't talked to Loren in some time and time seemed to fly when your busy raising your family. I had to call to get the update and he answered laughing with I was just thinking about calling you and my big head cousin. I of course asked how was Desiree? I could feel the warmth of his smile coming through the phone. I knew not to stay on too long because I didn't want to hear Bill's mouth about what did I do all day? Just talk on the phone?? Then add that's why we don't have a phone half the time. Loren calmly said again that they were doing fine, and he just didn't want to rush anything. She has her place and I have mine and we make time in between. Before I could ask, he must have read my mind about Fifi. He had to laugh with me saying why won't she go away? She tried that I'm pregnant routine. I laughed so hard then had to pause to get my own breath as she tried to convince me. I broke it down in a Fifi manner...

If you had baby Loren or Lorena they should be past the diaper and da-da stage and should be able to say daddy and just jump right here on my lap. Because I haven't been with you in years. So, bring me my walking, talking, potty trained child. Hell, Fifi I will save your ass a trip and swing by and pick up my seed. So, Mama Rosie Josey can see her grandchild. I told her let me thank you for taking care of our grown ass child and don't be trying to pass off one of your bad ass nieces or nephews, alright! I could feel his smile coming through with a slight laughter saying as proper as he could talk to his imaginary baby's mama. Loren added because I trust you so, Miss Fifi you don't need, "do need assistance" or the acronym "DNA" to determine who the daddy is. I heard dead air. I don't know if she was in ah, but there was a pause before I heard the dial tone. Rita could it have been something I said? I had to laugh on his version of DNA," do need assistance". Well for now there will be no diapers, no dada and no grandbaby for Mama Rosie Josey.

He told me again that there's no baby, but he had to be heading out to pick up his lady. They were going to Desil's wedding and hope that beard and mustache is trimmed. He said he did his and just hoping she got hers lined/cleaned up. I chuckled with oops. Desil cleaned his up just saying and she is pretty but, just had than lip thing going in form of a mustache. He asked with sincerity with don't you guys use tweezers or wax and shift, maybe I could sneak that in as a wedding present uh. I could only say ooh and no that's not a good move. Loren agreed with love talking to you cuz, but I got to pick up my lady. Those words sounded so good and I hope that is what Bill says about me minus old. I think back on Henray Luis thinking he had gotten the ramp, (as Courtney Diane called her), pregnant with her favorite words with your dumb ass. He did dodge that bullet. Miss Box Shape had three children in tote sitting with her on the bus stop. I hope that he appreciated his mom like Naylene did some years later with her family and her bobwired twin brothers, this one and that one. They called in their buddies/partners to show unknowingly formed a village to raise their baby sister. I think that expression fits this situation can't see the forest for the trees.

Time passed, and Bill came home, and he set at the dinner table which had become so routine at times it seemed boring to me. I could only think how this made Bill feel confined and wanting some type of freedom but not at the expense of losing his family. Talking with Naylene I did miss going to church. As our family grew Miss May ran out of car space and then Jack got sick. Our car was working with a prayer and managed to crank up and take off. The car especially, when it comes to Bill needing to get to work and other destinations. Although I wasn't making it to church, I still had my hometown values and Bill was watching me pray every night before bedtime. Prayer has and will be a part of my life.

One day I was taking Sonnyboy to the park and stopped at the little corner store. He managed to draw without saying yipes. I didn't know where he picked up that word up but, for some reason he manages to say yipes often and earned himself a time out. So, since the yipes stopped he needed to be rewarded. On the way back, Sonny/BJ wanted to blow his bubbles outside, which was fine with me. Just like the rain and the calm taste of Chai tea. Funny as I look back the bubbles were nice clean outside fun. This one time we were out Date came over watching and laughing at BJ as he blows and runs after the bubbles. Our conversation was small, because I didn't ever get away from the fear of talking to a male figure when Bill was or wasn't at home. This just didn't sit right with me. I don't know if he noticed behind the smile how much fear I had shivering inside. He said he noticed that things were looking better with us. Then he added an unknown slap your wig back on statement. He said I guess ordering Bill to see a counselor or lose his rank plus hitting the billfold helped. I tried to hold my surprise from his statement. Well that explains why the money is low and he sometimes he gives me convenient or accommodating affections.

I thought this was real and he was into making us work. On this one I had to give Bill the Oscar for his performance. I nervously laughed it off as he starts playing bubbles with BJ. I wanted to run around the yard myself screaming. A net would had arrived, and they would wrap me up and take me away to Bellvue. I chuckle with the thought of maybe I might have a seat next to Fifi. Here we go timing again worked. Naylene came out and true to her word gave her brother a hug as she greets me with the news that her bank had a part- time opening and wondered if I was interested. All in timing and this was my outlet back to working with people. Now it's time for me to start my maybe last performance. My father always said have some mad money and this time I'm mad! So, time to say and prepare for whatever move I'm or we are going to make, but again it's all in timing. I didn't have time to look back it was now time for me to look forward. How did Naylene's mom say it? Stop thinking about what people think all the time. You need to evict those people in your head they're not paying no kind of rent. So, move your ass on and look ahead there's nothing behind you but your ass, and that is everywhere. I guess that was an interesting way to say keep it moving. Bill eventually stopped the nice guy routine after we received our counseling completion. It was just a matter of five, four, three, two, one and now your on. I wonder if that goes with, (I'm still trying to figure out), the office hours. I know that I had to, (like Momo said), wait until his heart is open and talk to him about that bank opening. For some reason my life almost seems like Toni and Jovan but the middle or in between I hope doesn't happen. They took a rough road before they had their happy ending. Well our road has been bumpy but there must be a smoother road somewhere around the corner. DA smiled maybe it was the same way he did with his sister as he calls her Lene. DT was like Clarence and Keith just showing that smile of being careful with concern and love. Funny didn't realize it at the time but I do now. I'm thankful that during missing my family and friends, God blessed and reached out and provided additional family and friends.

Chapter 59
Something About Tuesdays

It's something with Tuesdays that strange things actions happen. Sierra wanted to go next door and play with Joshann and I told her it was too late, and she had homework. History repeated itself. Those beautiful almond shaped eyes closed slightly. As she burst out with I wanna go see JoJo, and if you don't let me, I'm going tell daddy to hit you in the eye and make you cry. Inside I was embarrassed and wanted to snatch this sawed-off mouthy child, this wasn't the child I raised. As I tried to re-group myself as her siblings in shock looked at what might be the outcome. I told her to go to her room and think about what she just said and that it was mean. I watched her stomp off, but one move she didn't do was slam that bedroom door. She might have said something crazy, but I know she wasn't trying to lose her breath. What happened to our child? Did our children see and hear what we thought were whispers? Did they actually see the marks on me or hear the shouting words from Bill? I had to come to my reality, did they see or hear and was practicing what they saw and knew that act would get the results they wanted?

Here I am taking care of my family and this house. Although the night went slow, I didn't tell Bill what happened. Fear set in and I just didn't want to be hurt anymore than I was with Sierra showing disrepect. A word her limited vocabulary didn't quite understand. I do know I'm losing the respect of the ones I love so much. This time I had to change the game and my starring role as mom, featuring "Rita". A name my children don't call me they just look at me and start talking, asking and wanting. Now it's time to get my name back and not that special noun that Bill calls me. Once everything settled down, I went next door hoping that Lene was home. Date answered the door and told me she was out with some girlfriends. I smiled and asked if he could ask if that position was still open and that I would like to be interviewed. He had such a beautiful smile and sense of humor. Date asked does Mr. Bill know you're getting ready to creep out and pray tell as he puts his hand to his mouth that you're going to leave the confines of your home and join the living again? My response was I pray that you don't tell. He daps me with a heads-up and just be careful. When Lene strolls her butt in, I will inform her that she has filled that postion.

Now the next step was to talk to Bill. Ironic that I knew how Toni felt when she finally had an opportunity to have some form of freedom from their apartment to employment. I want to use my social security number on a check and not just for taxes. How did Reva say it in nine months you're going to need a name for that indigestion and a social security number. Indigestion well I had and need that big burp four times, no more indigestion. Now the time has come for an Oscar performance. I rehearsed so many times what to say with not knowing what type emotion that may enter the door attached to Bill. I have convinced courage to stay and fear to just rest. I called on my ancestral strength to talk to Bill. He's not drunk because he doesn't really drink. Hmmm he might be still be getting high. I don't know because lately I haven't been rolling his special brand of cigarettes. He would have me drive him to work fussing that he was late and as he spills his special blend, he would cuss me out for spilling. He's not here smoking so is that the reason for the late work nights and who was he with as he smoked. Maybe that's one of the reasons he was bored with me and our marriage.

I did enough damage to my body with food. Food was my comforter and it sure didn't help the situation when he complained and critized my weight. That just made me eat more. He wasn't perfect but in my eyes he was. Bill managed to keep the same size he was when we met. It was me that gained the weight and more so after four children. Maybe it is me! Charlotte had two carts full of children and she just picked up a tad bit of weight. Reva was more attractive and slimmer than the first time I met her. Catrice had a bus load of children and she looks like she's still in high school. I had to stop finding my refuge in food and stop hiding behind my glasses. That's probably why he looks right through me, because I'm invisible to him and our marriage. Actually, what marriage in his eyes? As his wife I'm invisible to Bill. Maybe I have that little caption or ticker-tape saying for entertainment purposes only, wow!

Dinner is ready, and the table is set and the only thing missing is my husband sitting at the head of the table. The children in their own way stopped asking if dad was coming home. That was one question I had come to not have an immediate answer. I had stopped rolling over to his side of the bed wondering when he would come home. One thing he did do was eventually come home. I just didn't know when because after dealing with children all day cleaning, cooking and as soon as my head hit the bed snoring and I had something in common. His routine had become so old it actually became boring. I guess we both have something in common, boredom. My life will begin, and courage will accompany me, as I become employed again. I kissed Bill in which he acted as if he was in some type of shock. I guess here I go again being the other women. There must be a mental calendar in Bill's head on the time frame that I will convert into the other woman. Then maybe after thirty to sixty days I become his wife again. I asked if we could talk, because we haven't sat down and talked or communicated in any form or fashion. It was as if we were just roommates. I remembered how there was hesitation in his voice. This was a tone and look he probably hasn't seen in me. Heck this was an act that I 've never done except, when I found the courage to talk to my parents asking for a different form of punishment. I was at the age and stage in my life that you could talk to me and I would fully understand the consequence of my actions.

I set across from Bill at our kitchen table that way there would be no distractions and direct eye contact. I told him with a straight face that he has been pulling a lot of weight in supporting our family. I can't sit around continuing watching you work long hours and I see your frustration. And as your wife I'm here to support and stand by you. We've been married for some time where we should trust and continue to be committed to each other. Bill sat in silence as I spoke from the heart and verses that were reherased. Naylene is a manager at a bank and they have a part-time opening. I would like to apply and accept the postion. As his eyebrows rose my debate enhanced with the extra income this would help and take some the pressure off you. There is no need for us to struggle if I'm willing to work and sacrifice my time away from home. Inside I was laughing, heck I wanted to run out, while laughing on my performance. I chuckle inside that I would volunteer my time but, the pay is a bonus plus. My insides high five me with, you got him girl. I took his hand and added a convincing smile telling Bill that Miss Mayla babysits and she's right next door. There is a bus route and I can drop the kids off next door and keep it moving. I watched his eyebrows relax and a smile come on his face. This was an accepted deal without a hand shake.

Bill was relaxed that whole night as I anxiously waited for Lene to contact me. Well she did in a way. I wasn't prepared for her to tell me I will start Monday. Her mom said she got you and look forward to watching and spoilng another set of the next generation. With joy and reality set in my wardrobe was very limited. But no worries Lene had called saying that they wear uniforms and she had some that I could fit for now. The hours I worked allowed enough time to drop off my children and catch the bus to my new-found freedom. Leaving my children with Miss May was a big relief. I caught the bus and looked out the window with a different type of excitement. I felt as if this was my first day of school and my parents seeing me off. With so much excitement I couldn't believe that that I'm riding solo. This is actually my first time riding the bus solo! My mind was fresh and at ease as I looked out the window with so much joy!! My heart didn't skip a beat. I mentally felt the blood flowing and my mind was relaxed.

My work wasn't hard; I just had to re-adjust to being around working people. Although it has been years since I worked at a bank it was all coming back, including the smile that surfaced from my heart. On my way to work, I would see the ocean waves as I walked down the hill. I wanted to run through the water and play in the sand because, that was how much joy I was experiencing. The workers were nice but just like any where else, they tried to pry into my life. As usual I kept private- private and my children were not a topic other than I had three beautiful girls and one handsome boy. Oh yes, I 'm married and moved from Oakwood. Other than that, my parents and Bill taught me well on sharing my life. What life did I have? I started to breathe again and hear my name, (minus the added noun), and I'm employed. I have arrived at work, and I'm back to being employed.

Funny, at first, I didn't respond because I wasn't used to hearing my name. But now it sounds so pleasant to my ears and the sound of adult conversations. I was versatile in all areas of the bank which made Naylene feel good that the other em-ployees were impressed with her choice for the position. I'm thankful that I didn't forget my banking skills. Coming home felt better because, I had refuge outside the doors of our house. When I received my first check it said pay to the order of me, Rita!! That check had me dancing and celebrating my workforce independence. Bill and I had agreed that I would pay for the babysitting, phone bill, (in which I kept down with frequent calls to just a few), and a few groceries. With my paycheck combined with my $120.00 allotment, I felt rich. This seemed like a lot but there was no price to freeing myself from the confines of the house to breathing the fresh air by myself enroute to work. Bill seemed to enjoy the thoughts of having more money and less responsibilties. Our relationship seemed to become better because we weren't around each other that much. Plus, we were able to talk about, (can't believe this word exsist myself), "work". This also gave Bill more freedom to work late, (ha-ha), and have more money. I went to work with ease and a solo bus ride. By time I made it home I had time to see Bill helping the girls with their homework, while I prepared dinner. The physical abuse faded away into more verbal. But just like no emotions from his hits, the verbal didn't penetrate my spirit, soul or thoughts anymore.

Momo would be so proud to know that my cooking has gotten better from the recipes I found in the paper and from co-workers. This was a big change from the routine meals they had become accustomed to. Not quite mystery but just different for all of us. No one complained just enjoyed and left the table full. I didn't make much but manage to buy a couple of outfits for just in case. I also upgraded our children's attire. Didn't have much money but I knew how to mix and match from many sales. Naylene was leaving early and asked if I wanted a ride home. Although, I became accustomed to the long bus ride with the long-distance walk, a quick ride without stops at every other corner along with transfers the answer of yes came very easy! I lisented to the gospel music as the wind was hitting myself while we drove on the freeway. She talked about the good job I was doing and was wondering if I would like to work full- time. One of her workers was being transferred and before she opened that position, she was offering me the position. She said that since you're working everyday anyway, just add a few more hours with benefits. I'm sure my mom Miss Mary wouldn't mind spending more time with your children that she loves to spoil and now will have more time. I could feel her waiting for my answer and I went into deep thoughts that took me in so many directions on how this would be a benefit. I mouthed thank you Jesus as I told her I would take the position. I didn't tell Bill about the promotion just told him that I would be working more hours because they were short staff and Miss Mary was okay with the extended time with the kids. Plus, I wouldn't have to take the bus often because I could ride in with Naylene from time to time. I didn't want to depend on her for transportation it was my reponsibility to get to work. I was used to long rides. The longest rides were taking my children in tote to church.

I was so thankful that my prayers were being answered. I tried to keep my children in church as much as I could. Sometimes the car wasn't always running, and Bill needed to have the car rest so, he would have transportation during the week. The paychecks increase tremendously. Since I was working at the bank, I opened an account in my maiden name and had direct deposit going to my work account. I deposited half of my check to that account and kept the statements there. No information would find itself open to the eyes of I didn't know we had this much saved. We didn't know?? This was my mad money my father always told me to save, and Miss Vicki told me to have a bankcard that' s available anytime I needed some money. Robin always said plan your act and act on your plan. Courtney Diane's would be don't talk, just walk your ass on out and let him see what's leaving. I've only seen a few women that depended on their husbands to balance the bank account and take care of bills to be left empty when they either passed or left them.

I knew that I had to establish me and keep our marriage working in the right direction. One was the finacial support I wanted to provide for my family and not see the stress of struggling on my husbands' face. After all this was new to him as well. Our families didn't sit down and plan a budget or talk about bills or saving money. We just knew they were taken care of because the lights were on and food was in the refrigerator. We didn't have a care in the world. We just knew; how to play outside, don't run in and out of the house, don't let the door slam and the universal rule was be home in the house before the streets came on. That was the only clock or silent alarm we needed and there was no embarrassment. On my breaks I would look in the paper for ads and my eyes wandered onto apartments for rent and small homes too. I felt inside as if my thoughts took a seat at the table and asked me to join in with courage, faith and strength. We talked about our future. The beatings had stopped but the words came faster than the blows. I had to ask myself did I want my girls to marry someone that treated me this way or did I want my son to be raised to treat someone that way? Was I going to show them to do as I say and not what you see me do? That was a huge contradiciton and that's not what I wanted for my family. I couldn't save myself, but I could save my family. Naylene joined me in the lounge and just smiled saying she supports me and will help me in any way that she could. I felt her compassion and believed her heart. We didn't talk much about her exit from her husband, but we had banded together from just mere experience.

I've found a three-bedroom house not too far from the bank and schools were within walking distance. Since I didn't have transportation this would make the children drop off easy, plus I didn't work on the weekends. The ironic part when I spoke to the owner, I didn't know anything other than I was speaking to my future hopefully landlord. I asked Naylene if she would take me over to this location and she readily agreed. The house was small yet large enough for my small family. I met a nice lady that showed me through the house as I had joy with each room we looked into. This was going to be our new home. This place was full of life and the smell of a new freedom. She wanted a deposit, plus first months rent. Hmm that seemed not too impossible but probable. I had managed to save enough money that I felt good to say I had a comma. I looked at Naylene and she smiled giving my shaking spirit confirmation that this was the right move.

The house would be ready in about seven weeks. I paid the deposit plus I still had a comma with my bank account. This was feeling good as I arrived home happier than Bill has ever seen me. Not even Bill could take this joy away. I watched him stare at me wondering why I was so happy. I told him that work was going fine, and they enjoyed my work. In other words, Bill they appreciated me. Since some of the boxes hadn't been unpacked just relocated to the garage and some boxes were empty, I started filling them with some of the kid's clothes and toys. Not many just enough for them to play with and not bring any attention to whining or asking for any favorite toy. I would look around on my break for items on sale and put them, in the garage of my new place. I had my own set of new shining keys and just kept them hidden at my desk at work, for just in case. I ran into the twins Date and Dutton and they smiled as if they knew what was going on. They again warned me on being careful and they were there if I needed any help. Angels come in many forms and mine were about 6"4" and strong. I started having my mail come to my new place. One thing my father stressed was don't have your mail looking for you.

Now as I sit here looking at the rain each drop flows so freely and this hot cup of Chai tea is soothing just like my thoughts of a new beginning. Time is everything and time was approaching for Bill's two-week training. I didn't debate with myself was this the right move or should I give this a try again move. But how many agains do I need to try. One day he loves me and more of the other days I'm a stranger or the other woman. I want to help them both out, she can be the woman and let my shoes slide right onto her feet. So many women want to be, try to be but can't become the wife just a scant, that they snatched up just because. I'm ready this time my wounds have healed, and my brain cells have been regenerated with fresh air. The numbness now has feelings, but no emotions to cry, that has long been gone. Just warmth that reminds me that I'm still alive and when I hear my children 's laughter reminds me of my responsiblities.

The management company represented by Miss Lolita met me with her children Kayla and CJ and the warmth of their smiles and energy again provided confirmation that this was the right move. She was just checking on us and making sure everything was working and happy that I was moving in some of my items. She didn't question if there was a husband and made sure that everything was taken care of. Her smile was angelic and warm as she addressed any of my concerns. She said that her daughter, Kayla had just finished first in her long-distance run and her son, CJ made the running touch down. They laughed as they said that track paid off. So, they were patiently waiting to go out and celebrate their victories. Kayla winning her long distance runs and her journal class report and CJ relay run, first place and he scored the running touch down. Her kids proudly said that their dad was proud of both and they had to be leaving so they could meet him. I had to mentally step back and re-examine my children's talents.

Sierra could play music by ear and sing, Sabrina was good in management and sales, Shaurice hmm good listener with compassion and there was the crayon eating Charles that would be a good artist. Sierra and Sabrina reminded me of Denise the hurdler and Nicole the relay, long jumper with all the around star athlete. I kept up with their talents through Robin and I'm as proud of them as she would speak proudly of them. I'm proud of my little ones and pray that I can help them achieve their talents too and hoping that Bill would be there to celebrate their victories. Maybe I should think this out more, but I had to think about the safety of our family. Trying to hold on to our memories while doing that, bad thoughts invade the memories that I try and generate. I need to stop looking at what I'm losing and flip to what I'm gaining. One thing I will be re-gaining is my real birth name back. No hidden scants or thoughts of why or what I did to pick up his anger that he had from them. Maybe one day he will realize how much love I had for him. It had become harder sharing a heart. Miss Mary said get those thoughts out of your head evict them they are not paying any rent. You need to look forward because the only thing behind you is your ass.

I didn't have much to take. I just took the kitchen and the children's bedroom items. We didn't have too much furniture because the house had some furniture. I left the car. I caught the bus so much that it was just easier to catch the bus and plus Bill needed to get to work. At least I'm not leaving him a green Pacer. I'm just leaving. Bill's life will go on as I move on into a new life with new adventures. DA and DT picked up a truck to help me move. I took the front room television. I made this move to the children as a new adventure. They didn't ask about their dad and I didn't say anything. That was a conversation I wasn't ready to have. I was still talking to myself of why I was leaving and allowed confusion to enter a mental debate. Was it Kennitta's family or Leah that family talk to themselves, then end up arguing with themselves?? I needed to be entertained but not at the expense of arguing with myself. When I looked at the children in Naylene's car I knew it was all worth the move. As I left the house of horrors, I didn't look back not to even close the door. Like Robin once said it takes two in situations one to open the door and the other one to close it. I was looking forward to a new life and I was the other one closing the door. I laughed to myself thinking about what Courtney Diane said about "BIC" and her slightly laughing saying you thought the "B" stood for something else but no it means "Being in ControL". I guess her online anger management' classes were working. Right now, I'm feeling "BIC" and we will become more acquainted...

When we arrived at the house there was a Mercedes in the driveway. I thought it might be Miss Lolita returning to welcome us into our new home or the first lady I meant by the name of Miss Jamie. I walked in to see Miss Mary and Robin. I haven't seen Robin in a while, and I didn't know she knew Naylene's mom Miss Mary. She reminded me that she had leased a house from her with the option to buy. Then in that instant I remembered the story Robin told me when we first met but didn't put the two together. As I looked around the room it was furnished. This furniture looked so familiar because it was Robin's, but why was it here. Robin smiled with her pretty dimples showing saying that she had good news and not so good news. She and the girls were moving back to northern California. She had bought a house and transferred to the new office that the company she was contracted with. Robin laughed with I didn't want you to be cold in an empty house. So little sister I gave you a fresh start and I wanted to travel light into my new beginnings. She told me to close my eyes and open my hand. I felt giddy just like a little girl as the children cheered me on close to your eye's mom!!

Now that was a first, they all called me mom!! Another confirmation, that this was a new beginning. She placed in my hand's keys to her Mercedes as Miss Mary handed me an envelope full of money. She had returned my deposit but smiled saying child care is not free with a huge smile. Sierra comes from the kitchen with capri sun. Funny because through it all I hadn't went to the store. Courtney Diane had sent some money to fill up our refrigerator and cabinets. This was so overwhelming, that the bed of my eyes filled with tears. But the normal for me wouldn't have allowed me to cry but overwhelmed my heart with joy. I could only praise and thank God for such a blessing of more angels. We set down and talked as the children ran into their rooms. When I look into my room and I saw that a large television was in my room! Your neighbors Linsy and Pito are my good friends and they will help you get adjusted. I enjoyed their company but wanted to enjoy the new freedom and my fully furnished house and my new car! Robin had set me up with a year of service at Robier's. I just knew he was happier taking care of the Mercedes instead of a lime green Pacer.

When they left, we took a comfortable seat on the couch all of us crowded on the couch and fell asleep. Warmth comfort and the best sleep I had in years. We awakened to breakfast and not the need to rush for fear of missing the bus. Miss Mary and Miss Vicki asked if the children could come over to Joshann's birthday party and her cousin Maryann was bringing the other set of twin cousins Gabino and Gautam with their sister Connie tagging along. Then she added their Aunts Terri, Teresa and Sandi with their grandchldren in tote too. I thought my nephew Tony and his wife Chante would be bringing their newborn Poet, but little Anthony and Deja stood us up for Disney field trip and Beautiful was invited to a slumber party, heck they have more of a life than I do. But either way there will be a full house and backyard. While I listened, I had a quick flash of Mr. Woodson shouting the names out to Shanta on their dinner parties and making sure the fire department doesn't site them again for the overflow. I didn't see a problem because Bill was still away at training. When I passed the house, it didn't seem as large as I remembered, and I didn't feel any regrets as I passed the house to go next door. My little ones jumped out and ran to the backyard as the twins, Date and Dutton asked is this you. I smiled as they told me that was a good look and fit for me. Inside I couldn't believe that I received a compliment with no consequences.

Well, when Bill returned, he found an empty house with no noise, no laughter and no family. Now he had the freedom to do him and stay where he had the shiny keys too. He came to the bank, which was a first. When I saw him, my heart skipped a beat as he bought me flowers in trying to convince me to come back. When Bill entered the bank again, my heart didn't stop or skip a beat because it was now beating for me. He wanted to talk, and I wanted to listen. But I had a few thoughts I wanted to share with him. I had time and made time for him. I wasn't mad for those feelings had left long ago. It was a Tuesday, (something about Tuesday hmmm), the sun was shining, the skies were clear, and the bank was slow. I asked Naylene if I could take my lunch early. She responded back with a warm smile asking if I needed to take the rest of the day off. Although I appreciated her heart, I knew that I had to work for my family. Now it was my time to be back in the workforce. I waited many years to see my full name on a paycheck.

I walked out the bank slowly looking and feeling the fresh air of freedom and the sounds of people walking and talking. I set inside the car that I once called ours. This was now Bill's time. I would listen and absorb his words and thoughts without any interruptions. I wanted to actively and openly listen to Bill's thoughts and his heart.

I allowed Bill time, so he wouldn't rush his thoughts because I had plenty of time to listen. I was giving him time, but I knew deep inside I was saying good bye. I waited and wanted to hear Bill's thoughts. I wanted and had always long to hear his intimate thoughts on us and our family. This was his time to share and my time for input. I watched Bill's eye beds fill up with tears and watched them slowly roll down his cheeks. The twinkle in his eyes were there but the sparkle had faded into his tears. I wish that I could have joined him, but my tears had all dried up. They wouldn't come out. I no longer had the towel on the couch or the first aid kit or the wet facecloth in the bathroom. I no longer had any tears, no more tears stains. All stains had faded away. I continued to listen and hear the words and his thoughts. The thoughts that I had long to hear. I gave Bill my youth, my body, my soul, my heart and my life.

Bill then called me by my name, with no attachments. His voice was clear with his thoughts saying Rita, I knew you were the one when I saw you going into our Psychology class, and walking around the campus. Then fate happened when you came into the library. Your smile, walk, demeanor with brains and was and still fine. Inside I didn't realize that Bill thought that I was still fine. I smiled at him saying that I had seen him around, but my mind was in so many places. We both smiled at each other sharing laughter saying that we were both young. Bill continued, I had to marry you before someone snatched you up. That day that I came over to your parents' house and saw someone else holding our daughter straightened my ass straight up. It was then I knew I had to do my part and accept responsibilities. He said I had jobs, but knew he needed more for his family, his wife and his daughter. I asked what he felt when I told him I was pregnant. He said he felt fear, scared and left Chicago to get a new start. Being a husband and father was not part of his plan. He just didn't want to be tied down to anyone. Just wanted to be free. Hell, he said I just barely made it out of high school. I smiled with that wasn't my plan either. I wanted to finish up with school. Husband and babies weren't part of my plan, either. I love kids but being someones', mama wasn't for me. Bill smiled yep but it happened. I smiled yep it happened. He said he told his parents that he was going to marry me, because he knew that I was the one. I smiled as I listened a watched his dimples showing as he looked like a little boy telling his parents a story with excitement. I listened as he went on to say that there was one thing missing. He told them that he didn't have any money for the rings. I can picture Naomi laughing through her smiles saying "boy" and his father Richard just looking at him. I had a quick flashback on how Jovan used his savings to get a ring for Toni out of the gum ball machine. Bill look at my hand smiling that I still had on my wedding rings. The rings had more meaning and were beautiful.

I chuckled with the boyish comparison with the sincere innocent heart. He went on to say that he shared his love for me and Sierra with his family and friends. But he was still scared. When he joined the service, his thoughts were getting his family out here. He had to admit that he did party but kept his heart on bringing his family to their new home. But being in California added more stress than I could imagine. I ask where did his imagination take him? Because I didn't imagine me ever leaving Oakwood, married and with a daughter. But I did imagine California with palm trees and beaches. Bill said the women, activities, being in the service was a lot. My buddies had girlfriends, but they were back home, and that was the reason why they like coming over to a home cook meal and family environment. I really got tired of hearing it. I knew what I came home to, but I was looking at their freedom. I felt like I was missing out on me. I looked at him don't you think that I wanted to enjoy my youth too and reminded him that I was three years younger and graduated early. I was only sixteen what life did I have? We both moved from the comforts of our parents' house and into being married. Bill change his smile to that he was sorry that he isolated me while he enjoyed California's scenery. I didn't want to ask but we were talking and listening to each other. I asked the question again and we both knew what I was asking. His eyes were telling the truth as he spoke the words. Words that I had to embrace my heart for. He said that he had a few affairs. I asked what was his definition of a few?? He hesitated with around thirteen. I asked him since when did a few meanings two turn into around a dozen. Bill went on to say that he didn't know why. They just had a special look. I wanted to scream and cry, but it didn't happen. I just took a big sigh and ask if you had all those women then why you stayed with me? I didn't have the look, was I still hometown ugly? He said no they could never add up to me. I could have detoured after all you worked a lot of hours. And you said yourself that some of the service wives detoured. I watch his expressions change as if he was dissecting my words and thoughts. I listened as he talked. Now I'm finally hearing Bill's thoughts and answers to my many years of what did I do?

Bill thoughts and words were expressed with so much passion. He said through his tears that he had fears, and this was all new to him. I told him that we should have been sharing our fears together as husband and wife and as best friends. He was mine and I was all his. I never ran away from him. I was in all ways there for him. He shared his fears, heart and concerns outside the doors of our apartment. I didn't ever share or tell anyone what happened behind our closed doors. Bill should have shared all those thoughts for our family with me and not with his family, friends, co-workers or his scenery.

Bill short changed me, and he didn't give me all of him, but I gave Bill all of me. I thought I was giving my best, but I guess me, and my best wasn't good enough. As time and his thoughts continued the words and thoughts that I had long to hear were now just words. I realized that we were unbalanced. Bill took my hands and I didn't feel the warmth penetrate my heart. His lips no longer warm my soul. That warm embrace no longer had my heart skip a beat. My heart was now beating for me. Bill's eyes cleared and the many questions I had were no longer an issue. Those questions had cleared by thoughts and faded into the freedom of fresh air breeze.

One thing that we both experienced that day was our eyes were both open and now we see clearly. Now Bill can continue with California scenery as I enjoy the fresh air hitting my face. I left Bill with the fears that he would have to face. Bill did try to come around and tried to plead for his family. I told him, he will always have his children and now it's my turn to enjoy the scenery. He didn't know that my perception was so different from his. For years I was inside now I'm on the outside learning how to be Rita. The love I have for Bill will always be there, but I need to learn to love my family and myself...

The words he said my heart and ears longed to hear and feel, but it was too late, and my insides told me no deal. Bill tried the whole routine with more flowers, and romantic words that again I longed to hear, but again it was too late. There were times when I had lonely moments to feel his touch and hear his voice, but the screams came in and reminded me of why I couldn't show emotion no "s." I'm now behind the wheel, steering in the direction I want to finally go. There were times where I longed for just a gentle touch from Bill. We were so separated and sleeping so far apart in the bed that I lost my spot on his chest and if I turned just a quarter I would have landed on the floor. We were just sleeping partners, just friends with the benefits of taking care of our children and keeping the place clean. The rain has finally lightened up.

I stopped to pick up a bite to eat since I didn't have the children with me. As I came out of the resturant Shanta, Sheree' and Alan 's mom, Robin Denise comes out the same place. I look at her and stare at her because now her face looks so familiar. We have similar smiles and I could be a younger her and she could be an older me, hmmm how ironic. She looks at me as if she was trying to figure out who I was? We smiled as I greeted her and told her I met her at her daughter's resturant. She smiles saying hi and we both in sync said the sun finally came out and now we both see clearly since the rain had stopped. I now understand that old saying of you don't miss the well until the water runs dry. Bill had the thirst of thirteen women, and all the put downs of my weight and looks and he ended up temporarily with large Marge, humph. Thirteen women hmm when he had a full glass that would have quenched his thirst from his loving supportive wife, Rita.

Miss Joe Ann, a close Aunt to Momo, said that when you get married you change your last name and life, but you still maintain your first name because that's the only idenity that will remind you that you still exist. It's up to you if you decide to stay or go. Understand that you have more than the reflection in the mirror to tend to. You have the reflecitons of your daughters looking over your shoulder as you glaze into the mirror. Never gave much thought as it faded away at the time to resurface. Mr. Jack said one time he held a conversation with me while he was thinking with his cars said about his sister Sharron. That he thought he was asleep and when he woke up, he thought he was standing and found out that he was upside down. Didn't know if he had a sister by the name of Sharron or he was sharing a concern without saying and it was directed at me. Miss Mary never mentioned her, but I'm glad that I woke up standing and no longer sleeping. I have always enjoyed the rain as it slowly fades away just like my problems. They went away, and I finally saw the rainbow as the sun was breaking through. hmm, just like this last drop of Chai tea is always good. The clouds are going away, and the rainbow is ready to smile. What a nice break through. I love the rain! The sun was just being shy, but not any more and "Now I Can See Clearly".

I had a good talk with myself on how to be me and accept being me. I would look at other women and compare myself to them. Hoping that I could take what they have and just add it to myself. Once I saw clearly, I realized that I was creating a monster. A little of this from her and a little of that would make me look okay. Once I worked from the inside out, I found my inner beauty and accepted and embraced what I was blessed with from God through my parents. Everytime I looked into the mirror my reflections see the real me and I like that. I like it so much that I smile, and the reflections smile back at me. I guess we both agree with what we see in the mirror. This didn't happen over night, but it did happen and that is all that counts. When that happens, you will see clearly too.

I'm so thankful for my beautiful blessings of Shanta, Sheree and Alan. I watched them grow into their own unique style/character. While not shivering in their siblings' shadows. They taught me and inspired me to grow. I pray that they continue to be obedient to the footsteps that have been ordained. I appreciate the spreading of their blessings in being a light for themselves and others. I also want to thank my mom, dad and many of mothers that stepped up in prayers and raised me and others that they selfishly adopted into their hearts and prayers. I also want to thank the mothers that gave birth through the genuine love they provided. to God be the glory for our unique blessings and Happy Everyday is Mother's Day.

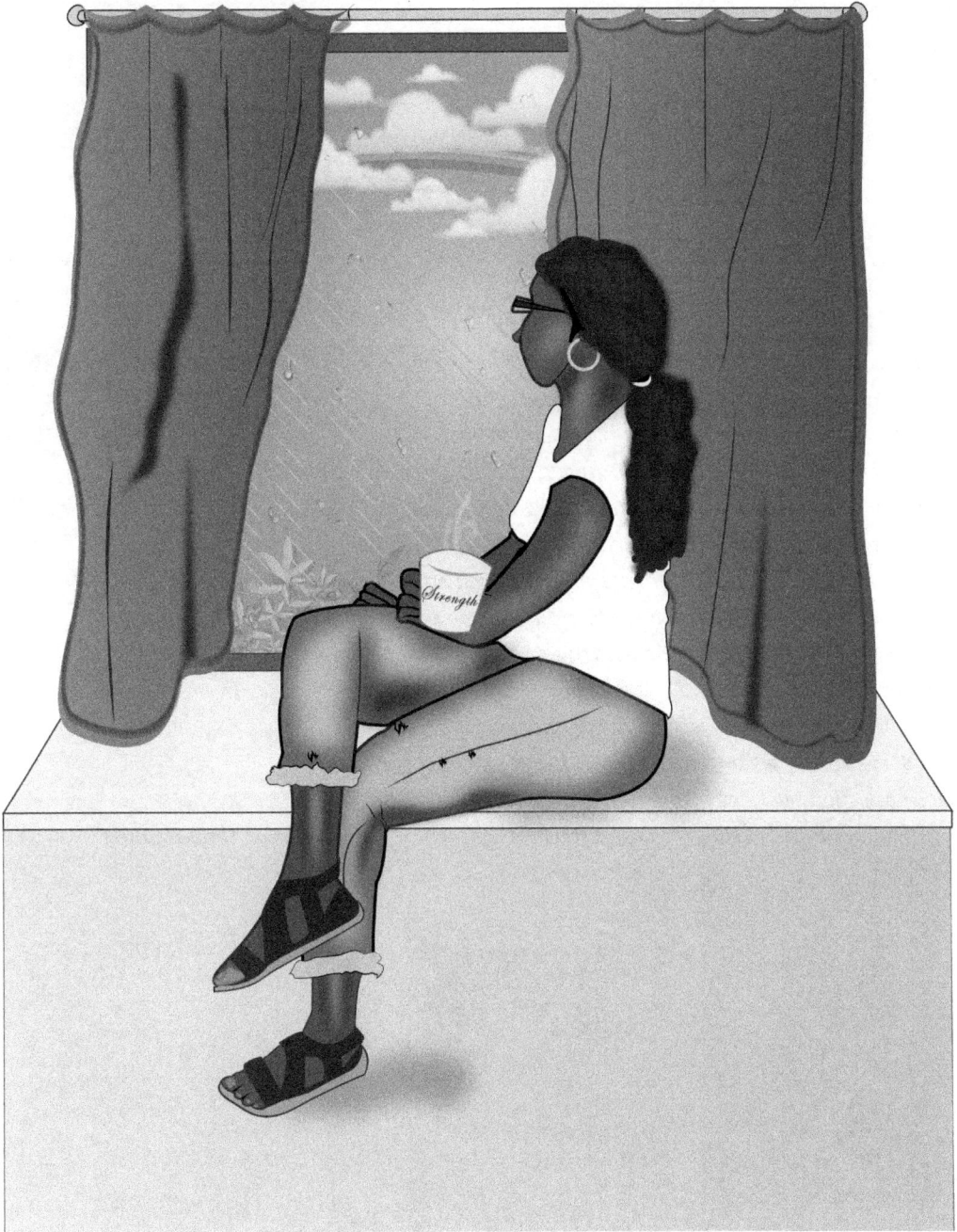

SECTION 4

Rita's Thoughts

My Mirror My Reflections

I looked into the mirror and tried to wipe her tears
I wiped, wiped and wiped, but the tears would not disappear
The reflections seemed to know my every move
So I tried to close my eyes and change from that teary view
Her tears flowed like a river running so deep
I wanted to help but I felt so weak
I asked the reflection if I embrace you, will you embrace me
I told her I would try to help so she could escape her misery
No longer tossing, turning or holding on to those bad dreams
If you take my hand and I take yours
Together we will not have to fear no more
She opened her eyes and smiled and I told her that each day
God will guide her way, so continue to pray
I smiled back and we both could see that the woman in the mirror was actually
Me

Robin Reed-Poindexter

Now I See Clearly

Wow I can't believe I opened my eyes
No longer in bondage to Bill's innocent lies
Now I see clearly to finally be me
My mind, soul and heart can feel the freedom breeze
The words that were said I admit they did hurt
And through my abuse I was building courage
I finally have back my name and added new friends
I'm so very thankful for the village for letting my family in
I told fear to take a seat
Because strength and faith said it was time to meet
Now is the time for us to get reacquainted
Because it's time and we patiently waited
For you finally opened both eyes to see
That you have arrived to now see clearly

Robin Reed-Poindexter

I Feel My Tears

I no longer feel the pain
The tears are flowing to erase the tear stains
My heart can feel the release
And now my soul and thoughts are at peace
When I close my eyes I embrace
The path that the tear stains had to take
But now the pain has gone away
I feel my warmth and know that I no longer have to convince myself that
I'm really okay
My tears allowed my spirit to grow
I'm on solid ground but I have to take it slow
I may stumble and might sometimes fall
But whatever steps I take I'll still stand tall
So my tears are now flowing from my joy
No constant reminders of what they were before
God has blessed me to survive
I feel my tears and they remind me that I'm still alive
I'm thankful that I feel my tears
They help me know that I'm no longer trapped or shivering in my hidden fears

Robin Reed-Poindexter

Don't Judge Me

Don't judge me if you don't see my smile
I've hit some curves and had some trials
I closed my eyes to take a break
So many choices and decisions I had to make
While my eyes were closed
I heard a voice and it was the Lord
I really needed to hear from Him
My soul, mind, and heart had His full attention
He's not an author of confusion
But I had stop praying and I found myself loosing
A battle that I could not win
All because I didn't listen
I didn't think He heard my cries
I thought I had been pushed aside
But it was me that left Him
And now through prayer and faith I'm listening

Robin Reed-Poindexter

Know Your Self Worth

My Rainbow Smiled
It feels so good to stand
I feel the warmth of my rainbow that finally smiled
I love all the joy I now have in me
I just feel like running as I feel the breeze
Every now and then I might hum or sing my special song
Lifting my sprits because my life has just begun
My heart, mind, and soul are now at ease
Because they too love that cool freedom breeze

Robin Reed-Poindexter

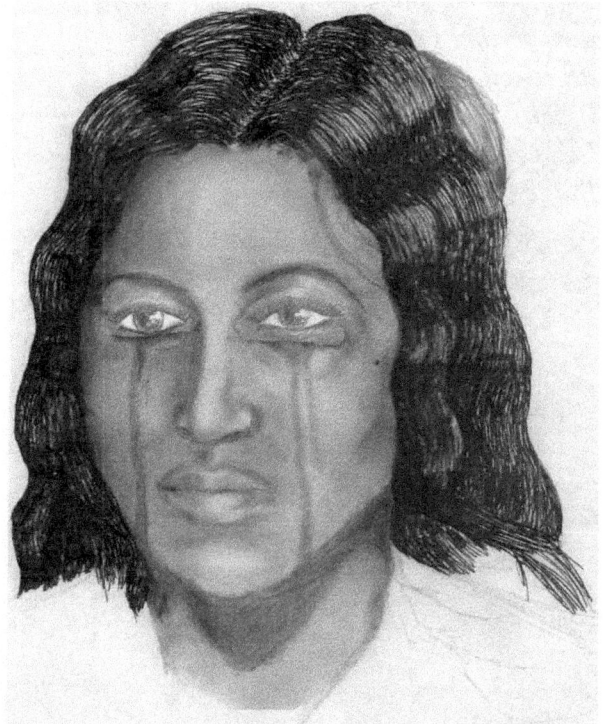

We Are All Together

Now I see clearly, I've opened both eyes
I see my reflections and I feel the joy inside
My tears flow from the depth of my soul
To God be the Glory for now I know
I can feel the breeze of freedom and embrace my peace
And I love the strength that gives me a sigh of relief

Robin Reed-Poindexter

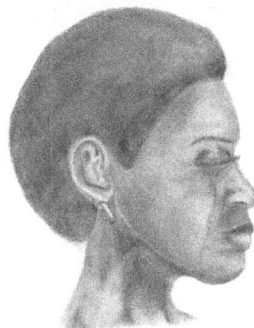

My Rainbow Smiled

It feels so good to stand so tall
I feel the warmth of my rainbow that finally smiled
I love all the joy I now have in me
I just feel like running as I feel the breeze
Every now and then I might hum or sing my special song
Lifting my sprits because my life has just begun
My heart, mind, and soul are now at ease
Because they too love that cool freedom breeze

Robin Reed-Poindexter

CPSIA information can be obtained
at www.ICGtesting.com
Printed in the USA
BVHW012252280719
554531BV00008B/218/P

9 781977 205513